The Charles Bridge

Book and cover design by Riki Moss

By Michael Gruber:

The Long Con
An Active Shooter
Amnesia Dreams
The Charles Bridge
Tropic of Night
Valley of Bones
Night of the Jaguar
The Book of Air and Shadows
The Forgery of Venus
The Good Son
The Return

YA   The Witch's Boy

Ghostwritten/published under the name of
Robert K. Tanenbaum

No Lesser Plea
Depraved Indifference
Immoral Certainty
Reversible Error
Corruption of Blood
Material Witness
Justice Denied
Falsely Accused
True Justice
Reckless Endangerment
Irresistible Impulse
Act of Revenge
Enemy Within
Absolute Rage
Resolved

The Charles Bridge

A Novel of 1848

Michael Gruber

The Charles Bridge

For
Aliceanne

1848 remains a seed-plot of history. It crystallized ideas and projected the pattern of things to come; it determined the course of the following century.

--Lewis Namier

A Note On Money

The ordinary money of the Austrian empire during the two periods described in this novel was the florin, also called the gulden. Accounts were ordinarily settled in thalers, but there were also thaler coins, of gold. Two florins made a thaler. There were thirty kreutzers, a silver coin, in a florin, and four pfennigs in a kreutzer. The minimum wage in Bohemia in 1848 was 15 kreutzers per day. Bread cost two kreutzers a loaf. As a comparison across time, in 1786, Mozart lived on about 500 florins a year. For those comparing across novels, a pound sterling was worth about eight florins in 1848.

One

One summer's night in the year 1786 a boy of seventeen walked onto the Charles Bridge of Prague from the Little Quarter side. It was late, the bridge was deserted, the moon was full, its light casting the youth's shadow before him on the roadway. A mist rose from the river, as it often did on these summer nights, and it gave a halo to the moon and to the Tower and to the lighted windows of Prague in the distance the look of the land of dreams. The youth wore a blue coat and fawn breeches, tucked into polished top-boots. A plain cambric neck-cloth was loosely tied about his throat, his hair was gathered behind, but unpowdered. A sword hung at his left side, for he was of gentle birth. In his right hand, in violation of the custom that gentlemen never carried anything in the street, was a length of stout rope, with which he intended to hang himself from the bridge.

At the center of the bridge, on the north side near the statue of St. Augustine, he stopped and looked down over the balustrade at the Moldau below. The river retained much of the power of its vernal spate. It threw up little waves and wound out oily ripples, each crest reflecting the bright moon. It was . . . what is the word? Yes, *mesmerizing*: and mesmerized he stared down at it for some time, thinking of eternity. He had considered simply filling his pockets with stones and leaping in, but the thought of the choking water repelled him, and repulsive also was the thought of how his corpse would be battered by the current and the rocks downstream and what the fish would do to it. He was vain enough to desire a lovely corpse.

He owned pistols as well, a fine pair, and he had thought of that way too, the muzzle to the breast, like Young Werther, but had abandoned that idea, for the thing had to be public, everyone must see it, the dawn must play on his swinging body, so that she and everyone she knew would know why he had done it, and grieve. Inspiring grief was

1

nearly as satisfying as inspiring love, he thought, and that was another reason for not going into the Moldau, besides the nibbling fishes: he had written a last letter, tucked carefully into his breast, and this would become known as well. He named her in it, and the wrongs she had done, her cruelties, her betrayal of true love. He hoped she would suffer, but he did not really know if girls suffered; he knew very little of girls.

He realized he was delaying it, staring like a dog at the moon-play on the river. With a snort of self-contempt, he uncoiled the rope and threw a bight around the base of St. Augustine. Some of his schooling floated to the surface of his mind: St. Augustine had invented Original Sin, he recalled, but he did not believe very much in Original Sin. He thought Mankind was born to be good and to love and be happy, and Sublime, like Nature, and not all gloomy. But these thoughts were not well- developed in him and they soon faded before the solemnity of his present plan. Although he understood that what he contemplated was a mortal sin, he had no thought of judgment or the nearness of his Maker. All his mind was consumed with pain and a shame that could not be borne. Since it could not be borne he had to stop it, and this was the method he had selected.

He tugged at the rope and found it secure; he was the kind of boy who was good with knots, though a gentleman, and he knew about climbing too. In an instant he was up on the plinth and had coiled the end of the rope into a service-able noose. Not a true hangman's noose, to be sure, for he had never seen one of those, but such a slip-noose as boys in the country use to snare rabbits. This he placed around his neck. Again, he stared down at the Moldau, this time be-tween the toes of his polished top-boots. He had just bent his knees to make his final leap when a woman's voice cried out, "Stop! What on earth are you doing? Come down from there at once!"

Startled, he nearly fell to his death, but managed to grip the rope he had tied around the base of the saint and goggled at what he saw. Standing in the roadway was a handsome Hungarian closed coach with two fine white horses in the traces and a liveried coachman on the box, who looked at him without interest, as if he had been another statue. The door of the carriage had been flung open. On the step stood a woman in a yellow ball gown and a court wig glittering with brilliants. A line of emeralds shone at her throat. The lad was stunned; his mouth gaped. How had he not heard the carriage approaching? Was this real at all? The woman gestured, a quick motion of her hand, as people did to summon a lackey.

"Come here this instant!" she called.

He clambered down and moved forward obediently until the noose around his neck pulled up short and he choked and fell to the cobblestones. He thrashed around in the filth of the road clutching at his neck. When he finally tugged the noose off, he stood and walked to the coach, feeling the blood of shame rush to his cheeks.

"The devil!" she exclaimed. "You're just a boy. And were you really trying to murder yourself? For shame! What could have made you contemplate such an act?"

He stared at her like a peasant at a country fair. She was beyond question the most exquisite adult woman he had ever beheld face to face. She spoke German with a court accent, the true Schönbrunn drawl, the words slightly nasal but preternaturally clear, as if declaiming to an army. He was arranging a response in his toppled mind when she added, "No, don't tell me! It was about a girl, was it not? The most beautiful and desirable creature in the world, and you swore if you could not have her you would die, and you could not have her. Why? That scarred face? You have not learned how little that matters to women of spirit. Besides that, you are well-looking enough in your blue coat, and you carry yourself high. A sprig of the nobility without doubt, but not from the court. Your neckcloth is years out of fashion, and your hair is a bird's nest. She is in love with another? No? A better marriage then? Yes, that is it. A little countlet pursues a girl of higher station, a few kisses shared, yes? Love plighted, only she is playing and you are serious. You come to Prague, you make your offer and she laughs in your face. Yes, I can see I have won the bank. Dear Jesus! You must at all costs stay away from the card rooms, with your phiz that shows all. They would pluck you like a pullet."

The woman tilted her head, and studied him as if he were a dog she was thinking of buying. "And for this you mean to do away with yourself and lose your soul in the bargain. Tell me, young fellow, have you ever had a woman?"

He found his tongue now. "Of course, I have." He tried for an indignant tone, but she laughed merrily.

"Yes, with peasant girls in the straw or servants on the back stairs. I mean a real woman, who knows what she's about. And I answer myself: you have not, for if you ever had, there would have been no nonsense about love forever. All men love the odor of the rose, but only fools clutch at a particular blossom until the petals fall. And any rose will do. It is the same with women, although no one admits it. Step up here!"

As in a trance or dream he did so, and pulled the door shut behind him. The air in the carriage was dense with her perfume. He thought to himself, perhaps I am dead already and this is part of Hell.

"Where are you taking me?" he asked.

"To paradise, I suppose," she replied and threw her arms around his neck, pulled his face close and kissed him. It was not the sort of kiss he had shared with Marietta or with peasant girls in the straw, but a thing of art, having structure, rhythm and depth. He was clumsy at first, clacking teeth, but her mouth was a fine schoolmaster. It went on for a long time, and as it did, she unfastened the front of his breeches, reached in a cool hand and clasped with it his stiffened organ. She made a satisfied sound and lowered her face to it. Kissing continued in another fashion, one he had neither experienced before nor even imagined. And this was just the overture to what was to

The young man stopped writing. "Sir, I must protest! I engaged to take down your memoirs, not this . . . this, how shall I say, *picaresque* tale."

"It *is* my memoir, sir," replied the old gentleman from his bed. "It happened to me just as I told you. I could show you the spot in ten minutes if I had my legs—upon the Charles Bridge near the statue of St. Augustine."

"Then why are you using the third person, sir."

"What third person? It was just the two of us--unless you count the coachman, and why would you?"

"No, sir, I meant the term of grammar. In a memoir one writes, for example, *I* was born in such and such a place, of such and such parentage, *I* did this and that at various times. *I*, do you see? The first person singular. Whereas you are describing someone who might be a character in a novel: *he* did this and so, although you say it is yourself of whom you speak."

"It *was* who I was of whom I speak. That man no longer exists. So I use, as you point out, the third person."

"It is irregular. Memoirs are always first person."

"Then they are all lies. No one could tell the naked truth about their life without a veil to protect his honor and the honor of those he has to do with. The thing is impossible. Yet I wish to tell the truth, as much as I can recollect."

The young man picked up his pencil again, and observed, "Well, it is the case that some novels are written in the first person. Or they pretend to be letters. I suppose it can be done the other way around. But, sir, the, ah, matter of the story, memoir or novel is . . . such things, the intimacies you describe can never be published. No printer would risk it."

"I contemplate a private edition with a select readership. You will allow me to attend to that. At my age, you know, I hardly seek literary renown."

The old man closed his eyes. The young man waited. He could hear a clock ticking in another room, the sound of a carriage passing on Wanmelgasse and the stertorous breathing of the man in the bed. He studied the ancient face. It was a hard face, but noble: the brow was broad, the hair still thick and whiter than the linen of his night cap, the eyes, though sunken with age, were large, bright and the color of coffee without cream, the nose bold but disfigured with a remarkable scar that turned its straight bridge into a zig-zag. The man had clearly kept most of his teeth, for his mouth retained a firm line, firmer than the younger man's, for his tended towards a cupid's bow--a minor embarrassment. It was hard to tell stature in a recumbent man, but clearly he had been lithe and on the small side in earlier times rather than bulky.

The clock ticked on. Had the old fellow dropped off? Or died?

"Sir?"

The eyes popped open. "Forgive me, sir; I am no longer used to interlocutors. The memories sweep over me and I am someplace else. Apologies for my rudeness. I was saying, or meant to say, that I wish to leave a record behind. I knew some remarkable men and women, I traveled widely; and there are secrets I do not wish to carry to the grave. So call it a testament, if memoir sticks in your craw." The old man cleared his throat, adjusted his pillows, drank from a glass at his bedside.

"Where were we? Yes: the Charles Bridge."

The motion of her tongue, I say, the like of which I had never felt before, nor even imagined, brought me quickly to my crisis. I was abashed, not knowing the proper action in such cases, and attempted to pull away, yet she gripped my member like one grips the hilt of a sword and took my effusion down her throat. She rose, grinned, licked her lips like a cat.

"A liquor that preserves youth, they say, although there is in the stews of Bohnitz a brigade of toothless whores that have that as their specialty, and God knows they are withered enough. Now, your youth ensures this fallen grenadier..." (here she flicked my member with her fingers) "... will soon stand in ranks again. In the meanwhile, I will show you how to amuse a lady as the necessary time passes."

With that she performed certain adjustments to her garments, so quickly that it seemed magical, or perhaps she had done it many times in such a conveyance as that one. Her breasts were clear out of their enclosure, so that they could be touched as well as seen, and she had her legs cocked up and braced against the sides of the barouche, so that her entire equipage below was laid open. I reached out a hand to touch her breast, as a little boy might touch an iced cake on a tray, but she snorted and grasped my head with both hands, clenching my ears so tightly that I could do nothing but bring my face to where she wanted it. With this came every kind of advice, so that with my mouth and hands at her complete disposal she managed to bring herself to a pitch of pleasure so extreme that it was as if she were being racked—curses, cries, desperate imprecations, and at last a great shaking, her head thrown back, her eyes rolled up so that only the whites showed in the shafts of moonlight coursing through the rear window of the carriage.

I laughed then, and when she asked me at what I laughed, I said it felt exactly like a young horse being schooled, me the horse, and she laughed too, and said it was time for the rider to climb into the saddle for a run across country. My grenadier, as she called it, was already at strict attention, so she guided his shako into the place designed by nature to receive it; and we went to it, again with unceasing directions from my mistress: faster, slower, higher, lower, pull this, rub that, bite here and there. I must have been a good enough rider, for she thrashed like a gaffed pike, rattling the stacked heels of her shoes against the walls of our bower, and causing the well-sprung carriage to shake as if it were going full tilt down a stream-bed. At last, she announced with a strange cry that she was close, that she was going over, that she was dying, and shook like one with the ague all along her body, and this final paroxysm brought me also to my pleasure, so that I felt my heart would burst from my chest and my head explode.

It took some moments for the world to return, and when it did I saw she had gone all limp, with her wig crushed in a corner of the seat and a line of drool depending from her red lips. I knew not what to think, and it crossed my mind that, in fact, I might have killed her, but then she

7

stirred, and stretched like a cat, and smiling asked, "I fear we have not been properly introduced. May I know your name, sir?"

I told her that I was Johann Anton Ludwig von und zu Pannau von Kinsky. She raised an eyebrow. "A Kinsky, are you?"

"I am not one of *those* Kinskys," I said. "We have the name from a cadet branch, and while we are an old and distinguished family, we do not dispose of millions nor of palaces in Prague and Vienna."

"What a pity! It is so lovely to be extremely rich." she said and extended her hand languidly to me. I kissed it. "Clotilde Daumer," she said. "Very pleased to have made your acquaintance. Tell me, young Pannau-Kinsky, do you still wish to hang yourself from the Charles Bridge?"

"No, not at present," said I. She laughed aloud, and after a pause I did too.

I truly did not wish any longer to perish: the thoughts of the humiliation I had received at the hands of my Marietta, and my desire to make her regret it, together with the remains of what I had supposed a divine and deathless love, had quite flown from my head, which thoughts had utterly consumed me for the past several days. I was like a pot scrubbed shiny with sand. I admitted as much to the woman.

"Good," she said. "At least you have learned not to kill yourself for love." I watched as she efficiently rearranged her garments, and adjusted her wig with the aid of a small mirror set into the front wall of the compartment. As she did so, she observed, "I myself have been careful never to have my heart broken; well, I am an actress, and we are said to be heartless in any case. But as for you, it would be well for you to keep in mind that every woman possesses one of these…" here she patted at her gown where her legs came together … "and while I own they vary in quality as horses do, that quality has as little to do with the usual things men prize in women—bearing, an agreeable manner, a pretty face, station, a fine figure—as the speed of a horse does with its coat color or the length of its mane. I urge you to take the next one for a ride before you turn over your little heart. Now, off with you. I have an appointment with my lover, and I will be even later than usual. The gentleman is an Italian, and thus has no sense of time himself, but even *he* will notice an hour."

"But, I thought *I* was to be your lover?" This I managed to blurt out as she flung open the carriage door.

"No, my dear. Let me tell you how it is. I have the use of this carriage from Prince Clary-Aldringen, from whose palace I have just come. He is an old fellow and not up to much in the way of sport. He sucks at my bubs like a baby and tries to push his thing in me, but it is much like running a hank of boiled noodles through a keyhole. Of course, I groan and cry out and call him my stallion, and so forth. It is all for fun, and is always good for a jewel or a length of silk brocade. Wonderful manners, the prince, but stupid as the night is dark.

"My Italian, on the other hand, is a great genius, a writer for the theater, and will set me up with wonderful parts. He works all the time, and when he takes me it is as if in an absence of mind, and then rushes back to his lamp, still dripping the juices of love. I am mad about him, but it will not last—he will fight with the director and the composer or some royal patron and then he will be off again to Dresden or Paris or Berlin. His work is more important than I am, which suits me well, for that is how I am myself. As for you —have you ever been to a great banquet? Yes? Then you know that they often serve a delicious sherbet between the fish and the roast to cleanse the palate and leave it all a-tingle for the next course. Well, that is you, my sweet, and very well met too. Now, out!"

"When will I see you again?" I demanded, but only to the slammed door of the carriage and again, despairingly, to its rear, as the whip cracked and the conveyance drove away, quickly losing itself in the gloom under the tower on the Little Quarter side. So there I was on the bridge, alone with my rope, alive and not dead as I had intended. As you can imagine, my head was whirling.

I untied the rope from St. Augustine's statue, flung it out into the water, and watched it dive like a snake into the roiling Moldau and vanish. So my life would have vanished had I left my rooms ten minutes earlier, or had my darling savior delayed the same span with her ancient paramour. Thus is the course of our lives determined.

As I walked back to my lodging on Franzosichegasse, I felt myself overcome with a curious elation. I suppose a slave must feel so when he receives his freedom and stands alone at his master's gate, the whole world before him, and no one to tell him what to do. At that moment I resolved that I would not keep my appointment with Colonel von Kolowrat-Krakowski the next morning, despite still being alive, and so would not join the Kaiser Cuirassiers, my father's old regiment, or any other regiment. I would not see Marietta again, of course, nor would I maintain contact with my family, except perhaps for my aunt and Oskar. In my freedom, it had struck me as never before that no one cared about me, except servants, that I had no life in society, except on tolerance. I was without income, the son of a father who rued my existence. My fortune was some fifty thaler in coin. No wonder Marietta had laughed in my face!

"Sir, if you will allow me to interrupt you here," said the younger man, "this now demonstrates the difficulty I had predicted. Who is this Oskar? Who is this Colonel, who this Aunt? What is their importance in the story? And why does your father not care about you? Here is the problem with beginning a memoir *in media res*: characters must invariably be introduced who played a part in the earlier history, and unless one is to describe at ungainly length their relations to the principal, the reader is all at sea. Nor will the reader understand why you were on the bridge with such a desperate project in hand, unless he comprehends your origins and the quality of your soul. Absent that, it is a mere tavern tale, unhinged from any meaning."

"So you believe I must begin in the conventional manner—I was born at such and such a date, to such and such a family? I find myself reluctant to do that. My breeding was, shall we say, peculiar."

"In what manner peculiar, Herr Baron, if I may ask?"

"In every manner possible," replied the baron, with a fierce glare, and then, seeing he had startled the young man, added, "No, forgive me, sir. Of course, you must ask questions of me, and I am wrong to treat them as impertinent. But, Herr Moritz, for now I believe I must consider this further, and alone. Besides, I have grown weary: memory, I find is a fractious horse, ridden over broken country. Now, as to our business. I take it you are satisfied with the fee we discussed?"

"Oh, indeed, sir. It is more than generous."

"Then I suppose you stand ready to attend me when summoned? I will have my man come by with a note to that effect, when I feel well enough to receive you."

"Oh, yes, Herr Baron. Whenever you wish," said the younger man, rising and gathering his things. A servant appeared, led him from the bedroom to the hall, handed him his hat and stick, and ushered him out.

Emerging from the dimness of the house, Rudi Moritz experienced a moment of disorientation, not just from the brightness of the afternoon, but from the feeling that for the last hours he had inhabited a former time, and for a brief disturbing instant the people on the street and their accouterments seemed wrong, as if they should have been wearing the petticoats, curled wigs and long colored coats of the previous epoch, instead of the dull shades favored in modern Prague.

The house was in the Wanmelgasse, four storeys in rusticated pale stone, very narrow, as if it were being squeezed between St. Thomas's church and a wing of the sprawling Wallenstein Palace. Rudi studied the coat of arms set into the keystone of the arched doorway. The blazon had three fields: dexter, three claws; sinister, a Teutonic cross; below a line wavy, a tower. A coroneted helmet topped it and was itself crested by a grinning boar's head. The motto was engraved below: *Meine Ehre Heisst Treue,* and Rudi thought interesting that it should be in German rather than Latin. A certain primitive nationalism? A dislike of the church? My honor is called loyalty. A feudal and hence outdated sentiment, in his opinion, and he wondered to whom this loyalty was due when the thing was first inscribed.

He dismissed this thought—why bother with coats of arms? They were all antiques from an age that had already long overstayed its welcome. The people was now the only suitable repository of loyalty for any reasonable man. Still— was it decent for him to take money for recording the memoir of some aristocratic fossil? Yes, the money: an amazing, a preposterous sum had been offered—nearly half Rudi Moritz's annual salary as a government lawyer.

He turned down Wanmelgasse, anxious to leave the street and this disturbing thought behind. As he rounded the corner, he could not help seeing the Prague lair of the beast he served: on the one side, the Lichtenstein Palace, where he worked, on the other, the Royal and Imperial Military headquarters. It was after office hours, of course, but the work of governing Bohemia went on. Fiacres and larger carriages crowded the edges of the square, and the horses of passing officers were tied to the guard stones around the Plague Column, its gilded spire tip catching the last of the day's light as it shone from the west down the Royal Way. He stood watching the square and its important businesses for a minute or so, as if to help recover the modern world. Then, swinging his stick, he walked down Bruckengasse toward the Old Town and his home.

Normally, he would have taken a cab but it was an unusually fine evening for March, and he felt like walking. He wanted especially to walk over the Charles Bridge. At this time of day the bridge was packed with cabs and carriages. A pair of gigantic black centipedes seemed to crawl past each other on the roadway, while on the sidewalks, the clerks, shop girls, students and the various poor jostled and chattered. All along the walk people were selling cheap goods--lavender sachets, wooden toys, coarse tobacco in paper twists, sugared almonds; and here and there, the bodies of women. Rudi was acutely conscious of the bodies he pushed through, and the hands that fluttered against his clothing, for the bridge was a prime locale for pick-pockets. He focused his attention on the weight of his watch and wallet: he wished it midnight and the bridge deserted, as in the story he had just heard.

At a certain point he left the right side of the bridge and threaded his way through the slowly moving traffic, stopping to regard the statue of St. Augustine. Augustine gazed sternly outward, holding his episcopal crook in one hand and a blazing heart in the other. Rudi had passed the figure innumerable times over the years and ignored it, as did every other Praguer: it was part of the scenery, like the Moldau beneath his feet.

But, now after that a remarkable story...! He would never pass this statue again without thinking of it, and of how a youth had nearly thrown his life away over a girl. What nonsense! But, on the other hand, how wonderful! To live life as if one were in the pages of a novel! What would that *feel* like? The thought was followed by a peculiar weakness in his limbs; his brow bloomed sweat and he sought a stone bench. How odd, he thought, it is almost as if I am experiencing the antique emotions of that old man!

As Rudi sat musing, a troop of cavalry clopped and jingled by him. Without conscious thought he identified them as being of the Franzes, formally the 1st Chevauxleger, green jackets, red facings, red and gold shabraques, probably coming from the cavalry barracks on Jedwabnegasse en route to Hradčany Castle. Rudi had never been a soldier but was something of a military connoisseur, and had been from an early age. As a boy, he had doted on toy soldiers, and as his father could afford to fund all the little armies Rudi desired, he had a lot of them, all of the finest quality, cleverly painted in the gaudy colors favored by the age just past, accurate in every detail. For much of his childhood, these figures had been very nearly his only pastime, and his absorption in them nearly the only act of defiance he had ever presented to his father. For although Karl-Ludwig Moritz was as kind and generous a father as any boy could wish, his temperament grated on that of his son.

A scene from Rudi's childhood seized his mind, perhaps stimulated by the cavalry passing. He was about twelve, in his large, well-furnished bedroom in the family's Vienna mansion. He had arranged all his several thousand lead soldiers on the Persian carpet, using the intricate woven designs to indicate terrain in a convention long practiced. He had advanced to the study of tactical formations based on the battles of the late war against Bonaparte. This was his first attempt at Austerlitz. He worked delicately, placing the hussars and infantry columns just so, close enough to satisfy history, but wary of the uncertain footing offered by the fuzzy ground. It had taken hours of painstaking delight.

The door opened. A shadow fell on the armies. His father said, in what was meant as a kindly tone, "Still with the toy soldiers. Aren't you a little old for that sort of thing? I am going to the bank now. I thought it would be pleasant if we went together. When I was your age I was already working as a clerk in my father's business."

No answer. The man said, "You know, you should rise when your father enters a room."

Rudi had replied, "I'm not going to work in a bank. I am going to be a soldier."

Kindly or not, Karl-Ludwig had a temper when vexed and his habit then was to stamp his foot. He did so, and domino-like, the serried ranks collapsed. After that there was a period of shouting and tears. Rudi was informed that Karl-Ludwig Moritz paid the bills, including the cost of all those expensive soldiers, and that Rudi must put all absurd thoughts of a military career out of his mind. Can you imagine? *It would kill your mother.*

Rudi had not thought of this. As a sentimental and responsible child, the idea appalled him. After he stopped weeping, he returned the soldiers to their boxes and did not play much with them after that. He did resolve, however, that he would never have anything to do with banking. As he grew, his resistance to Karl-Ludwig became subtler, based on his belief that were his father ever to confront something not measureable in money, he would be at a loss, helpless as a puppy. But life could not be like that, all bullying and arithmetic; he knew that, and knew it was not mere fancy, because, as he had learned quite early, the girl who was to become his wife shared his views. It was the age: they were both romantics, although their love was the farthest thing from what anyone would have called a romance. And by the time they were ready to be wed, each had chosen a pure blue flower from the garden of the Romantics. Berthe's was Beauty; Rudi's, Freedom. He smiled to think of it.

Now another thought came, even more disturbing, although in a different way. He imagined the fortunate carriage and the enticing actress and what had happened inside to make the springs jiggle and he felt himself suffused with the most intense sexual feelings, these tinged with longing, for nothing like that had ever happened to him. A beautiful actress beckoning from a carriage! Such things didn't occur any more, they were relics of a former age, that, in the main, the world was well rid of. But still . . . his smile turned rueful.

A tug at his sleeve: he looked down into the face of a young girl, a face thin and smudged, framed by a dingy flowered bonnet. A small crusted sore bloomed on the side of her painted mouth. She smiled and said, "You must be a stranger in our town. Would you like me to show you some of the sights?"

This is what we have instead, he thought. He fetched out a kreutzer from his pocket and offered it to the girl. She regarded the coin dubiously but took it. "Usually it is three, you know."

Rudi laughed and replied, "I am not buying your services, my girl. I am buying you a sausage. Go and get one at that stand under the tower. You look half starved."

He turned away from her and strode rapidly across the bridge to the Old Town side. Entering the great square, he did not pass through it in the direction of his house on Zeitnergasse, but proceeded south toward the Carolinium, the famous Charles, the university of Prague.

As he passed its buildings, his thoughts turned gloomy. He had come here at seventeen in the revolutionary year of 1830, when Paris rose against the Bourbon king Charles and threw him out. Rudi had been part of an absurd group of students who had tried the same trick in Vienna, an effort that had been quickly and easily suppressed by the police. He had run home from the futile march and thrown himself on his family. He still recalled the moment with deep shame, he'd hid quivering in his bedroom while Karl-Ludwig spoke amiably with the police agent below. Perhaps some gold changed hands. The next day he'd been shipped off to the Charles, while many of his comrades had been drafted into the army to serve as common soldiers. He had named himself a coward then and the sting of it remained.

Now he recalled his very first day at the university. He had paused to get his direction in the brief tangled streets around the uni, sick of himself and fearful, when he became aware that someone was staring at him. He glanced at the man, then away, then again a minute later. Still staring. The fellow was dressed in a dark frock coat, tight black trousers and boots, with a soft hat, worn tilted. All these garments bore the unmistakable look of having been bought second-hand.

Could the fellow possibly be a police spy? An absurd thought, yet Rudi had crossed the street, entering the doorway of a tavern there, At the Golden Swan. He sat at a table and called for wine. The bottle had just been delivered, a good Tokay, when Rudi became aware that the staring man had followed him inside and was sitting at an adjoining table. Now Rudi returned the stare.

"Do I know you, sir?"

"Never saw you before in my life."

"Then why are you staring at me?"

"If you honestly want to know, I will tell you. But I warn you, it will be perfectly honest, and free of any subterfuge or hypocrisy. This may prove a unique experience for you.'

"Oh, go ahead," said Rudi lightly.

"Very well," said the other. "I was staring at you because you glow with wealth, privilege, and self-satisfaction, and I wished to warm myself at that hearth. I ask myself how to do this. My answer: I see a young fellow dressed in expensive Vienna clothes, obviously at a loss, who has not been at the Charles before, and perhaps has been sent here to insulate him from the recent broils in the capital. Ah, yes, I see from your face that this is true. So, says I to myself, let me offer my services to this lad. I know Prague; I am a native of the place. I will sponge off him, diverting a trickle of his wealth. In return I will keep him out of serious trouble, and get him into amusing trouble, and perhaps become his friend, because I observe in his face something that is not yet completely corrupt. You agree? For if not, I will walk out and you will not see me again."

Stupefied, Rudi had mumbled an affirmative. They introduced themselves. His man was named Paul Novotny, a fellow made all of bones and angles, knitted together by electricity, always moving, looking, poking, without regard to persons or social propriety. He was one of the dark Slavs, with a hawk nose and a curiously sensual mouth, a lush anomaly. His hair was blue-black, worn long, with a gloss on it that stopped just short of greasy. His head was round, borne on a long neck, and he moved it about aggressively as if it were one of those medieval weapons consisting of a weighty ball, occasionally with spikes, strung on a chain. He had remarkable blue eyes, ordinarily slitted, that would in response to some stimulus (a remark, the sight of a person, a thought passing) seem to double in size, as if to devour the scene.

On that afternoon, Novotny had immediately moved his chair, clapped his hands and called, "Barmaid! Another glass for this table!"

That was their first evening together, and it had lasted until three in the morning. Rudi had never heard such talk: about literature, and girls, history and politics, and most of all, their plans. Rudi could not recall what he had offered, but what Novotny had said remained in memory: "I want to write, to be a great writer. I wish to set Europe aflame."

They had been best friends ever since, and it was to meet him that Rudi now turned onto Parizgasse and entered a doorway under a sign showing a top-heavy knight slaying a Turk: this was the Café Zum Ritter, At the Knight. He often stopped here for a drink before going home of an evening, rather more often recently, given what was going on in the world, for the Knight was a liberal café.

Every morning and afternoon a lad would dash out and race to the post office in the Little Quarter and back with a copy of an Augsburg newspaper, Augsburg being outside the empire and thus free from the censorship that prevented news unwelcome to the authorities from reaching Bohemia. One paper was allowed per café. There were other sources of news too, travelers from Germany and even France, brought in larger numbers than formerly by the new railways, travelers who knew where gentlemen of a certain tendency would be most welcome in Prague. The beer at the Knight was very good, but Rudi came for the news.

Two

The place was crowded, smoky, smelling of fried dumplings, roasted coffee, and spilled beer. As Rudi entered, he felt a familiar stir, a pulse in the crowd, as if the men there were children waiting for a treat, or children of a certain age desperate for the forbidden secrets of sex, impatient, resentful. This was what they felt was their status here in Prague, in the Empire, treated like children, feeling themselves pathetic, desperate for a look at what anyone in Paris or London or even Frankfurt could have for a penny—news!

Rudi ordered a brandy. Jonas Babka, the proprietor of At the Knight brought it out himself. Rudi drank a great gulp of it, coughed, wiped his mouth with his handkerchief, and took a smaller sip.

Babka was looking at him with benign interest: favor shone out his small blue eyes, for Rudi was one of the patrons of the Knight who paid his tab with ready cash, and also the tabs of a number of others. Rudi asked him for news and Babka bent closer and looked conspiratorially from side to side before saying in a confidential tone, "It's spreading. Frankfurt, Berlin, Milan, Venice. They will never be able to stop it without reform from one end of Europe to the other."

"And from Vienna?"

"The usual. The students are up. We'll see if they go past writing respectful petitions to our overlords."

"The last time the students rioted they inducted them all into the army as common soldiers," Rudi said. "Do you think it will be any different this time?"

"Yes, because this time the workers are up as well. Strong arms and iron bars. They're not going to be satisfied with petitions that the Hofburg uses for crap paper. And they have the example of Paris before them. *Paris!*"

Rudi nodded at the magic word. Two months before this, the students and workers of Paris had brought down the corrupt regime of King Louis Phillipe. The royal troops had refused to fire on marching workers. No one had imagined that such an event could have happened with such rapidity, yet there it was—France was now a republic.

Yes, it could happen now, the great change they had been waiting for these thirty groaning years. All liberal Europe had been waiting for it, some break in the dull, constrained life they'd been forced to lead; a great change that might even penetrate the Austrian Empire, what the English called the China of Europe. It would be a colossal event, a new life. Just to be able to sit in a café like this one, and read anything published anywhere, and speak freely without worrying that someone would denounce you to the secret police; to vote for a legislative candidate, to change your tedious round, the dusty office, the pudding faces of your peers, the tepid tea parties, the unexciting ballrooms, to be young once more, to triumph this time, to wipe out the shame.

Thinking thus, Rudy was struck once again by the image the old baron had drawn of the events on the bridge. How many years ago, was it? Forty-eight plus what? From seventeen eighty-six to the year nought makes fourteen, so, sixty-two years ago, nearly twice as long as he'd been alive. Aside from his family, he thought it an unsatisfactory life, so far. At the university, Rudi had done what was required, had studied hard and joylessly become a lawyer. His father naturally assumed he would become the bank's lawyer, but no: in a measly and perfectly safe act of defiance he'd chosen the Imperial civil service, and so spent his days on contract negotiations of excruciating dullness, a petty cog in the instruments of oppression.

The brandy was fuming up from his empty belly—he really had no head for the stuff. His mind drifted back to the tale of the passionate suicidal youth and the beauty in the coach and what had happened in the Charles Bridge under the statue of Augustine, and the wretched girl pulling at his sleeve. He felt a stab of extraordinary lechery.

A pull at his sleeve caused him to jump violently in his chair, making the little table jump too and nearly oversetting his drink. He looked up, there was Paul Novotny.

"Really, Moritz," said Novotny, "I thought you were having a fit. I have been trying to attract your attention for some time now." Not waiting to be asked, he sat down, folded his long, ink-stained fingers, and grinned in a way that hid his bad teeth. "You'll stand me a drink and a pie, won't you, my dear fellow?"

Novotny had indeed become a writer, but Europe remained as yet damp to his spark. He assembled a slender living as a feuillitoniste, with a speciality in guarded sarcasm directed toward the ruling classes, in which group (unfortunately for his career) he placed newspaper editors. Clandestinely, he was Fax, the fire-brand, and wrote under that name for a four-sheet entitled *The Torch*, that was printed in Dresden, smuggled into the empire, and circulated privately throughout Bohemia.

There were a number of such papers, but *The Torch* was perhaps the most sought after in Prague at the time, especially for the songs and comic pieces written by one Jiskra, a personage whose true identity Novotny had clothed in utter secrecy. Even Rudi did not know who the man was. The authorities wished very much to know this person's name and who Fax was and just as assiduously sought the paper's military correspondent, who, under the name Miles, exposed to the world the corruption and stupidity of the Austrian army. This was Rudi, and his pocket contained his latest dispatch.

Rudi recovered himself, feeling a blush whose origin he could not have explained to anyone, and motioned for a waiter.

"I'm glad you're here," said Novotny. "We need a position on the Frankfurt proposal."

"Which one is that?"

"I mean summoning a Congress of all the Germanies to Frankfurt, to propose an all-German union with a liberal constitution."

"Obviously we support it."

Novotny raised his thick eyebrows in a look that suggested a different opinion. "Perhaps. I smell an over-sufficiency of lawyers."

"Well, if one wishes to replace arbitrary tyranny with the rule of law, lawyers you must have."

"Oh, the devil with your rule of law. Your spirit is stifled by your stifling profession. What is this rule of law? It amounts to mere rule by lawyers, and what do lawyers do? Why, sir, they make laws. I had rather have ironworkers rule. At least there would be a great deal of iron about, which is a demonstrably useful substance. Or why not farmers? A statue of a cow in every square and plenty of food."

At this moment the food arrived, the two men laughed at the coincidence and the journalist set to his plate. Rudi turned his attention to the room, which had become even more crowded, and hummed with anticipation. There were men here who were rarely seen in the Knight except on occasions such as this. They were prosperous men in the main, who knew one another, whom Rudi knew in fact. He nodded cordially to several of them.

Novotny paused in his eating, gesturing with a chunk of dripping meat stuck on his fork.

"And? How does the lawyer answer that?"

"Thus: it is a fact that society must be ordered through law alone. The alternative is to be ruled through the mere caprice of the rulers, and that is outrageous. An independent judicial arm is therefore one of our revolutionary aims."

Novotny leaned across the table. "My dear Moritz, the sad fact is that no one will face grapeshot over an independent judiciary. They *may* dare it if it leads to more food on the table. There is a man I met in Frankfurt who has laid it all out in a little pamphlet, which I will share with you another time. Meanwhile, have you anything for me?"

Rudi dropped a tightly folded square of foolscap under the table and said, "I believe a paper has fallen to the floor from your pocket."

Novotny looked at where Rudi was pointing, leaned over and made the little packet vanish. Were there police spies at the Knight? The thought gave Rudi a strange frisson of fear mixed with pleasurable excitement. He had to do something to expunge the shame of having quaked on his bed while his stepfather bought off the police, and his skillful pen was the weapon at hand. In fact, he had become known in recent years among the liberals of Prague for this talent, not as yet a Palacký or a Brauner, but known and respected by them and the other paladins of liberalism. He was good at political writing, and not only in German. Unusually for a German of Prague, he had studied Czech and could write decently enough to compose some of his articles in that language. He could read English as well and had supplied *The Torch* with translations of forbidden articles from the British press. He did not, however, speak either language with any fluency.

"Is Moritz buying food? God be thanked!"

This was from Jacob Liebig, another friend from university days. Liebig was short and slight with a head that seemed too large for his body and a vast broad forehead that seemed too large for that head. He wore a glittering pince-nez and his hair in untidy ringlets that framed a heavy-featured face set with dark, intelligent eyes. Both Novotny and Rudi (Novotny only if pressed) agreed that they would not have passed their examinations at the Charles without Liebig's help. He pulled up a chair, sat down, and signaled to the barmaid.

Novotny remarked, "Liebig, I thought you people couldn't eat this food. Don't you have laws against it?"

"You always say that when I cadge a meal off Moritz, especially when you are cadging yourself. You must teach yourself to be generous with the charity of your friends."

"I only fear you will drain poor Moritz dry, the rapacity of the Jews being well-known," said Novotny. "Are you feeling drained, Moritz? If so, I will organize a pogrom on the instant."

Liebig smiled blandly and flicked a finger of foam from his beer at Novotny.

"Even if the Jews should refrain from grasping," said Liebig, "the Czechs would still complain. The whine is your national song. How terribly we all feel for your ancient wrongs! But really, Moritz, are you pinched? I would be happy to sponge elsewhere."

"No, no, dear friend, I am well in coin," said Rudi. "I am rich, in fact. I have just been engaged to take down the memoirs of a decrepit nobleman and he is profligate with his gold."

"Damn you, Moritz!" exclaimed Novotny. "Why do I never get such commissions? I am far the superior writer. Who is this foolish fellow?"

"His name is von Pannau and he is as old as Prague Castle."

"I suppose his story is a tedious drone of marriages and connections," said Novotny. "You will earn every kreutzer in tears of boredom. How much is he paying you?"

"Five hundred thalers."

They stared at him; Liebig's mouth actually gaped for an instant, before he said, "That's absurd, Moritz. You are pulling our legs."

"I swear not. I was astounded myself, but it is true. A note of hand for the full amount, delivered at my bank. The whole thing was arranged by letter and I just left him after our first interview."

Novotny said, "My dear fellow, a court stenographer, as you must know, can be had for twenty kreutzer the hour; five hundred thalers would suffice to take down the life of Methuselah himself. There is something amiss here."

"Yes," said Liebig, "who is this baron and what are his politics?"

"Politics have not come up as yet. I have been taking down a saucy tale, and I must say that the aristocracy of the former age certainly knew how to enjoy life." He told them about the courtesan and the boy on the bridge.

"Yes," said Liebig, after they had all had a laugh, "A sweet life at the expense of everyone else. On the other hand, I detect among the revolutionary brethren a tendency to dourness and the rejection of life's pleasures. The art of revolution must surely be to create a society where everyone enjoys the life of an aristocrat, but how it is to be done remains a mystery to me."

"It is obvious how," said Novotny. "The French have done it--expropriate the property of the rich and the church and give it to those in need."

"Yet France was unhappy with it," countered Liebig, "and the poor did not disappear in their revolution, nor in the one in 1830, hence the current revolt. No, it is puzzle that has not been solved, unless you agree with Bakunin."

"Who is Bakunin?" Rudi asked.

"A Russian philosopher. If you look past my right shoulder you will see him. A large man with a beard."

Rudi looked. A large man indeed, holding forth to a group of students in university caps.

"And what pray is his plan for after the revolution?"

"You will have to ask him directly," said Liebig. "But he always says that anyone who asks what will be the case after the revolution is a counter-revolutionary."

"How very Russian," said Novotny. "What is he doing in Prague?"

Liebig started to answer but at that moment the door burst open and Babka's potboy, Joscha, burst in, holding the Augsburg paper like a battle flag. It was the great moment of his day. Thereupon a table was cleared. Liebig took the paper and, mounting the table, read out the news. He had a fine, mellifluous voice and had served as the regular newsreader at the Knight for many years.

The paper read, a torrent of discussion followed, for the news had been good to liberal ears. Vienna was entirely in the hands of rebellious students, the Hofburg seemed stunned, the government yielding on all points. The fever had spread throughout Germany; a popular parliament was organizing in Frankfurt.

"Yet Metternich holds on, damn him," observed Novotny. "How long will he plague us? Months? Years?"

"Days, no more," said Liebig confidently.

"How do you know that, Liebig? Do you have sources of information restricted to your race?"

"You may believe that, if you wish, Paul. I had an interesting conversation with some Vienna men the other night. He cannot last the week."

"Can I be introduced to these men?"

"Come by this evening and I will arrange something."

"Excellent! I shall cancel the pogrom in that case. Meanwhile, I am due home, for my children cry for bread. Moritz, since you are flush with gold, might I impose....?"

"Of course, Novotny. Will a florin suffice? I believe that makes seventeen thousand thirty one you owe me." He handed over a coin. Novotny took it, flipped it shining into the air and caught it.

"Thus I despoil the bourgeoisie! Thus you advance the revolution, dear Moritz." With a laugh, the journalist departed.

Liebig sighed. "Do you suppose when the new order is in place, Novotny will cease his Jew-baiting? At length I find it grows tedious."

"Oh, you know it is just his way. He does the same to me as regards my father's wealth."

"Not the same thing at all. But since you are dispensing aristocrat's loot, might I trouble you, too? I must send off a package to Josef."

This was the elder brother, caught up in the disturbances of '44 and condemned since then to the dread fortress of Munkasch. Liebig was constantly begging funds for bribes and comforts and liberal Prague knew that any conversation with Liebig was apt to end in a solicitation for the revolutionary hero.

Rudi extracted a ten-thaler note from his case, feeling less guilty than usual. He was by no means personally wealthy, as he took pride in living on his salary and taking nothing from his father.

Liebig bowed his thanks and said, "Although I batten on your good fortune, I would beg you to have a care. Such largesse must have little to do with your skills as a penman. You are obviously being paid to bind you to your baron, but for what purpose?"

Rudi was about to speculate on the subject, when Liebig exclaimed, "My word! I wonder who that can be!"

Into the tavern had come a man in a worn overcoat and a battered old-fashioned stumpy gray hat, carrying a small leather traveling case. This man paused in the doorway like a cat does, and his sharp blue eyes cast rapidly up and down the room as if seeking someone he knew. A stiffness in his face, the intensity of the look suggested moreover that he was not looking for a friend but scouting for enemies. He entered, however, and removed his hat.

His dark hair was cropped short, like a convict's or a fever victim's, and he wore a beard of about the same length. He had the look of a minor functionary or a superannuated student, quite unremarkable except for those eyes. They met Rudi's and the man held the glance for somewhat longer than was polite between strangers; then a small, correct nod before he walked over to where the Russian, Bakunin sat. They seemed to be acquainted.

"Another Russian, perhaps," said Rudi.

"Yes, but this one no philosopher," replied Liebig thoughtfully. "You know, Moritz, in our pride we believe that revolutions can be controlled by the wise and just—ourselves, in other words. But suppose they cannot. Suppose they must fall inevitably into the hands of such fellows as that, cold, grim-faced Robespierres, who do not despise terror. What then?"

"Oh, have courage, my friend!" said Rudi. "After all, what have we to do with Russian villains? Bohemia is a civilized country."

"So was France," said Liebig.

Three

The next day, having been summoned by note to the narrow house on the Wanmelgasse, Rudi opened his notebook and the old baron began, as if no time at all had passed between their first interview and this one.

You say you wish me to start at the beginning. So . . . I first saw the light of this world on the tenth day of May in the year 1769. Some weeks after my birth, my mother ran away with her music instructor, a Frenchman named Rambouillet. Subsequently, my father spoke with me directly on only two occasions, otherwise ignoring me completely. Despite this treatment I never harbored any resentment against the man, but loved and respected him as well as I could, from a distance, rather as I loved and respected God. Indeed, in Pannau there is not much difference between almighty God and the Count, so my child's mind was easy enough with having two objects of distant worship.

Our family is ancient in that land. The original ancestor was Johann Maximillian von Aargau. At the battle of the Marchfeld in 1278, he contrived to rescue the person of Rudolf von Hapsburg, the founder of the present imperial line, and the fief of Pannau was his reward. He had asked boldly to be a king, but Rudolf was parsimonious with crowns. According to family legend, the emperor clapped him on the back and said, "I will make you a king, if only of a very little country. And if the world should see you as only a count, to my house you will be a king forever."

On the present demesne is the last remnant of the schloss of that era, what we call the Old Tower. Upon is inscribed a little verse:

All that people Pannau call, Valley, river, schloss and town,
The Count of Pannau rules it all, A king is he, without a crown.

Rudolf and his descendants have been true to their ancestor's word, for, you know, while the Hapsburgs may learn little, they forget nothing. Pannau has been nearly immune to change for over six centuries. The Count's sway remains absolute, and as an extra mark of favor, the imperial crown decreed that every son of the house should be granted the dignity of barony at birth. All the emperors have asked of us is loyalty and that we have freely given."

"Yes," said Rudi, "it is on your coat of arms: my honor is called loyalty."

"Oh you saw that, did you?"

"It is hard to miss, Herr Baron, sitting as it does above your doorway."

Well, we take it seriously, you can be sure. In any case, once installed in our out-of-the-way corner in the shadow of the Erzgebirge, we flourished moderately. The valley produces plums in prodigious quantity and from this we distill the finest slivovic in the empire. We were Catholic in the Hussite wars and Catholic in the wars of religion in the seventeenth century. Our forefather, Johann Anton, the twentieth Count, fought with distinction at the White Mountain. In 1701, my great-grandfather, Johann Friedrich Wilhelm von Pannau, married a grand-daughter of Prince Stephan Wilhelm von Kinsky, and we were allowed to join our name with that distinguished one, and became thereafter, formally, von und zu Pannau von Kinsky.

My father, so let us at last reach him, was a colonel of cuirassiers in the Prussian wars of the last century. At a ball in Vienna he met the woman who bore me. I can hardly call her my mother, since of mothering she gave me not a whit. She was Maria-Louisa von Neipperg, of a distinguished Viennese family long active at court. I suppose he liked her looks, and I suppose she liked the idea of being a countess, or perhaps it was his wonderful uniform and the ribbons. She may have been pretty in her youth or not; I could not tell, for she was not spoken of, nor were there any images of her around the place during my childhood.

I know she was musical, as the Viennese women tend to be, and the Count supplied her with a harpsichord and a man, that Rambouillet, to instruct her on it, with dreadful result, as I have said. My father married her in 1764, when she was seventeen and he was thirty-one. My brother Anton was born a little over a year later, during which confinement my father was with the colors. He must have taken a furlough long enough to engender me thereafter, then returned to his troops, leaving the gates of her body open to the other enemy. My father thus returned home to find not a welcoming wife, but an empty bed, a band of terrified servants, a sturdy four-year-old, who was the image of his sire, and a squalling, swarthy little brat, myself. Whom he ignored, then and thereafter.

Here Rudi interrupted. "Forgive me if this seems impertinent, Herr Baron, but was your father of the opinion that you were not, how shall I say . . . "

"A bastard? Not at all. He had proof positive I was his son. What proof this was will emerge in due course. In any case, if someone of name runs off with one's wife, one calls him out and kills him, or dies in the attempt. But if she runs off with a servant, the shame can never be expunged. The only thing to do is what he did—excise her from the life of the family.

According to what I later was told, he made a bonfire in the courtyard of the schloss and into it threw all her possessions: the harpsichord, a cello, her sheet music, all her garments, a portrait of her, her books and letters, even her wigs. Beyond that, he conceived that music itself was to be banished from the schloss, as being too sharp a reminder of the tuneful whore, and so he gave orders: no singing, humming, or playing of instruments. The prohibition extended to Pannauburg itself, at least as far as public performance went. I suppose there were people who, to curry favor with the schloss, gave up private music as well. In any case, during my early life the only musical sound I ever heard was the tolling of the church bells. Even the organ in our chapel fell silent.

Madness, you may say, or something out of the Brothers Grimm, the little domain where there is no music, and I would agree. But a count in those days, especially a Count of Pannau, could do very much as he liked, only excepting scandal to the church or open murder. My father resigned from the army, of course, and devoted the remainder of his life to breeding horses for the cavalry, playing billiards, and insuring that no tune whatever polluted the air above his lands. I suppose his other eccentric project, if one can call it so, was ignoring my existence. I was not brought into his presence as my brother was. When contact occurred, as it inevitably must when two people live in the same house, however large it may be, he simply looked through me, as if I was a chair or a servant.

But, nonetheless, I was satisfactorily reared . . .

At that moment, the door opened and a man-servant entered, carrying a tray laden with coffee things. He laid these out on a small table, gilt, carved and painted in the manner of the former age. The servant paused, glanced at the old man, and then cast on Rudi a cool blue-eyed look such as he could not recall ever having received from a footman. Turning to his master, he said, "Does the Herr Baron wish to be moved, or will I prepare a tray for the bed?"

"Oh, let me sit up like a gentleman, Pavlic," said the baron, at which remark the servant took a heavy, quilted dressing gown from a wardrobe, wrapped his master in it and carried him to a leather armchair that faced Rudi's across the coffee table. The servant fussed, the master slapped and uttered low imprecations, the servant relented, poured out the coffee and departed.

The coffee was thick, very hot, very sweet. Rudi commented on this, and his host said, "Yes, I was out east during the early part of my career. One forms habits then, and I came to like my coffee the way the fucking Turks drink it. The only good thing they ever invented, God damn them. Where were we?"

"Your father ignored you," said Rudi.

Yes, he ignored me entirely. Still one does not let a little baron waste away, unless one is a God-damned French Jacobin swine. I was raised by two people and educated by two others, no, three others, and a horse; had fate disposed differently and deprived me of any of them, I would not have become the man I am. Who raised me was a servant, Ljuba Budic, and her man, Janos, a steward. Ljuba nursed me at her hogshead teats, ear-to-ear with her own child. This was, as you will observe, a common thing. Uncommon thing: instead of being transferred to the nursery and put in charge of a proper English nurse, I was left in the servants' hall and there brought up until I was, I suppose, four or five, along with my milk brother, Lennart, Ljuba's boy. One does not remember much of those years, of course, a mercy that saves us embarrassment when we grow to men. I was a strong enough infant, I am told, and forward. I was ever leading poor Lennart into scrapes, and he got the blame, as was only right, me being a tiny baron and him only a Böhmer servant brat.

I suppose it would have ruined my character, had it not been for Ljuba and Janos. They knew my tricks, and they gave me to know they knew. And so, although they beat their own child in my stead, the blows fell on my inner being and chastised me worse than him. For I was a proud little mite, and wanted the world to think well of me, and most of all Ljuba and Janos.

Ljuba was of course a Czech peasant, God-fearing, rough and of unstained decency and propriety, if devoid of any imagination whatsoever. "Evil doers are evil dreaders," was one of her sayings. "Greed which hath the longest arms, is the father of all harms," was another. In fact, almost every word that came from her mouth was such a saying. I think she would have been shocked had she ever heard an original phrase. No, that is not quite accurate. She spoke the usual proverbs, of course, but some were such as I have never heard from anyone else. All's well, soonest mended. Little by little serves nine. He who digs a pit will fall from a tower. And my favorite: when the devil rides, horses are cheap. I absorbed all these in the way any child takes in what his elders say, and if I didn't understand them quite, it was all one with the rest of the world's confusion. Later, when I had reached the age of reason, I assumed that this was part of the deep folk wisdom of the Czechs, inaccessible to those of other races. So in that at least she had originality—of a sort. But originality is not a quality to be prized in mothers, I believe; my natural mother was, by reports, entirely brilliant.

She had the kindest eyes, my Ljuba, bright eyes, of china blue. And there was no grain of falseness in her, I remember that well. All household servants pilfer, you know, they regard it as a perquisite of office, but she never, although her man, Janos, was as canny a thief as we had on the place. So I trusted in her, and absorbed her nonsense as I did her milk, by which reason I am as tough as a Czech in my body, but I suppose my faculties of reason are less supple than might be desired. Of course, I did not pursue a learned career and I suppose my brains proved adequate to the tasks I set them. Among cavalry officers, that renowned college of stupidity, I was considered sharp as a new tack.

I would have been perfectly happy in that vast warm kitchen, dense with smells both fragrant and foul, had it not been fated otherwise by my birth and also by the peculiar nature of Anton, my elder brother. To a little boy, a boy four years older is a kind of god. From the time that I could walk and had enough comprehension to be aware of human connections, he was my sun. I followed him everywhere he would allow, with Lennart following close behind us two. As to Lennart, I paid him no regard, or only such regard as we pay to our own limbs. They are there to use; and Lennart was less than a limb to me, because I had no need to heed his feelings. I knew not to place my own hand in the fire, but I would happily command Lennart to do so, and he would. I speak in figures only, of course.

It is no figure, though, to say that Anton hated me and wished me dead. He tried to kill me on three occasions. Once he threw me into a stall containing a stallion that was known as a savage kicker. Fortunately I had filched a sugar lump from the kitchen, and by this I kept the beast content while Lennart ran to bring the groom. On another occasion—I must have been six or so—he pushed me off the bridge into the mill-race and I would have been dashed to pieces in the wheel had not some peasants happened by and dragged me out. Lennart was whipped for the infraction of allowing me to fall into the stream. He told me that my brother had pushed me in, but I told him to shut his mouth, as did his father and mother. A still tongue makes a wise head was what she said.

"What was the third occasion?" Rudi asked.

"That comes later in the story. It is your rule, sir, to tell things as they occur and I will keep to it."

"But why did he hate you so, Herr Baron? Surely, you were no rival for your father's affections."

"Oh, as to that, my father had been a sociable man before the catastrophe, and so all of his natural desire for company was loaded upon the shoulders of one little boy. And that little boy had better be perfect, for look what had happened to the mother! Neglected, she went to the bad, and this the count resolved would not happen to Anton. So: riding, fencing, hunting, billiards, the count took all in hand personally. It is not a good thing to have God Almighty as one's tutor, which is why God in His wisdom dwells far away in heaven and lets us get on however we may. Anton suffered much, and what he suffered he passed on, as much as possible, to me. The ingenious cruelty of little boys is well known, and is an argument stronger than those of the pernicious Calvin for the reality of Original Sin. From following Anton, I therefore had by the age of seven or so, become skilled at avoiding him. But let me go on."

I was forbidden the town, lest I be stolen by gypsies, but I was made free of the countryside, and there I would escape at every opportunity, with Lennart, my second self, at my side. Perhaps you know little of the delights available to a boy in the woodland. After escaping from chores and lessons, we would range out among the trails we had by heart from infancy. Sometimes, especially in the winter, we would go out in the morning and not return until after dark, soaked, chilled, howling for food and drink. We set traps, and fished, and killed everything that crossed our path, with sticks and our slings. Country boys love to kill things, you know; or, now I think on it, perhaps you do not. It is their nature, and a good thing too, or we would lack for armies. Sometimes when we were out we heard the sound of a hunt, and from a safe distance would watch the beaters and my father and Anton mounted or on foot with their guns. I would have given anything on earth for a gun, but there was no chance of me getting one. Whom could I ask? As for horses . . .

Did you know that Pannau was a stud for the royal and imperial army? Yes, the Kinsky, you know, is one of the great imperial studs, the equal to those at Lipica in Slovenia or Mezöhegyes, in Hungary. Through some family arrangement early in the last century we began to breed Kinsky horses. The Golden Horses of Bohemia, they call them, wonderful animals, loyal, hardy, courageous, the best possible mounts for heavy cavalry. They have fine, noble heads, black manes and tails, and their coats are the palest golden brown, like oak leaves in autumn. The man who became after Ljuba my second teacher, was a Böhmer named Emil Neckar. He had been a wachtmeister in my father's old regiment, the Kaiser Franz Cuirassiers, and left the service when my father did. Over the years he became the man most responsible for the running the stud.

"And so we come to horses, which is a large part of the life story you were so eager to hear. I presume you ride?"

"I can indeed. I was taught to sit a horse at our country place. An old groom instructed me. He had been in the Second Cuirassiers in the late war."

"Ah, the old black-and-whites! A very fine regiment. He taught the old long stirrup seat, I presume."

"He did. He also taught me to handle a saber. Secretly, I confess. I bribed him with brandy drained from the tantalus in my father's study. I was mad for the army in those days, but my family forbade it."

"Well, it is a hard service, and tedious beyond imagining in peacetime. Is that where you got your scar? A mishap, perhaps?"

Rudi raised his hand instinctively to touch the livid red line that marked the angle of his jaw. "No, sir—that was got at university. Mensur, with the basket-hilt saber. I was in the Corps Carinthia."

"Were you really? Of course, I did not attend university, but in my day they did not allow bourgeois in the dueling fraternities."

"My father--that is, my stepfather--is immensely wealthy," said Rudi, "and so I could buy my way into a rather minor one by purchasing hogsheads of champagne and windrows of theater tickets and making frequent personal loans to boys of impeccable family; of course, I never asked them about repaying and few, alas, did. That is the done thing. You would be amazed at how many of our best families haven't got a kreutzer. Ah, there is my father speaking. Still, it was remarkable to associate with them. They regarded me as a sort of superior hound, not an actual person, naturally, but a useful creature to be treated kindly and never abused. And if I did not much like my brothers, I liked the mensur. I was good at it, too, except for the day of the scar. May I inquire where you got yours, Herr Baron?"

"You may, but I shan't tell you until the proper time in the story. Your rules, sir. Where had I got to?"

Rudi consulted his papers. "Now we come to the horses …"

The baron smiled. "Yes, the horses."

I was not yet six, I think, and my brother Anton had been riding for some years, but no one had thought to put me on a horse. It was often like that at Schloss Pannau, where I was concerned. On Sundays, for example, Ljuba would dress me correctly in my little velvet suit and then I would have to walk by myself during the introit down the aisle of our chapel from where the house servants sat to the family pew and slide in next to my brother. Shameful that; it's a wonder I am not a pagan.

In any case, my infant eyes took in my brother's riding lessons as he trotted and walked around the stable yard on a longe line, with the end in the hands of the Wachtmeister. That was what everyone called him, even his wife.

I recall the day. Anton had finished the longe work by then and was let to ride with the groom on Flora, the mildest of our hunters. I stood staring at the Wachtmeister as he held Barnabas, a very old and sleepy gelding. I thought he would call a groom to lead it away, as he did after lessons, but this day he did not. He looked at me, as if for the first time. Perhaps it *was* the first time.

He made a peculiar little bow and said, "Would the young baron care to mount?"

I walked over, he cupped his hands, hoisted me into the saddle, adjusted the stirrups, placed my feet, adjusted my buttocks, my legs, placed the reins in my hands and adjusted them too. Then he backed off, and, holding the longe, said, "Very well. Walk your horse!"

I said, "Walk on, Barnabas!" and tapped his flank with my little heels. He walked a few steps and then stopped. I tapped him again and the same thing. After a few of these stops and starts I was yelling and slapping at him with my in-effectual heels and trying to hold back my tears. Finally, Barnabas would not budge.

"Little Baron," said the Wachtmeister then, "listen to me! What is the very most important thing concerning the art of riding?"

I thought for a moment. "Not to fall off?"

He laughed at that. "Not at all. That is like saying that the most important thing about planting barley is not to be struck by a comet while out in the fields. We do not fall off horses at Schloss Pannau, sir, as we are not struck by comets. Now I will tell you what is the most important thing about riding."

He leaned close to me and said in a loud whisper, "To cause your horse to go forward."

"That does not seem like a very great secret, Herr Wachtmeister," I said.

"No, but it is true.   Everything in riding descends from this simple act: you tell your animal to go, and he goes. And this secret is but a gateway to a greater secret, the knowledge of which separates the greater horseman from the lesser."

"And what is that secret?" I asked him.

"A horse will tell you it when you are ready. But for now, I ask you, Little Baron: why have you not been able to make our Barnabas go?"

"Because I had neither whip nor spurs?"

He stroked his mustache as if considering this remark. "Do you really think Barnabas needs a whip and spurs to make him go forward?"

I had no reply to this. He stood up and took me by the hand. "Let us find out," he said. He brought over a stool, and standing on it, adjusted my hands, wrists and elbows as he had before, but also my body, back, neck, head, and legs.

When this was done, he said, "The way you are sitting now is the way you must sit a horse always. Look, even now your heels slide forward! There must be a ruler line from the back of your neck through your heel, and from your elbow to the bit in his mouth. You must do this without thinking, as you can walk and talk without thinking, always the same way. If you cannot control your body at least this much, you will never be able to control a horse, and we must wait until you are older.   And some never learn this, however old they are. Now, listen close! You must move your tail bones forward, so, changing your balance, and therefore the balance of the horse in response. Now you move your legs slightly against the grain of his coat; and see, he moves forward! You have helped him to understand what you want, and this is why we call the signs we give to horses, 'helps'. This, you see, is why we must always sit the same way, for that is like being in a quiet room to a horse. If your legs and hands are all a-fiddle, it's as if he were in a room with all kinds of shouting, telling him to do all different things."

Let us now move on: for although I find horses and horsemanship a source of endless fascination, not all men are with me on this, and I perceive you are one of these. To be brief, I learned to ride a horse. By the age of ten, I was a perfect centaur. I do not boast, it is simply the case that I could ride as well as anyone the Wachtmeister had ever taught. Better than my brother, who was a good enough rider; he was older, yet I surpassed him.

There were, of course, many, many horses at Schloss Pannau and I suppose I rode on most of them. It was a changing herd, as horses came in from the traders, or were foaled in our stables. I learned to school horses, as the Wachtmeister taught me: how to tie a foal so it did not struggle, how to lead it on a foal slip, how to longe a yearling, how to back a horse, so that it slowly became used to the weight of a rider. These were tasks that were beneath my brother, being, as he said, groom's work, but I did them gladly, for I loved horses. I read once a strange book by a mad English parson, in which the horses were civilized and the men were beasts. It was meant to shock, but it did not shock me, for I always had more love and good faith from horses than I ever did from my family, or from the greater part of mankind, for that matter.

What a mystery there is in a horse! I recall once when I was just starting out, asking the Wachtmeister why it was that horses allowed themselves to be used so by men, when they were so much bigger and stronger than we were. Why did they not just kick us to bits and run free? We were in the stable yard and Anton was there too, for as I had followed him about in the past, now he seemed to want to follow me, especially when I was with the Wachtmeister. It was as if he, having everything, our father's regard and enjoying the privileges of Pannau's heir, begrudged me the attention of a retired sergeant, which was nearly all I had, besides the horses. Perhaps he begrudged even that--I never understood the motives of my brother's heart.

When I asked that question, the Wachtmeister smoothed his long mustaches, as he did when considering a serious matter, and said, "In the olden times, I have heard, men worshipped horses for their strength, beauty and nobility. Then God said, Worship none but me. But as to the horses, I will make you their servants, to teach you humility. You will feed and house and protect them from ravening beasts, and in return they will carry you, out of charity, as Christ bore His cross, and die for you in battle, as Christ died to save us all. My grandmother told me that story."

Anton said, "But that is just a tale. In fact, we do as we like with them, for we are men and they are brutes. This is how the world is arranged. The lower serves the higher. Men are higher than beasts, as nobles are higher than commoners, and Germans are higher than Czechs."

This was one of those opinions held by everyone one knew, but never so baldly stated, especially not to a Czech. It was unconscionably rude, like calling a woman stupid to her face, the actual stupidity of women being neither here nor there.

The Wachtmeister's eyes met mine, and I blushed for shame and looked down, and in the next instant he was saying, "Just so, young baron, just so," and arranging on his face that look of false, ironic geniality we were used to seeing on the faces of our Czech servants, but which I had never seen before on his.

Anton was blind to this. After a few moments of uncomfortable silence he gestured with his crop and ordered the Wachtmeister to have his horse saddled. The man bowed and called out for a groom, and so the incident ended; but here it is, over seventy years passed, and while wounds and girls, friends and battles have disappeared into the sink of memory, I still recall that little play in the afternoon in the stable yard at Pannau.

Which brings me to my horse. Anton had received his own horse at the age of ten, as was our custom, a pretty little Arab named Rosamond, and horse and rider were being schooled to jump. I was near eleven by then, and had heard nothing about a horse of my own. I asked the Wachtmeister about this and he said that it was up to the Count; the Count was the one who bought horses. He seemed uncomfortable with this reply, especially since it was he and not the Count who was in charge of buying horses, and as I did not wish to embarrass him, I said nothing more to him about this desire. I spoke to Ljuba too: her response was, all things come to him who waits; and also, a broken cup holds no water.

Although I do recall that something extraordinary happened during that week. We had gone out early in the morning, Lennart and I, on horseback. He had learned to ride after a fashion—one could hardly help it, living on a stud—and we were out to check our snares for birds. How I delighted to be on horseback in the morning, with the dew still glistening on every leaf, and the fields sparkling with the same dew gilt by the rising sun, breathing fresh cool air, and feeling half a god with a great bronze horse under me, treading the paths of my home country.

Returning from this expedition, we heard the baying of our pack. A hunt was setting, and as we approached the gates of the schloss we saw the hunters assembled on the drive. I rode slowly by, saluting the riders as I passed, including my father, mounted on his big black hunter, Jupiter. I doffed my hat, my insides writhing, for I feared he would cut me in front of the assembly, but no, his manners took precedence over his anti-paternal fancy, and he gave me the nod. As I passed him, he said, "Hands."

I thought he had called my name. I checked my horse and swiveled in the saddle. I was so startled that I could barely croak out, "Yes, Father?"

But he only twitched his wrists and moved on to take his place in the van of the hunt, by which gesture I understood that, in the panic of seeing him, I had let my hands fall from the prescribed angle, which he had just corrected. That one word buoyed me for days; one word in all my years, yet it was proof my father knew of my presence, and cared that I rode properly.

Still there was no horse for me. That summer I grew morose. I felt that if I could not have my father's regard, the regard of the rest of the world was ashes. I suppose I was a dreadful brat, and I grew in my churlishness because no one could give me any discipline. Poor Lennart was my only companion in these jaunts, although I abused him disgracefully, in the way that only those who feel unloved can abuse those so unfortunate as to love them. And, strangely, at the same time we were the best of friends. The woods rang with our boy's laughter, for although I had resolved to be grim, like many boyish resolutions this could be reversed in an instant, by catching a fish, for example, or winning a horse race, or even the sight of a goshawk against the pink clouds of morning.

It was just such a morning in fact when we set out after boar on the first hunt of the season, always the sixth of October, St. Bruno's day. My father was the farthest thing from a sociable man after his disgrace, but he was conscious of his obligations and heritage. There had always been a St. Bruno's boar hunt at Schloss Pannau and so would there always be; but just the hunt, mind you, not the balls and breakfasts and feasts that went with the hunting season in those parts. People came, of course: an invitation from Count von Pannau-Kinsky could not well be refused, and besides, people were curious about the old hermit, they wanted to see the monster in his lair. Besides the local gentry, his old comrades attended, grizzled veterans of the Turkish campaigns and King Frederick's War, and these were the men he mainly conversed with, on horseback, their breath clouds and their horses' mingling in the frosty air as they gathered in the drive.

Anton was now twelve and according to our tradition could hunt boar for the first time on horseback. There he sat on Rosamond in his frogged green coat, and I wished he would fall off into a mire, but he did not. The people of the estate, men and boys, armed with sticks and noisemakers, and a few with spears, would sweep up the back or northern flank of the mountain in a line, hundreds I say, summoned and directed by the huntsmen with horns. They would be over the crest and into the beech-hangar by mid-morning, driving all the animals before them. At the same time, the hunt proper would rise up from the south on these forest paths, the bright-coated hunters, the huntsmen and spear carriers, servants carrying refreshments in the rear, the kennelers and dog-boys in the van, crying out or baying according to their kind. The aim here is to gather your prey in the center of the hangar, position your hunters in a rough circle and press inward. At a certain point the boars will try to break out, running like blazes down the paths and onto the spears of the hunters. It was not unusual at Pannau to take half a dozen great boars in an afternoon. But some old boars, having been hunted many times, knew well where the hunters were, and thus understood that their best chance to see another winter was to break north, through the lines of beaters.

Of these old boars, the most famous in that time was the one we called Frederick the Great. He had ruled the mountain for nearly as long as my father had been alive— some said longer, some said he was a hundred years old, or that he was a spirit, an enchanted knight, all that nonsense peasants make up. In truth, he was just a very large and canny animal, and every year he escaped the circle. He had maimed a dozen men in his time, and nearly as many horses. As the hunt started, it must have been on the minds of every hunter and every beater, what they would do if the great Frederick showed himself in his pride and came at 'em, all red eyes and saber tushes.

I was with the beaters that day, on the northern flank, where I had no business being, since beating is a menial task, and part of the *robot* owed by peasants to their lord. But Lennart was beating that day along with his father, Janoś, and I decided that I would not be left behind. Janoś objected; we argued; he said that if I was hurt the Count would hang him and turn out his family, but I said that all Pannau knew that my father cared not a whit for me, and would be happy to see me dead, and would give Janoś a gold thaler for the favor of my mangled corpse. Nor could a servant give me any order I was bound to obey.

Argument proving futile, he strode off carrying his boar spear on his shoulder. This spear was something of a joke at the schloss. It was a huge thing, thick as a man's wrist and near as tall as its owner, with a foot-long blade equipped with four quillions, so that if the boar impaled itself, it could not ride up the shaft to gore the spearman in its final agony. God alone knew where Janoś had obtained the thing, but he had carried it manfully on many hunts. Although it had never tasted the blood of any pig, he cherished the weapon, and always boasted that "All-Slayer," as he had named it, was preserving its virginity for the mightiest of all boars.

Lennart and I joined the line of beaters and marched in column through the yellow woods, around the west flank of the mountain. The horns sounded from afar and we began our upward climb. When we reached the ridgeline, they passed around sacks of noisemakers—rattles, tin trumpets and the like, and at the horn's signal we started down the slope making a hellish cacophony, to which was soon added the whirrings and crashings of fleeing animals: rabbits, deer and partridge, woodcock and weasel. We boys were in paradise, blowing, running, rattling, shouting; for sheer excitement it was far better than a carnival. And now we saw the pigs racing out, and we would clump together screaming and rattling to try to turn them back into the circle, toward the killing ground.

We paused to catch our breath and as often happens, even in great battles, there was a lull in our sector of the line. We were in a small clearing ringed by giant beeches, marked in the center by small outcrops of pale rock where the mountain showed its bones. Janoś was in front of me, gasping and leaning on his spear, Lennart was off to one side and there were several other men at some distance, all of us waiting for the commanding horns. Instead, we heard the thump of heavy hoofbeats and a crashing in a deadfall not too distant. Janoś turned to look at me, a puzzled frown on his face. Was it possible that the hunters had come so far already? But it was not, alas, a horse at all.

The boar shot into the clearing, moving impossibly fast, swifter than a horse at full gallop, an immense black beast that looked to our startled eyes nearly the size of a pony. Everyone froze. It was for an instant like a *tableau vi-*

vant at a court play. Then I heard a cry and the boar was upon Janoś, knocking him over, sending his futile spear in an arc, to land point down, quivering in the earth a few yards from where I stood frozen in horror.

Moving as in a nightmare, slowly, slowly, I plucked the spear from the earth. The boar Frederick (for it was surely he) stood over Janoś, savaging him, I saw gouts of blood and bits of his clothing flying. He screamed once, twice—a sound I will carry to my grave--and then the boar raised its muzzle, dripping foam and gore. It looked at me. I began to back away, holding the spear at the balance, as one holds the handle of a valise. I did not even point it at the animal, so stunned was my mind. I did not think of fleeing, or of anything else. No, I tell a lie: I was mortified because I had wet myself and I was thinking about how to conceal it from the others.

The boar charged. Its bulk seemed to fill the whole world, it blotted out the sun. I felt myself flying through the air. There was no pain, just a floating feeling and a roaring in my ears.

When next I came to my senses, I found myself looking into the face of a woman I had never seen before. She had on a low round hat and a veil pushed back. Gray eyes, and she wore a grey riding habit with silver buttons and frogs across the breast. I thought, ah, my mother has returned and all will be well with me again, and I also thought, I am dead, and my mother has died also and I am reunited with her in heaven. But it was not my mother. It was my first sight of Vera Wolanska.

Four

Here the old man sighed and lay back on his pillows, closing his eyes.

"Who is Vera Wolanska?" Rudi asked.

"A Polish noblewoman, the next of my teachers; her and Kíslang, my horse."

"So you did get your horse."

"Yes, and I will soon relate to you how I came to get her, but it is now time for certain medical necessities attendant on my decrepitude. Will you wait in the library?"

"Of course, Herr Baron. I am sorry you are feeling ill."

"Not at all. It is a mere vomit ordered by my physician. In fact, I have been feeling stronger recently. Do you think speaking of my youth imbues me with the sap of those bygone days? Or perhaps it is you yourself. I have heard that some old men like to surround themselves with young people, to batten on their life-force, this animal magnetic they talk about. Or is that theory exploded? One is hard pressed to keep up with the philosophers. Have you perhaps felt a diminution of your own forces? A draining?"

"Not at all," Rudi hastened to say, but looking at the baron, he added, "But you are being facetious, I believe."

"Perhaps. Or perhaps I am like that Hungarian woman--what was her name? Who drained the blood from virgins and lived centuries. Bathory! Yes, and a Hungarian, it almost goes without saying. An unreliable people. I will ring for Joska."

A gangling youth in livery appeared, who had the same blunt, bony look that Pavlic bore, and his blue eyes showed the same veiled intelligence. Rudi imagined them bred for service at Pannau like the famous Kinsky horses.

Some minutes thereafter, Rudi was ushered downstairs into a long room with coffered ceilings, lined with bookshelves and a long mahogany table at its center, flanked by dark, heavy chairs upholstered in tufted leather. The room also held a couch and armchairs done in yellow silk, a painted fireplace, a large globe of the world on a wooden stand, and a pewter chandelier with ten candles. Windows set in the two interstices available between the ranks of bookcases gave a view of a tiny orchard, a brick wall with an espaliered rose, and beyond this the gardens of the Wallenstein Palace, a haze of spring green.

What is this feeling? Rudi thought. Can it be envy? Yes, damn me! What a wonderful room, spacious, with good light, and, were it mine there would be a place for all my books, where I could shut the door against the dear children, and not have to put every single thing away in a chest before I work on something else. Yet I could have had such a room and more, had I allowed my father to pay for it; which I would never do.

Joska was moving about, quietly for one so large, arranging the fire and lighting the candles. After his silent departure, Rudi toured the room. The taste ran heavily to the classics, to religious and philosophical works of the past century, and, more than any other category, to history, especially its military branch. There were books in English, he was surprised to see: Swift, Defoe, and Johnson, and Burke's *Reflections on the Revolution in France,* as well as a set of Gibbon in six volumes, all showing signs of much use.

So: Herr Baron was a reading man, which rather surprised him, for Rudi believed that reading meant enlightenment and therefore an acceptance of the ideas enlightened men ought to hold. The notion that an intelligent, decent, and well-read man might not share his own political liberality was foreign to him, and disturbing.

He paced, warmed his hands at the fire, spun the globe. The Europe on it, he noted, was still the Europe of the age before Bonaparte had redrawn its maps. His irritation grew, and grew more annoying because he could not precisely locate its cause. What is it about this room and this house that so upsets me? he asked himself. The globe of the former world, those books that ought not to be in the library of the unenlightened, the seductive comfort of the place, the deference of the servants . . . it is almost like I am being seduced. Does he really imagine I will change my ideas because of that unreasonable shower of gold coins, a wonderful library and a lackey's bow?   He paced further, he opened cabinet doors: in one he found a cardboard portfolio. To his amazement it contained not drawings or prints, but newspapers, recent ones, from all the great cities of Europe, including Amsterdam, Paris and London. There was even one from Boston in North America, not a month old.

For a moment he sat and gaped. English newspapers in the house of a reactionary aristocrat? It was like finding a naked whore in a bishop's pantry. For one moment he considered theft, folding the *Times of London* small and stuffing it into his coat, taking it to that night's meeting, reading it aloud in a café, and then immediately shuddered at the shame of such a thought. He felt his face flush and sweat break upon his brow. But, really, what harm would it do? A newspaper was not a silver spoon, or even a book; they were used to wrap fish when past their date after all, and besides it was the fault of this accursed regime and its censorship, to lower a gentleman thus in his own eyes by depriving him of the uncensored truth, which was his right . . .

He heard a door slam at the front of the house and the sound of a carriage. This broke the spell and he placed the papers back into their portfolio, just as the door opened to reveal Pavlic. The man conducted him back to his master.

"Forgive me for making you wait so long in that library," said the baron, when Rudi was again seated. "I daresay you found nothing of interest. One tries to keep up with the latest thought, but all I see in the catalogues are shocking novels about the goodness of immorality or political books bent on improving the world. Oh, and reports about the mammals of Zanzibar. Although I suppose the mammals are at least harmless to the reader."

"Oh, no, I found it quite interesting, actually," said Rudi. "Would it be insulting to say I was pleasantly surprised? One thinks of cavalry officers as . . ." He searched for a word and felt his ears heating.

"Stupid? Not a thought in our heads but girls and gambling?"

"Well, since you put it so . . ."

The old man laughed in a curiously soundless manner, his mouth stretched broad and tight with barely a gleam of tooth. "Yes, blockheads all. One has to be quite stupid, you know, to ride a horse full-tilt at people who are shooting cannons at one, armed only with an oversized carving knife. And the tedium of a mess in the usual cavalry regiment is beyond description. If one introduced such a thing as an *idea*, why they'd throw you right out. It'd be like cheating at cards, almost."

"Then how did you get on, sir? You are an educated man. Your shelves hold the best philosophy of former ages. You have read Hegel and Hume, Gibbon and Herder."

"Yes, but not when I was twenty, I can assure you. So you had a look round the shelves, did you? What did you find interesting, I wonder."

"Frankly, sir, I found the most remarkable things not on the shelves, but in a portfolio. I admit to peeping where perhaps I should not have, for which I beg your indulgence. But I could not help but observe that you receive newspapers from London and Paris."

"I do. Although I am afraid they merely pile up nowadays, and go unread to start fires and line shelves. But you are interested in the news, are you?"

"Yes, I am, and so is everyone I know. And you must be aware, sir, that not one of the newspapers in your portfolio is available to the general public. It is a wonder to me how you ever got hold of them."

"Oh, you know, friends in high office. I expect the government believes I can be trusted not to entertain revolutionary notions or attempt to suborn the state."

"With the implication that I cannot be so trusted?"

The baron favored him with a long, searching look. "Oh, *you* can be trusted, I believe. Do take as many as you like. Do you read English? Good for you! I will have the boy wrap up a bundle to carry off. But you must promise not to overthrow the royal and imperial government by violent revolt."

"You have my word. But may I not improve it?"

"You may try, sir. But the last man so to try was the Emperor Joseph II himself, and a sad botch he made of it all. And if an emperor failed, how will a gaggle of lawyers and journalists succeed? I mean no offense—to your profession, that is."

"It succeeds in England well enough. And France, and America."

"All lands ruled by lawyers. I can see why they excite your admiration. Men seek power for the class to which they belong. Animals do the same for their own kinds. This is only natural, although why a law of nature should be taken up as the rule for society I do not know. We are artificial creatures, are we not ? We wear clothing, we dwell in houses, and so forth. And from the earliest memory of man it has been thought good by almost all men, lawyers aside, that society should be ruled by those trained to rule from their infancy: we nobles, in fact. And were that not obvious enough, think of the chaos unleashed on Europe by the unraveling of that rule. A twenty-years' war of unparalleled savagery, in which my only son lost his life."

"I am sorry to learn of it, Herr Baron. Yet that war was bred of tyranny, sir, and not by representative government. Bonaparte was no lawyer."

"No, but it was lawyers who murdered an innocent king, and his yet more innocent queen, our own Austrian princess, damn them all to hell! Thus they paved a pathway in blood for the tyrant to walk. But we digress from our task, for our subject is not politics but me. Tell me, sir, what do you make of my story thus far?"

Rudi had not expected the question. In his surprise he blurted out, "I could not have stood it, sir. Forgive me, but I cannot see how anyone of spirit could."

"Stood it? You mean, I suppose, the peculiar way in which my father and my brother behaved toward me."

"Yes, sir. And it is a wonder to me that you were not ground into powder under such unwarranted abuse."

"What would you have had me do then? Rebel, I suppose?"

"Yes, sir! Rebellion is the only moral response to such tyranny."

Now the baron fixed Rudi with a look difficult of interpretation—not anger; could it be pity? He said, "But you know I abused Lennart as badly, yet he did not rebel. Is there perhaps a lesson there? I mean that once one starts to rebel against established order, where does one stop?"

"When all are free, obviously."

"Yes, freedom is your great maggot. Tell me, would you wish for such rebellion from your own dear wife, or from your children?"

"Of course not, nor would I expect it, for my rule is mild and loving. And I am as ruled by love as I rule with it. My case is thus entirely different."

"Is it indeed? Well, perhaps my story will further illuminate this interesting question."

Again came that curious look on the baron's harsh face. Rudi felt his own cheeks warm and found he wished very much for a change of subject.

"Perhaps," he said. "But to return to what we have already heard of your story, I wonder, did they ever catch that great boar, Frederick the Great?"

"Frederick? Oh, dear me, yes. He died that day, and I suppose it was me that killed him, with poor Janos's spear. The merest luck, you see: I was not grasping it at all, just frozen with fear. Old Fritz had dodged many spears in his time, but this one he didn't see. Limp as it was in my hand, he ran right on it. The butt caught against a stone and impaled him like a Serb. They found him on the other side of the clearing, on his knees, spitting blood, and the huntsman gave him the quietus."

"What a remarkable experience! It seems like something from an epic."

"An epic, you say! Well, perhaps something from another age. I doubt that there are any boars like Frederick left. Shall I tell the rest? Or shall I wait for the notebook?"

"Oh, no, sir! I am certain to recall so vivid an event. Do proceed, I beg you!"

"Very well. As I have said, I came up out of my swoon to find Vera Wolanska looking down at me. She brought a silver flask of eau-de-vie to my lips, and I drank and coughed—my first drink of that divine essence of plum. Then came a clatter of hoof beats that meant many horses arriving, and there was my father on his black hunter.

He looked down at Vera, not at me, and asked, "He lives?"

She said, "Battered, but he will mend."

I heaved myself to my feet and made my bow. There was a moment when our eyes met, I believe for the first time; then the Count acknowledged the bow with a barely visible nod and turned his horse away. I saw Anton there, too, with a peculiar pinched, white look on his face, as if he had received some grave insult. I heard a howl and crying then: Lennart at his father's corpse. His great spear had saved me, but not him. A moment later our huntsman came up, bowed to me, and with the boar's tail marked a blood cross on both my cheeks to honor the kill, as is our custom. Then I fainted again.

I was taken off on a litter and put to bed, the doctor called, my ribs bandaged, my wrist splinted and set in a sling. Lennart came to visit me. His mother was inconsolable, he said. No one had expected this, for she had never seen an opera or read a book, nor was extravagant wailing the style of our people. Had you asked me before the event I would have ventured that the marriage was like the other peasant marriages I knew of: workmanlike unsentimental affairs, similar to a couple of neighbors going snacks on a cow. Although there is always venery to consider: Ljuba was well-known throughout the schloss for the remarkable sounds she produced when Janoś was at her, and Cook used to say it was the only case she knew where planting the child produced as much racket as the child coming out the other way. She said this often enough—it was nearly her only particle of wit--and Ljuba would blush every time. Perhaps that was the case, or perhaps her faculties were less balanced than we knew--those strange un-proverbial proverbs! The saddest part, for me, was that she had got it into her head that I was to blame for the boar killing Janoś, that somehow I had taken away his spear, or that he had given it to me, leaving him defenseless. She would not see me or hear my name—this report I had from Lennart, who told it with the tears streaming from his eyes. Nor were mine dry, for I had lost at one blow both my foster parents. That winter, in fact, she walked into the river with a stone-filled sack about her neck.

Lennart was of that disposition, which I have always envied, that takes the world as it comes, so that though he had lost his father to death and his mother through a derangement of her wits, he brought to my sick-room a ready smile and the news of the schloss below stairs and above—who was on the outs with whom, what dalliances, what fights, what sports, how the horses were getting on, who had been whipped and who had escaped whipping, but deserved it.

My only other visitor was Vera Wolanska. Mme. Wolanska, I should tell you, was a *szlachianka*, an aristocrat of the first water through her father, the famous savant and philosopher, Count Ignatz Casimir Jaroński, and also the relict of one of my father's brother officers, a gentleman with whom he had been particularly close. This officer, Adrian Wolanski, having recently died, his estate had passed to his son, who had married a woman not to Mme. Wolanska's taste. a parvenu, of great wealth but, let us say, uncertain blood.

Such connections are always fraught and in the end the wife made life unbearable to Mme. Wolanska, and she wrote to my father asking if there was not some little corner at Pannau where she could subsist and perhaps be of some use. My father responded as a gentleman ought, and she arrived on the evening before the hunt with a single trunk and a saddle. Of course she hunted—a wonderful horsewoman, as I later learned; and that was what had occasioned our unusual first meeting.

Well, of course, it was in the nature of my previous existence that I had never before had conversation with a cultivated woman; nor could I even begin, for she had but a few words of Czech and although she could read German well enough she found it clumsy in her mouth. She expected to speak French to me and did for some time before she comprehended that I had never been taught to speak it.

"Why, that is monstrous," she exclaimed. "Not to speak French! How else can one think? Or converse in society?"

I explained that we had no society at Pannau and I was not expected to think very much. In fact, it was the opinion of our tutor that I was a blockhead and could not get past the first book in Latin.

At this, she assumed a look that I was to see many times on her face and which I have tried unsuccessfully to wear on my own. Perhaps you had to look like her. Regal is a word much overused, but apt here. Poland, she once told me, is a slice of France stuck between the sane barbarity of Prussia and the maniacal barbarity of the Tsar's empire, and so Poles of birth strive to be more French than France—their faces are set on Paris. And Mme. Wolanska had one of those faces, something that seemed carved out of ivory with a chisel, flat planes like the stonework on a fortress. Her nose was thin and fine-boned and rose a little at the tip. Also, silky hair, blonde, of course, that she wore parted in the center and pulled back in a chignon, with little ringlets hanging pendant before her ears. It was the kind of face that only aristocratic Polish women seem to possess, at least in my experience.

Well, that was how I began with Mme. Wolanska—imagine if you will a seed long hidden at the bottom of a dry well and then carried up for the first time to sunlight, air and water. I had enjoyed rough love from the servants, of course, but servants, while they can be faithful and caring, are not capable of love for their masters. Love is only possible between equals. I never had it before then, and now I did.

I blossomed like a young rose. It was the best year of my life thus far, I suppose, although it must be dull to hear it. To begin, with, she stayed with me during my convalescence, talking French and making me answer her in the same language. We read *Candide* to each other, and we read La Fontaine, and Perrault, and we performed parts in the plays of Molière, of which she had a folio book, laughing together like children. I had not thought that a book could make one laugh, but found it so in her company, and even alone; which, you will admit, is something strange, laughing to oneself in bed, and the man who thought up the joke perhaps long dead. It was never known before in Pannau, I assure you.

Two other great things happened that year. The first was that Anton, my brother, was sent off to school in Vienna. Perhaps Mme. Wolanska had something to do with this, as it happened shortly after her arrival. Anton despised her from the first moment, and as he could never learn to control his face or manner, I suppose my father believed that the peace of the house required that he leave. Then--and this was scarce a week after I could get around by myself--I went for my first visit to the stables to see if I could still sit a horse.

The Wachtmeister inquired as to how the young baron was getting on and I said I was learning French, and he said *pain, vin, espèce de salaud,* and *merde* was the only French he had learned in the wars and was most of what a soldier needed, not counting some other phrases I was too young to hear in any language. He asked me if I wanted to ride and when I told him I did he left and came back with an unfamiliar horse. She was a smallish bay mare, just under fourteen hands, with a white mark on her forehead in the shape of a candle flame.

She was altogether a different sort of horse than I had seen before, not at all like the golden cavalry chargers we bred on the place.

"She is a Mezöhegyes horse," the Wachtmeister told me. "From the imperial stud, in Hungary. What do you think of her?"

This was a serious question, and so I examined the horse with some care, feeling her legs, examining her hooves, taking her halter and walking her back and forth in the yard. Steely hooves, I observed, unshod, sloping withers, short back, close-coupled and well ribbed-up; ears short, a smallish head like an Arab, long arched neck; knees wide and flat; a broad chest, a deep girth, rounded flanks, hocks well under, straight forelegs. I looked in her eyes, and stroked her head. You can tell a lot about a horse from its glance, whether it is bold or furtive, intelligent or dull, fiery or steady. This one was intelligent, and if you think it is possible for a horse to have an amused look, this one had it. But when I made to roll back her lips to see her teeth, the Wachtmeister stopped me.

"No, sir," he said, with a smile, an expression so rare on his face that it was almost startling, "we never look a gift horse in the mouth. This is your own horse, young baron. Her name is Kíslang. It means 'little flame' in Hungarian."

I gaped at him; I gaped at the horse; I could barely speak. "My father has given me a horse?"

His smile faded somewhat and he said, "No, not your father, young baron, but another."

"Who?"

"One who does not wish to be named. But it is an honorable gift; you have my assurance on that, and your father does not object. Let us put a saddle on her and see if she will go forward when you tell her."

Of course it was a gift from Wolanska—who else could it have been?

The old baron had barely begun to describe that first ride, when the window flashed white with a strike of lighting, thunder rolled, and sheets of rain began to beat against roof and panes.

"Ah, I have been expecting this," said von Pannau. "My knees are an infallible harbinger of the downpour."

The bells of St. Thomas, sounding the hour, could barely be heard through the sound of wind and falling water. Rudi put down his pen, exclaiming, "Good Lord! Can it be six o'clock already?" He rose, and said, "Herr Baron, I fear I must leave you precipitously and unceremoniously. I am due at the Rossmarkt this moment."

"Are you? Well, you will never get a cab in this drench. Stay a while and I will have one of my people take you over in my carriage."

But Rudi, desperate to avoid the enormity of arriving at a liberal meeting in a nobleman's crested coach, made so strenuous an objection to this proposal that the old baron did not insist more than courtesy demanded, and Rudi departed into the watery evening with a portfolio of foreign newspapers clutched under his arm. As foretold, no cabs were on offer, and so he reached the great rectangular square of the Rossmarkt entirely waterlogged but filled with the kind of virtue attendant on doing something stupid in service of a good cause.

Five

The Red Goose, or *U Červený Husa* as it was known to
its denizens, was a Czech nationalist tavern at the southern
end of the Rossmarkt, occupying a four story brick structure
marked with the eponymous fowl on a hanging sign. At the
Red Goose, the carters and other workmen drank at long
trestle tables in the basement, the shopkeepers and clerks
used the bar-room on the ground floor, and the more refined
patrons, and ladies, of course, used the upper floor, which
was furnished with round tables and chairs. Over the bar
hung a fanciful portrait of Libussa, the Wise Woman of the
Czechs, summoning Přemysl from his plow to found the dy-
nasty that bore his name. Another painting supposedly
showed Jan Hus in flames, but it had become so blackened by
the soot of ages that this identification was mainly tradition.
This top floor also boasted four private rooms, used for the
various amusements that required privacy.

Rudi's meeting was being held in one of these, a
small, windowless chamber, smelling of beer and smoke, with
faint ghosts of perfume lingering. It was furnished with a
round table, miscellaneous chairs, a bad painting of a buxom
woman in her bath, and a wide, worn, baize-covered sofa
used in those various amusements. Novotny was the only
one of the group who would sit on it, and he was sitting on it
now as Rudi entered and flung off his dripping coat and hat.

"See, Jasny," cried Novotny, " I told you a little rain
would not defeat our Moritz. You owe me a stein."

Jasny was the fourth member of their little group,
besides Novotny, Liebig and Rudi himself. He was a schoolteacher, a passionate Czech nationalist, the possessor of a
great mass of bright red hair, like a bed of copper wire, and a
fierce military mustache of the same shade. He wore small,

rectangular spectacles that always seemed to dart fire from the reflections of their surround.

"But late, as usual," replied Jasny. "What have you got in that portfolio Moritz?"

"I have treasures from abroad. But first, for the love of God, shout down to the girl to bring me a brandy and a couple of dry towels!"

"And my beer," said Novotny.

Liebig opened the door, admitting the noise of the upper bar room, and shouted out an order. Upon returning, he opened the damp portfolio. "What is this!" he cried. "Foreign papers! From Paris? My God, from *London!* Man, where did you get these?"

Before Rudi could form an answer, Jasny and the other two descended upon the papers like ravens upon a battlefield, grabbing each a sheaf of newsprint and falling into chairs (Novotny onto the horrible couch) to read, to exclaim, to comment on the progress of politics outside the Chinese wall that isolated the liberals of the Empire from what was happening now across Europe. Rudi drank his brandy, rubbed himself dry with the beer-fragranced towels, and fondly watched his comrades devour the elixir of news.

A considerable time passed in this manner; beer and brandy flowed, pages rustled, passages were read aloud. Then Liebig folded his paper neatly and rapped on the table.

"Friends, we can read to our hearts' content later. Now we must take up the issue of the petition. It is time we made some news instead of reading about it. Moritz, the floor is yours."

The petition! Some weeks previously, encouraged by the revolution in France and the happenings in Vienna, the liberals of Prague had organized the first open political meeting in nearly two centuries. It had been held at Wencelaus Hall, across the square from where the four friends now sat, and the attendees, Czech and German alike, had agreed that a petition must be drafted proposing remedies for the ancient ills of the Bohemian nation, written in both Czech and German, of course, and sent to the Emperor. A draft had been produced amid great contention and found unsatisfactory—turgid, over-legalistic, and far too timorous. The people involved, now calling themselves the Wenceslaus Committee, had looked around for a skilled writer of impeccable liberal credentials, literate in both tongues, to turn the document into a clarion. Rudi Moritz had been duly impressed into the service of his nation, and had labored all week on the thing.

Now he read out the great demands, more boldly stated: the restoration of Bohemian crown lands to full self-government; a freely elected diet to constitute such a government; the abolition of serfdom; full equality of the Czech and German languages in schools and administration; freedom of the press and assembly; a national guard to protect the peoples' liberty and property. Liebig's eyes were shining. When the last words were out he applauded, as at a show. Novotny applauded too, four short, spaced, ironic claps.

"Well, Moritz," he said, "a great improvement on the previous pusillanimous screed. This is revolution indeed. In future ages painters will treat this scene—the first reading of the Bohemian petition of rights, although they will make me handsomer and Liebig larger, one hopes. I will copy out your closing, if I may. I have an illegal poster in mind that it will suit." He paused. "This business about languages, though. Are we really to be concerned with the squabbles of school-teachers and clerks?"

"Nonsense!" cried Jasny. "That is a vital point for the Czechs. The Czech political clubs won't sign on to any petition that does not address the language issue."

"Oh, Jasny, the Czechs! The Czechs will be with you in anything that weakens the empire, and beyond that not at all." Novotny picked up the petition and gestured at Rudi with it. "My dear Moritz, pray do not mistake me. This is a wonderful document, and it will be cheered to the echo at the next meeting, I have no doubt. And if we were all Russians or even Spaniards I would be first among those cheering. For nations like that, the bourgeois revolution is a necessary stage, I agree, and the situation in England and America confirms it. But not here. Once the iron grip of the aristocracy is released, the whole trumpery show of empire will collapse. And then what? On what basis will Germans and Czechs live together, not to mention Hungarians and Ruthenians and Poles? There has to be a completely new way of organizing society, a nineteenth century way that attends to the actual conditions of modern life. And this," again indicating the manuscript, "this is not it."

"Then what *is* it, Novotny?" said Liebig with some heat. "Fourier's mad schemes? Must we all live in phalansteries and have everything in common?"

"I don't know, to be frank. But I will tell you something. The plague of the bourgeoisie is ignorance, willful ignorance. You walk every day in a narrow path through our city of Prague, from your comfortable home to your comfortable office, never deviating, never seeing anything that does not offend your sense of your own decency and good faith. We must take a journey to Karlin, one time, to visit with the workers. It will be good for your soul."

"But the poor you have always with you," said Liebig. "Some will always get farther in the race of life than others."

"Ah, thank you for that penetrating, and may I say *Jewish,* observation, dear Liebig. The poor you have always with you, indeed. But it not a question of rich and poor. It has to do with the nature of property, with capital itself. Have you met Bakunin yet?"

"That Russian at the Knight? I did not; but what of him?"

"He has some interesting ideas about property. We should have a talk with him. In any case, whatever happens with this petition, it is clear to me that the general situation with respect to industry and the workers cannot go on indefinitely. Everyone knows slavery in America cannot go on, and everyone knew that the old church in Hus's day could not go on as it had before. Jan Hus tried to reform it and the Church burned him alive for his pains. There are tides in history, my friends, and they cannot be resisted, only channeled by those who understand the true methods of history. And there is this."

He took a thin pamphlet from inside his coat and laid it on the sideboard. Rudi picked it up. It was printed on cheap paper and smelled unpleasantly of sweat and tobacco.

"This is your Cologne editor, is it?" asked Rudi, looking at the title page. "*The Communist Manifesto.* Well, certainly bold enough. And who is this Engels?"

"A German living in England. A capitalist, of all things! He owns a cotton mill. He's written a study of English workers. Those who admire the English system as a shining tower of liberalism should read it. It turns out that the shining tower is built upon a cesspit of exploitation and cruelty. I could let you borrow my copy."

"Oh God, not communism again!" said Liebig. "If you please, Novotny, perhaps we should have our little inconsiderable revolution first, before we think of turning society upside down."

"The workers may not want to stop at your little revolution, my dear. In fact, I can virtually assure you of the opposite."

"Then you can lead the workers yourself," said Rudi, "and perhaps you might start by becoming one of them. Seek employment! In the meantime, this draft it what is going to the committee."

"Then let it!" said Novotny. "Metternich will use it in the jakes, I dare say, and then we will be back to where we began—precisely nowhere."

The two men stared at each other angrily, until Liebig broke the tension by saying quietly, "I have told you--Metternich will not last the week."

"Yes, your wishful thinking," said Jasny. "The Army will shoot them down. It will be another '44."

"It will not," Liebig insisted. "Vienna is full of angry workers. The students are united in their demands. The Burger Guard—fourteen thousand men, armed indifferently but still armed—will act for once as a true national guard, and the Army will not fight them in the alleys of Vienna. And without the support of bourgeoisie the government has no money. You will see. I say again, he cannot last a week. Less, I should say!"

"I believe him," said Novotny. "By God, this is the hour we have waited for. We should get out a special edition of *The Torch*, just two pages will do it, and print a thousand, no, five thousand copies and scatter them through every inn and tavern in Prague. I will have Jiskra write the leader, which will be a brilliant appreciation of the political situation in Vienna. Jasny, you will do a piece on the effect of these events on the nationalities. You can crib from Moritz's petition for noble language. Liebig must write on the constitutional issues—how will we govern when the monster has fled. Copy by noon tomorrow at the Knight—we can have it printed and distributed by Tuesday morning."

"And what will be my role, dear Novotny?" Rudi asked. As always, he found himself fascinated by his friend's mercurial temper—one moment cynical—oh, woe, nothing will ever change—and the next full of revolutionary fervor.

He was musing on what it must be like within the mind of such a fellow, when the fellow answered, "Oh, you have done enough already, your petition will be hailed, you will be acclaimed as the liberal titan you are. Meanwhile, you can pay for the printing with your aristocrat's gold." He raised his glass. "Down with the Prince and oppression!"

The friends all echoed this sentiment and then Jasny said, "We are out of beer. Are we finished? Then let us then go out to the tavern for more!"

The friends left the private room and descended to the upper floor, which they found crowded, with the barmaids rushing by, their brows damp with sweat, in each red fist four frothing steins.

"It seems there is nowhere to sit," said Rudi. "Perhaps we had better go …."

"Nonsense," said Novotny, "Look, there lurks Bakunin with an empty chair at his table. Sit you down, and I will find some other chairs."

It was indeed the big Russian sitting with the cold-eyed young man that Rudi and Liebig had observed entering the Knight. Rudi drank deeply of the Red Goose's famous beer, and quickly perused *The Communist Manifesto*. Well, the man could write! But determining whether it was a real program or a radical fever dream needed more attention than he had at the moment, for he thought it more interesting to study the two actual radicals before him. As to the younger, whom he called in his mind the Revolutionary, no particular feature of his face was distinguished, but taken together they created a curious effect, both animal and noble by turns. It was like looking at a wolf: if captive, one admired its fierce beauty, but it made a different impression when it chased one through the snows, slathering for blood. An unpleasant face in all, full of self-regard—that beard a little too neatly trimmed—and the large, bright hazel eyes full of a superiority of the sort that turns easily to contempt. Yet the man had an attractive energy, and it was easy to imagine him doing desperate deeds, grabbing a falling banner and leaping defiantly upon a barricade to wave it in the face of Reaction. Rudi thought that the man had spent a good deal of time imagining such an exploit himself.

Bakunin seemed made of weightier stuff than his comrade, Rudi thought, and watched as the man downed a tumbler of brandy and raised his glass in the air, calling out for another. His costume was in poor repair, as if he had been on the road for some time, but he carried himself like a lord. He probably *was* a lord, Rudi thought: you only saw that combination of vaunting confidence and infantile self-indulgence in the scions of the Tsarist aristocracy. Bakunin reached out and grabbed a brandy from the tray of a passing barmaid, took a drink from it, smacked his fleshy lips, withdrew a cigar from his coat, lit it from the lamp on the table, blew a plume of smoke, and turned his gaze on Rudi.

"I don't know you, sir," he said in accented German, "but I detect you are no Slav. Allow me to introduce myself. I am Mikhail Alexandrovitch Bakunin. And may I also present . . ."

"No, you may not!" said the Revolutionary in a low grating tone.

"Oh, well, he prefers to be known simply as Bors. We are lately from Dresden, where the agents of our gracious majesty, Nicholas the Hangman, were close on our trail: this fills him with fear, but not me."

Rudi introduced himself.

"So, Moritz," said Bakunin, "what brings you to this den of Slavism? Perhaps *you* are a policeman?"

"The police of our country are often stupid," said Rudi, grinning, "but not so stupid as to try to infiltrate the pan-Slavic movement with someone who looks like me and can barely speak Czech. It is far more likely that Bors, here, is the spy. He is the image of someone bent on destroying the empire, and would be welcome in any cabal."

Bakunin laughed, but Bors did not, saying. "Yes, it is my curse. If I only looked like you, sir, I could cut the throats of half the kings in Europe and walk away whistling."

"Bors is working up to royal throat slicing," said Bakunin. "In Dresden recently, he . . . "

"Damn you, can you not learn to keep your mouth shut!"

They looked at Bors, whose face had gone pale, with red blotches showing on his cheeks.

Bakunin smiled and patted Bors on the shoulder. "Truly, Bors, we are perfectly safe here."

"We are *never* perfectly safe. It is very well for you to play the cavalier, because if you are taken, you will lie at ease in a comfortable suite in the Petropavlosk, where your family will provide as many comforts as you desire, while at best I will be at Irkutsk, dragging logs through the mud. At worst, against a wall."

But Bakunin continued to smile, a little foolishly, Rudi thought, and drank again from his glass. "We will not be taken, my friend, not in Prague, and not now."

"Why do you say that?" Rudi asked.

"Because Vienna is at the point of explosion, as you must know, and Prague will take the spark. I can feel it in the streets, and Bors, who is by way of being a professional at this, agrees. This is why we have come here, you see."

"You are not connected with the pan-Slavic conference?"

"Indeed. I am. An academic fellow of my acquaintance offered me lodging and keep, if I would attend, as the representative of All the Russias. I believe I am large enough to suit the role. Also, we can never tell what will be the spark that sets the whole affair off. It might well be pan-Slavism. The main thing is to find the lever that will work against the rotten stone of society. It matters not which crack you shove your handspike into—the thing is to bring down the wall."

"To what end, sir?" asked Rudi. He had occasionally heard such talk from Novotny, but he suspected that for Novotny it was all fancy, and the desire to show how shockingly modern he was. This great bear seemed to be serious in another way. But perhaps it was a difficulty with the language. Or that he was a Russian. And who could understand Russians?

Bors, who might or might not be Russian, returned with a black bottle and sat, looking pale and gloomy. He seemed to be matching drams with Bakunin, which could not have been a feasible venture—the man was three times his size.

"To what end?" said Bakunin. "Why nothing less than the creation of a just society. Why else do we live, for what else do we struggle?"

"Then I detect you are a socialist, like Fourier, or Marx."

"Not at all like Fourier, and only a little like Marx. You've read Marx, I take it?"

"Only his *Communist Manifesto.*" Rudi tapped his bosom. "In fact, I have it right here. Perhaps it is the only copy in Prague."

"Besides mine. What did you think of it?"

"I found it thrilling—the vigor of his language, his passion—but also dismaying. The warfare of the classes: well, I mean to say—perhaps he goes too far."

"No, not at all," replied Bakunin with force. "He does not go far *enough*! You must always remember that Marx is a revolutionary philosopher and not a revolutionist. This is an important distinction! The revolution will be made by people like Bors here, and myself, although I am a philosopher as well. Bors does not hold our Marx in highest regard."

"He is a petty bourgeois scribbler," said Bors, "who knows nothing of how revolutions are made. The whole point of revolutionary activity is to provoke the authorities into greater oppressions, which create more revolutionaries, and to disarm those who pretend that amelioration is the goal, for their own selfish ends. It is only when everyone feels the oppression in its fullness—*everyone*—that everyone will join the revolution."

"That is a tactical quibble, Bors. Herr Marx proposes that the state, under the control of the proletariat, expropriates all property from the expropriating classes and the church. The state now administers this property in the interests of the proletariat. This is paradise, yes? But let us observe history another way. In France, as we have seen, the bourgeoisie contested with church and aristocracy in 'eighty-nine and triumphed. They could vote. They could read newspapers. And what transpired then?"

Rudi answered, "They descended into terror and tyranny."

"Correct! Whatever class takes control of the state becomes the *ruling* class, and the ruling class always acts to preserve its prerogatives. It is an inevitability determined by the immutable laws of history. No, my friend, the aim of the true revolutionary can only be the *destruction* of the state and all its dreadful appurtenances: laws, police, armies, prisons and the rest. Then it will be relatively simple to abolish property and the tyranny of families, and for the first time man will be able to breathe free in a world without compulsion."

"But . . . that's impossible!" cried Rudi. "You would have chaos, the war of all against all. In a generation or so the few people who survived would be dressed in rags and planting potatoes with sharpened sticks."

Bakunin released a theatrical sigh. "Yes, the chaos argument. I could dismiss it in an instant, were I not to drunk too recall the main points. You must take it on your faith in my genius that when property is abolished, men will live in harmony, not conflict."

Bors now stood abruptly and showed his watch to Bakunin. "We must leave. Our meeting with . . ." Here he looked around in a dramatic show of suspicion.

"Ah, yes, yes," Bakunin sighed as he rose to his remarkable height and smiled down at Rudi. "Well, sir, an amusing conversation, but we revolutionaries never have a moment to ourselves. Yet another meeting! It appears that such is the chief defect of anarchism. We cannot give orders in anarchism, oh no. We must convince, and this requires innumerable meetings. Farewell, then: perhaps we will meet, on the barricades by preference, but if not, then at some meeting or other." The great head swiveled sharply. "My soul, but that is a remarkable-looking woman!"

Bors stared too, but in what seemed to Rudi a strange way, like a man who sees his wife walk into a unsavory tavern. As the pair departed, they brushed past a party that was just entering, a party full of laughter and high spirits, a party that included the remarkable woman. At the sight of her, Novotny stood up and called out, "Sisi!"

The woman turned and smiled at Novotny, but this smile was like a charge of grapeshot, it struck down those on the edges of the target, one of whom who was Rudi Moritz.

Six

Her name was Svetlana Zbyhneva Vasová, called Sisi, according to Novotny, who apparently knew her well. He told Rudi that she earned a fragile living as a singer, but was also, of all things, a writer, and a reasonably famous one in Czech literary circles. Rudi had never heard of her. He had never met a woman who wrote for publication. Nor had he seen a woman who was not a prostitute come laughing like that into a tavern with a group of men.

She swept off her bonnet and he saw a glossy pile of black hair, a strong angular face with heavy brows that nearly touched over the blade-thin nose. High Slavic cheekbones. And that smile. She sat at another table with her companions. He would have had to crane his neck to stare at her, so he forbore and addressed himself to the remains of Bakunin's bottle. He was terribly drunk, flushed, dizzy. Novotny leaned over the woman, placing his hand familiarly on the back of her chair. He must have said something amusing because a roar of laughter went up from the company. The woman threw her head back and laughed like a man, a hearty guffaw rather than a screech or a polite titter. The laugh only added to Rudi's fascination.

Now Novotny was talking into her ear. She was nodding. Then she shifted in her seat and stared boldly into Rudi's face; Novotny continued to talk, grinning slyly. Rudi met her eyes, which were large and green. The woman laughed again. Could they be talking about him? He turned away and took another drink. He had not been this drunk since his days as an undergraduate, when he had first discovered oblivion and disgrace and crapulous regret, the secret trivium of the Charles University.

More loud steps on the stairs, more people pressed in, although it seemed the room could hardly hold them. The newcomers had brought instruments, a concertina, a fiddle, a flute. Shouts rang out: "Sisi, Sisi, sing for us!" She mounted a table, laughing like a man. Music arose, unsteady at first and then lilting into a familiar folk tune, *Teče voda*, flowing waters. She sang, others joined in: the rippling brook, the blue-eyed darling at her window and the rest, and Rudi added his voice, surprised that he was singing aloud in a tavern, but enjoying it. He was a Bohemian among his fellow countrymen, united in song across the barriers of language, as they would be united in freedom.

Vasová was looking right at him as she sang, or so it seemed. She sang several other tunes of the same traditional sort and then spoke to the musicians. They struck up the familiar strains of *Kdož jste Boží bojovníc*-- warriors who for God are fighting--the old Hussite battle hymn, which in recent years had become almost the Bohemian national anthem, at least among Czechs. Everyone stood, doffed their hats and joined in lustily, after which came waves of cheers and applause, along with some cries of "out with the *skopčáky*!" Rudi resumed his chair, and considered leaving, a thought instantly extinguished when Sisi Vasová sat down next to him, in the chair recently occupied by the Russian anarchist.

She said, leaning close, "You are Moritz. I have heard about you for years from Novotny, and now we meet."

Perfume enveloped him, almost masking the beery, smoky stink of the tavern. Attar of roses, of good quality; it was like stepping into a warm summer garden. His wife, Berthe, did not wear scent, she smelled only of her soap, vaguely lilac, and of her own skin, which bore a toasty odor Rudi had known nearly all his life, and which had as a result faded from his sensory consciousness, like the odor of himself. He thought this, wondered why he was making comparisons, and resolved to stop it.

Pulling slightly away, but not enough to imply a rejection of her attention, he said, "You have the advantage of me then, Madame. Having seen you, I am astounded that your fame has not reached me, but such is the case. And I trust what you have heard of me pleases you?"

"Oh, indeed yes! It is from Paul that I have heard. He and I are old friends. He talks of you often and with great affection. Furthermore, he admires you; and if you know Novotny, you know he does not admire many. He admires your writing especially; I mean the political articles, the precision of expression, the inspired language. He thinks your words could move the world could you only nerve yourself to become truly revolutionary."

"Only that? Well, I must endeavor to expand my bump of bloodthirstiness, which I fear is but an exiguous promontory."

"Still, you have written the draft of our petition."

"You have read it?"

"Not I. But Paul said in my ear the peroration. I trembled."

"Did you indeed? I am flattered, Madame."

"Oh, don't call me madame, I beg you! I am no bourgeois. Everyone calls me Sisi, since I was a young girl, and you must do the same."

Her German was accented, grammatically correct but unidiomatic, clearly not her cradle tongue. It was not *quite* the accent of a Czech chambermaid. This thought embarrassed him.

"Sisi, then. And do you have an interest in politics?"

"Not so much, or only what everyone thinks, which is that the Czechs are oppressed by the Germans and must struggle for the freedom due every nation. People say, Oh, Sisi, you must lend your pen to our cause, but I am no Havlíček. I am just a poor singer and a country girl telling stories."

"Like those of the Grimms?"

"Not in the least like. The Grimms are important scholars, while I have no education at all. A peasant girl am I, and that's the plain truth. Were I not, we would not be sitting here together conversing in my bad German, me with my head uncovered in a tavern and showing my teeth whenever I laugh."

"Your teeth are fine and white. Pearly. They do not offend me in the least. But I will swear you are no peasant."

"No? Then pray tell me what I am." Without a gap, she had switched from German to Czech, and it seemed to him that her eyes grew brighter and her face even more animated.

"In a word, you are a bohemian."

"Of course I am a Bohemian. I was born in Dobrany, near Plzen, and reared in that town. I've been for some time in Vienna and now I've come to live in Prague. What else could I be?"

"No, you mistake me. Don't you know that when the inhabitants of London or Paris wish to indicate a free spirit, an artist, an unconventional type, a person of uncertain morals even, they use the word 'bohemian?'"

"Do they? What an odd choice! Surely nothing is less like a free spirit than a Bohemian peasant."

"I believe they confused us with the Gypsies."

"I dare say. But no one could confuse you with a gypsy, Moritz. You are bourgeois German from your pomaded hair to the tips of your polished boots."

"Things are not always as they appear."

"Really. If that is meant to be a mysterious comment, you have me, sir. I love a mystery. Say that you were found by the wayside as a babe, wrapped in a curiously worked tapestry, with an amulet about your neck inscribed with runes that none, not even the wisest in the land, could interpret."

"Oh, not nearly as gothic as all that, dear lady," replied Rudi, laughing. "You have pinned me to the board—I am as ordinary a bourgeois as you could find in Prague. My father is a banker! Yes, you roll your eyes to heaven—what could be more boring! Yet, I have recently heard a tale that might suit your fancy. "

Then he told her the story of Baron von Pannau. To his delight, she cast an admiring gaze on him throughout, and when he had closed, she remarked, "Wonderful, sir! Of course, the tale of the noble youth brought up by simple people is a commonplace in peasant stories; but the aristocrats do not tell them, as a rule. And the land without music! Wonderfully mythic! Encountering such a fable told as truth in real life, why it is like finding a magical ring in a fish, even without the fish talking. Tell me, what is he like, this prodigy of the last age?."

"Surprisingly well. He is somewhat frail, of course, and must be carried to meals. But he says he has gained strength since I began coming to him. He jested that he was sucking in my youthful energy . . ."

"Yes, like a vampire. Better and better! The story forms itself in my mind already. And that girl in the coach— he must meet with her again, of course and fight duels. People love stories of the former epoch; they dote upon the clothes, the balls, the luxuries, the courtly folderol. Every little shopkeeper's wife imagines herself a marquise with a secret lover. Shall he die of love, do you think?"

"My baron? Well, he did not, in fact, and I daresay he had any number of opportunities. What a very wicked world was the *ancien regime*, as he tells it! Not to mention the rank oppression that supported all the wonderful balls. Well, we mean to get rid of it once and for all, don't we?"

"The balls? Or the oppression? Or both at once? I suppose I would suffer under a little oppression could I have a few balls. Or does your system not allow that?"

"I shall insist on at least one, let oppression do its worst! Are you very fond of balls?"

"I expect I should be, if ever I were asked to one. Oh, student balls and artist's balls, but never a great one, in a real ballroom with an orchestra. I did peek at one such when I was very young and in service at Plzen. It looked marvelous, and I assure you I would have oppressed my own mother down to the ground, and refused my father the vote forever, could I have whirled around that polished floor in the arms of a dashing young captain of hussars. By the way, this is why you liberals will fail, for you can never abolish oppression. For why? Because what chiefly drives the great mass of mankind is power over other men, and what proves the case is that the lowliest, who commands no other man, still has the command of woman, and exercises it the more he is crushed by his betters. But I see you find me tedious now . . ."

"What! No, not at all. Very interesting I am sure, and in a moment I hope to demolish your argument root and branch. But do you know that feeling, when someone is staring hard at one's back and one receives from who knows what magnetic influences a prickle down one's spine? I felt just such a prickle while you were talking and looked around and there he was, just over my right shoulder, that enormous fellow. He's been looking daggers at me, I imagine for some time."

She looked past his shoulder, raised her eyebrows to heaven, rolled her eyes, and laughed. "Oh, that is only Novak. Pay no attention to him, I beg you. In half an hour he will be insensible."

"Do you know this person?"

"For years. He works at the flour depot. When we were younger, we were lovers, but now he has a wife and four, and he would still like to tip me over. In the meantime, he does not approve of me talking to German gentlemen. He is a good fellow when he is not too drunk. As a rule I despise drunken men. I believe you are drunk at this moment, Moritz. I call you Moritz, although properly I should address you as Herr Moritz. Or would 'Rudi' be offensive?"

"Oh, never in life! Please feel free: we shall be Rudi and Sisi. I'm am sure we will be great friends." He leaned toward her as he said this, a nearly involuntary movement in his present state of intoxication; for a moment he bathed once more in her cloud of rose essence.

"Will we really? I have said I was in service as a child. My mother was a cook in a great house, the Hildebrands at Plzen, and I was brought along as a slavey. One gets a different view of our fine German bourgeois if one is so placed, I assure you. They *all* want to be one's friend: on the back stairs, in the butler's pantry, in one's wretched little garret. But I see you are gripping your gold-headed cane so tightly your knuckles have gone white. Can you be contemplating a blow? No, I see you are repulsed by my innuendo. You have fine eyes, and they reveal all when you are stung. You must forgive me, Moritz. When I am in wine and speaking my native tongue my heart and its wounds are too exposed for polite company."

"It is not a gold-headed cane," said Rudi, inanely. "It is only gilt brass. My father has a real gold-headed cane. But I am not, not that sort of man. Unless you think that there can be no friendship between a man and a woman, except the sort to which you advise."

"You mean 'advert.' Your Czech is terrible. It does me good to hear it. So--you swear you will be different from the others. *They all say that—at first.*" This line was delivered in German, which she henceforth spoke. "But I tell you what, Moritz: I like you and believe you have a good heart, although you are fool to think that such will suffice to make friendship between a Böhmer peasant girl and a bourgeois. You are also fool to imagine that you can create free Bohemia with a piece of paper, but that is food for another discussion, which we may have another time. However, as now it stands, I am an artist and it is permissible for artists to have rich patrons. Tell me, do you know Madame von Silber?"

The band had taken up some kind of wild folk dance, with many a whoop, and the company was keeping rough time by stamping their feet and pounding their steins on the board. Rudi had to lean toward her and ask her to repeat her question. Once more, that cloud of roses. "We have not been introduced," he said. "I know the name, of course. Do *you* know her?"

"Yes, well may you wonder why the keeper of an elegant salon in Prague should know *me*. In fact, I am a pet of hers, a bit of outré decoration. There is a dwarf who comes too, quite a learned man, but not there for his learning. La Silber collects oddities and I am one—a woman who writes for publication, and beds whomever she wishes, but does not take money for it. You must come as my guest, and tell your strange story for the amusement of high bourgeois with liberal pretensions."

At that moment a huge figure loomed over them. It swayed, and from it came a dense odor of schnapps. A hand whitened by flour fell heavily on Sisi's shoulder. Rudi saw that it was Novak, the former and would-be lover.

"I want to go now. Get up!" he said, and then repeated the demand, his voice sulky and the words slurred.

"Oh, Novak, do sit down," said Sisi. "I am just finishing my conversation with this gentleman."

"The conversation is over," said Novak, not releasing his grip.

Rudi surprised himself by saying, in a voice he barely recognized as his own,

"The conversation is over when the lady says it is, fellow. And take your hands off her!"

Novak stepped back, swaying slightly. He clenched his enormous fists and raised them. "I'll breaking your fucking *skopčak* head," he declared, and cocked back his right. Rudi shot to his feet and brought up his own hands into a protective stance, quite forgetting that he had his cane gripped in the right one. The heavy metal knob collided with the point of Novak's jaw with a sound like splitting firewood, a report easily lost beneath the pounding music. The workman's eyes rolled up, blood welled and dripped down his loose neck cloth, his legs gave way and he fell to the floor. There was a stir among his companions, all rough-looking Czechs. Several of them rose to their feet.

Rudi stood dumbfounded, quite incapable of thinking what to do next. He had never knocked a man flat in a tavern before. While he was lost in this thought, he felt his arm gripped, his hat plopped onto his head, and heard a voice hissing in his ear, "Out! Out! We must leave this instant!"

Then a long stumble down the stairs, racketing from side to side in the narrow stairwell, and at last the welcome damp of the night. The rain had stopped for the moment, replaced by a windless mist flavored with coal smoke and the faint yeasty odor of the flour depot, which on still, wet nights like this one overhung the entire southwest side of the Old Town.

She was standing close to him, still holding his sleeve. She had thrown her shawl up over her head, and now she really did look like a peasant woman; but her eyes were lit with an entirely urban sensibility.

"Well, that was nicely done," she said, catching her breath. "You are a man of unexpected parts, Moritz, I swear it! Poor Novak! Well, he deserved the comeuppance, the lout!   But you know, we can't have any accursed *skopčák* knocking down good *Česki* boys in the Red Goose, which was why I dragged you out of it. You were standing there like a man who has just stepped in a cow pie, and wonders what to do with the mess."

"I was considering whether to clear the whole room with my stick-fighting skill; but forbore out of respect for you, dear lady."

She bowed, "And it is appreciated, sir. I believe I saw enough heads broken in Plzen to last me my time. And now, you will put me in a cab . . ."

"I will accompany you home, of course."

"Put me in a cab, I say, which will take me to my dwelling place, not quite a garret and not quite on top of the new railway station.   It is clean, warm, and a tissue on the good side of respectability, but it is not a place I would care to show someone like you. Meanwhile another cab will take you to your comfortable home, with your piano and the smell of roast chicken. No, not another word!"

Here she pressed herself to him and placed a hand over his mouth. They held that position for a moment. He thought he could actually hear the beating of his heart.

There came the clatter of shod hooves on cobbles: a cab was passing on the St. Heinrikegasse. She grinned at him, pulled away, stuck two fingers in her mouth and produced a piercingly loud whistle. It echoed sharply off the buildings, and the cab, well-beckoned, swung into a turn. Rudi had never seen a woman do that before and he let out a bark of a laugh.

She laughed too, and said, "Yes, I too have skills not obvious to the casual glance, nor expected in a female. Now you may hand me up, and give me the money for my fare too, and if you come to Mme. von Silber's some Thursday evening I may see you there."

They approached the cab. He handed her up. All he could think about was the old baron and his coach with the courtesan in it on the Moldau bridge in the year 1786. The air was damp enough but that was not what produced the shiver that shook his body as he watched the red lantern of the cab recede.

How strange, he thought, a day comes and I discover I am not the person I thought I was the day before. In all my years of thinking about revolution, it has never occurred to me that I myself might be revolutionized, that I would become the sort of man who drinks himself silly in Czech taverns, and converses with men who propose assassination and the overthrow of religion and property, and—what was the word?—"flirted" was not quite right, but anyhow engaged in the most intense way with a . . . I can't even think of the proper word for her, but anyway, a woman unlike any I've ever met, no boundaries at all, doesn't care what she says— and, God help me, I have actually fought over such a creature and knocked a man down with my stick!

The mist now thickened again into rain. Rudi stirred himself and began walking up the Rossmarkt in search of a cab. The few that appeared were either full or too far away to hail, even could he whistle like Sisi Vasová. Therefore he walked home in a growing downpour that soaked through his boots and the shoulders of his coat.

Squelchingly, he entered his home and as he did all energy deserted him. After Hilda had taken his coat, hat and stick, he sat on the bench in the hall and dripped and gasped like a dog splashed by a passing wagon. Gregor arrived a moment later with towels, robe and slippers. His boots were pulled off and he was dried and sent up to bed. He took

Gregor's candle, but refused   the man's offers of help un-
dressing, a warming pan, and so on, for he wished to be
without servants upstairs.

Because, as he had expected, Berte was up and waiting in their dressing room-study, in her gown and cap,
wrapped in a cashmere and curled in an arm-chair with her
feet tucked under, like a small girl waiting to be read a story.

"You are late home," she observed as he entered. He
leaned to kiss her cheek.

"And smelling of the tavern," she added. "Well, after
such a long time I suppose the revolution is a done thing."

"All but the shouting, my dear."

"And did your friends like your petition?"

"Indeed they did, but much tedious work remains for
your husband.   Still it was a good start and we drank the
health of the infant with more glasses than I am used to taking. You see a weary, tipsy fellow who could not get a cab in
this rain and is chilled through.   Perhaps we should both
make our way to bed."

"Yes, we could. And I could resolve myself to be one
of those wives who live like the stuffed birds inside glass jars.
Is that indeed what you desire?"

"Why, whatever do you mean?" he said, looking into
her face, observing the narrowed eye, the flared nostril, the
lower lip curled under and trembling.

"I mean," she continued in a strained tone, "that
while I may have only the education that the sisters thought
adequate for a girl, I am not a fool. I suppose you must do
what men do, but I had hoped you might have the courtesy
of discretion, and the decency not to disguise it behind a
show of civic virtue."

"My dear, in all honesty, I cannot comprehend your
meaning."

"My meaning is: you reek of . . . of some woman's
scent!"

Rudi bent his head and sniffed at himself. "By God,
I do reek! The roses of perdition. It was my bluestocking.

Must you hear this now, while I am fainting from exhaustion, or can it wait until the morning?"

"This instant, if you please," she said, her face looking more like that of her father than Rudi would have believed possible. "What bluestocking?" she asked, and he told her, without, however, describing the effect on him of Sisi Vasová's smile, voice and manner. Berthe seemed satisfied with this, to his somewhat shameful relief, and they went off to bed reconciled.

Seven

The following day being Sunday, the family attended church, the church bells more irritating than usual to Rudi, for his head ached from the dissipation of the previous night and the bells kept ringing in that head even when they had stopped ringing for the town. The family proceeded down St. Jakobusgasse, the parents walking ahead, arm in arm, followed by plump Hana the nursemaid with the two children, Fritz, aged seven, in a little soldier's outfit and Reni, five, upholstered like a tiny chair in a red velvet coat adorned with little ermine tails. Following at decent interval came the servants, except for Cook, who had to prepare the Sunday dinner and had for that reason fulfilled her religious obligation the previous evening. Missing also was her new scullion, who was from some distant precinct of Litomerice and who was, as far as anyone knew, a mere heathen.

They were joined by other similar parades, respectable Prague burghers with their households. Rudi nodded politely to those he knew and received nods in return. He nodded also to the clumps of working families in rusty black Sunday best, from whom he received only an occasional nod in return, and a good number of startled looks and averted eyes. Would this awful class business change after the revolution? He devoutly wished it.

St. Jacobus, like many of Prague's churches, was a monument to the Counter-Reformation, graced with an interior that writhed with cherubim and statues of saints, exalted or in the process of martyrdom, but with wonderful draperies either way, every inch of wall space painted with Biblical accounts (or fairy tales, as Rudi thought them) and floating above all, the corpus on the great crucifix, doleful, bone-pale, spouting bright rivulets of scarlet from His wounds.

After church they had to pass through the usual cluster of beggars. Rudi sent Gregor ahead to clear a path, and he did so as gently as he could. Rudi deplored the necessity for this, but some of the sturdier beggars would thrust themselves forward in the most frightening manner, showing their filth, rags and sores, if any, and disturbing the children.

Where was Berthe? He stopped and looked around him. She *would* drift off after church to speak to her friends, although he often pressed upon her that it was essential to keep the whole family together, because of the beggars. Rudi resented beggary entirely, it made his blood boil, so unnecessary in a well-ordered state, and of course there would be no beggars at all after the revolution. How this would be arranged was still obscure in his mind. These people here, his neighbors and fellow bourgeois, having just heard a homily on the virtues of charity, were now ignoring the beggars, as if their fellow human beings were some noisome gas, invisible and unpleasant, something to be pushed through on the way to their comfortable homes and their Sunday dinners. But was he any better? And where the devil was his wife?

A tug at his sleeve. His Reni. "Papa, look, there is a little girl with no shoes. Why doesn't she put her shoes on in the street?"

"Perhaps because she does not have any," Rudi answered. The child in question, a dark rat-like creature of eight or ten with her hair in filthy tangles, squatted in the road with her palm out. She was wrapped like a parcel in various rags, held on to her emaciated frame by strings. Every so often she cried out "For the love of God please help me!" in a shrill voice like the creak of a rusted hinge, mindless and repetitive as a bird call.

"Then her mama should buy her some at the shop," said Reni. "I shall give her a pfennig and she will give it to her mama and then, and then she will have shoes. And stockings, too, but I hope she will wash her feet first."

Rudi was just beginning a small lecture on the price of shoes when Reni left his side, darted across the road, and stood before the beggar girl. Carefully, she opened her tiny purse, an article of blue leather with nickel clasps in which she kept all the coins she had been given from time to time, along with the various small treasures that little girls accumulate. The family referred to it as her life savings. From this purse now she extracted a copper pfennig and placed it on the beggar's palm, saying, "Little girl without shoes, here is a pfennig for you."

As when old ladies scatter crumbs for the birds in public gardens and flocks arrive from nowhere, now instantly, as if by some mystical communion of the miserable, little Reni was completely surrounded by screaming ragged children. Rudi looked around wildly for Gregor, for Berthe, for Hana and Fritz, but none of these was visible through the crowd. He heard a shrill cry—his child! Without further thought he plunged into the mob of urchins, shoving them from his path, using his stick when they wouldn't move. His hat came off. He struck harder at the ragged backs, kicking with his booted feet at naked legs, until he reached his wailing child, whom he found sprawled on the filthy cobblestones, her bonnet gone, her ermine trim besmirched, her scarlet coat torn at the shoulder.

He snatched her up, held her close, then away from him, inspecting her. Her face was red and she was blubbering, but she seemed otherwise unhurt. "There, there," he said, "It's all right, Papa's here. You're safe now."

"I was frightened, Papa," she said when she had recovered a little. "I gave them, and I gave them, but they were so many. I gave them my *whole life's savings*. And my little silver lion from Venice. I didn't want to, but they *took* it, a big boy took it. That was very wicked of him, wasn't it, Papa?"

"Yes, my dear, it was very wicked indeed," answered Rudi, looking out past his daughter's head at the crowd. Remarkably, some of the beggar children were still there, pleading and holding out their hands. The churchgoers glided by in dark-clothed clots, their faces shuttered. No one met Rudi's eye or offered help, as if the mobbing of a little girl on a respectable street like St. Jakobusgasse could not possibly have happened and so had not actually happened.

Hana now appeared, her face pale, looking terrified, with Fritz in hand. Rudi felt incapable of speech; it would not do to upset the children by screaming at a servant in the street. He handed the little girl over to the nursemaid and went off, on shaking legs to find his wife.

Home, and Sunday dinner, the eternal brisket and dumplings. The children dined with their parents at this meal, and it was usually Rudi's favorite of the week, for he liked brisket and dumplings and he liked his children. But on this particular Sunday he found the meal oppressive and endless. Reni was naturally the center of attention, doted over extremely, and needed little prompting to tell her tale of robbery again and again. Rudi had to strain for his paternal smile, and left the table feeling like a fraud, although what sort of fraud he could not have said.

Later, also as usual, with the children put to bed, there was music. Berthe played Mozart's C Major sonata. Rudi felt tears spring into his eyes and he rose from the sofa and embraced his wife right on the piano bench. He told her he loved her above all earthly things, asked for her forgiveness.

"For what, my dear? You have done nothing wrong."

"I endangered my child out of some preposterous sentimental notion—how darling, I thought, for her to practice charity, a pfennig to a starving child. And of course she was attacked, demonstrating in miniscule exactly what is wrong with charity of the giving-a-pfennig type. Then what did I do? I behaved like any Cossack; I actually beat starving children with my stick. Had I a saber in hand the street would have run with blood. Consumed with rage—an expression I had not fully appreciated until the phenomenon itself lodged in my own breast. I spoke to a man last night whose plan is merely an infinite expansion of what happened with Reni and the beggars. Take the pfennigs from those who have them, by all means, but what then? Where will more pfennigs come from when all the little girls are despoiled?"

"I am sure I don't know," said Berthe. "Poor Rudi! Your revolutions! You know very well that whatever happens the important things in life will go on as before. Four pfennigs will still make a kreutzer, and if you give one to the baker he will hand you a loaf of bread. I tell you what: I will play some more Mozart. That always makes you feel better."

Berthe chose to play the Allegro from the Piano Sonata Number 15, in F Major, and after a pause went on to the Andante. Rudi moved to the sofa and listened as the notes painted a lost age, the baron's era: ordered, assured, full of delight, an era where one knew within certain limits what was coming next. A refuge from the present, which was all crashing chords and unexpected changes of key. She was right. It *did* make him feel better, and also somewhat ashamed of that fact.

She finished the Rondeau movement with a fine flourish, then sat next to him, massaging her long white fingers. "That is enough, I believe. I wish for bed." She stretched, stifled a yawn, gave him a certain look.

"I suppose," she said, "that you will be soliciting my favors tonight."

"Soliciting indeed! I shall demand them. Am I not the husband?"

"Oh, la! My ogre! A liberal without the house and a Metternich in the boudoir. You men!"

She skipped off like a girl, with him close behind.

The following morning Rudi set off for his office, his heart lighter than it had been for some time. Berthe was right: the most important things could not be touched by revolution, most especially the relations of marriage.

He understood that his own marriage was an unusually close one, and unusually passionate. Unusual in another way too. Rudi's father, Karl-Ludwig Moritz (Kalo to his family) had long been a business partner of his younger cousin Franz Ludwig (Franzl), a widower with a single daughter. The partners had shared a home, the two children had been raised together, the expectation had always been that when the time came they would marry, and they duly did. The men of Rudi's acquaintance seemed to regard their wives as troublesome domestic animals, a sort of servant that one could not easily fire. But Berthe was like a second self, and, moreover, had not had to go through the trying experience, common to most women, of taking a virtual stranger into intimate congress on the wedding night. He had heard that the princes of ancient Egypt had married their sisters, and perhaps the builders of the Pyramids were no fools. The couple referred to them collectively as The Fathers.

On the street, he paused as usual to inspect himself in the plate-glass window of Trevigliani's next door, under the guise of examining the display. The place was a stationers, carrying the usual run of writing paper, envelopes, ledgers, pens and ink, and thus convenient for a lawyer and writer.

As he was so engaged, Herr Trevigliani emerged in his gray shop-coat and round cap to lower his awning.

"Have you heard the news?" he asked Rudi, skimping the usual pleasantries and weather commentary.

"What news would that be, Herr Trevigliani?"

"My nephew has been arrested. Josef, or Giuseppe as he now styles himself. Snatched off the street right in front of the Týn church."

"Whatever for?"

"Some political foolishness. Sixteen years old and he has decided that Italy must be free, and so he has a picture of Mazzini in his room, and he walks about with a tri-color in his button hole, and shouts out 'Viva Italia!' in the streets. Insane!"   "That's very sad," said Rudi.   "Still, if he's done nothing else and since he's merely a boy . . ."

"Yes, sir, but the family don't know where he is, you see. He has disappeared. The family go to the city jail, they go to the military prison, they go to the castle and there is no word of him." He paused and his voice took on a more confidential tone. "And we thought, seeing as how you're an advocate and well in with the military, perhaps you could make inquiries? It would mean so much to them, sir."

"I will make inquiries. I'm sure that it's nothing serious—perhaps a policeman was over-zealous."

There followed effusive thanks, in the Italianate manner, and Rudi went on his way. He walked briskly down

Zeletnergasse, past Old Town Square just as the famous clock was striking nine, then through Jesuiterstrasse to the bridge. He navigated that thoroughfare like a born Praguer, avoiding the filth where he could, ignoring the beggars and whores, keeping a close hand on his valuables against the cutpurses and pickpockets, and in general gliding efficiently along over the sparkling Moldau, while closeted with his thoughts.

Thoughts about work: Rudi held the rank of Amtsrat in the imperial civil service and his office had charge of all the procurement contracts for the royal and imperial army in Bohemia. A stab of shame, quickly suppressed: what is one to do, must earn a living, can't take from the Fathers, unbearable oppression close to home, worse than the notional oppression the office represents. Hypocrisy? Of course—but all will be made right. Details of contracts, cheating purveyors, how to outwit, perhaps better not to, let the whole thing come crashing down. But the poor soldiers then, shoddy uniforms that dissolve in the first rain, boots of cardboard, rifles that misfire six times in ten; and Austria does have real enemies, so must keep the bastards honest, a quandary he has not solved.

Thoughts on revolution—Bakunin a fool here, one *must* think of what comes after, how the empire is to be governed. A constitution, obviously, but what goes in it? The nationality question, fair representation of all nationalities in a what? A congress of nations? The Americans with their Senate. But the Senate is a bastion against the liberation of the slaves, poor devils, that Boston paper from the old baron described it well, but still a forum to debate the great issues, not ruled by whim, that ancient spider in the Hofburg, will he never leave. Liebig confident, but what does he know? But Jews knew things through their own channels. No, what a thought! Absurd prejudice, like Jasny or Novotny. But Paul's is but a silly pose, no doubt, a more decent liberal never drew breath.

Jasny different, a real enmity there, teaching school, a Czech patriot having to teach Czech boys in German. Yet he loved German, knew vast stretches of Schiller by heart,

Holderlin, Novalis, would he give all that up for the scant repository of Czech verse? Broke his heart, why he drank, why he had that absurd Jew-baiting reflex. That evening with Paul and, yes the woman, a friend, perhaps an old lover, they seemed intimate; she a poet, remarkable!. No poetry in his life, tried his hand, no talent, a prosy man only, but he did have talent there, he was a better writer than Novotny, he thought, who was a professional—some envy from that corner? One could never tell with Paul, would he were more serious, but he loves to mock.

That woman—why did I say bluestocking? Not a bluestocking in the least, right to call her bohemian in the metaphoric sense. Her scent.

The awful scene on the street when Reni was mobbed, striking that huge lout with his stick, striking at the beggars, what was that, could he own the feelings? Dear God, if he lusted after violence, *him,* steeped as he was in liberality, what hope was there for the nation?

And this wretched memoir business, the baron's reactionary ideas, could these infect, like bad air was supposed to infect with fevers? Perhaps he should end the connection, make excuses, plead the pressures of work. No, the old fellow would see through that at once, had been in the imperial service himself, would understand that there *were* no pressures of work for the emperor's coin—that was part of the trouble of Austria: the imperial service was ruled by Talleyrand's famous advice--above all, no excess of zeal. And by God, his money was welcome!

Now he was approaching the Lichtenstein Palace, where the courts had their slow existence, and massing there were the usual early crowd of lawyers, petitioners, witnesses, functionaries and policemen, these latter engaged as always in an effort to keep the ways clear, to prevent the entering officials from being overly importuned by people calling out and waving fluttering papers in their impassive faces. Rudi's face was impassive, too, for what could one do? The law was so tortuous, the system so recondite, and not in any case designed to mete out justice at all, but to maintain the monstrous weight of the regime. He pushed through the crowd unheeding and after passing through many a dreary corridor gained the sanctuary of his private office.

This office was charged with contracting purchases for the royal and imperial army in Bohemia. Every bullet fired, every bale of hay consumed had its ultimate origin and official existence as a charge against the treasury in a floridly stamped and engrossed document traveling through the wicker basket on Rudi's desk. The work was tedious, the process corrupt; luckily, it did not require long hours. Occasionally, the army would be supplied with goods so inferior that the long-suffering soldiers rejected them. In such cases, Rudi would supply a requisition by which the peccant supplies would be removed from regimental depots and shipped to a central location where they could be inspected and officially condemned.

There were several of these this morning: foul hay, shoddy boots, percussion caps that popped too feebly. Rudi wrote out the forms and drafted the necessary letters. The forms had to be sealed with a red paper seal and stamped with his official stamp. When he had done this, the work of an hour or so, he lifted a small brass bell from his desk and sent forth a ding. Immediately there appeared from out of a closet in the corner of the office a tall, thin, tow-headed youth dressed in a shabby black suit, the cuffs of which showed rather more wrist than was conventional. He had a long nose, red and damp at the tip, and a pair of quizzical, intelligent eyes. He stood attentively before Rudi's desk, his long white fingers surreptitiously brushing what appeared to be pastry crumbs from his waistcoat. This was Jerzy Havel, the private secretary.

"You rang, sir?"

"Yes, get these out to the clerks for copying and let's have them out of here today. I don't want our masters complaining that we ignore their incompetence."

"If we did, we would have little work to do, Herr Amtsrat."

"An excellent observation, Havel. But never forget that it is *schlamperei* like this that puts bread in the mouths of all his imperial majesty's servants. How do we do on the carting contracts, speaking of *schlamperei*?"

"They inch forward, Herr Amtsrat. But we will prevail, I believe, and within the month. I am happy to report, sir, that only a minimum of actual forgery was required to set the Austrian contracts in order. The army in particular seems to lose things."

"Including virtually every battle it fought during the late war. It is the fate of our nation, Havel, to have an army just powerful enough to insure that we will still be accounted a great power. That it is not powerful enough to actually win is accounted less important than its wonderful parsimony. Do forget you heard me say that, or at least soften it when you make your report to the police."

"Oh, sir, the police would never bother with someone as small as me."

Rudi rose from his desk. "In fact, I shall visit the police this instant, to report myself for insulting the army, and you for not reporting me."

"Really, Herr Amtsrat?" Havel was used to his master's antics, but there was a limit.

"Not really. It is just to see Major Speyr on a matter of imperial security."

"Very good, Herr Amtsrat. Oh, and here is a note for you, just come this minute."

Havel handed him a folded paper sealed with a familiar crest. Rudi read it and said, "And I believe I will absent myself for some hours after that."

He left the office and walked to another part of the vast building, down stairways and through dim corridors redolent of dust and wood smoke, until he arrived at a tall door, guarded by an armed sentry. A sergeant ushered him through this room into an inner office. Within was a desk and a major behind it, who rose to greet Rudi, a smile on his face.

Wulf-Eric Speyr was the younger son of Berthe's father's older sister and thus Rudi's cousin by marriage. He was also the head of the imperial political police in Prague. He looked the part, being beefy, with a set of yellow bristles under his large nose, a match for the shorter bristles on his cropped head. His eyes were as blue as those of his pretty cousin, and as intelligent, but chilly where Berthe's were warmed by affection. Major Speyr was utterly devoted to the extirpation of everything Rudi believed in, while Rudi despised the whole idea of a secret political police, yet the two were on cordial terms, and had been since childhood. Perhaps their most significant area of agreement was that Berthe Moritz was one of the finest women presently upon earth.

They sat, engaged in family gossip for the usual amount of time, and then, when this had run down, Major Speyr said, "So, Rudi, what is the latest from the subversive elements?"

Rudi looked to the four corners of the office and raised his hands. "We have obviously made small progress, for it seems you are still here."

Speyr snorted out a laugh. "Yes, we are, and so will remain, for surely you are not such a goose as to believe that you will not need police after your revolution. In fact, I expect my profession will wax great, if the empire is so unfortunate as to succumb to your liberal phantasms."

"Oh? Why would that be?"

"My dear fellow, isn't it obvious? The mob will have little patience with being thwarted when their political darlings happen to be in the minority. Having overthrown legitimacy, why should they bow to their own creation? They will not. They will riot and conspire, and that is why a republic requires more policing than a monarchy. Good Lord, have we learned nothing at all from the French? There was one prisoner in the Bastille when it fell, and barely a corporal's guard of policemen in all of France. Five years later, every other Frenchman was an informer and the country groaned under a police tyranny worse than anything the Tsar imagined. I don't see how any decent man can countenance it."

"But we *have* learned from the French. Even the *French* have learned from the French. No one, for example, expects the present new republic there to descend into terror."

"Don't be so sure," said Major Speyr darkly, and then he leaned back in his chair, clasped his arms behind his neck, and smiled engagingly. "Ah, Rudi, God grant that I don't have to toss you into a cell someday. But now that we have had our obligatory argument and discussed the beauty of our children and the accomplishments of our wives, perhaps you will be good enough to tell me why you have decided to lighten my day."

"Oh, I was just wondering. When I work, I am constantly soiling my cuffs with ink and my waistcoat as well. It seems an inevitability of office labor. Yet you soldiers are always turned out in immaculate white uniforms with never a spot. How do you manage it? It cannot be mere discipline or the superiority of your pen points . . ."

Major Speyr threw back his head and laughed, a genuine one this time. "Rudi, Rudi, what an amusing fellow you are! If only all the damned liberals were as entertaining! Well, since you ask, and although I suppose it is a military secret, the answer is this. We splatter and blot as much as anyone, but we are able to cover up the damage with . . ." here he feigned a secretive whisper ". . . pipe clay."

"How symbolic of our empire—all the discontents and injustices covered over by the blank whiteness of censorship and oppression to make a pretty show."

Major Speyr did not acknowledge this remark. After a moment, he said, "But now, seriously: you did not come all across the palace to discuss ink blots . . . "

Whereupon Rudi recounted the story of Josef Mosca's arrest and asked if something might be done. "It seems innocent enough," he concluded. "A little youthful enthusiasm. A decent lad--perhaps a night or two in jail is sufficient to the crime."

Major Speyr made a note in a small black commonplace book he extracted from his tunic. "Yes, well, since you vouch for him, I'll have a man find the little wretch and send him off with a kick in the rear. But you'll tell him to steer clear of all this Mazzini nonsense. There are boys just like him down in Milan yelling 'Viva Italia' and flinging stones at Austrian soldiers, who are also decent lads, serving emperor and nation."

He returned the notebook to his breast, folded his hands under his chin, and said casually, "And what did you make of that Russian fellow, Bakunin?"

A chill, a pulse of resentment. Someone had reported his conversation with Bakunin, and this was the payment for the favor. Rudi asked very few from his cousin, and they were invariably granted, but then came the innocent questions. Have you seen so and so lately? What's he up to? Is he still close to that fellow what's-his-name? The inquiries were expertly judged so as not to smack of informing or betrayal, mere little tidbits that anyone in Prague might know, but it was, of course, significant that Speyr was asking Rudi, the liberal paragon. He'd been that way as a boy, Rudi recalled. He would be happy to let you play with his ball, say, and then, inevitably, he would ask for the loan of your most precious toy, which you could not well refuse. And he would keep it for a good long time, too.

"A great talker," Rudi replied after a pause, feeling his face flush as if he were a thief caught in a hencoop, "well-bred, genial. A typical Russian, I would say, grand ideas, but essentially toothless. A creature of the tavern and salon."

The policeman grunted and extended his lower lip.

Seeing this, Rudi said, "Why, you don't think so? You think that fat bear is here to foment revolution? Really, Wulfi, it's ludicrous. Have you talked to the man?"

"Oh, the man himself is shit. But just like shit, when you spread it on a field it encourages many, many green shoots. I am particularly interested in one of these. We don't know his name, but he is an adherent of this Bakunin. Mid-twenties, thin, a little ginger beard, hazel eyes, a furtive look. Do you know him?"

Rudi managed an almost life-like chuckle. "Wulfi, I appreciate the favor, but you know very well that I do not permit myself to be interrogated about my associates."

There was a brief unpleasant look from Speyr; then his face grew jovial again and he laughed. "Very well---but I certainly hope that this fellow is *not* one of your associates. Our information has it that he has outfitted himself with a Patterson Colt pistol."

"A what?"

"An American invention. It fires six bullets without reloading."

"Good Lord! I had no idea such things existed."

"Oh, yes. Five hundred determined men so armed could snap up a city. But I dare say in thirty years or so the Hofkriegsrat will get around to issuing them to us, so everything will be fine again. God help Austria!" He rose and smiled and threw his arm around Rudi's shoulder, a habit of his that Rudi did not care for, but endured.

"God help you, Rudi. I pray you, do be careful!"

Eight

Pavlic greeted Rudi at the door of the baron's house and led him not to the bedroom, as he expected, but up a different staircase to a room he had never before entered.

"The Green Room," Pavlic announced as he held open the door.

It was a kind of drawing room, furnished in the taste of the last age. It was warm there, perhaps too warm. Rudi saw that a substantial fire blazed in the large marble fireplace, and there was a German tile stove in operation in one corner. Despite the warmth, the impression the room gave was of watery coolness. The walls had been covered with pale green silk and the furniture was of gilt wood, covered in striped silk to match the walls. The windows, which gave on the street, were draped with forest-green velvet, but the drapes had been drawn back, flooding the room with sunlight. The floor was covered by a large Turkey carpet depicting an impossible garden, leaves and tendrils looping in arabesques, flaunting every possible shade of foliage, bearing yellow and pink flowers.

For a room of such size it was sparsely furnished—a sofa, the gilt chairs, a few side tables, and one round table covered in green baize of the kind brought out for cards, at which sat the baron. As he walked toward the man, Rudi had the peculiar sensation that, as he had facetiously told his clerk, he was traveling backward in time, that somehow the interior of this room had preserved the atmosphere of eighty years ago, gelid, ordered, dense with the exhalations of people long dead. That was why there were so few pieces of furniture, Rudi realized: the room had been designed to hold a party of women wearing huge panniers and men bearing swords at their sides.

"I thought we would meet here today," said the old baron as Rudi approached. "I am feeling so much better that

I resent having to speak from my bed, as if I were some kind of invalid. Do sit down now, and let me collect my thoughts. You have your notebooks? Let us resume."

Well, you were to hear about my horse, and my first ride upon her. In fact, I have been contemplating how best to express her qualities and what it was like to be a boy up on her with the knowledge that she was mine, mine, mine. I had late been in despair of ever having a horse of my own, and I would have been in paradise upon a spavined nag, but to be up on Kíslang, who was the cream of the greatest stud in the empire, was divinity itself. It would take a poet to get it across to you and that I am not, nor are you a real horseman.

But to try: *item*, at the outset, I rode her as I rode other horses, not roughly of course, but using my helps with enough force to be clear and precise. Yet we had not gone two furlongs before she gave me to understand--I cannot quite say how--that I was, in a sense shouting at her, and that she would take helps with far more subtle a touch. *Item.* She had a mouth like a girl, she could have been reined with spiderweb. A flick of the fingers was all it took to make her stop, or go or turn. *Item*, her speed--she was by far the fastest horse I had ever been on, and she had a heart that never failed. The best goer I ever saw.

Item. She was an artist. You think me mad to call a horse an artist, but it is the case that some horses desire to learn, to improve their art, which is perfect obedience to the will of the rider, nay, to even anticipate the rider's wishes. She learned to jump, for one example, as if she had known it in the womb, as if she had wings. She could walk sideways and backwards at command and she learned the airs above the ground as well.

But not that first day. That day was devoted to the purest pleasure I had ever experienced, simply riding on the road to our upper meadows and across them. I did not experience anything near as consuming until the night I got into that coach with Clotilde Daumer.

My education, such as it was, proceeded over the next several years. As I have told you, this was the happiest time of my youth, for though I was gaining knowledge, it was of the sort most agreeable to a boy, and I was not at school. Each morning except Sunday I would rise early and be in the saddle while the sun was still low in the sky, and Kíslang would carry me through our demesne and beyond. Sometimes Lennart came along, but I preferred being alone. The nags he rode could not keep up, and in any case, I found I would rather talk to the horse than to him. You are surprised that I talked my horse, I see, and you will be even more surprised when I tell you that the horse talked back. Childish fantasy, you may say, and perhaps so; but I have a clear recollection of conversations I had with dear Kíslang."

"Upon what subjects, if I may inquire?"

"Oh, in the main I told her what it was like to be a boy and she told me what it is like to be a horse. They believe they are the masters, you know, and that they gallop where they will, although being far more good-natured than we, they are happy to oblige us when we suggest a direction. In the afternoons, after our supper, the Wachtmeister would school us in jumping and the other fine points of riding, that is to say, other than merely going forward. I say he schooled us, but, of course, it is the horse that schools us, and the best riders understand this. I have broken a good many horses in my day—it is necessary in the cavalry, you understand—but I kept always in my mind the lessons taught me by that horse."

"What, for example?"

"Courtesy," said the baron. "And decisiveness. Control of impulses and attendance to duty. Above all, loyalty."

"Remarkable. Perhaps we should dismiss the schoolmasters and put horses in their places."

"It would be a better world if we did, sir, I do assure you. For one thing, the young would not learn *sarcasm*. The horse is a sincere creature, and demands sincerity in others. A horse will throw you, sir, and he may kill you, but he will not pass remarks. No, please, do not trouble to apologize, for I am not offended in the least. It is natural for the young to bait the old, and make fun at their expense, just as it is natural that the old see their juniors as the worst generation of fools and scoundrels ever to burden the earth with their feckless antics. Beyond that, sir, I confess am a bore on the subject. I have always been so, but since I have spent the main part of my life with others of the same breed, I believe I have not unduly burdened society. But let me move on to other facets of my education.

Having got me through the first book of Euclid, not without sighs and tears, and having insured that if, in society, someone used a Latin tag I would not gape in ignorance like a peasant, Vera Wolanska now turned her attention to manners. These lessons were naturally conducted in French. It seemed that although I had been walking and sitting for some years, I could not walk or sit like a gentleman, for I had never been taught. It was nearly as difficult as learning to ride a horse, I discovered. I was taught to bow, another complicated subject, with all the situations a gentleman might encounter: the bow to an equal on the street, in a dwelling, to an inferior in the same situations, to a lady, to a lady of a certain age, to a lady in whom one has an interest, to a count, a prince, the emperor.

She taught me to dance, too, a singular achievement, as we had no music, nor did she even dare to hum a tune. Instead, we clumped around her apartment when we knew the Count was from the house, her calling softly one-and-two-and-a-two-and-a-three, or some such, teaching me the figures of the principle dances of the age. It was part of the equipage of a gentleman, you see, and she dared not omit it.

"And do you, in fact, dance, sir?"

"Well, not at present, when I can barely essay a walk. But you mean in my youth. I did dance; never very willingly, but well, enough, I suppose, not to be thought a boor. Yet having been reared to associate music with disgrace and shame, I never grew to enjoy it. One gathers such breeding at a particular age, I suppose, or not at all. No, I have but four skills, all learned at about the epoch we are discussing: I can ride, I can shoot, I can handle a saber, and I can play at billiards. That seems to have been sufficient."

"Did Mme. Wolanska teach you to handle a saber too?"

"This faceity does you no credit, sir. Of course she did not, but in fact it was she who insisted that I learn the art of fencing. A gentleman must defend his honor with his sword, she said, and she arranged with the Wachtmeister that I should begin fencing lessons immediately. The Wachtmeister was at first reluctant to do so. 'I am no Italian, Madame,' he said, but she insisted and cajoled. I sensed at the time that they had some connection in the past, for she was more familiar with him than with the other servants. His point was well taken, for he was nothing of a real fencing-master. His point was therefore *not* well-taken! Do you catch it, sir? Ha ha! Well. He taught me to use a saber on horseback with enough skill that I am still here before you alive, if barely, while some scores of Turks and Frenchies have been sent into the clay by my blade. But one does not defend one's honor with a saber upon a horse. On the occasions when I went out, save one sad time, I used pistols.

Did I mention I am a dead shot? You will recall I complained about not having a gun. She had one and instructed me in its use. It was a pretty little Frwy of Munich rifled fowling piece, two barrels, light as a feather, practically aimed itself. Thereafter, all those afternoons out on my horse I took it along and shot at everything that moved. Here is but another example of the value of early exposure in the gaining of skills and the development of taste. So: music a cipher; mediocre with the blade; a dead shot; upon a horse, sublime—there you have me at, say, fourteen, and it has not varied much since.

"And billiards? Did the Wachtmeister also take that on, or had you another teacher?"

"Ah, billiards! Well, there I was taught by an expert indeed. Will you guess who it was?"

"I could not begin, sir."

"It was Mme. Wolanska! I have surprised you, I see. It was her father taught her the art. I have said he was a savant and as savants do, he had peculiar notions about how women should comport themselves. He was by all accounts the billiards wizard of Krakow and she an apt pupil. She played with her husband and, of course, with my father, who was mad for billiards, but had no one to play with on account of his shame, besides Anton, who was ever a useless stick and so nervous with his sire that he could barely score a point. I imagined then that his desire for a billiards partner was in large measure the reason he allowed Mme. Wolanska permanent residence in the schloss. I was wrong, as it turned out, but here is not the place for that.

In any case, my father a man of regular habits, rode every day from ten in the morning until almost one, when he took his dinner. During that time we had our mute dancing, as I've told you, and could also invade the billiard room and play to our heart's content. Do you play, by any chance?"

"I have played," said Rudi, " but I cannot seem to make the balls go in the right direction, which I gather is essential to the game."

"That is the opinion of the finest players, to be sure. Now, I am aware that the bore at billiards is even more oppressive than the bore at horses, so I will compress several score wondrous afternoons under some general heads. First, if you ever wish to learn billiards, secure for your teacher a beautiful woman. This will ensure that your zeal for learning will be encouraged by the natural desire of all young men to look well in the eyes of such women and not be thwarted by the competition that must exist between any two men of spirit; for winning has nothing to do with rivalry between the players. Rather, each player must play only against Newton, by which I mean against the eternal laws of motion.

Second, billiards is one part physical skill and five parts strategy, rather like war itself in this regard. By strategy I mean a complete knowledge of the table in any conceivable positioning of the balls. The player must have in mind precisely what strike will make either a winning or losing hazard, with carombole or no. I came to see, in my mind's eye, as it were, glowing lines extending from each ball, wheresoever placed, to each hazard both direct or off a carombole from any cushion, or any ball, or a combination of the two. Can you follow me, sir?"

"I believe I can, although I could not do the same for a thousand gulden. My mind is not so ordered, I fear."

"Well, it is a gift. She had it and so did I, as we discovered. It is the case that besides recalling all the angles that I have described, there is another skill in billiards; this was an art little known in the empire in those days. It happens that one can strike the ball at different quadrants—oh, it is damnably difficult to describe in words, where I could make it clear in a moment were we at the table—I mean that if the ball is struck with a well-roughed cue at a point other that at its center, the motion of such a ball, its path, that is, will vary from the perfectly straight, and in this way one can work miracles. The ball can be made to curve, or roll back along its path, or change the angle of its rebound from the cushion. It is called 'english,' I suppose after the quality of perfidy and crook-dealing peculiar to that nation. Mme. Wolanska had in fact learned it from a French officer when the regiment was stationed in Brussels. At this english I excelled; she called me 'the infant Mozart,' which I supposed a Polish expression, for at the time I had no idea who Mozart was or what he had accomplished in infancy. But it pleased me, for I desired to be praised. Years later, when at billiards with him, I related the anecdote, which occasioned much laughter from the company. So we continued in this way. . ."

"Wait, you played billiards with *Mozart?*" The remark burst from Rudi spontaneously, and the interruption drew a severe glance from the baron.

"Indeed, and rode with him too; he was a fair enough player, but could not ride worth a French fart."

"But how? Where? I mean how came you to play billiards . . ."

"No, sir, not a word until we come to the proper place. To resume: the months passed and I grew in skill.

One afternoon—we were playing doublet hazards, the winning-and-losing game—and I had the shot. I suppose you know that it is the aim of the player in this game to strike the opponent's ball in such manner as to sink both that ball and one's own, having first made a carom off the opposite cushion. Here, I will show you just how the balls lay."

(With a brusque motion, the old man whipped one of the maps on the table over onto its blank side and with a pencil drew a rectangle, marked the position of two balls and explained the shot in detail.)

I see I grow tedious, and you will forgive me, but after over sixty years it is still fresh in my mind. Why, you may ask? I have performed far greater feats on the table than that in the years since, but at that moment, with the cry of triumph still fresh on my lips, I heard from Mme. Wolanska a small gasp. I looked up at her, grinning, but she was not looking at me. No, she was staring at the door, where stood my father.

I was ice; she was not. "Play on," she whispered. I breathed deeply, controlled my trembling after a little, and studied my next shot. I did not dare to look at the doorway until the game was over, but by then my father was gone. The following day, I had to be urged by my dear friend to play at our usual time. We played for some hours, and then as the clocks began to strike the hour of one, a noise that continued for some little time, as they were all somewhat out of adjustment, my father entered. He took his stick from the rack, and said to La Wolanska, "Madame, if you please, we will play bricole, the winning game, to twenty points."

They played; he won. I stood watching in silence. I might have been a chair—neither of them paid me any attention as they took their shots. She leaned over the table like a man, showing her lower limbs. I quite often looked away. When they were done, my father went to the bottom of the table with his ball and shot it, to string for lead. I looked at her. She was still, but with the tiniest motion of her head she indicated that I should play. With thumping heart I moved to my position and shot. I did not play as well as I could, as you may well imagine, but I did not disgrace myself; I own I gave him a good game, losing by only two. We passed the rest of the afternoon in this wise, playing winners in turns. He lost once to Mme. Wolanska, which shows something about her character, as she played to win, with no thought for his rank or that he was her sole refuge. And during this whole long session, not a word was spoken that did not have to do with the game, no sound for scores of minutes but the click of the balls and the thud of them falling into the bags.

Then, without a comment, my father racked his cue-stick, bowed to Madame, and left. My knees gave way and I fell to the carpet, sobbing like a girl, I who never cried, who had not cried when knocked down by a giant boar or at losing my foster parents. But I could not help it. She knelt to comfort me and I pressed my face into her bosom.

"Why?" I said over and over through my tears. "Why does he use me so? What have I done? What have I done?"

After I had cried all the tears I had and the front of her gown was sodden with them, she held me away from her and looked me in the face. "You are blameless," she said, "you are a wonderful boy, and would be the pride of any father. It is his fault, and I assure you he recognizes it."

"But what *is* it? Do you know?"

"I know," she said.

"Then for the love of God, tell me! I am dying from this."

"Stop that! You are not dying. Indeed, you flourish. It is he who dies, but he cannot help it. Look, do you know Liliane, the dun filly I sometimes ride?"

"Yes," I replied, "what of her?"

"Then you know she must be close barred in her stall when the weather threatens, and by no means used when there is any chance of thunder. Otherwise she is a perfectly good riding horse, but that one thing she cannot bear. It is the same with him. He shies from you as Liliane shies from the thunderclap, and nothing can be done about it. Nor can I help her, nor can I help you, for on my oath I have promised never to speak of it with you while he lives. And surely you would not have me break my oath?"

105

We never spoke of this again while he drew breath, nor did we ever mention my disgraceful discountenance on that afternoon.

The old man stopped talking and cocked his head. "What is that bell? It has been ringing these five minutes, and there is the noise of some crowd or other coming from the square."

"It must be some revelry—it is carnival, you know," said Rudi. "The bell seems to be coming from the university quarter, but the church bells are silent."

"Yes, that is what is strange. Ring for the boy, would you?"

Rudi got up and pulled the cord. In less than a minute the lad appeared, smoothing his livery coat.

The baron said, "Jani, be a good lad and run down to the square and see what all that noise is about. If it is the Turks, fetch me my saber and pistols. Go!"

Where were we? Yes. Well, now we are at the summer of my fifteenth year, of our Lord seventeen seventy-five, and in this summer occurred a most singular event. I have not before spoken of my extended family, because I had not had any relations with them. As I have noted, my father was something of a hermit. But he did have two brothers and a sister who survived childhood. The younger brother, Anton Johann Nepomuk, was bishop at Brünn. I only met him once. The middle brother, Karl Rupert, married Marie Angelica von Kuenenhauer. She had five children, one of whom . . . but no, this union and its fruits will be interesting later in the story. My father's sister, who was also the first born, was my aunt Augusta Frederike, called Fredi in our family, and she married Ferdinand Felix Graf von Hohenberg, rather a grand marriage actually.

Unlike us, the Hohenbergs are a political family— generals, ministers, a sprinkle of cardinals, and for the entirety of my existence the current Hohenbergs had been serving abroad. The count was minister at Baden, then Stockholm, then London, and finally Paris. Now he was to take the foreign ministry in Vienna, and it had been arranged that he and his family would spend the summer at Pannau.

It had been a long time between guests at Pannau, except for Mme. W., who being in the way of a permanent inhabitant did not count. Accordingly, the old schloss experienced a revolution in its affairs. In an amazingly short time the castle was made new, the place stank appallingly of paint, varnish, bleach, and polishes of various sorts, but although I saw it happening,   still it was like one of those tales in Grimm, where a curse is lifted and a castle that had been frozen with all its people for years on end comes back to life. Some of the servants were old enough to recall Aunt Fredi as a girl and I asked these what she was like.   Beautiful but something of a tartar was the opinion, and also the sense that my father, who had faced the cannons in a dozen fights, was nevertheless shy when his sister thundered.

But the servants were no longer as frank with me as they had once been.   My manners had changed, thanks to Mme. W., and I was a Herr Baron now. The neglected little boy rolling around on the kitchen floor was long forgotten, except by me. And of course I did not truly believe my father was frightened of his sister.   My father frightened of a woman!   It would have been unnatural, like spilled water creeping back into the pot.

At last the great day arrived: sunny, warm, with a strong breeze from the north. Riders had been stationed on the Dresden road and in Pannauburg, so we had ample warning of their progress. We were all out on the steps to greet them: my father foremost, wearing his orders and medals; behind him me, stiff   in my new suit,; and, standing somewhat in front of me and just as stiff, my brother in his student uniform and cap. Mme. Wolanska, resplendent in a pink silk dress I had not seen before, was a little to the rear, and behind us gentlefolk were ranked the servants, row upon row of them, scrubbed all to an unnatural brightness.

In came the cavalcade in a cloud of dust, which rose and fell, marring our perfection. Yet none of us ventured to brush ourselves off, lest we spoil the tableau, and I suppose we all looked like statues kept for ages in a lumber room.

There were three closed carriages, with postilions and outriders, and liveried footmen clinging on to the carriage backs, followed by a wagon loaded high with trunks and boxes. From the first of the carriages emerged the splendid figure of the Count. He turned and handed down his lady, my aunt. The second carriage exuded my cousins, three small girls and a large boy. The third contained only maids and other servants.

Greetings nowadays are not so ceremonious as they were then. We engaged in a good deal of bowing and curtseying according to our rank and status. My uncle, Count von Hohenberg, was the smoothest man I have ever met--and I have met both Metternich and Talleyrand--a charmer in a perfect wig, dressed in pink silk and yards of dangling lace, clanking with glittering orders. My aunt was a short woman inclining to flesh. She had the bold Pannau chin and nose and our blue eyes, which looked about her sharply, as if searching for some fault. I made my bow and kissed her hand as I had been taught. She looked me up and down as if at a horse, and I concluded that, had I been a horse, she would not have made an offer. She seemed more satisfied with Anton, and bestowed on him a smile that had doubtless illuminated the Hall of Mirrors at Versailles, and which quite obviously dazzled my brother.

Her disapproval, however, fell most heavily upon Mme. Wolanska, though my dear friend dropped a curtsey to the pair of them that would not have insulted the Holy Roman Emperor. Aunt Fredi responded to my father's introduction as if she had, through the mistake of some boorish host, been introduced to a servant. I saw Mme. Wolanska's flush and the flare of her nostrils, but she said nothing.

Next came the cousins. Three little girls in white, all with long blond tresses, aged ten, eight and six, of no conceivable use or interest to me, and one male cousin, just about my own age. He was taller than I was, but with his mother's tendency to fleshiness. Otherwise, he resembled his father, but as a roughed-out block of stone resembles the polished statue. The first words he said to me after we had shaken hands were, "That river—do you suppose there are any newts in it?" This was Oskar, who afterward became my bosom friend.

"My word, what *is* all that noise. And where the devil is the boy?"

The clamor had waxed amazingly, and it was clearly a cheering throng that had gathered in the Little Quarter Square, of the sort that might have greeted the arrival of a crowned head, or several. Other bells had taken up the clanging, now joined by the crackle of fireworks. Rudi was just thinking that it was after all the day before Shrove Tuesday and such noisy demonstrations were a common feature of the season, when the door flew open and there was Jan, red-faced and all asweat. He stood in the doorway, panting and heaving.

"Well," said the old baron, "what is it? Speak up, lad!"

"Your honor, sir: the news has come in by the telegraph (gasp, gasp) the news from Vienna, sir. The government has fallen. Prince Metternich left the city yesterday and . . . the students have formed a guard and are keeping order. That's all the bulletin said, sir, but they expect more to come soon."

"And the Emperor," asked the baron after a certain stunned pause. "Is he safe?"

"The bulletin didn't say, your honor."

"Very well, Jani. Good work. Stay outside the door; I may need you to go forth again."

The boy left. As soon as the door closed, the baron said, "Well, he always was an expert at self-preservation; not a martyr, our prince. And I suppose his famous promise to the dying Emperor that he would care for the imbecile heir forever was worth just as much as all the other professional promises he made. So, what do you think?"

"I think it is stupendous," answered Rudi. "A new age now begins."

"Yes," the baron replied, "you have your revolution. Let us see how you will like it."

Nine

This ended the interview: a hurried farewell and Rudi was out on the street among the growing crowds.

Prague had gone mad with joy. A mass of humanity extended from Little Quarter Square, across the bridge and into the Old Town, moving back and forth along the bridge like the tides of the sea and making an ecstatic oceanic roar. Everywhere people were decked with the red and white colors of Bohemia, with ribbons pinned to their coats, around their hats, around their arms, flying on sticks, wrapped around the saints on the bridge. Rudi had to wonder where all the ribbons came from—had all the people hidden banners in their homes and shops against this day? A plump girl was standing at the foot of the bridge pressing red-and-white boutonnieres on gentlemen passing by and giving a kiss to those who accepted. Rudi allowed her to pin one to his lapel and accepted a beery smack on the cheek. The bridge itself was packed with cheering people waving banners and singing Czech songs, this crowd roiled at intervals by gangs of white-capped students joined arm in arm and singing *Kde Domov Muj* in four part harmony. The few police Rudi saw looked upon this scene with bemused expressions, but made no move at all to interfere with the demonstrations.

Upon reaching home, Rudi walked into his hall, handed his hat and stick to Hilda, sniffed, and said, "A chicken."

"Yes sir, all roasted fine as you like, and cabbage with poppy seeds. Cook made bread rolls, too, sir, the kind you like, with bits of onion."

"Well, that sounds divine, Hilda, but I won't be at table tonight. Have cook make up a plate for me in, oh, about two hours."

"Does mistress know, sir?" the maid asked, somewhat darkly.

"I dare say she will find out. I'll be up in the study."

There he went, and brought from his files the portfolio with the petition drafts in. He had just begun to mark the surviving sentences with a pencil when his wife entered.

"What I this I hear?" she asked. "You are not at table tonight? It is a *chicken*, have you heard?"

"I have heard and smelled, too, but there is no help for it, my love. I must work away without cease. And I am out to a meeting tonight and will doubtless be gone till all hours."

"But whatever for? Can you not endeavor to complete your work in the day?"

"This is not my ordinary work—I have been asked by Herr Lörner and the members of the Wenceslaus Committee to prepare a final draft of our petition to the emperor and it must be done tonight."

"My word! Do you have any idea how much such a chicken costs? And I wished to enjoy it with you, with wine and all the rest. It will be Lent tomorrow and you will not see another chicken for a good long time. What is so special about tonight that you must leave your family?"

"Special? Haven't you heard? It is all over the city-- Prince Metternich has fallen!"

Her eyes widened and she put her hands to her cheeks. "Fallen! How terrible! Is he badly hurt?"

"No, darling, it is only a figure," said Rudi after a brief, astonished pause. "I mean he has left office. He is gone from Vienna. The revolution has started. This is why I must finish the draft of our petition immediately."

"But you have waited for this revolution for years. What difference can a few hours make?"

Rudi sighed. "Because it will be chaos in Vienna, and we can obtain concessions that we could not hope to gain under normal circumstances. Don't you understand that this is the moment? Bohemia will be free after more than two hundred years." He examined her lovely face, which was blank and confused. Then he sighed again, took her hand

and patted it. "It will be fine, my dear. Go now and enjoy your supper."

"I intend to, and more fool you for not joining me. I bought the best Moselle too. And don't think you shall have a drumstick! I shall consume both and laugh."

Nestled among the contracts in Rudi's basket the next morning was a small envelope with a *Secret* stamp on it. He opened it, read the few lines and uttered a curse. It was from Wulf-Eric Speyr, and read: "Found your Italian, freed same. I hear you have been invited to Mme. Von Silber's. I was not invited. Let us come together next week and you can let me know, in a general way, what transpired among the glittering liberals.. Yours, Speyr."

"God damn his insolence!"

"Sir?" said Havel, eyes alight with curiosity above his station. "Something amiss?"

"It is nothing, Havel. Go about your business."

The lad slid away in his oddly noiseless fashion. Rudi tore the note into small pieces, went to the window and flung the fragments into the breeze. How the devil did the man know he was going to the von Silber salon on Thursday? He had told no one. Only Sisi Vasová knew, although she herself was no sphinx. Half the town might know by now. He suppressed the irritation and thought for a few pleasant moments about Vasová herself. He recalled her face, and her startling smile and her clever eyes . . .

What! Am I sinking into reveries about a woman no better than . . . well, a woman of indifferent morals. I'm going to Mme. von Silber's salon to catch the political gossip, he told himself, to make myself known to notables there; not an assignation by any means. But should I go? Novotny's down on Mme. von Silber; says his political opinions, far less his wit, were not meant for the amusement of a lot of fat bourgeois—of course, he had not been invited nor was likely to be. Treat it as a lark, and if he ran into Vasová, he would be as cool as a bucket of champagne.

Thinking of champagne, and of that wretched woman, whose face and laugh he *still* could not quite expunge from his mind, Rudi rang his bell.

"Sir?"

"Havel, would you go find out what is playing at the German theater tonight?"

"Why, I know that already, sir. They are doing Iffland's *Compulsory Service*. Somewhat old-fashioned, but quite amusing all the same."

"You have seen it?"

"Several times, yes. I, ah, have a connection to a young person employed there."

"An actress? You astound me, Havel."

"Oh, no, sir, not an *actress*. No actress would look at me for one second. They all have their hearts set on an archduke at the very least. No, she is with the theater itself, checking cloaks, fetching coffee, and so forth. But she is sometimes able to slip me in, informally, that is, and so I may observe the play."

"Well, I wish to attend tonight. I have not had a night out with my wife in some time. Could you secure a pair of tickets?"

"Nothing easier, sir."

"Splendid! And find a boy to take a message to my wife. I will write it out for him right now."

"This is a lovely surprise," said Berthe, when they were settled in their seats. They were orchestra seats, somewhat to the side, of the sort that theater managers let their staffs have at a discount, in lieu of a living wage. They were not loge, to be sure, but Rudi was happy to have any seats at all. The theater was quite packed.

"Whatever made you think of it?" Berthe continued. "I count you an excellent husband, mind, but you are not famous for romantic surprises."

"Perhaps I have changed. We live in revolutionary times, after all."

"Times that seem to require all *your* time at any rate."

"And my wife has delivered a witticism. Yet another surprise this evening."

She slapped his arm with her fan. "Beast! I was quite nearly famous at the convent for my remarks."

"My dear, that sally leaves you so open that no gentleman, far less a husband, would take advantage of it."

Berthe smiled and took his hand. "I do thank you for this, my dear, and you may call me grateful that your revolution will not require me to read tedious pamphlets. Or vote!"

The play was, as promised, amusing, and Berthe did laugh, covering her face properly with her fan as she did so; not a bit like a bar-maid, not, in fact, like Sisi Vasová, a thought that Rudi was quick to suppress. Midway through the second act, however, the revolution arrived in a theatrical stroke greater than any that old Iffland had ever devised.

It started with a murmur, that grew into a babble. A light shone down from the royal loge and all eyes turned upwards toward it. In the glow of a lamp held by an aide stood Rudolf Graf Stadion, the governor of Bohemia, dressed in immaculate white, with all his orders and decorations glinting color and throwing sparkles. He held up his hand; the babble cut off, the actors fell silent on the stage. Then he announced that he had just received a telegram from the Hofburg announcing that the Emperor had decided to grant a constitution, and that furthermore all censorship was abolished throughout the empire. In the moment of silence that greeted this speech, the leading man stepped into the footlights and cried, "God bless his imperial and royal majesty, and hurrah for our constitution!"

With that, pandemonium. The play was forgotten. The cheering rang louder than any ever yielded by a play, strangers embraced, friends kissed, strangers kissed. Berthe found herself lifted and twirled by a stout gentleman, who had tears of joy running down his face and had to be tapped on the ear several times by Berthe's fan before he would put her down. Rudi threw his arm around his wife and allowed himself to be drawn along with the crowd, all of them shouting Vivat! and Long live the Emperor! and more than any other cry the dear word, *constitution*. Constitution! they shouted as they passed through the lobby, constitution! they shouted as they gathered in the street.

The crowd moved, no one could resist it; it was like a deep current of the sea; and it grew by the minute as word of the wonder spread through the whole city. At length, they found themselves in the great plaza of the Horse Market. Somehow a band appeared and the vast crowd started singing, Czech songs and German songs, often at the same time, making a delirious cacophony. With something of a thrill, Rudi realized that among the songs was one from *The Torch*, by the cryptic genius Jiskra, a scabrous ditty about the well-known deficiencies of his imperial majesty. Now actual torches appeared--a group had marched from the railway station bearing them, and soon other torches were found and householders rushed from their doors with handfuls of candles. One was thrust into Rudi's hand. The band struck up the *Deutschlandlied* and Rudi sang out lustily, and to his surprise he saw by the light of a thousand flames that his wife was singing too, although he knew she had been taught, and knew she had taught their children that singing in the street was low.

The crowd started to move like an immense glow-worm; though brainless, it had sense, and direction. It moved from the Horse Market to the house of the archduke Karl Ferdinand, where it sang a raucous serenade, and then to Count Stadion's house, and then to the city hall and the burgomaster's house. No one could pay for a drink in Prague that night. The celebrations utterly eclipsed those after Metternich's fall, every tavern contributed kegs and bottles, the mood of the crowd, fueled by this cheer, grew even more enthusiastic. Rudi lost his hat, but somehow another one appeared on his head. Time contracted, seemed to vanish--they felt they had always existed in this universal joy, torchlit and roaring with song.

At last, after who knew how many hours, they found themselves at the Carolinium, at Crusaders Square, with the great bronze statue of Charles IV looking sternly, greenly, down at the joy of Bohemia. The crowd had stopped moving, but the thousands seemed reluctant to end the night. The great mass pulsed and swirled, like herring in a net. Their torches and candles made it light enough for each man to see his neighbor's face and smile into it. Rudi smiled at his wife and saw that her cheeks were wet with tears.

"Why what is wrong, my love? Why do you weep? Has some brute trod on your foot?"

"Oh, no! It is just all this, and . . . oh, you know I have not been a good wife. All your dabbling in politics, and dabbling was how I thought of it, some silly thing that men did, a sort of hobby, like your collecting tin soldiers. But all this, tonight--I see I was wrong and that the revolution is real, and that I was indeed an idiot, and I am so happy to know I was wrong. I am as proud of you as any wife could possibly be."

"Proud of me? But I had nothing to do with all this."

"Oh, yes, you and all your friends. You never gave in; all those years, all that time you were the yeast for this great thing. Honestly, I never thought . . . because I was raised such a dunce by my dear parents, to care for children and manage a house and think only about that, and meals of course, and what people thought of one, and the fashions. Oh, Rudschen, I am so happy for you and the country and all these happy people. That is why I am crying."

He kissed her there on the street, which he had never done in his life, grasping her around the waist with one hand and holding up his candle high with the other.

But now there was a stirring in the crowd, a great heave, that made Rudi stagger and shift his stance. Some men were pushing their way toward the statue, large men, carrying a door. The peristalsis of the throng had impelled Rudi and Berthe forward, so that they ended at the forward edge of the square right in front of the statue. Then there sounded a chant, one-two-three; and the door rose onto the shoulders of four big men.

On the door stood a woman. She was hatless, glove-less, dressed in a plain stuff gown whose color could not quite be made out in the flicker of the torches, but which bared her neck and shoulders. These glowed ruddy in the same light. A red and white sash was tied around her waist and a wreath of red and white roses ringed her head. She raised her face to the heavens and began to sing *Kdo domov muj?*

It was only then that Rudi recognized the singer as Sisi Vasová. At first her voice was lost in the noise of the crowd, but soon the people in the immediate area fell silent to listen. The passion in her voice seemed to silence them, and then, like a ripple spreading across still water, the ring of silence expanded until it had covered the whole crowd. In that uncanny silence the thousands listened to her sing the first verse of Tyl's great anthem: *Where is my home? Where is my home? Waters murmur across the meadows, pines rustle on the cliffs, spring blooms in the orchards, paradise on earth to see, and that is the beautiful land, my Czech land, my home.*

She sang into the silence; but when she started the second verse, the song burst forth from the thousands, or from all who knew the words, which did not include most of the Germans in the crowd, and Rudi felt a slight chill when he heard how fiercely they sang the line, *"and with a strength that brooks all defiance, this is the glorious Czech race."*

The song ended with a vast cheer. Someone passed a wine bottle up to Sisi, from which she drank deeply, and then, laughing, knelt on her trestle to pour wine splashing down the throats of her caryatids.

"What was that song they were singing?" asked Berthe.

"It is a sort of Czech anthem, all about how beautiful the land is and how nice it is to live in it."

"Well, we should sing a German song, to show how happy we are to live here, too."

"Perhaps not just now, my dear," said Rudi. "And perhaps we should be getting along home. It is not so very far. I believe I have revolutionized all I can tonight."

He took her arm and was about to turn away, when someone by chance swung a torch closer to his face and illuminated it, just as he sent a final look toward Vasová, and she saw him, and having seen him gave a coarse shout and slipped down from the trestle like a cat. Two great bounds brought her to Rudi; she called him "my darling Moritz," flung her arms around him and kissed him on the mouth. He tasted the wine on her tongue and it produced an intoxication so intense and paralyzing that a shameful number of seconds expired before he managed to thrust her away.

Vasová was talking at him, but he could not comprehend what she was saying. He looked at Berthe. Her mouth hung open, a black oval, and then it snapped shut and she spun on her heel and plunged into the crowd. He lost her for a terrible minute, found her, grasped her arm.

"Berthe, stop!"

"Why should I stop? Why should I not go home, snatch up the children and flee to Vienna on the earliest train?"

"Oh, for the love of God, have some sense! That was just Sisi Vasová. She bestows kisses like clouds drop rain. Being kissed by Sisi is as culpable as getting soaked in a downpour."

"But she knew you. She called you by name"

"I do know her—slightly."

"Oh, *that* is her? I had imagined a more homely creature, with a dumpy figure, a large head, and spectacles."

"Well, you can't condemn her for her looks."

"It is not *her* I am condemning. I thought you were going to stand there kissing her all night. Disgusting! I don't believe I have ever been so mortified in my life."

"I don't know," said Rudi. "There was that time before we were married when we were invited to a fancy dress ball at the Kastrups and your parents were to give a ball at the

Winter Garden the same week and I mixed up the dates and appeared at the Winter Garden as Pierrot. How they stared! You turned pink as a radish and fled in horror."

He watched her fight a smile, with fair success. She tapped him on his forehead with her fan and said, "That is not the same thing at all. We are married now, and I believe I know when a man is enjoying a kiss."

"What can I say, my dear? The revolution has quite overthrown my morals, and here we must own the reactionaries have a point. Society will come to ruin and kissing on the streets will spread sans limits. I *did* enjoy it, and I *do* enjoy the antics of La Vasová."

"So you confess it?"

"I confess you are my heart, my second soul, the one love of my life, forever. Vasová is the anti-you, and thus she exerts a strange, dark fascination. I believe such things are natural in life, as, for example, yourself and Lazlo."

"Lazlo? Who is this Lazlo?"

Oh, don't play the innocent with me, madame! Lazlo the baker's lad. Lazlo of the smooth limbs, the tight trousers, the flashing eyes, the hyacinthine locks. How often, upon the occasions when I have stayed home to work, have I heard gales of laughter from my dear wife arising from the kitchen where he has delivered his bread! How remarkable that you should so very often find yourself in the kitchen when he arrives! How amusing to be flirted with by a young god, while the dour, aged husband is upstairs with his fusty papers! I would not be a bit surprised to learn that our Lazlo has delivered other delights, forbidden, but just as warm and yeasty as his bread, to the matrons of the district."

"Oh, monster!" she cried, "how can you entertain such vile thoughts?"

"That is just the point, my darling love. I do *not* entertain them, nor should *you* entertain any thoughts of me having amour with Vasová. It is just as likely as you running wild with the baker's laddy."

***

"Something has exploded in the kitchen," said the old baron, when Rudi was shown into the conservatory the following day. "Or a problem with the flue. Maurice is reduced to making custard on a spirit lamp while it is being repaired, so there is nothing but a bacon pie and some fresh asparagus. Do sit yourself and take a slice! I have had a bottle of my best Montrachet brought up to make amends. A glass with you, sir! Wonderful! The bastards! God gave them the ability to bottle up a summer's afternoon in all its glory, and yet they persist in remaining disgustingly French."

"It is a wonderful vintage, sir," said Rudi, after a sip. "I don't believe I have ever had its like."

"It's the 'thirteen. I put up a good bit of it, and unless I live a great deal longer than the doctor gives me, some fortunate fellow will have the largest portion, and . . . my God, I am rambling---that is because I got no rest last night. Hubbub and riot until nearly dawn! Damned fools, rioting because that poor fool in the Hofburg has promised to grant them the power to scratch out upon paper what everyone already knows. The Emperor rules and the subjects obey."

"With respect, sir, I submit that such is not exactly the purpose of a constitution."

"Is it not? Pray, what is it, then? Oh, yes, I suppose you were out there, too, yelling your head off with the *canaille* and *enlightening* the night with torches and fireworks. That was a fragment of wit, sir; I dare say you grasped it."

"Very droll, sir, I am sure. Well, since you ask, a constitution is simply a compact between ruler and ruled, delineating the powers, rights and responsibilities of each, and stating what may and may not be done in the state. It asserts the primacy of the law over the caprices of whoever may hold the supreme position in the state."

"So the king cannot do as he pleases?"

"By no means. He can only act within the law."

"And who says what is the law? I have not been much in court, for which I thank God, but as I understand it, the law is by no means perfectly limpid. Lawyers grow fat on arguing its points, this way and that, and it may mean one thing at a certain season and something quite different at another. Is this not the case?"

"It is. And that is why we have judges to interpret the law and say what it means."

"So it is the judges who rule, the same as ruled the old Jews in the Bible story. As I recall, there were some troubles with the arrangement at the time. But in any event, I suppose your judges will be chosen by the mob."

"Not at all. It is considered most advanced if the judges are appointed by the sovereign, so as to shield their decisions from undue influence."

"So the king may not do as he pleases, but he appoints some lawyer who tells him if he can do as he pleases or not? I never heard such foolishness!"

"But Herr Baron, it is the rule in all modern nations. England, America . . ."

"Oh, the devil with them! Grocers and savages!" The old man's face was growing red, like a ripening plum, and he stopped abruptly, swallowed a draught of wine, took a breath and collected himself. "Damn me, I am getting upset, and I have broken my rule about politics at table. But let me leave you with this. Austria is *not* an advanced nation. It has certain peculiarities. Do you know the expression, 'Let others make war, you, fortunate Austria, marry'?"

"A very famous tag: *Bella gerunt alli, tu felix Austria nube.* Yes, what of it?"

"*This* of it, sir: nations have each a distinct nature, and their rule must be suited to it. The English love trade and lucre, so they are ruled by shopkeepers. The Americans live by slavery and land theft, so they are content to be ruled by blackguards."

"I protest, sir! Surely Washington was no blackguard."

"I did not know the gentleman, but he was a traitor to his king, and as I understand it he lived by slaves, not serfs, mind you, but human creatures bought like cattle, just like the fucking Turks, and if that is not blackguardry, I should like to know what is.

To resume: the Russian does not feel comfortable without a boot on his neck, the Prussian loves order above all things, and the Frenchie loves riot. Therefore all those nations have each their own, let us say, *style* of government. But it is Austria's character, which is both its bane and its glory, to be, unlike those other nations, a composition of many different peoples, who have but one thing in common, which is that at one time or another their crowns got married into the House of Hapsburg. What else do all these Germans and Hungarians and Croats and Ruthenians and Italians have in common? Nothing but their king and emperor; and I tell you, Herr Moritz, you must have a care when you propose to weaken the throne with your judges and constitutions."

"I will surely keep that in mind, sir."

The old man gave Rudi a sharp look to see if he were being mocked, but Rudi kept his face as bland as he could manage, the moment passed, and the baron shifted in his chair and continued his story.

Where did we leave off? Oh, yes, the arrival of my Aunt Fredi and her family. And Oskar and his newts. The coming of Oskar struck me as a revelation as great as that of Vera Wolanska's. You will have gathered that the peculiarities my father had imposed upon Pannau had prevented me from having friends of my own age.

We had a long luncheon to mark their arrival. I suppose we ate well enough at the schloss, although my personal meals had been rough occasions before the arrival of Mme. Wolanska. I had all my table manners from her. This was, however, the first time I had sat at table with my father, and I could barely swallow my food.

I cannot recall what we ate, probably game, baked grouse, or well-hung venison, and vegetables from the garden. My father was at the head of the table, of course, with his sister and my uncle on either side and then Anton, me and

Oskar and the little girls. Though I was not an habitué of my father's board, still I knew enough of how such things were arranged to understand that Mme. Wolanska had been placed where normally a bailiff or steward would sit, on those rare occasions when such folk were invited to dine with their lord. I was inexpressibly shocked and could not meet her eye. She sat like a ramrod and picked at her meat. None of the adults spoke to her or acknowledged her presence in any way.

This was clearly my Aunt Fredi's doing, and a foretaste of the changes that were shortly to overturn my life at Schloss Pannau and beyond. To my surprise, Aunt Fredi made an effort to charm me. I had never been charmed before. I had barely been paid the courtesy of attention, and now this splendid women, lately an ornament of the most magnificent court in Europe, was speaking to me, drawing me out--although there was precious little to draw, I own. I was bowled over, and to my shame I quite forgot my dear Wolanska and babbled like a brook. Well, more of that later.

After lunch, Oskar and I donned rough clothes and I took him down to a placid eddy of our river, along with Lennart to carry things, and I had Lennart wade out and dredge up buckets of ooze, which Oskar poured into an enamel pan he had brought and probed the black slime with his fingers. After a few minutes of this he cried out triumphantly and held up a tiny wriggling thing, bright orange in color.

"We call them manikins," I said. "They make a good bait for perch or chub. Your brown trout will take one on occasion. Do you intend to go angling? It is the wrong time of day, you know."

"Not today, I think," he replied, placing the creature in a glass jar with a little water, and tying some muslin over the top of it with twine.

"Then why, pray, are you after newts?"

"Oh, newts are very philosophical creatures. Did you know that if you cut off a newt's tail, or even a limb, it will grow back, exactly the same as before?"

"Nonsense!" said I.

"Why nonsense? Have you ever tried it?"

I owned I had not, and asked why anyone should ever want to do such a thing, and he explained that enlightened people, of whom he considered himself one, aimed at studying nature directly, by experiment, and then he explained what this entailed, in rather more detail than I required. Indeed, he was a phenomenon of knowledge, more like a tome than a boy, and it grew vexing to be told, for example, that the names of all the living creatures, that I knew in both Czech and German, were not their true names at all—these had to be Latin. Growing vexed with his *nodosas* and *hirsutas* I suggested that we go for a ride up the mountain.

I gave him Caesar, renowned as a frisky one, and Oskar fell off twice, which gave me great pleasure, I am ashamed to say; but he had provoked me.

Ah, me, once again I must reflect how remarkable that a day spent seventy years ago should live so vividly in memory! Ten thousand days condemned to oblivion, and that one lives still. I remember we found a place to tie the horses, by a little rill, with water and grass aplenty, and set out on foot, climbing the ever steeper path. Lennart bounded ahead, a true goat of the mountain; I followed close behind while Oskar puffed and stumbled far to our rear.

We waited for him at the edge of a little stream that had made a sunny aisle in the pines. He came clumping up to us, cheerful despite his red and dripping face. We followed the course of the stream to its source, a pretty little waterfall gushing out from the rocks. We climbed the rocks then, along a route familiar to generations of Pannau boys, until we emerged above the tree line onto a stony dome, the top of what we called the Kahlstein. The great blue casque of the sky, loaded with thick, fleecy summer clouds, reached above us, the sun behind one of these, shooting shafts of light through gaps in its gilded fabric, gilding too the vast plain below, upon which towns and villages sat like toys.

Oskar clutched his hands to his breast and exclaimed, "Oh! Oh, but it is sublime!"

"Not at all," said I. "It is Saxony. That smudge on the horizon is Chemnitz."

In his bag Lennart had a flagon of beer, a loaf of bread, liver sausage and cheese, and he set out our dinner on a flat rock. We ate, and afterward Oskar and I sat in the sun and talked, while Lennart stood at the lip of a precipice and hurled stones out into the void. Of course, my cousin had to explain about *sublime*.

I should tell you that what became known later as the romantic--Goethe and Herder, Schiller and all that--had never yet been dreamt of in Pannau. Oskar was its first ambassador, and I suppose that, coming from ambassadorial stock, he was very good at it indeed. He talked and I listened, and found what he said far more fascinating than the newts.

After a while the conversation turned, as such boyish conversations will do, but which they had not for me before that day, to love. He wished to be in love. He wished to be in love like young Werther. I asked him who that might be. He was amazed. "What!" said he, "is it possible that you have never heard of the greatest book of the age!" So saying, he brought from the pocket of his coat an octavo volume bound in blue leather.

"*The Sorrows of Young Werther*," he announced. "I cannot believe you have never read it. It has taken all Europe by storm."

"Well, we are backward here in Pannau, to be sure, but we do not fall off our horses." I turned that fateful volume over in my hands with a doubtful look. "Is it about love?"

"Oh, yes! It is about love and longing and tragic fate and every wonderful thing. It tears at one's heart and makes one want to seek the keenest emotion. Tell me, have *you* ever been in love?"

Well, this was a poser. Of course, I had by then tumbled in the hay with the peasant girls, although I was not an absolute rake, like my brother. Such play eased the juicy rigors, so to speak, but it made me feel a little foolish, as if the girls were making game of me. It was not to be compared with a good gallop on a fine horse.

"I don't think so," I answered. "There are no suitable girls on the estate and my father is not social with others of our class. Have you?"

"Oh, not I, I regret to say, although I did try once with Marietta. But it was no good, for she is my cousin, the daughter of my father's brother." He brightened. "But she would do for *you*. There is no bar to a cousin by marriage. And oh, she is the loveliest thing imaginable. Her laugh is music itself, and she has the grace of a swan. How I regretted our cousinage! But I expect you will meet her soon enough," he added

"How so? Is she coming to Pannau, too?"

"Oh, no, but she will certainly be at Hohenberg when we travel there. My mother wants you to come out there after the summer. The house is being prepared for us--a substantial task after our long absence."

"Why does my aunt wish to have me at Hohenberg? She has barely met me."

"For just the reason you have already expressed. There are no suitable girls for you to meet here, given your father's disinclination for society."

"And what concern is that of your mother's?"

"Why, she is concerned for the family and the preservation of its name. Your brother, Anton, is of course the heir, and will have no trouble finding a bride. But as for you . . . Well, the short of it is, she means to bring you out into society. She would have had you come to Paris but forbore. It was that your father never referred to you in his letters all those years. You might have been a . . . oh, unpresentable in some way. In fact, I heard her remark earlier, upon first meeting you, 'Thanks to all the saints--not a monster.' So you will come."

"If my father permits," I added.

"Oh, he will permit it. My mother always gets her way, certainly with my father and doubtless it will be the same with yours. Besides, I could not help but notice at our meal that your father pays you no attention at all, does not deign to even notice you. Pray, may I inquire what you have done to displease him?"

"Nothing that I know of. He despises me, as you observed, but for a secret reason. Mme. Wolanska knows but is sworn not to tell me."

At this his face brightened. "How unutterably romantic! Perhaps it is a mysterious curse. But this Wolanska person--some sort of governess, is she? How do you suppose she came to know a mystery forbidden to the son of the house?"

"She is no governess," I replied and told him who she was and her antecedents and quality.

His reaction was not what I had expected.

"My God! You mean to tell me that you have Ignatz Casimir Borowski's daughter here at the narrow end of nowhere! Borowski, the monarch of Carpathian geology! Borowski, the comrade of Voltaire! The inventor of the modern process for refining mercury, the greatest botanist, the greatest zoologist of Central Europe, a second Humboldt, the savant known as the Light from the East! I am stunned. And you say he educated her with his own hand? Then tell me, why ever are we here on this barren peak when we could be at her feet, supping at the Elysian Spring? Let us be off this instant!"

Ten

"And were you off that instant?" Rudi prompted, for the old man had fallen into one of his trances.

"What! Oh, yes—do forgive me, sir! I was lost in fond memory. The introduction of Oskar and La Wolanska went very well. He had wonderful manners and showered her with respect in impeccable French. Thereafter we spent every day together, Oskar gulping from that spring in great draughts while I sipped from the puddles like a sparrow.

Oh, those days! Even the weather blessed us, mild endless mornings, afternoons filled with merry talk and laughter, discussions of everything under the sun and beyond it, with a small rain at night to lay the dust.

This arrangement, this new closeness, did not please my aunt, however. She was a woman with a talent for rivalry and a taste for power, and ought to have been a monarch rather than an ambassador's wife. Like all autocrats, she could not brook a rival, and supposed that Mme. Wolanska was one, although my dear friend never gave her the slightest cause for reproach. I suppose she intuited that my father respected her; rather, that is what I believed then. We fail to observe what we do not wish to know.

One example will suffice. We had all gathered in the breakfast room on a fine morning and Aunt Fredi entered. Observing the beauty of the day, she ordered that the breakfast be served on the terrace. This was agreed, the servants began shifting the salvers and so on, and we all began moving out through the French doors, when my Aunt said "Just the family, I think." Wolanska stopped as if shot; there was a silence. I stared at my father, but he said nothing, his face like stone. He strode through the doors, and we all followed him.

There is no point in detailing her other slights to that noble and harmless woman. It was only later that I discovered the real cause of Aunt Fredi's enmity, and in any case that incident marked the end of our idyll, for the next day my brother Anton returned. He had been on maneuvers with the Neustadt cadets and he brought with him a friend, one Gerhard Von Leiningen-Skorczy, a great handsome blond bear of a lad, and clearly one with a great future in the imperial cavalry, for, as we soon learned, he was brave, a *soi-disant* judge of horseflesh, rude, loud, and completely brainless.

Now, as you may have heard, the inmates of Neustadt are notorious for their outrageous antics when released from the harsh discipline of that place. These two were no exception; indeed, they seemed to delight in being obnoxious. They terrorized the peasant maids, rode through crops, drank themselves roaring every night, and devoted themselves especially to discomforting Oskar and me.

Gerhard made so bold as to take Kíslang from the stable without leave and ride her into a lather; worse, he used a heavy cavalry snaffle on her, on that tender mouth that could be bitted on a reed. I remonstrated with him, was laughed at, mocked even, and my brother took his side.

Anton made up fulsomely to Aunt Fredi, complimenting her on her dress, on her French airs, listening by the hour to her stories of Versailles and the high life there. Nor did my father check him, for he seemed under a spell, as if his sere life were in abeyance before the more vigorous existence of his older sister. And Anton made no secret of his disdain for Mme. W., nor was he discouraged in this by my aunt.

Life at the Schloss became increasingly intolerable for we three, who had lately been so content, and so we took to riding out every day and staying out past dinner, well supplied with portable victuals by Cook, and devoting ourselves to the pursuit of natural philosophy in all its aspects. I do not know that we made much contribution to learning, but at the least Oskar improved his seat on horseback, and many such a day passed without his falling off, or not more than once.

On one of these fair days, we were returning, me upon Kíslang, Oskar on a harmless gelding named Gypsy, and Mme. W. on her little sorrel mare, Artemis, a fine pure-bred Arab, when we chanced upon Anton and his friend coming down the path in the opposite direction. I greeted them cordially--me being in the lead--but received no answer. Instead, as he rode by Mme. W., Leiningen-Skorczy said in a loud voice, "Anton, I see your father knows how to mount his whore," at which both of them broke out in coarse laughter, Anton repeating, "So to speak, so to speak!"

At which I spun my horse around and placed it to block Leiningen-Skorczy in his path. "How dare you offer insult to a lady under my protection!" I cried. "You pig, you disgrace to your uniform! Apologize this instant!"

He laughed in my face, and remarked in a voice loud enough for all to hear, "It is not necessary to apologize to kept sluts or bastard puppies."

"Very well," I said. "You may name your friend."

"What! You challenge me? You are a child."

"I do, sir. And I am no child, as you will soon see. I tell you now, sir, if you refuse, all Neustadt will hear of it, and I would not be surprised if you were struck off the rolls in disgrace."

With that, I turned Kíslang and rode off. Oskar had never arranged a duel before, but in those days everyone of rank understood what was to be done. As the challenged party, the cadet had choice of weapons, and like the churl he was, he chose the sword, as it was common knowledge at the schloss that I was a dead shot with any firearm. The rencontre was arranged for the following morning at dawn, in a clearing in a little copse of trees west of the mill, the sound of which we imagined would help cover the clash of steel.

That evening I had a note from Mme. Wolanska, asking me to see her in her apartment, but I sent a note back saying that she had no part in the affair, and while any protestations she might have, or any concern she had about my safety, surely did her honor, the thing was fixed, absent a formal apology. Of, course, when one is young, one is immortal in one's imagination. I fell asleep that night without trouble, and awoke the next morning in good spirits.

Oskar and I rode out to the place in silence except for the sounds our horses made. Kíslang, I recall, was restless, perhaps she sensed something from us, or thought it was a fine morning for a gallop and was puzzled as to why I reined her in. And it *was* a fair morning, cool but not chill, the sky clear, a few stars still glimmering in the west, and just coming robin's egg blue on the other side of the sky. I was calm, far calmer than poor Oskar, who looked as if he might break out weeping at any moment. It simply never occurred to me that this fine dawn was the last I would ever see. I have always been like that, you know, before rencontres and battles and such; it is no credit to me, mere temperament, and a lack of imagination.

They were already there, with Anton acting as my rival's second, which I did not think quite proper, a brother after all, but so it was. The formalities being accomplished, we stripped to our shirts and took up our weapons. These were small swords, of course, not sabers, light as wands with little round bells. Leiningen-Skorczy had near a foot's advantage in height and a consequent reach, and he was a far better fencer than I was. Perhaps I would have given him a fight were we mounted and armed with sabers, but as it was I was completely outmatched.

He toyed with me for some time, me backing away from his blade all around the clearing, until at last, in his overconfidence, he did not set his footing properly and slid on a damp patch, and, quite by accident, I managed to pink his thigh.

This set him into a rage and he attacked in earnest—degagé, coupé, degagé—well, in all honesty, his attacks came too quickly for me to truly recall, but I believe it was a doublé in quarte that did me. When I parried, his point slipped from my blade and was heading for a killing thrust at my neck.

Perhaps the shout distracted him, or I may have leaned back, in some brute instinct of preservation, but, in the event, I was not killed; he merely sliced off my nose.

It was the Wachtmeister's shout. I was holding the pieces of my nose onto my face, gushing blood through my fingers, when he came galloping out of the wood line on one of our cavalry mounts, a saber in his hand. I thought he was going to ride Leiningen-Skorczy down, and apparently Leiningen-Skorczy thought so too, for he ran like a rabbit.

How did the Wachtmeister know to intervene? The servants know everything on a place, sometimes well before their masters, even if the thing concerns only their masters; especially then, I should say.

My brother was not, of course, frightened of the Wachtmeister, whom he must have regarded as part of the furniture of the schloss, like a butter churn. His face turned red, and he brandished his riding whip. "How dare you interfere, you dog!" he shouted. "I shall have you flogged for this."

"For shame, baron!" cried the Wachtmeister in reply. "Your own little brother against that big lout, and you standing by, grinning. For shame! And you can have me flogged when you are Count, and please God I will be long in the clay when that happens."

I report this, but only at second hand. Oskar told me later, for by then I had fainted. The Wachtmeister and Oskar heaved me up across the horse's saddle. When next I came to my senses, I was in the Wachtmeister's cottage, on a bed, my head cradled in his arm, and he was holding a cup of slivovic to my lips. I coughed and sputtered, but managed to get down a draught that would have felled a hussar. My face grew numb. It was the Wachtmeister's wife, Mecka, who sewed my nose back on, and she did as good a job as any surgeon. She had been a camp follower with the cuirassiers for many years and there was little that she did not know about repairing wounds. Later, they must have moved me to my room in the schloss. I awoke some hours later, in the most grievous pain, and was sick into my chamber pot.

Further hours must have passed, and then the curtains of my bed were drawn aside and there was Mme. Wolanska. She asked me how I did and I said I was well, that it was a mere scratch, and she said, "Nonsense. You are lucky to be alive, and your lovely face is all ruined. I deeply regret it, and I beg your pardon. It is all my fault."

"How your fault? He insulted you and I took your part, as a gentleman should."

"There was no insult. As he pointed out, quite correctly there on the road, one cannot insult a whore. And that must be how the world regards me. I have been your father's mistress for many years, now and for long before I came to live here. We used to meet in Chemnitz, in Dresden, once in Krakow near my home. We deceived my husband while he was alive. Did I wish to justify myself, I would say that I love him. I have always loved him, from before you were born. Therefore I must accept the scorn of the world, even an insult from a loutish boy.

"I ask myself, how could you not have known? The scullions know, the peasants know, they snicker as they plough. In Paris, in London, Vienna, even Prague, in any civilized place, no one of quality would think it much amiss—it is the done thing in those places, but not here, where scandal grows rank, fed by the unyielding shame that makes this place a tomb. Imagine, a great and famous schloss, with no music! Who ever heard of such a thing? Yet I would do more, I would stop my ears with wax if I could see his face every day. And I thought that was to be my life when I came here. What other life did I have? My three children were dead-- they died in two days, one after the other from the black croup.

"And I said to myself, this is my punishment for loving Jani von Pannau, for Jani I called him. It was our love name. I betrayed my marriage and God deprived me of its fruits; truly, it is said, just are the ways of The Lord. So when my husband died I came here, the dog returneth to its vomit, but I thought at least I could be of some final use in this world, at least I might offer the comfort of my body to this destroyed man, in just the way that a bundle of love letters may serve to fill a chink in the wall, to keep out the chill winds, when the writer and his lover are dead. But, my dear, instead of a living tomb I found you."

I should say that while she was speaking, my heart was dying in me. I did not want to hear her terrible story; I could not find within me a particle of sympathy, for I was consumed with disgrace, which banishes all human feelings; and now for the first time I understood my father, and why he lived as he did. Oh, the common people look at us with their envious eyes and they see only what we have, our wealth, our power, but they can never understand what it is to lose honor, that turns all of it to ashes; for that is one thing they do not have and thus can never lose.

She went on now, pouring her words into my reluctant ears: how her heart was reborn in her when she saw me broken in the mud where the boar had left me, how she thought it was a gift from the God who had abandoned her, that she could once again mother a child, raise him up and give him the gifts that only a mother such as she was could convey. She was weeping then, which appalled me--what could I do with these tears!

When at length she stopped all I said was, "Does he love you?"

I saw her recoil. She drew a handkerchief from her sleeve and wiped her tears. Then she said, "No. He is fond of me, and he needs me, I think. But your father has loved only two things in his life besides his honor: this place, Pannau, and Maria-Louisa Von Neipperg, your mother."

Now I did the cruelest thing I have ever done. I turned away from her on the bed and I said, "Go away!"

I heard a gasping sigh and a few moments later the sounds of her departure.

Silence now in the cheerful room, but for the scratching of Rudi's pencil. The man Pavlic entered with a maid servant and they began to clear the dishes. Pavlic leaned over and said something to the old man that Rudi did not catch. The baron waited until the maidservant had left and said to Rudi, "My doctor has arrived. Yet I feel the need to conclude this chapter of my story. Can I impose upon you to tarry a little longer? I will have coffee and cakes brought in to you.

Pavlic can carry me elsewhere. Most people do not enjoy the sight of this treatment, I fear."

Rudi spent the next half hour in the wonderful library, reading the latest news from Paris, from one of the hundreds of newspapers that had sprung up there after the fall of the king and censorship. He felt himself smiling as he read, this smile caused, he knew, by the expectation that soon his own Prague would have scores of free journals and he would not have to get the news in a baron's chamber.

"I have no idea what he puts in that needle," said the old baron when the doctor had departed. "I only hope it is not distilled from the blood of Christian babies, but even if it were, I do not know that I would brook at tossing a baby, a scrawny ill-favored one, mind, into his alembic for the relief it gives me. You will doubtless say it is only my selfish and brutal aristocratic propensities speaking."

"Not at all, Herr Baron," said Rudi. "I am happy you are feeling better. If he is a Jew, that is neither here nor there, in my view."

The remark, though sincere, engendered a troubling thought: could it be that the old man was *challenging* him and his ideas? He now recalled similar provocations: it almost felt as if Herr Baron imagined he was putting his temporary secretary to school. Could that be his fancy? Pay an absurd sum to have a liberal sit at his feet and absorb the out-worn politics of a former age? Some near-Gothic aristocratic lunacy? If so, it was a challenge Rudi would gladly face. The work from that moment became more interesting.

"A very liberal sentiment," said the baron "I supposed you mingle with heaps of Jews. Still, one must move with the times, although we do dig in our heels. The old emperor liked 'em well enough, and that should suffice for any loyal subject. Well, have you got your notebook ready? I believe we are about to close the first act of this adventure."

I recall we left the little me in the deepest misery of his life so far. It was not the pain in my face, or even the thought that I might have to live out my life with a ghastly visage. No it was the thought of them together, my dear

Wolanska in the carnal act with my father, and that the picture of the world I had constructed was false. Now, we all understand from whence we are engendered, but a natural delicacy in all men prevents us from dwelling much on the details, for we know our parents *as* parents, and this must draw a veil, so to speak, else we could never look them in the face. But this was not my case. I did not know my father at all, by his own desire, and I had, in my boyish imagination, and my thirst for love, imagined Mme. Wolanska as a type of angel, sent by heaven itself to rescue me from a life of loneliness and brute existence. To learn the truth now was therefore intolerable. And the worst of it was that I had nowhere to unburden my heart, for you know that a pain told is halved.

Thus I was prey to all the poisonous phantasms of which the boyish mind is liable. What boy, thwarted by parents, friends, kin or cruel necessity, has not dreamed of an entirely new life? I daresay you have yourself. When we are hurt we all wish to be robbers in the woods, ship captains, bear-leaders or what-have-you, anything that will dismay our tormentors and cast our wonderful selves in a flattering light. Such were my thoughts, and while it would be too much to call these hectic fancies a plan, still I was at heart a practical fellow—having been raised by peasants, after all--and had always known that I must someday have means to earn my bread. Now that day had come. I took stock of myself as I have told: pistol, saber, riding, billiards. The answer was not far to seek, given this scant list. No one cares what a soldier looks like, and I could say I got my face from the Turks. As good as a written character! So I decided that I would ride to Saxony, to Dresden, and offer my sword to the king.

Yes, an absurd notion, but you must see things from the perspective of that boy. It speaks to the depth of my despair, for in all the history of our house, none had drawn steel for any service but that of Hapsburg, and for me to think of serving the Wittelsbach—well, that was a grave step indeed, even if only in the mind. You know our motto: our honor is called loyalty, a sentiment carved on every surface that would take a mark throughout the schloss. But, you see, I wanted to hurt my father, and this was the only way I could think to do it that was in my slight power.

I dressed, I took my little bag of coins, I slipped from the house and walked to the stables. Not to drag out my flight for longer than it took itself: I got lost in the mountains, struck my head against an overhanging limb and the next thing I knew I was lying on a pallet, in a stone room, daylight streaming in through cracks in the door and wall and one small high window, with an ache in my noggin to match the hellish pain in my face. At first I thought I had been thrown into prison, but the room did not resemble any jail I had heard about. It was damp, yes, but the dampness was the cool of a larder rather than the close rancid chill of a cell. I have been imprisoned since, and I know. Besides that, the window lacked bars and the door was latched on the inside. A crude table and a pair of benches stood at the far end, and a set of shelves of the same rough manufacture.

I heard the bleating of goats. The door swung open and a man of peculiar aspect entered, carrying a small tin pail. He poured a stream of what must have been milk into a crock, which he covered and placed beneath a grating that he raised from the floor. Then he stood and faced me.

To find his features was like looking for a rabbit in a hedge, so thickly did the growth of russet hair obscure them. His sunburnt nose was like a plum fallen beneath that hedge, and his eyes a pair of gooseberries. So pale those eyes were that at first I thought he was blind. Of his mouth there was no sign, so heavy sprouted his beard and mustaches. He was dressed in a peasant smock, with wool stockings crusted with mud, and clogs, the same.

His first words to me were, "Would you like some goat's milk?" He held out a brimming bowl.

He did not use a proper form of address, which irked me, so I ignored the offer and demanded to know where I was and to whom I was speaking.

He answered, "You are at what used to be the abbey of Our Lady of Loretto, although it is all ruins now. Where you now lie was the creamery of the place, the only building left with a proper roof. I brought you here because you were feverish and it is cool. A stream runs there, under the grating. My name is Hugh. How are you feeling?"

"How did I come here?" I asked him instead of answering, for I bridled at his damnable familiarity—*du* and *dein*, when he could see I was a gentleman!

"I found you on the road, insensible, with a great bruise on your forehead and your nose all squashed. I saw that your nose had been sewn together and so must not have been injured in your fall, but earlier. I straightened it some, and put in a stitch or two. However did you come by such an awful wound?"

At this I grew angry, and said, "Look, fellow, I am not to be interrogated by a goatherd, and especially not one who does not know how to address a gentleman. I am Baron von Pannau-Kinsky, you churl! Where is my horse? Bring me my horse! I wish to leave this hovel instantly!"

I stood then, and reeled, and he caught me before I could fall--a grip of steel he had--and lowered me gently to the pallet.
"There is no horse," he said, and, "Please, you must rest."

For you will comprehend I was not entirely in my right mind, from the blow, of course, and also from what had happened before. Otherwise I would not have spoken so to a kind man who had probably saved my life. I raved for a while and then fell back in a swoon. When I awoke again it was dark, and the room was full of a wonderful odor of cooked meat. Goat it was, but welcome, made with potatoes and mountain herbs. He fed me, and I allowed it, for I felt myself at the very bottom of life, my dear horse lost, as was my honor and my place. As I ate, I thought I would ask him if I could stay and be a goatherd myself, so low had I fallen in my own eyes, and after I had eaten I turned my face to the wall and wept as silently as I could manage.

Well, not to drag on. I stayed. Some days passed. I grew stronger. He spoke infrequently, and adopted, it seemed to me, the proper manner of a peasant. One morning I rose and Hugh was not there. I sought him in the little hut he had constructed where two ruined walls of the old abbey met. The single room held nothing but a rope bed, a broad shelf supported by two legs, and a small chest. Of course I looked into the chest--a boy's curiosity--and what I found amazed me. It was full of books! And I found a leather case containing fleames and other medical instruments. Later that evening, as we ate our meal--potatoes in goat milk--I made my confession, or rather a confrontation, for I felt I had been badly used.

"I have seen your chest, sir," said I. "Why did you not tell me you were an educated man? I have disgraced myself in the way I have treated you."

"There is no disgrace, for I am no longer the man who bought those books. And it is I who should beg your pardon, for my native tongue does not distinguish classes."

"But where are you from, sir, and how did you come to be a goatherd in the woods of Saxony?"

"And do they not teach young gentlemen of Pannau that one does not interrogate a man in his own home?"

At this I was still decent enough to blush. I begged his pardon; and he regarded me for a few long seconds with his white eyes. But now that I saw him as a man like myself and not a peasant I could for the first time observe the suffering that marked them. At last, his glance softened, became even humorous.

"Well," he said, "tit for tat is fair play. If you will tell me how you came to be riding break-neck through the Saxon forest in the middle of a raining night, I will attempt to satisfy your curiosity about my antecedents. But it is a long, sad story, perhaps even sadder than yours."

"My tale is shameful," I said, "and involves a lady."

"Yet however shameful," he said, "it will not make you unfit for the company of goatherds. And the lady need not, of course, be named."

With that, I began to recount my recent adventures, and I fear I was at pains to show myself in a better light than was the case. When I was done, Hugh let fall on me an appraising regard, and his hidden mouth made the mass of hair that concealed it curve into a secret smile. He said, "That is quite a tale, sir. I wonder it was able to enter in here, the doorway being so low."

"What!" said I, "Do you question my word?"

"Oh, come sir," he answered, "we are not upon oath here. And it is no sin to put our experiences in a better light when offering them up to the view of others. Were we to ban all such self-flatteries there would be no conversation at all, no, nor any commerce either. But what I shall now relate is true in every particular, or at least as well as memory serves. For I do not wish myself seen in a better light. Far from it! Indeed, I must be careful not to show myself in a worse light than the facts support. This is a sin, you know, to see ourselves as too depraved to deserve God's mercy."

So he began his tale, the most doleful I had ever heard, or ever did hear in my life. I shall not burden you with the whole thing, for this is my story, not his, but I will tell one part of it, for it has marched with me through my life. Nor will you easily forget it. He had been in the slave trade, you see, carrying poor brutes of Negroes from Africa to the sugar islands. As he was at heart a decent fellow, the barbarity of this commerce drove him to drink, then despair, then near to madness.

After one voyage, his ship arriving safe at a port on the Slave Coast, he ran from it, and wandered into the interior, hoping, he said, to be eaten by a wild beast, or taken by a fever, or slain by savages, he did not care which, but instead he came across a party led by a priest of our faith, a missionary traveling to a distant province. This party he joined and after many days' travel arrived at the sort of town they have in those parts, huts made of sticks and mud, and were made welcome by the people there, who had never before seen a European.

The natives seemed prosperous enough, but not rich, their clothing simple, their implements few. Their chief luxury seemed to be meat, and more and finer of it than was common in those parts, or indeed in much of Europe. The natives gave feast to the priest's party for two days, and then they were shown about the town. The streets ran in circles, like a target. In the very center was established a kind of fort made of closely joined logs, with a tower rising above it, and the priest, inquiring of the natives whether they feared depredation by their neighbors, was told that the tribe feared no one, and that the construction was not a fort but a prison.

At first they thought that it was a kind of barracoon for keeping slaves to be sold on the coast, but they were assured this was not the case, and the king of the town asked if the guests desired to inspect it; for they seemed proud of the forbidding pile. Within the walls they were amazed to find a small village, very comfortable-looking, as finely built as the homes of the people outside, or even better. The prisoners were more richly attired after the local fashion than were the free subjects, the women comely, the men of fine appearance and all those imprisoned seemed well-fed, even sleek. Numerous children dashed about, all of them fat and healthy.

The mission party was soon surrounded by the imprisoned, who greeted them warmly and proposed a feast in honor of the visit. The priest, who had learned the lingua-franca of the district, inquired of the prisoners' headman how came it to be that the people were so generous to their prisoners, a phenomenon not known in other lands, where prisoners were treated with contempt and given poor accommodation and short rations. To this the headman answered that this seemed foolish to him, since prisoners poorly treated in such fashion would never thrive, would not put on flesh and hence would be very poor eating.

"What!" cried the priest, "do they eat you?"

"Of course," answered the headman. "That is our purpose. Years ago, our ancestors were captured and since then, generation on generation, we have served as food for our captors."

"But that is monstrous," replied the priest. "I swear that henceforth my only thought shall be to secure your liberty. I have no doubt that when the world hears of your plight an expedition will be raised to strike down your oppressors and accomplish that deed."

At this the headman assumed a look of horror. "Please, I pray you, put all such thoughts from your mind! Within these walls we are the most contented people imaginable. We have the best of housing, raiment, and food, all without working or taking any trouble whatever. Whatever we demand is freely given to us by our enemies. What situation could be more delightful?"

"Yet you are eaten!" exclaimed the priest.

"That is so," said the headman, "but all men are eaten eventually, by worms and crawling things. What difference does it make? And, of course, some of us survive for quite a long time. I myself have seen two kings of our enemy go down to death, and here I am, still living off their work, enjoying my comfort and leisure."

Here they enquired as to how this was possible, and the headman explained that at the dark of each moon there was a lottery of the prisoners and one in ten was selected for consumption by the people in the town. These chosen were housed in a kind of palace and laden with honors and let eat their fill of the choicest viands the country afforded.

"But what of women, the pregnant, nursing mothers, the little children?" asked the priest.

"No matter," replied the headman, "all must take their chances. Suckling babe is considered a great delicacy on the other side of the wall, and unborn young are so much so as to be reserved for the king and the high priest." Seeing their horrified expressions, the man laughed, saying, "What, do not babies die in your country, or women in childbed? It is no different from our case, yet we thrive at our ease and you must struggle mightily to get your meat."

Then Hugh spoke up, saying, "If it is all so well with you, why is there a stockade and guards to keep you from escaping your paradise?"

The headman burst out laughing. "Is that what you think?" said he. "If so, you have misjudged. The wall is to keep the people in the town from *joining* us, of course, or the king would soon have no subjects, and then who would work to make us all rich?" When this was explained to the people standing about us, he said, there ensued a great roar of merriment.

Hugh paused here and asked me what I thought of the tale.

I answered that it was the most remarkable I had heard, and would have doubted it from any lips but his. With the impertinence of youth, I then asked him if he considered himself a cannibal, too, having feasted on the meats served up in that village, and he nodded, saying, "Yes, that is added to my list of sins, but at the time I had such contempt for my person that it was all one to me, no further darkness could show against the stygian of my soul."

After this he related the remainder of his journey: many hard miles by land and sea, after which, so he said, he felt like that antique sailor who, hoisting an oar upon his shoulder, resolved to walk inland until the inhabitants knew not the purpose of an oar, and there settle. Thus he had come to the dry heart of Europe and resolved there to stay, forsaking the company of men, whom he considered to be like those in the cannibal prison, living a heedless life, though in their hearts they understood that at some future time, demons would be feasting upon them. This was the moral he drew from his tale, d'you see?

He was a strange man, Hugh the goatherd. I have never met one so deeply estranged from what we are pleased to call the world, for he believed that the cannibal town was the very type of every human society, in that each consisted of the eaters and the eaten, with this difference: in Europe we had not the charity to make life easy for those consumed, and therefore those vile cannibals of Africa were our moral superiors. He said, "The only difference is that we Christians consume our human flesh in the form of sugar cakes."

I was happy enough with him, for despite his hatred of humanity in general, he was, man to man, perhaps the kindest person I have known, and mild of temper, amusing, and well-spoken with it. I might have stayed with him longer, and been a penitent goatherd and not had my life—how wonderful is fate! But one morning we awoke to the sound of horses, and it was my Lennart and cousin Oskar. After embracing me warmly (Lennart frankly weeping with joy) they told me that they had been searching assiduously every day since Kíslang had made her way back to the stables.

From them I gathered that things had changed mightily at the schloss since my precipitate departure. First, upon hearing what had happened, the Count sent for Anton, questioned him strictly, beat him with his own hand, both for his part in the duel and for lying about it to his father's face—for he knew all from Mme. Wolanska—and packed him off back to Neustadt with his friend. Then he had raised the whole place and sent every available man out to search for me, which I counted a wonder, for I had thought my father cared not a fig if I lived or died.

Oskar added, "And the great news is you are to come live with us at Hohenberg. Where it was merely projected, now it is settled."

I was amazed to hear it and asked how it had come about.

"It was my mother, of course. When she heard what had happened, she upbraided your father for his unnatural neglect of you, and blamed him alone for the disaster. I listened at the door. She called you 'dear boy,' 'lost babe,' 'precious darling,' and owned that the Count was no better than those antique gentleman who exposed their infants for the delectation of wild beasts. Oh, I do assure you, it was better than an Italian opera."

"But your mother hates me," I objected.

"At one time, perhaps, but my mother's hates and loves are like the weather--however violent, they soon pass away, often to be replaced by the opposite. Besides, it was, you will admit, a dramatic occurrence and my mother cannot bear a dramatic occurrence wherein she does not take the stage in the leading role. She may despise you this fortnight, but for the moment you are her jewel, and of course, the Count can refuse her nothing."

I confess I was sensible of some resentment at being so packed for shipment away without even the ghost of a consultation, but when I voiced this, with heat, Oskar replied, "Oh, tosh! You have been too long in that grim pile. And while I say nothing against your father as a man, you will admit he has been something of an ogre with regards to you. Oh, and Hohenberg is lovely-- the house is full of light and you shall have the room next to mine and there will be music. You shall hear Marietta play on the pianoforte, and I on the cello . . . ah, sweet Marietta! To be in her presence is alone worth leaving home."

This last settled my doubts, for Oskar had expatiated upon the points of Marietta like a gypsy touting a blood mare almost since he'd first stopped down from his coach onto the gravel of Schloss Pannau, and I greatly desired to view this paragon myself. I recalled what he had said about there being no bar to our being in love, if this sweet fate should befall us.

Having set my mind on leaving, I looked around the place for Hugh, but found him not, and had to be content with a scribbled note left on his table. I felt the obligation to give him some token of my gratitude, but could not think of any he could use or would respect. Having nothing, as he once told me, he had everything, and was besides closer to God for his poverty. I saw he was happy enough in this state, but I was not bred to think likewise, and I do not; yet I have honored the man and his memory my whole life, a nice paradox for the philosophers.

Eleven

The old gentleman paused and took several deep swallows of wine. "I shall rush ahead somewhat now, for I see you fidget."

"Oh, not at all, Herr Baron," said Rudi. "It is a most fascinating tale. It is better than a play for drama and romance."

"Very well, but to be frank, imagining my youth begins to sicken me, like eating too large a quantity of nougat. One recalls vaguely that one was a fool and callow, but reliving it, as I have done with you, does bring up the bile. But let me resume, for there remains a good deal of that youth to tell."

So, back we three went, joyous greetings and so on, swooned over by Aunt Fredi as foretold, a tearful farewell to the Wachtmeister and his wife, to Cook and all the servants who had been my only human comfort as a child. Mme. Wolanska kept to her room, and would not see me. I wrote out a note and slipped it under her door, behind which came the sound of weeping. In my note, I begged her forgiveness and pledged my friendship anew, for I was utterly ashamed of how I had treated that dearest of women.

My father had absented himself on some pretext, hunting, I suppose, and the next day we had packed up and were on the road.

Have you seen Hohenberg? You must visit it someday. It is in the Egerland, not far from Karlsbad, a very fine estate, Nothing near the size of Pannau, of course, but richer. Count Hohenberg and his brother owned a great slice of fertile valley, and the two schlosses overlook the river, one on either side, with the Duppau mountains edging the horizon—very green and picturesque.

The house was, as described, a structure of the former age, entirely Frenchified, formal gardens, playing fountains, everything all gilt, little chairs that would tip over or crack if a man sat on them. Carpets. Well, I dare say you've seen houses before, even been inside one or two. The servants were in livery--that I recall, and powder. At Pannau we didn't bother with that, having no one to impress, and our servants were a comfortable homely lot, not at all stiff and on their guard like the ones at Hohenberg.

We arrived at night, I was shown to a comfortable room and a deep bed, slept soundly with Lennart on a pallet at the foot of that bed: he insisted, although it was not the custom of that house. I awakened quite late the next morning and was served in bed: chocolate and little cakes with powdered sugar on 'em, and I was hungry enough to gobble two down before I recalled what Hugh had said about sugar and the cannibals and we civilized folk and did not eat another. I dressed in the clothes Lennart laid out for me and went to find Oskar.

As I strode though the halls—and here there were enough mirrors to make a dozen me's at every passage—I heard the noise. It startled me because I thought it was the sound of a mill wheel that had not been well greased, a kind of low groaning, and there was a clanging sound behind it, very regular, as if the wheel of the mill were striking a hanging chain. I could not compass it, for although I knew the place had a several mills, they were down at the river, and this sound seemed to be coming from inside the house.

Curious and baffled, I followed the sound and came to a room. A footman opened the door for me. I am afraid I gaped like a peasant, for, of course, I had never seen such a sight. Oskar, seated, held a sort of churn between his knees, stroking it with a stick and pressing on the churn's handle—for so I saw his violincello. This and not a mill was the source of the groaning drone I had heard. I stepped further into the room. Next to Oskar was set a sort of crate on legs, brightly painted with figures, angels and so forth, and tossing above this, partly concealed behind a vertical board, was a mass of reddish-gold curls.

Another step: and there is my first sight of Marietta, who was to be my ruin.

"Am I boring you, sir?"

"What?" Rudi's eyes, which had been gazing sight-lessly at a spot of sunlight on the wall, re-focused on baron's face, and took in its expression of annoyance.

"I have been speaking these five minutes and your pencil has not moved. Do you then consider my experiences at Hohenberg to be beneath your talents? Shall I break our compact and move on to the Battle of Austerlitz, or my meeting with Prince Metternich at Paris?"

"I beg you forgive me, sir. I did hear what you were saying— the music and your Marietta, but I was momentarily distract-ed by concerns of my own. Pray continue, sir. It will not happen again."

"What concerns, if I may be so bold? You have been twitching like a sleeping hound this past hour. Your face is an open book, sir--I wonder that you are involved in politics at all, as I had understood such is considered fatal in the chan-celleries. But is it indeed politics that interferes with your concentration?"

"Sir, you have me pinned," Rudi said. "Guilty and damned for it. But let us go on. Your first sight of Mariet-ta—and was she as beautiful as Oskar had promised?"

"That and more. But she will keep for the moment. You have intrigued me, sir. Will you not share your troubles? I am a bluff soldier as you know, but I have spent my hours among the great of this world, and may be of service, save it is a plot against the person of his imperial majesty."

"Oh, no, nothing so dire. In fact, it is an embarrass-ment more than anything of moment." And here Rudi laid out for the old man his involvement with von Speyr, the Ital-ian boy, and the invitation to spy.

The baron heard him out and, after a considerate pause, said, "This fellow, Speyr, you say he is related to you?"

"By marriage. We were playmates when children."

"And yet he uses you so? It would never have been countenanced in my day. It is French! How we copy the fell practices of our enemies, to our everlasting disgrace! Imagine, spying in a private home to which you go by invitation! Here is a dictum: never become obliged to scoundrels. Whatever instant satisfaction you derive from the obligation will be taxed four times its worth before long. In any case, you must put it out of your mind! I still know one or two figures in that line. I will have a word and the obligation will vanish."

"You astound me, sir," said Rudi. "I mean that you are familiar with the secret state police." As he said it, he felt a shiver of apprehension, but did not allow this discomfort to show on his face.

"Oh, well, as to that, you know there were dragoons before there were police, and we functioned as a kind of field-gendarmerie, and part of that work is to search out enemy spies. As I have been in the imperial service since a boy, I suppose I am tolerably familiar with the hidden levers."

So, to continue . . . I walked into the music room, caught my first sight of Marietta and was lost completely, knocked over like a shot hare. Well, I had hardly seen a girl of my own age and class in my whole existence and was unprepared when she looked up at me and smiled. She was a pretty girl enough--I see that now looking back-- although I have seen women since that would put her into deep shade, couldn't share a room with 'em. But that mattered not a whit at the instant. I had never been smiled upon by a pretty girl, and it went to my marrow.

Oskar introduced us. I made my bow as I had been taught. She asked me if I enjoyed music and--here you will gather what was the depth of my boordom at the time--I blurted out a no, which would have been bad enough, but then dug myself further into the pit by adding that I had never heard music before this, and that I had thought it was the sound of an un-greased mill.

But the angel was not offended in the least; no, she gave a merry laugh and conveyed to me that dear Oskar had told them all of the strange ways of Pannau, and the exile of music therefrom, but now that I was within the precincts of civilization perhaps I would learn to enjoy it. I hastened to assure her I would, as I would have had she proposed to tear out my fingernails in the manner of the Iroquois. They played some more. I kept my expression rapt, although in truth I would almost have preferred the Iroquois.

After this, a servant appeared and called Marietta off to attend her aunt.

Oskar could not stop laughing, though I shook him and called him names.

"You are already in love with her," he says, "It is as plain as a pikestaff. Dear Lord, the sound of a mill! Did I not tell you that you would love her? Is she not everything I foretold you?"

"You have arranged it very well," says I, "but now what am I to do? I am a worse fool with a girl than you are on horseback."

"It is not so hard," he said, "and if unsuccessful, at least one does not break bones. Here is what you must do. First, you must pay compliments. You say her hair is like gold, her cheeks like damask roses, her lips like cherries, eyes like stars, and so forth. Yet, she hears that from everyone, and to distinguish yourself in her eyes you must also praise her accomplishments. As graceful as a fawn is good. She dances like an angel, light as swan's down, and so forth, and also her playing. She is as proud as Lucifer of her playing upon the pianoforte. I will tell you the names of her pieces and you must say, I have never heard that Cherubini played with such feeling. The andante especially was divine. And so forth. She does not after all know many pieces, so this will be easily accomplished."

"That is absurd," I objected. "I know nothing of music nor do I care to learn the difference between one drone and another."

"Oh, but it is *all* show in love. Were I to dote upon a maiden who cared for horses above all else, which God forbid, I assure you, sir, I would be all fetlocks and withers, cruppers and blood mares. So must you exhibit connoisseurship of music, art, poetry--for that is what wins a girl's heart nowadays. And the sublime, a word that should trip often from your tongue: at the rising of the sun and its setting, should there happen to be any colors involved, at a thunderstorm or a bright moon, at the singing of a linnet. It shows deep feeling, you see. And you should write billets doux in numbers and slip them under her door, or pass them privily to her when walking in the gardens."

"We might ride out together," I said half despairingly, for if Oskar was right I would have to become quite a different boy from the one I was, and my pride griped at so doing, even for Marietta.

"Oh, no," says he, "she deprecates horses. They frighten her, and she will not venture a ride without she travels by carriage."

My face must have fallen at this intelligence, because Oskar gripped my shoulder and said, "But not to worry, for I have the key that will surely open her heart," with which he brought out his little blue leather book.

"*The Sorrows of Young Werther?*" said I.

"Just so," he replied. "As I have said, but you failed to heed it, it is the talk of Europe. Every young fellow of spirit has read it, and young ladies would love to do the same, especially the young lady of interest, but can she? Not at all, for it is depraved, and in no wise suitable, or so says my mama, who rules despotically in these things. As there is nothing like such a prohibition to engender desire, she is mad to have a look, and I have teased her mightily on the subject, for she knows well I have a copy.

"Now, what if you were to compose a billet doux in which you speak with enthusiasm of this book and let on you have a copy, and if she will slip out one evening late, you will be waiting in--let me see--the small walled garden would be best. She comes on noiseless slippers, perhaps uncorseted in her wrapper--oh, my! You read to her from the book. Her pulse quickens, her cheeks flush, she is swept up in Werther's passion--what could be more romantic!

"A few letters read from it per night, for you know it is epistolary, yes? Of course you do not. But a few evenings of this, and you have hooked your little fish. Nothing on earth will keep her from the rendezvous. You will have her all to yourself, in the moonlight, with the scent of blossoms--if she is not yours in a fortnight, I will eat my shoe."

"What if it rains?" I said, but in my heart I had already resolved to follow his plan. At the least it did not involve an excess of music.

Here the old baron seemed to fade into a memorious trance. After a few minutes, Rudi spoke. "And did it all transpire as Oskar foretold?"

"Oh, well, that Oskar! Make no mistake, my cousin was a good friend to me, according to his lights. But to Oskar, everything was an experiment. We were all newts to him, and as he was curious to see what would happen when a certain powder mixed with a certain liquid, so he wished to observe what transpired when a certain boy and a certain girl and a certain book were placed together in his alembic, which in this case was a walled garden under an espaliered pear tree decked with blossoms, under moonlight. Do you catch the figure?"

"Oh, it is plain, sir. And what was the result?"

"As to that, we advanced our scheme; and down she came upon a fair evening, decked in darling white ruffles, treading soundless, as he had foretold, on little slippers trimmed with fur. I read to her from the book. Have you read it?"

"Of course, Herr Baron," said Rudi. "Everyone has read *The Sorrows of Young Werther*. It is taught in all the schools as one of the great works of German literature."

"Is it now? Well, you know that they who think any book can be read by anyone with the coin to pay for it, which I suppose includes you, sir, may say all they like that there is no such thing as a bad book, and that no girl was ever ruined by a book, but I say that yon damned Weimaraner wrote a bad book, and a noose might better have been dropped over his head than any laurel wreath. As a story, you know, it is a mere nothing and of no interest to any man of breeding. A little bourgeois clerk infatuates himself with a married woman, makes a nuisance of himself to friends and family, disgraces himself before his duke, and, when the married lady--who, to make things worse, is married to the fellow's best friend-- when, I say, the married lady quite properly shows him the door, what does the fool do but shoot himself? And even that not done decently. A man blows his brains out, you know; only women shoot themselves in the breast. It is their vanity, sir, that outlives even their deaths. I only knew but one woman without it . . . but all that in its time. I am wandering, I find. Let us resume."

The short of it is, sir, that I was ensnared. The figure is exact, for I was caught in an actual snare when a boy. Lennart set it and forgot to tell me he had, the churl! And I had a deal of trouble freeing myself, I do assure you.

So, as I read the book, with that dear golden head bowing closer and closer, so that tendrils of her hair brushed against my cheek, and I could feel on my skin the heat of her breath, and as I saw how she was caught by the tale, how the poet made her heart beat in tune with the travails of his fancied clerk, why I tell you I was myself entranced. Not by the book, mind, but by the book-and-she, if you will allow that. By degrees the sorrows of Werther became my sorrows, and from a miserable whining fellow who wished only to debauch his friend's wife, blossomed a hero and a beau ideal of manhood.

Have you ever been taken over in that way? Yes, you have, by that damned fellow Voltaire and that rascal Rousseau, and this was quite the same. The world that had been one way was now the other. Music became a less unpleasant drone; I could at last tell one piece from another, this one doleful, that sprightly, and their names and parts. I was able to announce that the scherzo was brilliantly accomplished and see the nods of the assembly and the delight in my Marietta's eyes. The moon was sublime, or rather sublime was her little sigh when I named it so.

Thus from being interested in a variety of things, I became the devoté of but one. Marietta naturally spent much of her time in the house I dwelt in, since she had lost her mother at a young age and her father was much caught up in his own affairs. He was a drunk and a gambler, not to put too fine a point on it, but so were many men of our class in those days. It was hardly thought worth a comment. In any case, Aunt Fredi had become her effective guardian, and liked to have the girl under her eye.

I recall that it was wonderful being in love; of the object of this love I recall somewhat less. We talked, we walked through the gardens, we played bezique on inclement days. There were balls. I danced with her and looked daggers at any man who presumed to do the same. Did she love *me*? I suppose she did, but only as she loved her latest gown or the little reddish dog she owned, small enough to fit in a shako. She would send me on ridiculous errands . . . well, this grows tedious. Old love, especially ancient youthful love, is like a bottle of wine that has corked, and those who persist in pouring it out and tasting it are fools.

The family had the habit of decamping to Prague for the season, from, say. November to March, to the palace the Hohenbergs had in the Karlgasse, not so grand as the Clam-Gallas pile, but grand enough. Here more balls, and interminable concerts and theatricals, in which my beloved delighted, and so perforce the creature I had become must delight, too. I suppose I was in love, to a greater or lesser degree, for most of the period between my fourteenth and sixteenth years, during which time I considered it a done thing that when we were of age we would marry. I often spoke of this to Marietta, and she responded as a young girl ought. We would have an apartment at Pannau, and Mme. Wolanska would share it with us and be her companion while I was away at the wars. For it was the opinion of my aunt and uncle, which I came to share, that I was mere food for powder, having no discernable interests or abilities suitable for making my way in the professions of peace. We decorated that apartment, we bought airy furnishings, fancied horses and coaches, and bred imaginary children.

Then, upon a June day in 1786, a rider came pelting up to the Hohenberg palace in Prague with a message. I was slaughtering Oskar at billiards when the footman handed it to me. I slit the seal right there in the billiard room, my heart in my throat, for I could not conceive anything to my advantage in a letter from Pannau.

Oskar saw the look on my face when I had read it, and I must have looked like the plague, for he called out, "What is it! What has happened?"

"It is my father," said I. "He is dying and wishes to see me."

"The coach is out and will not be back until this evening. Will you wait, or take the post-coach?"

"Neither. I will ride Kíslang."

"But Pannau is near one hundred miles distant from Prague. It will take you days."

"I do not have days," I said, "I may have little more than *one*. Mme. Wolanska writes he is very near to it."

I raced out of the billiard room to my suite and donned boots and breeches, while Oskar stood and explained why I would be better advised to take the mail and how no one could possibly travel on horseback a hundred miles in a day.

"Give me some money," was all I said, and left for the stables. In half an hour I was clattering over the bridge to the Little Quarter, then out the Auguste Gate and the road to the north. It was a little after noon—I recollect the bells of St. Vitus ringing me from the town. Leaning over, I spoke earnestly to my horse: "My dear, we must ride now as we have never ridden before, without rest and little food, until we

reach Pannau. My father who has never spoken to me, wishes me to hear his final words, and if I am late I will deem my
life worth nothing. So stretch out, my love, let us canter and
let us gallop as the road permits, eat up the miles for me, Kíslang, my little flame."

And more to that effect. You will think it sentimental
to speak thus to a horse, but mind, I was asking her to do
something that no horse I ever heard of had done, and horses will not be whipped into feats such as that, but offer them
only for love and the pride of their blood. And she spoke
back to me, for in a ride such as that one falls into a rapture
of sorts, where you can understand the language of horses. I
cannot recall what she said, however.

Now a ride of an hour is a delight--horse, ground and
weather permitting, and a ride of six is an ordeal that leaves
one sore and the horse blown. Imagine then what a ride of
over twice that length is like! I ignored the physical pain, for
it is ignoble for a man to carp at this. Have you had the
toothache? Well, imagine a toothache in every joint, and a
flaming agony where the seat meets the saddle and along the
thighs. And yet in a strange way one moves in such cases beyond pain—I just spoke of rapture, and it is so, one departs
from the unbearable and seems to float outside the mortal
carcass. Thought ceases, one descends into the animal realm,
and I have a kind of memory of what that was like, but I
could never put it into words. It is too strange, too—if I may
be allowed the term—*mystical.*

On the other hand, we were blessed with good
weather and firm roads. It had rained in the district a few
days prior and so the dust was laid to an extent; I gagged
upon it, that is, but did not absolutely choke. We stopped
only for food and water, for though I was insane, my horse
was not; if I recollect, we made halts at Melnik, Dauba, and
Haida and we rode into the stable yard at Pannau in time to
hear the echoes of the clock in Pannauburg striking the hour
of one, making thirteen hours almost continuously in the
saddle and near one hundred and twenty miles on the road.

I found the Wachtmeister awake and dressed; I fell from the saddle into his arms.

"Does he live yet?" I asked.

"I have not heard the tolling-bell," said he. "Go! I will take care of your horse."

It was like walking through treacle. I could barely put one foot in front of the other and the scant few dozen yards that concluded my journey seemed like something in a nightmare, impossibly slow. A footman was waiting at the door with a lit lantern; he greeted me and led me to a hall I had scarcely passed through in all my years at the schloss, the region of our home where the Count had his apartments. I followed clumsily in his wake, up the stairs and down the dark hallway, past the invisible portraits of my ancestors, to where Mme. Wolanska sat in a chair by his door under a sconce with lit candles. She rose and put down the book she was reading. A moment's hesitation here, her face held stiff, as if expecting a slight, but I pulled her into my arms, we embraced, she kissed me thrice as was our old custom.

"How is he? I asked. "I came as soon as I received your message and have been in the saddle all night. What happened? You said a fall…"

"My child, I am so happy to see you! I feared you would not arrive on time and I have been praying as I have not for some years." Here she indicated the book, which was a breviary. "But I should not have doubted you, my valiant boy! Yes, a fall. He has been hunting every day since you left, in all weathers, it has always been his way when distressed. He is a magnificent horseman, as you know, but those mountain trails in the rain—his horse went down, he plunged into a ravine, and they had some difficulty getting him out. This can wait—go to him now. He has been asking for you by the hour."

I passed through the door. Attending him were a doctor from town, with an old woman I did not know, and Grodic, my father's valet.

I took this last aside and asked him to leave me alone with the Count, which, with a bow, he did, taking the others with him. A tough old bastard, Grodic, a soldier too; he had been weeping, I observed.

Now I stood by the head of the bed. The Count looked as he had always looked to me, although the cheeks were somewhat shrunk and his eyes shone out of dark sumps. These eyes stared at me; they were blue, unlike mine, and the absurd thought flew into my head that until this instant I had not really known their color. The silence hung, I cannot tell you how long, but a fearful long time, until at last he sighed deeply and said, "Oh, Christ, what have I done, what have I done! I will burn in hell for this, condemned for my pride. Oh wretched man!"

I said, "Pray, do not torment yourself, father. You must husband your strength for your recovery."

My first sentence to him, almost.

He said, "There will be no recovery. A jagged rib has pierced my vitals and I am bleeding inside. I have observed it often enough before. I will not see the dawn, so we have no time for anything but truth between us. Do you comprehend, boy? Good. You will want to know why your father has been a monster to you your whole life. On that marble credenza is a blue plush box. Bring it here, and bring that candelabra too. Light the candles, all of them. You will need the light to see this."

I did as I was told. He handled the box, a thing not much larger than a deck of cards. By the light of the six new candles I could see how very pale he had become, fish-belly pale with his lips turned blue as slate.

He opened the box, stared at it for a moment, and then handed it to me.

In it was an oval portrait done in enamel, surrounded by a rim of carved gold set with small brilliants. It depicted a lovely, dark haired woman in a white gown. I stared at her, gaping. Her face was my own.

I could hardly speak. "This is my mother?" I asked at length.

"It is, the whore! I am sorry, but there is no time for dissembling. She was in bed with that French Casanova before the dust of my leaving had settled. It killed me. Oh, it is a mere figure, I know, but true for all that. My heart was dead in my bosom, and so it has remained, and this now, this other dying, you must take as a mercy and a release. But, you know, I was still Count of Pannau, and obliged to live that life, although the man who carried the title was but a husk; nor can any man say I did not do my duty by my station and my name. I say I did my duty, save in one respect, which you know well to your awful cost. It was simply more than I could bear to have you in my presence. It is not merely that you are her living image. Your smile is hers, your laugh is hers, your carriage and your manner are so like, even the peasants saw it, and no one said a word. It was the great secret of the place, a curse of God, some said, that the image of the wanton bride would walk living through the halls of Pannau. You know I avoided you; and for why? So that I would not draw my sword and slay you, blameless though you are, and then fall myself upon a blade still wet with your innocent blood."

Here he fell to coughing, great wracking spasms, horribly liquid to the ear. I seized him about the shoulders and held his torso upright while he spewed bright gouts of crimson on the counterpane. After I wiped his mouth with a napkin, he resumed.

"Yes, it is close now, close as that cannonball at Leutzen that clipped my hat and took off the head of a corporal in the rank behind mine. By Christ, I have wished many a time the Prussian gunner had aimed lower. I would have come home a headless hero and saved much trouble to myself and others."

Another spasm of coughing, after which, he said, "Now let us speak of the future--yours, not mine, thank God at last! Your brother—well, he will be Count, of course, and you know he bears you no great love; nay, let us stay frank: he hates you and your life will not be worth living here. We are not Italians, thank God, but some would seek to please the lord of Pannau by arranging your departure from this world.

You know it has near enough happened already. Advocate Winkelmann has my will in hand. You will have five hundred florins a year. It is the tradition of our house that the younger sons make their own way in the world; for Pannau must be preserved and not cut into pieces every generation. Grodic will give you my red leather campaign chest. In it you will find my brace of rifle-pistols. They are by Hauschka of Woltenbüttel, and your man is dead at fifty yards. Aim low and to the left of your mark, but only a little, mind. You will have my service sword as well. Anton must have the jeweled one. And my portable billiard cue, the Mingaud. It has a leather bouton. You are a wonderful shot. I so wanted to embrace you when we were playing. I had to bite my lip so that blood came. Also there is a letter to Colonel von Kolowrat-Krakowski. You will buy a commission in the Kaiser Cuirassiers, although you are small for a cuirassier. But no matter, God willing, you will grow a little more; the colonel will see you right. He was rittmeister under me in 'sixty-two. There is a roll of ducats for the purchase. I cannot ask you to forgive me--only God can forgive such a father--but I hope you can pray for me sometime."

Now he clutched my hand and coughed again, worse than before. I called out for the doctor and nurse, and they came, but aside from cleaning him and changing his linen, they could, of course, do nothing. I stayed by his side until the dawn, when he gave up the ghost, saying nothing more than mumbles. Once I thought I heard my mother's name— Marie-Louise—and the words honor and loyalty. I think he was saying our family motto. He last words were, 'vedettes north and south of this line.' His mind had gone back to the battlefields of his youth.

So died Johann Anton Ludwig von und zu Pannau von Kinsky, twenty-sixth Count of Pannau, may he rest in peace, and may God forgive him, as surely have I. I had only a few moments of fathering from him, but I believe it was sufficient.

Well, there is not much more to tell before we find me on the Charles Bridge with my rope. I left my father's corpse and the bedroom, my sight obscured by tears. In the corridor outside I flung myself upon the bosom of Mme. Wolanska. We clutched each other, wailing, scandalizing the servants, I suppose, but little we cared.

When we had somewhat recovered, we walked down the hall to her apartment, where I was surprised to see preparations being made for a departure. Her maid was in the midst of folding a gown with tissue paper into a portmanteau. Madame W. dismissed the girl and I asked her where she was going. Surely she would stay for the funeral?

"Not I," she said with that familiar determined look on her face, "I would not be welcome and I wish to avoid any further slights. My time here is done, I believe. Horrible old place, yet I remember . . . well, none of that! I have said good-bye to my dear Jani in my own way, and that's the end of it."

"But where will you go?" said I. "How will you live?"

"I will manage, my dear. Decayed gentlewomen are thick on the ground where I come from. I shall be another pea to the pod. Your father was absurdly generous to me. I have traveling money and a modest bit of capital, the evil wage of my whoredom, as they will doubtless say in Krakow. But I have many friends left among the enlightened in Poland and I will not be entirely neglected. Perhaps I will open a public house, as I gather retired whores are wont to do."

"You? Never!"

"Come, it is a charming idea. I could call it, 'The Fallen Woman.' Speaking of which, I presume your father has revealed the secret behind his neglect—you have seen the enamel?"

"Yes. And I forgave him. If only my face had been ruined in infancy, none of this would have befallen me."

"If you had died in infancy you would have been even better off, by that calculation. Don't talk nonsense! Your father received a blow from Maria-Louisa from which he never recovered. Such things happen."

"Did you know her at all?"

"Did I? Why, we were the best of friends. Our husbands were, and so were we, when we were young."

Well, not to draw this out, but she described her life and how my mother fit into it, the balls, the traveling between estates, and so on. Apparently the two women were much in each other's company during the war. She said she had never seen a man so smitten by a woman as my father was with my mother. "For," she said, "I loved my Adrian well enough, as a wife should, but the marriage had been arranged by our parents, as was usual for those of our class. It was not a love match. Dangerous to let romance interfere with marriage, but such were the times. I was there when they met, a musical evening at the Khuen-Balasi palace in Vienna. Esterhazy was there, and he'd brought his man Haydn along. Your father was mad for music, you know."

"What! But my father despised music," I cried.

"Oh, no, not in those days. He doted upon it, I do assure you. In any case, after the musicians had played their pieces, old Khuen-Balasi asked Maria-Louisa if she would sing and she did. A voice like an angel, and you have seen her portrait—by the time she had finished, Jan was a cooked goose. And, like the stout cuirassier he was, he moved immediately to the assault—all flags and bugles. In two weeks the thing was done, engaged, the banns read, married that spring. Old von Neipperg, her father, was a fiend for faro, not a kreutzer in his purse, barely a crust in the house. You may believe he made no objection to his girl marrying the Count of Pannau."

"But didn't my grandparents object? He should have married a gräfin, or at least a woman of substance."

"Oh, no, his parents had both died before that."

"Yes, I recall now. Ljuba told me. Well, so he was an orphan. As am I now."

"As to that: I have not heard of her death She might live still."

"I don't care if she does. To me she is dead forever."

"Forever is a long while, my child. In the meantime, what are we to do with you? For you know you cannot remain under your brother's roof."

"I know. My father has arranged for me to join the cuirassiers."

At that she gave me a long, considering look, as one looks at a horse, and said, "I suppose it cannot be helped. With that face you would not be welcome as a diplomat, besides which your frankness of manner would tell against you. You have no vocation for the church, nor can I imagine you toiling at the law. You were born to be on horseback, charging into shot and shell, I am afraid. Well, it can be a jolly life, and I'd wager your poor face will be impressive, even in the Kaiser Cuirassiers--a duel at fifteen! And now you must rest. I will see you in the morning; and you will oblige me by taking me to the diligence at Pannauburg, where we will make our farewells."

Rudi completed his line and waited. But no more came from the old colonel but a buzzing snore, little louder than the purr of a cat. He had fallen sound asleep in his chair.

He left the house strangely disturbed, not so much by the tale but by the baron's talk of hidden levers. He did not care for the expression. In a proper state, the levers of power should be worked openly, not controlled by some cabal but by the representatives of the people.

It struck him forcibly then that he really knew nothing about Baron von Pannau-Kinsky, that is, the present man. A reactionary he could bear, but one connected to the secret police? A vague doubt only, but as he strode across the bridge he resolved to find out something about the man. He would ask Novotny. Meanwhile, speaking of absurd infatuations, it was Thursday, and that night he would attend the salon at Mme. von Silber's.

Twelve

The evening being fine, Rudi dispensed with a cab and walked rapidly, knocking his stick against railings with some vehemence as he passed through the streets. An unpleasant tension roiled his inner man, and he had found that physical activity tended to relieve it.

Why had Berthe implied that attending a salon was in some way a betrayal of their marriage? It must be the pregnancy, he concluded: that state, especially in its early stages, makes women half-mad, and as he thought this, he thought of a solution, and the further thought of the delight on the faces of his family when he told them lightened his heart, so that he arrived at his destination in far better spirits than when he had left his house.

Mme. Marina von Silber had her residence in a large stone-faced house on St. Annagasse, not far from the bridge. As he approached, a cab pulled up and two men alighted, conversing loudly in German, both well-fleshed men with an air of entitlement about their jowls. Rudi recognized one as the chairman of the Wenceslaus Committee, Alois Lörner, and bid him good evening.

Lörner turned his plate of a face upon Rudi with the searching, even intimidating look of a man not used to being accosted by strangers. But when he saw it was no stranger, he smiled and held out his hand.

"Is that you, Moritz? You are attending tonight, I see."

"Yes, sir, I have that honor."

"Not been before, have you? I have not observed you in the company here, I believe."

"No, sir. It is my initial visit"

Lörner indicated his companion. "Allow me to make you known to Alderman Borosch. It is his first visit as well, coming in as my guest."

Rudi shook the chill hand of the alderman, a broad beamed fellow with a complexion like raw pork.

Lörner said, "Let us go in together, shall we? By the way, who invited you? One of the Committee, I dare say."

"Actually, it was Sisi Vasová," said Rudi, with satisfaction. The two men exchanged a startled look and said nothing more as they went through the door into a well-lit vestibule. Greeting them was a butler of grave mien, in powder and a wasp-striped waistcoat, who, after extracting their names, engaged with a gesture a similarly liveried under-butler to take their hats, coats and sticks.

"The way it is done here, Borosch, " Rudi heard Lörner saying, "is I will make an introduction, you kiss her on the hand, a little chat and then off. Don't hover! She detests being monopolized."

They moved off, left the vestibule, and entered a large room, bright with the light of innumerable candles, crowded with chattering people. Rudi looked for Vasová, but she was not in evidence.

A few yards in from the door stood their hostess. Marina Von Silber was in her early sixties, or some said seventies, but her age was as indistinct as her other antecedents. Her enemies said she was spawned in some Galician slum, whored her way to Prague and there captured the heart of the wealthy military purveyor, Samuel Silber, via means better left unmentioned by Christian tongues. Another party, a somewhat larger one, claimed she was an unacknowledged daughter of the aristocracy, raised by respectable secular-leaning Jews of Pressburg, highly educated, and, if the truth be known, the brains behind Silber and thus the reason he had been made a baron for his services to the army and nation. Baron von Silber was conveniently dead. His relict did not use the title formally, but she was never displeased to be addressed as Baroness.

Tonight Mme. von Silber was wearing a black silk gown, into the fabric of which had been sewn thousands of jet beads, so that when the wearer moved, the impression was of roils in dark oily water. Pearls hung thick on her long neck, diamonds glittered from her headdress and ears, and one ring, an immense canary diamond, shone from a finger.

"Baroness, allow me to express my sincere delight at once again being invited into your home and your presence." This from Lörner, now bowing over the lady's hand.

"Dear Lörner," said she, "welcome, sincere delight as well. And who is this?"

She turned her gaze on Borosch, who essayed a smile, snatched at Mme Von Silber's hand and planted an audible kiss upon it.

"Ah, let me present to you Alderman Richard Borosch. He has long been an admirer of yours."

"Has he indeed? What exactly do you admire in me, Alderman?"

Alderman Borosch faltered, reddened, gaped. "Why, everyone admires your . . . hospitality, the wines and, ah, the foods are reputed to be excellent."

Are they? That is a surprise to me, since I serve only coffee and buttered bread. Feel free to indulge yourself in these, however. Oh, and as an alderman, I suppose you know all about the public sewers? In this regard, we have noticed some unpleasant odors in the cellars. Where we store the excellent wine? Can something be done, do you suppose?"

"I will attend to it myself, dear madam," said Borosch.

Mme. Von Silber cast a bright smile at the alderman and dismissed him from her attention. He opened his mouth to say something, but a tug on his arm from Lörner drew him away.

Rudi had been discretely studying Mme. Von Silber during this colloquy. What he saw was the attractive ruin of a woman once beautiful. The shriveling of youthful flesh had given prominence to the underlying architecture--the high cheekbones, the long, barely convex nose—and to the famous eyes, which were preternaturally large. These, though somewhat sunken, sparkled in the candlelight like the jet on her costume.

They turned now on Rudi. "And who might you be, sir?" She inquired. "Please God, not another alderman."

"Not even so high as that, madam. My name is Moritz, and I appear before you with some embarrassment. I am here at the invitation of Sisi Vasová, but she is not here to present me. Perhaps I must withdraw?"

"Not at all. Vasová is in the music room, singing in that wonderfully vulgar voice of hers and breaking hearts. She has told me all about you, and you are therefore most welcome. In any case, I would have desired to make the acquaintance of the author of our magnificent Bohemian petition. What sentiments! What noble periods! Everyone declares the great Kossuth could not have bested it for style. And not only brilliant, but dashing. I have heard how you knock rival lovers to and fro with your stick! I like some dash in a man. Deplorable as is any violence, still I must confess it manly."

"Un-aldermanly certainly."

She opened her mouth and laughed, a series of dry barks.

"Very good. Although I hope you will not lay about you here."

"Never fear, madam. My stick is safely racked, and in general I am not disposed to cause havoc in drawing rooms. Aside from anything else, it would be tortious."

"Worse, tedious. But enough of you, Herr Moritz. What about me? Have you, like the alderman, long been an admirer of mine?"

Only through hearsay, madam, for until this moment I had not the honor of knowing you. Say I admired you as I admire the Atlantic, which I have also yet to see, but know to be unfathomably deep, cool, sublime and at times dangerous."

She laughed again, snapped her fan shut and tapped him on the chest with it.

"I find you have a ready tongue, Herr Moritz. It will make your fortune, I dare say, or ruin you."

"Surely nothing I say here can ruin me, madam," Rudi answered, but Mme. Von Silber was already looking past him at what must have been the next arrival. Rudi turned his head and saw a handsome, elegantly dressed, dark-bearded man of about his own age.

Mme. Von Silber extended her hand to this gentleman, and dipped an elegant curtsey.

"Ah, Count, how good of you to honor my house this evening!"

"Charmed, madam," said the man, "really, is there anywhere else in Prague to be when it is open for soirée?"

Rudi sensed a dismissal and turned to move away, when Madame detained him with a touch of her fan against his shoulder. "Count, if I may--here is someone you should know. Allow me to present Herr Moritz, author of the petition to his majesty from the Bohemian Estates? Herr Moritz, Leopold Graf von Thun."

Rudi bowed stiffly from the neck. "Honored, Sir."

Thun acknowledged the bow with a nod and a smile, made an intelligent comment or two about the petition, voiced his hope that a constitution for Bohemia might soon be written, and seemed inclined to enter into a serious political conversation with Rudi, except that he and his hostess were soon surrounded by a number of people who wished an introduction to the nobleman, and Rudi found himself edged away and then completely out of the circle around Thun.

Rudi moved into the drawing room, a large, high-ceilinged well-lit chamber, furnished with a number of small tables and one quite large, round one. The small tables were occupied, crowded even, with more chairs stuck beneath them than their circumference suggested might fit. The large table and its attendant chairs stood quite empty.

Lörner sat at one of the small tables with Borosch, Alois Trojan, the most prominent Czech on the Committee, and several others sat a nearby table, drinking coffee and consuming quantities of Mme. Von Silber's bread and butter. An empty chair beckoned, but Rudi was reluctant to sit. Instead he leaned over Lörner and said, "Excuse me, Herr Lörner, I am curious as to why no one uses that large round table. Is it some superstition of the house?"

"Not at all. At seven, Madam is accustomed to sit herself there and assemble around her the choicest conversationalists present. There they hold forth, often for some hours. Then, if there are musicians at hand, the party moves to the music room next door. Do you know Liszt once played there?"

"Yes, I have been so informed."

"None so fine, tonight, I fear. I hear your Vasová is at large somewhere, so we will probably have to sit through her Czech warbling. Can that be her music we hear now?"

The playing of a piano could be heard from the next room, powerfully struck chords and startlingly rapid runs of notes.

"No," Lörner concluded, "that is someone else, perhaps the ghost of Liszt. A fine hand, whoever it is. Do not hover, Moritz, but sit yourself down."

Rudi took the only vacant chair, and Lörner made the inductions.

"Herr Baumer here, who heads our casino, has long desired to make your acquaintance. I believe you already know Herr Trojan, our Czech friend; here is Alderman Borosch of course, and this is Herr Schnee, the wheat king, as we like to call him, and Herr Voss, who is involved in the manufacture of steam engines. Herr Maisel, the banker."

Rudi nodded to each these gentlemen and shook hands. Except for Trojan, who was about Rudi's age, they all seemed of a type: heavy, firm-jawed, narrow-eyed German gentlemen in their fifties. Even Maisel had managed to submerge whatever Jewish identity he might have inherited under that thick confident plaster. They reminded him of his father, and he was conscious of a demonic urge to treat them as he treated Kalo.

"I believe I know your father," Maisel said, as if reading his mind. "We have often done business with him, the railway bonds and so forth. An excellent fellow."

"I will tell him you said so," Rudi replied, "when I see him in Vienna after his imperial majesty has received our petition and agreed to every single point."

A heavy chuckle from the group, and then a discussion of the fluid situation in the Hofburg, the shifting alliances, the danger that the forces of reaction, knocked off balance for the moment, might recover.

"Oh, you can be sure the reactionaries will do something," said Maisel. "Rumor has it that Prince Windischgratz is to be military commander in Bohemia."

"What! " said Rudi, genuinely shocked. "They cannot suppose the butcher of '44 will be acceptable to the people. They will take to the streets."

"Some will want to," said Trojan, "But as leaders of the people, we must do all we can to retain calm. Calm is what will bring the revolution to a successful conclusion, by which I mean a constitutional Bohemian state within the empire."

"The constitutional issues in such a state would be a nice puzzle," Rudi observed.

"What do you mean, constitutional issues?" asked Lörner.

"Well, sir, the great thing about an absolute monarchy is its simplicity . . ."

"There is no great thing about any absolute monarchy," called a low growling voice. "I know you, sir, and as I suspected, you are a secret lover of tyranny. Admit it, and be damned!"

Thus Mikhail Bakunin made his entrance. Standing next to him was their hostess, on the other side of whom stood Count Thun.

Rudi observed the look of satisfaction on the woman's face. This is what she loves, he thought, to bring together deadly enemies and render them tame for a few hours, with only the power of hospitality as a weapon in her hands.

When they were all seated and coffee and buttered toast had been served out, Mme. von Silber addressed Rudi. "Herr Moritz, I was interested in what you started to say about the constitutional question before the Russian hordes invaded."

"There are no Russian hordes," said Bakunin.

"You are a horde in yourself, Bakunin. Do be quiet for a moment, would you! Herr Moritz?"

Rudi felt all eyes turn to him, not only those seated but also most of the other people in the house, who it now seemed clear had gathered around the hostess's table, sitting on chairs they had pulled over, or standing in groups. Two chairs remained empty, but no one moved to take them.

"Yes, I was saying that the autocratic state is simple compared to the constitutional state that may succeed it. Power is distributed by design, many share it, negotiations must precede its exercise, and so on; here in Bohemia the situation is made more complicated by nationality, and by the peculiar and unique nature of the Austrian empire of which it is a part."

"Why peculiar, sir?" asked Thun.

"I advert to its scarcity of actual Austrians, my lord. Fewer than one in four in the empire is a German by birth. And yet everywhere Germans rule, to the eternal resentment of everyone else. Any electoral system we devise under the new constitution will have to account for the nationality issue. This issue also makes difficult or impossible any opening to Frankfurt. It is all very well for the men of Frankfurt to call for a parliament of all the Germans, but were we to join them as an empire, we would face revolt in every corner of our Slavic lands. Aside from that, Europe absolutely *requires* an Austria. It is the diplomatic balance wheel of the continent, and Bohemia is the balance wheel of the empire. If we cannot form a state here in which the nationalities can live together as one, then the empire is doomed, Europe with it."

"And the solution is . . . ?" said Mme. Von Silber. "I wish you all to remember that the salvation of Europe was first voiced at my table."

Everyone laughed, including Rudi. "Madam, you have me there. I look around for models, of course. The American system merits notice in this regard."

"Yes," said Bakunin. "Perhaps we could import black slaves. That is what seems to hold their system together."

"Such is the case in only a part of that nation," Rudi answered, "and the least important part. No one who has studied the issue doubts that the Americans will deal with the slavery question as Britain has, and abolish the practice peacefully through popular legislation. But my point was that the American constitution makes provision in its Senate for the equal representation of both weak and powerful states. It is most ingenious at protecting the rights of smaller powers from the tyranny of majorities . I imagine we could devise something similar so that all nationalities in the empire would feel safe from the oppression of the others."

"No, no, you have not understood the problem," said Bakunin. "Your constitution and your senates are a mere sleight of hand, sir, to salve consciences and distract from the gross injustice that lies at the heart of any bourgeois society. You are an intelligent and well-meaning man, Moritz. How is it that you do not see this?"

"No one sees this, Herr Bakunin," said Maisel. "No system that does not respect private property has ever nor can ever exist in the real world. I wonder that you persist in proposing yours."

Bakunin persisted, and launched another tirade, advancing notions that Rudi had already heard. Rudi recalled Speyr's opinion of the man—harmless in himself but deadly as an inspirer of others. That Bors, for example, he of the supposedly prodigious weapon.

The music from the other room stopped then, and soon a familiar voice broke through the Russian's spate.

"Oh, God help us, Bakunin is at it again. Bakunin, tell us, what is the place of music in your new world? Can we at least sing in your classless, Godless, propertyless paradise?"

Sisi Vasová pushed through the circle, towing by the arm a slight youth whose intense yearning expression shone through the distractions of mustache, chin beard and thick oval spectacles.

"You all know Smetana?" she asked, as if they all should. "A wonderful musician! He will play for us later."

Everyone nodded at the youth, who bobbed his head in response. Atop his wide, slightly bulging, pale brow sat a mass of coarse brown hair like a miniature shako, and this seemed to wiggle with each bob.
Vasová slipped into the seat next to Bindermann and pulled the young man down on her other side.

"Of course there will be music," said Bakunin, "all the arts will flourish, for everyone will be trained in them, not just a select few, as now. How many artists and composers have had to sweat their lives away in field and factory, with no opportunity to give voice to their talent?"

"None," said Vasová. "Genius cannot be suppressed by any system devised by man, and I present myself as an example. No one was ever born lower, and yet here I am, conversing with the aristocratic Bakunin in an elegant salon. But can we not talk about music now? Are we always to live suspended in waiting for the new revolutionary order? How terribly tedious to drain the life from the moment in slavery to the future! Don't you find it so, madame?"

Mme. von Silber smiled indulgently at the singer. "Tedious but necessary. For we must change things."

"Must we? Oh, I suppose so. It is dreadful always to feel a stranger in one's own land, German in one's ears every minute."

"Hear her, hear her!" said Trojan, and two Czechs on the fringes of the group and a woman clapped their hands.

"But must it be done through these tedious *systems*? Could not art lead the way? Art changes the souls of people, and once changed, they must naturally create forms of government allowing a better and freer life for the nation."

Trojan spoke up. "But what sort of art would that be, dear lady?"

"Oh, you know, poetry and painting, novels, of course, and especially opera. Think of what Mozart's *Figaro* did for the liberal cause! The rulers wished to ban it, I mean the original play, but with that glorious music attached they could not. It was put on and lifted every heart that saw it against the oppression of our masters, even if the libretto was Italian. Why are operas always in Italian?"

"Because it is the most beautiful language for singing?" Rudi offered. She seemed to notice him for the first time.

"Moritz! You came! " she cried, and gave him one of her smiles. He felt his face flush with pleasure.

"Oh, that it what everyone says," she continued, "but that is only because the Italians invented it and have the most libretti. Yet when people's hearts yearn for song, they sing in their own language. Even the Russians sing, I am told, and the Africans. Mozart wrote an opera to a German libretto, after all, and no one thought it very bad of him. Don't we all love *The Magic Flute*? But now we must also have operas in Czech."

At this, laughter rang around the table.

"What! You laugh?" said Vasová. "Why is this amusing?"

Maisel said, "No offense is meant, Fraulein Vasová—but, you will forgive me, an opera in *Czech*?"

"And why not?"

"Because opera is a refined art and operatic libretti require a certain poetical refinement in their language. An Italian libretto has centuries of poetical diction behind it, and German poetry, if not so ancient as that, still has a considerable tradition. But Czech is a folk language—you yourself mentioned Africa, and while I suppose the Hottentots have their chants and so forth, they do not make operas."

How remarkably her face transforms when she stops smiling and her eyes stop emitting their sweet radiance, thought Rudi: something positively witchlike there, quite frightening!

"I know nothing of Africa, sir," replied Vasová in a chilly tone, "but the Czech of Bohemia was as sophisticated a literary language as any in Europe in the sixteenth century, certainly the equivalent of English or German of the same era. This language was systematically destroyed by our Hapsburg conquerors as an act of state. *Finis Bohemiae!* as the saying goes: our libraries were burned, our schools were closed, our children were forced to read and write only German, our poets and teachers and philosophers were killed or driven into exile. Our religion was banned, so that even when we spoke to God we had to do it in an alien tongue. So you crushed us; and as crushed beings we were worthy of contempt. But no more. We have writers now as good as any in Europe, writing in Czech—Palacký, Havlíček, the great Mácha . . . "

"You!" cried Trojan. Rudi noted that the lawyer's face had taken on a most un-lawyerly glow, as if he were watching a circus act or a horse race.

"Not me! I am no more than the little woman who takes the coats at the music hall, knows all the tunes, and hums. But we will make a Czech literature in your despite, O Germans, and we will sing opera in Czech too."

"Yes, yes," said Bakunin, "and you will all speak Czech, and in Czech the bourgeois will order the continued immiseration of the workers, and the workers will rebel in Czech and the bourgeois will order the Czech soldiers in Czech to shoot them down when they rebel, and Czech judges will sentence the miserables to hard labor. In perfect Czech, of course. Do you really imagine, Vasová, that oppression and brutality will be more difficult under one language than another? I did not think you so silly. Has the dominance of the German tongue made the plight of German laborers any easier? I assure you, in Russia everyone is oppressed in perfect Russian."

"I thought you all spoke French when you ruled the peasants," said Maisel slyly, at which Bakunin shot him a fuming glance and said something inaudible, so although they could not tell if it were French or Russian, its tone was unmistakable.

There was a brief, unpleasant silence, into which Count Thun spoke. "Madam Vasová, allow me to speak as one of your conquerors. It is true that many dreadful acts were accomplished during the suppression of Bohemian nationality and religion in the years after 1618, and these I do regret. But history moves on and we must move with it. Next week the Bohemian people present a petition to his imperial majesty, calling for full freedom for the Czech language and full freedom of religion. I have every confidence that it will be accepted and that these principles will be embodied in the constitution he has also recently granted. We can then move forward, German and Czech Bohemians together, to deal with the many problems of the nineteenth century, and leave those of the seventeenth to molder in the grave. It seems to me that a constitutional Bohemian state within the empire, protected by that empire from powers far more despotic than Austria at its worst, is the best solution for the unpleasant occurrences of long ago. Would you not agree, madame?"

Vasová responded, "Yes, Count, it is well enough when you have burned down a man's house to propose to let him build another, but make sure it is not a dollhouse, but a real one that he can live in and have his human life. So is your Bohemia within the empire a real house or not? That I don't know. But of one thing I am sure: if ever the Czech people can find it in them to reach out their hand to the Germans, it will be standing on their feet, not kneeling to take a gift from a sovereign. And how can a people stand on its feet without their own culture, at the highest levels, I might add? Which is why we must have Czech operas."

Now she smiled around the table and raised her hands in a theatrical gesture, like a conjurer concluding a trick. There was a burst of applause, mainly from the Czechs in the group. Rudi himself applauded vigorously.

Bakunin deliberately crossed his arms upon his chest and frowned, lowering his head, bull-like. "Bah! What nonsense!" he exclaimed. "Operas! I thought to find intelligent political discussion here, and what do I find? Operas in Czech!"

Rudi observed that witch's look on Vasová's face once more—how she transforms herself with her changing passions, he thought, and also how she seemed to combine and intensify all that was alien to him about the Czech people! He had often felt it with Havel in the office, something a little uncanny, and it was not just the language.

"Oh, Bakunin," she replied. "Do you think anyone will ever live in an anarchist society? Don't you sometimes shrink before the utter futility of your work, the meetings, the arguments, all wasted laboring for a system that no possible revolution can bring about? Whereas, it is perfectly possible to have an opera in Czech, and we will, and all of us can see it and partake of real pleasure in our lives, nor need anyone be shot or imprisoned before it can occur."

Here she clapped the thin young man on the back. "Perhaps Smetana here will write it. Perhaps he has one already tucked in his portfolio."

The young man blushed and emitted a strangled sort of giggle. "Oh, no, I am just . . . I mean to say, an opera! Well, I have just a few small pieces. I am too young to have composed an opera."

"He has performed his G Minor Sonata before the Schumanns," said Mme. von Silber. "At the home of our own Count Thun. A very promising Czech musician. And still so young!"

"Although he hardly speaks Czech at all," added Vasová. "But he will learn in time for his opera, won't you, Herr Smetana?"

Smetana nodded vigorously, and seemed ready to rush off to lessons. Count Thun said, "Of course, age is no bar to genius. Didn't Mozart write an opera at ten?"

At this question the conversation turned to that safest of subjects, with some relief, Rudi thought, at shoving the great bogey of nationality back, for the moment, into its fetid cave. Talk of Mozart was nearly as delightful as his music; the familiar anecdotes were displayed for some minutes, before Maisel cleared his throat for attention and said, "Not ten, I believe, but he did produce a little thing called *Apollo and Hyacinth* for the archbishop in Salzburg in 1767, when he was eleven. I suppose his first real opera was *Mitridate* in 'seventy. It does not hold the boards today, of course: a style too antique for modern tastes. His first, we might say, immortal opera was *Idomeno,* composed during his twenty-fourth and twenty-fifth years. I suppose Herr Smetana is of that age at present. You must begin your labors, sir, and astound us with an *Idomeno,* an *Idomenov,* that is, in Czech."

Here titters broke out, rather louder among the Germans than the Czechs, but still, good humor had been restored. Count Thun said, "Herr Maisel, I compliment you on your musicological knowledge. You have made it your study, have you?"

"In a small way, my lord. I have a man assembling notes for a biography. There is a great deal of material—the master was famed throughout Europe for decades. Although one longs to speak directly to those who knew him. I believe one son survives at Naples, but it seems there is no one left in Prague who recalls his visit to our city."

Some talk now of ancients still residing in town, and the possibilities that they had been present and aware in 1786, and then Rudi casually announced, "I know a man who knew him. Played billiards with him, in fact, and taught him riding as well. I am happy to say he is still with us, and with his faculties intact. He is called Johann Anton Ludwig Freiherr von und zu Pannau von Kinsky, and I am helping him with his memoirs."

Expressions of fascination and interest from all. Rudi observed a look of satisfaction on the face of his hostess. Political talk, musical talk was all very well, but nothing could match gossip for illuminating a salon.

"Tell us all!" she demanded. "Is it like a visit from a ghost? What did he have to say of Mozart? Did this Herr Baron attend the concerts? Did Mozart pass on to him the secrets of the *Requiem*'s composition?"

"Not at all, madam. It was with the keenest disappointment you may be sure that, despite this connection, my baron has no interest at all in music."

Thirteen

"I always leave when she brings out the cards," said Sisi Vasová. They were walking rapidly down St. Annasgasse toward the square, she clutching Rudi's arm in a tight grip, as if she feared he would run from her. "Am I imposing? Did you dreadfully wish to play boston? By the Virgin, I am famished—I had half a bread roll and a coffee at dawn, it seems, and nothing since except two of those miserable thin slices of bread and butter she serves . . . and Christ Jesus, I need a drink. I am awash in that cheap coffee. I thought Jews dined well—I know they do, although no pork, the poor wretches! I adore a pork chop. Moritz, let us find a tavern and you will buy me a brace of chops and a stein of Pilsner!"

Rudi was not entirely sure how he had been inveigled out of Madame von Silber's, for he had been looking forward to sitting around a card table with some of the most astute and influential people in Prague, it being well known that the real politics of reform were hammered out between deals at those very tables.   Nevertheless, when Vasová had come up to him, placed her hand meaningfully upon his arm, and said that it was absolutely necessary for her to leave, and that, since she had invited him, it was his duty to escort her home, he had acquiesced. He had bid farewell to the assembly, individually if of rank or standing, and taking especial care to remain in the good graces of his hostess. She assured him that he was welcome at any time, meanwhile casting significant glances at his companion.   With that, Vasová had whisked him away; he recalled their retreat from the Red Goose the previous week—the woman had a genius for precipitate exits.

"Since you mention it, I do rather enjoy a game of boston, if the stakes are not too high. Do you truly despise the table?"

"As to that, I am indifferent to the play itself, but stakes of any height are too high for me, and I am far from indifferent to shame. I thank you for this indulgence, Moritz. You are exceedingly kind."

"Well . . . I confess it was a bit awkward. What can they all be thinking?"

"Oh, an easy question: they are all sure you have taken me off to bed."

"Do you really think so?" replied Rudi with as much aplomb as he could manage. "Do I exhibit the character of a rake?"

"Not in the least--a mien of perfect chastity, as you would of course assume in distinguished company, were I in fact your mistress. I wager you that more than half of those exalted gentlemen have a little Czech femme de chambre or, if noble, an actress, stabled in a neat apartment in Mala Strana, convenient to the courts. It is the done thing, Moritz."

She paused and regarded him quizzically. "Can you really be so pure of heart? If so, it would be the wonder of Prague. They should place you in a glass case next to the Infant in the Church of Our Lady of Victory."

He had nothing to say to that, as he felt his heart was very far from pure at the moment, polluted indeed, whenever he was in Vasová's presence.

"Ah, there is a place," she cried, pointing to a sign hanging in an alley off the Jesuitergasse. "Let us go in, Moritz. I am positively fainting!"

He let her pull him along into the tavern. At the Stork was not the sort of place he would have entered himself: low-ceilinged, dim, smelling of old beer and boiling, with the signs in Czech only.

The waiter put them at a table in the back, behind an angle of wall, although there was plenty of room in the front. Rudi understood what the fellow must have thought: a gentleman in beautifully cut evening clothes in the company of a handsome, bold-faced woman in a cheap dress. It was obvious what was going on, and that the gentleman would value discretion.

"Yes, he thinks I'm a whore," Vasová confirmed when the waiter had departed with their order. "No, don't deny it—it is the natural order of things, that a fine German gentleman should have a Czech whore. This is what it means for one nation to have domination over another."

"But we can change that. Isn't that the purpose of the revolution? Surely you cannot believe that this is permanent in our land, like the rivers and mountains?"

"No, not as permanent at that. In truth, I look forward to the day when fine Czech gentleman have German whores. Oh, wonderful, here is the beer!"

She drank from the stein in great gulps, like a carter, then banged the stein down half drained, saw his face, and laughed.

"Your face! You look like you are watching a catastrophe—a coach has tumbled off a bridge. Yes, I am a vulgar person without manners, although you have witnessed that I know how to comport myself in a salon. But with friends I can be myself, and you are a friend, Moritz, though a dirty *skopčák*—are you not?"

"I very much wish to be," said Rudi, fervently.

"I know you do. And as a friend I will show you the real Bohemia and the real Prague, which you do not for a moment suspect. I mean the depths, the pillars of the society whose upper frothy levels we have just left, the lows where the subject peoples sweat and toil to maintain the glittering empire of Hapsburg. In return . . . in return, you will buy me pork chops and best Pilsner. Do you like that bargain? I assure you it is better than the one we usually strike with the Germans—you will be accounted a saint among both peoples."

The waiter came by and asked her a question, and they had a conversation, the Czech too rapid and muffled by dialect for Rudi to follow, at the end of which the man burst into laughter and walked off, still chuckling.

"What was that all about?" Rudi asked.

"An untranslatable colloquy between peasants, far too crude for your bourgeois ears. We will have to give all that up when the great day dawns and the little Germans must learn Czech in the schools. No more the secret insult as our masters look on uncomprehending, our pathetic revenges Oh, your mouth droops so when I rail against the Teutonic boot on my neck. And you have such a sweet mouth."

She took his hand in both of hers. "Perhaps you alone have not your boot on my neck; perhaps it is a naked foot only. Oh, alleluia! Here is my supper!"

The waiter unloaded three platters and a bread basket from his tray: two thick pork chops in steaming gravy, a pile of small potatoes doused in butter, garlic, and parsley, and a bowl of boiled cabbage flecked with poppy-seeds. It was a meal fit for a foundry-man, but this did not seem to daunt the poet. She set to like a starveling, forking dripping chunks of food into her mouth as if it were about to be snatched away, pausing only to call for another stein of beer.

Rudi sat in silence, drinking bad brandy with a soft smile on his face, fascinated. She was right, it was very like watching a catastrophe of nature or a display of exotic beasts at a circus. She cleaned all three plates, wiping them thoroughly with lumps of bread, which she stuffed into her mouth—something Rudi had been taught was the final infamy at table—and when the last scrap had vanished, and the bones actually *sucked clean*, sat back, sighed, belched mildly, giggled at this, and grinned, her face shiny with grease.

"Oh, *ty vole*, but that was good! Moritz, you have saved my life and I will never forget it, never! But now we must go—what time has it got to? What were the last bells for?"

Rudi consulted his watch. "It must have been ten. It is getting on for eleven."

"*Sacra*! We must fly!" Rudi settled the bill and they were out in the street walking rapidly towards the Square. Rudi had to hurry his pace to keep up with her.

"Can we have a fiacre?" she asked. "I am late."

"You have an engagement?"

"Yes, I . . . I give lessons."

"In what, may I ask, at eleven in the evening?"

Instantly the witch face appeared. "Oh, do not interrogate me, sir! I cannot bear to be interrogated, especially not in German. I will not stand it!"

"You are right that it is none of my business—a friendly curiosity merely. I do beg your pardon."

"You have it. I will count one cutlet against your score. Oh, see, there is a cab. Can you . . . no, let me." Again she produced a whistle like a steam engine. The fiacre came trotting up to the curb at the head of Jesuitergasse at the entry to the Old Town Square.

Rudi told the driver to go to his house on Zeitnergasse. "He will take you home from there," he said, "although, perhaps you would like to show me where you live. I would try not to interfere with your lesson."

"Another time perhaps. Perhaps after the revolution we will live in the same phalanastery, and salute each other as we trudge to work in our smocks."

"But really . . . "

"I don't know what *really* is, dear Moritz. I am a poet, after all. Really is for you lawyers. Oh, it is fine to ride in a fiacre, is it not, and see all the lowly Czechs stumping by in their worn-out clogs."

"Some of them may be lowly Germans stumping, you know."

"Again you introduce reality where it is not wanted. Do not become tedious in that way, Moritz, for I wish to like you! Ah, are we here already? Well, that is not so fine a house as I imagined the son of Moritz the banker would occupy."

"Thus in at least one regard your imagination proves deficient. Dear lady, I will bid you a good night."

As if in answer, she leaned toward him, clutched his thigh, threw her other arm around his neck and drove her mouth against his. Her tongue, heavy with the taste of meat and garlic, writhed like a trapped animal and withdrew. He was aware of the most powerful carnal feeling he had ever enjoyed, if enjoyed was the word.

"Ah, you have a good mouth, Moritz. That was a most pleasant aperitif. But look here, have you any money on you?"

"Why, yes, a little. You mean for the fare?"

"That, and besides I must have ten florins immediately. Have you got it?"

"Ten florins?" It was a month's wage for his clerk. "What do you need ten . . . oh, pardon me, madame, I am not to interrogate." He withdrew his note case and handed her some currency, and a few coins for the cab.

"I will see you again," she said, releasing her grip on his thigh, which continued to tingle. "Now, be off!" She sat back on the seat and looked away from him, made a little shooing motion with her hand.

Exiting, he watched the cab disappear around a corner and thought, I am in danger of becoming another Hans von Pannau, if on a smaller scale of venery.

The next morning, the Friday, Rudi announced to his family that they were all going to Vienna Sunday. On the train! They would visit the grandparents, they would ride in the Prater, it would be such fun! Fritz cheered and clapped his hands and Reni did too, although she was not entirely sure what Vienna was. As for Berthe, she went so far as to throw her arms around him and give him an enthusiastic kiss, making the children giggle and the maidservant blush.

"Have I made up for my neglect a little?" he said when he caught his breath.

"Oh yes, and with interest, as the Fathers always say. Oh, Rudi, please say we can visit Kunningshelm! The children have not been there since they were babies. And they can see their grandparents and all their relations, the cousins —oh, it will be grand!"

He had not seen such a look of delight on her face for too long. It was her natural look, something that grew out of her nature. He warmed himself at it, and said, "Well, perhaps for a short visit. This business with the petition should not take very long."

At his first free moment at work the next day, Rudi went to Major Speyr's office, past the clerks and the guards, and found the policeman at his desk.

"Well, Rudi," said Speyr, rising and shaking his hand. "Do have a chair! I have just been thinking about you."

"And why is that, Wulfi?" asked Rudi as he sat.

"Because I have received a minute from my superiors. You are to be given special handling, it seems."

"And what is meant by that, if I may ask?"

"You may, but will get no answer. I could befuddle you by citing reasons of state, but since you are an old friend, I will be frank. I have no idea, except I have an impression that it arose at the highest levels."

"Really. And what does special handling mean?"

"Why, only that I am to desist from trying to pry from you information about your many disloyal acquaintances. I have no interest in what occurred at Mme. von Silber's last night, at least not from your lips. By the way, what did happen, since you're here?"

"We spoke of nothing but his imperial majesty, and praised his virtue and wisdom to the heavens."

Speyr uttered a short, barking laugh, just the same one as Rudi recalled him voicing when he was a large and overbearing boy up to mischief. "That's very good. But I care not; I didn't hear it, your doings are a closed book to me henceforth."

"Shall I take that as an insult? Have I really fallen beneath the contempt of the secret state police?"

Ignoring this, Speyr said, "I understand you are working, if that's the word, for Baron von Pannau-Kinsky."

"What of it? What's he to do with all this?"

Speyr put on a bland smile. "You have no idea how infrequently people in that chair are allowed to ask questions. In that way too, you are a special case. Are you truly as ignorant as you profess? Well, you must at least know that your baron was a dragoon. Yes, in certain quarters, while you and I were just getting into long trousers, he was quite famous as *the* Dragoon. I suppose it was a secret fame, if that is possible—a what d'you call it . . ."

"An oxymoron," said Rudi. "In what did this fame consist?"

"Oh, well, if you had pesky rebels in some godforsaken corner of the empire and you wanted someone to carry out a dragonnade—go in there with fire and sword and root the bastards out—then Pannau-Kinsky was your man. He suppressed the Parmese when they rose up in 'thirty, did you know that? They still shudder at his name, I'm told, and frighten the children with it. Of course he knows everyone in the service, including Count von Pencheg. I expect you know who he is."

"The police minister of Bohemia and I are strangers, so far.

"By him I am directed to remove one Rudolf Moritz from my lists and forever ignore his doings with respect to the internal security of the empire, so long as said Rudolf does not commit acts of treason with a foreign power or murder officials of the empire about their lawful duty or raise his hand against the person of his imperial majesty. Can I count on you to resist these temptations?"

"You have my word. But I had not realized I was on lists."

"Oh, Rudi, of course you are on lists. This is Austria. Everyone is on some list. You are a prominent liberal. That is one list.   You are well in with Czechs of uncertain loyalty. . ."

"Who, may I ask?"

"You may not. That is another list. And you are also on the most select list of all, those who hobnob with the most dangerous men in Europe."

"You must be mistaken in your hobnobbery. Signor Garibaldi is as much a stranger to me as the police minister,."

"Oh, don't play the fool, Rudschen! You know very well I mean Bakunin and his invisible familiar, Bors. Help me here, my old friend—do you know anything at all about their movements or plans?"

"I do not, and would not tell you if I did, save in case of the three situations you have noted."

"Then I have done my duty. The old Dragoon, my word! I understand he has you writing his memoirs. That should be an interesting tale. I wonder why, of all the scribes in Prague, he chose Rudi Moritz."

"I have wondered that myself."

"Enjoyable work?"

"Remunerative, at least. And as you say, he tells an interesting tale."

"I'll wager," said Speyr, "and by the way, to what do I owe the pleasure? Did you have business with the police to-day?"

"Not at all, Wulfi. I happened to find myself in your hall and thought I would just drop by to see an old friend." With a broad grin, Rudi rose and departed. He returned to his office, bemused and troubled by the information Speyr had conveyed, and was not surprised to find a note with the famil-iar seal upon it sitting on the middle of his desk.

Some hours later, Rudi was in a comfortable chair in the green room at the baron's house, listening to his talk, and making notes in shorthand. The old man was arranged upon

189

a chaise, with a throw over his legs. His voice sounded strained to Rudi, and he supposed it was because the events he was now recounting remained painful, even after the passage of many decades.

He described how he accompanied Mme. Wolanska to the post coach and saw her comfortably upon it, and quite disgraced himself before the assembled common folk, blubbing and covering her hand with kisses, until she sternly called him back into countenance.

There departed the woman who had formed my soul, as my wretched mother had formed my body in her womb. Ever after she was the standard against which I measured all women, and, save one, I never found her like again. This parting proved permanent; in two years' time she would follow her Jan, my father, into the grave.

My father's funeral then swept me up in its panoply, for the funeral of a Count of Pannau is a significant event, and certainly it was among the most significant of my young life. It had, as I discovered later, much in common with the movement of an army across country. My Aunt Fredi was, of course, the field marshal, and all the hundreds of servants and guests marched to her orders. We sons had nothing whatsoever to do, being thought of rather as large artillery pieces, twelve-pounders at least, to be moved by bustling lackeys into the proper position, unlimbered into battery, discharged at the proper moment, and limbered again to be moved onto the next bastion. There could not have been fewer than a thousand people attending.

There was even an entourage from Vienna, an archduke and the usual sort who accompany archdukes on these occasions. I recall the uniforms. My father was laid out in his own uniform, with all his decorations. I had never seen these, of course, and I was stunned by their number and prestige.

The Charles Bridge

I wept like a child, not just for the man, but for the two people I loved and had lost by that death--Mme. Wolanska and the Wachtmeister. And perhaps also for what might have been, had my family not been ruined. For depend upon it, sir: the happiness of a happy family of the nobility is the greatest happiness that can be obtained from any earthly source. The true sweetness of life, as that French serpent Talleyrand said; but he was right.

The new Count von Pannau-Kinsky, my brother Anton, did not speak at all to me during this time, except as required by ceremony. I pledged my fealty to him with the usual formulas, and announced that I would be entering the army as soon as that could be arranged, but would in any case not trouble him with my presence at the schloss. I could see by his face that he was torn between satisfaction and disappointment, that I had begged no favor from him that he could refuse.

During these days I spent every minute I could with Marietta, who had made one of the Hohenberg party. I wish I could relate that she was a comfort to me, but the case was otherwise. She denied me the small familiarities to which I had been accustomed and seemed ill at ease in my presence; nor would she respond to my entreaties, begging her to tell me in what fashion I had offended her, and what I could do to win back her favor. In the end, she refused my billets doux, and departed whenever she saw me approach, sending me into the deepest hell I had known, not excluding the duel and madcap flight to which I have previously adverted.

For it was this, and not my father's death, nor the loss of my home and dearest friends, that drove me maddest. Or perhaps that is only how it seemed to me. When we are drowning, we clutch at any plank, and place all our hopes upon it. Young men unhappy with their lot often clutch in this fashion upon romance with young ladies. The world may be lost to me, one thinks, but still I have you, my dearest one, and so on and so forth, absurd in the telling, as here, but in the event the very heart of one's existence. It is a shame to me, even now, that absurd lunacy!

So I suffered; and Oskar took pity on me, or at least what might have been called pity in a less philosophical fellow. I recall long conversations with him on the subject. He wanted to know how it felt; and in fact, he wished to make experiment upon my person—was my vision quite clear, had my hearing some fault, was my temperature elevated? These I violently refused, until he ventured that he could arrange a private meeting with Marietta. So I was measured and palped in the fashion of natural philosophers, although whether he made progress in revealing the mysteries of love *in corporea* I cannot tell.

In any event, I met her one night, in a corner of what we called the statue garden. Our ancestor, one of several Johann Anton Leopolds, had gone to Italy some century before and returned with a quantity of marble gods and heroes, which he had placed in neat military lines, on high plinths. One of these was a favorite of mine, a handsome youth, naked save for a fig-leafed groin. When I was a child, and lonely for a friend, I would sit in his shadow and hold conversation with him as if he were alive. The life of lonely boys is stranger than most people imagine. Perhaps I thought he would bring me good fortune when I chose him as our trysting place.

I met her there under a waning moon, the remains of that which had lit my way on that desperate gallop only a few nights ago. I will say she was at least frank. I could not have borne coquetry and this she spared me. She said that romance was all very well but she was seventeen and her father had to think about betrothal, and that I was not to be considered, quite aside from any personal feelings she might have. It was true that I was the scion of a famous house, but I was the younger son, and now that Anton was installed as Count of Pannau, it was likely that he would marry and have children of his own. There was thus little hope that I would ever succeed to the estate, and there were any number of men with secure estates or who were heirs apparent to them who would be glad to vie for the hand of a von Hohenberg girl.

I do not recall how I left that interview. I suppose I
was in a kind of daze. I went to my room. I was not then in
the habit of drinking spirits, or I would have drunk myself
into insensibility. As it was I had to bear all. Oskar knocked
on my door, but I told him to go away. During these hours I
hatched the plan for self-destruction that I have already described.

I packed my clothes and my inheritance: the pistols,
the billiard cue, the roll of money, the portrait of my mother
that my father had shown me, and whatever else would fit
into one modest valise. I went to the stables and saddled Kíslang, secured my valise to the cantle of my saddle, and rode
down the path to the post road leading south. For some reason I was set on ending everything in Prague in the most
grandiose way conceivable. Such is youth!

The southern boundary of our demesne is marked by
a stone wall and a gate with high columns erected by the Johann Anton Leopold I have mentioned, and there were statues on it too, antique deities whom no one had bothered to
identify. As I passed it, one of them seemed to come alive.

I felt a chill of fear, for I suspected in some wise that
my reason was not what it should be, and here was a proof;
but my horse was calm, and so I called out boldly and was
answered in a familiar voice.

"It is only Lennart, your honor." He came out of the
shadows and took Kíslang's reins in his hand.

"Lennart?" I exclaimed, "Whatever are you doing
abroad at this hour?"

In answer he replied, "I was waiting for you, sir. I
hope you had not intended to leave without me."

"That is just what I intended."

"But that can never be, your honor. The Count has
told me with his own lips, that I am to serve you and look
after you."

"Ha! The Count would be happy to see me dead in a
ditch."

"I don't mean Anton, sir. I mean the *Count*, your late
father. Before we left Pannau he told me I was to 'list with

the colors alongside of you, and be your servant and a sword on your right hand. I have brought Silenus to ride on. The Wachtmeister gave him to me before he left. And he told me the same order, although him being just a Wachtmeister it don't bite so deep as from the Count."

"Let go the reins, Lennart," I said wearily. "I shall not require a servant."

"I can't do that, sir," he said in his mulish way, and though I railed at him he would not let go. Finally, I drew my saber, raised it over his head and repeated my demand.

He stood fast, though, saying, "Well, you can strike me down, sir, and cut off my head if you like, and I would die a happy man knowing I did my duty to my lord and you until the end. But don't you kill me, sir, for it would be the break of your oath as well. For when you were hurt bad with that old boar pig, the one killed my Dad, you swore you would see me raised up if you could do it, and cutting me down would be the contrary of that, and it would be against the honor of Pannau to carry a broke oath, even to such as me."

At this, I relented, and said, "Mount your horse!" Lennart heaved his vastness up upon Silenus and off we rode to Prague. We stayed at the Hohenberg palace, but of course I could not possible stay there for more than a day or two, for the wedding party would be returning and I could not share a roof with her. To get rid of Lennart, I sent him out to find a place to stay. He found us lodgings on Franzosichegasse, with stabling for the horses and everything proper, two rooms and a cupboard. I told him that before I left the palace he must stay a night there to make sure it was quiet and that there were no vermin.

He complained about this, as calling into question his good sense, as if he would ever put a Baron of Pannau in a lousy bed, but grumbling he went off, and so it was easy for me to rummage the tack room of the palace stables for a length of rope. The rest you know; and now at long last we can proceed with the remainder of my story. I trust it has not been too tedious thus far.

"Not at all," replied Rudi. "What passions! What adventures! But I did have a question. If you were bent on destroying yourself, why did you carefully pack your possessions and take them with you?"

"Ha! I knew you would catch that. Well, tell me, why do *you* think I should have done so odd a thing?"

"Sir, I can only conclude that in some deep warren of your spirit the urge for self-murder did not penetrate. And as you pointed out, you had pistols to hand. If you wanted to make a show of your suicide, you could have blown your brains out on her doorstep at Pannau. There was no need to travel to Prague and hang yourself from the Charles Bridge."

"An excellent conclusion, and one I have come to believe myself. It was reading about that churl Werther put it in my head. Boys were killing themselves all over Europe after reading that damned story, but the fellow that wrote it, that Goethe, was never brought to book."

"But he himself brought many books thereafter."

The old man stared at Rudi for a moment and then uttered a series of creaky barks, slapping at his knees. "Oh, very good! Brought many books indeed! I see you are a wit, sir, and will have a career among the ladies. They do love wit, I find, although I never had much of it myself. But my point, sir, was that books have been the ruin of many a good young man. I was no exception, as we have seen; yet I became harder-headed thereafter. Take that as a lesson: books are very well in their place, but a man learns what he needs from life itself."

Yes, Herr Baron, thought Rudi, and I have yet another question, although I will wait a little to ask it. Who the devil *are* you, sir, and what do you want with Rudi Moritz?

Fourteen

An enormous crowd had gathered on Sunday to see the Bohemian delegation off to Vienna. Vast marquees had been erected in the Rossmarkt, and the archbishop officiated at a high Mass under one of them. Everyone who owned a uniform had donned it. The delegates were all in sober black with white and red sashes, these trimmed discretely with black and gold to show loyalty to the empire. Flanked by a guard of honor, the procession wound slowly through Heinrichsgasse and Herrengasse and down Kolowratsgasse to the station.

Rudi recalled the baron's words as he viewed this panoply of civic enthusiasm: not books, but life indeed. Words had at last become action, his own words in fact were the source of the present enthusiasm, and he wondered if a slave should not have been provided, as for the Roman emperor in his triumph, to whisper in his ear, "Remember, oh Rudi, thou art mortal."

They were received at the station by uniformed national guards and firemen, and there were two bands, one German, one Czech, blaring away at national airs, occasionally the same one at the same time, although this quite accidentally. People thrust bouquets at Rudi through the windows of the carriage, until the giggling children were near buried in the blooms. Everywhere there were cries of "Glory to you! Go with God! Return with a good reply!"

It was only with difficult that Rudi was able to see his family settled in their first-class carriage. The children bubbled with excitement, and had to be strictly prohibited from dancing upon the plush seats or dashing madly up the corridors, and Berthe, though she did not dash, was as excited as any child.

Rudi felt obliged after this to spend some time in the carriage in which the other delegates had gathered, which was packed to bursting with these and their well-wishers. He was pummeled and caressed and had his hand shaken until it was sore. Bobka the tavern-keeper was there, reveling in his moment, his round face shining with simple pleasure, as if he had served a tasty dinner. He shook Rudi's hand for longer than a handshake ordinarily lasted, pumping and intoning, "A great day for Bohemia, is it not, is it not, a very great day...."

Rudi agreed that it was. After this, he made brief visits with the other dignitaries in the first-class carriages, and then returned to his own just as the trainman blew his horn for the departure.

Seated again with his family, he had to contend with Fritz's questions about the trip and railroading in general: how powerful was the locomotive, how fast could it go at top speed, how fast was the fastest run on this route, did the train run all night or did it stop, and if it did run all night, how did the engineer sleep, when would they get to Vienna...

In this catechism Rudi proved an unsatisfactory tutor. He had avoided any detailed knowledge of rail travel (rather foolishly, he now realized) as one of the petty defiances he had adopted to irritate the Fathers. He regretted this. Railroads were obviously going to be important to any modern state and he would have to make an effort to understand them, even if humbling himself before the superior knowledge of the Fathers should be required.

His wife and daughter were meanwhile having a fine time, squealing with delight when the train jerked, jerked again, and began to move from the station. Berthe smiled at him and asked, "Do you suppose we will be in Vienna this very day?"

"Oh, not a chance of it, I am afraid. The regular run is something like seventeen hours and we will be stopping frequently. I believe every town along the route will wish to fete us and hear a speech. It will be deep into Monday, I fear, before we find our beds."

So it proved. The train halted at Karlin, at Pardubice and, some hours later, at Česka Trebova. At these stops the delegates had to leave the train, endure band music and both hear and present speeches. Bobka spoke first, promising the dawn of freedom and prosperity without dwelling overmuch upon the fine points. Trojan took over during the next few stops, speaking in both German and Czech, to loud applause.

By the time they reached Brunn it was supper time. The townsfolk had arranged a banquet outdoors by the railway, trestles set out under a bright red and white awning. It was Bobka's turn again and he, finding he had run out of things to say, or perhaps even his celebrated capacity to absorb beer had been exceeded some towns ago, mentioned that they had in their midst the author of the wonderful petition they were carrying to his imperial majesty. At this his imperial majesty was cheered madly and so was Rudi. A speech was demanded and Rudi, who, having expected and perhaps even desired the occasion, had jotted some notes down, acquitted himself well. He was not exactly carried upon shoulders, but every worthy of Brunn wanted a word and a handshake, and some little girls stepped forward with bouquets.

When he was back with his family, collapsed in his seat, curiously exhausted, he heard Reni ask, "Mama, is Papa the king now?"

"No, darling, the king is in Vienna," said Berthe, "where we are going on the train. Why do you think Papa is the king?"

"Because he spoke and everyone listened and those girls gave him flowers. And we have had a revolution, which is when they make the old king go to his room and then we have a new one. If Papa were king, I would be a princess, wouldn't I?"

"My dear," said Rudi, "we think you are a princess already, and I believe we treat you so, but the truth of the matter is that the people cheer me because they are happy that at long last our country is to receive once more its ancient rights, and because your papa has written down what those rights must be on a paper. The day after tomorrow the emperor will look over my paper and find it good and grant those rights. This is why the people cheer."

"But Papa, will I have some ancient rights too?"

"Every right to which the law entitles you. Item: The right to be kissed. Item: and tickled. . ." The child becoming overly hilarious under this treatment, her mother exercised her veto and restored order with stern phrases.

"You must not bring your revolution to the nursery at any rate," she said, "or our children will be spoilt and run riot. Tyranny is our rule there, the knout and the lash."

"True enough," said Rudi, "and I expect our current masters feel the same about everyone below the barons. But we will prove them wrong in the end."

The children being settled, Rudi walked out into the corridor and paced there, thinking. At the next stop he put these thoughts into action: after the usual greetings and speeches, he did not return to his own carriage but entered one of the second class. There he found Paul Novotny.

"How gracious of you to visit the peasantry in their hovels," his friend said, looking up from his notebook. He had taken a commission as a reporter for a paper called the *Czech Bee,* which was paying his way to Vienna. "I hope you are not offended by our crude manners."

"In fact, I travel with children, which is considered fourth class in the railway business, and find most will raise questions. If I did not know you from a babe and were we not having this conversation, I might suspect you of having been turned."

"But others, who do not know me, might be suspicious? Yes, a possible motive, but I am hardly significant enough in the revolution to become a target of so apparently august a figure in the political police. No, there is more to it than that, I am sure, but we require more information about this von Pannau to uncover it. It is just the sort of thing a journalist such as yourself could find out. If that person uncovered a plot . . . well, what a coup of a story!"

"I will need money for expenses," said Novotny.

"Of course you will. Fortunately, the baron has en-
sured I am in funds, a nice irony there. Besides that, I have
been thinking of you in another way. With the ending of
censorship, our little Torch has become de trop. What would
you say to establishing it as a genuine newspaper, with a salary
for the staff and printing costs all paid?"

Novotny laughed. "I would say, yes, please, sir! Why,
are you now rich enough to become a publisher?"

"Not I. But I was thinking of the banker, Maisel. I
heard him complain at Mme. von Silber's the other night
about how all the Czech papers seemed to regard Jew-baiting
as the chief advantage of freedom from the censor. A Czech
paper that did not so indulge in that vice might well look for
funding from a grateful Israel. What would you say to me
approaching him with *The Torch* in mind?"

"Oh, I would say let the rain of gold begin! But,
Rudi, do you really think it's possible? We may lose Jasny, I
fear, but as for me, I can resist the urge to blame the Jew for
every evil."

"What about Jiskra? Maisel said he particularly enjoyed his
work."

"Oh, Jiskra is philo-Semitic to a fault. He will be
happy to write and even happier to receive pay for it. Moritz,
you are a good friend to help me so. I will never forget it.
And I will find out more about your old baron than he knows
about himself. Trust me on this!" Here his face lit with a
smile such as Rudi had rarely seen on it, the smile of a delighted boy, absent any cynicism or guile. Rudi returned to
his first-class compartment with a fine feeling of content: it
was rare that the service of the revolution and the satisfaction
of personal feelings so aligned—it was more often the opposite—and he thought it an excellent omen.

The train drove on through the night. Rudi rested his
head against the cool glass and considered how pleasant and
smooth this ride was compared with a post coach over the
same distance: absent was the dust, oppressive heat or biting
chill, the many inconveniences, the miserable food, the continuous jouncing, the grinding duration. This in contrast was

hardly travel at all, a comfortably swaying box, suffused with a gentle rhythmic clacking, with the country rushing by at a steady twenty-two miles in every hour. Rudi's family slept peacefully, curled up under rugs and shawls, but Rudi only dozed, waking into the separated world of the train as if into another dream.

The passing scene was lit like a stage-set by a full, creamy moon, which gave a chill dignity to the passing villages, the occasional schloss on its eminence, the sprouting fields and barns. At one point the train slowed, then rolled forward at a walking pace, with intermittent full stops. During one of these, Rudi observed that a road ran parallel to the tracks, and upon this road was a group of peasants accompanying an ox-cart, a vehicle that, to Rudi's amusement, was at the moment gaining distance on the train. Several peasants rode on the cart itself, having made themselves seats or beds amongst the piles of sacks. For one uncanny moment Rudi was able to look directly into the faces of these riders, separated only by a pane of glass and ten feet of air.

They regarded him incuriously as the cart moved slowly by, and Rudi was shocked at this, at the dullness he read on their faces, at the notion that these men, who lacked all understanding or education, would soon be given liberty and the right to vote. Of course universal manhood suffrage was a principal that all liberals must espouse, but it appeared in a different light when one observed these actual universal men. He thought of what Vasová had said about the real Bohemia. It struck him forcibly how little he knew about the nation he aspired to govern, how scant his knowledge beyond his thin circle of liberal acquaintance in Prague. Did he know a worker? A peasant? Von Pannau perhaps understood the Bohemians better than he himself did; and understanding them, how could he be so wrong?

The train jerked into motion again, adding speed. Rudi watched the peasant group slide backwards into obscurity. Once they were no longer in sight, it became somewhat easier for him to think of Peasants abstractly again.

Bands played for them at Vienna too, better, larger, more magnificently caparisoned bands, since this was Vienna and not mere Prague, and magnificent too, were the committees of welcome, the officials with plumed hats and the students in their new uniforms.   Among the first wave of greeters was the Moritz family, with a number of servants. Without bothering to entertain any argument to the contrary, they swept up Berthe and the children and carried them off, though not before informing Rudi that he was a brute for subjecting a woman in Berthe's delicate condition to the jostling of the mob.

In truth, Rudi was happy to shed such responsibilities. The revolution in Prague was all very well, but this was the capital, the heart of the empire, and here the revolution seemed to have taken irresistible hold.   The air he breathed, the true air of freedom, seemed to flow more sweetly in his nostrils.   To inhale it now was enough to convince even a skeptic that the revolution was a fact.

Or perhaps not quite enough.

Here was Novotny at his side, making acid comments as some student leader spoke. "I tell you what it is, Moritz: it is romantic.   It is the fever dream of the romantic brought to life.   Youth triumphant! Freedom reigning!   And I am not romantic.   You are, but I am not, and was not, even when I was young alongside you.   For the romantic is not to be trusted.   The romantic does not trust power and knows not how to wield it."

He paused to attend the speaker, but after a few moments, sniffed and made a sour face.

"These uniforms, I mean, really . . . I grow bored with yon popinjay haranguing me about our glorious revolution.   I will take a cab to my hotel on the newspaper's kreutzer.   How wonderful to have expenses paid!   There I will have a wash, a beer and a nap, and rise fresh as a new chick to attend the great event at the Hofburg.   It is at three, I believe?   Yes, and then I will spend some hours in the state archives looking for the spoor of your baron."

Rudi found that carriage had been arranged to take him to the Moritz mansion. Riding through the familiar streets, he was astounded to observe the extent to which the students of the university controlled the life of the city. There was more gaiety in the streets than he recalled, and on every hoarding posters in black, red and gold announced a meeting on some issue of the day, or a reading or concert in aid of some new and liberal enterprise. Decrees were posted too, pronounced by students gathered in the Aula, the student assembly, and made into imperial policy by the docile emperor. The streets were patrolled by student-soldiers in bright uniforms.

The revolution had not quite reached the Moritz family home, however. This was a noble pile in the Renngasse, constructed at the end of the previous century but one, reportedly by the same architect who had done the Schönbrun-Báthorý palace just down the street. It was large and white and convenient to the Bourse. On the few occasions on which Rudi had returned to his childhood home since leaving for university, he had experienced, as he did now, a peculiar sense that the scale of things was wrong. The great mansion seemed shrunken, all the secret places he had hidden, the niches behind the statues, the balustrade of the great marble staircase, felt impossibly small. He had grown out of it, as was natural; and yet the moment Rudi entered through the shining black door and passed the bewigged and liveried footman holding it for him, he felt a child again, fearing oppression and the displeasure of his elders.

"Good afternoon, Marcus," he said to the footman who took his things. "How are you keeping?" The fellow had been a staple of Rudi's childhood, a prime dispenser of horse rides and treats filched from the kitchen. Rudi was dismayed to see how he had aged

"Oh, well enough, sir. You are a glad sight, Herr Rudi. Welcome home to you!"

"Thank you, Marcus. I believe I have grown too large to ride upon your back."

"Oh, no, sir. Climb up and I will run you up and down the big stairs as quick as we used to."

Rudi laughed. "I believe you. But just now I suppose I must go in to dine."

"They're waiting in the small dining room, sir. Impatiently waiting, sir."

Sighing, Rudi went out of the hall, walked through familiar passages, past the oil portraits of his family (including one of Berthe and himself as children, which made him pause for a moment and stare) and entered the dining room. Here the family took its meals, except for great occasions, when they used the large dining room, with its paneled wainscoting and crystal chandeliers. The small dining room was a pretty chamber, sunlit and well-proportioned, its walls covered in pale blue silk, its furnishings all in the heavy, carved, gilt and brocade style of Louis XV that was favored by the late empress Maria Theresa.

There were seven at table and they all looked up at him when he entered. The Fathers, Kalo and Franzl, wore similar expression of displeasure. As usual, Kalo was at the head of the table, Franzl at the foot. At Kalo's left was Karoline Augusta Moritz, neé Hetzen, Rudi's mother, and then the eldest Moritz sister, Aunt Klara Schmeller, a stout widow of fifty or so. She bore on her doughy face the Moritz frown of disappointment; next to her was a man named Otto Gerhardt, the exiguous husband of the younger sister, Tettie, who sat across from him. Aunt Tettie was the prettier, and sillier, of the two sisters, although all agreed she had made the worse marriage. A talented musician, like Berthe, she was always happy to see the younger Moritz family, and passed Rudi a quick, secret smile. Gerhardt did something small and obscure for the Moritz bank, but today the important thing about him to Rudi was that he had a sister, and this sister had a son, who was Major Wulf-Eric Speyr of the political police, who sat on Franzl's left, grinning like an ape at having brought off this surprise.

Or so Rudi imagined. It might have been mere coincidence. Wulf-Eric had every right to travel to Vienna, and when there he might expect to call on his relatives and be received as a luncheon guest. Rudi knew the Fathers liked the man, in a way that suggested that they regarded him as a model of what a bright young fellow might achieve. Not to mention his comfortable politics.

On the other side of Speyr sat Berthe. She smiled at Rudi too, not the usual Berthe dazzle, her husband observed with a sinking heart, but the sort one puts on to keep from crying.

Rudi bowed to the company, apologized for being late, pleaded affairs of state as the excuse, and took his seat, the place of honor at Kalo's right hand. Kalo gestured to the waiting maidservant. In came the soup.

"I am happy to see you looking well, mother," said Rudi. "It has been a long time. Reni's christening, was it?"

"No, you joined us for the summer at Kunningshelm, three years ago. Henrietta was just two."

"Ah, yes, we came by coach before the railway was done. I had forgotten."

"You are very good at that, dear. As all of us know."

"Now, mother . . . " Rudi began, hoping to forestall, at least for the length of this meal, the usual nagging complaints, but his father now grumbled forcefully,

"Affairs of state! What nonsense! I suppose you intend to give more encouragement to those maniacs in the Aula. Insolent puppies!"

"I am sure you would like to give them a good thrashing, father," said Rudi mildly. It was wonderful soup, celery and cream and chicken dumplings and some flavor Rudi could not identify. He ate well enough at home, but his father's table was in another class. He hoped that at least he would be able to enjoy the meal. He was peckish from his journey: one never ate well at official banquets.

"I would," said Kalo. "I would warm their bottoms and send them back to their books. And I would levy a fine on their parents, that's who I blame . . ." He stopped short, suddenly aware of having been baited, and turned again to his soup.

Aunt Klara said, "It should not be allowed!" which is what she always said when she sensed that her elder brother was exercised about something.

"No, Aunt, it should not, and neither should discussing politics at table. How are your cats nowadays?"

A dependable topic, and Aunt Klara rose to the occasion, describing the antics, ills, and feats of Grishka, Happy, Growler, and Silky until the soup was removed.

Rudi turned now to Franzl as the fish was brought in, turbot in a lemon-green onion sauce. "We enjoyed our train journey, sir. Thank you for arranging the carriage. Remarkably comfortable. Far nicer than I had expected. The miles simply flew by."

"Well, they're supposed to. That's the point of a railway. And I don't wonder at your surprise. You have positively prided yourself on ignorance of the great wonder of this age."

"I have," said Rudi, "and I am ashamed to admit it. My excuse is that unlike you and Franzl I have no imagination, so I had to experience the delights of rail travel for myself.

It was our Fritz who exposed my ignorance--I could not answer a single one of his intelligent questions. It shamed me as a father and I have resolved to do better in future. A future, I have concluded, in which the railroad will be of paramount importance in the fate of nations. As I am by way of being, in a small way, a national leader, it is my duty to positively immerse myself in railroad lore. Fortunately for me, I possess expert instructors in my own family."

Both Kalo and Franzl stared at him, suspecting some sort of joke or gibe. But Rudi's face bore no sign of this and while Kalo merely grunted an acknowledgement, Franzl positively beamed.

He said, "Well, out of the mouths of babes, as the saying goes. I am happy to see this, may I say it, revolution in your attitude, and to share with you any knowledge I possess on the subject."

"Thank you, sir. I would be most grateful to be allowed to sit at your feet. Perhaps you are free tomorrow."

It was quickly arranged and while this was happening
Rudi cast a glance upon his wife. Her face bore a sweeter, but
still uncertain, smile. I will be good, and accommodating, was
his determined thought, and not make a scene or occasion an
argument; or not until I find out what is going on here.

The conversation had just turned general when the
sound of a throat being cleared and the ding of a spoon on a
wine glass was heard, and Speyr rose in his place.

"My dear family, may I propose a toast to the return
of Rudi and Berthe?"

He raised his glass and so did the company, save the
couple in question. Rudi looked at his wife but she would not
meet his eye. His resolve of amity cracked a little.

"Thank you, dear Wulfi," he said, "but we are not
returning. Alas, we live in Prague, a city far off, though ever
closer thanks to the rails. We shall be back there in a few days
at most."

After this, a strange brief silence; and then Karoline
Augusta said, "Oh, Tettie, tell everyone your news!"

Aunt Tettie's news was that her eldest son, Gerd, had
received his commission in the army.

"He is an engineer, you know, bridges and fortifica-
tions and so on. It is all very mathematical, but of course
Gerd was so successful at the university." The paean to Gerd
continued for some time, interrupted only by the arrival of a
roast suckling pig, and the appropriate expressions of delight.

Rudi liked his younger cousin well enough and was
happy at his achievements, yet he was sensible of a peculiar
feeling of contempt for the commission being with the engineers. He understood he would have felt differently had the
commission been for a cavalry regiment and this surprised
him.

My God, he thought, is this *snobbery* invading my
mind? It is that wicked old man infiltrating his reactionary
notions into me, and yet, is it not the case that I have always
felt a stranger among these people, my family, who should be

the dearest to me? How wretched of me that I can love people so well, as long as they are strangers! What a notion! How does it lodge in my brain?

Look at Franzl there, his jowls full of pork, his lips and chin shiny with grease. What did he think a napkin was for? As for his politics, as long as whoever ruled Austria let him conduct his business and grow wealthy, that person might be a democratic assembly, or Ferdinand von Hapsburg or the Mikado of Japan, he cared not which. Gerhardt is one of them as if born, whereas I who was born in this family feel myself distinctly alien. And there is Berthe, my heart, my ally, yet she will not meet my eye. Still, this is my family, chained to me by bonds of familiarity and affection. I must learn to suppress these thoughts, to crush them out. I shall stick a smile on my phiz and say something pleasant to Tettie.

He did, something anodyne about opportunities among the engineers, and turned to his excellent roast pork. As they ate their meat, the Fathers began to talk across the board about their business, who was up, who down, and who among their wealthy comperes was the greatest fool and the cleverest operator, with Gerhardt at pains to add his little wisdom to the flow.

It was vulgar to talk business at table, Rudi thought, and wondered again how this notion, too, had come into his head. The Fathers always talked business, at table and everywhere else, for it was nearly their only topic. Well they *were* vulgar, that was a fact. Their father, the original Karl Ludwig, had been born in a farmhouse with an earthen floor before becoming one of the wealthiest men in the grain trade of Moravia. At fifty, he had died of a stroke in one of his warehouses, angrily demonstrating to a lackey the proper way to heave a sack of grain.

Of course, he had brought both his sons into the business, training them in tightness with each kreutzer and in never putting money into anything but wheat and the land to grow it, because whatever happened (as he often remarked) people would always need bread. Immediately upon inheriting, however, the sons liquidated the firm and removed to Vienna, where they opened their bank.

For they were forward-looking, modern young men. They knew that the real money to be made was not in agriculture but in industry. They subsequently made a fortune in British railroad bonds, and when the Rothschilds underwrote the German railways they climbed aboard while other Viennese bankers hesitated.

Rudi's mind was brought back into the present when he heard Franzl ask, "Did you hear Rothschild bought up most of Saxe-Weimar's six per cents?"

Kalo stopped a forkful in mid-air. "No! Where did you hear that?"

"Old Samuelsohn told me, at the Bourse."

"Saxe-Weimar, eh? Well, that's yet another province they own."

"Oh, they'll have everything before long," said Franzl. "Remarkable people nonetheless, curse them! But there's one thing they can never get."

"What is that, Franzl," asked Tettie.

Franzl held up a loaded fork. "Suckling pig. That's what!"

This provoked general laughter; even Rudi laughed, and everyone agreed that it was quite the cleverest thing Franzl had ever said.

Fifteen

It was the custom of the Moritz household on the conclusion of an afternoon meal for the gentlemen to assemble on the terrace that overlooked the garden at the rear of the house and smoke cigars. Once out in the thin sunshine, the Fathers began a conversation with Gerhardt about railroad bonds. This pleased Rudi, for he had nothing to contribute and was able to throw an arm around Major Speyr and lead him a distance away, where he said, in as friendly a tone as his anger allowed, "How surprised I was to see you at table, Wulfi! I thought you would have your hands full with the revolutionaries in Prague. Should I feel pursued?"

Speyr answered with a chuckle, "Pursued? What a notion! I am in Vienna for consultations with my superiors. Naturally enough, I called at your father's house, and was asked to luncheon."

It was plausible, Rudi had to admit, but something was still wrong. Berthe had been upset, not her usual self, and there had been veiled looks around the table.

Speyr continued, "Perhaps you are not cut out to be a revolutionary after all, for, you know, a fear of conspiracy is the great menace of such work, and in sensitive souls can wreak awful damage. I have seen it before. Speaking of conspirators, how is your friend Novotny?"

"He is perfectly well. I will tell him you inquired."

"Do that. Rudi, a word to the wise: I know he is your friend, but in these times we must be particularly careful of our associates. Novotny is not someone you should know."

"Oh? And why is that, pray?"

Speyr blew out a long plume of smoke and watched it vanish into the garden.

"Of course, I am not at liberty to reveal details," he said. "Only that he is not what he seems. Not a reliable person, shall we say?"

"I remember when we were children; you used to delight in lying in wait and leaping out to frighten the younger ones. It is a habit you have retained, I find. I, however, am no longer a child. My best regards to your family, Wulfi, and now I believe I will visit my own."

Rudi bowed, walked off the terrace and climbed the stairs to the upper floor. He stopped first at the nursery—his own nursery of long ago—to see how his children were getting on.

The place seemed unchanged since he and Berthe had occupied it, a comfortable suite with its own pottery stove in the corner, engravings hanging on the walls, The Vow of the Horatii and The Flight Into Egypt, and the worn, comfortable furniture. Dozing in an easy chair was Hana, the nurse, who sprang awake and rose when Rudi entered, nervous lest the father think she was neglecting her charges. The two children were playing cards with their older cousin Gussie, Otto and Tettie's youngest, a knowing child of twelve.

"Don't show me your cards, Reni!" Fritz was saying when Rudi walked in. "Then I shall know what you have and win all your buttons."

"I don't care about silly buttons," said Reni loftily. "When I am a princess I shall have all the buttons I wish, and some shall be silver and gold."

"That is not the point, Reni," said Gussie mildly, but with authority. "You must pretend to want them or there is no game." She caught sight of Rudi standing in the doorway, beaming paternally. "Oh, and here is your papa," she said. "He will tell you that you must care."

The Moritz children rushed to embrace their sire. He scooped them up, one in each arm. Reni still fit snugly. Fritz was nearly too heavy to carry.

"Papa," Fritz cried, "we are having such a lovely time here. There is cake every day, cook says, and one can have two pieces. And Grandfather Kalo has promised to take us to ride in the Prater, in a carriage and four. And I am to have my very own pony, Grandfather Kalo has said it!"

"Has he?"

"Yes, and Grandfather Franzl has said he will take me to the train yards and I can stand inside the locomotive and the driver will let me blow the whistle. Grandfather Franzl runs the railroad for the emperor, did you know that?"

"I did indeed. And have you thought of where your pony will live when we return to Prague? In the nursery, perhaps?"

"Oh, no, papa. We shall stay here. There are stables and everything is so much nicer."

Reni said, "Yes, it is, papa. And I am to have a kitty and a puppy. The kitty will be called Fluff and the puppy will be called Bumpa. And we will all live together with Grandmother Karoline and Grandfather Kalo and Grandfather Franzl and you and Mama. And Gussie will visit every day and I will let her play with my puppy and kitty, if she is gentle."

"I am sure she will be," said Rudi, putting the children down. "Where is your mother, my dears?"

He found her in their bedroom, reading a book. The Fathers had given them the Yellow Suite, a set of rooms with walls clothed in striped silk of that color and furnished in the manner of Louis XV with such opulence and slavish devotion to style that one expected that monarch to emerge from the corridor at any moment, wig flying, in pursuit of a mistress. As a symbol of all Rudi had left Vienna to avoid, the rooms could not have been bettered.

"The children seem happy," he observed. "And are you, my dear?"

"I am. I had not realized how much I missed this place."

"And its denizens?"

"Oh, the Fathers are different creatures on their home grounds. They are always uncomfortable when they come to Prague and they do so snap and bite there. Here in their own kingdom they are inclined toward cordiality and generosity. They cannot do enough for me and the children. It is quite touching."

"Yes, I heard of their generosity from the children. What is all this talk about ponies and kitties?"

"Oh, well, you know my father. With the children it is ask and you shall receive. We must take care they are not spoilt into little beasts."

She smiled at him and looked away. He felt ice in his heart, for it was a false smile, a dissembling smile, the first he could recall seeing on her face, for Berthe was the soul of honesty.

"Yes, we must. You know, Berthe, since I have been active in politics, where prevarication is a way of life, I have become more sensitive than formerly to obfuscation and to the ways in which those not privy to decisions are kept in the dark. Thus I am fully aware that something is going on that is purposely being kept from me. And I think, can it be that my Berthe is a conspirator?"

He saw broad flashes of scarlet appear on her cheeks, which confirmed his suspicions.

Quickly she said, "The Fathers have asked us if we will not stay for longer. Rudi, really, it would be so pleasant for them; the old people never have a chance to see their grandchildren . . ."

"They asked you? Why did they not ask me? Am I not the father?"

"Yes, of course, you are, but you have been so busy since we arrived I had not got the chance. I am asking you now."

"For how long, pray?" he asked coldly.

"From now until the end of the summer. Oh, Rudi, they could spend the summer at Kunningshelm, just as we did when we were children. Don't you remember how glorious that was? The woods and the river at Krems, the picnics and . . . they could get to know their grandparents, Rudi. They will not be with us forever, and these years can never be recaptured. I think of my poor mother, who never knew them at all, and I do not wish the same fate to befall Papa. Do say you will allow it!"

"You propose that I not see my wife or children for near six months? It is unheard of."

"It is heard of all over the world, when a man has business abroad. He takes ship and leaves his wife to manage as best she can."

"That is not the same thing at all. A man must work at his trade or business. No, no, it is impossible! Prague is our home, and to home we shall repair when this delivery of the petition is concluded."

"Very well," said Berthe after a moment, in a quiet, harsh voice, quite unlike her ordinary tone. "It shall be as the Herr Amtsrat wishes. I trust you will tell the children."

"Berthe, I beg you! Can you not understand the un-reasonableness of this request? We decided long ago that for us to have a true and free life together, it was necessary to remove from under the eye of our parents, and we did so, and settled in Prague, where I have my career. I thought we were happy."

"Indeed, we were happy, when we were a family all together. But you are not with us anymore. Your head is full of this revolution, and I do understand. I understood completely the night the constitution was granted, when we walked with that great throng through the streets, singing. But the revolution has come. All that you hoped for has happened. And still the politics grinds on, and still there is no room in your head for anything else. I speak and you do not hear me. The children ask for your attention and you shoo them away. So I think to myself, let him devote his all to establishing freedom, let him bend every nerve to this great purpose, and let us remove to a place where the children can be surrounded by people who do have time for them. It is only until these tumults in the state have died down. Surely in six months the situation will have resolved and normal life can resume."

"I don't know. No one knows, for Christ's sake! It is not like a pregnancy, dearest."

Berthe looked at the carpet and said nothing.

Rudi pulled out his watch. "I have not time to discuss this with you now. I am due at the Hofburg in little over an hour. Shall we not kiss and make up?"

In answer, she merely hung her head and was still. He waited. Nothing. He felt an unaccustomed snarl rise in his throat, suppressed it, and strode from the room, slamming the door. He had not slammed a door in a quarrel before this, had barely had a single quarrel with Berthe in the course of a year. He was furious—with her, with himself, with . . . he knew not what—things. The damned spying, the false faces he had to wear, and now the poison had infected the heart of his family. Berthe was slipping away, withdrawing from him, and he could not see how he could bear it. He hung outside the door for a moment in an agony of indecision. Then the press of his accursed duty pried him away, and he dashed back to his dressing room, crying out for Gregor.

The valet had already laid out Rudi's formal attire, not court dress exactly, but the clothes one wore to the opera. The delegation had not discussed questions of style at all, natural in a group representing all the classes, and Rudi did not look forward to observing what was sure to be a rag-tag assemblage, nor did he care to think about how the court officials would see them. He bathed, had himself shaved close, dressed in his suit--shirt front, tie and waistcoat fresh laundered dazzling white and starched stiff as tin—took up his hat and stick in the hall and left the house. The Moritz phaeton drove him to the Hofburg.

Nearly all the other delegates had arrived and were milling around the street in front of the Michaelerkuppel, the immense gateway that led to the state apartments. Rudi saw that they had worn what they had worn upon leaving Prague, which he supposed could not be helped, although Trojan, for another, had chosen formal dress.

"Well, Trojan," said Rudi, "I cannot but admire your sartorial display. I suppose it is wrong and unreasonable to wish the others had thought to dress for this historic occasion."

"I suppose they think they *have* dressed for it. In any case, it conveys the picture of a whole people coming to petition the monarch, each appearing in his native pelt, as it were."

"Yes, I'm sure it will be fine, so long as someone remembered to bring the actual petition. Have you got it?"

"No, Bobka insisted on carrying the engrossed copy himself. And he has not yet arrived. I trust he has not become lost, although if anyone could get lost seeking the Hofburg in Vienna, it would be Bobka. My chief anxiety now is that we will be fobbed off with a minor chamberlain and not see the chancellor at all, far less his imperial . . . oh, good, that must be Bobka and his cronies now."

Rudi turned to see a shiny landau drawing up to the curb. It was indeed Bobka and three of his friends—a butcher, a brewer and a fishmonger. Rudi heard Trojan exclaim, "Oh, Jesus, Maria, will you look!"

Bobka and his friends had chosen to array themselves in Bohemian style: collarless white linen shirts, embroidered red waistcoats, serge trousers stuffed into knee-boots, and round black hats adorned with ribbons.

Rudi felt a laugh building in his throat, but choked it down. "*Surgo Bohemiae!*" he said, and advanced toward Bobka with a smile on his face and his hand out in greeting.

"As you feared," said Alois Trojan to Rudi, "we are about to be fobbed off."

"We shall see about that," Rudi replied.

The delegates of Bohemia had been led by a uniformed gentleman into a large, literally palatial, room: carpeted floors, paintings of mythological or religious scenes on the walls, the gilt furnishings slightly worn from hard use and dating from the early portion of the previous century. The uniformed gentleman had left them to cool their heels in that noble space for going on an hour now. Rudi wondered if this was a calculated insult or if everyone was so handled, and concluded it did not matter. The world might have turned upside down, but clearly the protocols of the Hofburg had yet to respond.

A tall door swung open, and out popped the official who had bid them wait. This person, uniformed in immaculate white with a watered silk sash, and a lush red aiguillette growing from his left shoulder, wore on his pretty face the standard expression of supercilious ennui. He announced to the delegation that while the Minister of the Interior, Count Pillersdorf, was not available, he had graciously consented to read their petition and respond to it in short order, perhaps next week. If they would kindly hand it over . . . ?

Bobka, who was holding the engrossed copy in its red leather portfolio, advanced, but Rudi stepped forward and detained him.

"We will not, sir," said Rudi. His face flushed and he heard murmuring behind him.

"Excuse me?"

"We will not place our petition in any hands but those of our monarch, the King of Bohemia."

"The King of Bohemia?" said the equerry. "But that is his imperial majesty."

"We are well aware who the King of Bohemia is, sir," answered Rudi. "And we are his Bohemian people. This petition is our voice and we will speak it only to our king himself. I suggest you take us to him at once."

The man shook his head and smiled, as at a small child who has requested the moon. "Sir, I see you are unfamiliar with our ways. You petition will be dealt with in the usual fashion. I assure you . . . "

"Sir, I care not a fig for your assurances. Perhaps you are not aware of it, but the usual ways are quite overthrown. In any case, this is not a petition by a group of draymen requesting improvements to the road between Mollnitz and Zollnitz. It is the petition of a whole people for redress of historic grievances and for improvements in governance designed to increase the prosperity and happiness of the most important kingdom of the empire. The Bohemian people demand that it be presented to the person of the king and emperor. Now, sir, if you are not competent to perform that duty, I suggest you find someone who is."

The equerry opened his mouth, closed it, said, "I will enquire of my superiors," and left through the same door.

After twenty minutes the official returned with a man in a frock coat and spectacles, a rather more intelligent-looking fellow than his subordinates. He looked the delegation over and asked in a quiet, humorous voice, "Who is the trouble-maker?"

"That would be me, sir," said Rudi.

The man extended his hand, "Pillersdorf, Minister of the Interior. What is all this about demanding to see his imperial majesty?"

When Rudi placed his hand in the other's grip, he was drawn by a subtle pressure a little distance away from the others.

"It is necessary, Count," said Rudi.

"It is impossible. I assume you know the emperor's condition."

"It is well known, sir. Believe me, discommoding you is the farthest thing from my mind, but if I am not able to stand up in Prague and say that I have seen our king and given him our petition, I cannot answer for the consequences. In any case, we will not leave unless this occurs."

"That is bold, sir. I can have you escorted out, of course."

"You can, sir. In which case the students will learn of it and who can tell what they will do? Perhaps on the morrow we will be back here with a few thousand students, all in uniform and bearing arms."

"I hope that is not a threat, sir."

"Not in the least, my lord. But these are perilous and unpredictable times. The wise do what they can to control the various elements. It is you who must decide between a trivial inconvenience to palace protocol and a possibly disastrous emeut. For we will on no account leave without an interview with his majesty."

Pillersdorf considered this for a moment, then gave an acquiescent nod.

"Very well. You have your document?"

Rudi went over and took the portfolio from Bobka's hands, who was wise enough not to protest.

"Follow along," said Count Pillersdorf, and they all, the two uniformed officials, the minister, and Rudi, (trailed at a discrete distance by the rest of the delegation) passed through the tall doors. They marched along corridors variously magnificent and shabby in the elegant way that only magnificence becomes shabby, until Rudi had quite lost his sense of direction. Down a flight of marble stairs and through a set of doors and another hallway that ended in a pair of immense carved portals, heavily gilt, that were thrown open at their approach by a matched pair of white-wigged footmen, via which, to Rudi's surprise, they emerged into sunlight and the astringent smell of boxwood.

They were in the great private gardens of the Hofburg, built in the space previously occupied by the city walls. Bonaparte had razed these in an act of contempt; the Hapsburgs had constructed a garden over the rubble, a typical act of theirs. "Let others make war, you, Austria, marry!" And plant gardens. These were Rudi's somewhat incoherent thoughts as he strode beside the minister down the tan graveled path; also he wished he could show these gardens to his wife, who doted upon any careful patch of greenery.

The equerries halted and Rudi saw them bow. The minister gestured him forward. Seated on a bench was a man in a white uniform, with an over-large, egg-shaped head upon which thin brown hair spread like moss on a statue, this moss concluding in a peculiar spit-curl on the forehead. He had a silver bowl next to him filled with crusts of bread, and he was feeding the birds. Two aides stood at a slight distance, watching the approaching party disapprovingly. Pillersdorf walked two steps forward and bowed deeply; this was enough to flutter all the birds into the air. The man on the bench, His Imperial Apostolic Majesty, Ferdinand I of Austria, also King Ferdinand V of Bohemia, clapped his hands and giggled.

Count Pillersdorf cleared his throat and said, "Your Majesty, may I present a gentleman from your kingdom of Bohemia. He has a petition for you."

"Ah, ah, Bohemia! I love Bohemia," the emperor said. "I was in Prague once. They have that wonderful clock, they took me to show the workings." He had a slow, overloud voice, and his impaired version of the court accent was difficult to follow.

"Pray, deliver your petition," said the minister in a low, tight voice.

Rudi stepped forward and bowed. The emperor smiled. Spit pooled on his pendulous lower lip; one of the attendants stepped forward and in a smooth, clearly practiced motion, dabbed it dry with a white handkerchief, then resumed his position.

Rudi said, "Your Majesty, the Bohemian people send you their loyal greetings and present you with this humble petition from your loving and faithful Bohemian subjects. We hope that you will agree to grant the requests therein inscribed."

He handed the emperor the portfolio. The emperor smiled delightedly in just the open and innocent fashion in which a child receives a sweet.

"Oh, I grant everything. I love my Bohemian people. That wonderful clock!" A little frown appeared on his face and he looked to Count Pillersdorf. "Oh, but may I grant them? I wish I might, Kolowrat, I do!"

"I beg your Majesty's pardon, but I am Pillersdorf."

"Of course you are, and I am Ferdinand. You must take care of this. Whatever must be done should be done. If it is allowed." He handed the portfolio to the minister, and reached again for the crusts. "It was charming making your acquaintance," he said to Rudi, smiling broadly. Then a look of alarm appeared. "Must I sign something?"

"No, Majesty," said Pillersdorf, already backing away. "Not at this time."

The emperor nodded and smiled, the royal hand flung out some bread and the birds descended again.

What was he like close up, they all wanted to know.

Rudi answered blandly that the emperor was a fine Christian gentleman who had graciously accepted the petition from Rudi's own hands.

"But did you discuss affairs with him?" Trojan wished to know. "Does he share our ideas?"

"I believe he does," said Rudi. "Or did at that moment. His Majesty tends to share the ideas of the last man he spoke with."

"Yes, so I have heard. I had hoped this was a canard, but if it is not, if the emperor is indeed *non compos*, why were you so adamant about seeing him?"

"Oh, that was mere theater," Rudi answered, "which I find is as essential to politics as the ideas. It will play very well in Prague."

"As to ideas," said Bobka, "I have one I should like to propose to the group."

They all stared at the innkeeper in wonder. "An idea, good Bobka?"
Trojan said. "Pray share it with us this minute!"

"I have discovered a tavern that pours good Pilsner. My idea is that we should all repair there as soon as we can and drink to our success."

The tavern was called At the Bohemian Crown, and it was as Böhmer as anything in Bohemia, perhaps even more so. The barmaids were all dressed in peasant finery from various districts and they greeted the delegates who had chosen to wear similar costumes with the blend of delight and contempt that city girls everywhere reserve for yokels with money. The beer was real Pils, however, and very nearly as strong as wine. Rudi was on his second stein when Novotny slipped onto the bench beside him.

"I understand you had a royal audience, Herr Kanzler. Would you care to share it with the press?"

"I would. Say that his imperial majesty exhibited the loving care for his people that has long endeared him to every decent citizen of the empire and immediately granted all the articles of the Bohemian petition."

"Every decent citizen except those currently in armed rebellion in Italy and Hungary. Or perhaps only the indecent ones are up in arms. But really--did he actually drool in your presence?"

"Not drool as such. The thick lower lip that is a glorious inheritance of the Hapsburgs is difficult to keep dry."

"May I quote you on that?"

"No. Make something up, as you always do. Or have a beer. It is really quite good."

"f you're paying, then thank you, I will."

He flagged down a barmaid, who gave him one of the ten steins she was carrying. After a long pull, he smacked his lips and said, "I heard about your demonstration at the Hofburg, the way you faced down the lackeys and then Pillersdorf. Very impressive. Now, off the record and between friends, how do you see the situation developing? I mean in Prague."

"I won't be quoted, Paul."

"Do you see my notebook out? Talk freely by all means."

Tongue loosened by the strong beer, Rudi did so. The petition would be answered after a time, the answer would not suffice, there would be another petition, more strongly worded, and negotiations would continue. In the meantime, Prague would increasingly be ruled by the Wenceslaus committee, reforms would be put in place, and gradually the empire would have to acquiesce to the existing situation. With Hungary and Italy aflame, the Hofburg would never chance provoking a state that *wanted* to be in the empire, no, that *required* the empire both to retain its integrity as a nation in the face of Russian and Prussian expansionism and to prevent civil strife between Czechs and Germans.

"You look doubtful, my friend," said Rudi when he had concluded. "Why is that?"

"Oh, not doubt as such. For all I know your happy tale of national comity and a supine Hofburg may come to pass. But a somewhat happier enslaved Bohemia is not a revolution by any means."

"Then what is, pray tell? Do you require the head of that poor fool in the Hofburg? Sans-culottes running riot in the streets?"

"He can keep his empty noggin, and all of us now wear long trousers; but a real revolution must cut a good deal deeper into the dispositions of power than what you propose."

"Then what? What is your program? What are the lineaments of the society your revolution will establish? Yes, grin at me! But I am serious. It is the height of irresponsibility to condemn the possible in favor of the fantastic. You know, I have been warned against you just today, by the police."

At this comment a look of startled terror flashed across Novotny's face, a look so unusual that Rudi, in his current state of mild drunkenness, thought he had imagined it. Then Novotny laughed, and said, "That is good news. It means I am a success. And will you heed this warning, dear Moritz?"

"Oh, don't be stupid! Yet I wonder why you were singled out for particular mention."

"It has no significance. I have been warned against you, as a matter of fact."

"What! By whom? And whatever for?"

Novotny continued as if he had not spoken. "And others have been warned against poor Liebig, the perfidious Jew. It is mere tactic. The police wish to sow suspicion and dissention in our ranks. I advise you to put it and all such provocations out of your mind. Let us instead discuss plans for the first edition of our *Torch*. I have sent to Jiskra to ask him to write some verse lampooning the reactionaries. I hope

I can count on you to produce a few lines on the Italian and Hungarian situations."

"As 'Miles,' I trust. Even with the current situation, I will not be forgiven for releasing military information in defiance of regulations."

"Oh, by all means shelter under your pseudonym. I in contrast will have my true name in bold letters on the second page masthead. As will Liebig and Jasny."

"Neither of whom is employed by the army. Forgive me if I desire to keep my job, so as to be able to lend all of you money and buy your beers. But what of our Jiskra? Will he at last emerge from the shadows? I would very much like to meet him and shake him by the hand."

"As would many others; but it is not to be. Herr Jiskra has a situation comparable to your own and desires the most complete discretion. Any investigation into his identity would be resented in the extreme."

"I quite understand. How vexing this need to work in shadow! But as to shadowy figures, have you learned anything of Baron von Pannau-Kinsky?"

"In fact, I have. I spent the afternoon in the Hofkriegsrat archives while you were bearding the emperor. Your colonel, I learned, has had a distinguished career—service in the Thirteenth Chevauxleger, formerly the Thirteenth Light Dragoons, mentioned in dispatches innumerable times, awarded the Theresienkreuz at Leipzig—here it is, all copied out. After 1820, however, his service record is a blank. He continues to draw his pay but is attached to no regiment or staff. Interesting, don't you think?"

"I don't know. He may have been seconded to a staff somewhere, when he got too old to take the field. But there should be a memorandum to that effect."

"None that I could find. Combined with what you have told me about a possible influence on your case, I conclude that your old fellow ended his public career in the secret state police. And may still be so employed: perhaps his duties involve becoming close to certain liberal personages via a pretense of memoir writing."

"But to what purpose?" said Rudi in a voice loud enough to draw attention from the surrounding tables. In a more moderate tone he added, "Does he think to suborn me with his gold? I shall confront him and throw it in his face."

"Please, Moritz, if you fling gold, do throw it in *my* face instead. No, what you should do is continue on as you have, scribbling down his senile maunderings until we have a clearer picture of the plot. For rest assured, it *is* a plot, although your baron may be a mere cat's paw of someone more significant. Perhaps he will let something slip—he is a dotard, after all—or perhaps he will think he has you pocketed and will then reveal whatever scheme there may be. In the meantime, peruse what I have copied."

Here Novotny pushed across the table a neat stack of foolscap, closely written. "Something may strike you that I missed."

"Thank you, Paul. But by God, I hate this dissembling! It makes my skin crawl to be false to any man."

"Yes, it is one of your charms. But if you stay long in politics, I dare say you will learn to bear it."

Rudi laughed along with his friend at this, and said, "I expect it is like beer. Good going down, but then one must repair to a stinking jakes. Which, if you will excuse me, I now do."

When Rudi returned there was no sign of Novotny. He went out of the place and was just in time to see his friend enter a fiacre and drive off.

For the remainder of the evening, the beer flowed on. The conversation flowed as well, but into less demanding channels, singing began, steins were slammed in time to the songs, and a general drunkenness overcame the representatives of the Bohemian people. It was therefore quite late when Rudi alighted from a cab in front of the Moritz mansion. He had dined informally at the tavern and hoped to slip quietly up to bed, but the footman who took his things at the door told him that his father and his father-in-law urgently required to speak with him and were at this moment awaiting him in the library.

Sixteen

Rudi found them sitting across a low table from one another, in their comfortable leather chairs, a bottle of Madeira on the table, much depleted. The library was a smallish room, befitting the status of letters in the eyes of the owners, yet it contained everything necessary for a library—a tantalus or two containing decanters of madeira, Tokay, sauterne and cognac, Persian carpets, sconces thick with beeswax candles, a plaster copy of the Aphrodite of Praxiteles to demonstrate culture, and matched, leather-bound sets of all the classics, their pages uncut.

The Fathers were not as drunk as Rudi but significantly mellowed nonetheless. They rose, shook his hand, invited him to sit, poured him a glass of wine. They questioned Rudi closely about the events at the palace and appeared more than content that one of their family had met and conversed with his royal and imperial majesty. The Moritz cousins were both as apolitical as salted herring, but anything that seemed to redound to the status of the family was welcomed. Yet they seemed to Rudi curiously ill at ease, a condition hitherto unknown in their home or, perhaps, anywhere else.

Kalo began by saying, "My boy, I, that is, we, have a great favor to ask of you."

"Yes, I will," said Rudi, and had the satisfaction of seeing his father utterly nonplused.

"But . . . but, dear Rudi, you don't know what we are asking."

"I believe I do, father. You want me to permit my family to stay here with you, perhaps until the end of the summer. I have already spoken of it with my wife. I own I was vexed when I heard, and refused out of hand, but now I have seen a monarch with my own eyes, I prefer not to be of his company and have resolved to surrender my tyranny. Berthe once taxed me for being liberal in public and a tyrant at home, and I now confess it as a shame. Berthe may stay where she pleases. For myself, I am happy that the children will come to know their grandparents better. It is also the case that in the coming months I will be pressed with affairs of state in Prague, and will therefore not fulfill as I would like the duties of husband and father. This period should pass after a while, things will settle, and we can go on as before, although I believe that your magnificent railroad will make more frequent visits a reality."

"That is wonderful, Rudi, truly it is," said Franzl. "I am deeply grateful, as I know Kalo is, too."

Kalo nodded in agreement and added, "Your mother in particular will be delighted. How she dotes on those little ones! But Rudi, there is something else."

"Oh?"

Kalo's expression grew heavier: his brows crumpled, the lines around his mouth deepened into dark gullies. "Yes. These political broils . . . we are extremely concerned with your involvement, your prominence, and fear that you and your family will come to great harm."

"I detect you have been discussing my affairs with Wulfi Speyr."

"What of it?" said Kalo. "It is no disadvantage to have a policeman in the family, and he gives us a good deal of information to our benefit. He says you are mixing with dangerous characters."

"What of it? Dangerous characters are wont to gather around civic tumult, as flies gather around a stable. One brushes them aside and takes one's horse for a canter. In any case, the revolution is won. A constitution is promised. The heavy hand of the police is slapped back, including that of our cousin Wulfi. All is over but the scratching of pens; this is my own profession and, save an occasional paper cut or the damage from a slipped pen-knife, I foresee no possibility of harm."

Kalo's frown deepened and his eyes grew popping wide. "You jest about it; but I tell you, my son, there is no cause for levity. And there is no revolution."

"What do you mean, no revolution? Have you been out in the streets?"

"That is a show, a sort of carnival at the wrong time of year. The government is demoralized and shocked. The emperor--well, you have seen him, and losing Prince Metternich could not but have an ill effect, but this is only the first act. The levers of power are still in place and the same hands are upon them. You are an intelligent man, Rudi. Surely you can see that a revolution without the army firmly in hand and without a source of funds is little more than a phantasm."

"The French would not agree," said Rudi. "Their revolution…"

"The French are not relevant to us," said Kalo. "Everyone in France, irrespective of their politics, is French, which is not the case…"

"Yes, Father, I am aware of the nationalities issue. I struggle with it every day. Yet I believe the analogy holds. The old order is clearly dying, absolutism is finished, and it only remains to order the new dispensation."

To Rudi's surprise, Franzl now spoke. "Where are the cannons?"

Rudi stared at his father-in-law. The younger Moritz cousin rarely contributed anything to a discussion in which Kalo was a participant, except to offer agreement and support, and Rudi understood that the latter was now in play.

"Cannons? Why should I be concerned with cannons? Do you expect a war?"

"There is already a war, in Italy," said Franzl, "and I cannot see how it will not spread to Hungary and to other parts of the empire. I mention cannon, because if you do not control cannon, you have no revolution. You cannot defend yourself in Prague or anywhere else. And you cannot really think that a class and an empire that has existed for centuries will surrender its rights and privileges without a bloody fight. There are already signs…"

"What signs? The students seem perfectly in control..."

"Oh, the students! The students are not important. I will tell you what has happened. When Prince Metternich was forced from office, you could not sell a government short bond on the Bourse except at a ruinous discount, forty or even sixty percent below par. Now, however, the men of business look around and they ignore what is said and what is written and the fools in the streets. What they want to know is, who has the cannon? The Army has them? Yes. Is the Army of a liberal opinion? Far from it. Do they continue to send Italian regiments to Hungary and Hungarian regiments to Italy? They do. Then all is secure. Those who understand such things believe it, which is why one can buy five and a half percent 1850s at a mere six below. Six percent under par! So one thing is the cannon, the army that is, and for another there is the money. What does the money say? It agrees."

"Whatever it says is voiced in an obscure tongue," Rudi replied. "Or, better, it is the evidence of a flock of sheep or of pigeons. You have said it yourself, many times. The Duke of Mecklenburg stubs his toe and wheat drops three kreutzer the bushel on the Bourse. I think you are made nervous by these changes and have woven this imagined catastrophe. Now you wish to tug me into it, with Wulfi's help. I am a prominent liberal, he wishes to discommode me, and he uses you as his lever. The problem is that you do not understand the people. When the people want change--as I assure you they do--then change must come. It was true in '89, it was true in America, and also in the Year Fourteen when we overcame the French."

Rudi smiled jovially at the two. The drink had made him happy to instruct the Fathers on the subject of constitutional politics.

"So you see, at this juncture the revolution is irresistible," he continued. "Your cannon will stay in their parks, and a Minister of War will be appointed who represents the people as well as the crown. I implore you, dear fathers, not to be so worried."

There was a silence. Kalo let out a deep sigh. "No, Rudi," he said. "I believe you have missed the point of Franzl's story. We are *not* worried about the political situation, not at all. That is *why* bonds have recovered. And believe me, that kind of fall and recovery is not something that happens every day. Rudi, I know you think you know everything, but we really *do* know everything. It is our business. You would be shocked to learn how much it costs, how many archdukes and counts we are keeping in women, racehorses, and Chateau Yquem, all for information, intelligence about the plans of the government, and, of course, to assure us that the government will act in ways that benefit our concerns. I can therefore inform you, based on this information, that the aristocratic forces are not remotely defeated. They were taken by surprise by the recent events, and they lost their leadership. . ."

"Again, father, you do not understand the depth of the changes now taking place in Europe . . . "

"Oh, speak to me not of Europe!" cried Kalo. "I care not a fig for your Europe, nor your German freedoms, nor your Bohemian nation. I care only for my family and my fortune. I have taken care that the latter will flourish whoever sits in the Hofburg, and now I turn to the former, which is similarly secured except for you and yours. Berthe and the children are safe with us for the moment, and all that is necessary for our complete happiness is that you should abandon these wretched politics and remove to Vienna, where there is scope for your talents enough. I have told you before, you could easily achieve ministerial rank with our help . . ."

"I don't want your help, Father. Why can you not grasp this simple truth? You have contempt for my ideals—fair enough! I have contempt for yours, and your boasts of how you bribe the government. I look forward to a government that does not take bribes at all, that is of and by the people . . ."

"And you will still be looking forward when Judgment Day comes! What nonsense!"

Here Franzl said soothingly, "Gentlemen, you know very well we shall never agree about political questions. These, however, are not at issue. It is just that you are dear to us, Rudi, and we wish to keep you from harm. As much as we are not worried about politics, so much are we worried about you, personally. As is Berthe, of course, although she will never admit it. We have intelligence, as Kalo said, and we wished to warn you. This affair of the students cannot last. Either the workers and radicals will take over, and we will have civil war, or the students will commit some outrage and lose the support of the Viennese, in which case the generals will strike back. In either event, you will be in grave personal danger. Be extremely careful in Prague, and put your trust in no one but yourself. And observe the cannons—that is most important. Will you at least do that?"

Rudi had an acerbic remark on his lips in response to Kalo, but the sight of Franzl's genuinely pleading look stifled it in his throat. Instead, he said, "I promise to be careful and to run to the bosom of my family should calamity strike. Is that sufficient or must we call the notary?"

"Oh, Rudi," said Franzl with a small sigh. "Do be serious!"

"That is odd," said Rudi, and finished his wine in a gulp and rose. "All my friends tell me I am far *too* serious."

"You have made me the happiest woman in Vienna, my Rudschen."

Rudi was in bed with his wife, both of them naked, he having told her she could remain in Vienna and having afterward received the fleshly attentions naturally arising from the renewal of marital concord.

"And you have made me the happiest man, my dearest. After all, it is a small thing, yes? As you have just observed, we have had forever and will have more of it. What is six months to that? And it might not even be so long."

"Not so long, you say?"

"Yes, I have been thinking about our future. I have obligated myself to the revolution in Bohemia. I must see the Bohemian state through its current transformation, which I suspect will be resolved within the year. After that, it may be that we will find it more convenient to remove from Prague and settle here."

"Truly? Dearest Rudi, you know I love our life in Prague and our little house, but in fact we only settled there because you wished to escape the overbearing of the Fathers and...."

"What is that 'you,' my dear? I was under the impression that your desire in this was the equal of mine."

"Perhaps not *quite* equal. But I saw how you chafed and wished to support you as a wife should. And how could I not be happy anywhere, with you and the children? Still, Vienna I regard as home, and in my current condition I am glad of the opportunity to stay and bear our child in the heart of my family. But Rudi, what if you are made chancellor?"

He laughed and hugged her more closely. "And what if a stone should fall from the sky onto Prague, or a previously unknown volcano should bubble up in the Vienna Woods? Let me say this: should I be named chancellor I will say, 'Gentlemen, I thank you for this great honor, but I must decline. I find I am not after all a politician."

"But Rudi, you are indeed a politician. I can see how politics excites you and brings a glow to your face."

"I beg to disagree, my sweet. It is revolution that excites me, and the establishment of a more just order in society. The actual operation of the political machinery, the canvassing for support, the arguing with fools, the flattery required, the false smiling one must learn--all this is tedious to me. No, once the new state is established and running itself, your Rudi will fade away and become a mere footnote in the history of this great year, 1848. The fancy once took me of being a power in the state, I admit. But since then I have seen how power operates and I have decided it is not to my taste. It is like your music, I think."

"My music? How so?"

"Just that you are a talented musician with no resolve for doing the things one must do and making the sacrifices one must make to reach the level required to appear upon the concert stage. Your interest in music is driven solely by the pleasure you and your intimate circle derive from it. Similarly, my interest in politics is driven by necessity. Things must be done, and I have the talent to do them. But real politicians are driven by elements in their own spirits, a lust for preeminence, glory, authority, and the imposition of their will upon others. These I lack. So I hope to be like Cincinnatus or Washington, who, after saving their nations, retired to their farms and welcome obscurity."

"You wish to become a *farmer*?"

"No, no, my dear. I meant it as a figure only. I have no idea of what I will do, except perhaps leech upon the fathers until they throw me out in the street."

"Now you do amaze me, after how you have chafed the Fathers. Independency has ever been your watchword."

"Well, I doubt it will come to actual indolence. And yes, I have mocked them. I held myself as being more pure than men of business because I was in government, and not under the thrall of lucre. But now that I have come to know a little about how we are in fact governed, I see that the Fathers are like innocent babes in comparison to those who rule us. Power is a drug like laudanum, it seems, and I am far from immune to its effects. Besides, I have come to see our private lives in a different light as well. You are so brave and loyal that I failed to see how you missed the places and faces of our childhood. I suppose the revolution has awakened me not only to the defects of the present state but to defects in how I have governed our little lives."

"Oh, you men! How tedious to have to decide your destiny at every turn, and how frightening! I am sure I could never manage it. Women are the lucky sex, I believe, for our destiny is given to us with our bodies. And therefore we are calm where men are frenzied, practical where men are fantastic, and rational where men are prey to every flibbertigibbet that drifts into their minds. This is why in the main homes are run more satisfactorily than governments, and require neither armies, courts, or jails. Yet, one must have men, and I believe, if I must have one, you are the best one ever made. I thank God every day that He has given you to me."

At this she delivered to him a passionate kiss, with the usual sequelae.

"What again?" she demanded. "I imagined your lusts were slaked by our recent encounter, barely half an hour past."

"You forget that we will soon be parted. I must leave you with my lustful tuns and hogsheads drained to the lees, lest I be discommoded while alone."

"Is that truly how it works? Well, then, there is another advantage women possess."

"Nonsense! Women are infamous sinks of venery. All philosophers agree on this point, not to mention Scripture.""

"Men have these fantastical notions, as I have just said, and this an example."

"What--do you deny lust in females?"

"Pleasure I do not deny--how could I, given what is occurring at this instant? But the practice of . . . *accumulation*, the bedding of this one and that one, this sniffing like dogs about skirts, I do deny that is common among women. Oh, there are a few, and men make much of them, as well as of any number of silly women who manage to get themselves entangled, because they have discovered that some strange man is superior to the one they have. And I suppose a woman could set up to imitate the male sex, in the way that mountebanks dress little dogs in clothes and teach them to prance about like men. But I believe that for most of us, those of us, I should say, who are happy with our lot, passion grows out of love, for husband, home and family, as a plant grows from rich soil."

Some touch of his produced here a gasp and a wriggle. "No more talk," she said, "But the thing itself."

It was delightful, of course, a familiar delight, even more delightful, in that when pregnant Berthe seemed more abandoned to ecstasy. Rudi thoroughly enjoyed it then as always, especially given what had stood dolefully between them mere hours before. Yet the moment Berthe had mentioned the women who set up to imitate the male sex, the image of Sisi Vasová had strolled unbidden and unwanted across the theater of his mind, and it took real effort to banish it while he made love to his wife.

Upon arriving back in Prague, Rudi soon found that obscurity was not yet his fate, for the news of what he had accomplished at the Hofburg had preceded him. From the time the train rolled into the station, he was the toast of the city.

Arriving at his home, he discovered stacks of cards left by visitors, and even taller stacks of invitations to soirees and dinners and assemblies of all kinds. Apparently there was not a hostess in town who thought her gathering complete without an appearance by Rudi Moritz, defier of imperial grandees.

One invitation, however, took precedence over all the others, was rather more like a command. For the first time, a certain dread was attached to the sight of the familiar sealed envelope. Briefly Rudi considered refusing the interview, returning the money, and resigning his appointment, but then he recalled Novotny's words. There was a plot here and he meant to ferret it out.

The morning after he returned from Vienna, a Thursday, Rudi therefore went to the house on Wammelgasse first thing, ignoring his office. The lad Joska opened the door.

"Is the Herr Baron at liberty?" Rudi asked.

"Oh, yes, Herr Moritz. He has left instructions that you are to be sent up whenever you call."
He ushered Rudi into the library, where they found the master of the house on the sofa, his legs covered by a rug and a small book in his hands.

"You are back from Vienna, Herr Moritz   I find I have missed you," he said when Rudi entered.

"And I you, Herr Baron. How have you been keeping?"

"Splendidly, I must say. My Jew has been feeding me his elixir of Christian babies and profaned sacraments. It is like grease to my old joints, but I must not imagine it is the return of youth. Oh, no! It is like the flare of a candle before it sputters out. But no matter! I shall enjoy it all the more knowing it is the last of the good brandy. How are you? You look well: confident, full of yourself, even. I suppose your journey had a satisfactory outcome?"

"I saw the emperor, if that is what you call satisfactory."

"Ah, yes, dear Ferdinand! I saw him last some years ago, at court, and we had a pleasant chat. He is more intelligent than people think, although he has those fits. His trouble is he loves everyone too much and wishes their love in return."

"You say that as though it were a defect."

"In an emperor? Of course it is a defect. In you or I, or, *a forteriori*, a priest or mother, it would be an admirable trait, but in a ruler it is a fault. As is hate. The strong emotions breed favoritism and enmity, which are both evil in the state. The ruler must model himself upon the Deity, whose representative he is on earth, and exercise dispassionate judgment, wanting nothing for himself as a man and everything for the nation. A heart of ice may be a bad thing in a man, but it is an excellence in a king."

"And why is that, Herr Baron?"

The baron frowned and replied, "Oh, it has to do with the Fall of Man. The argument is unanswerable, but I have forgot its points. But we are here to speak of me, and not emperors and the Lord God. Is that a fresh notebook I see?"

"It is indeed. We are on volume two of your life story."

"Well, I daresay we will not reach the canonical four, although I am a good bit older than Jesus was when they nailed him up. Where were we?"

"I believe you had just refrained from hanging yourself."

Yes indeed, walking back on quaking legs to my new lodgings, which I had not yet seen, to continue with my life, which I had thought forfeit. Such peculiar feelings in my breast—I can recall them without the least difficulty even now. I suppose they may be common in failed suicides, especially when the reason for the attempt has, we may say, dissipated with the failure. The great clock struck four as I passed the square and I was the only person out to observe the famous parade of the apostles, and Death, of course, swinging his scythe.

I looked at it in passing and thought, I have been saved from death by a libertine woman; henceforth, my life will be different. All the dreadful events of the recent past acted as a kind of vitriol on my spirit, dissolving away my boyhood, the beliefs, the sense of right and wrong, and all attachments. Or so I believed at the moment. In their place remained a sense of freedom and power such as I had never felt before, except perhaps when galloping Kíslang at top speed across a field on a fine morning. This freedom was, of course, perfectly hollow, the freedom of a bubble or balloon to fly in any direction. Which, by the way, is what you lovers of liberty do not understand—but let me not pontificate, oh, no. The lessons will come later.

What was most in my mind, of course, was Clotilde, my savior, and my chief desire was to find her, and taste again in fuller measure the delights that she had offered me *en passant*, as it were. She had had me, as she observed, like a dish of sherbet between courses, but I resolved I would one day have *her*, and of that dish take my fill, as the main course of a banquet. That this lecherous madness was but a different style of that romantic madness I had previously endured, and worse for being devoid of any tenderness, did not, of course, occur to me at the time.

How I would accomplish this feat was obscure at that moment, for you will collect that I was a country boy, raised in a country possessed by my family, and had no knowledge, apart from what I had gathered from books, of how to conduct myself in debauchery. Yet it is not a skill difficult to learn, and any city has willing tutors in abundance. I thought I would begin by getting drunk in a tavern, since I had heard this was a habit of the libertine set.

I had not previously been anything of a tippler, nothing like my brother, at any rate. I took beer, of course, and wine at meals, and slivovic on occasion. Now, as I entered the Kohlmarkt, I looked for a tavern in which to begin my life of dissipation. It was still quite dark, but the square was already full of wagons and horses and men, the latter shouting and bustling and unloading crates of cabbages and potatoes, their straining faces rendered demonic by lantern-light. No one paid me any mind, for it is not unheard of for gentlemen to stop for a drink at a Kohlmarkt tavern after a night of gambling and fornication. But this I learned only later.

The place I chose, or rather stumbled upon, was called At the Wheel. For a sign it had an old wagon wheel, painted red and stuck on a rod fixed into the wall. The barrow boys used to make a game of standing on each other's shoulders and giving it a spin, for luck.

To be brief, I managed to get drunk, and boisterous, on sour beer and brandy, supposed brandy, that is to say, made of potatoes in the back room and flavored with brown sugar and sawdust. I believe I was making love to the barmaid, a woman twice my size and thrice my age. I pinched her backside and asked her to come back to my lodgings with me. I would shower her with gold and treat her like a queen upon sheets of silk She laughed and took it in good part and the tavern keeper called out that if such a little fellow ever got into Katia's *thing* they would have to send a party of men with torches down there to find him. There are taverns in Prague where such a silly sprig as I was then would have been knocked on the head, to awaken naked in an alley, but, by God's grace, At the Wheel was not one of them. Katia loomed her great bosom over me and inquired, "Well, little gentleman, where'll we go for these silk sheets?"

I told her number ten Franzosichegasse. It was a wonder I recalled it. Everything that had happened prior to my attempt at death had taken on a strange insubstantial quality. My memory offers nothing as to the remains of the evening. I suppose I slid to the floor and they sent to the address I had named for Lennart, who carried me home. There is an image--I can see it clear, the dark sky, the stars, a wash of smoke, and all on a bounce, for Lennart is carrying me home like a babe in arms. Yet I cannot say if it was this or another time, for there were so many.

I awakened late the next morning in an unfamiliar bed, believing I had caught the plague. I wept and cried and behaved in a disgraceful manner. Lennart treated me as I deserved--that is, like a puling infant, and brought me coffee and warm rolls and jam and made me drink and eat, and after a while, I felt myself again.

The lodgings Lennart had chosen consisted of a large sitting room that gave on a courtyard and a small bedroom that gave on nothing at all, its window opening on a narrow alley and the windows of the house next door. It was furnished in the taste of former years with items that no one particularly desired—the chairs and sofa and tables unmatched, but oddly enough it all seemed to fit together and it pleased me anyhow, an establishment that reflected my own condition. No one wanted me, either. The walls had been freshly papered in the gray-blue color popular in that era, with wreathing in white near the ceiling, and the floors were furnished with worn Turkey carpets. It did not smell, or not very much, and then only from the bakery below, nor was it excessively warm, being on a middle floor. Both rooms had small fireplaces. I had never lived elsewhere than in a palace, of course, but I was not dismayed by the humility of my new lodgings. When one is young, one wishes the world to reflect one's feelings; and so I, lost, discounted, abandoned, liked the notion of living, so to speak, without style.

How Lennart had found the place and secured it so quickly I did not know, nor did I ask. One does not, you understand, for I own that peasants and servants have skills we lack. I dare say that neither you nor I, set down in a strange city, could negotiate such comfortable quarters. We would be all at sea, but not Lennart, nor his breed. I have seen it a thousand times. One is on campaign, the countryside is barren and raked by war, all are on short rations, and yet, somehow, a roast chicken appears, or a stew of beef. Truly, are we not babes in their hands?

It was a rhetorical question but Rudi chose to answer it. He stopped his pencil and said, "Yet, despite this undoubted competence, you assert that the class of persons you name are unfit to rule themselves. How is that? How is it that the government of the empire is reserved for the helpless babes?"

The old man passed a sharp look, sniffed, and then smiled a hooded smile. "A lawyerly question, sir. You suppose you have caught me out, but I answer you thus: the talents necessary to procure a roasted chicken in a barren country are not what we desire in the management of the state. Those who steal chickens are not to be trusted with government, however we may enjoy the chickens thus obtained. Your peasant who shows clever in small ways invariably proves as great a fool when confronted with large questions. It is all breeding, sir, and only breeding that makes a man capable of command."

"Bonaparte's marshals might beg to differ, sir," replied Rudi. "Was not Ney a cooper's boy and Massena the spawn of a shopkeeper?"

Yes, and Davout and Kellerman were of noble birth, as was Bonaparte himself. Exceptions are to be expected in exceptional times. I do not say it is impossible to breed leaders in the cauldron of revolution and war, but it is far from the rule. And the damned bastards lost in the end, as I seem to recall. May I continue?" Rudi bowed and took up his pencil again.

As I was finishing my coffee, Lennart announced that he had shined my boots and set my best suit in good order, but that I had no lace fichu for my neck cloth.

"Why the devil should I have a lace neck cloth?" I asked.

"Because you are going to see Colonel Kolowrat-Krakowski, sir, are you not? We are to be enlisted in the Kaisers, as the Count desired."

"I have no such intention," said I. "The Kaiser cuirassiers will have to make do without me."

He said, "But the Count..."

And I said, "The Count is dead and buried. What he wished is no longer of concern. Do dead men order you about?"

"Why yes, your honor. I always try to do what my old Dad would have wished. That is how I was raised."

"Well that is not how I was raised, as you very well know. Let us hear no more about the Count, if you please!"

"Then what will you do, baron, if I may make so bold? We have a roll of thalers, true, but they will hardly last out a year, with things dear as they are in these parts. A bread loaf costs a whole kreuzer, if you can believe it. And nothing found, as it is on the demesne—we must buy with coin every drop of wine, every scrap of meat. The very soap must be bought, imagine! And these rooms are twelve kreuzer the week. Where it is all to come from I don't know. I have heard that all gentlemen have an income--I mean money for doing no work at all. So it may be Lennart plays the fool again, for your honor is surely a gentleman and must have one, as every dog has its tail."

"A fool for certain," says I, "but correct in this: I have my five hundred a year. Look now: I have decided to turn libertine. "

"Oh," cries he, "must I do the same, your honor? For I was taught to stay with the old Church, and have no truck with heretics. For you must leave the dance with the same girl you brought, as my mam used to say."

"No, Lennart, you country oaf," says I. "A libertine is one who does as he pleases and lives for pleasure. He is clever, and gold flows into his purse, and he breaks hearts left and right, and has a jolly time of it."

"Well, then," says Lennart. "I shall be one too, according to my station, though only copper shall flow into my purse, I suppose. But, your honor, how does a man start out at it? Are there tools and a bench?"

I laughed and ignored this, and had him lay out what I wore in those days, a costume I had aped from Oskar, who had it from the English bloods. It was very nearly the equipage of a groom, for it was considered dashing then to dress below one's station. It had got into all our heads that the world would be better for being turned upside down, and that defying convention and shocking our elders was delicious. And shortly thereafter the world was turned upside down, in earnest; to prevent which, had I but known it, I should have dressed in oceans of lace, and the highest, snowiest wigs, and everything gilt and brocade. As it was, I took to the streets in a plain blue frock coat, with a black stock, a plain black tricorne hat without lace, top boots, and my own hair, powdered and clubbed behind. And my sword, of course, so no one would take me for an actual groom.

Out upon the town, I made haste to seek out the woman Clotilde, frequenting the places where actors congregated: taverns, brothels, gambling hells, and so on. I found many who knew her, but gathered that she had gone from Prague, somewhat precipitously, as actors and musicians are wont to do, leaving a trail of yearning lovers and unpaid bills. Some said she was in Vienna, appearing at the Burgtheater, others that she had gone with her lover to Munich.

In any case, I had her not, nor was likely to obtain her favors, unless I should search every bedroom in Europe. Meantime, I had my lust to contend with, whose wellsprings she had opened. For a young man in my position there are two possibilities only—to seduce with charm and wit or to buy the thing outright from a whore, or quasi-outright, by consorting with the women of the theater. As for charm, I had this face of mine. The scar you see today is but a shadow of what it was when fresh. It looked, one young lady took the trouble to inform me, as if my visage had cracked apart down the middle like a pasteboard mask and then been stuck together hastily by a child, so that the halves did not quite align.

My wit, I suppose, was ready enough. I had practiced upon Marietta, although the wit one uses when one wishes a maiden to fall in love and that which is required to get her merely to open her thighs are of different sorts. But I would have had to have been Voltaire and Lichtenberg all in one to overcome my face, whereas money makes the greatest fool a gallant, and, as another young person once told me, a girl can always close her eyes. I believe a certain sort of gentleman writes a memoir in which he enumerates all his conquests in detail. What could be more boring, not to say indelicate? Besides, as the Emperor Marcus says, it is absurd to place so much importance and endure so much agony over what is, after all, only a fleeting spasm and the emission of a tea-spoonful of slime. Reading the stoics is a habit of young men wounded in love, I believe, and perhaps you have. Or no--your romantic life has been a special case, so I suppose you have been preserved from both the blight and the cure.

Seventeen

Rudi continued to write, but this last comment disturbed. How did the old man know anything about his domestic affairs? A *special case*? He forbore to question, however, and after a pause, the baron continued his account of ancient fornications.

If seduction be an art, as many a coxcomb professes, then it is much akin to the art of riding a horse. That is, one listens to the mount, one is sensitive to its balance, and, through a combination of subtle touches one leads the horse to believe that it wants to go where the rider chooses. I do not speak here of mere brutes who must use force in both instances. It is simply the case that one can have any woman one chooses if one will only listen to her. I had that from the greatest seducer of the former age. You have heard the name Casanova? Yes. He also said the ear is the most potent organ of lasciviousness, and it is true. But more of that in its proper place.

One instance will stand for two dozen. The house I occupied was owned and managed as apartments by a Frau Oslinger, a widow in her middle years. I believe Lennart had exaggerated the magnificence of my breeding and prospects, for the first time I met her in the hallway she paid me the sort of obeisance with which prince-archbishops must be familiar, and I responded with the haughty condescension she desired and expected. A certain type of wealthy bourgeoise dotes upon every sprig of aristocracy and I am sure that having a baron in her establishment, even a poorish one, was thought greatly to her credit among her peers in the neighborhood. She was a buxom woman, high colored, red haired without, I thought, any help from the dyer's art, clever in business matters, mean with tradesmen and her inferiors, obsequious, as I have said, to those she thought above her. She employed a chambermaid, Valeska by name, a saucy girl about my own age, a blonde with a passing resemblance to my Marietta, but only as the mark made by a new coin pressed in clay recalls the golden visage of the original.

I had not been in the place more than a week before her charms were mine, an occurrence barely qualifying as a seduction. I was lying late abed after a night of drinking and gaming when she entered, Lennart being out on some errand. Seeing me there she hesitated, blushed prettily, excused herself, said she would return later. I said she might come in when she pleased and not to mind me at all. She did as I asked—to a point, for I soon observed she was putting on a kind of dumb show performance, stretching, bending, leaning, and doing all the things that pretty young girls do when displaying their bodies to men, although they would throw a jug at the head of anyone who dared suggest they were doing so.

Thus, it seemed that the framed engraving of the *Ride of Mazeppa* above the head of my bed was deeply filthy and required to be brought to a high polish, which necessitated her leaning over me so that her breasts were inches from my face, nor did the threadbare smock she wore do much to conceal their shape. Again, while scrubbing my floor, she arranged her skirts, I know not how, so that her buttocks were all on show, as well as the cleft between. As for me, it being early in the morning, and this exhibition going forward, nature took command and there grew in the middle of the counterpane a demonstration of my parts, so that it appeared that a pavilion had been pitched upon the bed. I lay watching her, my hands behind my head, and failed not to observe her casting sly looks at the pavilion; the back of her neck, I observed, was pink as a ham.

At last she had cleaned the place to a fare-thee-well and stood by the door.

"Does your honor wish anything more," she asked.

"No," said I. "Is there anything you would wish of me?"

Her eyes dropped to the tent pole, then rose to meet mine. "What happened to your face," she asked, then gaped in shock and put her hand over her mouth.

"A duel," said I. "Shut that door and take off your clothes."

In two shakes she was under the quilts in her shift, hot as a fresh biscuit and squirming like a tench in a boat. Well, a chambermaid, after all; I made myself imagine it was Marietta bouncing under me. For her part, she said she liked me for being young and gentry, and with a nice smell, not like the last one, a brewer who stank and who forced himself on her whenever he could catch her unawares. And did not give a kreutzer, imagine! I gave her five kreutzer for the convenience of it: thus my first conquest! So many to follow!

Let me sketch for you the life of a libertine and idler of the former age. One rises late, one's servant brings coffee and a crescent or tart. One takes horse and rides in the royal park, then clatters back over the bridge to the stable, sees the horse fed and rubbed down. Then the café. Mine was Skober's. I believe it is still in business. One sees acquaintances there and engages in idle chatter. Subjects: who is bedding whom; who has fought a duel; the fashions, who sells the most desirable coats, pantaloons, hats, cravats; what is appearing on the stage, the actresses, how pretty, how available; who is likely banking at faro this evening chez Monferrato and how much they gained or lost the previous evening; blood horses, for sale or wishing to buy, their speed and points; how drunk on prior occasions and what outrages committed; money, not enough, how to obtain more; projects to invest in for that purpose; cheats and swindles, who was gulled and who carried it off. Also musical performances, what singers, how pretty and which available and for what price. In all this not an idea, not a fragment of wit beyond vile clenches or bawdry, nothing that would tax the intellect of a goose.

One drinks, of course, and buys drinks and has drinks bought for one. It is known one is a baron, hence rich, hence to not be thought low one must lay out spirits for anyone with a decent coat and clean linen that might pretend to a tincture of gentility. The kreutzers fly, and the florins too, and few enough fly back, especially when one repairs of an evening to Monferrato's. Faro was my doom. Have you played? I see not. It is difficult to remember the details of those days, so similar they all were, and besides, one is always, save the morning, a little in cups, not staggering precisely, but without judgment.

Lennart kept my purse, the principle being that it would be a bold thief who tried to rob a man-mountain like him. He would count out when I left each day and I would return to his keeping any coins that remained when I staggered in before dawn, or, as was more frequently the case, after he carried me into our apartment.

So my days went on, and I moved through them without thought, like that automaton Turk once displayed in Vienna that could play chess, but not as interesting. And one morning, or it may have been early in the afternoon—when I suppose I had been at this business for perhaps four months —there came a change. I asked Lennart for twenty florins as I usually did, and to my surprise he said that he could not.

"What!" said I. "You refuse me my own money?"

"Not I, your honor, but the purse itself. You may have four with all my heart, for that is what is left in it."

"Just four? But that is impossible. I had five hundred thalers from my father in June."

"Yes, sir. And each one turned into florins and kreutzers and went their way. It is a habit of purses to empty in this fashion when all is expense with no income. As our old Mam used to say, when gold is the husband, starvation is the widow. I have the figures here in my copybook. I can show them to your honor. "

This was the odd thing about my Lennart. He looked the most oafish of men, an ox on two legs, you would have said. Yet he was bred from a man who was the steward of a great schloss, with all the schloss's accounts in his head, a dealer with dozens of merchants, all wishing to cheat the Count in some wise, and rarely bested. Lennart was not to be doubted on the subject of money and what it bought.

"But we must have money," said I. "How will we live? I do not get my income until Lady Day, six months hence. We will be thrown out into the street."

"Not for some time, your honor. We are paid through the quarter--that is, through the end of September. Our accounts at the baker and grocer are in good order, so you will have rolls and coffee at least. The tailor's bill we cannot pay, but he can be avoided as you have a closet full of clothing almost new. The stable man will want his twenty kreutzers this Friday. You could sell your horse."

I stared at him, dumbfounded. "Sell Kíslang? Never!"

"Then, sir, if we are to remain here, we must change our ways."

"How do you mean?"

"Your Honor, I mean we must pursue a different profession; for libertine is a fine thing, but it is all outgo, if you take my meaning, sir."

"Give me the four florins!" said I, and took my leave.

But out upon the street I was at a loss, for I could no longer cut a figure at my usual haunts; what I had in my purse would barely furnish a decent meal and a round of drinks of the quality demanded by my cronies. So I went to the stables, had my horse saddled, and rode out of the town in the direction of Karlín.

I galloped both of us into a sweat and afterward, as we went back at an easy trot, I considered what Lennart had said.

Money. How to get it--what a mystery! I have always been astounded at the way bourgeois seem to have no trouble with this art and we nobility flail about while all we own falls into ruin. No one has been able to explain it to me satisfactorily during a long life. I believe it has to do with buying cheap and selling dear, but beyond that my mind stalls like a green hunter at a hedge. I asked Kíslang, but she had no useful advice, for never was there a horse that set up as an economist.

So I saw her comfortably in her stall and then strolled through the Kohlmarkt, where I spied the sign of The Wheel and thought that it was a good place to secrete myself until I could arrive at a solution to my troubles. Now for the first time in my life I became aware of what I was spending, a peculiar feeling, as when we try consciously to control our breath instead of leaving it to the body's devices. How delightful cheap was The Wheel! A big stein of beer, a dish of eels, a half-pound of black bread with lard, and all for two kreutzers!

As I sat there, I noticed a procession of fellows passing through the room to a door at the back. These were rogues in the main, flash, soi-disant gentlemen with silk cravats and embroidered waistcoats, some few of whom I recognized from the faro rooms at Signor Monferrato's, as well as a number of macaronis of the town--punters all.

Strange as it will sound, I regretted my expulsion from this fellowship, although in truth not one of them was worth a clipped pfennig as a man; and so my attention was drawn to that door. It opened upon a time, and I heard floating out of the room beyond a familiar, even dear, sound: the click of billiard balls. You will wonder, sir, at my stupidity, my yokeldom, for until that moment I had not imagined that there were public places to play at billiards. For all I knew, my father and Madame had invented the game between them. I was fainting with curiosity, so I rose and went through the door.

There were three tables, two of the common type, with holes and bags, and one set up to play fortification billiards, with the various forts, passes, batteries and flags arranged in accord with the rules. No one was playing on this, but all clustered around one table, at which a match was in progress. They were playing white winning hazard, which is everyone's first game. Do you understand me when I speak of a winning hazard?

"Yes, Herr Baron. The aim of the strike is to sink the other man's ball without your own ball sinking."

"Indeed. And the losing hazard is the opposite. Your own ball must strike the other's and then go in pocket, without causing the other ball to sink. I watched as one of the players prepared to shoot from the baulk-line at a ball on the rail a little up the corner pocket, not a simple shot, especially if he wished to return the ball to play. As I watched him set up, I felt a tug at my sleeve. A curly-headed fellow with a squint, wearing a long redingote that had once been green, held up a sheaf of small paper slips.

"Bet bet bet," he mumbled, "good odds! Fine sir, what's your bet?"

I shrugged him off and watched the game. The player, a meagre fellow with a phiz like a grinning ferret's, made his shot, using backspin to return his ball to the center of the table and then ran through, winning ten to two. There was a rustle of paper and clink of coin as people settled bets and a drift of discarded slips to the floor, which was quite covered with them, as a forest path is by leaves in autumn.

They played two more games and then took a break for beer and tobacco. I asked the redingote about the players and about betting on the outcome of the matches. He told me that not only did they bet winners, but also upon each stroke, whether he would make it or no, and also upon every score, odds being fixed for each combination. You will wonder at this, sir, but I was so country-bred that, while I was familiar enough with horse race betting, it had never occurred to me that one could bet upon billiards.

"And do you play, sir?" the redingote asked me.

"I have played," I answered, "and I believe I will take it up again."

For, of course, I now saw that my troubles over money would soon be over.

Baron von Pannau closed his eyes and rubbed a hand over his face. "Now begins a most tiring part of my story. It is exhausting to recount the follies of youth, far more, I find, than the accounts of how one was abused, which are almost pleasant in the retelling. So you will excuse me --I feel the need for a short nap."

With that Rudi was dismissed and found himself again on the Wanmelgasse, from which he made his way back to his office. He felt oddly disturbed by this last session. Even with the excitement of revolution, the Baron's life seemed so much richer than his own, the difference between a spicy goulash and watery gruel, and Rudi felt less of a man for it. Of course he knew it was all in the telling; he realized that such a life was politically suspect, depending as it did on a corrupt system. Suffering and injustice imposed on thousands supported the life of young Hans von Pannau, all this was perfectly clear, and yet . . . Rudi didn't know what came after "and yet," but he understood that there was something that the liberals he spent his days with could not understand.

And was this shame he felt about not playing the rake? How the devil did the old monster know about his, what did he say, special case? The blight and the cure? Here was a secret thought that Rudi rarely let emerge: although Berthe was a treasure to be sure and he was more fortunate than any man he knew in having had her dropped into his lap while still a youth, still there was something unsatisfactory about having been given the cure before experiencing the blight, a few clumsy encounters with whores not really being of any account. Again the fantasy of some consuming affair, the failure of which would prompt suicide. Absurd nonsense, he knew; but some part of the inner man ached for it, and the ache put him in a bad mood.

Which was not at all improved when he threw open the door of his office and found Havel rifling through the drawers of his desk.

"Havel! What the devil are you doing!"

The clerk shot to his feet with such alacrity that the chair he was using went over with a crash. His panicked efforts to right it caused a stumble. His hand grasped wildly for support, which toppled the stack of papers in the wicker basket that held outgoing correspondence.

"Well?"

Havel's voice came from the other side of the desk, where he crouched and gathered documents. "I'm awfully sorry, Herr Amstrat, but I could not find the . . . the latest contracts with the Meissinger concern, and the Herr Praktikant asked for them while you were out, he desired them instantly. And so . . ."

"What nonsense! The Meissinger contracts are in my out-basket, or were until you knocked it over. They are probably in your hand at this moment."

Havel flushed beet-soup. He stammered out another apology as he riffled through the documents in his hand; then he stopped and there appeared on his blazing face a patently false look of dumbfounded surprise.

"Why, here it is! And I swear I looked through this basket half a dozen times or more."

"Well now you have it," said Rudi mildly, "take it to the Praktikant! Off you go."

When the young man was gone, Rudi examined the drawer of his desk. It had been carefully and thoroughly searched and the papers and seals arranged so much as they had been that Rudi would never have noticed had he not caught Havel in the act. The story about not being able to find a contract half as thick as a brick was a patent fable: Havel had never misplaced so much as a memo in his life, and the part about the Praktikant was laughable. The superannuated general who governed the entire legal department could barely tell a contract from a deposition and had never asked for anything at all from Rudi's office, much less instantly.

So Havel was a spy; it hurt Rudi to think this, for he liked the lad and thought him talented. But why spy? Rudi never kept anything incriminating in his desk, not a scrap connected with his secret journalism or political work. He would have been a fool to do so; and Havel, who was no fool, knew that his chief was not one either. It must have been something to do with the work of the office, but what that could have been eluded him.

Another, more disturbing, thought came: who was Havel spying for? The police? Would a bright young Czech, a sincere nationalist, work for the police? It was possible--he knew well what pressure the authorities could bring to bear, and suborning a clerk would be trivial for them.

But what had Havel been seeking? He racked his brains and came up with nothing that bore scrutiny. He required advice. Novotny? No! Why? Because Novotny was a Czech. Perhaps it was *he* who had suborned Havel. Insane thoughts. Rudi shook his head violently to scatter them. How he despised conspiracy! The whole point of a liberal state was that there would be no room for it, for this vile spy craft, that the business of politics would be done in the open by free men . . .

He let out a snarling sound. Havel entered, glanced briefly at his master, uttered a low obsequious noise that might have been a greeting, and retreated to his cubby. Rudi took up his work. It was complicated, requiring close reading of tedious contractual language and before long it damped those other thoughts, although not before he had fixed upon whom to consult.

Rudi left work early and took a fiacre to the eastern end of the Tandelmarkt. The neighborhood consisted of older tenements, largely occupied by Jews who had left the old ghetto after Emperor Joseph's famous emancipation. Liebig was at home but busy with a student, so Rudi spent an uncomfortable half-hour being entertained over weak coffee and cheap store biscuits by his friend's mother and the older sister, both of whom looked remarkably like Liebig.

The talk was all of the recent events, and one would have thought from their conversation that the prime purpose of the enormous changes racking the empire was to engineer the release from prison of Josef Liebig. Papers were pressed on Rudi, all letters to and from the authorities concerning this deliverance, and his legal opinion was solicited. He could not but agree that some weeks would see their angel home--to suggest the contrary would have been rank cruelty--and when he confirmed their beliefs he saw tears of joy stream across the two homely faces.

The student appeared, a pimply, disheveled youth, who almost raced from the apartment and then Liebig stepped through, in waistcoat and shirtsleeves, looking spent, as if he had just wrestled a calf to the ground.

"Moritz? What on earth....?"

"Ah, dear Liebig, I am so sorry to disturb you at home, but I wished for a private conversation."

Liebig raised his eyebrows in a quizzical expression and mutely gestured Rudi into his room. This was small and close, smelling of old paper and Liebig's cheap cigars. Books in stacks filled every corner and the remaining space was jammed tight by a day bed, a plain deal table, and two rickety spindle chairs.

"Shall you take the student chair or shall I?" asked Liebig. "No, take the master's seat, for it is the more comfortable and I detect you wish to instruct me on some matter."

They sat so, whereupon Rudi told the tale not only of Havel's rummaging but also what he had learned of Baron von Pannau's history with the police. Liebig had listened without comment. After a considerate pause he said, "An interesting story, Moritz, but why come to me?"

"Because you are intelligent, you have a devious mind, and you are not a Czech."

"Distinguishing me from Novotny on one point in three. Or perhaps two. Very well. Let me begin by asking *you* a question. Have you noticed anything odd about Novotny recently?"

"Not odd. He seems to have become, well, more of an adult since he procured funds to start a real paper. I was quite pleased with our conversations at Vienna."

"You don't find him somewhat evasive, running off to meet people he does not name, for example?"

"No, although he affects a radical view, talks about defending the revolution with armed workers and so on. But

255

you know Paul. He is somewhat fantastic, especially with beer in him."

"True, but let me share some observations. I was in the jakes behind the Knight yesterday afternoon. I heard two men talking in the alley. One of the voices was Novotny's; the other spoke German with a Russian accent. The door there you know is cracked, and by peering through I could see that it was indeed our friend. His interlocutor was that odd little fellow who accompanies Bakunin."

"You mean Bors?"

"Himself."

"What of it? There is no harm in . . ."

'Wait! That evening I was walking to Paul's place on Wassergasse to deliver some copy when I saw him step from the front door and look both ways down the street. I was in shadow so he failed to notice me. He crossed the street and climbed into a black berlin drawn by two black horses. He was there for ten minutes and then went back to his house. I delivered my copy, we spoke for a time, but he did not mention the carriage. What do you make of that?"

"Of that I make nothing. What do you infer?"

"Just that such a rig is typical of the police."

"And of a thousand who are not police. Liebig, if we start spying on each other and nursing suspicions, we are doomed, along with our revolution."

"Yes, but you come to me with a tale of spying by a young man whom you name as a Czech nationalist, and you ask me, what was he seeking? I supply you with sufficient background to guess at an answer."

Liebig waited; Rudi frowned, then let out a laugh.

"Dear Liebig, you are a tutor to your bones, but I am too old to be tutored. If you have an idea, toss it out!"

"Very well, but you are sure to object. Rudi, there are but two factors that can destroy the current revolution. One is national enmity, and our masters, you can be sure, will labor hard to set Czech against German and both against the Jews. This is their familiar game, but because familiar, we are at least partially on guard against it. For the moment at least, the elites of all three nations are working toward a common cause, embodied in your famous petition. The second is the possibility that the working class will rise up, arm themselves, and threaten the property of those same elites, and if that occurs you may be sure that the bourgeoisie will instantly abandon all their revolutionary fervor and throw themselves on the mercy of the nobility and its army. Therefore, anyone who wishes to destroy the revolution will move to arm the workers, produce an emeut that will alienate the bourgeoisie, and thus stifle any reform."

"That's absurd, Liebig! Why would the regime secretly arm the workers? They would be cutting their own throats. Look at Paris!"

"Yes indeed, look at Paris! And look too at the numbers: there are vastly more proletarians in Paris than there are in Prague. Bohemia is a peasant nation after all, and the peasants, God bless them, have just as much political awareness as their cattle. As long as the *robot* is abolished they will lean on their spades and do nothing. There are just enough workers in Prague to terrify the industrialists, but not nearly enough to carry off an armed uprising of any real effect. Thus, any effort to arm workers must only be a provocation meant to bring in the troops and destroy the revolution."

"Liebig, this is absurd . . . "

But Liebig raised a cautionary hand. "Let me finish, if you please. That is but the first point. The second speaks to your original question—what was your clerk searching for in your desk? Let me hazard a guess. The function of your office is to procure military goods. Clearly there must be a system of paperwork that, when presented at a purveyor's warehouse will authorize the transfer of so many harnesses, or bales of hay—or stands of arms and the ammunition to shoot from them."

Rudi felt his stomach knot at these words.
"My God! The seals! That damned boy was after my seals."
"Please explain. What seals?"

"For the requisitions! It is when received goods are defective. Look, let us say the 22nd infantry regiment stationed at Czernowitz reports one hundred fifty two muskets defective. But before they send them to the depot at Pressburg, they must be supplied with replacements, for they cannot stave off the Russians with broomsticks. And since we would have a claim against the manufacturer for the defects, the courts have ordered that all such transactions be dealt with not by the ordinary quartermaster, but by the legal department, so that the entire cost may be laid upon the responsible party. My office handles this. The regiment sends in its report, and we issue a requisition for replacement weapons. The requisition is invalid without an official seal. I keep them in a box in my desk."

"You don't use wax?"

"No, a paper seal, stamped with a metal stamp. Good Christ, he must have forged a requisition. Someone with such a document in hand could present himself at any depot in the land and waltz away with armaments for a brigade. That stupid boy! I will have to sack him, of course."

"Do no such thing!"

"Why not?"

"Because if whoever did this knows you are on to them, it will be exceedingly hard to find the weapons. They have been very clever so far--let them stay confident in their cleverness."

"What should I do, then?"

"Let it be known to both Novotny and Jasny and any other hothead you meet that you have weapons at your disposal--and would it not be a capital idea to steal them from the state and give them to the workers? Before long you will be drawn into the conspiracy and will learn where the weapons are stored. At that point you may take appropriate action."

He paused, removed his spectacles, and rubbed his eyes. These now took on an expression of sad sympathy. "And you will not like to hear this, I know, but it is clear as daylight that Paul Novotny is behind this scheme."

"Oh, that is too much! I know you don't like him, but Novotny is a journalist and as far from a man of action as it is possible to be. He positively prides himself on his timidity."

"So he wishes the world to believe. In fact, he is a police spy and an agent provocateur. This is the only explanation for the facts I have laid before you. I know he is your dear friend and your loyalty does you credit, but it is so. Nevertheless, if you don't believe me, go offer him guns. See what he does."

"I will," said Rudi, rising. His head felt hot, as if a kettle inside it was coming to a boil, and he could not bear to stay in this stuffy room a moment more.

Liebig rose too, and, reaching into his waistcoat pocket, brought out some coins.

"What is this?" asked Rudi when Liebig made to pass him the money.

"I owe you fifty kreutzer. Take this twenty on account. For a wonder, my stupidest pupil paid me today. Ah, I see you are amazed. You believed Jews are so tight with money that you had virtually written off the debt."

"I thought no such thing."

"You did. You are a fine fellow, Moritz, but as subject to bias as the next man. I daresay you will never get a heller back from Novotny, but will go on expecting it. I suppose you will see him this evening."

"Yes, the Wenceslaus Committee. You will be there, I suppose?"

"Oh, yes. And as for what we have just discussed-- I beg you, do not delay."

Out on the great square Rudi consulted his watch and found he had an hour or so to spend before the meeting at the Baths. His cook would have prepared a meal for him, but he did not want to eat alone in his empty house. He felt hollow and shaken by his conversation with Liebig and needed to sit by himself for a time. He walked past the Red Goose, already crowded with after-work drinkers. Not there! Instead he found a small restaurant, a German place—At the Silver Stag—went in, ordered schnitzel and a beer. A rack of newspapers on sticks beckoned and he took one, Havlíček's paper, *The Prague News.*

The leader, he found, was written in a familiar style and described the events surrounding the presentation of the Bohemian petition to the emperor. Rudi had never seen himself described in the public press before and he felt his face heat as he read. Yes, he had done those things, but the author—obviously Novotny—had made him almost grotesquely heroic. His meal came, but he now found he had little appetite. He picked at it, and downed two beers, then a brandy, and went across to his meeting, feeling dulled and not quite himself.

The Wenceslaus Committee was much expanded by an influx of notables, especially Czech notables, who had previously shunned it. Rudi noticed Palacký, the great historian of Bohemia, and Havlíček. The meeting was held in a room at the Baths usually devoted to parties. It smelled faintly of old beer; someone's broom had missed bits of confetti and smears of candle wax.

Rudi saw Novotny sitting and writing in a notebook, went to him, and said, "I read your leader in the *News.* An interesting report. Much of it was nearly true."

"You liked it, did you?"

"Had I not been its subject I would have admired it unreservedly. A beautifully composed two thousand words."

"Nineteen hundred and sixty-two, at a guess. Havlíček offered me a position I would have jumped at a few weeks ago, but now that I am awash in Jew money and have my own paper, I graciously declined. Excuse me, but why are you staring at me as if you'd never seen me before?"

"Perhaps I have not," said Rudi, almost to himself.

"What do you mean?" said Novotny, still with a smile on his mouth.

"Oh, nothing. We have known each other a long time, Paul, but in our present situation people change--haven't you noticed? We do things we have not done before. Our ideas, becoming real, push back at us and make us different men."

"But not you, Moritz. You are the still center about which the wild tarantella spins. You will not change. Solid as the Hrad itself is our Moritz."

"You might be surprised. I have been talking to Liebig. He has heard some interesting rumors."

"Oh, Liebig! He has a tendency to hysteria, as do all his kind. There is always some pogrom in the offing . . ."

"No, nothing like that. He'd heard that some people were trying to assemble armaments with a mind to organizing a workers' uprising. Have you heard anything like that?"

"There are always rumors, and people who spread rumors, and people who are paid to spread rumors."

"What are you saying?"

"Only that if I had to pick someone in our circle particularly likely to be a police informer, it would be Liebig."

"Because he's a Jew? You know, you should have a care, Paul. The money that backs you can easily remove itself if you don't drop this kind of baiting."

"It has nothing whatsoever to do with his race," replied Novotny with some heat. "It's to do with his brother. Can you imagine the pressure the authorities could use upon the brother of a man locked up in Munkasch? For an extra blanket or a bowl of soup, a man might sell his soul, much less a few of his old friends. I wouldn't believe any provocative tales from our Liebig, if I were you."

"I won't argue the point, and in any case that situation will soon resolve, with the release of political prisoners. But as to arms—you yourself suggested that these might be diverted to supply a workers' militia. You recall too that I disparaged the notion. I have reconsidered. Let us say that if someone did wish to supply arms, to workers or any other revolutionary group, I would be someone to talk to."

Rudi watched Novotny's face closely as he said this, but no obvious mark of treason appeared. Instead, only a slow, mischievous smile. "I never thought I would see the day, Moritz. You have become dangerous."

"As I said, people change. And the times require it. Have you any interest, or do you know any who might have?"

"Me? I would not know which end of a musket is which. You might talk to Jasny, though. He is your real fire-brand."

"Perhaps I will," said Rudi as he studied his friend's face. Could he really be such a liar? Or was that mere fantasy from Liebig, who did not like him?

"But for now I must go to my meeting. Herr Lörner will be vexed if I am late."

"Your master calls?"

Rudi managed a grin he did not feel. "It's hard to know who serves whom anymore, don't you find? It seems to be another revolutionary difficulty."

Eighteen

The meeting took place in what was known as the Painted Room, owing to a large mural depicting the defense of the town of Prague against the Swedes in 1648, the last major hostility of the Thirty Years War. Under the command of the valiant Field Marshal Colloredo, here shown sword in hand upon the canonical white steed, a tiny imperial force, swelled by a citizen army of burghers, Jews and students of the Academic Legion, had fought three Swedish armies to a standstill. The invaders took Hradčany Castle but they could not win their way across the Charles Bridge. The mural was cracked and faded now, perhaps a suggestion, thought Rudi, of the current state of Prague's martial spirit.

He had been the first to arrive and was idly perusing the mural when a voice behind him said, "And now we face a different sort of crisis, but as great. And mere valor will not suffice."

Rudi turned; it was Lörner.

"Well, valor is always useful," said Rudi, "even if not entirely sufficient. I wonder if Prague would turn out like that again, to oppose an invasion, I mean."

"Let us pray we can arrange things so that we do not have to find out. You've seen the plaque commemorating the battle? I mean the one on the bridge. No? Well, this shows you are not a native Praguer. My father took me to see it when I was six or so. The Latin says, 'Rest here, walker, and be happy: you can stop here willing, but unwilling were stopped the Goths and their Vandalic ferocity.' I fear the Goths and Vandals are now somewhat closer to home than they were in 1648."

"Your meaning?"

"Oh, I suppose I refer to our Czech friends and the radical workers. You think it inept?"

"I confess I do, dear Lörner. Look here, we are small fry in a sea of sharks. If most Bohemians cannot agree on how they may live in peace together, then the revolution is doomed and Bohemia will remain a pawn of the great powers. That is the fact. The *only* issue in which I am at all interested is that one—how Germans and Czechs are to agree and forge one nation. That solved, everything else will fall into place and we can have the independent constitutional monarchy of our dreams. That unsolved, nothing we otherwise do will be of any avail."

"Oh, believe me, sir, I grasp the point. But the damned thing is, they won't listen. We invite them to our meetings and they don't come."

"They certainly came to the last Wenceslaus Committee meeting."

"Oh, yes, but that was just to make sure their precious language issue was raised to a higher station of importance. My God, why choose to limit themselves by keeping to such an obscure tongue? German is a language of culture and philosophy. It should be seen as a gift to such people. If they all learned and used German every day they would soon abandon Czech, I assure you. But they are a mule-headed people."

"Yes, and this is what they say about the Germans. Let us try to keep nationalistic speech to a minimum and see if we can all work together in pursuit of common interests."

"Yes, and in the meantime, we want you to take over the Academic Legion, with appropriate military rank."

"Me? But I am a lawyer."

"And I run a shipping company, but now am a damned politico. Revolutionary times, sir. We must all do our part. We need a solid man in charge of those hotheaded boys, and that scar on your face is better than a breast of medals."

After a moment, Rudi acquiesced and found himself unaccountably pleased. The boyhood dream of arms was, it seemed not entirely buried under the freight of briefs and procedures that had been his life.

"Good," said Lörner, "you will do well. And perhaps we can expand your authority later, over the full National Guard and those Czech militias."

"Oh, I don't think the Guard will take kindly to being ruled by someone like me. Not to mention the Czechs taking orders from a German."

Lörner rubbed finger and thumb together. "They may, if they wish to get their pay and bullets for their muskets. In politics, I am finding, money is quite as effective a goad to action as it is in trade. And may I say it, while your modesty does you credit, sir, let us not see any of this self-denigration in public. You have the makings of a great figure in our future state, if you will only thrust yourself forward."

Other people came into the room then and sat in the chairs that lined both sides of a long central table. Some opened portfolios of papers, the rest stood talking in small groups.

"And as to that state," said Lörner quietly, "a substantial number of prominent Germans in the country believe that our fate lies with the Frankfurt parliament rather than with the enlightenment of the Böhmers."

Rudi stared at him. "Then you must make it your business to dissuade them. Whatever may happen in Frankfurt or the other German states, our responsibility is entirely to secure the revolution here. Any motion that advances this cause will have my support; any that does not, though praised by the entire German nation from Lübeck to Linz, I will oppose with all my strength. That would include, for example, any effort to join the Germans of Bohemia to the Frankfurt parliament. Have I made myself clear, sir?"

A look passed briefly over Lörner's face, one remarkably combining surprise, irritation and calculation. Rudi caught this and thought: no, sir, flatter me as you like, but I am not your tool and it is past time you learned it.

"Very well," Lörner said abruptly, and looking about the room, observed, "We seem to be all present. Let us begin."

265

The meeting now commenced under Lörner's chairmanship, and the leading figures of German Prague had their say about the future. Two motions were brought, both of which Rudi vigorously opposed. The first, to which he was actually indifferent, was to draft a second petition to the Hofburg, stronger than the first. He yielded here, which gave him an edge in the debate on the second, which was to send a delegation to Frankfurt toward uniting with the all-German parliament. This narrowly failed. Almost as an afterthought, the committee appointed Rudi Military Commissioner of the Academic Legion, the loose militia that had lately been formed by the students at the Charles and the Polytechnic.

"Herr Maisel is not pleased with us," observed Rudi as he watched the banker leave the room without any expression of cordiality. "It would be unfortunate to lose him and his florins."

"Oh, Maisel will accommodate," said Lörner. "He has to."

"Why so?"

"Because we are the only play in town for him and his tribe. He cannot possibly ally with the Czechs, given how the Czechs feel about the people who own the factories where they toil. Besides, putting his race to one side for a moment, he is as German as it is possible to be. No, no, you can be sure the Jews will stand with us, in that they stand with anyone except themselves. Let me allow that you played your hand well just now—you have a real future as a politician. You might even come to replace Herr Borosch as alderman."

Rudi glanced over to where the ox-like alderman was gathering his papers and bestowing smiles.

"I thought Herr Borosch was an ally of yours," Rudi said.

"Herr Borosch, whom God preserve, is a capable man as regards a city ward, but lacks, shall we say, the vision to lead a nation. He is yesterday's man as you are tomorrow's. I am happy, by the way, that you accepted the military commission. I cannot think of anyone I would rather have in that place."

"Thank you. I suppose the first order of business in that line is to see what is what with the Academic Legion."

"As soon as you can, after your uniforms are prepared. I would recommend Levinsohn's. He does for the guard officers and will whip you up something without delay."

"Good God, I had not thought uniforms would be necessary!"

"Oh, yes. One cannot command in a frock coat and tall hat. I suppose you are coming to coffee at Mme. von Silber's day after tomorrow? Yes? Good. You might wear your uniform there. With a sword. As for rank, I believe two silver pips will serve."

"A major? I am sorry, Lörner, but this seems ludicrous. A sword and silver pips?"

"Perhaps, but it is a fact that to exert any authority in this field, one must look fit for the role. Politics is part circus, as you will have already learned. You must lead with sword in hand, from horseback. I suppose you can ride?"

"I don't often fall off," answered Rudi and the other man laughed louder than the remark required.

Two days later, Rudi stood in front of the cheval glass in his bedroom and studied his image, while Gregor fussed at the new uniform, tugging here and there and brushing quasi-invisible specks from the blue cloth. Two rows of gleaming brass buttons adorned the chest of the tunic. Glowing gold epaulettes sat jauntily upon each shoulder, both bearing the two silver pips of a major. Rudi supposed the uniform had been modeled on the National Guard uniforms of France; old Levinsohn had probably found an engraving in a newspaper, or someone had, and made the decision that the defenders of the March revolution should be dressed so. No one had extended that decision to the equipage of Rudi's troops, who were dressed more or less as the fancy took them, the

Academic Legion appearing in the main like a gaggle of dressed-up children.

He placed the peaked cap upon his head and grimaced.

"I look like an idiot," he said to his image. "Do I not, Gregor?"

"You look quite distinguished, sir--the fit is just so," said the valet, standing back a little. "The equipage wants only a sword, if I may be so bold."

"There *is* a sword, as a matter of fact. The town has supplied one, a tarnished item from the last age. I am disinclined to wear it and besides, just now I must visit the headquarters of the Academic Legion. Presenting myself unarmed may be taken, I hope, as an overture of peace. Hail me a cab, would you??"

Gregor dashed out. Rudi fiddled with his hat, adjusting the angle, making faces at himself, wishing Berthe were here to see him and tell him it was all right.

"It is here, sir," said breathless Gregor, and stooping with a rag, extinguished a blemish from the toe of one of Rudi's shining boots. As he left the room, Gregor held out a book. "Don't you want to take this, sir?"

Rudi smiled and shook his head. The book was one he had picked up at a used-book stall on the Moldau embankment: Jacobi's *Description of the Material and Organization of the Royal and Imperial Army.* He had been reading almost nothing else in the last twenty-four hours. Rudi knew he was an infant with regard to the actual operation of armed forces, but on the other hand he knew himself to be an effective absorber of knowledge and perhaps somewhat brighter than the typical Austrian officer, so that he was able to add to his juvenile study a knowledge of arms and army sufficient to prevent him appearing an idiot when discussing military topics. But he did not need to actually clutch the pony in his hands.

Rudi's cab pulled into the courtyard of the Carolinium. He emerged, gave the driver some coins, told him to wait. Today the Charles University appeared less a shrine of education than a fortress. Students in colored caps and arm-bands, some with cross belts and booted breeches, others in the ordinary garb of students, the short jacket and the loose collar, milled about the famous space, the Stare Mesto, as it was known, the ancient heart of the university. The faces he saw were full of enthusiasm and the sort of self-importance found among the young when they have thrown off the authority of the old, a category Rudi now realized included himself.

Observing a student who seemed to be giving commands to a small group drilling with muskets of a type that might have been used at Marengo (and a few actual pikes) Rudi approached and said, "Excuse me, do you know where I might find Herr Popp?"

"Who the devil are you?" was the reply.

"I see you have not read the proclamation."

"What proclamation?"

"The one from the revolutionary government of Bohemia and the City of Prague proclaiming one Rudolf Moritz as Major commanding the Academic Legion. There is a lot more in it about the supply of weapons and pay. I'm sure a copy is pinned to a board in some hallway of the Aula."

"We'll, that's good news about the weapons and pay. But I've never seen this Moritz."

"Yes, you have, sir. He stands before you."

The lad had the presence of mind to draw himself up, click his heels, salute, and command his miscellaneous band to order. This took some little time, after which Rudi returned the salute, his very first, but nonetheless credible, for he had practiced saluting at his glass twenty minutes that morning.

A pimpled youth was told to guide the new commander to the headquarters of the Legion, which occupied a classroom off the square. A certain laxness reigned. The space was full of young men in caps and cross belts, who lounged and sported and smoked, as young men will when no one is making them do anything in particular. Andrej Popp, the captain of the Academic Legion, appeared to be actually working on something at a desk when Rudi approached and introduced himself.

"It's about time, sir!" Popp exclaimed, shooting to his feet and saluting. "We have been pestering the provisional government for weeks, asking for weapons and materiel, and being ignored. If you can make some advances in that department, you are a welcome arrival."

Popp, it emerged during their conversation, was of mixed Slavic and German parentage, a tall engineering student with a mass of unruly black curls, an exiguous mustache and passionate blue eyes. Rudi liked him immediately and they conversed affably for an hour or so, Rudi making notes of the Legion's dispositions, strengths and requirements.

Rudi closed his notebook after this, and said, "I'm impressed by what you have made out of virtually nothing, yet I venture to suggest that you are stronger in enthusiasm than in the military arts. Perhaps some drill sergeants might be found who would instruct you. If it comes to a fight, you will need to know your business."

"Do you think it will, sir? I suppose we can guard public buildings well enough, but an actual battle . . . We had not thought..." He brightened. "But we will do our duty to the revolution whatever the cost."

They shook hands warmly. "I'm sure you will. But muskets will help a fighting spirit immeasurably, not to mention bullets and powder. I will try my best to procure what you require."

As his cab drove away, Rudi thought, Oh, yes, I will try my best! What a hypocrite! And what, after all, constitutes hypocrisy in this grand new age? Try my best? I shy like a virgin aunt passing a brothel when it is suggested that I divert muskets to the revolution, then I pretend to wish to do so to catch the people who are actually doing it. Now the thought appears in my mind that I might actually do so in service to that band of hopeless children. Arriving at the von Silber house on St. Annagasse, he had to strain to place a congenial smile on his face. And he felt like a fool in uniform.

Once inside, a butler ushered him into a drawing room he had not seen before, decorated all in pale blue, and in the Chinese fashion: azure shot-silk on the walls, upon which hung several framed scrolls with landscapes and calligraphy. Against the far wall stood a glass-windowed cabinet displaying a collection of chinoiserie. Arranged around a low bamboo table were an assortment of comfortable-looking chairs and sofas, upholstered in ultramarine silk. On one of these sofas reclined his hostess, dressed in a plain afternoon-dress in bright canary yellow. She stood out like the running lights of a ship at night.

Rudi bent and kissed her hand. She gestured with a painted fan to an armchair and he sat.

"I am happy to see you again, Herr Moritz. After all this time I was beginning to think you had forgotten us."

"Never, madam. Only affairs of state could have kept me from your door."

"Or affairs of the heart, an even better excuse. Your family has stayed in Vienna, I hear."

"They have. I am all alone in Prague."

"Yes. But we shall improve upon that, sir, before too long. Ah, here are Palacký and Father Bolzano. Father, I am so happy that you could come. Are you well at last?"

The elderly man so addressed wore shabby clerical garb, and had a deeply-lined and gentle face, from the eyes of which shone a lambent, humorous intelligence.

"I am dying, Madame," he replied, "although not, I hope, before taking coffee with you."

"Herr Moritz," said Madame von Silber, ignoring this remark, "allow me to make you known to the distinguished philosopher, Father Bernhard Bolzano, our own Descartes. Father, this is Rudolf Moritz, the author of our great petition and now the commander of the Academic Legion."

The priest regarded him benignly. "A military man, I see. We have not had a military man for coffee before this, have we Madame? I hope it is not a presagement that chez von Silber is girding for war."

"Oh, it is mere show, Father," replied Rudi. "I am but a chocolate soldier, and there is the fellow who put me in this uniform. You may lay any discomfort occasioned by my martial appearance upon his head."

This was directed at Lörner, who had just entered the room along with Count Thun.

"Not I," replied Lörner, "but the Bohemian people, speaking through their provisional government. And it is a fine choice, if the discomfiture of several of our so-called student leaders is any witness. I have had several on my hands this last half-hour. Our Major Moritz has apparently brought them a revolution they did not expect."

"Why, what has he done?" asked Madame von Silber. "Surely not commanded them to shine their boots?"

"That will come later, Madame," replied Rudi. "First we must supply them with boots to shine as well as the other paraphernalia soldiers require."

"Including arms?" asked a familiar voice.

Rudi turned to the speaker. "Wulfi? I am amazed. This is the last place I expected to find you."

"Major Speyr is a new guest," said Mme. von Silber. "Now we have had our revolution and can speak freely, we need have no fear of dear Major Speyr in his official capacity."

"Yes, indeed," said Speyr with an unctuous grin, "as I recall remarking to my cousin Moritz on another occasion, a liberal state requires more, not less, policing than a despotic one. And all of us must change with the times, mustn't we?"

Rudi perceived a certain awkwardness in the room, for it was clear that Speyr's point was not one that these good people had ever considered; but their hostess launched into a discussion of just how the functions of the police would change under the new regime and a lively discussion ensued, in which Rudi was largely silent.

As this was proceeding, the company increased, each new addition a notable of town or nation. Among these were Maisel the banker, the editor Havlíček and several others of distinction, including the Chancellor of the Carolinium and a Monsignor reputed to be the brains of the archiepiscopal palace. As he looked at his audience, Rudi could not help but think that every significant power in Prague--church and state, the press, money and nobility, Czech, Jew and German--was here represented, and they were all listening to Speyr expatiate with expressions of interest and good humor.

When he had done and the conversation had moved on, Speyr drew Rudi aside.

"Just a word, cousin. I know you don't like to discuss your associates, but this now moves out of the realm of normal politics and into actual criminal activity."

"Oh?"

"Yes. A matter of stolen arms, new muskets diverted from the depots and hidden away. Do you know anything at all about such a plot?"

"I do not," replied Rudi, feeling his mouth go suddenly dry. "And what does such a plot, assuming it exists, have to do with me?"

Speyr let out a dramatic sigh. "Rudi, please, let us not fence. We have informants, of course, and putting together information received from these, we have concluded that the plot is real. Thousands of muskets and the ammunition to go with them, spirited off and hidden here in Prague. I know we have political differences, but I beg you, if you know anything at all about this, please do not let considerations of loyalty prevent you from your duty as an agent of the state. Your name need never come up. An investigation is already being planned—I tell you this, although I should not, out of friendship and concern for our family."

"I appreciate that, Wulfi, but in all honesty, I know nothing of such a plot. I would tell you if I did."

Speyr looked long into his face, shrugged and said, "Well, then, that's good," and turned to sit down.

They were a dozen at table now, settling themselves while Madame's efficient servants poured coffee and laid out plates of little cakes.

"But to return to the Academic Legion," said Maisel, "I do wonder about arming students? Are you certain they may be controlled? Many of them have wild ideas about property and so forth."

"I daresay they have all sorts of ideas, but the point of putting them under discipline is to unite them behind the aegis of a *single* idea, which is the establishment of a new constitutional order in Bohemia. That firmly established, I care not what other thoughts they may have. Like the police, for example. The police may be hidebound reactionaries, the students may be flaming radicals, but henceforth they will be bound by the will of the people as reflected in the law."

Everyone looked at Major Speyr, who laughed and said, "As a hidebound reactionary myself, I cannot but concur, and remind the revolutionary government that it does not represent only the liberals. The 'people' you talk about all the time include many who prize order above all things."

"Indeed , sir," said Maisel. "Herr Moritz seems to have moved energetically, I must say. But what of the armed bodies now assembling on behalf of our Czech friends? Are they also to be incorporated under your command?"

A little stir ran around the table. Rudi replied after a moment. "Unity of command is a military principal of the highest importance, I believe."

"So I have always heard," said Maisel. "The question is, will you demand of the Czech student militias that they serve under you? And what will you do if they refuse?"

"I fear you are too hypothetical for me, sir," answered Rudi. "We have enough immediate problems without inventing ones that may never transpire."

Maisel looked like he was ready to continue the argument and Palacký had on his face a look, familiar to his intimates, that indicated the gestation of a telling point, when Father Bolzano said, "This is an interesting case of how fantasy is incorporated into our view of the world which, by engendering action not in accordance with reality, actually brings into being some new and perhaps undesired reality."

"To which fantasy do you refer, dear Father?" asked Madame. "Do you so name the possibility of armed conflict in our day?"

"Oh, not at all," said Bolzano with a little smile, "I could not begin to have an opinion on such a matter. I am only a philosopher, as you know, but my work engages those mental processes through which we beget certain knowledge of the world: I mean the sciences. Regrettably, natural philosophy has not progressed very far with respect to the affairs of men in congregation, politics and so forth. This is why religion remains useful."

"Speaking of fantasy," said someone Rudi could not see, and there was startled laughter. A woman's voice, familiar. Sisi Vasová entered the room and sat in the chair across the table from Rudi and gave him what seemed an especially warm smile. Rudi felt his heart shift, but could not easily tell if it were apprehension or anticipation or some of both.

"Oh, not at all," the cleric said. "Were it fantasy, it would not be in the least useful. I own it may attract fantasy, but so does patriotism, so does politics, which are real in their core, as is faith, although they arise from different sets of perceptions and possess a different epistemology."

"To what patriotic fantasies do you refer then?" asked Palacký, frowning.

"Nationalism, of course, if we make it an idol, and worship it in the place of God. In such a case, we begin to define ourselves not through the God-given qualities that make up what we are, but only in terms of what we are not. This road must lead to civil catastrophe."

"Hear hear," said Rudi. He would have applauded too, but, looking at the faces around the table he saw only closed expressions and eyes that would not meet his, and so did nothing. But one person had no fear and did clap enthusiastically. Of course, it would be Sisi Vasová. There followed a long and, to Rudi, quite interesting conversation about the role of coercion in constitutional state. It was just getting to some conclusions, when Rudi felt the sharp blow to his ankle that indicated that Vasová wished to leave.

As they both walked down Jesuitergasse toward the square, she asked Rudi, "What did you think of Bolzano? I suppose you had never met him before."

"I suppose you have?" he replied, pausing in the street and turning to look in her face. It was twilight now, but he could see her expression had stiffened.

"What, you think that I cannot know the greatest philosopher in Bohemia? I am too low, too uneducated...?"

"Not at all. Why must you lay upon me that I attempt to denigrate you? It is simple friendly curiosity. How do you come to know him?"

"He enjoys that I sing folksongs to him in Czech. And we speak afterwards of philosophy and the lost culture of Bohemia. Ordinarily I do not like conversing with educated Germans. So many little insults pass their lips, perhaps they are not even aware, but still it irks me; but not him."

"Nor me, I trust," said Rudi.

"Oh, you! You are perfectly oblivious to Czech sensibilities, although perhaps you have a good heart. Yet you think that a good heart will be sufficient to prevent Father Bolzano's civil catastrophe, you think if we are all good little liberals with free press and a vote, all will be well. But all will not be well."

"Ah, the famous Bohemian gloom. Novotny gave me a dose of it when we were in Vienna. Really, why must you doubt that things can change for the better? You have no difficulty at all imagining things will change for the worse."

She clutched his arm. Yet another odd thing about Vasová—if he offered his arm, she refused it, , but from time to time, to demand his attention, to make a point, to emphasize a joke, she would grasp his arm in a claw-like grip, briefly and hard. It gave him a peculiar thrill.

"You know, Moritz, you are an intelligent man and yet you can say stupid things like that. You say Bohemian gloom, as if it were a vice we chose. But believe me, there is a good reason for this."

"Oh, let us not have 1618 again!" he said after a great sigh. "Must we drag that doleful year behind us forever, into the age of telegraphs and railways and beyond?"

"Not in the least. Banish it from your thoughts and we shall think only of 1848, of current relations among Czech, Jew and German in this wonder era of telegraphs and railways. You will recall that on the first night we met at Mme. Von Silber's I promised I would show you a Bohemia you had not seen, a Prague even, that does not know the soireés of rich Jewesses in which our rulers are made deliciously uncomfortable for an hour by chewing radical ideas along with their toast. Tonight is fair and mild; you have no pressing engagements, I think. Now begins this course of instruction."

Rudi was willing, but insisted that he must return home and change his uniform. He did not intend to crawl the lower depths dressed so. She agreed but suggested she accompany him to his home.

"I could watch you dress," she said, "and undress, if you like. I like to watch a man dress; I like the expressions that arise upon their faces when they pose before the glass, like boys pretending. And I could poke through your drawers and wardrobes and find secrets. It was one of my chief pleasures when I was a chambermaid."

Rudi refused this, offering to meet her somewhere when he had changed clothes.

"Yes, you do not wish the servants or neighbors to see you have acquired a Czech slut," she said.

"I beg your pardon!"

"Even if you have not acquired. Very well. You shall give me two florins and you will seat me at a table . . . there." She pointed at a café, the Golden Swan, right on the north side of the great square. "This will be proper and I will drink your florins away while you excuse yourself and return dressed in mufti. Truly, your German prudence is as irritating as Slavic gloom; more, if I am the judge."

He left, he reappeared, dressed in his oldest clothing, the things he would have worn at Kunningshelm for a ramble in the wet springtime woods: rough wool trousers, sturdy boots, a leather waistcoat over a check shirt with a loose cravat at the neck and a soft, brimmed hat. In his hand he carried a stick he had never borne before. It actually belonged to Liebig's famous brother. Liebig had deposited it with him on the dreadful night in '44 when they had come for Josef. It was a sword-cane—pushing a button put thirty inches of needle-pointed steel in your hand. He had no idea what had possessed him to take it.

He arrived at Sisi's table swinging it jauntily. She looked him over. He could see by the mark the barmaid had scrawled on the lid of her mug that she had consumed three steins. The stack of small plates at her elbow indicated she had added food to her drink. He placed some banknotes on the table.

"These are your slumming togs, I take it," she remarked after her inspection. "You will fool no one, for your face has the typical German look, and no Czech would wear such a hat. However, I doubt you will be beaten as long as you stay by me, keep your mouth shut, and smile in as stupid a fashion as you can arrange. Let us go!"

He wanted to take a fiacre from the Little Square but she mocked him and said he must get used to trudging as part of his expedition to the real Böhmers, "and you are to imagine," she added, ""that we are not strolling on a pleasant spring evening in our good boots, but that it is winter with freezing rain coming down and your boots are more newspaper than leather and you can no longer feel your toes."

"I suppose you yourself need not rely entirely on imagination."

"You are correct, Moritz, and believe me, I cared not whether the newspaper had been censored or not, but only wished I could squeeze in another few thicknesses of the stuff. Insulation is the chief concern regarding the press among the laboring classes, I do assure you."

Through the darkening square, crowded with people hurrying about their lives, the two strolled, and Rudi reflected that, without the red-and-white ribbons on display and the youths marching about officiously with militia brassards on their arms, one would never imagine that a revolution had taken place. He wished she would take his arm. It felt unnatural walking next to a lady in the street who did not, as if she were a housemaid, but unlike a housemaid she did not travel some paces behind him. An unnatural situation, but one that the strange woman appeared positively to cultivate.

"That was wretched beer in that place," she observed presently. "And the sausage roll was garbage fit only for Saxon tourists. I wish for a true Czech blood sausage and real Pils. They will have that where we are going. And I believe I will ask you to buy me a slivovic, although I rarely take spirits."

"I take them rather more frequently than I once did," he said, and they spoke lightly of drinking, how often they were drunk, the most drunk they ever were, effects thereof, stupid actions contemplated and performed, hangovers suffered. They walked along laughing, she often seizing his arm in that peculiar way and loosing from time to time her raucous guffaws. He thought, how odd that there is no one else in the world with whom I could have this conversation in this manner!

"We are going to the old ghetto, I see," Rudi observed as they entered Heiligegeistgasse. Here was a street scene hardly to be matched in the western regions of the Empire, a mass of dark-clad people, shouting their wares, arguing, gesticulating in an outlandish fashion, wearing the dress they had carried on their backs when they left the muddy towns of Galicia. "Josefov. I have not been in many a year, not since my student days, really."

"You came for the girls," she said confidently.

A moment of embarrassment and then a releasing laugh. How could he feel shame in the presence of one to whom shame was a stranger?

"Yes, there was a brothel a little further up on Heiligegeist. A large house. I daresay it must have belonged to a wealthy Jewish family when the Jews were still confined here. After emancipation, of course, the Jews prospered but their district became as now we may observe, a cesspit full of the sweepings of the east, as the gutter press calls them, poor souls."

Several of these souls now attracted their attention. A drayman's wagon with two stout horses stood in front of a tavern, and workmen were rolling barrels down a ramp. Idlers watched this operation as entertainment: there was always a chance of a bloody accident, and (faint hope) a barrel might slip and crack and spurt beer, in which case there would be a riot of the desperately poor swarming with cups, jugs and even rags to sop up the wastage. Among these idlers Rudi noticed a half-dozen young children, whose attention seemed fixed not on the beer but on the two horses, specifically their nether ends. Most of the children were young boys, their pale wrists and ankles staring through the filth that crusted them, uncovered by their outgrown rags. But there was a little girl there too, a dark creature of six or so with a feral stare, and as Rudi watched, the off-nag lifted its tail and deposited a mound of steaming ordure on the cobbles, at which moment this child darted under the horse and with her hand scooped the droppings into a sack.

Screams of outrage issued from the boys and one of them, a lad of twelve or so, hideously thin, fell upon the girl and knocked her flat with a blow. As she shrieked, he pulled at her sack, and had just secured it, when two other boys attacked him. The bag went flying. The three boys rolled in the filth of the street fighting and screaming curses, to the amusement of the crowd. Meanwhile, the little girl snatched up her sack and ran off, followed by a mob of howling urchins. A waiter emerged from the tavern and threw a bucket of greasy water on the fighting boys. Amid great hilarity they slunk away, but not too far, as they clearly wished to observe whether the other horse might also deliver.

"I suppose you send your own children out in the street to fight for lumps of horse-shit," said Vasová.

"Perhaps I should. I expect it would please you and it could not help but improve their characters. I assume the stuff has some economic value."

"Oh, there must be a Jew hereabouts who gives them a few pfennigs the bag and sells sacks of it to the market gardeners. Josefov boasts a somewhat lower sort of Jew than the Maisels or the von Silbers, and a good deal of the district is now Czech. The Jews converted the property they vacated in the last age into tenements for their factory workers, forty families packed into a space that once held four or even one, and on the ground floor the workshops. But come, did you like the girls?" She pointed to a two-story house on the corner. "That is a brothel still. You may drop in, if you like."

"It was your friend Novotny who took me," said Rudi. "He seemed to take a personal interest and delight in debauching me."

"Did he succeed?"

"Not to any great extent. I fear I am entirely too dull to be a proper rake. I found it fairly repugnant, if you must know, and of course, I have been engaged to my Berthe almost since I was breeched. The fleshpots of Prague will have to stretch if they wish to lure me in. I was surprised to learn that the inmates of this particular establishment were neither Czech nor German, but Jewesses in the main."

"Yes, and they all have the same story. They caught the eye of some Gentile boy, with the usual consequences. Their families throw them out, declare them dead, in fact; they are on the street with a baby coming and their pretty boys all drink and beat them, which makes a change from home, I can tell you, and some nice woman approaches when they are spending their last kreutzer on day-old bread and offers a place to stay that is warm and arranges about the baby. As with the little horse-shit hawks we just saw, it is a tradition of long standing, and one which your revolution will not affect in the least."

"You can never tell what might happen in a revolution."

"Oh, that we *can* tell. Here Bakunin is correct. There will always be top and bottom, and should the bottom become the top—for why else do we call them revolutions?—they will behave just the same way as when they were oppressed, or worse. It is the nature of man, and beyond the power of any constitution to improve. Here—we have arrived. What do you think of the Sack of Meal?"

She indicated a black doorway in the middle of one of the small twisted streets to the east of Rabbinergasse. A burlap meal-bag had been nailed up over this door, from which the stink of beer, frying meat, and packed humanity emerged to unpleasant effect. Stairs led down to darkness and the noise of men drinking.

Rudi looked and replied, "Ah, these must be the lower depths about which you have spoken so often. I am delighted to find that they are indeed lower."

With that, he accompanied her down the greasy stairway. Inside, despite four struggling candle lanterns, gloom prevailed amid a richer stench of grease and stale beer. Two trestles stretched the length of the room, flanked on their sides by benches, and these were occupied almost shoulder to shoulder by roughly dressed workmen all engaged in the business of seeking what oblivion they could afford.

Vasová strode into the room like a habitué and immediately called out, in Czech, "Oh, good! There is the big man. Ho, Stefan Novak, what news!"

With Rudi trailing behind she pushed further into the stew and clapped her hand on the thick shoulder of a drinker, a massy shoulder that rose near a foot higher than those of his neighbors. With a shock Rudi realized that the man was the same depot worker whom he had knocked senseless at the Red Goose the night he had met Vasová.

Nineteen

Novak looked over his shoulder. At the sight of Vasová, his hard face lit and strangely enough seemed to acquire intelligence. He got to his feet and embraced her, laying a loud kiss on each cheek.

"Sisi, you crazy girl, where have you been? We hear you have been consorting with the quality, dining on champagne and quail eggs. Shame on you!"

"Yes, and I need some Pils and blood sausage to restore my soul. Is there still a seat for me at the Sack of Meal?"

"For you, always," said Novak. Placing a hand on the shoulders of the two men on either side of him, he pushed and cleared a considerable space, which resulted in the dumping on the floor of the drinkers at either end of the bench. Amid general hilarity, Vasová sat down, and Rudi managed to squeeze in beside her. The Czech giant gave him a passing glance, cold, touched with contempt, but showing no recognition, and Rudi, feeling a sense of relief, was careful not to look the man in the face. He seemed one who would not disdain vengeance.

He inspected the company, trying to breathe just enough to support life, for the stench was appalling. So, these were the People, he thought, and they dwell in this stink every moment of their lives. How could they? Don't they even notice it anymore? Vasová was speaking privately with Novak. He tried to listen in, but following the low patter of rapid colloquial Czech proved beyond him. It was easier with the conversation of the other surrounding denizens, which was loud enough, but unspeakably dull, consisting mainly of oaths and mutual insults, complaints and boasts.

The barmaid, a dough-faced slattern, came by to replace the drained beer-steins, and, observing Rudi had no
stein before him, asked if he wanted a beer. He did not. He
was breathing beer already and the sour, yeasty stink had
turned his stomach. So he said, "No, thank you. Can you
bring me a slivovic instead?"

The girl's forehead creased, her mouth opened. After a
moment's staring she called out, "Hoy, Bogya, this man wants
slivovic."

"Then give him some, you stupid girl!" came a voice
from the gloom. "Three kreutzers."

The noise in the place diminished perceptibly. Rudi
said, "I detect that slivovic is not a common tipple at the Sack
of Meal."

Novak shifted in his seat so that he could bring Rudi
fully into view.

"No, not common," he said. "Who is this fellow,
Sisi?"

"This is Rudi Moritz, who wrote the great petition to
the emperor and is in charge of defending the revolution.
Rudi, this is an old friend, Stefan Novak."

Rudi rose in his seat and held his hand out; Novak
looked at it as if it were a pool of vomit, and said, "We have
not yet had the revolution, and when we do I doubt that this
type will be much engaged in defending it. I detect you are
German, Pan Rudi. Perhaps you do not care for honest
Czech beer. This is why you drink slivovic."

The barmaid plunked a clear label-less bottle and a
small, dirty glass on the table.

"As a matter of fact," said Rudi, "I am a Bohemian of
German tongue. As such I can drink the national spirit of
Bohemia without a blush. Will you have one with me? All of
you," he added after a moment.

"Oh, Moritz!" he heard Vasová say, but sotto voce.

Twenty minutes later, the four bottles of slivovic the
place possessed were in circulation, the men taking huge

swigs directly from them, and the proprietor had sent out a boy for more.

"I know you," said Novak to Rudi abruptly. "I have seen you before, but I can't recall when."

"It was on Constitution Night," said Vasová quickly. "I gave him a kiss, in the interest of Bohemia unity."

"Oh, you did, did you?"

"Yes, and now you get one too, you oaf—let it not be yet another grievance of the Czechs!"

With which she threw her arms around his neck and planted a good one on his mouth. The assembly hooted and whistled and stamped their feet.

But Novak continued to glower at Rudi, saying, "Yes, but it was something else too. No matter. So you think a kiss from Sisi is a ticket into our company, do you? You are drinking slivovic with us to show you are a true Bohemian. Drinking from your little glass like a gent. How generous! You steal our country and buy us a drink. Is that fair?" He raised his voice to a roar. "Is that fair?"

"No, no!" shouted the assembly, pounding their mugs on the tables. Someone shouted, "Pour a bottle down his throat!" and another, "Stick one up his ass!" Men were getting to their feet, staggering, hooting, moving toward where Rudi sat.

Heat flowed up Rudi's neck and sweat sprang out upon his forehead. They were about to manhandle him. It was not to be borne, especially not in front of the woman.

He shot upright, staggered a moment, jumped over the bench and set his back against the wall. The laughing men closed in on him. Without thinking at all he drew his sword cane and pointed the blade directly at Novak, who grinned at him around big misshapen teeth and said, "Oh, little *skopčák*, you will need more than that toy." He picked up an empty bottle, flipped it neatly so that the neck was in his fist and smashed it against the table. He pointed the glittering jagged mace at Rudi and advanced.

But Vasová leapt to her feet, stood between the two men, and shouted at Novak to sit down, to have another drink, to not be so stupid. Did he want to end up in prison? Or this was all that Rudi could derive from the harangue, for it was delivered in the demotic Czech of Prague and seemed to contain a remarkable number of obscenities. Rudi slid against the wall, keeping his sword pointed at the milling drunks, none of whom seemed anxious to assault a man so armed, and by this means reached the stairs.

Out on the street he strode blindly away from the Sack of Meal, his sword still in hand, like an officer about to command a firing squad. He heard running steps behind him, stopped and spun about, coming within an ace of skewering Sisi Vasová, the sword tip halting just short of her breast.

She said, "Put that thing away before you hurt someone! Unless you wish to dispatch me here and now. Perhaps I would not blame you overmuch."

He clumsily returned the blade to its cane. "I beg your pardon. I thought it was...."

"Yes, the Czech mob, out for vengeance. And we note yet again it is the German who first draws steel."

"You will forgive me, madam, but they meant to abuse me, and I was not going to tolerate it, even at the price of shed blood. I cannot bear being so mauled."

She favored him with one of her sardonic looks. "My God, Moritz, you know nothing at all! It will be my great pleasure to educate you about real life. What in Christ's name possessed you to buy spirits for a room full of Czech workers?"

"Why ever should I not? I was attempting to be congenial."

"My lamb, these are men who drink nothing but beer, because your government taxes spirits beyond their ability to pay. Slivovic they drink at weddings, christenings and funerals, if they are lucky, a tiny ceremonial glass. Vodka they make on the farm and smuggle into the cities, but it is not common. So of course they became instantly unruly. But at least you have seen some real Czechs."

"There were Czechs aplenty at Mme. von Silber's."

"Bah! Half of them cannot hold a conversation in Czech. They are bourgeois poseurs, envious of the sway of the Germans, pretending to wax enthusiastic at the thought of a constitution. Ah, look, here we are at the Golden Spoons, Pan Palacki's favorite tavern, a place for a very different kind of Czech than the company we have just left. You might wish to go upstairs and converse about the rule of law."

"No, thank you. I have been promised squalor; let us not mingle tonight with the unsqualid. But why do you say pretending? And how otherwise do you propose we shall be ruled? How shall the three communities relate, and how shall Bohemia be tied to the Hapsburg crowns? How can these questions be decided without a constitution?"

"Bah again! I will tell you one thing, Moritz, which you must never forget. We will talk, and negotiate and cut the cards for a better deal than we have now, but every Czech desires in his heart only one thing: that there be a Czech in the Hrad, ruling his ancestral lands in his ancestral tongue. On this ultimate goal there will never be a compromise, whatever supposed arrangements we may agree to in the meantime."

"And the Germans?"

"The Germans have many lands. You have Saxony and Silesia, Prussia and the Palatinate. You have Bavaria, Thuringia, Württemberg, Mecklenburg, and other burgs beyond counting. Go thence and flourish, and leave us Czechs to enjoy our one small country in peace!"

"What! You would expel people who have lived here near a thousand years?"

"A thousand years is long enough, we say. And no one talks of expulsion, ninny! We are an hospitable people and anyone can live among us; but as guests, not masters. Look, there is Bakunin."

Rudi turned his head and saw the big Russian approach, the man Bors following at his heels like a guard-dog.

"Is that Moritz?" said Bakunin. "I hear you have been busy since last we spoke. You have engaged to shoot down workers, if need be. I congratulate you, sir. You prove my point that the liberal, for all his fine talk of freedom and the law, is in the end just another assassin of the people."

Rudi ignored the provocation and said, "I suppose you are going to meet with your fellow Slavs, above."

"And are you particularly concerned with whom I meet? Would you like a list of names? You may report I conspired with Herr Schnitzel and Herr Beer. Good day to you, sir. And Madame," he said, touching his hat to Vasová.

He entered The Golden Spoons. Bors followed, but paused on the threshold to favor Rudi with a long, cold stare. As they moved down the street, Rudi said, "My soul, but that man gives me the shivers. He has the look of an assassin."

"That is because he *is* an assassin. I heard he shot a general in Katowice in Galicia. Or a colonel, it might have been."

"Truly? Seeing him, I do not doubt it for a moment. I wonder he is not taken up in Prague."

"You wonder? If you think him dangerous, arrest him yourself, after donning your new uniform and providing yourself with a troop of dragoons."

He could not help smiling. "That is what is so amusing about you, Vasová. Every encounter becomes the seed for a grand romance. I suppose it is your métier."

"As dull pettifogging is yours, dear Moritz. What o'clock has it got to?"

Consulting his watch, Rudi told her it had just gone eight.

"We could attend the puppet theater in the Ziegengasse," she said. "Have you been?"

"Not often. The children enjoy it."

"Yes, there are some made for children, but I myself have written puppet plays. It is the genius of a subject people, deprived of a literary culture for generations, and in it we can say rude things, we can speak of our little agonies, and no one bothers to stop us, because they are only puppets."

She seized his arm. "Yes, indeed, we must see the puppets. They are doing *Don Giovanni* tonight. Don't you adore *Don Giovanni*? The musicians and singers are all students and some of them are quite good; the puppets themselves are charming. Afterward, you will buy me dessert and chocolate in a silver pot at the Pariz and I will expatiate for you upon how the Czechs have brought the art of the puppet to its present high level, excelling all other nations. I assure you that you will be entirely rapt, and will understand your subject people better than ever you did before."

Rudi allowed himself to be taken to the puppet theater, where, to his surprise, he felt himself carried off by the artfulness of the puppetry: he accepted that glorious song was emerging from the little painted mouths and that the great drama of the seducer destroyed was entirely native to this tiny theater. So much was he entranced that he felt a definite shock when, after the last chord, amid the applause, a curtain was drawn back and the puppeteers were exposed above the tiny stage. Another drawn curtain revealed the musicians and singers, who took shy bows (they were all ridiculously young) and smiled ingenuously at the audience.

"I see you were ravished," she said as they walked out into the street again. "I am happy to observe it. I do not believe I would keep up friendship with a man who did not enjoy the puppets."

"You will doubtless cover the reasons in the expatiation you have promised."

"When I have drunk chocolate in luxury," she replied. "Which direction do we go? Oh, I know! There is a shortcut through here that will bring us right up to the hotel."

With that she tripped off down a nameless alley that led eastward off the Ziegengasse. Rudi followed her into a gloom lit only by a single lantern hanging above a doorway at the head of the narrow street. He had not gone ten paces when he heard steps behind him, hurrying heavy steps: a pursuit.

Rudi whirled about, in the same instant freeing his sword, stabbing it at the pursuer, who was Bors, frozen in the act of drawing his huge pistol from his belt, its barrel just visible as a silvery gleam.

"Drop that pistol!" Rudi ordered, the point of his sword inches from the other's neck.

"Drop that sword!" replied Bors.   Neither man moved.

"We are at a stand, it seems," said Rudi.   "Why are you following us?"

"You are spying," Bors said.   "Who are you spying for?"

"I am not spying for anyone," said Rudi, keeping his eye on the pistol.

"Oh? Then why is this the third time you just happen to appear where Bakunin goes?"

Rudi heard the click of heels. "What is this?" cried Sisi Vasovà. "A footpad? Oh, no, it is the little Russian assassin. What do you want with us?"

"He thinks I am spying on Bakunin," said Rudi.

"You! What nonsense! Moritz is a member of the national committee and the commander of the Academic Legion in Prague. Can you imagine that he would be employed to spy upon a Russian philosopher of no political importance? Even a crazy person such as yourself must conclude that this is nonsense."

Bors cried out an obscenity and raised his pistol. Rudi struck with his sword at the hand that held it, and the pistol fired.

The noise in the narrow lane was colossal, deafening, the gout of flame from the muzzle unexpectedly bright. In the instant, Rudi saw the woman's face as if lit for the stage, her eyes dark pits, a spark within each, her mouth wide with shock. The face of Bors was nearly as amazed. Rudi struck again, with greater force, at Bors's extended wrist. The man cried out and the weapon clattered upon the cobbles.

Rudi directed his point at the man's face, and, backing slowly away, knelt and retrieved the pistol. He spied a water barrel against the wall, brim full from the recent rains. The pistol made a loud splash as it went in, and a moment later, Rudi had taken Vasovà by the arm and hustled her unresisting down the alley to the busy street beyond.

"Stop, stop, for God's sake, I can't breathe!"

They had run through the Old Town Square and now were at its margins, where Plattnergasse ran into the Little Ring. Still clutching her arm, Rudi led her into a tavern, sat her down, and ordered a pair of brandies.

She drank hers in gulps, her teeth chattering on the glass. At last she let out a long gasp and said, "I was never so surprised in my life as when that thing went off. I could hear the snap of the ball; I felt its heat on my cheek. A hand's breadth to one side and I would have been stone dead, such a little distance! But...why would that fellow desire to shoot me? I am a harmless poet with no real politics."

"I do not believe that was his intent," said Rudi. "I think he was himself trembling with excitement. I saw his face when the pistol fired--he was every bit as surprised as you. Perhaps he has not fired it often. Perhaps he is not a cold-blooded assassin as you imagine, but a mere passionate youth with a terrible weapon."

"And you confronted him with your little sword, disarmed one of the most dangerous men in Europe, and threw his terrible weapon into a water butt. This is almost a song. I shall dine out on the story for months."

"Oh, must you? I would prefer the whole matter to be kept close. It will not do for the commander of the Academic Legion in Prague to be brawling in the streets."

"What nonsense! Of course it must be shouted out. Who ever heard of a political leader without a romantic legend? We must make of you a pocket Garibaldi."

"Now you mock. But in all sincerity, my brandishing naked steel to both Czech nationalists and Russian anarchists in a single evening cannot endear me to the Czechs of the Golden Spoons."

"Bah! No one despises Czech workers as much as the Czech bourgeoisie. They will cheer you to the echo. And I will say further: men such as Steffi will admire you for your show of spirit. As, of course, do I."

Here one of her infrequent blazing smiles. He smiled back, delighted, and said, "I suppose the only way to round out the evening would be a challenge from an aristocrat. The German opera must be letting out now. I could go there and tread upon some noble toes, a Schwartzenberg or a Kolowrat perhaps."

"Christ Jesu, no! No more violence, if you please. I must return home instantly in any case."

"Another appointment?"

A frown, that immediately transformed into an embarrassed giggle. "No, my cavalier. Not to put too fine a point on it, I have wet myself in terror. And tonight you may accompany me home, if you can bear it."

He could. Sisi Vasovà lived on Spiegelgasse, a tiny street near the railroad tracks, in the one house that remained standing amid a general demolition, the result of clearances meant for an expansion of the train station and its ancillary structures. Rudi could not help thinking of what Franzl had told him about the fortunes to be made in real estate speculation around the growth of the railways. He supposed that this devastation would put money in his family's coffers.

He declined to mention this, for Vasovà was carrying on about the rich bastards ruining a decent working-class neighborhood as she clumped up the dark, narrow stairs. The smell was cabbage and potato water and that fetid human stink that wafted about the dwellings of the poor. The peeling door opened on a large, untidy room, with a stove in one corner and the side opposite masked by a shabby green velvet curtain, hung up on a wire. Here, however, there was the scent of roses.

"This is how I live," she said with an expansive gesture, "cramped, filthy and falling down around my ears. Impossible to keep clean, of course, if the windows are opened to the railway smoke. How strange that those who love the railroads and profit from them should in general decline to dwell near their darlings! Anneke! Are you there, girl?"

From behind the curtain stepped a child of about eleven, who might have been pretty had she ever been well fed in her life. She had boy's boots on her feet and a check cotton dress that had been cut down to fit her. The bosom of this dress sported a large red-and-white Czech cockade.

"Is there a fire, please the good God?" asked Vasovà.

"Yes," said the girl, "we were out all day on the tracks picking coals. Who is this?"

"A friend of mine. We call him Moritz. Moritz, this is Anna-Magda Smolka, who lives with me. She will keep you amused, I trust, while I attend to myself, and she will serve you tea and delicious small cakes, or would do, surely, if we had any. Sit on that sofa, Moritz. Anneke, show him the end with the bad spring. Good. Now help me unbutton, child."

Rudi watched, spellbound, as the woman and the girl prepared for the toilette. The soiled dress fell to the floor. Off came the corset, helped by strong, tiny fingers. A tin bath was dragged from a cupboard, a cloth screen depicting oriental ladies appeared from a corner and was placed before this bath, behind this screen Vasovà vanished, but not before placing a large kettle on the hob of the stove.

The child sat on a little stool and stared at him. "You are a *skopčák*," she said after some moments of silent study. "Usually, she does not bring *skopčáky* home. Once there was a Jew, but he didn't last. You are for the revolution, I suppose? Yes, you must be, for she would not have a reactionary, even a rich one. But why are the Germans for the revolution? The revolution must sweep away all the masters and the Germans are the masters, them and the Jews. My father was actually killed by a train. He built the railroad, it killed him for a thank-you. Isn't that comedic?"

"I would say it is tragic instead. And where is your mother and the rest of your family?"

"Killed, all killed or dead or don't care. I am all alone in the world, except for my dear Sisi. Have you ever killed anyone?"

"No, thank God," said Rudi. He was somewhat distracted from this conversation by the sounds arising on the other side of the screen. Clanks and rattles, the sound of water transferred, the more interesting slithering sound of flesh escaping fabric and finally the characteristic burble of a human body lowering itself into water. And a sigh.

"I have not either," the girl said, "but I hope to soon, when the workers take back what is theirs. We will hang the Jews first and then the *skopčáky*, and then the other *skopčáky* will run back to Germany and we will have no more masters and every person will have enough to eat. I will have a cake all to myself on that day."

"But I am a *skopčák*. Will you kill me too?"

"Oh, no, because you are her friend. Do you know Maria Velitcá?"

"No, I'm afraid I do not."

"She is my especial friend. She lives on the first floor and loves the revolution as well. Perhaps she will kill you and I will kill the *skopčák* who visits her mother."

A pause here. Rudi said, "So, Anneke, do you go to school? Are you able to read and write?"

"Of course I can. I am already an accomplished poet. Would you care to enjoy one of my verses?"

Rudi was just parsing an excuse, when Vasová, wrapped in a sheet, emerged from the other side of the screen along with a waft of steamy rose-water.

"Child, you must go down to visit with Frau Grossbart for a while," she said to the girl. "She will be happy to give you some soup."

"I was going to read him my poem."

"Another time. Hurry along, please."

The child left grumbling and soon they heard the thump of her booted passage down the stairs.

"Who is she?" Rudi asked.

"No one. A Czech, a child of the poor. I found her crying in the hallway below some years ago. Her mother was a whore beaten to death by a client. Four days she stayed in a freezing room with a corpse."

"Dreadful! And is she an accomplished poet?"

"Suppose I fling this sheet aside." She flung. "Now we need not talk of Anneke or poetry or anything else. Well, do you like this?"

She stood boldly, with her hands fisted on her hips, her legs wide, her chest thrust upward, a thick mass of pubic hair presented a foot from his face.

He found he could not form a word.

"Now you must remove your slumming clothes. Or I could tear them off you with my teeth. Would you like *that*, my darling German pig?"

"You seem peaked, sir, if I may make so intimate a remark," said the Baron when Rudi was shown into the Green Room the next morning. "Revolutionizing must be arduous; or perhaps you disport yourself at the tavern. No, no, do not reply, sir. It is none of my business, to be sure. You have your materials, I see; well, let us begin. If you would but recollect me where we had stopped . . . "

"I believe you had just set up as a billiard shark, sir."

"A billiard shark, d'you say? How I deplore the term! Rather say, 'a sporting gentleman,' for it is no offense against manners to play billiards in a public hall, and if other gentlemen wish to place wagers upon one's skill, that is their affair. It is like horse racing in this regard; nothing more wholesome than a horse race, nor do we call the gentlemen of the turf 'horse sharks.' "

"Forgive me, Herr Baron. "I meant no offense."

"None taken," replied the old man, and proceeded.

You will recall that, on first entering the billiard room at The Wheel I was amazed at the betting and had resolved that this would be my source of income. I did not prosper as I had expected, however, and one afternoon, as I was taking shots by myself, I was approached by the same man who had introduced me to the idea of betting on billiards in the first place, and learned why. He was a short, pot-bellied figure, always with a broad smile on his face, and a free hand with drinks. A Jew, by the way, as are many in this business. His name was Horovitz.

He had handled much of my betting and I had reason to trust him. One day, he said to me, after I had been complaining about the thinness of my purse, "Sir, if I may be so bold, you are going about this business all wrong."

"How do you mean?"

"I mean, sir, that you flaunt your skill. This is considerable, I must add: I do not believe that I have seen your match, lest it be that Hanneker the Keg."

"I have never played the Keg, although I have long desired to."

"But you have observed his play. I do not mean his grand tournaments, when he goes against the best sticks in Prague, but his living."

"How do you mean?"

"I mean how he skins the *patzers*. This is what we call players who presume to challenge him, not knowing his skill. Your young bravo, let us say, comes into a billiard room with a heavy purse, and, fancying his chances against a fat, down-at-heels seeming gent, of no obvious talent, offers a bet on the game. Our Keg first refuses--he is no match for the bravo, he protests. But the bravo thinks himself clever. He muffs his play; the Keg takes a few games, and at last he agrees to go for a florin, with a one-ball handicap. The bravo readily agrees, plays and wins. Naturally, he must offer the fat man a chance to win his money back, so they play for two florins, at evens. The Keg loses again and again. He sweats, his eye takes on a desperate look. The stakes grow ever higher.

"Now, remarkably, the Keg takes a game, but in such a manner that it seems a stroke of luck. As if to confirm this, the bravo wins once more, which, though he knows it not, is the last time he will triumph. Towards dawn, we shall imagine, the Keg announces he is dead on his feet and must leave, and offers a bet of all he has won against all that is left in the bravo's purse. The bravo now plays in earnest, and at first he succeeds, ahead by four balls, by five, by six! And then, without seeming effort, clumsily, scratching the cloth, tossing balls off the table, the Keg gains, and with the score ten-all, he makes a ridiculous shot, missing the object ball entirely and then, oh, it seems the merest chance, the cue ball rebounds from the cushion, clips another ball, spins away and kisses the target ball into the bag for the winning hazard. The bravo stands there without a kreutzer to his name and thinks, 'What rotten luck I have had tonight!' That is the true art of fleecing a *patzer*, sir. So the great Keg plays and so must you also, if you wish to prosper."

"But such feigning play would be dishonorable for any gentleman," I protested. "It is mere cheating."

"Not at all, sir, not in the least.," answered Horovitz. "Moving a man's ball or your own when he is not looking-- that is cheating. Double counting one's score upon the buttons is cheating. But concealing your skill from a fool is no more cheating than keeping your cards close at boston whist. Do you show your aces and courts to your rival? Of course not, and this is the same. Now, I believe we can make a good deal of money together, with your skill and my knowledge of the game and how it is played in this city. For believe me, sir, there are games in our Prague in which ten thousand florins may dance from one purse to another and back again, games in palaces, I say, in which only the nobility may engage; and as to that, I believe you could pass for a baron dressed in a proper suit of clothes. You certainly speak fine enough."

"I *am* a baron," I said and gave him my name.

297

He bowed, smiled a crafty smile, and said, "That is as good a name as any I have heard concocted. Well, are we agreed, Herr Baron? Shall we grow rich together?"

We began this enterprise by playing a remarkable number of games of billiards. Of necessity, I quite abandoned my dissolute life, and entered one of extraordinary discipline, not unlike that of a training Jesuit. Horovitz would arrive at my apartment in the morning, take breakfast with me, and then we would repair to the billiard room, not the one at the Wheel, but another one, on Plattnergasse in the Jewish quarter, a place called the Black Horse. This was by way of being Horovitz's home ground, and he had made some arrangement with the host to have the single table always in reserve for us, a convenience to be sure, but the real reason was so that no casual player could observe our work, or even the connection between us two.

There we played, with interruption only for meals and calls of nature, until nightfall. We played every sort of game, the white winning and losing, the red carombole, winning and losing, even fortification billiards, because Horovitz said a professional player must know them all, not only how to win but how to feign the oaf at each one.

As a player, he had only indifferent skill, but as a teacher and driver, he was nonpareil. I cursed and railed against him at times, to be sure, insulted his race, said I would be damned if I stood this abuse a moment longer, and at these outbursts he would smile and, handing me again the cue-stick I had flung into a corner, say, "Do take the shot again, Herr Baron, and this time not so tight a grip on the shaft."

After a month or so of this, I began to play for money. We did indeed prosper, and I was often able to place a neat stack of florins or even thalers in the Bank of Lennart. In this wise I was able to resume my character as a bon viveur and lecher. So the summer passed into autumn until, on October 21, 1786, I had an encounter that would change my life, and introduce into this story first one, and then another, of its most memorable characters. I recall I was in the Wheel, at the table, practicing a trick. You would not think it possible to knock a ball from one table to an adjoining one and strike any ball upon it into a bag, but it can be done and Horovitz had taught me how. One can always win a few florins on trick shots and I was accumulating a small repertoire of these.

It was tedious work and had to be accomplished early in the morning or very late at night, when I might arrange to have a billiard room at some tavern to myself. It was a Saturday, I recall, and I had been working all night until I could scarcely hold the cue. I went out just an hour or so after sunrise to stretch my limbs and find some coffee and sustenance.

There was a market that day and the Kohlmarkt was full of carts and people setting out tables and booths. October, as you know, is a great time for festivals in Bohemia, and this was something of a fair, with peasants having come from miles around to sell their produce and crafts.

Two girls passed me, a pair of pretty misses, blond and pert. I smiled at them and wished them a good morning and they giggled and bobbed in reply and it was only after a minute or so that I grasped they were from Pannau!

Twenty

"However did you know that, sir?" said Rudi.

"Oh, well, every dorp and valley in Bohemia, has its own style of headdress, and this little velvet pot with the trim of lace and ribbons in red and gold was one I had seen all my life. I followed these two girls through the market, threading the aisles of cabbages, potatoes, and beets, past crates of squawking chickens, past pigs and sheep and every other thing sold in such a place, until I saw what I had expected: a wagon decked with the gold-striped scarlet of Pannau, bearing a great oaken tun. Pannau slivovic is famous, and I well knew that at this time every year, Hrubal our stillerer took a load of it to Prague and other places for the October fairs, and here he was with his white hair a-flying as he handed down crates of bottles from the cart to his boy. I watched him from the shadow of an awning as he broached the tun and let the water-clear essence pour into the first bottle.

I had thought I would rush out to embrace him and renew, even at second-hand, my connection with my native place, but as I was about to leave my station, a waft of the slivovic struck my nostrils, and . . . well, I cannot account for it but that odor, which had filled all Pannau at certain seasons . . . that odor and the season itself, for the autumn had ever been my favorite, the harvest and the fairs and the merchants coming through and the horse sales, glorious for a boy such as I . . . I tell you, it utterly unmanned me. Tears sprang from my eyes and my knees refused their duty. I collapsed upon an upturned barrel, held my handkerchief to my face, and sobbed.

It was the loneliness, you see. I dare say you have never felt the like, surrounded as you have been by a loving family and having a family of your own. I was cut off from all I had known, an orphan, without a respectable profession, exiled from the one place I loved. Nor did I have a single friend of my own rank with whom I could share my heart.

At that moment, however, as if an angel had taken mercy upon my despair, a voice spoke behind me.

"Sir, I observe you are in distress. May I be of service?"

I turned and saw that the speaker was a young man in uniform: green coat with yellow cuffs and facings, a white waistcoat, yellow breeches tucked into knee boots, a black bicorn hat worn flat-side forward. A dragoon, then, with a somewhat unusual equipage, but not near as remarkable as the visage that smiled at me from under the shadow of the hat. I thought at that moment of the statue of the young god at Pannau, which had overlooked the miserable scene of my last parting with Marietta. I felt at first a flash of envy at his extraordinary beauty, but the sweetness and openness of his expression instantly flushed it away.

Although I was at that time extremely reticent, I felt an immediate confidence in him, and so I said, "I thank you, sir, but the distress you observe is not a woe that any man can repair," and told him what had brought on the fit.

"Ah, yes, it is a dreadful thing to lose home and family," he replied. "As it happens, I am similarly afflicted, an orphan and far from home. Just the other week, I heard a beggar girl, a Galician, singing a song I knew in Polish, and my eyes filled so that I had to stop and turn into a doorway to regain my countenance."

"You are Polish, then, sir?"

His smile increased. And let me assure you, sir, I have smiled and you have smiled, but ours do not, I think, shed light like his did. Being there before it was like stepping out of a dank shed into full sun; it seemed to cast actual warmth.

"I have that honor," he replied, and extended his hand. "Allow me to introduce myself. Unterleutnant Miroslaw Victor Fabian Paradowski, of the Kinski Light Dragoons."

I grasped the offered hand warmly and gave my own name.

"Kinski? Are you by any chance a connection of our inhaber, Clemens von Kinski?"

"I dare say, but only distantly," I answered. "Our names were joined by marriage in the last century, and while we are a military family, we do not run to the founding and maintenance of regiments. We have always served in the Kaiser Cuirassiers, and I was meant to serve there too, but events unfortunately worked against that connection. Forgive me for saying I have not heard of your regiment."

At this he laughed merrily and said, "I do not wonder, sir, for we are monstrously obscure and without prestige, the sweepings of the army, if some are to be believed. They keep us out in the Banat mainly, on the border, where we are employed chasing bashi-bazouks and other ruffians of that region. We are only here in Prague to refit and collect remounts. In a month or so, back we go to that restive province."

"It sounds a doleful occupation. Why are you so employed? Are you deemed incompetent for higher service? I am sorry if I seem to insult your regiment, but you yourself appear to be a fine officer, alert and all correct in your uniform."

"Oh, no, far from being incompetent, we are surely the finest light dragoons in the royal and imperial army. The reason is our Colonel Max. We deem him a military genius; the Hofkriegsrat does not agree. Besides which, Colonel Max does not suffer fools, a species in which the Hofkriegsrat is inordinately rich. So we languish in distant lands, and fight inglorious skirmishes and leave our bones in nameless places. It is a fine life, if one does not require dances, music, the sight of fine ladies, tasty food, or wines easily distinguishable from vinegar. Speaking of which, I have not yet breakfasted . . ."

I took him immediately to Skober's. We sat in that table to the left of the door, under the large window, and began to talk, as strangers do, to tell each other our stories, but also not as strangers from the first moment, because we soon discovered that our lives were nearly twins. We laughed at this as we spoke. We were speaking French, it goes without saying, although his German was perfectly adequate and he spoke Czech fluently--he often observed it was much like Polish. Like Polish, it was also a language he was used to speaking only to servants. He was an aristocrat, one of the szlatcha, as they call their nobility, of a family hardly less ancient than mine.

Did his father reject him? Yes, indeed--a violent man, a drinker, an officer un-promoted to the level he felt appropriate to his birth and disappointed with life, who took out his grief on the person of his younger son.

Did he have an older brother who despised him and who, after inheriting the estate, made it clear that he was not welcome in it? Yes, indeed, and his Tadeusz seemed an equal to my Anton in spite and intemperance.

Did he lose his mother early, and in a disgraceful fashion? Assuredly. She took a lover, a local landowner, but later spurned him, saying that it was wrong to carry on so, that she had to stick with his father, though he treated her so ill, all of it within the hearing of the ten-year-old boy, you understand. One day, the poor devil rode into the stable yard of the Paradowski chateau at the moment Paradowski's mother was preparing to go out on her daily ride. The man drew a double-barreled pistol and shot her dead at the feet of her horse. Dismounting then, he held the corpse in his arms, kissed its mouth and, taking up his pistol again, blew out his own brains. Paradowski had watched this horror from his own horse nearby.

But this story came later, much later, in my rooms. Before that, perhaps even as a predicate to that, we drank: first beer, then wine, and after some hours, he called for brandy. I believe this was just after I had mentioned being educated by the daughter of the great Ignatz Casimir Borowski. At this he gave a great whoop, and warmly clasped my hand, saying that an engraving of the man had hung in the study of his own tutor, who had studied under the savant at Kraków.

I said that brandy was all well and good, but for such a meeting as ours, which could hardly be matched in a lifetime, there was only one drink worthy of the occasion, the special reserve slivovic of Pannau. He asked if it could be ordered at Skober's and I said no, not at all, but that I knew where some could be had, with which I rose and, urging him to follow, dashed from the place.

It was already dusk and the marketers were packing their stalls. Old Hrubal was directing his people to load their wagon. I approached him and asked if he had for sale a bottle of what we called Kaisersfreude, which was slivovic aged twenty years in oaken barrels. It was so called because each year, for six centuries, we had shipped a case containing twelve engraved crystal magnums of it to the Hofburg.

He glanced indifferently at me and went on with his work, "You have expensive tastes, laddy," he said, "but I have none for sale, unless you are the emperor himself. It is not for common tipplers."

I said, "And yet you draw off a gill or two every Saturday and drink it on the white rock behind the millhouse. And while I am not an emperor, I am yet a baron of Pannau. Hrubal, don't you know me?"

He looked, he squinted, he gaped, gasped, and then, the light dawning, he swept off his hat and bowed.

"By God, it's the young baron. Christ of a whore! What a trick to play! Forgive me, sir, but you did look so . . . so . . . "

He stopped and reddened.

"Damned ugly? Well, so I am, but no matter. I am happy to see you, who are at least entirely unchanged. But do you have a bottle?"

"I do, by Jesus! It is meant for the governor, but I will gull him with a bottle of mere Premium. The fucking skopčák will never tell the difference."

He rummaged in the depths of his cart, the Pannau people all the while staring at me and smiling shyly, and soon handed me a boxwood crate with our arms stamped on the cover. I made to pay, but he stopped that with a gesture and a frown. "You pay for your own slivovic? Nonsense! Take it and drink a health to those who make it! By Christ, it is good to see a familiar face in this nasty town."

"Though an unfamiliar familiar face," I said and then seeing his discomfiture at that remark, I embraced him, called him a good fellow, and reminded him that it was my brother's liquor.

He frowned. "Oh, him. Well, you know there is a lot of breakage on these long journeys."

We repaired to my rooms, called for Lennart: no answer. I found some glasses and drew the cork myself, with apologies. The dense scent filled the space around us. That alone made me happier than a purse of a thousand.

We drank. Our vitals melted, our eyes blazed, we became merrier than ever and pledged our new friendship in the essence of my homeland. "Like plums turned to flame," he said and swore he had never tasted the like. After half the bottle was gone, there were no secrets between us. I told him about my father and mother, about the duel, about fleeing in shame, about Marietta, the summit of love, the depths of despair, and so forth--by Christ, it is embarrassing as the devil to reflect on youthful antics, ain't it? Although how would you know—you are still in the flush! And I ventured further, about the rope and the Charles Bridge and the coach and the woman, my wastrel ways, my present libertinage. And billiards, of course.

Alongside this tale, weaving it in and out of mine, he told me his own story, as I have related. We both sobbed and embraced, so great was the emotion that I could not stand it. It touched on things that were still tender and raw within my soul, which I had bricked up, if you will allow the figure, and which I wished the wall to hide.

Coming back to myself, I shot to my feet, "And suiting the action to the word, to billiards we shall go! I have an engagement tonight—what with you and our elixir I had almost forgot it. It is at the Kinski Palace, of all places. Prince

Josef is of course not in residence at this season; rather, a sprig of the clan, our clan I should say, a second cousin of the present Count, keeps the house warm. This cousin—Rollo is his name—fancies himself a billiard player and it has all been arranged. It will amaze me if I do not take a thousand florins from him."

"But you are drunk," he said. "How can you hope to win?"

I replied, "Were I twice as drunk as I am now, I would take him. He is a mere patzer. Besides, I will refresh myself with coffee when we arrive. Let us be off!"

Well, everyone knows the Kinski palace on the Old Town Square, that great white cake. As we approached it, we heard a hissing call from the shadows near the porch of the Týn church. It was Horovitz.

"Horovitz," said I, "why do you lurk out here?"

"Oh, my lord, such as I are not admitted into your fine palaces. I am happy to see you arrive, however, for we can do well for ourselves this evening. I suppose you intend to fleece the young Kinsky?"

"I suppose I might. What is it to you?"

"Are we not partners, my lord? Do I not watch out for your interests as carefully as I do my own?"

"You batten off me when I win, you mean," I replied, for while I liked Horovitz well enough, and while he had never positively cheated me, I found I was embarrassed to be confronted by such a character while in company with my new friend.

"That is what I wished to speak to you about," he said, moving closer and lowering his voice. "Yon Kinsky has a trick up his sleeve. He has brought in a ringer."

I asked what he meant by this and he explained that Rollo, knowing full well that he could not beat me in a fair match, had invited a man named Ferenczi, reputedly the premier player in Buda, and lately arrived in Prague. The plan was for Rollo to play a few matches, lose small sums, then suggest in a friendly manner that his Hungarian friend play a match or two with me, the intent being to out-shark the shark. Rollo would, of course, bet heavily on his ringer, and thus gain his revenge.

I said, "Thank you for the warning, Horovitz, but I am in no way dismayed. I shall trounce the Hungarian champion as I would his impresario. Will you back me?"

He looked doubtful. "The man is very good, sir. I would be inclined to bet against you, were I to bet at all. But I am always willing to advance money, if you are so sure of yourself."

"As much as five thousand florins?"

"Willingly, sir. At five, shall we say?"

"At three," said I and we agreed upon four per centum. He gave me a note of hand for four thousand eight hundred and wrote down a debt of five thousand in his pocket-book, saying he would meet me at this spot in the morning. I bid him farewell; he gave Paradowski a quizzing look, but said nothing to him. After he departed I took my new friend by the arm and entered the great house.

Have you been inside? It is one of those palaces in the style of the former age, all gilt and plaster icing, silk walls and Aubusson on the floors. The billiard room was as one would expect, brightly lit by great chandeliers, one over each of the two tables.

The company was the usual mixture: sporting gentlemen, a few officers from good regiments, and a few distinctly louche fellows I knew from the billiard rooms about town. I say usual, because at the time it was not uncommon for the well-born to play with fellows of all sorts in their homes, if they had the necessary skill with the cue stick. We took some coffee from the buffet and as we drank, I noticed that Paradowski was somewhat out of countenance.

I inquired of him whether anything was the matter and he replied, "Of course, I am not to comment on your private business, only that I am an officer of Galician breeding, and I have seen enough good fellows ruined by Jews to make me wary of them to the present moment."

I clapped him on the back and bid him dismiss all such worries. Horovitz might be a Jew, yet his game was not lending money but betting on billiards, and in this we were on the same side. And he had never played me false yet.

"That you know of," Paradowski replied glumly. "And to be fair, I once saw a stuffed leopard in a Wunderkammer in Warsaw that was all white, with not a spot upon him, so I suppose you may have found an honest Jew."

Rollo hailed me and shook me by the hand. He was a tall and remarkably broad man, wigged in the fashion, jowly, a face wider at the bottom than the top, dressed in a silk suit of malachite green, so that he resembled an ambulatory billiard table. He was playing the white losing hazard with the promised Hungarian, a saturnine fellow in his middle years. I watched their play. Rollo, as I said, was a patzer, but he won the game handily; Ferenczi was playing below his level so obviously that it was near an insult.

After that, I played him. I should say here that a battle between two sharks is quite a different affair from a match between a shark and his gull. After a certain amount of false play to accumulate the bets, we run our true flags up the mast and play in dead earnest. I soon found that we were equally matched. We played game after game, alternating victories, hour after hour until we had consumed the whole night. We played in near silence, the only sounds the click of the balls and the low murmur of the company making side bets.

Near the end it had become quite warm in the room, the chandeliers seemed to burn above us like the sun, though by then the candles were mere stumps. Gradually the crowd dispersed, until there were left in that room only the two players, my Paradowski, slumped in a chair, sipping cool coffee, still alert; and our host, leaning against the wall in his shirtsleeves, a frozen startled look on his doughy face. Between two equal players, in a long match, youth tends to take the palm. Ferenczi's game faltered, mine did not; I won two in a row at the red losing-and-winning hazard, and the match was over. We settled up. I found I had won over sixteen thousand florins. Ferenczi bowed, took up his coat, his cue, and walked out, without a word to his patron, who looked as if he had just had his foot trodden upon by an ox.

Out on the street, the sky was just promising the new day, providing enough light to avoid filth on the streets, and the air was delightfully fresh after the waxy fug of the billiard room. Paradowski and I almost danced across the cobbles, giddy as we were with the coolness we sucked into our lungs and the exultation of victory. He owned he had never seen such a game of billiards, said that they would talk of nothing else in Prague for a week.

I said, "Yes, for Prague is a very dull town."
We reached the Týn church, but no Horovitz appeared. And then we heard the cry, high and shrill, seeming to originate from an nearby alley. We looked into that dark passage and in the feeble glow from a window's candle we saw three men with round hats pulled low and mufflers wrapped around their faces. Two were cudgeling a figure on the ground, while a third, much smaller than the other two, was picking at the prostrate man's clothes.

I shouted, "What is going on here? Leave that man alone instantly!"

At my words, the victim cried out, "Oh, save me, my lord, save me!"

It was Horovitz.

Paradowski stepped forward and drew his saber. "Get away from that man," he commanded in a voice quite unlike the conversational tone he had used previously.

The two left their victim and approached us, cudgels raised. The larger of the two said, "This is no concern of fine gents like yourselves. We are just relieving a dirty Jew of his thievings. Move on, now, little soldier boy, and you won't be hurt."

He extended his cudgel and pushed it against my friend's chest. It took a second for my mind to register what happened next, so wonderfully swift was the motion of Paradowski's saber. One instant the menacing cudgel was held high; the next it was rattling upon the paving stones, and the robber was staring unbelieving at the stump of his right arm, which was spurting jets of black into a puddle at his feet, in which lay his former hand and right arm to the elbow. He fell to his knees and again the blade flashed out, almost too quick for sight, and the man lay dead with a cloven skull. This was the first time I heard the wood-chopping sound of a saber cracking a head, but far from the last, and also the first time I had seen a man killed by a sword, ditto. All this in a fraction of the time it takes to relate it.

My friend was already moving upon the other footpad, who aimed a great swinging blow at Paradowski's head that I thought could not but dash out his brains. Yet somehow the little dragoon was no longer in its path. The cudgel dropped to the ground with a clatter as the man clutched at his throat, from which the blood poured around his futile grip.

By that time, the third robber had run off. We raised Horovitz to his feet and left the alley and the two footpads lying in their gore. At the square we found a fiacre post, awakened the driver, and bundled the poor fellow in. He was overcome with gratitude, more so when I handed over his loan.

"Here is your money," I said, holding up a roll of florins.

But he cried, "Oh, my dear, keep it, keep it for heaven's sake! I have earned twenty times that on your play tonight, which sum the robbers would have had. And my life saved in the bargain: blessings upon you, blessing upon you," and he began to jabber in their barbarous tongue, at which point I signed to the cab to be off.

When it had clattered away, I said to my companion, "We have done a good deed, Paradowski, or *you* have. I never saw such work with a saber. You are a virtuoso of the blade, it seems."

"I cannot but admit it, in the teeth of all modesty," he replied, "I was brought up to it from an early age, as you were to billiards. It hardly needs saying that it is handy in a dragoon."

"Indeed. But I wonder at you using that skill to save a Jew. I thought you hated the race."

"Not in the least. I was always taught that it was vulgar to despise Jews more than strictly necessary. They are wonderfully useful people. In Galicia, you know, we could not get on without 'em. No estate could possibly run without its Jew, no more than it could sans cattle or peasants. As for trade and business, they would come to a halt without our Jews. And besides, I hate bandits with a passion."

He looked up at the pinking sky. "Well, this night of wonders is over. I shall not soon forget seeing a Jew part willingly with money in gratitude to a Christian. It is a pity it is dawn--I should have liked to have seen the Phoenix bird or the circle squared."

We went back to my rooms, where we finished the rest of the bottle and he left, promising to meet me again on the morrow.

So ended my first evening with the valiant Pole who would become my best friend and was to influence the course of my life unto the present day.

Rudi finished a few lines of his scribbled shorthand and asked, "The present day? Then does he still live? Do you maintain your connection?"

"Oh, no—we lost touch eons ago."

"Then what influence can he have? Unless you mean some moral lesson you learned at his feet..."

"Nothing moral about it," the old man replied in a peculiar tone, "but that shall come in its proper place. We will hear a great deal more of Paradowski--on the morrow, however, for I believe I must rest now. Come a little earlier next time. I will tell you of my meeting with Mozart. That should bring you running, eh?"

Rudi left the baron's house thinking about friendship—how formed, its pleasures and trials, and then his thoughts ran naturally to thinking about his own, about the three friends he had made at university and how they still constituted the pillars of his own life. How peculiar that so many men of his university fraternity had drifted away, that he was left with this odd assortment: Novotny, Liebig, and Jasny. I should call on Jasny, he thought. Something fanatical has crept into his character in recent days—well, we have all changed in response to these great events, but surely the success of our dreams should bring us closer together.

Or what if the opposite is true? What if the prospect of actual power drives us apart? Certainly the reactionaries would love that outcome. That is what all this suspicion being sown must be about. And Wulfi Speyr, appearing like a bogeyman in a puppet show at Mme. von Silber's and trailing his cloak! Speaking of long-time friends. Was he sincere? Of course not. But what to do about those damned muskets?

Rudi considered this for the remainder of the day, and it troubled his sleep in his solitary bed. Yes, that too! He had suppressed any consideration of what had happened at Vasová's. It could not have happened that way, since he was not that sort of man, and so via some mental alchemy, he had concluded that it had not *really* happened. In any case, he had been drunk. It certainly would not happen again.

By the time Rudi reached his office the following day he had come up with a sketch of a plan. He waited until noon, when Havel was absent for his lunch, whereupon Rudi took the opportunity to search the boy's onion-scented closet of an office. The drawers—nothing. Papers on the desk—the same. Law books on the shelf? Rudi held each thick volume spine upward, shook. . .

And uttered an oath. Fluttering down from volume three of the *Code of Civil Law* came half a dozen red paper seals. He picked them up and left in a rush, grabbing his hat and coat. Out of the building, across the square, down Bruckegasse he went, heading for the sausage stand under the bridge tower, unconsciously touching as he went the pink marble column set in the center of the roadway. Every real Praguer did this, no one knew why, but as a result the top of the column had been worn away and shone like glass.

As expected, he found his clerk sitting on a convenient ledge along with a crowd of other clerks and menial employees of the government. Havel stood up as he saw his superior approach, and swallowed with a noisy gulp the large bite of sausage roll in his mouth.

"Herr Amtsrat!" he said. "What are you . . . I mean, can I be of service?"

"You can, Havel. You can come back to the office. I have something to discuss with you."

A few minutes later, Rudi was behind his desk, Havel standing rigidly before it. He stiffened and grew pale when Rudi placed the purloined red seals one by one on his blotter.

"Havel, listen to me," Rudi said, "and please do not deny what you have done. I caught you rifling my desk the other day, and just now I found these seals hidden in your office. There is only one reason for you to have done this—someone wished to present a false requisition to a purveyor. I have since learned that a quantity of arms has indeed been stolen. I would be amazed were you not the source of the false requisitions."

The clerk's face had gone paper white except for the staring red pimples. He remained silent.

"Have you nothing to say? This is not like hiding your sausages, my lad. This is a crime, for which you could be dismissed and even sent to Munkasch. Munkasch! What possessed you to do such a damned foolish thing?"

Havel's features contorted in a way familiar to Rudi from observing his own little boy struggling not to weep.

"I did it for the revolution, Herr Amtsrat. I am ready to take my punishment."

"Oh, don't be a little fool, Havel! Think of your mother! There will be no punishment, if I can help it. But you must tell me everything. First of all, who put you up to this?"

A silence, the lad's head hung down. "I don't wish . . . sir, oh please don't ask me to betray. I could not live with myself."

"I am not asking you to betray," said Rudi. "Do I look like a policeman? See here, Havel, my interest in this matter aligns with yours." He paused to let that sink in. Now a modest lie. "I too have done some discrete diversion of weaponry. The revolution requires arms and the present situation is convenient. You know as well as I that the Hofkriegsrat has no idea where all its weapons reside and they never will—unless certain irresponsible parties clumsily expose their depredations. That is what I fear, and so I require you to identify those parties."

The boy's eyes widened and color came back into his face."Oh, truly, Herr Amtsrat? I told him you would be agreeable to the plan, but he did not listen. He said you were a . . ." Havel choked on his words.

"He said I was a what, Havel?"

"A . . . he said you were in with the police and not a true patriot. And a German. The muskets are for the Czech workers."

"Of course they are. And whom do you imagine they will be used against? Me? Do you really want to foment civil war in Bohemia? Now you will give me the name of this fellow and I will find him and talk sense to him. Arms the revolution must have, but these must be controlled by a lawful authority representing both peoples and used, if need be, only against the forces of reaction. "

"But I don't know his name," cried Havel. "I only met him twice, and he said he was called Jiskra." Weakly, he added, "But I don't think that was his real name."

"I daresay. What was his appearance and manner?"

"He was taller than me, with red hair and a big mustache, and small squarish spectacles. He was an educated man, a Praguer, I think, from his speech."

Rudi cursed inwardly. Who else could it be?

"Yes. And where has he stored the weapons?"

"That I don't know, sir. I swear it! I just gave him the sealed requisitions."

"Very well, Havel. Now I want you to put this whole affair from your mind, seals, requisitions, guns—you are innocent and nothing, including this interview, ever happened. And you would not be such a dunce as to go to your Jiskra or any other of your firebrand cronies and chat about what we have just discussed, would you? For if I cannot stop this foolishness, the police surely will, and that would spell your doom."

Havel scurried back to his closet. Rudi attempted to return to his tasks, but found it impossible to concentrate after what he had just learned. This soi-disant Jiskra was obviously no one else but Emil Jasny, but Jasny could not be Jiskra the writer. Rudi had read Jasny's writing and he had read Jiskra's, and while he might be confused about many things, his understanding of literary style made it impossible for him to believe that the two could be the same man.

So why had Jasny used the Jiskra name? Could there be two of them? Jiskra was "spark" in Czech and anyone could use the word as a pseudonym or nom de guerre, but Rudi thought it unlikely that any Czech revolutionary would poach that particular, well-known one. A more dire possibility: someone must have launched the plan to steal muskets. He doubted very much that it was Novotny or Jasny. If Jiskra was one person, he had to be a brilliant political writer with a bloodthirsty streak and a deep allegiance to the lower orders. And an irresponsible fool as well. Who could it be? Rudi ran his mind across every liberal and radical writer he knew and remained baffled.

A messenger arrived. Havel dutifully appeared and handed a familiar envelope to his chief. With a certain relief,

Rudi left his office for the von Pannau house on Wammel-gasse.

There, in the Green Room, he found the baron reading a letter, holding it close to his nose, and for an instant, as Rudi entered, an odd look appeared on his face, so that Rudi had the bizarre notion that the letter concerned him. Then the old man thrust the missive behind his back in the chair, and, as usual, without preliminaries, resumed his story.

"Yes. Well, I recall I had just told you about meeting Paradowski. Did I mention I ran into my cousin Oskar again at about this time? No, I see I did not. And also Mozart, since you seem so interested in him. And that woman, Daumer, who brought me almost to ruin. I see I will have to pick out the threads so as to make sense of the story, although when one is living such a life one does not require that sense should be made, one day following another, the juices of youth flowing in one's veins. Ah!"

Twenty-one

Yes, the juices of youth. They flowed amply in Lennart's veins too, that scamp! You will recall that my chambermaid, Valeska, had from the start of my residence at Frau Oslinger's house been offering me comforts not strictly under the heads of cleaning and polishing; a most convenient arrangement, you will agree. Upon an evening--I suppose it was by now early October and I had known Paradowski for perhaps two weeks--I had engaged to meet him and some of his friends for supper. We were to gather at a place called The Mounted Man, which was in Jezdeckágasse, by the cavalry barracks. Mirek—for so I had now come to call Paradowski—came by to carry me there, and we had gone but a few streets when I recalled that I had not taken any money from Lennart that evening. Of course I was in funds at the time from my great coup at billiards.

Mirek protested that he would be glad to treat for the evening, but I would not hear of it, for I had learned the poor fellow had only his pay upon which to live. Therefore we returned to my lodgings, and I was about to call for Lennart when I heard a familiar sound: the creaking of bed-ropes, the groan and thump of a bed frame, and rhythmic gasping cries in a voice I knew well.

I flung open the bedroom door. There on my bed I saw a set of white buttocks flying up and down between two stockinged legs ending in black boots sticking straight up. I seized my razor-strop off its hook on the commode and laid a good one across the heaving flesh. To no apparent effect, except a scream from the girl, who was, of course, my own Valeska. Again and again I struck with no effect except for screams and violent bucking from the servant girl, pinned beneath my man. She kept up a continual wail to which Lennart seemed deaf, although it might have driven him to a higher pitch of lubricity.

At last, Lennart gave a mighty groan, not from the beating at all but from the natural climax of his fornication, then immediately rolled off the girl (who dropped her skirts and dashed out, her face flushed red as her petticoats). Rising to his feet, he yanked up his trousers, smiled at me, and said, "You are returned before time, sir. May I be of service?"

I could barely speak from rage, especially as Mirek was standing there trying with indifferent success to stifle his amusement.

"Service?" I cried. "Why, you blackguard, you treasonous wretch, I saw how you served that filly. Insolent pig of a Böhmer, how dare you mount your master's girl! Get out of my rooms this minute! I don't care to see your face ever again."

He didn't move an inch, but regarded me mildly. "Oh, no, baron dear, that can never be. I swore to the old Count on his death bed I would look after you, and so I must, and you swore you would see me raised up, and so we two are tied together, tail to tail, like those two cats, if you recall that time we tried to do with old Cook's tabbies and were whipped for it. Or I was. An oath is an oath, you know, whatever may befall. As our old Mam used to say, oaths plant no turnips but shame the devil. You forgot your florins, sir. I will get them for you now."

"But Valeska, you lout," I cried, "what of that?"

"Oh, sir, she is a comfortable girl and means nothing by it. You remember back in our dear Pannau, we servants had the use of the Count's broken meats after he'd had his fill, and this is very like. Let me get you your purse."

With that he bowed, to me and to Mirek, and slid out of the room to his own closet.

Whereupon, Mirek let out a hearty laugh. After an unsure interval, I joined him in hilarity. When we had recovered ourselves, he said, "Be content, friend Hans, for never was a valet who could not run rings around his master. It is the nature of the world; and besides, yon fellow is a Versailles chamberlain next to my Wojtek. But in the end, they are faithful as spaniels after their fashion."

The Mounted Man was a three-story house, spacious and well appointed. The sign showed a dashing dragoon upon a white steed, but when we entered, we came face to face in the hall with a saucy painting that showed the same dragoon mounted in quite another fashion. I had imagined it a tavern. It was a brothel as well. I looked around the room, which was large, clean, whitewashed, with a black-beamed ceiling. Benches and tables were arranged around three sides, the fourth being occupied by the tapster, his kegs, the usual shelves of bottles, and a staircase. I was not at the time a frequenter of brothels, not from any moral or physical delicacy, but because my situation did not require it. If one has chilled hock delivered at need, one has no occasion the take a pail to the public fountain. I mentioned this, lightly, to Mirek. He laughed and said, "Yes, but now your valet has spit in your hock, you will be looking for a different tipple, I suppose. This is a fine house, I should tell you, finer by far than the ones we poor soldiers must frequent out in the empire. The girls are clean and above the common sort in intellect. They can hold a conversation, if one so desires. If not, I know that One-Eye Margo keeps a dummy for those who cannot abide a woman's chatter."

Barmaids with painted faces ran gaily about the room with their trays, all dressed alike in frilled blouses with low cut fronts that displayed their breasts as they leaned over tables. They wore long white aprons down to their boots, which I though surprisingly modest for whores at first, but as one of them turned her back I saw that she had nothing on below but a chemise and a pair of high stockings held up by fancy garters.

A hail came from a far table, returned by my friend. Four men sat there drinking wine from a black bottle. Now I first met those who would be my comrades in arms for much of my youth, although at that moment nothing was further from my mind. They were all in the same green coat that Mirek wore and all were clean-shaven. I can see them in my mind's eye now, in their golden youth. Fritz Von Waldstein, a tub of a man, red haired and red-faced with jollity; Hanno von Hoth, a tall fellow from the wilds of Moravia, dark-complected and somber of mood; Albrecht Freiherr von Silmaringen, a scion of the great Carinthian family, pale, quiet and austere, and Wilhelm de Cavriani, a cornet and the youngest of the group, with black curls spilling around his head and an antic look in his dark eyes.

Introductions made, we called for more wine, and ordered food. As the meal progressed, I found it a most congenial company. Among men such as these, antecedents and breeding soon arise in conversation. I discovered that all of us were younger sons of noble houses, and all had a touch of the black sheep. No details as yet, but there was a sense that the Kinsky was in the nature of a last chance, and that its colonel did not mind it, in fact encouraged such recruits, for reasons I would learn much later. Soon I felt comfortable in asking a question that had been teasing at me: why none of them wore mustaches, for I had thought a hairy lip de rigeur for all soldiers, *a forteriori* cavalrymen.

De Cavriani began to explain that it was an ancient tradition of the regiment, but Waldstein broke in and said, "Pippet, you have no mustache because you are too little to sprout one. As for the rest of us, you should understand that the Kinski Dragoons, the so-called Thirteenth Chevauxleger, are known as the *blanche-becs,* and we wear no hair on our lips because . . . well, I will relate to you our story."

"You will fuck it up," said Hoth. "You are too drunk by far."

"I beg your pardon, sir," replied Waldstein with heavy dignity. "I am pleased with the world to be sure, but I am not drunk. I never become drunk when plotting venery. Well, sir, to resume: we, the Thirteenth that is, now the Kinsky dragoons, was originally a Netherlandish regiment, based in Tournai, and we had our school there as well, with some hundreds of young cadets in attendance. That was well before the imperial military academy had been thought of, and officers were schooled at their regiments. And so they still should be, in my opinion. They should be introduced to their regiments at the earliest possible..."

"You wander, dear Fritz," said Hoth. "Can you not manage a simple tale? Drunk without doubt!"

"As I was saying, by your leave, sir, during the French assault on Tournai in 1676 . . ."

"Seventy-three," said Hoth sotto voce.

"Seventy-three, there were some two-hundred and twenty cadets in the town. Observing that one of the two bastions that covered the main gate of the town was about to give way, and with no orders, they saddled their mounts and dashed out into the storm of shot and shell, rode right over the assaulting columns, and scattered them, doing great slaughter, although only boys. The town commander, General Lodron, observing this feat from the battlements, desired to know who those *blanche-becs* might be, and blanche have been our becs ever since. The cadet uniform of the time included yellow breeches and therefore we are still so clad."

"It hides the urination, you see," said Paradowski, "as we attempt to slip by the pickets of our enemies and penetrate his deployments."

"Pisspants we are called," said de Cavriani, "but never to our faces."

"No, never," said Waldstein in a loud voice, raising his glass, and all of them raised their glasses and shouted "Nederlands!" for that, I learned, was their battle cry.

We drank and japed in this fashion for an hour, I suppose, at which point Mirek drained his glass, smacked it down on the table, and said, "We have fed and drunk, gentlemen. Let us now repair to the upper room, and there refresh our nether parts before wine robs us of the capability."

Silmaringen said, "Thank you, Paradowski--it is always you who recalls us to Venus." Amid much laughter, we stumbled up the stairs. The upper room was a parlor of sorts, and just the sort one would expect to find in a brothel-- velvet drapes, deep carpets, soft lighting from candles in red glass shades, lounges along the walls upon which sat the girls, in their shifts and silk stockings. Mirek went right to one of these, a fragile-looking blonde, who, instantly he came into view, let out a whoop and threw her arms about his neck. They vanished through a door.

Waldstein said, "Your friend is a famous swordsman."

"Yes," I said, "I have seen him use his sword, and never did I see the like."

"Indeed, but I meant in the other sense of the word; he is renowned as a whoremonger, even among cavalrymen; although with that face of his, he scarcely requires to pay a kreutzer for a piece. Nor can we tell what he sees in that little thing, but he always picks her. Makes her howl too, as you'll hear. A bit distracting when one is in the saddle, I do say. Oh, and it don't do to mention these things to our Apollo. It makes him testy and when he's testy, holes somehow appear in the body of the offending party. A good fellow, Paradowski, you know, but... a word to the wise."

The others paired off swiftly and departed, and I had just made my choice, and by God I can no more remember her than what I had for breakfast the day after Michaelmas in the year Ten. I do recall the sounds. A heavy thumping and a shrill repeated cry as if someone were chasing a bird around a room with a maul. My girl giggled beneath me and informed me that they were ever like this; poor Bretka was sore for a day after her time with the pretty Polack; she says his thing is hardly inferior to the one on his horse.

When I was done I left the little bedroom and, as I entered the hallway, out of the room opposite popped my cousin Oskar. The two of us blushed but a little, I suppose, as we both wished to think ourselves swell bucks sunk in depravity. We embraced cordially, Oskar demonstrating both astonishment and relief. Then we repaired to the tavern downstairs, and over brandy we spoke.

"We had no idea where you had got to," said he, "for we imagined you a cuirassier with the Kaisers. But when no word of you came, my father inquired of Colonel von Kolowrat and learned that you had never arrived at the regiment. Wherever have you been hiding and why did you not write us of your plans?"

"Oh, upon thought," said I in the most casual manner, "I found that the prospect of military life did not suit me."

"But, my dear Hans, how do you live? Surely Anton is not . . . "

"No, Anton would not give me a herring bone if I were starving naked in a ditch. I had some few thalers my father gave me and I have put them out with the Jews. It is sufficient to my needs for the moment."

"But . . . how distasteful! It is almost trade."

"But not quite, you'll agree," said I. "Yet you can now see why I was not anxious to make known my situation to the family. Besides which there was the shame, my face, Marietta, and so on." I was anxious to change the subject, so I went on, "But what of you, Oskar? How do you do? I presume that since you are in Prague you are at the Carolinium and staying in the Karlgasse house."

"I am indeed at the Carolinium. I have taken up a course in natural philosophy, which will not surprise you in the least, but I am not at Karlgasse. Mother has thrown me out. I have a place on the Krankengasse in the New Town. You must come visit me. Number twelve."

"Thrown you out? For depravity perhaps?"

"Oh, mother doesn't give a fig for depravity," he said with a grin on his round face. "No, it was the stinks."

I visited him the next day at his house, a large handsome structure in the modern style, such as were building in the New Town at that time. The servant who admitted me had a rag tied across her nose and mouth and I dearly wished I had one too, for the stench was mephitic. I found my cousin in a large room on the first floor. He was holding brass tongs and roasting something over a brazier set upon a stand, from which issued a copious smoke, and that stench. When he saw me, he said, "Take a chair, Hans, I will be but a moment."

There may have been chairs in that room, but so great was the drift of books, papers, and pieces of what I supposed were philosophical apparatus, cast upon every level surface, chairs included, that I gave it up.

When we were settled with our coffee, he said, "So, cousin, how have you been keeping since the doleful occasion of our last meeting? I trust you have recovered from your disappointment. "

"Quite recovered," said I. "It seems there is more than one girl in the world."

He laughed and said, "That is hard won wisdom, to be sure. And as long as The Mounted Man is open, what is a requirement of nature need not become an obsession. Are you an habitué?"

"Not I. Last night was my first occasion. And yourself?"

"Dear me, yes! It has become my venereal mainstay; indeed, I own it the best house in Prague. I commend it to all my acquaintances who cannot afford to keep an actress. Have you met One-Eye Margo yet?"

"The bawd? I have not. She did not show her face in the parlor. I thought it odd, for though I have no experience with such establishments I had imagined it a necessary thing for the proprietress to have all under her eye."

"Oh, I do assure you, nothing whatever in the Mounted Man escapes her eye, although she has but one of 'em. There are said to be peep-holes throughout the place."

"But why does she not show herself?"

"Oh, there is a tale! It seems that in her youth she had a lover, a passionate fellow, who, being consumed with jealousy, threw a pot of boiling oil at her face, turning her from a famous beauty into a horror, and costing her that one eye. This was in France, *il va sans dire*. When she does appear in public she goes masked. I have seen her but once."

"You amaze me, cousin. What is she like?"

"Well, her conversation is fine enough—a woman of some culture and wit, it seems, possibly noble. And agreeable even, after one becomes used to talking to a painted face that does not move with her thoughts. But I will say what will

strike you as uncanny. As the only motile feature is the remaining eye, one's whole attention is inevitably drawn to it.
Large and lustrous, it captivates until--I know not how to
express it--the artificial face seems to animate until one believes one converses with a beautiful woman without blemish.
As to the body, it is in the full bloom of her sex--nonpareil!
Those arms, those breasts, that skin, that hair!"

"Does she ever . . . engage with her customers?"

"I have heard of it. She will send for one she fancies
from time to time, but none from the common ruck. I have
often wondered what it would be like. Her room is supposed
to be entirely lightless, black walls, black hangings, bedclothes
of sable silk. It would be the experience of a lifetime to be
sure. She charges, it is said, one hundred florins for the
night."

"Then we must save our kreutzers and hope," said I,
laughing.

"Yes, and meantime we must keep up our manly
strength. I tell you what--it is past one and I have been with
my stinks since dawn. Let us to my club and we shall see
what they have that's hot."

"Your club?"

"Yes, a group of young gentleman about town *club*
together, you see, to lease a house, furnish a number of
suites, procure a wine-cellar, set up a kitchen and so on. We
ape the English here, as in so many things. Besides that, we
may play cards among gentlemen we know, without fear of
sharpers, and we have a billiard table kept free of sharks. Do
you play?"

"I have played," I admitted.

"Splendid!" he said, and we left at once.

The clubhouse was on Kurzstrasse, hard by the Little
Ring in the Old Town, a four-story building of some age but
in passing good condition. A brass plaque affixed to the wall
announced this this was the Philosophical Club of Prague, in
English and German. Inside, an oval hall, very pretty, a dining room with a view of a little yard and the stables, a stair-

case on either side. Oskar hailed and greeted some of the members. An odd flock, as I recollect, much like Oskar they seemed, well-fed, clothed in the English style, most plain, all with the same distracted look, as if instead of watching where they trod, they contemplated the heavens or the secrets of the beetles.

There was a collation offered *en buffet*, cold chicken, liver paste, potato salad and such. One pointed and a man made up a plate for you, a novelty I had not before seen. The Mosel was very good. No conversation at table, or none that I could follow: had you read this paper or that, and Latin names of bugs. And the electrical fluid, a topic of great interest to most of them. I saw a pair of fools rubbing their feet vigorously upon the carpet and causing little sparks to fly at each other from spoons. This, spark, they told me, was the cousin to the lightning bolt, a thing impossible to believe, and yet Oskar assured me it was so. A mental transport back to that summer in Pannau, chasing newts. He had not changed much; I was a different person altogether. And who was the better for it, I wondered?

Our repast concluded, Oskar suggested that we tour the place, and so we did--the library, the card rooms--all very proper and well-lit--and finally the billiard room.
"Let us have a game," he said as we entered, "a florin to win and twenty kreutzer each point over. Ah, too bad--the table is in use."
It was, and by a most peculiar pair of players. One was tall, portly, florid, who from his clothes and bearing I judged was one of our sort. The other was a meager little fellow, quite homely, and sporting a cheap wig on top, who had the look and manner of a valet. The big man took his shot, missed, mumbled a mild curse and then hailed Oskar.
"Ah, Hohenberg, I am glad to see you. This table is wretched, you know, the cloth in very tatters and if it is at all true in the lower corner there, you may call me Jew. Why cannot we have a decent billiard table, I'd like to know."

"I shall take it up with the committee, my lord," said Oskar, smoothly. "My lord, may I present my cousin, Johannes Freiherr von und zu Pannau von Kinsky. Cousin, make your bow to his honor, the Count Thun-Belaczy, the patron of our club."

He stared. It had become a common thing, of course--stares at my face. Barrow boys would mock me, I knew, if only behind my back, and I had cultivated a fierce countenance in return that served to stifle the ordinary person's curiosity. A Count, however, may stare at what he likes.

"What the devil did you do to your face?" he asked.

"An affair of honor, sir," I replied in as cold a manner as was consistent with our respective ranks.

He did not enquire further. After we had made our bows, Oskar and I looked discretely at the little man, who was standing, cue-stick in hand, with an uncertain smile on his face. There was a silence. Was he really to be snubbed openly?

But Thun-Belaczy noticed and said, "Oh, this is Mozart. The musician, you know? He is in town to put on an opera. What is the matter of it again, Mozart? I have forgotten."

"It concerns Don Giovanni, my lord," the little man replied.

"Yes, that's it. Mind you make it just as good as your *Figaro*! Oh, that was a fine thing. Gentleman, a pleasure, but I must be off. I have an engagement on the Hrad, tedious business; Mozart, back to your scribbling, ha ha!"

And he walked off, humming a tune.

"Figaro's *Non più andrai*," said Mozart. "A useful tune. I have used it again in the new one. Well, I suppose I must return to my lodgings. I am staying at the Three Lions-- do you know it?"

We did not. Mozart shrugged and made to leave, at which moment I had a thought.

I said, "Herr Mozart, do you by any chance know a singer or actress by the name of Daumer? Clotilde Daumer."

"Daumer? Oh, there are so many singers! Let me think. Ah, yes, I believe so. She tends to flat her B's in the higher registers."

"Beg pardon?"

"Flat her B's. It is a fault in a singer, you see. Odd, because her A's are perfectly fine." Here he actually sang a little tune, fa's and la's, to show me the difference, but the two were one to my hearing.

I said, "I haven't a notion of what you are talking about. Do you know the woman or not, sir?"

"Oh, yes. She is attempting the part of Donna Elvira, but whether she will succeed remains a question. Da Ponte, of course, is her slave, but there is that unfortunate B. Do you then know nothing of music, sir?"

"Nothing. Nor do I desire a closer acquaintance with such noise."

Now he stared at me, with an expression that I read as pity, and naturally I assumed he had become aware of my disfigurement. I almost said, 'or with musicians,' but I forbore: one cannot insult a guest of the Count, after all.

In a lowering tone I said, "Do you stare at me, fellow? Is there something about me that intrigues you?"

He started as if kicked and answered, "You mean your face? No, not at all. It was what you said about music. I never met anyone who did not love music, who was not also impaired in his hearing. Even the peasants have their little dances. Unless there is some defect . . . I beg your pardon, sir, I am intruding unconscionably. . . but not to love music! It is almost not to love life itself."

The man, I could see, was affected by the thought, and showed the marks of real distress on his peculiar face. Indeed he pitied me, but not for what I had thought.

Then Oskar spoke up. "Shall we have a game? Mozart, will you risk a florin at the white winning game? The victor will challenge my cousin here."

They agreed and began to play. Oskar proved to be a confident player, but with little reason. He struck every ball as if he intended to shoot to the moon, or to smash the object ball into fragments. That cloth would not soon recover. Mozart, however, was a fine player with a delicate touch and a degree of finesse, although sadly deficient in the art of english. He won by six, and then I took up a cue and we played. Of course, I did not reveal my true skill and strung out the game, eking out a victory of one ball.

As one does, we talked of the game whilst playing. I said in passing that my game was off because I was used to playing with my own cue, a Mingaud.

"Yes," he said, "the French do the best sticks nowadays. I have always desired one but if I paid out so much, my dear wife would stick it you know where. Did you get it in France?"

"No, but my late father did. I have never been to France."

"You miss little, sir. Paris is filthy and they know nothing of music." After this, much talk of Paris, of the French, and so on, and of the court there, which everyone owned was the most magnificent in the world. Mozart seemed to know a good deal about that court and its personages, so I inquired as to whether its manners had changed since our Austrian princess had become its queen.

"That I do not know," he replied, "the last time I was there I did not visit the court. I was last at Versailles in 'sixty-four, when the late king reigned and I played the harpsichord for them. But Maria-Antoinetta could not but ornament any court. So lovely and gracious and not in the least overbearing or proud! I knew her as a girl, you see. I kissed her once and said we would be married one day. She laughed sweetly and was not in the least offended. As it happened, I married someone else." He laughed at his joke: a man who liked to laugh.

I responded somewhat coldly to this sally, now regarding my late opponent as some kind of fantastick. Playing at court! Why, thought I, he must have been a mere child in 'sixty-four! And kissing a princess of the imperial house! What a notion!

We played further. He quizzed me on how I managed to make the cue ball take a curving path, and I condescended to instruct him a little in the art. He was a fellow hard to dislike. At about three o'clock he begged our leave, saying he was due at the opera house to hear auditions and rehearse the parts of his opera he had already written. I suggested we accompany him there, as I had never seen such a thing. In truth, I cared not a fart for his opera, but only hoped to gain an interview with the woman who had obsessed my mind, even in the midst of my many subsequent fornications. In truth, and you must forgive my vulgarity, I had never had a fuck such as the one she had given me in that damned coach, and I wanted one just like it again, at all hazards.

We walked, all three of us, to the new theater Count Nostitz had built a few years prior. I will not describe it, as it is still there in its place on the Fruit Market Square and you can see it any day. Inside, a great deal of confusion, people shouting in Italian, musicians sawing away. I remarked to Oskar, "Do you know, Oskar, I have tried to understand music—I have, but this still sounds like mere caterwauling."

"That is because it *is* mere caterwauling," he replied. "The musicians are tuning their instruments. That gentleman over there is Bondini, the impresario of the Italian opera."

Mozart went to speak with this personage and Oskar and I sat down in the parterre. Many young ladies of the theater were about the place, chattering gaily, but I had no eyes for them, for my Clotilde was not about. There seemed to be some delay in the proceedings. Mozart finished what business he had with Bondini and sat down at a pianoforte. He was passing remarks with the musicians and the singers, and then he played; some of them laughed, although for what reason I could not say.

What was remarkable to me, though, was the way everyone in the theater acted toward our little man. The great Louis of France or the Pope himself could not have been treated with more deference or respect. They seemed to worship at his feet. I mentioned this to Oskar, and he told me something of the man's career. It turned out that I had been mistaken when I thought him a fantastick. Indeed he had played at Versailles *aetat* seven and at the Schonbrun palace even earlier, a wonder of the age, and I no longer doubted the kiss with Maria Antoinetta. I recalled with a pang the time La Wolanska had named me the infant Mozart at billiards, and at last comprehended the remark. While he was only a musician to me, I saw that he was a king in this small realm. He was not aping the manners of his betters as valets do, and as I had thought, but carried himself nobly because he reigned in fact among the musical of that era. And I thought that if kings and emperors could show him courtesy because of his genius, I could hardly do less. Besides, he was an amusing fellow, if you set aside the noises.

Some music now began, instead of mere tuning, as they called it. To my surprise, I could just tell the difference. A fellow played upon the violin, and Mozart played that tune and then played another tune that was like the first and then a good deal of music less like, first louder then softer . . .

"What is the matter with you? That look! Like you bit upon a bad nut."

"Oh, sir!" cried Rudi. "To have seen and heard Mozart inventing variations on a theme, for his own amusement and that of his orchestra! And at the rehearsal for *Don Giovanni*! I writhe with envy, and my dear Berthe would do the same, in even greater measure, for she is a true musician. And yet it was lost upon you!"

"So it was, although I did not feel the loss, I can tell you. In any case, there was a distraction at the door and in strode a large man with a flowing mane of hair and the presuming carriage of a mountebank."

"That is Da Ponte," said Oskar. "He wrote the libretto and will direct the players while Mozart directs the musicians."

But I cared not a pin for any mountebank or musician at the moment, because there she was. She had arrived on Da Ponte's arm, looking even more wonderful than she had in the moonlight in the coach. Instantly, I was aflame.

Twenty-two

This word *aflame* worked upon Rudi like the catch-word of a mesmerist. He continued to wield his pencil but his mind was elsewhere. He was no longer in the comfortable antique room but climbing a set of rotting stairs toward the apartment of that woman. In that instant he discovered that it was not so easy to keep Sisi Vasová from his thoughts. The long-dead passion of the old baron acted like a taper to fire his own.

The baron had stopped talking. "Excuse me, sir," he said after a pause, "but are you ill?"

Rudi started and almost lost his notebook and pencil. "What? Oh, no, sir, not I. Why do you enquire?"

"Because for the last five minutes you have been writing and I have been telling a most interesting little anecdote and yet I believe you were not at all here. And then you let out a great groan."

"It is nothing, sir. Do forgive me. I have been working on . . . personal activities until very late."

"Personal activities, eh? I remember those. And they do tire a man out, to be sure. But read me where you have got to."

Rudi consulted his page and replied, "La Daumer was even more magnificent than I recalled, and you will remember that I had only seen her in a coach in the dark of a summer's night."

"Yes. You wrote it down correctly, yet certainly you were elsewhere. I recall the experience well from a thousand nights on sentry. Well, let us continue. Clotilde was wearing a dress the color of wine foam. She seemed to me to sparkle like that airy stuff does under candlelight. Standing by Da Ponte's side as he spoke to Mozart, she looked out over the theater to see who was attending the rehearsal. Our eyes met, I stood and made my bow; she affected not to see me. What was this? I left my seat and went to her. I smiled and made another bow. She looked through me as if I had been a post, whispered to Da Ponte, and departed to speak to a group of performers. Da Ponte soon followed and began to arrange the players about the stage, to marshal them, as it were, for the next scene. I was staring after Clotilde, wondering what to do, when Mozart noticed my discomfiture and said, "So you have found your Daumer—but I observe you do not go to her, nor she to you. Do you perhaps require an introduction?"

"Oh, not at all," I replied. "I know the lady. I saw her perform once."

"Oh? In what role, may I ask?"

"The lead part in a tragi-comedy, *A Lad Saved From Hanging*. She was stupendous."

He frowned and said, "I do not know the piece. Pray, who composed it?"

I replied, "You have me there, sir. I fear I pay little attention to musicians."

With that, I went back to Oskar, took my leave, left the theater, and went around the side of the building. I found a doorway and waited like a footpad, wretched as any beggar, no, more wretched, for folk feel sorry for the beggar, but everyone mocks a thwarted lover. Eventually, she emerged and I followed her back to her lodgings--the Golden Keys, near the Horse Market, an establishment well known for catering to actors, demi-reps, gamblers, and mountebanks. A bribe let me past the doorkeeper and supplied me with the number of her room. Another bribe let me into the room opposite, which happened to be vacant.

I lay in wait for her for some measureless period, feeling a fool, yet helpless to resist. At last I heard the rustle of her dress, the tap of her shoes, and I sprang out like a footpad to block her path.

"Well, and what do you want?" she demanded, with an affected sigh.

"Do you know me, Madame?"

"Of course I know you. Who could forget such a face! You are the sherbet from the Charles Bridge. I see you are still with us and have not found another girl to kill yourself for. But again, I ask, what do you want with me?"

"Only to know you, to be with you, to make you happy, to shower you with affection, and to complete the education whose first lesson you conducted in that coach to which you advert."

Now she favored me with a charming smile and an appraising look.

"Very prettily managed. I see you have not been idle at the libertine academy. And there is a different look to you, less the rude hedge-baron boy and more a gentleman of parts. You have done well these last months, I perceive. That is a fine coat you wear, your linen is new and of the best quality, as are your shoes--those buckles are real silver without doubt. A subvention from home? I think not--you do not have the flaccid air of a sponger. Nay, you have tapped some source of florins all on your own. What is it?"

"I am a billiards shark," said I.

"Are you really?" Now came a broader smile and a hearty laugh, too. "This makes you somewhat more interesting a fellow than you were. Come into my room. I am famished, but we will send out."

We entered the chamber. I expected that this would be but prelude to what I chiefly desired, but after a futile effort at embrace, all I gained was a box on the ears.

"Listen well, my little sherbet," she said, with steel in her address. "Do you recollect Da Ponte, the gentleman with whom I entered the theater? In opera, the librettist directs and chooses the actors, subject to the approval of the composer and impresario. Da Ponte and Bondini, the impresario, are agreed on the cast for this new work, with one exception--the role of Donna Elvira. Bondini favors Caterina Miceli,

Mozart is largely indifferent between us, although he would prefer Miceli

because he has worked with her before now. Da Ponte will settle the matter by choosing me."

"But it is an Italian company and you are German," I objected.

"Nonsense ! I am as Italian as Bondini or the others: born in Milan, of an Austrian officer and an Italian singer, whom he declined to --oh, but that does not matter. What matters is that I must keep Da Ponte sweet until he secures me that part, and thus I must have macaroni day and night and not a spoonful of sherbet. Do you catch my meaning? Oh, Jesu, let us have some food!"

She pulled the bell rope. In a few minutes a young slavey appeared at the door. Daumer said to her, "Bring a supper for my cousin Hans and me. Greta in the kitchen knows my tastes--a meat pie, new peas, and a bottle from that case Signor Da Ponte left for me."

The girl dropped a clumsy curtsy and left.

"Your cousin? No one will believe that."

"They will, because no one would dream I would choose a lover with a face like yours. Oh, do not pout, for heaven's sake! Your face has nothing to do with what we are to one another."

"And what is that, if I may make so bold?"

"Oh, well, I am the summit of your desire, I haunt your sleep, and so on. I have not had a hopeless devotee in some time and it is very pleasant, I assure you. I send you hither and yon on errands for trifles; I borrow money, which I have no hope of repaying; and yet I am unobtainable. Every actress must have at least one, and you shall be mine for a season. As for my part, when the proper time comes, you shall be again my delicious young sherbet, for I assure you, it is far beyond tedious to let these old men paw at one, and in the end I almost always have to rub them off with my hand, for they can never get stiff enough to give me a proper fucking. It is too long since my toes curled and I gasped in ecstasy in truth and not for show. Still one must secure one's future, as I hope to do before I reach the dread shoals of thirty. A little house and a modest competence is all I am after, although I would not say no to an archducal palace, if offered. But to attract this rich protector I must have a solo part, and Da Ponte is the key to it. I do admit he gets it well up for an old fellow, bigger than yours as I recall, but not near as rampant."

And much more in this saucy line, and while she talked her little warm hand snaked its way past my belt and grasped that rampant member in the most casual way, as if toying with a handkerchief. I made to embrace her, but she pushed me away and clamped my parts so tightly that I gasped.

"None of that now, be nice, for I have told you my situation and require that you respect it. You must wait for the part to be mine and for Da Ponte to finish his work and depart for Vienna or somewhere. Then we will have a fine warm time together. I will drain you so dry you will be like a eunuch in the streets and ignore all other women entirely."

Steps sounded outside; she withdrew her hand and said, "Oh, good, here is the food."

We ate, and drank, and though we grew tipsy, she was careful to rebuff my ardent advances, for she swore that her Italian was mad with jealousy and could smell another man on her.

"Besides that, he is very clever, and we could never outwit him. He is a Jew, you know, besides being a priest and a famous whoremonger. It is a combination not found every day, you will agree! I believe he ran a brothel in Venice and was expelled from the Republic for that cause. The Venetians don't mind brothels, but they deplore them being operated by priests, not to say Jew priests. He once wrote three operas at once, or so he says. He is certainly a genius and admirable, though I wish he smelled better. I would like a taste of Mozart, of course, all the girls would, but he is beyond reach--I never saw a man more enslaved to a wife. He will talk bawdy, but it is all cry and no wool. Why are you looking at me like that?"

"That is a look of love, my dear, and also of amazement, for although you are as false and corrupt as any whore in the city, yet you glow like a girl new in from the farm."

"Oh, that is just my stock in trade. Aside from a few nice gems and a paltry voice, that look is all I possess, and it is as quick to spoil as fresh milk. It rots away as we speak. Nor do I have family or fortune to sustain me--I am no baroness, unless you care to marry me? Ah, I see you do not. That being the case, Herr Billiard Shark, let us be rid of our scruples--they don't suit such as we, and I do assure you that when you are upon me and plunged all steaming to the hilt, these concerns are unlikely to occupy your mind. But not just now. Get off me, you beast, or I will send you away!"

There were many such scenes in the ensuing days. I haunted the theater, attending her like a pet monkey, and like a monkey's keeper she showed me off and made me do any trick that struck her fancy. The worst thing about being so enslaved is that it cuts one off from the rest of humanity and, indeed, from the fullness of life. You quite give up your friends, for example, for your behavior distresses them and they wish you to reform, some even going so far as to denigrate the object of your desire, which may prove fatal to the friendship. I was fortunate in both Lennart and Paradowski, for neither of them adverted to my madness.

Horovitz, however, quite threw me over, for I had no interest in billiards and disappointed him in several matches he had troubled to arrange. No money was coming in and I was spending ruinously on Clotilde; she had many more than a few nice gems now.

My lust was incessant, of course, and as it could not be slaked in the body of Clotilde, I naturally carried it to the Mounted Man, becoming at last a true habitué of the place. There was a girl there, one Trudl, a coarser version of my inamorata, and she stood-in, as they say in the theater. Yet as often occurs in such cases, the mere expulsion of seed served more to enhance the desire for the true object than to diminish it. Of course, all Prague knew of my plight, or so it seemed, for one comes to believe that the desire to stick one's schwanz in the quim of a particular woman is the axis about which the world turns. The girls at the Mounted Man knew all and made whorish fun of me, and as a result of this notoriety, I one evening received a summons from the place's mistress, Margo of the one eye.

She dwelt in the cellar, which she had transformed into a sumptuous apartment. It boasted walnut-paneled walls, carpets thick and soft as a loaf of white bread, ceilings painted with the amours of gods. Glass cases held fine bibelots; all the furnishings were comfortable, à la mode, and included a vast leather sofa that had once, according to local tales, adorned the seraglio of the Grand Turk. In brief, the place was delightful enough to obviate for the visitor the complete absence of windows. It was not the black cave that Oskar had described, but dim enough. The only light came from a six-armed gilt-bronze candelabra that stood just to the left of the aforesaid sofa. The servant who had guided me to the room begged me to sit on this prodigy. I did so, and waited. Then, in my very ear it seemed, a voice said, "I have studied you, sir."

I started, and looked around the room. Nothing!

The voice resumed. It was a lovely and intriguing voice, low, cultured, well- articulated, the sort of voice one desires in a lover.

"You are making a fool of yourself over a singer; this is not unusual in young gentlemen, but I detect you are not entirely a fool."

"You are behind that panel," said I, for I had seen that the panels were purposely set not flush, so that there was a clear gap of about two inches, from which the voice emerged and also a cooler air, smelling of a musky perfume.

"I have been interested in you for some time," the voice continued. "Your face interests me."

"What about it?" I said, although of course I knew.

She ignored the question and said, "Our faces are how we show ourselves to the world. They can be false or honest, lovely or homely, and behind these fronts we live the secret life of the heart. Some faces show easily what is going on inside; others veil it, or present a false image. Those who have been given beauty take the plaudits of the world as their due, unconsciously for the most part, and never think how brief is the season of loveliness. You will have observed the differences between the deportment common among the ugly and that of the handsome."

"Yes, the ugly man often acts as if the world has played him false and he must take revenge."

"Or, being despised for his looks, he may adopt a humble mien and thereby become a saint. I note as an instance the philosopher Lichtenberg, once a client of mine. Or he may come to feel that he owes the world some wonderful feat, as if to make up for the insult his appearance imposes upon it. But the case is different with those who have been deprived of beauty through violence, like you and me. We may hide it or flaunt it, but we never own it, and it imposes a dark glory, the power of which we may use for good or ill."

"How did you lose your eye?" I asked abruptly, for I was growing annoyed with this talk. There was a silence, so I added, "If you tell me, I will relate how I lost my nose."

At that she laughed, a surprisingly girlish sound. "You are bold, sir. The great advantage of a brothel, you know, is that it is a place of perfect anonymity. We have no names, nor do our clients, and it is often a struggle to preserve this, for men in lust wish for tales. The body is not enough for them; they demand to know the woman in full. Where are you from, they ask, how did you begin in this life? We can offer this service as well, although, of course, we never tell the truth. Men often fall in love with whores, or imagine they do. Some need this illusion as part of their pleasure."

"I do not. So you can tell me the truth if you choose. It is all the same to me."

"Very well, but let it be for your ears alone; I will be frank with you as I am not with others, because you are a fellow member of the confraternity of the mutilated."

She told her tale at length. I supply a précis: she was married, she took a lover, the husband discovered them in flagrante and slashed her face with a knife, taking her eye; and the lover killed the husband. She fled.

"And from that passage," I inquired after a decent pause. "How did you come to occupy your present station?"

"No, first your nose."

"A duel."

"Yes, and…"

"And nothing. The great advantage of a brothel is that it is a place of perfect anonymity."

Again came that tinkling laugh. "Very good, you! I believe we shall be friends hereafter. And now, goodnight."

I returned to the brothel the next evening, and was immediately summoned into that subterranean parlor. Again I smelt the waft and heard that charming voice. We conversed as usual, but this night she directed the conversation toward a consideration of the delights of the flesh. She quizzed me about my experience and tastes. Our talk grew warm indeed, and my parts grew warm with it. At last she bade me blow out all the candles in the candelabra but one, and also to remove all my clothing. This done, I waited in the dimness for some time. Then the sound of a sliding panel, and she emerged, naked but for the famous mask. She blew out the last candle.

The room became perfectly dark, dark as the inside of a horse. I felt her approach. I reached out; she slapped my hands away and made me lie down on the sultan's sofa. "Make no resistance, my boy," she said, "for I know more of this art than you do."

With that she bound my hands and feet to the couch with silken cords. It is said that the blind acquire heightened senses to replace the one they have lost, and I can vouch for the truth of this, if only in small part. Being bound and helpless also seemed to add to the intensity of the pleasure she bestowed. A hundred florins! I would have paid a thousand for that night, I do assure you, sir. Unendurable pleasure indefinitely prolonged was her art—I shall not trouble you with the details—and it went on through that long night. But never again, never again, and perhaps a good thing, too."

Rudi lifted his pencil and inquired, "Why was that, sir? Did you displease her?"

"Oh, no! At least I don't think so. But at dawn, a silly maid opened the outer door of our crypt and a beam of light fell on the bed. She had released me from my bonds and I was lying prone, naked as a bird. She gave a strange cry and left in an instant through the secret panel. She never sent for me again."

"Did you never find out why?"

A long silence here. Then: "I will share a notion that may shock you."

"I suppose I am not easily shocked, sir."

"Well . . . I have always believed that she left in such haste, never to resume our friendship, because she spied the wolf mark on my back. Which can only mean . . . that is to say, what other woman would know that mark?"

"I beg pardon—the wolf mark?"

"Yes, and here you discover why my father could have no doubt at all that I was his son. Every male in my family, time out of mind, has borne a small triangular brown mark at the base of the spine, in which fancy has descried the face of a wolf. It is the inerrant sigil of a male von Pannau."

"But, sir, many a man might have such a mark. I myself am told I have one, although given its position I cannot see it. And I am no von Pannau."

The baron cast on him then an odd look, which changed in a flash to his thin smile.

"You are correct, sir, many a man could, but a woman knows the flesh of her babe and its markings."

The baron's meaning now struck Rudi, and he gaped.

"Good God! You suppose Margo was your *mother*?"

"I can think of no other explanation. You will note I have not clawed out my eyes like old Oedipus in the tale, so the fact of our intimate congress did not appall as it is supposed to. She was never my mother, except as an accident, only a woman; and indeed, she gave me more mothering and good advice during our trysts through that panel than any woman ever did, save La Wolanska. But let us not dwell on what is, after all, mere speculation. It is not the done thing to fuck one's mother, so let us there end the story."

Quite aside from this connection, it was a strange time, now I look back on it. I divided my hours between Mirek and the dragoon officers at the Mounted Man and, to be close to Clotilde, with the musicians and their acolytes at the Nostitz theater--and two more different ensembles could hardly be imagined. The dragoons talked about horses, girls, games and never enough money, while the opera people talked about who was in love with whom, who had succeeded in gaining or granting the final favors, who was making it impossible to perform well because they didn't have any idea of how to do their parts; and never enough money. Trivial gossip, yes, but there was something else, too, in both assemblies. One forgave the soldiers their silly conversation because they lived beneath the shadow of death, ever ready to kill and to lay down their lives for the king and emperor. They were thus noble, and therefore arms is a noble profession. Music is not a noble profession, but the opera people treated music as if it conferred nobility upon those who practiced the art. And there *was* a nobility there: one could feel it in their manners, and in this nobility, as I have said, there was one king and that was Mozart.

I don't say that I became friends with him: our differing ranks and interests made too wide a gulf. But I found in him a certain fascination, as I believe he did in me. We often met for coffee before he went to the theater, repairing for this to a small, shabby place on the Strahöferplatz, unfrequented by either musicians or billiard fiends. In an odd way he prized, I think, converse with one who set at naught the supreme value of his life.

I suppose there were two reasons for this. First there was his, you may say, philosophical curiosity. All the world loves music, especially we Germans, and so one who was indifferent to that jangling and tweedle posed a puzzle for him, as the blind fish and monsters of the womb, who reside murkily in philosophical carboys, do for the savants. He determined that I could hear the differences between the notes well enough, and could distinguish tempi, one from another, but that I was incapable of experiencing delight from hearing a piece played. We speculated upon the reasons for this, whether a defect of nature or the result of my peculiar rearing, but came to no firm conclusion.

The other reason was subtler. He had famously been a prodigy and immersed in music from an early age, as he still was, and I suppose he enjoyed the company of one who did not dote upon his talent, rather in the way that a bite of plain bread clears the palate between two high-flavored dishes at table. Or a sherbet, I might have said.

As for my interest in him, I suppose there were two reasons as well. First, I wished to pump him for intelligence about the politics of the opera, especially that concerning the choice of singers, for with some tidbit in hand I could send a note to my inamorata and suggest a rendezvous for the purpose of communicating it. But he was not free with many of these; he seemed to think all such affairs beneath him.

The other reason was a curiosity akin to his own about me. I wished to learn about vocations. Having no strong one of my own, I desired to learn what such a calling felt like, and who better to so inform me than one whose vocation had dazzled kings? It was a pleasant encounter for both of us, I believe, but beyond this, the connection led to an adventure, in the course of which my life changed once again, and set the mold of the man I became, whose ruin you see now before you.

Let me now relate how it came about. One evening, I suppose it was mid-October by now, Mirek had the guard that night, and I had gathered in his absence with my soldier friends. As it sometimes does in small, close-knit groups of men, the conversation turned to the virtues and foibles of our missing brother.

I believe all in the dragoons were a little afraid of Mirek Paradowski, and this tempered their deep love for him, for truly, he was the most splendid man, madly brave, loyal unto death, fanatically honest, an Achilles, but one who never sulked, who had a joke in the direst circumstances. His only flaw was an excess of punctilio concerning his honor, as a result of which he was out more than any ten men in the regiment, and the Kinsky, everyone acknowledged, was a regiment unusually quick to fight.

At first I thought they were trying me, to find if I was worthy of the company, for they knew him so much better than I did, and they wanted to be sure I knew what kind of man I had chosen as a friend. Because it is so--there are those who would be uneasy in the company of one who had slain two dozen or so men with cold steel, in duels. But I was not, as they soon found. I believe also that my hideous scar lent me a certain credence as a man not prone to squeamishness.

This tale-telling concerned mainly swordplay and lecherousness, in both of which Mirek was named a prodigy. To support the former quality I added my own recollections of the fight with the footpads, which they applauded, saying it was just the sort of thing Paradowski would have done. As to the latter attribute, each of the friends had a story, some of perhaps doubtful provenance, of how the handsome lieutenant had won this or that reluctant maiden.

"But he never tarries long, you know," said Waldstein, "Never an actual engagement, or even a fortnight in love. I suppose with that face and figure he can play the bee among the flowers."

"Although he always goes with the same whore," observed Hoth. "That Bretka. I have always wondered why."

"You always use the same saddle, Hoth," said Silmaringen. "I have always wondered why."

"I suppose you mean that he is used to her," replied Hoth a little coldly. "Still, inconstancy among ladies and fidelity to whores is not the usual thing."

"Well, why not quiz him on it?" asked de Cavriani in an innocent voice, which caused some laughter, because, as it was explained to me, Paradowski would tolerate no inquisition as to his personal habits, and as he was able to enforce this ban with steel, he was uniquely shielded from the prurient raillery that marks every assembly of vigorous young men. For this reason, they often referred to him (but never, never to his face) as The Princess.

Did he have any defects at all, I wondered, and asked.

"Oh, he wears a corset," said de Cavriani.

"That hardly signifies," answered Waldstein. "*I* wear a corset and it does not make the ladies flock to me as to Paradowski. We should all hate him and wish him ill, but we do not, for he never boasts, and never poaches a brother's lady, and is liberal with a florin when a fellow is short, although God knows he hasn't a pfennig from home. Let us drink to our absent friend!"

We hoisted our glasses and cried out, "The Princess!" and then Waldstein said, "But as to coxcombs, we have a prize one staying at our house in town. Do any of you know the Chevalier de Seingalt?"

None of us did. "He is a remarkable old fellow. I suppose he was the premiere adventurer and seducer of the former age. He is the only man ever to escape from the Leads prison of Venice. That tale alone is worth a visit."

"How does he come to be at your house?" asked de Cavriani.

"Oh, the Count my uncle met him at the Venetian ambassador's table—the Prince de Ligne introduced them—and they struck up a warm acquaintance. My uncle has a place up at Dux where he keeps his girls—a rather nice one just now—and he installed Seingalt as librarian. A sad end for such a man, used to mingling in the most distinguished company—I mean to say, if the fellow is to be believed, he has supped with both Louis XV of France and Voltaire. And Dux, as I know to my horror, is a wasteland. But he is here in Prague for a few days, and . . . yes! You shall all dine with me tonight and he shall make one of the company. Do come —I pledge my honor he is most entertaining."

Given my history, as you may imagine, I had no wish to sit at table with a famous seducer. I was about to plead a prior appointment when Waldstein happened to mention that the reason Seingalt had come to town was to meet with an old friend, a man who required advice on an opera he was writing about just such a great lecher. This was, of course, Lorenzo Da Ponte, my rival for the affections of Clotilde. Later, and privily, I suggested to Waldstein that Da Ponte ought also to attend and that he should be encouraged to bring along his mistress.

"Ah, a complot!" he exclaimed, his round face aglow. "I adore complots, the more farcical the better. How wonderful if you should seduce your lady under the nose of her protector, all in the presence of the master of seduction. I daresay he would be happy to lend a hand in the enterprise."

"I believe I am capable enough," I said. "Besides, I wonder that this prodigy has not more of a reputation. None of us knew this Seingalt."

"Yes, but what of the name Casanova?"

"Of course. It is like Don Juan, a byword for arrant lechery, a myth of sorts, I suppose."

"Not at all. It is an actual man: the veritable Giacomo Casanova! He likes us to use his title, the old pantaloon, as tenuous as it is. Until eight then! Oh, this will be rich!"

He walked away, chuckling, leaving me amazed. The last time I had heard that name, it was in my father's mouth, and for a time I had imagined that it was the name of the man who had stolen my mother and brought our family to ruin.

"But now," said the baron, "I see it is growing late, and my eyes are drooping. The next part of my story involves my closest connection with your Mozart, and it is not a tale to be interrupted. Go off, if you please. Return tomorrow and I will complete it all in one swoop."

Twenty-three

I am insane, thought Rudi, as his fiacre drove across the bridge. That old man's bawdy tales, that mad-woman the other night . . . this is not who I am, and I must resolve it, must return to who I was. I must apologize, I must . . . regularize our connection. I was very drunk, I will tell her, they had both been in other than their right minds; I don't wish to lose your friendship, he would say, but he wanted to make clear that an error like that could not be repeated.

But when he arrived at the shabby building Sisi was not at home. The child Anneke opened the door and grudgingly admitted him. He entered the sitting room, as he supposed he must call it, and looked around. Now that he was sober, and with clear light of day coming in through the windows, he could see details that had been obscure during his earlier visit. A sofa draped in shawls, propped up with bricks where one leg had gone missing; a square table with a cloth on it, much patched and stained; three mismatched wooden chairs; a window pane missing, the gap stuffed with rags; a brownish carpet, curling at the edges; a pallet in a corner, where the child must sleep; a screen in the other corner, painted with a pastoral scene, dulled by grime; on the walls, a portrait of Sisi, in some barbaric costume, incomplete, energetic, but an unconvincing likeness; a framed steel engraving of the martyrdom of Jan Hus, and in place of honor over the bed, a ferocious mask, some demon, perhaps oriental.

Rudi sat on the couch. The girl perched on a chair and regarded him unsmiling, gnawing on a heel of bread.

After some silence, he asked, "Are you hungry? I could give you some money and you could go down the street and . . . "

"You cannot buy me with your German gold," she replied. "I am not a whore."

"Of course you are not! I only meant . . . "

"Nor is *she* a whore. She is a poet. A poet may have a lover. She is not a goddamned bourgeoise, you know."

"Yes, I am well aware of that. You told me you were a poet as well."

"I was, but I have sacrificed my art for the revolution. Now I am a revolutionary."

"Are you indeed? Tell me, do you go to school?"

"There is no need. She has taught me to read and write and figure to the rule of three. I have also suspended my education to help with the revolution. It is a sacrifice to me."

"I'm sure it is. And if not school, how do you spend your revolutionary days?"

"Conspiring against the authorities, marking walls with slogans, and writing manifestos. I can show you a manifesto, if you like. It may enrage you."

"Certainly; I shall attempt to control my ire."

She clomped over to her corner and from a herring box at the foot of her pallet took a sheet of brown paper that had clearly been used by the butcher. She thrust it at him. It was in Czech, penciled in a clear, round schoolgirl's hand. He read:

A REVOLUTION MANIFESTO OF THE CZECH PEOPLE

We Czechs are oppressed! There is nothing in the house to eat and we have not nice clothes or anything! The Germans make us talk German! What a crime! So down with the Germans!! They must leave us alone!!
We have nothing to eat because the Jews ruin us by paying to much rent and not enough pay at the factory! Why do not the Czechs own the factory? This is the question. Soon we will wade in the blood of the Jews and all will be fine for THE DAY IS COMING!!! RISE UP O CZECHS!

"It is very forceful," Rudi said, handing it back.

"You may beat me and throw me in prison," she declared, "I care not. I will   suffer and die for the Czech people."

"It would be better if you did not have to suffer and die, however, and we brought about a peaceful revolution. That is what I am trying to do, you know."

She gave him a startled look and barked a short laugh. "How can there be any such thing? You are a silly man as well as a goddamned *skopčák*. A peaceful revolution? That would be like quiet noise or clean dirt."

She giggled and pointed her finger. Meanwhile, steps sounded on the stair and into the room walked Sisi, carrying a straw bag. She took no particular notice of Rudi; her glance slid past him, as if he were always there on her sofa.

She handed the bag to Anneke.

"Take this down to Frau Grossbart's, my girl. There is a bit of brisket and some potatoes and bread and greens. Have her make your dinner and stay there until I come for you."

The child complained briefly but a snarling hiss put a stop to that and she stamped out.

The door closed. They listened as the child's steps retreated down the stair. He opened his mouth to speak and got out a few bland words, but she flung herself at him without warning, like a tiger upon a staked goat, her mouth crushing his, her tongue stiff in his mouth. She bore him back upon the sofa, her hands tore at his trousers, a button snapped free. She freed his sex, she rucked up her skirt, she sank down on him, enveloping him with that greasy heat, she rode him violently, breathing like a locomotive, cursing in Czech, she hates him, she cannot live without him--the ravings of a mad-woman. The supporting bricks slid, the sofa collapsed with a crash, but this didn't stop her, oh no, they coupled on the splintery boards, on the soiled rug, she never stopped moving, even after he has squirted it into her, it seemed to madden her more, she ground painfully against him until with a cry like a woman being strangled she reached her own climax.

After that, she collapsed upon him for the space of a dozen ragged breaths and then she stood, adjusted her clothing and said, "By Christ, I am famished. Let us go downstairs and get some of my food before it is all gone."

He made an excuse. He could not stay—he had revolutionary business. She shrugged and went her way without another word.

It was not a convenient lie. The bells were ringing three o'clock, and he did have someplace he had to be. Limbs still slightly trembling, he found a cab at the train station and directed it to a small street near the Charles University. As he paid the cab, he heard the glad sound of boys released from school and soon he was passed by mobs of these, in caps and swinging satchels. He followed their spoor back to a substantial building on the other side of Kolowratsgasse, the King Leopold Gymnasium, and entered. After inquiring of a porter, he soon found his man in an empty classroom, stuffing books and papers into a satchel.

Jasny looked up at the sound of Rudi's step on the creaking old floor.

"Moritz? What are you doing here?"

"I had some difficulties with a quotation. I thought I would come to the source."

"Oh? What quotation would that be?"

"In every tyrant's heart there springs in the end this poison, that he cannot trust a friend."

"That is Aeschylus, the *Prometheus*, line 224."

"Yes, now I remember. You got us all through classics at university--I assumed you would still have it all by heart. But, you know, tyrants, being incapable of trust themselves, seek to destroy trust among their subjects. It is a sovereign elixir in the practice of oppression."

"Humph. What are you getting at?"

Jasny was having difficulty with the clasp on his briefcase. He muttered a curse and let the cover flap as he took his coat and hat from a stand and prepared to leave.

"An observation merely. Let us walk together a while, Jasny. We have not been as close recently as we once were. I regret it. The revolution has taxed all of us with new responsibilities and we have not as much time to spend with old friends."

Jasny strode from the room without comment, Rudi keeping to his heels.

On the street, they walked in the direction of the university. Jasny said, "I am not in a convivial mood today, Moritz. You will excuse me. I had to punish two boys this morning for speaking Czech in school. Can you imagine? No, you cannot. You were never punished for speaking your native tongue. Yet this I must do in order to keep my place and feed my family, or tattlers will inform the authorities."

"Yet that will change. You know I support the Czech position on language "

"Yes, everyone supports but nothing changes, and still I must flog little Czech boys."

They were passing the gate that led to the campus. The Academic Legion was out and marching on the turf. Perhaps one in three carried an actual firearm. The rest shouldered poles.

"There is change for you, though," said Rudi. "Students of both nations training to defend the revolution."

"With what? Their teeth?"

"Yes, I agree. They should all have weapons. For example, the muskets that someone has diverted from the Imperial stores. One or more of those friends have taken advantage of Jerzy Havel, a clerk in my employ, convincing him to steal stamps and requisitions that enabled such friends to obtain perhaps twelve hundred new percussion-cap muskets. When I confronted Havel with this defalcation, he described the person who put him up to it. And so I demand of this person, which is you, dear Jasny, what the devil are you about, and where are those damned weapons?"

Jasny's face had grown bright red. His mouth worked up and down, like a gaffed pike. "I don't know what you are talking about," he spluttered.

"Yes, you do. You are the man, and you are more of a fool than I thought. Who put you up to this? No answer? By Christ, Jasny, don't you see that while the army is stupid, it is not *that* stupid? They will eventually notice the weapons are missing, my office will be the first place they look, and young Havel will give you up to them as he did to me."

"They don't need Havel when they have you," Jasny said bitterly.

"What do you mean?"

"That you are a police spy! Everyone knows it. A spy for the Germans and a spy for the police. Who are at this moment watching us."

"Jasny, please! I have known you since our days at university. I saved your life on the roofs."

"You never did!"

"You have forgotten, have you? The three of us, you and me and Paul, drunk as lords and racing across the tiles, with poor Liebig down in the quadrangle howling up at us not to be fools." Rudi grasped his friend's lapel and pointed. "Look! Right up there. Paul leaped the gap and I followed. You slipped and would have rolled down the slates to your death had I not clutched your coat. You trusted me with your life, and not in vain. Do you now accuse me of treason?"

Jasny pulled away and said, "People change. Now *you* look! There are your friends in the police. You may denounce me this minute, but never will I admit to anything or tell you where we have . . . Damn you, Moritz! I am a Czech patriot and will do what I must to defend my people. What you are I have no idea. Look at them! They follow me everywhere."

With that, Jasny darted into the university gate and vanished. Rudi looked where he had pointed and saw a black coach with two black horses and two hard-looking men up on the box. From the window of this vehicle extended a white-clad arm with a hand that beckoned.

Rudi approached. The door swung open. Wulf-Eric Speyr said. "A word, Rudi. Step in for one moment, if you please."

Rudi climbed in; Speyr extended his hand. After a short pause, Rudi took it.

"Why are you following Jasny?" he demanded.

Speyr seemed genuinely surprised at this. "Jasny? But I am not following Jasny. Jasny is of no interest. Or rather, he is of the same interest as any dangerous tool, like a bayonet. Or a musket. The interest is in him who wields it. No, actually, I was following you. Your peregrinations about our Prague are far more interesting."

"I thought you had been commanded to leave me alone." exclaimed Rudi in a tone embarrassingly shrill.

"You *are* being left alone. Have I asked you anything since then about your disloyal friends? I have not and will not. But following is another matter. I suppose you could complain to Baron von Pannau, but I doubt you will get any further relief in that quarter. Police work, you see, is all a matter of patterns and connections. We see who goes with whom, in order to chart the flow, let us say, of subversion. And you have such interesting connections: Novotny, Bakunin, Bors—yes, we can now put a name to the little wretch--Jasny, Liebig, all dangerous radicals of the first water. You don't visit Jiskra, for some reason, not that we would know if you did. Herr Jiskra keeps himself to himself, it would seem. But those others are bad enough. And then there is Vasovà."

A shock ran through Rudi's vitals, as of electrical fluid. He felt his face burn.

"I have no idea what you mean."

"Oh, come, Rudi! You are a public figure. Did you imagine that you could keep your dalliance private? I confess to some disappointment. Despite your disloyal political ideas, I had imagined that in the domestic sphere you might have retained a measure of fidelity to your most admirable wife. "

"Who have you told?"

Another look of astonishment appeared on the policeman's face. "Who have I . . . my Lord, can it be you don't know? Then look at this!"

With which Speyr drew a paper from his tunic and handed it to Rudi.

It was a cheaply printed handbill on rough newsprint, of the type that had circulated widely in town since the lifting of censorship. This one showed an officer in uniform with a huge plumed hat on his head and an expression of idiotic lasciviousness on his face. He was mounted on a horse, which was looking back upon its rider with gaping dismay, the object of which was clearly the naked woman mounted just in front of the soldier. The artist was a fair hand at caricature, but lest any mistake the personages represented, they were labeled. The coxcomb general was "Rudolf M.," the naked woman was "Svetlana V." and the horse was "Bohemia."

Words had been supplied for the *dramatis personae*. Rudolf said, "Here is how I stand up for the little Czechs. I am as stiff as a pikestaff!" Svetlana V. said, "O! This German sausage is doing me well, but then I shall do *in* the Germans!" The Bohemian horse said, "That fool is so busy with his mare that there is no one to handle my reins. I shall run wild in a minute!" It was unsigned. Beneath the drawing was a poem of twenty-four lines, a lampoon, the burden of which was that R. had discovered the charms of his German hausfrau (Brunhilda) were vastly inferior to those of the Czech temptress (Svetlana) and describing why, in salacious detail. This was signed—by Jiskra.

Rudi let out a groan and tore the paper into fragments.

"That helps but little," said Speyr, "there must be hundreds about the town. Can you imagine if one was sent to Berthe?"

Rudi could. Sweat blossomed on his face.

"Yes, it would make even a liberal such as yourself long for the golden days of censorship," said Speyr. "Still, as a friend, and stretching my official capacity, I suppose I could suppress it. The printer is known; we could lock him up and destroy the plate. I would certainly like to know who Jiskra is. Any ideas?"

Rudi wiped his face with a handkerchief and said, "Wulfi, have you always been this vile, or did they send you to a special school?"

"Vile, is it? To defend my emperor and country? And though you believe it or not, should a parliamentary regime eventually arise in Bohemia, I would defend that as well. Meanwhile, I will return every night to my wife and family with a clear conscience, unlike some. Let me tell you something else. Your Vasová is not what she seems. There is something going on in Prague, the workers are up to something, with the help of a party of idiots from the better classes, and your little thrush is in the thick of it. I know you will not listen to me, but I beg you—have a care!"

Rudi flung open the door of the carriage and jumped out, heading where Jasny had gone, into the passages of the university, where following would be difficult and where he would be surrounded by his Legion.

He was not followed that he could see, and soon made his way to the new offices of *The Torch*, on Bredauergasse, behind the Fruit Market.

"Have you seen that . . . thing yet?" he asked Novotny.

"Ah, I assume you mean this," said the other, plucking up a copy of the cartoon from his desk. "The artist has captured Vasová quite well, I think. Yourself, not so much, opting I believe for a stock-cut pompous, fat German . . ."
Rudi snatched the cartoon from his hands and tore it into confetti.

"Oh, be quiet! How long has this filth been on the streets?" he demanded.

"It has been out but a day or so. I am surprised someone did not tack one to your door."

"And why has Jiskra attacked me so? I thought we were comrades."

Novotny shrugged and said, "Jiskra is a satirist and you have rendered yourself satirical by your actions. And I daresay someone paid him."

"But why?" he demanded. "Whom have I offended enough to engender so vicious an attack? Or could it be Sisi who is the object?"

"Oh, no, rest assured it is you, my friend. As to why —well, you are prominent, and powerful, or potentially so. It is politics, after all, which is a form of war, and in war—you know the saying about fairness there. It is a shot across your bows, Herr Commander of the Legion. The message is clear. Stick with your tribe, or perish, for this explains to the vulgar mind why you favor Czech interests in the deliberations of the state."

"But I don't! I am for fair treatment of all the constituent peoples." He sniffed, aware suddenly of a strong smell of fish in the room. "And what is that odor? It smells like bad fish. I knew they used newspaper to wrap fish in, but I imagined it was not done before printing as well."

"Fish? I don't smell anything," said Novotny dismissively. "Fair treatment, of course--which threatens those who have had it all to themselves these past centuries, that is, the Germans. This is one response, and you opened yourself to the blow. Whatever possessed you to bed a Czech nationalist like Sisi Vasová?"

"Her political opinions had nothing to do with it. My God! What if *Berthe* should see that awful broadsheet! Or my father! Or *her* father! Oh, damn me for a fool, Paul, what must I do?"

Novotny said, "As to that, you will of course deny everything. Above all, you must resist the impulse to clear your conscience by confessing to your wife. Any easing of the soul that may result will be as nothing compared to the position of cad and wretch that you will occupy for the rest of your marriage. A woman can stand an affair if discrete, but not a public extravaganza such as this. Should it come to her attention through a cartoon or a story or gossip, simply deny the truth of the charge and explain that politics is a dirty business. Your enemies seized upon a casual acquaintance to besmirch your good name. As for their ability to do so--well, freedom has some unpleasant consequences and you can hardly demand a return to censorship.

"You might kill the man, of course. That could discourage such creativity in future, and I doubt you would be in much danger should you call the fellow out. We writers and artists are peaceable men in general, if nasty. You might even wring a public apology from him. Most important, you must not see the woman ever again. In fact, you must cut her in public, simply turn your back should you encounter her. Can you do that, or is there some compelling passion?"

"Of course not," said Rudi vehemently. "It was a moment's weakness. Berthe is the only woman I have ever wanted."

Novotny gave him one of those eye-popped looks. "Well, then, it should be easy for you to throw her over."

Rudi took the first opportunity that presented itself to do so. This was the coffee that afternoon at Mme. von Silber's, where his tension in anticipation of a meeting with Sisi, like that of a soldier on the eve of battle, rendered him dull in company. This was unfortunate, as it was a company that would have engaged him some months ago. There were men from Frankfurt, with news of the deliberations of the German parliament there, and a man who had marched with the Parisians when they threw out the king; he had heard Lamartine speak. The others in the rooms were the usual domestic luminaries—Palacký was there, and Havlíček, Lörner and Maisel, the burgomeister, Mohlmann, and Count Thun, newly appointed governor of Bohemia.

Yet Rudi could detect a subtle change in the atmosphere of the salon. It was as if having made a revolution, the liberals of Prague had run out of things to say. Perhaps, he thought, imagined governments in realms of fantasy were more interesting to a certain type of mind than running an actual state. One had not to deal with the consequences of one's decisions, nor could one any longer ignore the fact, so uncomfortable to the liberal mind, that power was necessary even when the old ruling class had been dismissed, and that, for all their talk about the popular will, power ultimately depended upon the point of the bayonet.

Surprisingly, Liebig was there, standing neglected in a corner, blinking at the illuminati circulating and chatting around him, like an explorer in a jungle teeming with unfamiliar, perhaps dangerous, beasts. Rudi greeted his friend and remarked, "Well, Liebig, what brings you to Madame's?"

"The bread and butter, of course. As for this invitation, I have no idea, except that I had a piece in *Svobodny Tisk* a few days ago that caused a slight stir. I suppose it was enough to earn me my cup of thin coffee."

"I have not seen it--what was its subject?"

"Oh, just *contra* Palacký--his letter refusing Czech involvement in Frankfurt. I said it was a grave, even deadly error."

"I concur. What was your argument?"

"That it was tactically stupid. As long as there was the possibility that the Czechs would join the German parliament, the government had to court Bohemia and offer it virtually any concession it demanded. The threat to join Frankfurt was our ace, and Palacký has let it be trumped. Absent the Czechs, who are the most advanced non-German people, Frankfurt becomes a mere talking-shop for Germans, and hence can never be taken seriously as a governing body. More significantly, reaction now has a free hand in Bohemia. The mere insertion of nationality into the debate dooms the revolution to defeat in detail--*divisio et imperae*, the old, old story. It is already happening, here in Prague, before our eyes, and we do nothing!"

"How was the article received?"

"The forty-two true liberals remaining in Bohemia uttered polite applause. The Czech press named me a traitor, and suggested that such was what we might expect from a Jew. I have had death threats slipped under my door at night, the same door having been spangled with bad eggs and rotten fruits on two occasions."

"A successful piece, then. Congratulations, Liebig!"

Liebig gave a sour laugh. "Yes, I am somebody now, and I must labor to secure my place among the notables of intellect."

"Perhaps you will take *my* place--I am a little unsure of my position. Madame's greeting was distinctly lukewarm this evening. Tell me, do you know that very fat gentleman speaking with our new governor? I have not seen him before."

Liebig adjusted his pince-nez, the better to peer at the indicated person.

"Why, that is General Prince Lobkowicz. He has just come with his brigade this week."

"A prince, no less," said Rudi. "I wonder what he does here, in a famous liberal salon?"

"Perhaps it is not as liberal as it once was. These are strange days in Prague, my friend. And may I say, dear Moritz, you do not look well, not well at all. Your eyes are hollow and your complexion . . . is there something the matter?"

Rudi tried a laugh, which sounded false even to his own ears. "Oh, it is just the revolution, you know, writing, my work, supervising the Legion . . . "

"And that cartoon. I cannot imagine why Jiskra would write that awful screed against you. If I were you . . . "

"I don't care to discuss it, if you please, Liebig."

"Very well. But since you are by way of being a military man, you might think about arranging your forces so as to forestall any outrage against the Jews of Prague."

"Forgive me, but I have not heard of any such."

"Not yet you haven't. But ancient instincts do not lie. All of us sense approaching disaster. So far there have been only broken windows, some scuffles at Jewish shops--because we cheat the people, you understand--an affair of low types in the main. But something builds. Ah, see there! I am being summoned by our hostess, who is anxious to feed me to Palacký and his cronies. I hear she loves a good fight in her parlors. Don't forget the Jews, Moritz!"

Yes, Liebig is right, I am out of sorts, thought Rudi as he watched his friend walk away—well, who wouldn't be? I am a laughingstock. I look up and I find people staring at me, as at a show on the street. My hand is shaking; the coffee cup rattles in its saucer. Intolerable! Well, let me at least be of some use!"

He put his cup down on a side table and walked boldly up the group speaking to Count Thun and Lobkowicz, tapped Lörner on the arm, and asked for a private word.

"What is it, Moritz?" asked the other. He sounded annoyed at having been drawn from the distinguished circle.

"It is the Academic Legion, Herr Lörner. You recall you put me in charge of it?"

"Yes, what of it?"

"They are organized, enthusiastic, and reasonably well-drilled. I managed to obtain some superannuated sergeants to whip them into shape. But they will be of little use if they are not properly armed. The town guard has given them enough bayonets and other gear, and some old flintlocks, but that is insufficient for my plan. I must have adequate arms and ammunition to carry it out."

"Your plan?"

"Yes. I have received intelligence concerning a plot to raise the lower orders in an assault against the Jews. If this proceeds without effective opposition, the German merchants will be attacked next. In the face of such civil disorder, the forces of reaction will be encouraged to send in the Army. The revolution will be over."

"What intelligence? You have been listening to tavern rumors, my boy. In any case, I have it on very good authority that General Prince Lobkowicz will soon be placed in command of the National Guard, and he has just assured me that any irruption by the rabble will be put down instantly."

"That would depend, sir, on what he means by the rabble. To a prince, perhaps *we* are rabble, too. In any case, look at the man! Do you see a face sympathetic to liberal ideals? No, sir, we must depend on ourselves. Arm the students, and you will have a force sure and agile, able to run to places of disorder and suppress it without the need to trouble Prince Lobkowicz, who does not seem to be an officer prone to rapid action. Beyond that, there is the problem of the heights."

"Heights? What are you talking about?"

"Just that Prague sits in a bowl surrounded by heights: on the Mala Strana to the east and at Vhesehrad to the north. Who controls those heights controls the city. We must occupy those heights with forces loyal to the revolution."

"Moritz, perhaps this little command has gone to your head. No one is threatening the revolution from any heights, and I am sure Prince Lobkowicz and the governor have taken all this into account. As for your arms, I will see what I can do. Now, if you will excuse me . . . "

Interesting, thought Rudi. A little scandal and I am no longer taken seriously in the councils of the mighty. Perhaps I should have stolen those muskets myself.

He had just decided to make his excuses and leave, when Mme. von Silber left the argument she had started and came to stand by him.

"You poor fellow," she said, touching his arm with her hand instead of her fan. "Well, you have my sympathy. It is the price one pays for renown. You can have no idea of what *I* must put up with from these broadsheet blackguards. But let me give you a word of advice, if I may. Moritz, you have the makings of a great man. You are well enough looking, bright, competent, and people like you. There is a superior quality to you, but you present it without the famous arrogance to which your talent, not to speak of your family's wealth, might entitle you. I like you, and this affection prompts me to be utterly frank--you will forgive me, I trust.

"No one cares if a great man keeps a mistress. We are not Ireland or America yet, thank God! But you must retain your status as a great man, for petty men will wish to pull you down and will use any supposed dereliction to do so. These cartoons! This gossip in the cheap journals! Ignore them all! Did not Metternich of cursed memory have more mistresses than hairs on his head? But you must pursue greatness and power without stint, you must sacrifice everything, you must not retreat, ever, to the comfort of bourgeois mediocrity. Your wife, if she is any kind of woman, will understand this, and if she does not, so much the worse for her.

As for our dear Sisi--well, she would not have been my choice for you. She is something of a genius, true, but passionate, unreliable, antic and vengeful. Be aware of these traits, while you take your pleasures with her."

"Thank you for your kind advice, Madame, but I believe it comes too late. I am even less like Metternich in passion than in politics, I find. I made an error that I am anxious to correct, and I believe I must discontinue my irregular connection with the person to whom you advert."

"What, you drop her! Well, well!" She tapped his chest with her fan and said, "I am happy I brought you into our little circle, Moritz. I knew you would supply brilliance; gossip I had not expected, but it is almost as good. As for dropping, you can begin this instant. Here she comes."

A familiar voice behind him called out his name.
He turned and there she was. His face flamed, his stomach soured, his breath caught in his throat. She smiled, not her usual smile, always a little touched with acid, but a girl's smile, of delight in seeing her lover. It could not be borne. He mumbled an excuse: he was late for an appointment. Then he rushed past her, down the hall, out into the mild spring night, taking great draughts of air, almost running.

He walked rapidly, heedless of his direction. By chance, he found himself at the Carolinium, near the plashing Lion Fountain and the gate to the Old Square. On impulse and to delay returning to the empty, condemning house on Zeitnergasse, he went in and inquired after Andrej Popp.

He found the young commander in a second-floor classroom refitted as a headquarters for the Carolinium branch of the Academic Legion. He was looking down at his troops drilling under the shouted orders of an imperial army sergeant.

He stood at attention when he saw Rudi, started a salute, but stopped when he saw Rudi was not in uniform.

"Be at ease, Popp. I am not officially here. How are things going? Are we up to strength today?"

"Barely. As you know, the lads not resident in Prague have gone away for the summer. I understand the Polytechnic is in better state, but their arms are also deficient. And . . . well, it is hard on them to drill and drill and never any action." With a hopeful look he added, "Do you suppose the reactionaries will try to crush the revolution by force?"

"The reactionaries have their hands full with Italy and Hungary. It will be some time, I believe, before they turn their attention to peaceful Bohemia. In the meantime, it is essential to show the National Guard is in control, to deprive our enemies of disorder and riot as an excuse to assault. In that regard, I believe I have a plan that will require your people, and will provide some action as well."

Twenty-four

The next morning, Rudi found on the silver plate reserved for personal mail a note that proved to be from Sisi Vasovà.

Dear Moritz--have I offended you in some way? You were so cold and abrupt at Mme. von Silber's, and I was so happy to see you with the memory of last night still warming my heart. I spoke with Mme. about it but she could add nothing. My dear, I am dying to see you alone--do come by tonight or the next day, or, really, anytime. I have missed you beyond telling. If I am not at home, the girl will find me. Yours ever true, S.

It having been a warm day, no fire had been laid in the parlor, so Rudi had to descend to the kitchen and toss the paper into the stove, all the while thinking, that silly woman, to write so intimate and incriminating a letter!

The next morning, there was another note, and that evening another two, of increasingly desperate and extravagant tone-- what have I done, why so cruel, I must see you, and so forth.

Insane woman! He was glad she was revealing herself as a lunatic. It made it far easier to be virtuous.

During this period, moreover, even had he a mind to dally, he would have been sore pressed to find the time. On a warm afternoon--it was now the twenty-eighth of April--Rudi sat drinking beer at the Knight and made just this point to his drinking companion.

"This is the paradox of constitutional government, Novotny," he said, "that when we groaned under the tyrant's heel, we had boundless leisure, but now that we are free men, we have less time for ourselves than galley slaves. How many hours have we spent in this very place, talking and planning, yearning for the day of liberty! I worked, if I can even use that word, at an office that made few demands; you hardly worked at all. Now you must scurry to meet deadlines--what a dreadful word!-- so that the citizens may know what the government does, while I am the slave of committees. I labor from dawn till past midnight nearly every day. Don't you dare laugh at me! I am on the committee to draft the Bohemian constitution, and the committee to draft the National Guard regulations, and the committee to bring the Moravian tax system into accord with that of Bohemia, and the one to establish what shall be the national banner--a very grave matter--and besides all that I must try to turn a gaggle of young fools into an effective military force. Even now, as I sit here drinking, a little voice in my head urges me to put down my stein and scribble, scribble for the good of the revolution."

"Yes, it was indeed a better world when we were treated like children," said Novotny. "Should you expire of exhaustion at your desk, I promise I will raise a subscription to erect a statue of you in the town hall."

"Really? That makes it all worthwhile. I aspire to a life-sized equestrian bronze, me in uniform, brandishing my sword."

"I fear you have not enough friends for that. Perhaps a modest bust, though, showing you thinking futilely, in a quiet corner by the janitor's closet. But speaking of your sword, how is your miniature army faring? Any muskets yet?"

"Not enough. To answer your question, I think it goes well, for early days. I wish I had more Czech boys--it is not a national guard if it is all German--but my lieutenant, Popp, is Czech and that may attract others in time."

"Certainly you must not crush the aspirations of the proletariat with a nationally-unbalanced force."

"Forgive me, Herr Marx, but we do not intend to crush at all; we intend to keep the reactionaries from using class rioting as an excuse to send in the army to restore order. Prague is a small city with few workers within the municipal bounds. A hundred men, ready to move quickly, well-trained and disciplined, should be sufficient to pinch off any riots before they can gather real force. My study of the issue suggests to me that alacrity and firmness, if applied in the earliest stages of disorder, can suppress it, and that relatively few troops are required for this, if they know what they are about. So we train, and wait."

"I wish you luck in that case," said Novotny, "although you know what I think of student soldiers." He drained his beer and added, "What do you make of the news from Vienna?"

"What news? There is nothing out of Vienna but the usual gavotte of changing cabinet posts and obfuscation on constitutional issues."

"That is my point. The reactionaries are quiet, although we find them sliding their men into high places, Baillet-Latour at the war ministry, for example. Latour insists that Windischgrätz will not be employed at Prague, but we see no move to employ him elsewhere, although the army is now hard-pressed in both Hungary and Lombardy, and Windischgrätz, though a reactionary bastard, is one of the best and most efficient soldiers they possess. When a rook remains in place on the board, and seems forgotten, I suspect a stratagem or gambit is about to be sprung."

Novotny turned to hail a barmaid and Rudi saw that he had a white mark on his back, the size of a coin.

"You have a white spot on your coat," said Rudi.

Novotny craned his neck to inspect it and grinned. "It is mere whitewash and will sponge off. Journalism requires a great deal of leaning against walls and observing life passing by—this is the dire result. I suppose it is better than a black mark, although I have plenty of those hidden from sight." Both men laughed and Rudi took his leave.

On the first of May, Rudi woke early, was served a leisurely breakfast, dressed in his uniform, and took a fiacre to Baron von Pannau's. He was somewhat curious as to what the old fellow's reaction to his brass buttons would be.

It was a long stare, and, "By God, I could have sworn carnival was over, unless I have slept for more than a year. Possible, I suppose, at my age. Yet if it is not a fancy-dress party, why the devil are you in that costume?"

"It is not a costume at all, Herr Baron," said Rudi. "It is a national guard uniform. The national committee has seen fit to put me in charge of the Academic Legion, which is to serve as part of that body."

"The national guard, you say! And a major! What is the nation, pray tell, that this body of yours will guard?"

"Why, *our* nation. Bohemia."

"You amaze me, sir! I had thought that guarding Bohemia from its enemies was the duty of its sovereign lord, the king and emperor, and the task of the royal and imperial army."

"But we have had a revolution, Herr Baron. The revolution cannot depend for protection on the forces of the authority against which it has revolted. Therefore the people have constituted a new kind of force, directly answerable to

The old man's mouth worked, fish-like, for a moment, his eyes stared, a red tincture flowed up his face from his neck.

"By Christ, I should have known when I saw that blue stuff on your back. You are aping the god-damned Frenchies!"

"I am sorry you are vexed, sir," said Rudi. Nor was the sentiment mere convention. He was sorry indeed.

"Oh, to hell with that! You are a grown man and you may dress as a Red Indian for all I care. But I admit that it would sadden me to see civil strife again in a land that has not known it for two centuries."

"We all pray it will not come to that."

"Don't be stupid, sir! How can it *not?* You cannot have two armies in the same country without a fight. But to speak of swords--you have not got one, I see. How can an officer, even a Frenchified damned rebel, go out on the street without a sword? It is a disgrace!"

Rudi felt the stirrings of an unaccustomed anger and spoke with heat. "I beg your pardon, Herr Baron, but, as you yourself have just said, what concern is it of yours how I accouter myself? I cannot believe our present connection gives you leave to comment upon my person."

To Rudi's surprise, this comment had a remarkable effect on the baron. He grew pale, with bars of scarlet on the cheeks; his fists clenched, his jaw gaped, his body grew rigid in the chair. For a moment Rudi imagined that the old fellow was about to leap from his seat and strike a blow. Then, all at once, he seemed to deflate and came back into countenance.

"Of course," he said, "you will forgive me, I beg. I am attached to the profession of arms, d'you see? It offends me deeply to see it slighted by . . . improper usage."

"Yes, sir," said Rudi, " I quite take your point, and it is you who must forgive me. I am something of an amphibian, you see—both soldier and politician—and as politician I imagined going swordless might exhibit a peaceable disposition to certain elements of the population. Perhaps I erred. I will obtain a sword at the first opportunity."

"You did err, sir, with your *amphibian*. But you may correct that error in the present moment. In that corner there you will find a brass canister with canes, sticks, and such, and also a serviceable dragoon palasche. Pray, fetch it now."

Rudi put aside his notebook, stood, and fetched the saber, drawing it from the scabbard. By habit, he flicked the edge against a thumbnail; it was horribly sharp, as if it had been honed on a strap. He felt the old man's eyes on him and let his body take charge. Although he had not swung a saber in fifteen years, he found that he could still perform the motions of guard, left and right protect, the assault in four cuts and the rest, in what he thought was a credible manner. He was starting to sweat when he was done.

The baron said nothing, and Rudi offered, "I am rusty, it seems. This blade is a good deal heavier than a mensur saber."

"Yes," said the other, "because it is made to lop the heads off damned blue-coat Frenchy revolutionaries, not scratch the cheeks of young university gentlemen. No, damn me, that was unmannerly, sir; I beg your pardon. Come here and I will help you belt it on."

Rudi watched the wrinkled hands affix the rings to the belt.

"There, now you look a little more like an officer, although if you don't keep your point well up in the fifth position, you will be a headless one should you get into a fight. Which God forbid! And I beg you, do not dishonor the blade. It belonged to one dear to me."

"May I enquire, sir . . . "

"You may not. It will come out in its proper place in the story. Where had we got to? Oh, yes. That dinner."

Fritz Waldstein was, as I have mentioned, a younger son, and worse, a son of a younger son, and so had to make his own way in the world. But he was still a von Waldstein, and with this came the right to live in the greatest house in Bohemia, perhaps the greatest in the empire, for the renowned Marshal Albrecht von Waldstein, or Wallenstein as some call him, the scourge of the heretics in the old wars of religion, had built his palace at Prague to compete with the Hofburg itself. On the evening appointed, I was as usual at the theater, observing the preparation of Mozart's opera, and Mirek was supposed to come by so we could share a carriage to the Little Quarter and the Waldstein Palace.

From what I could gather, the opera was not progressing well. For some reason, Herr Mozart had not completed the score, and Signor Da Ponte had still not decided upon the matter of the final aria by the wicked Don. The kapellmeister, Herr Kuchař, was not happy with his trombones, or some such. The rivalry between my darling and Mme. Miceli had divided the company entirely, and Signor Bondini was at his wit's end to keep actual fighting from breaking out between the partisans of one or the other.

Da Ponte could have settled the business with a nod, but nod he would not, as he enjoyed (so said my darling) the power this gave him over her in lubricious matters. All operas were like this when first arranged, said Clotilde, but this one especially so, since neither Mozart nor Da Ponte could quite puzzle out whether it was to be a happy work or a tragic one. Later I was to discover that Austrian military operations were similarly muddled; perhaps it is our national character.

Mirek arrived while I was speaking to Clotilde, and here I noticed a phenomenon I have often remarked upon—the bosom friend and the lover rarely agree. She found him stuffy, proud, and chilly; he never expressed an opinion regarding her, of course, but I could tell he thought her little better than the girls at the Mounted Man, and he disliked her singing. He himself—did I mention?—had a singing voice much appreciated by those who cared: a tenor, I believe it is called.

As we were leaving, we made way for a gentleman in uniform and several uniformed retainers coming into the theater. One could tell he was the sort of official for whom way must be made, and when he had passed, I asked one of the theater people who he was. I was told that this was Conrad Franz Graf von Leiningen-Skorczy, the minister of police in Bohemia, and he had an eye for one of the company, a young singer in the chorus; I have forgot her name, but the *gentleman's* name gave me a strange chill, for it was the name of the bastard who had marred my face. Mirek noted my discomfiture and asked what was its cause, and I told him. He remarked, "Then your man must be the son or nephew of that fellow just passed. The police minister, hey? You do know how to pick your enemies!" I did not respond to this sally, but walked from the room within a dark cloud.

We left for the palace by hired carriage thereafter, arrived, and were conducted to Fritz's apartment by footmen bearing candelabras. I was given to understand that these were not the most desirable rooms in the Waldstein, being rather too close to the stables, but I found them magnificent enough, outshining by many degrees anything I had experienced before, at Pannau certainly and even at the Kinsky Palace itself. If buildings were made of glass, by the way, you could look through that wall there and directly into the salon where we gathered, so close are we to the place. Those are the Waldstein gardens you see through my conservatory window.

On the ride, Paradowski was peevish, as he sometimes became when having to do something he did not particularly like to do, and he gave me to know that dining with Seingalt or Casanova or what d'you call the fellow was not to his taste. I asked why, and with a glower he replied that of all men, the two of us should be the most reluctant to share a table with a rake, as rakery had ruined both our families and made us exiles from our native places.

"I acknowledge that," I said, "but if we restricted our fellowship to those whose character was perfect, we would be lonely indeed. Besides, I am ever curious about the former age, its manners and great men."

"You are only curious about whether you can get that girl alone," he retorted. "If she comes. Whatever happens, I intend to drink as much of the Waldstein's famous cellar as I can and trust you to carry me home."

I recall the palace clearly enough, but I shall not bother to describe it, as you can see it any day. I doubt it has changed a minim--these old families never spend a kreutzer on new decoration, except perhaps once each age. It possessed the usual sumptuousness of the era—everything gilt, portraits on the walls, gods and goddesses behaving unruly on the ceilings, candles, lines of liveried footmen in full powder. You cannot give parties like that anymore, I think, something gone from the world. It was not mere expense either—your bourgeois may spend more and serve a nicer dish—but we understood splendor and we had *manners*.

Well, to continue: we were the last to arrive. In the salon, drinking Champagne from those silly shallow glasses that were all the fashion then, and sitting in a circle on little gilt chairs, were Waldstein and the rest of the party. I had eyes only for Clotilde, who was seated next to the guest of honor, on the other side of whom sat Da Ponte.

Waldstein rose and did the introductions, and I made my bow to the greatest lecher in Europe. In the pride of my youth, Seingalt seemed to me an aged man, although he was perhaps sixty or so at the time and in good health to the eye. He did not strike me as handsome, not remotely to be compared with Paradowski, but he had something in his eye that attracted. As to his appearance, well, one expected, even desired, to observe upon his face the marks of a lifetime of infamous sin, but instead he looked like anyone else—a broad brow under his antique wig, a great prow of a nose, a thick-lipped sensual mouth . . . the eyes, however, were large, dark and lustrous, not at all the rheumy sunken things we expect in an old man. No, they were bright and piercing, the eyes of a much younger fellow, somewhat disturbing, really, almost unnatural. These eyes met mine, took in my poor visage, slid away, and fixed upon the face of Paradowski, where they remained, on and off, for much of the evening.

Now, we had come on purpose to see him, and I will admit he gave us a good show. I am susceptible to charm, you know--it comes from having been neglected and not brought up in society. When someone takes the trouble to pay me attention, I must take care or I am lost. He talked, in a not unpleasant Italian accent, with rather more use of his hands than is our custom, but in the most fascinating manner. He had a thousand stories that would have defied credibility in another man, but from his lips they had the ring of truth--the escape from the dreadful Leads prison of the Signoria; his pandering of the famous beauty, La Belle Morphy, aged thirteen, to King Louis of France; the debauching of a nun in a closely guarded island convent. And on and on.

I say we were all fascinated, but no: my Paradowski was not fascinated, except, if you will allow, the sort of fascination presented by a dead baby in a ditch or a public execution. I thought then that only the advanced age of the famed libertine and Paradowski's manners as the guest of a brother officer prevented my friend from provoking an actual fight with the fellow. What he did do, was that after the story about the nun, he got up and turned his back on the speaker. There was a bad silence for a moment, it stretched, and then, thank God, in came the butler to announce dinner.

During this time I, of course, had not had occasion to address my beloved. I should have said that, interspersed among Casanova's tales, Da Ponte added his miscellany of whorehouse anecdotes and other scabrous matter, along with elevated discourse about writing and philosophy, a deal of it in Italian, so that general conversation was impossible. I resolved to look for an opening to speak to her, or make one.

Waldstein, as our host, had the honor of taking in the only lady of our company, and when we entered the dining room I found, to my further dismay, that I had been seated a good distance away from Clotilde. Waldstein was naturally at the head of the table, grinning like the moon at what he had wrought. To his right sat the guest of honor, to his left Da Ponte; next to Casanova (of course!) Clotilde, and opposite Clotilde, Paradowski, on whose other side I myself sat. The other three dragoons made up the foot of the table.

I suppose it was one of the most remarkable dinners I ever attended. Once the wine had begun its flow, and it flowed like the Moldau in April, a certain good cheer made its appearance. The two Italians again dominated the conversation. Da Ponte proved himself prodigious learned and was the sort of fellow who wished this acknowledged—Vergil, Dante, Tasso dropped from his lips in great clumps. Little de Cavriani said it was like being in school and wished to shoot a spitball at the fellow, but forbore.

Casanova was no more than polite to Clotilde, or so it appeared, and I supposed that even he could think of no way to make love to her, had he possessed the vigor for it, with her protector mere inches away. He divided his attention between complaining to Waldstein about the way he was treated by the other servants at Dux, begging him to use his influence with the count, his uncle, and attempting to engage Paradowski in conversation, a somewhat suggestive one, as far as I was able to hear, compliments on his look and bearing, attempting to draw him out about his antecedents and career. I thought it strange indeed, the great seducer sitting next to the loveliest woman in Prague and casting hot eyes on a dragoon. Was it possible, I thought, that the old roué was also a visitor at Sodom?

"No," said Paradowski, when I broached this possibility *sotto voce*, "he is simply mischievous. I have enough experience with these old debauchers, as you can imagine. When the capacity diminishes, as in such cases it must, they perforce content themselves with arranging the amours of others. He was attempting to make me an admirer of your girl. I suppose it would amuse him to put horns on that Da Ponte, even at second hand. I suppose he would arrange to watch."

Meanwhile, Clotilde turned her attention to Hoth, on her left. Hoth, I should tell you, was something of a chilled herring. He was a card player, but not a gambler; that is, he was the sort who remembers what card has been played. A hard man to charm, but my darling did so nicely. They talked of cards and what it was like to slice a Turk with a saber and soon the conversation turned to food, for the waiters had brought in a dish such as I had never seen before, an Italian mess in honor of Casanova, a kind of rice gruel with truffles in it, that he called a 'risotto.' At the same time was served a mess of boiled noodles with a red sauce that Waldstein proudly announced was made of love apples, or pomodoros, and he swore it was good to eat and not poison, as several of us had been brought up to believe. Apparently they dine so in Italy, rice gruels and love-apples!

Nevertheless, we Germans were all more than willing to eat such fare when washed down with gallons of Pomerol. A kind of bombe arrived for our sweet at the end, made with rum, and there was Chateau Yquem in private crystal bottles with the Waldstein arms etched on. Many toasts, to beauty (my darling managed a blush!) to love, to wives and mistresses (may they never meet!) to honor, to the host, the regiment, the king-emperor.

Da Ponte spoke of his opera, and told the tale of it, that it started with a duel, and that the spirit of the man slain later inhabited a stone statue and drove his killer to perdition in the final scene.

"Why perdition?" asked Paradowski. "For rape I can understand--a vile crime to force a girl--but what crime had your Don committed against that Commandatore? They met on a field of honor, is it not so? They fought and one lost his life. It could easily have been the other."

"I deplore duels," said Da Ponte, "as being both stupid and unjust. Stupid because there is no argument that cannot be settled with reason; and unjust, because it often happens that a brute triumphs over a decent man."

"Forgive me, sir," replied Paradowski, "but that is a bourgeois sentiment. Duels are not about arguments and have naught to do with justice. They are entirely about honor. If I may be allowed to invade your province by means of a poetic figure--honor is like a tender plant. It is uprooted by Insult and must be replanted, with Apology the gardener. Absent this, it requires manuring with blood."

"What! You would kill a human being because he trod on your toe? Infamous, sir, infamous! How can there ever be free social intercourse, or any exchange of ideas, if we all must fear that some point of punctilio will lead to the murder of one of the company?"

At this, Casanova said, "So, my friend, is it that you feel there is no such thing as honor, in the sense our young officer has just used it, or that, while it exists, it cannot be blemished by the actions of others, or if it can be so blemished, said blemish cannot be repaired with violent combat?"

"Oh, of course there is honor," replied the poet. "But honor must arise from within, from the human heart. For example, I am a poet--Signor Bondini contracts with me and my musical colleague to produce an opera of a certain scope and style by a date certain. Our honor is that we are true to our word, that the work is of the first quality and so on. What else? One pays one's bills when one is able. One does not force a girl. One does not betray one's friends. One is true to one's genius. You note that all of these forms spring from my own action or failure to act. Spit in my face, call me liar, I care not--you play the fool, not I, and thereby deprive me of not a particle of anything that I own as honor."

Paradowski had been shaking his head like an ox bothered by blowflies while this was flowing, and now he burst out. "But that is *not* what is meant by honor at all, sir! You describe mere duty, mere decency, mere pride. Love may arise from the heart, but honor is bestowed by others and travels with gentility. A common man may be decent, a bourgeois may have wonderful manners, but neither possess honor in the sense I mean. The rule for being received into the society of honorable men is simple: a gentleman's person is inviolate, and any violator must apologize or face death; a gentleman does not lie, and if given the lie, must fight; a gentleman may not suffer an insult offered in public, if not followed by a sincere apology. It is a spiritual thing in the end, I believe, and when it is gone the man is too, and must blow out his brains."

The dragoons all applauded vigorously at my friend's impassioned outburst, after which there was a moment of uncomfortable silence, broken by Clotilde, who said, "Then it is a good thing the society of women does not allow duels, or there would hardly be a woman left alive."

We all laughed heartily at this, which served to banish what tension there was, and Waldstein took it upon himself as host to introduce a topic more agreeable to the poet. Addressing Da Ponte, he said, "Sir, let us hear more of your opera. I collect that it concerns a great libertine and a rogue, who is nonetheless the hero of your work. Is it proper to set up such a fellow as a hero?"

"In opera buffa, certainly, although my *Don Giovanni* is not entirely an opera buffa. It begins with a murder—a duel as some would say—which is not at all the thing in opera buffa. And yet it is comic in essence, and thus there is a certain ambiguity to the hero's character. Although he is vile, he is still the hero, and the strange thing is that we accept this. For, whether they admit it or no, men must admire one who acts as they would, had they the nerve. Imagine being of such kidney that, upon seeing a desirable woman, you would instantly devote the entirety of your being to one object, to conquer her, to possess her, not merely the body, but the soul, to make that woman love you. And then, when passion stales, to betray her with another, without a tint of conscience."

"Do you think such a man is admirable to any but another blackguard of the same stripe?" asked Paradowski.

"Secretly, yes," answered Da Ponte. "You see a lovely woman--Clotilde would be an example--instantly the nerves are alight with desire, one fantasizes what the woman would look like in her shift, in bed, by candlelight. And you pass on by, because in the world as it is, our lusts are constrained by custom, law and manners. We say we are not beasts, but the beast lives on in us. In the libertine, this animal nature is let run. And decent men, who would never violate custom, law, or manners, delight in seeing such fellows depicted on the stage."

"And must you pander to this depraved delight?" asked Paradowski. "Mozart writes music that opens the heart —and what poison do you pour into it then?"

I observed that my friend was a little drunk and unusually angry, and I could not figure the reason why. He was a dragoon, not a monk or a blushing virgin; and besides, who could care what happened in a made-up exhibition?

I said, "But the villain is punished in the end, I seem to recall. Does the statue of the murdered man not come alive and drive Don Giovanni down to Hell?"

"Oh, yes, yes, he certainly goes to Hell," said Da Ponte, "which should satisfy even the sort of morality practiced by those who frequent operas, but this does not answer the artistic question, which is the reason I have not finished my libretto, even at this late hour. I refer, of course, to what our Don must express when he sees he cannot escape his fate. That is, should he repent or should he show defiance to the last?"

"He should repent, of course," replied Paradowski.

Here Casanova, who was now for the first time in close conversation with Clotilde, turned and said, "Why 'of course?' Why would the man who has lived his entire life outside the bounds of morality repent at the last moment?"

"Simple rationality, sir!" replied my friend. "While the certainty of infernal punishment remains in doubt, your man can pretend it is merely mythical, meant to frighten the simple into proper decorum. But confronted by the actuality of divine punishment, who but an idiot would not fall upon his knees and beg God for mercy?"

At this Casanova laughed and said, "Thank God for wonders! A moralizing dragoon I never thought to see. Sir, I believe you argue from mistaken premises. That is, you believe God is concerned with where we humans place our private parts, not with whether we are good to each other, and forgive our enemies, and are kind to the poor, the widow and orphan, but just that, nay, *mainly* that. For who condemns the monster of greed, of sloth, of wrath? They are respectable gentlemen or decent tradesmen all. They are captains and kings, whom all the world honors. Only the monster of lust is condemned. And this cannot be the case, for God is not a fool. He has decreed that the love of money and not the love of pleasure is the root of all evil, but this does not suit society in its present form, nor the church that is the servant of the great.

"You see I have read the manuscript you kindly sent me, dear Lorenzo, and may I say it? Bravo, bravissimo! What wit! What elegance of design! I adore how the thread of tragic consequence runs throughout the book. Though, if I may say it without offense, even the best libretto must rest entirely upon the music. I daresay Herr Mozart had a good deal to say about the details. As in your *Figaro*."

"Oh, well," said Da Ponte, "one writes with Mozart as a fish swims in the sea—his art surrounds and informs every line. Every syllable is tested so as to work in perfect accord with the genius of his music. The general themes, the characterization, the broad movements of the plot are, of course, from *my* genius."

Laughter at this, and then Casanova began to discourse on those subjects, in such detail as to leave the rest of us behind. De Cavriani and Hoch were tossing bread balls at one another when Waldstein interrupted by saying, "But look here, Seingalt, this whole damned opera is about *you*, isn't it? You are Don Giovanni in life, or were. We don't have Idomeno, or Orfeo or Julio Cesare to talk to, or the fantastic kings and heroes that stuff all the other operas, but here you are in the flesh. So we may ask, has he caught you with his art? Are you offended? Delighted? Or indifferent?"

"An interesting question," replied Casanova, "but perhaps ill-posed. The figure of Don Juan or Giovanni of course predates my own career and is as fantastic as any creature of myth. Nor am I a Don Juan at all. Allow me to explain. I am a man who loves women. Yes, you may laugh, but do consider what am saying! Most men do not, if love means the appreciation, the caressing, of the whole female person. Most men are interested in that one thing, the last favor, and having attained it, they lose interest.

"As for the woman, if a wife, she may be a partner and the mother of his children, but as an object of fascination or even of the ordinary engagement arising from friendship, she pales in comparison to her mate's male associates, connections or rivals. The world of most men consists entirely of other men, except when the physical itch engages him, and then he but seeks the torrid little clam beneath the skirt.

"Your Don Giovanni is such a one. He keeps score, a thing I have never done, by the way, and by this we know that he does not care a whit for the humanity of the women he beds. I, however, am not at all like that. I fall genuinely in love. If I were in love with Mlle. Daumer here, and she demanded that I risk my life, I would do it, as I have many times, for love. And the girl loves me back. Together in this selfless passion, we open every erotic joy, especially those that are restricted to true lovers.

"It is true that love of this sort does not last. How can it? It is a product of nature, and like all of Nature's products, mortal. Would you eat bread a month old, or last year's egg? But during that period it is divine, and I can assure you that I have kept the friendship of nearly every woman whose body I have enjoyed. There are no Donna Elviras in my life."

"But does not Donna Elvira still love her Don?" asked Paradowski. "How is this, if, as you propose, he cared only for her what d'you call it?"

"As to that," replied Casanova, "you might as well ask why there is counterfeit money, and why it is so readily accepted by the unwary? Don Giovanni certainly exhibits the simulacrum of caring as part of his seductive art, and while this is perfectly false, it can capture the heart of a certain kind of woman. Donna Elvira in your opera is such a one. Consider, my friends: she has been loved by Don Giovanni, and betrayed by him. And yet she comes, she travels long, she desires but one thing, to have him back. Absent that, of course she will conspire against him, but she remains, as to amorous matters, his slave. As Donna Anna--a more ambiguous figure—is not. Has she been raped? Leporello suggests yes, but rape is clearly not characteristic of a seducer like the Don."

"Or yourself, one presumes," said Paradowski.

"Oh, dear me, yes! There is no point to rape from the perspective of a sensualist. Could anything be more distasteful then holding down a screaming, struggling girl while trying to push oneself into an unready orifice? One desires only the willing gift, as an enlightened church must desire only true converts of the heart. So I prefer to read the Donna Anna sequence as a failed seduction. In fact, you know, Don Giovanni does not succeed in seducing anyone during the course of the play. I wondered at the meaning of that."

"The balked lover is a comic figure," Da Ponte responded.

"Yes, but Don Giovanni is no Altamira from your *Figaro*," Casanova objected. "He wishes his own pleasure, of course, but he also wishes to dispense pleasure. That is what he does, and the real reason why such men are abused and resented is because once with him, no woman will be satisfied with the erotic services of the typical husband, boor or bourgeois. This is why Donna Elvira has traveled from Spain--she wants more! The morality in whose name the Don is reproached by the other characters is a mere sham. We bind the erotic world in chains because women of a certain class are property, and property must go where its owners send it, and behave as its owners desire. The true libertine thus stands as a liberator. With him, the woman can throw off the chains of property and claim her birthright as a free person, giving and receiving love and transcendent pleasure."

"But no society could survive such doings," I objected. "You might as well tell a man in a market that any goods he can filch are rightfully his."

"You but make my point, sir," answered Casanova. "There is a great difference between a loaf on a market table and the body of a woman. The latter is animated by a will, and all persons wish mainly for their will to prevail. All desire freedom as the chief good in life; your laws merely restrict this good to those who rule or who own."

"Among some of us that may be true," I objected, "but it cannot be that freedom is universally recognized as the chief good, at least not the freedom proclaimed by the libertine. Look about this very table! Five of the company are soldiers, who must recognize authority as compromising their freedom. Signor Da Ponte subordinates his will, and hence his freedom, to the dictates of Herr Mozart and his music. All civilization must operate thus, for in a society of libertines all would starve or be at each other's throats."

The Baron paused for a considerate moment, and added, "You know, now that I reflect on this colloquy, I believe that I was not arguing with Casanova so much as with myself. I suppose it took meeting the greatest libertine of the past age to show up my petty libertinage for what it was: the waste of a life."

"And did Casanova have an answer?" Rudi asked.

"Oh, I daresay he did, but I have forgot it, and who cares anyway! The answer to that question must always be the same--liberty goes with rank and privilege. There is no right to it, no more than there is a right for one man to have as much money as the next. It is the nature of the world to have great and small persons, and the great will ever have more freedom. Yet it is a wonderful thing when someone free by birthright binds himself through his free will in service of a greater cause."

It was in that moment, looking into the rouged and powdered face of Casanova, that the libertine ideal first began to die in me. To demonstrate that freedom was not a universal desire, I told them Hugh of Scotland's story of the cannibal kingdom and the happy folk raised for meat.

They were amazed by it, I can tell you, and the conversation remained with the bizarre tale during the conclusion of the meal and our removal to another painted and paneled chamber for our coffee.

Paradowski and the other dragoons were now drunk enough to render fine discourse a strain, yet my friend retained enough wit to argue passionately. He said, "This tale is savage indeed, for only savages could conceive of such an arrangement. The argument that the cannibal prison is a model of our natural world, thus bearable and no prison, is entirely specious. For the actual world is ruled not by a hungry cannibal chieftain but by the good God, and whatever travails we endure on earth will be made good in the end through His goodness. In the meanwhile, our freedom is a gift from Him, to be used according to His will. None but a peasant knave would be satisfied with a life of gorging, drinking, and lechery."

"Unless a noble dragoon," said Waldstein. "What hypocrisy, Paradowski, in the chief rake of the regiment."

"If I debauch myself, sir, it is my personal failing and I regret it," answered my friend. "It is the east, sir, and what we must do there in the Emperor's service, that drives me thus to seek oblivion. But if I were in your cannibal prison, give me what delights so ever, I would still bend every nerve to make my escape, though I starved thereafter in the trackless jungles. It is a matter of honor."

"How you do go on about honor!" said Clotilde after the brief pause that Paradowski's remark occasioned. "I am glad I have none left, being an actress, although I must say that I would not countenance a man who shirked a duel. And as for drinking and gorging, it has a natural result, to which I must attend. Waldstein, I suppose you have such a thing as a jakes in your fine pile?"

We all laughed, and Waldstein signaled to a footman, who led Clotilde from the room, but not before she had caught my eye with a glance whose meaning I could not mistake.

I slipped out some minutes later. Da Ponte was in close converse with Seingalt, arguing about the ending to *Don Giovanni*, and the others had got up a game of boston, so I was unobserved. In the hallway outside was a lone footman, in livery and powder, who gave me a certain look and with a slight motion of his chin directed me to a nearby door. I went in, and found a small receiving room or study, furnished with a desk, a Turkey carpet, and a little silk sofa. On the sofa was Clotilde. I went to her; we embraced, I showered kisses, which were not at all rejected. When I could again draw breath, I said, "You have not got the part."

"It remains still in the air, curse them all!"

"Then why this? Are you not afraid of his Italian wrath?"

"Oh, fuck his Italian wrath and all Italians in the bargain."

"Because Casanova ignored you?"

"Oh, *ignored* do you say! By Christ, he had his hand up my dress from near the moment I took my seat. Oh, and those words of his! We have heard of men speaking from both sides of the mouth; I thought it a mere figure, but here was an example such as I never thought to see in life. No, really, Hans, it was uncanny. In the very midst of this elevated palaver about the opera or what-you-will, he was sending whispers trying for an assignation."

"Why did you not make an outcry? Or shift your seat?"

"Oh, you know a woman is always the guilty one, at least to men like Da Ponte. He would say I encouraged the beast. And I did encourage him; for I can now understand his reputation as the great rake of the age just past. He knows how to touch a woman, with voice and fingers."

"Do not I, mademoiselle?"

"Oh, you are well enough--when directed; but he knew things that I myself did not. With that and perhaps the thought of old Da Ponte sitting there pontificating while Casanova diddled his mistress, I can tell you, he had me dripping. And so hot was I by the *baba au rhum* that I thought to myself, a cooling sherbet would go well just now. Truly, despite his art, old Seingalt did not get his assignation; no, he merely basted the goose on which you shall dine."

She gave a laugh, lifted her petticoats, undid my front, and sank down upon it with a great sigh. "To the hilt," she said amidst the gasping, "because when I get a certain way there is no help for it but a young fellow with a stiff prick."

I see you blanch a little now. I cannot help it, sir: that was how she talked, well, that was how we all talked when around actresses and whores. To resume: of course we were discovered, for, though I bade her often be quiet, she made a good deal of noise.

By and by, I felt a draught on my bare fundament, looked over my shoulder and there stood Da Ponte, Seingalt and the others of our party. I don't know why, but it occurred to me to call out, "A few more strokes, gentlemen, and I am at your service," and this remark sent Clotilde into a spasm of hilarity that, commuted to her privy parts, brought on my emission in the most delightful manner imaginable.

Unfortunately, the poor fool in his rage laid hands upon me. There was no nonsense about carriages at dawn. We fought then and there on a path in the Waldstein garden. You can see the spot from the window of my conservatory, in winter when the trees are without leaf. Clotilde clutched my arm as we made ready and swore that if I harmed the man she would never speak to me again. I took this to mean a withdrawal of the favors I had so lately enjoyed; for I could have done with somewhat less talk from the woman.

Pistols at twenty paces, but a Moldau mist had descended in the evening, and we could barely see each other. I believe he shot out a window. I fired into the air. And some days later Caterina Miceli sang Donna Elvira at the premiere of Mozart's opera.

Rudi finished scratching a line and asked, "But why, after putting you off so definitely and for so long, did she yield in a circumstance sure to foil her plans to gain the part?"

"Oh, well, the mind of any woman is unfathomable to us. They are driven by whim. And lust, of course, as in this case. Recall too, she was an artiste, and thus doubly fractious and unpredictable. As you may learn, sir."

This last line was delivered sotto voce, so that Rudi could pretend he had not heard it. The old man waited, as if desiring some comment from his amanuensis. Not receiving it, he resumed.

This farcical duel was but a comic prelude to an actual duel, whose outcome would change my life and place it on the path it was to follow thereafter. This occurred on the evening of the first performance of that damned opera. Did I attend? Of course I attended. I could have hardly have stayed away. One of the difficulties of having an actress for a mistress is that you must attend when she treads the boards and clap like a madman, and glare at anyone who is not similarly noisy.

Rudi said, "But I thought she had lost the part."

"Oh, she did. But Mozart later told me she could never have managed it. That B, you know, going flat. It was only Da Ponte who had kept her in the race. In any case, he decamped for Vienna right after our duel, something about an appointment with Salieri to dash off an opera or two. Bondini and Mozart felt badly for Clotilde, so they made her a principle dancer. There is a scene in which the country swains and their maidens flit about the stage and she had a turn at the front. She was actually a better dancer than a singer, or so Mozart told me. As a voice, she was not a patch on Sra. Miceli, and Mozart thought it cruel for Da Ponte to keep her hopes up. It was a done thing for the principals of the stage to get girls like that, with promises of parts and so on. We talked of this when we went riding on the day before the first performance."

"You rode with Mozart?"

"Oh, yes. They were pressing him to complete the overture. That is the music they play before all the singing starts. I thought it odd that he had not written the thing from the beginning, but I know nothing of such affairs, as you well know. We had a nice ride, out the Hofs Thur toward Zikanka. He only fell off once and was not hurt. I took him back at a slow walk to the villa of some friends of his at Smichov where he was staying. His wife, I recall, was hugely with child and not pleased with me at all. In any case, I presume he finished his work thereafter, for the opera opened as scheduled, on the twenty-ninth of October."

"So you attended the premiere of *Don Giovanni,* with Mozart conducting. My God, to have been in your place! What joy! I supposed you were bored."

"If so, I was hardly alone. In those days people attended the opera to ogle the girls, or if women, to show off their clothes and jewels and gather gossip. Where I was sitting you could barely hear the music for the chatter and the cries of the vendors selling sweetmeats and almond milk. I recall the duel in the first act, which held some interest, although it was not the sort of duel one sees in real life. There was much applause at the end, and my little man took a good number of bows at his clavier.

What transpired after the performance was the important part of the evening as far as my own story goes. Count Thun—that is, the grandsire of the present governor, gave a soirée for Mozart and the principals of the company, with the gratin of Prague in attendance. I was not invited, nor was Clotilde, so we, the other dancers and choristers, and their followers and my dragoons repaired to the Three Lions for our own rout. You must know the Three Lions--it is still in business on the Rathausgasse, and you will recall the tavern there, one large room with a coffered ceiling, and at one end a place for musicians and a floor for dancing. There is the long center aisle and the tables are arranged in alcoves, two or three in each. It is a convivial arrangement. At times.

We all danced with Clotilde. I can dance when required, as I believe I have mentioned, but alas, it gives me little pleasure. Paradowski was a splendid dancer, however, and it was better than stomping about myself to see the two of them whirling in the waltz. In a strange way, perhaps because our companions of the evening were artistes and thus *déclassé*, it was like attending a dance with one's peers, while at the same time it was like attending a peasant dance at Pannau, after the harvest, with just that air of profound relief flavoring the joy.

We were five at table-- Waldstein, Seingalt, Clotilde, Paradowski and me, and after an interlude of some hours-- you know how time flies on such occasions--Mozart came and made us six. He had his rooms in town at this very inn and I suppose the splendid occasion at the Thun palace had ended or grown tedious. I have no memory of the conversation, in case you thought to ask. Mozart and Casanova were gabbing away with one another, like old friends. I believe it was part of Casanova's art to always seem so to any new acquaintance.

He proposed a toast, to *Don Giovanni* and its triumph, and with it gave an appreciation of the opera that I do not recall, but I do recall feeling rather less of a man for the first time regarding the matter of music. Waldstein told me later that the old rake confessed himself ravished by the thing. I almost envied the pleasure he expressed and the fine discrimination he applied to the different parts of the opera--the music, the acting, and so on. I felt like a eunuch in a brothel, if you get the figure, uncomfortable and yearning, yet stone bored at the thing itself. This did not improve during later life, I fear. How many times have I sat on a little gilt chair, knees together, hands, gloved in kid, clasping the hilt of my sabre, while someone tweedled or plinked, wishing myself at Damascus!

Just after this prodigious toast we heard shouts, snatches of male singing and bursting coarse laughter, and into our alcove came a party of Neustadt cadets, white tunics a little spotted so late in the evening, their shiny black caps askew. They threw themselves down at the other table and howled for beer and schnapps. There were six of them, one of whom was Gerhard von Leiningen-Skorczky.

"What is the matter, my friend?" said Paradowski. "You have gone white as a tomb."

"That is him," I answered, "that big cadet with the red plume on his cap." Here I touched my nose and he nodded and commenced to stare at the fellow's back. But not for long. Leiningen-Skorczky happened to be sitting facing away from us, but in a trice the others at his table informed him of the beauty sitting close by and he shifted his chair around so he was facing Clotilde directly.

With an ape-like grin on his red face, he extended his paw to my dear one, and said, "Come sit with us, my beauty and I'll buy you a brandy. In fact, come sit here on my lap! This is a more distinguished company than the one you now keep. And perhaps there will be a trinket for you, if you're kind." His companions laughed and cheered at this.

I said, in the coldest voice I could manage, "Sir, the lady is with me. She does not wish your attentions."

At this, the fellow stared at me most offensively and then burst into harsh laughter. "Why, I know you, boy. It is the little von Pannau. I see you have not learned proper respect since I improved your face with my sword, nor have you learned to distinguish a lady from a whore."

At this, the blood of fury rushed to my head and I made to rise, but was prevented by Paradowski's hand grasping my coat. He addressed the cadet, raising his voice over the tavern's din. "So you are the man who ruined the face of a harmless boy. I have long wished to make your acquaintance, sir. I am not disappointed: I expected an ill-bred, unmannerly, gross boor and that is what I find. Curious that— Leiningen-Skorczky is a distinguished name in the empire, and I would venture, on present evidence, that none of that fine blood flows through your veins. Perhaps your lady mother opened her thighs to her coachman."

The cadet-captain's face grew redder and he said, "I do not know you, sir."

"This is easily repaired. I am Miroslaw Victor Fabian Paradowski, a nobleman of Poland and lieutenant of the Kinsky Dragoons. I am this gentleman's particular friend and I must insist that you apologize to him and to the lady."

Leiningen-Skorczky smiled menacingly and answered, "Particular friend, eh? You look like a catamite, sir, and a man who keeps a catamite has no need of so lovely a piece. Get you gone, puppy, or I'll have one of the barmaids throw you out."

In an instant Paradowski was on his feet. His saber flew from the sheath.

"I believe we may dispense with the formalities, for you are hardly enough of a gentleman to warrant them. Draw, sir, or by Christ I will beat you like a dog out of this tavern and down the street."

The cadet-captain's smile grew broader and he rose slowly from his chair. Addressing his companions, who had grown silent at this turn of events, he said,

"Gentleman, you will now see a reprise of the lesson, of which I have often spoken, that I administered to that

Pannau lout not long since." He drew his own sword and advanced on my friend, who skipped backward until he stood in the center aisle of the tavern. The hubbub of carousing died away. People stood on chairs and tables. Someone shouted that they were calling the guard and that this was a respectable place that did not allow brawling.

I myself was on my feet now, fingering my own sword. I caught Waldstein's eye and said in a desperate tone, "Good Christ, Waldstein, he cannot fight with a palasche against a small-sword. He will be cut to ribbons."

"True in general," said Waldstein, "but not in the present case. Calm yourself, my dear, and observe."

I sat down. Paradowski had taken his stance and it was a clumsy one, with the saber drooping at the point as if it were already too heavy. Was he drunk? I glanced over at Waldstein, who appeared perfectly composed. Leiningen-Skorczy now began his attack: beat, beat, lunge on the low inside line, parried in prime, no riposte from Paradowski, a lunge to the low outside line parried in seconde, again no riposte. What was wrong with the man? The cadets were cheering their captain lustily; from our party, not a sound. Leiningen-Skorczky's tactic was clear, the very one he had used on me—under pressure on the low lines, the opponent's point naturally tends to droop, setting up a devastating fleche to the head after a low feint. Here was the feint—Paradowski's sword tip obediently drooped, and Leiningen-Skorczky launched himself through the air, his sword point heading unstoppably toward my friend's wonderful face.

You will be amazed at what happened next, sir: Paradowski simply vanished. I was looking at him, my heart in my teeth, and then he was not there but pressed up against his rival's belly with near a yard of saber sticking out of the bastard's back in the center of a growing circle of scarlet. On Leiningen-Skorczky's face, now blanched like any steam pudding, the usual expression of surprise: dead upon his feet. The defeated sword fell to the floor with a clatter, and then, slowly, its owner followed.

It was the *passata sotto* that did it, one of the most difficult and dangerous moves in fencing—one drops almost to the ground and shoots forward at knee-level, sword extended. If done right, the point goes in just over the belt and upward to the heart. If your man's sword is high, he has no defense, but if you do not perform it perfectly, you are a dead man yourself.

After that, we all made our escape, but if you wish to learn how, and what occurred as a result, you will have to come again. Tomorrow, if you can manage it, for I detect a fading of the strength I have lately received from my doctor's elixir. We will have to scurry, I believe, to get my whole story told before the long silence that cannot be far off.

Twenty-five

On his return, Rudi knocked on his own front door and to his surprise it was opened not by Hilda but by a thin blond girl in an apron and clogs. Mutely she held out her hands, and he deposited his hat and stick in them.

"Where is Hilde?" he inquired.

"Went to fetch eggs, sir. Cook dropped and broke 'em all and Hilde went off t'market. I can't be trusted with money, sir."

"I am sorry to hear that. What is your name? And how long have you worked for us? I do not recall seeing you here before."

She stared at him silently, her mouth slightly open.

"Your name?" he said again, in Czech this time, and slowly.

"Lidunka, sir," replied the child.

"Well, Lidunka, when you come in the hall, you should wear shoes, not clogs." Silence at this and a trembling of the lower lip.

"You do have shoes, do you not?"

"No, sir. Sorry, sir."

"There is nothing to be sorry about, child. I will tell cook to buy you a pair. Now, run along."

The girl vanished, clattering destructively across the parquet. Rudi walked through the parlor, as had long been his habit upon returning home. All was in good order, dusted, swept, mopped and polished, but there was a curious dullness to the place. It was serviceable but not a home, not without Berthe's presence and absent the stomping and cries of the children.

He stood for a moment before a Meissen figurine, the great treasure of the house, quite old and signed by Kändler himself. The Moritzs had purchased it for themselves on their honeymoon at a ridiculously high figure, rather as a gesture of defiance to the Fathers, who were bound to deprecate so much useful capital tied up in a breakable frippery.

The figure was large, nearly a foot high, and depicted a shepherdess of the disguised aristocratic sort bending at the waist, laughing, and dangling the blue ribbon of her straw hat for the amusement of a white cat. What was even more wonderful was that the shepherdess was the image of Berthe Moritz—the same blonde sausage curls, the same high curving forehead, the same little pointed nose and the same smooth, plump ivory line from the jaw to the neck. The same little round breasts as well, although this was not publicly remarked upon in the house. The children accepted without question that it was Mama.

Rudi touched its tiny face. Why am I here and not with her? he thought. Where they are is home, Berthe and the children, and this is a mausoleum without them. What a fool! But not for much longer.

He had his supper served at his desk and ate it in his dressing gown, smiling at what Berthe would have said had she witnessed this degenerate practice. He turned to his mail. A letter from Berthe! She wrote every day; he replied every day, sometimes twice in a day. He used all the eloquence in his power and it often took several drafts to create the effect he wanted. This writer was, of course, the other Rudi, the one who had not dallied with a Czech singer in low taverns, the man he had been all his previous life. This man was the faithful husband and father, the proper sane and domestic Rudi, who was working like fury to complete his work and be with them again. And this Rudi was successful! Prague was a beacon of freedom and amity. All was cooperation and peace between the nationalities and the classes.

A great many lines, a majority in some letters, was devoted to the theme of longing, and here Rudi used his not inconsiderable literary skill to portray a man separated from all he loved best in the world, to praise his wife, to expatiate upon her virtues, both moral and physical. Here he did not disdain the frankly erotic, calling up particular incidents in their mutual past when they had achieved marital ecstasy. The love poetry of Herder, Novalis, Schiller speckled these pages and he promised over and over that it was only for a little time, that his business here was near done, he would be at Kunningshelm in time for the roses of June.

In so writing, Rudi was not in the least conscious of dissembling. As the lines flowed onto the page, a smile touched his lips, for the writing enabled him to dwell for a time in the persona he had abandoned, and to forget his shame, his disappointment and his growing fear. An unsympathetic observer might have condemned this as hypocrisy. But Rudi had not a hypocritical bone in his body; what afflicted him was a form of insanity, the trading of lived reality for a world made of words on paper. After he wrote and sealed and kissed his letter, he made a quick copy and slipped it into the portfolio that held Berthe's, so that he might not forget what he had already covered when writing the next.

As he put the portfolio away in its drawer, he noticed a sheaf of papers lying there and recalled that it was the material Novotny had found in the military archives concerning Baron von Pannau-Kinsky, which he had put aside half-read. He now corrected that omission.

How odd, he thought, here is the paper man--the bureaucratic shadow of the opinionated, obstinate, but oh, so fascinating person whose life I have been taking down these past weeks. Can there be anything in this that might shed light on the peculiarity of our present connection?

The pay records stopped sometime in 1820, as Novotny noted—ah, here is the very memorandum--pay records transferred by order of the Hofkriegsrat to the confidential budget. Well, we supposed he had become a police official. But it is simply out of question that this connection is part of a plot to compromise Rudi Moritz. It must be something else, something deeper—but what?

He read on. Précis of correspondence, requests for leave, recommendations of junior officers, requests for registration of marriage, request for transfer of married officer to 13th Dragoons--wait, what was this? The fellow's name was Karl Rudolf Freiherr von Pannau-Kinsky, cornet, transferred in on May 14, 1812, listed as married. Unusual for an officer so junior to wed; the Colonel von Pannau-Kinsky, as he by then was, had clearly put himself out to help the young man. A nephew, perhaps, or someone from a distant branch of the family. Or the son? He did mention a son, did he not? Nepotism in any case, all too common.

He tossed the papers down, growing restless. The evenings were particularly empty. In the past he had gone out often enough, sometimes until quite late, talking politics with his friends at the Knight. He could do the same now, but something held him back. Somehow, while they all cheered freedom from the front door, a poison had seeped in from the window. Novotny thought Liebig was a spy, Liebig thought Novotny was, and Jasny thought Rudi was. He felt as if some great spider was squatting in the center of a vast web, that he and all his friends were being controlled and drawn slowly to their dooms. But who was this spider?

As he wracked his brain, his gaze fell on the sword given him by the baron, the ease with which Wulfi Speyr had been checked, and the answer came. Who else could it be?

He jumped up and paced. The damned room was too small for his angry energy. How dare they! How dare that old man think to work him like a puppet! It was clear now: he'd been played. The baron, under the guise of amiability, was using him as a stalking horse. He had made a great show of pulling Speyr's teeth—but had he? Speyr clearly still had him under observation and continued to seek information about the other revolutionaries, sowing discord as he did. *Divisio et imperae,* indeed! All considerations of legality sloughed off in that moment; if they wished to play a dark game, others could adopt the same rules. He paced, he thought violent, unfamiliar thoughts, and after a no more than five minutes, a plan sprang into his mind.

Throwing off his dressing gown, he donned his uniform, clipped on the borrowed sword, and hurried out of the house, using the tradesman's entrance in case Speyr had thought to post watchers. He found a fiacre and promised the man handfuls of kreutzers if he would hurry. The cab clattered over the Charles Bridge, stopped at the law courts, was told to wait. Rudi dashed into the entryway, startling the custodians, but no one dared to stop an officer in uniform. A few minutes in his own office—he knew just where to find what he required. Then out again, back over the bridge to the Charles University.

He found young Popp in his rooms, explained what he was about, stressed the necessity for security and speed, for unaccustomed, non-Austrian alacrity. None of the ten student-soldiers roused for the task were to be told what it was about—only to dress in uniform and to obtain—the means not specified, but naked theft not ruled out—a wagon with two horses to pull it.

While Popp dashed out to do his bidding, Rudi violated his oath of office and committed a criminal act at the student's desk. He had not long to contemplate the deed, for Popp had proven resourceful.

"We have a brewery wagon and two strong horses," he declared on his return. The young man's face was flushed with excitement. Rudi, in contrast, was remarkably cool, as if the whole affair had nothing to do with him. He wondered at this, briefly, before concluding that it was his anger that made him so, and that it was in all a good thing. Coolness would be required this evening.

Rudi's cab was trailed by the wagon loaded with ten uniformed students as it made its way to an obscure warehouse at the foot of Vhesehrad. The watchman might have been surprised at the arrival of a requisition for a company's worth of equipment at this hour, but the appearance of the major in charge of the detail and the perfection of the requisition order, with all necessary stamps and signatures, left him no choice. One hundred twenty 1843 model percussion-cap muskets, with all necessary ammunition and accouterments, were duly delivered into the hands of the young men.

Back at the Charles, cheering for their bold commander, the students deposited their new equipment in a basement storeroom amid piles of moldering books. Rudi swore them to secrecy and promised that, starting tomorrow, the Academic Legion would begin to drill in a new way.

He left for home with hurrahs filling his ears, feeling better than he had in a good long time. Whistling Mozart's *Non più andrai*, he walked through his front door and up to his bedroom, where he stripped off his uniform and donned a dressing gown and slippers. He was brought up short by peculiar noises coming from Berthe's bedroom. Was that weeping? It must be; and the scrape of furniture against floorboards.

He went to the door and flung it open. Sisi Vasovà, her face unattractively mottled with crying, was standing on a chair with a noose around her neck. The end of the rope was affixed to the finial atop Berthe's tall wardrobe. Their eyes met. Before he could say a word, she jumped off the chair.

"Should you wish to hang yourself," said Rudi a moment later, "you would fare better with a shorter rope or a higher chair."

Vasovà, who had delivered herself standing onto the rug rather than to Eternity, uttered a despairing cry, and with a poisonous look at her unwilling host, flung herself forward violently. The rope snapped taut, suspending her rigid body at an angle of about forty-five degrees to the ground. Her face grew dark, her tongue protruded, she began to hang in earnest. Rudi vaulted over his wife's bed, shoved Vasovà upright with one arm and with his free hand yanked the stiff rope downward with all his strength. The finial, not meant for such abuse, snapped clean off and Vasovà dropped face-down upon the carpet with a loud thump. Rudi loosened the noose, and turned her over.

"You silly woman! Whatever possessed you to try such a wicked thing? And why in my wife's bedroom? Who the devil let you into my house?"

Vasovà could not answer these questions for some time, as she was simultaneously coughing and weeping in the most energetic fashion, and in the intervals between coughs protesting the continuance of her life. Eventually, the sobs died away, and she heaved herself into a sitting position. A trickle of blood depended unattractively from her nostril to her chin.

In a cracked voice she said, "I did not know it was her bedroom. I wanted yours. But you had arrived. So I used the curtain cord."

"Why my bedroom, for God's sake?"

"Because there would have been a razor there, of course."

"A razor? You proposed to slit your throat in my bedroom?"

"Yes." She rubbed the red mark that encircled her throat. "I will go now."

With that, she rose to her feet and dashed toward the window, which had been opened, the day being fine, and she would have plunged thirty feet into the alley below had Rudi not sprung up and grabbed her from behind. She howled, they struggled, and in the end Rudi managed to fling her onto Berte's white counterpane, clutching both her wrists and pinning her under the weight of his body, but not before she had marked his face cruelly with her fingernails.

"Stop this," he cried, "stop this instant, you stupid woman!"

"Kill me!" she cried, "oh, kill me! Strangle me with your hands if you will not let me do away with myself!" The blood on her face had smeared and she had the look of some maenad just finished feasting on the flesh of Hippolytus.

"I said, stop it!" he shouted. "I thought you were a woman of the world, for God's sake. Did you really imagine our connection had a future? It had to end and I ended it. Did I ever give you any encouragement? Did I ever give you any hope that I would leave my wife and family for you? Have some sense, woman!"

She turned her head away and in the same cracked voice, but very low, she said, "No. I never dreamed that. I have that much sense. I only wished a little portion of you. To have it snatched away without cause . . . and I have given you no cause, Rudi. We have been good together, yes? When I saw you at Mme. von Silber's, my heart came alive in my breast and then you were so cold to me, Rudi, not the ghost of a smile, and you ignored my letters and I knew I was discarded. Truly, I did not think you would discard me in such a manner. It drove me mad to be thrown aside like that and I wished to live no longer. Let me up, please. I am quite collected."

Rudi relaxed his grip. The odor of roses filled his nostrils. He stared at her face, which had the expression of a child who has been slapped and does not know the reason.

"But why?" he demanded. "Do I really mean that much to you?"

She sat up on the bed and looked into his face. "You only ask that because you have no idea what the life of a woman like me is like, or of the swinishness of the men who wish to possess me, and here I include many who spring from fine families, rich men with that dear little tit on the front of their surnames. How I am treated you cannot imagine, the contempt they have for the skinny Böhmer with delusions of art. The Böhmers are worse. No respectable Czech lady would give me the time of day, and the men are as bad as their *skopčák* masters. And among the artists, where one would think there would at least be respect and fellowship, there is none, there is but mockery and denigration and astonishment that a *piča* would aspire to poetry. It doesn't matter if you say Sappho was a cunt too; they care not a whit for

Sappho and her unnatural ways." She sighed. "Ah, it was that cartoon, wasn't it, that made you hate me."

"I don't hate you," said Rudi. "It is Jiskra I despise, and if I ever get my hands on him . . ." He regarded her more closely. "Do *you* know who the damned fellow is? Or, more to the point, why he should want to blast me in print? I had thought we were comrades."

"What can I say? The man is mad for me, and I confess to a certain tendresse in return. Since I took up with you, however, he has been your enemy as well as your comrade."

"Who is he?"

"I really have no idea. He is always in disguise, a creature of dark places, ever in shadow. Not like you, who shines clear. What a pure heart you have, Moritz! Do you remember that night we met, at the Red Goose? The best conversation I ever had in my life--with a man. You do remember, don't you? My God, how I tormented you, mocked you, accused you of nefarious designs on my faded virtue. And you smiled and were happy to listen to this chatter, and I realized that you were listening to me, actually interested in what I had to say, and did not regard my conversation as something to be got through before you could get up my skirts. Christ in heaven! You even compared me to the Grimms! And then at von Silber's, you did not have that expression on your face when I spoke, as if watching a performing dog, that all the other men wore . . . My God, I would have loved you for that alone, but then you bought for me that lovely meal, and gave me just for the asking fifteen florins, without proposing, without *insisting* on the usual reward. Oh, my dear, how many times have I been pushed against a wall by a drunken bastard wanting payment for his fucking cutlet and stein of beer!

"And when I finally got you into my bed, oh, my good Christ! I was terrified and angry with myself, and I kept thinking, a married German bourgeois, Sisi, what are you doing! I cursed and abused you, do you recall, at the height of my passion . . . Oh, and what passion! Do you know, you make love like a young boy in the first flush of romance. It undid me, it drove me mad with love--and fear, because even in the moment of melting and consummation I foresaw this day."

"I am sorry," he said. "I did not mean you any harm."

"Of course you did not. It was I who seduced you, and not the other way round. This is all upon my head. You are the kindest, best man I have ever had anything to do with. And of course you are married and love your family and all that, and I tell you, from my deepest heart, for I am as far beyond shame as it is possible to be, that I care not a pin for all that. I wished only for a piece of you, a fragment of the roast such as poor peasants are given on Sundays at the kitchen doors of great estates. I would have been content with that, with such broken meats. But you snatched away even that.

"Let me up, please. I am myself again and will cause you no further trouble."

"Oh, do sit down!" said Rudi with a baleful glance at the pfennig of red blood on Berte's immaculate white coverlet, "you can't go with a bloody face. You look like Charlotte Corday."

"It is appropriate, somewhat, for I also thought of killing you. I imagined slipping in here at night, cutting your throat, and then my own. I had the note all written out, with a poem too."

"A pretty thought! And why did you not carry out that plan?"

"Lidunka. That is how I came to be here. Yes, I bribed your poor scullion. With a cream cake. Can you imagine? The child had never had a cream cake in her life. I enticed her with one, and then promised half a dozen if she would let me in through the back stairs. Had I done for you, my dear, the poor little beast would have been taken up as a conspirator and hanged! I was one much like her in my early life, except I was not stupid. And you bought her a pair of shoes! So you were saved by a flood of sentiment."

Rudi by this time had poured water from the ewer in his room into a basin and was using a dampened handkerchief to dab away the blood from Vasová's face. She sat unmoving, her eyes shut, a contented smile on her face. When the last livid spot was gone, he dried her, and said, "There! You can go greet the world unsullied with gore."

She opened her eyes, sighed and said. "Was that the last touch I will ever have of you? Oh no, it cannot be!" She seized his hand and pressed it to her lips.   W h a t Rudi felt at that moment he could not have described, for he had felt nothing like it before in his life. He had read, of course, of being carried away by love, and the Baron's narrative had demonstrated that it actually happened in life; now it happened to him. He still loved Berthe and his family: they were a permanent part of the man he was, like his left foot. But this man now understood that he would die if he could not also possess the half-mad woman covering his right hand with kisses and tears. It was if the old Rudi had walked into the inner house of his soul and found a stranger there, who insisted against all reason that he too was Rudi Moritz, and that he would be making some changes in the establishment.

It occurred now to Rudi that this new fellow was not the least like the bourgeois, uxorious Moritz: husband, lawyer, householder, and passionate liberal. He was more like the strange fellow who had just stolen ten dozen new muskets from the Royal and Imperial Army. This person was free to do as he pleased and, if the world as it existed did not allow this, could change the world to suit him. The former Rudi now seemed to retire to a comfortable seat in the parterre, content to watch the opera that had become his life.

The new man felt his heart pound, his breath quicken, his groin plump with desire. Without a word he grasped Sisi Vasová into his arms, pushed her back on the bed and pressed his lips to hers. They writhed there for some minutes, kissing, gasping, plucking one another's clothing away, baring their tumid flesh.

"No, no," she said, "not here, not on the *bed*."

She slid off, onto the carpet, raised her knees, lifted her skirts to her belly, smiled her crazy smile. "You monster," she said, "My kitchen scrap! I thought I'd lost you."

"I require a horse," said Rudi to Baron von Pannau the next time he was summoned. "I thought you could advise me."

There had been several summonses during the past week, which Rudi had ignored, but the old man had not adverted to this lapse, nor had Rudi offered any excuse. You old spider, thought Rudi: you may do your worst, but by no expression or word of mine will you discover that I am on to your tricks.

"I could," replied the baron. "When do you need it?"

"Now, actually."

"My first advice then is not to be in a hurry when buying a horse, unless you want a horse that can never hurry. Whence this urgency?"

"I am engaged in training the Academic Legion to suppress rioting and keep the peace. I require the ability to move rapidly from one formation to another, and I believe a horse is usual for officers in such circumstances."

"I see. Well, ordinarily I would send to my grand-nephew at Pannau and have him select a mount from our stud, but if time presses, I suppose we could visit the riding school at the Hrad. There is always some impecunious officer there anxious to get shot of some blood animal. We might go, say, the day after tomorrow."

"We? But, sir, I would not impose . . ."

"Nonsense. It is no imposition, and it will do me good to smell a horse again. It is settled. Now, where did we leave off?"

Rudi consulted his notebook and said, "Your friend Paradowski had just killed your tormentor in the Three Lions."

Yes, the scene at the tavern. Well, of course, an uproar ensued. The late Leiningen-Skorczky's friends were all on their feet shouting for blood, their swords out, and we, that is, myself, Mirek, and Waldstein, were also up, swords in hand.

I suppose there might have been a general bloodbath, had not Casanova jumped from his seat, cool as a damp stone, thrown his arm around Clotilde and marched her off toward the back of the tavern. Mozart, his face whiter than his neck cloth, followed them, and then the three of us followed, with our sword points menacing the cadets. The pursuit was not vigorous, since it was clear to our foes that Paradowski alone could have done for all of them in a trice. I had no notion of our direction, but Casanova clearly had a plan, and we followed him like sheep. Curious that: in a confused melee the advantage is always with whoever devises the first plan. It hardly matters if it is a good one, for it can be changed at need thereafter. But almost any plan is better than milling about. I took the lesson to heart.

He led us through the kitchen of the place out into an alley, down another alley and out into a street, which we discovered was the Fischlergasse. We heard hoof beats on cobblestones and the jingle of harness and withdrew into the shadows as a party of mounted police trotted by.

"The police already," Casanova remarked. "I am surprised. Who was the man you killed, Herr Leutnant?"

Paradowski told him and added, "He is a close relation of the police-president of Bohemia."

"Wonderful. I too had a habit of powerful enemies. It makes for a peripatetic life, and I advise you to make enemies only of the feeble hereafter. For now, we must manage our escape. Does anyone know how far away is the Nostitz theater?"

Clotilde answered at once: "This is Fischlergasse. If we follow it to Kolowratsgasse, then it is just across the Fruit Market square."

"We must go there at once."

"Nonsense!" cried Paradowski. "We must return to the regiment. Our colonel and two squadrons are at Řepý for field exercises. We must get our horses and ride there immediately."

"Yes, and be caught immediately," replied Casanova. "Think, man! You have been seen in your regimentals, so there will be no doubt as to where you belong, and the first thing our police-president will do is alert the sentries at the town gates. No, we must repair to the theater."

"Why there?"

"Because no one will think to look there, and because we will never get out of this town except in disguise. And the theater is the home of such illusions."

The argument was unanswerable and so we repaired thence, by stealth, moving in pairs from shadow to shadow. There were many such, for Prague at that time was not as well-lit as it is today. At last we reached the Nostitz. Knocking at the stage door brought a servant, whose irritation gave way to deference the moment he recognized Mozart. The musician then conducted us to the dressing room of the prima donna, as being the most capacious private chamber and convenient as well for Casanova's stratagems.

"A moment, sir," said Rudi. "Why was Mozart fleeing with you? He was a famous personage—why did he not simply return to his rooms?"

"You say that only because of the glow of honor that has attached to him in the years since. Back then we counted any musician little better than a servant. He had been seen, and had those cadets laid hands on him, they would have kicked him to death. May I continue?"

Yes, Casanova looked us over, like a fellow examining a string of horses. At last he rubbed his hands together and said, "We will be a merry group returning from the opera to a country estate in, let us say, Strodulk. We will have two servants with us. Herr Leutnant Waldstein--I believe a Figaro costume will fit you."

"What I, a servant? Never!"

Casanova ignored this. "I will be a priest, to provide countenance, nor will it be the first time I have played that role. But wait, is there an opera that requires the costume of a priest. Perhaps not . . . "

Mozart spoke up. "There is the opera Paisello wrote on *the Barber of Seville*, the Beaumarchais play. It has a character called Don Basillo, who is a kind of bad priest or charlatan and I believe they did it here some seasons past."

"Perfect!" said Casanova. "A bad priest and a charlatan! I will hardly need an actor's skill. As a reward, Herr Mozart, you will wear another servant's livery from the *Figaro*, to match Waldstein's. And please to find a violin! Fräulein Daumer will be a pious lady of the type that is always found alongside a certain kind of priest.

"It would take a very stupid sentry to believe me that," said Clotilde.

"Or one familiar with the ways of certain priests and pious ladies," said Casanova. He continued, "And then we must have another couple, which will serve to solve our most serious problem."

"What do you mean, 'another couple,' asked Paradowski, "for there is but one woman among us. And to what serious problem do you refer?"

"Look at the glass, sir!" replied Casanova, pointing to the mirror. "In all Prague are there two more unforgettable faces? Baron von Pannau has his unfortunate disfigurement, of course, while you, Lieutenant Paradowski, look like the Belvedere Apollo. But in a wig and a gown the case is different; make-up will give the baron a new face, suitable for the spouse of so lovely a girl."

"You are mad, sir," my friend responded, "if you think I would escape disguised as a woman. I fact, were our situation otherwise, I would have satisfaction from you for the mere suggestion."

A strained silence fell here, until I broke it by saying, "I will be the woman. Necessity demands it, for I am obliged to protect Fraulein Daumer, an obligation that must supersede any other claims on my honor. The Chevalier is correct—the authorities will be searching for two officers, two gentlemen, a musician, and a beautiful woman, and we must be entirely other than what we are in order to escape them. But, what of Clotilde, speaking of memorable faces?"

"Oh, that is nothing," said Clotilde lightly. "A wig, some paint, my art all together, and my own mother would not recognize me on the street. You would not credit it, I know, but I can seem as plain as a pancake at need."

"Very well," I said. "Where is my gown and head dress?"

"Oh, dear Pannau," said Paradowski, " I cannot possibly allow this. As Seingalt has said, look in the glass! The sacrifice is mine to make, another curse laid upon me by these pretty looks. Enough chatter! Now let us prepare ourselves!"

It took less time than I would have thought. We stood about in that room when it was done and gaped at each other and at ourselves reflected. I had a pale but unblemished face under a macaroni's plumed hat and a deep-blue costume that had once graced the back of Count Altamira. Casanova looked as authentic as most real priests do in a soutane and biretta. Waldstein and Mozart had, remarkably, achieved the mien of servants—the former being the officious interfering sort and the latter the kind who is diffident and obliging. Waldstein was sent off, still wanly protesting, to hire a closed coach for six and Mozart was dispatched to carry messages to Lennart and Paradowski's servant, Wojtek, telling them of our situation and arranging a rendezvous.

The last to emerge from transfiguration were Clotilde and Mirek, who had refused any help in dressing. I tell you, Rudi, it was uncanny. Clotilde had made herself into a plain, brown-haired woman with a too-long nose and a splotchy complexion. Mirek, in yellow ringlets and a mulberry satin gown, was enough like a pretty young woman to fool even a close observer. Casanova gave him just such an inspection, so near as to be offensive. I thought I could hear Mirek's teeth grinding. Casanova confessed himself satisfied with us all, but to Paradowski he said, "Your expression is altogether too masculine, sir; or mademoiselle, I should say. Relax your face, think only of dances and dress, smile winningly and let us hear a tinkling laugh."

Though I heard Mirek say to me, under his breath, "I will kill that man someday," still he was a good soldier and produced a smile and a tinkle with the same élan he would have used to charge a troop of Turkish *sipahis*.

Soon Waldstein returned with the coach, a musty berlin. We found some flags from a production of *Rodrigo*, cut the escutcheons from them and glued them to the panels of our coach with dry oil, to show that quality rode within. Mozart returned at last, breathless and red-faced, to tell us that our lodgings were as yet free of police and that he had encountered no difficulty in delivering the messages. Oddly enough, Lennart had been found with all our goods on a cart already, but we did not know the reason at the time.

It was nigh on midnight when we set off. Casanova, as the great escaper of the age, plotted a devious route. Because we intended to go south and west of the city, we headed north, through the great market square and the quiet streets of the New Town, up to the fortress of Vyšerad, that guards the northern approaches to Prague. It was a brilliant stroke, for Vyšerad was manned by the army rather than the police, and although they must have been alerted about the fugitives, they were not looking for a coach full of noisy revelers, with a servant up on the box fiddling away. They passed us through laughing, with wishes for a safe journey.

At the Moldau ferry, however, there was a patrol of mounted police. Their sergeant, a mustached, meat-faced villain, wished to take our two supposed servants and the coachman into the ferry-master's shed for questioning. This was how it is always done, as gentry cannot be so treated, of course, and for a moment we were all at a stand. We knew Waldstein was secure, but had no idea of Mozart or the coachman.

But as soon as the demand was uttered, Casanova produced out of his head a fantastic tale, told with the utmost gravity, involving an oppressive Moravian count, his lovely niece and ward (Paradowski), her betrothed (myself), who, as the son of the ogre count's deadly enemy, had been forbidden any society with the darling girl; a sympathetic noblewoman who had acted as the arranger of the plot (Clotilde) and himself as the priest engaged to perform the ceremony. He concluded by averring that we desired to get across the river and thence to Řepý, where a sympathetic kinsman had offered sanctuary, and where the wedding would take place.

"What is your name, Frelim?" asked the sergeant suspiciously of Paradowski, "and who is this kinsman?"

Here my heart leaped into my throat, for I thought that surely Paradowski's voice would give us away. But, miraculously, out of that mouth came the voice of a girl, and a high born one at that. In the accents typical of the Hofburg, Paradowski informed the policeman that he was Marie Augusta Federica Frelim von Ostfreisland-Rietberg. The noble kinsman was none other than the emperor's first minister, Prince von Kaunitz, whose mother was sister to her own grandmother.

"I will be seeing the prince, I am sure, within the next few days," he added in the same sweet tones, "and if you give me your name, sergeant, I will pass it on to him, recommending you as a man of deep discretion and suitable for promotion."

Even in the dim light I could see the contrary feelings race across that crude face—suspicion and ambition chief among them—but I turned the scales I believe with an appeal to avarice. I had a roll of thalers upon my person, a habit of us billiard sharks, for one can never tell when the opportunity for a game might appear, and from this I selected a half-dozen.

"Sergeant," said I, "we have distracted you from your duty with our petty domestic broils. Please accept this token in recompense."

Gold! In minutes, the bar was raised and we rolled onto the ferry. The old blind horse was whipped up, the mechanism engaged with many a creak and groan, the cables tightened and we were drawn across the river, laughing like the mad, with Mozart up on top giving us a tune from his *Figaro*.

From the crossing we looped back north and reached Smichov in the small hours. There we let off Mozart at Villa Bertramka, the establishment of his friends, the Dusseks, where Frau Mozart was staying. On parting, we embraced warmly. I begged his pardon for not appreciating his music and he, putting that aside as graciously as if he had been well born, expressed his gratitude to me.

"For what?" I asked. "I nearly had you killed or clapped in chains."

"For allowing me to experience a life like an opera. What remarkable tunes have been engendered in my head this night! Your existence should be accompanied by a full orchestra and chorus at every minute."

Then Waldstein woke the house with his pounding upon the door. Shutters flew open, lights glared, and Frau Mozart cried out, demanding to know what foolery her spouse had gotten himself into and what did he mean by arriving at this hour.

We shook hands and off he went. Of all the bourgeois I have met in my life, he came closest to having the manners of a gentleman. Of his famous gifts I have, of course, no opinion at all.

From there we proceeded west, through Skalka and Katlářkau and into the hills. The gibbous moon had risen and cast enough light to see the orchards of plum in their blossom glowing white as snowfall on the slopes. Through the windows of the coach wafted the familiar odor of the flowers, and I felt a pang of homesickness so severe that tears sprang to my eyes. I said it was the dust, when Paradowski asked how I did.

Past Motol, the land rose into the famous plateau known as the Weissenberg, where many years ago our ancestors conquered the heretics and secured Bohemia for the true religion. By and by, as we rattled along, the sun rose, shining pink beams upon the trees, one of those wonderful dawns when the world seems cast within a pearl. As we drew closer to Řepý, however, Paradowski became increasingly agitated, insisting we find somewhere to stop so that he could change out of his gown and into his uniform again. He had a positive horror of being seen by his comrades in that disgraceful equipage.

We had stopped in an orchard in order to suit Paradowski and to answer calls of nature, and we all scattered to the shelter of the flowering trees as people do in such circumstances. When I returned to our berlin, I found Casanova and my Clotilde sitting together in close conversation. Her cheeks were flushed and her eyes were bright when she looked up at me upon my entering. Odd how the young are not suspicious of venery in the old—I say old, although what I would not give to again be as young as Casanova was that morning!

I said, "Come sit by me, my dear," and she did, and very close, too, and gave me a kiss, whispering that I was a good old sherbet and she liked me much and I responded that we were past all danger and would now have a life together, such as I had often dreamed of, and she said she believed we would indeed be as happy as could be wished.

Now we heard the clatter and snorting of many horses, the creak and jingle of harness, the unmistakable noise a troop of cavalry makes approaching on a road. I leaned out the carriage window and spied for the first time what would, though I knew it not, soon become my moveable home, a troop of the Kinsky Dragoons in route order, a column of threes. I did not find it an impressive martial display, for the dragoons were in their gray overalls, their helmets covered in the same color, and their harness brass, instead of shining bright in the morning sun, had all been blackened. Of course, I was most interested in the mounts. They were all black and variously starred and stockinged in white, small, neat, tight-knit animals and curiously alike, as if all bred from the same mating. They reminded me of Kíslang.

The troopers filed by, raising a thin dust that hung sparkling in the still morning air. The coachman and Waldstein, still in his borrowed livery, returned and climbed up on the box. But where was Paradowski?

A flashing of gold braid attracted the eye. It was the rittmeister, that is, the senior captain commanding the troop, with his bugler, cover men, and guidon-bearer. As he rode by our carriage his head turned sharply and he reined in. A quick order, a short blast on the bugle, and the cavalcade stopped short. The rittmeister stared up at Waldstein on the box, who was feigning indifference in a most ludicrous manner.

"Unter-Leutnant von Waldstein!" The rittmeister bellowed. "What are you doing here? Why are you not with your squadron at Prague? And why are you dressed like a God-damned lackey?"

Waldstein leaped down from the box, approached the mounted officer, and saluted.

"Herr Rittmeister," he said, "there is an explanation. This is a costume from an opera. There was an affair of honor, you see..."

"Christ's blood! Do not tell me that fucking Paradowski has stuck someone again! Dead, I suppose?"

"Yes, sir. The fellow drew first. After impugning Lieutenant Paradowski's manhood, sir. I was there."

"And what is this about an opera? Oh, never mind! We are engaged on a tactical problem and I have a rendezvous that I cannot miss. You both must report to the colonel instantly. Where is that Polish nincompoop?"

But before Waldstein could respond, the question answered itself, as the Polish nincompoop walked out of the orchard on the right and onto the road. He was half-dressed in his uniform, stock untied, hatless, with his tunic hanging open, carrying his lady's wig in one hand and with the mulberry gown flung over a shoulder.

He too came to attention before the rittmeister and saluted.

The officer gave him a look that might have rotted apples. "Well, Paradowski, I hear you have done for another man. Not cavalry, I hope. You must have lowered the empire's strength by half a troop so far."

"No, Herr Rittmeister," replied the other, "only a Neustadt cadet."

"Oh, well, a cadet," said the rittmeister dismissively. "Still, the emperor has forbidden officers to go out and you must answer for it. Repair to headquarters at Řepý instantly, you and Waldstein, and for God's sake, dress yourself! Where is the woman?"

"The woman, sir?"

"Yes, you fool! The one who lately filled that gown and wore that wig"

"Ran off in her shift, sir."

Even from where I stood, I could see the rittmeister was struggling to keep the required stern expression on his face, and the bugler was frankly grinning.

"By God, Paradowski, between sticking men and fucking women I cannot see how you have the time to do your duty. In any case, thank Christ, you are none of my affair. I only lay it upon you strictly to report to the colonel."

He turned to the bugler: a word, a brief tune, and the column took up its march again.

Paradowski insisted on waiting for our servants to catch up to us, as he refused to ride into the camp of the dragoons in a coach. So the four of us wiled away the morning playing bezique for small stakes on a rug spread on a bit of grass at the roadside. Just after noon, we saw two carts coming down the road, a horse tethered to the tail of each. Upon one cart was Lennart and the horse behind was my dear Kislang; the other, leading Mirek's charger, was driven by his servant, Wojtek. This was a surly fellow, thick as a barrel with long, lank gray hair, his face brown and rough as a potato, decorated by a sparse mustache.

"Well, you took your time," I said to Lennart when they had drawn up.

"We were ditched, sir," he replied, "and it took both of us some time to get back on wheels."

"And after that exercise you repaired to a tavern. You stink of beer."

"The fault is Wojtek's, baron. He had brought a little, a small keg, and I thought it uncivil to refuse, though he did not offer. And once a keg is breached, you know, one must drink it all up, lest it spoil."

"And did you converse on the journey with old Wojtek? Was his famously close tongue loosened at all?"

"I conversed, but he did not answer, so it was like talking to the birds, but without the songs. He is no mute, sir, for he cried 'heave-ho' several times as we were levering the wheel, but no word else. Nor did he laugh at my jokes, sir," he added in an aggrieved tone.

"That is to his credit," I said, "since they are old and foul. But tell me--how was it that you had the cart packed with all our baggage before you knew we had to flee Prague?"

"Oh, we was evicted, sir, tossed out on the street that evening."

"To the pfennig, sir. Nay, it was because of a difference of opinion between me and Frau Oslinger. I believe she heard the squeals I was bringing forth out of little Valeska, and she desired the same, having not had that pleasure for some years. Accordingly, I endeavored to give good service and I suppose I did, though she is so stout it was a puzzle to locate her treasure."

"And did you manage? And, if so, did she howl?"

"Not howl, sir. I would not say *howl*; more of a whining cry, sir, like a new farrow, you could say, and the mention of the Blessed Virgin, God, Christ, and the saints. It was the whole litany, sir, before we were done."

"Then why the eviction?"

"Oh, I believe she objected to sharing, sir, with Valeska, for I felt that having begun it was not fair to cut her off, so to speak. Her and the baker's girl, the redhead, d'you recall? Both together, as it happened, and Frau Oslinger burst into the room and said she would not have a brothel in her house, and we had to leave, though I invited her to join us. But she would not. In any case, we cannot return to Prague. I never saw so many policemen about, and your description and that of Herr Leutnant Paradowski and Herr Unter-Leutnant von Waldstein are published and a reward offered, five hundred kreutzers apiece. Perhaps we will return to dear Pannau."

"Not while my brother lives."

"Then where, sir?"

At the moment, however, I could give him no answer. I was thinking that Dresden might be a good stop. There was a theater of some repute there, which would gladden Clotilde. Of course, I believed that I would spend my days with her, and that we would be happy in just the way we had been happy before this. I supposed there were billiard rooms aplenty in Dresden, but in any case, I had a good deal of gold put by, aside from what Lennart normally carried for expenses. How my darling's eyes shone when I showed her the leather rolls of reichsthalers!

Meanwhile, Paradowski and Waldstein had dressed in their uniforms, and Paradowski had mounted his charger, Rogue. He suggested I accompany him to the dragoon camp, while Waldstein rode in the carriage to Řepý to help the chevalier and my dearest secure what lodgings there were in that place. I did not wish to leave her, but my friend insisted, for, he asserted, a meeting with Colonel Max von O'Neill was not to be missed.

Twenty-six

All the talk I had heard from Mirek and the others had engendered in me a strong desire to meet this Colonel Max and take his measure. He obliged me with an interview that very afternoon, in his campaign tent. A pavilion, I suppose I should call it, for it was large, made with dyed panels in green and red and lined inside with green silk. It was a trophy of war, I was told, from the Turks. When the adjutant ushered me in, I beheld for the first time the man, who, though I knew it not, was to be my guide and mentor for the next fifteen years of my life. I bear his mark yet.

He was sitting behind a campaign desk drinking Madeira and eating from a dish of nuts and raisins. He always had these by him and it was rumored that he ate nothing beyond this, save for a plump subaltern on occasion. I made my bow, he bade me sit. We looked at one another with interest. I suppose he was fifty-some at the time, and meagre with it, about my size or even smaller, a thin face with red knobs at the cheeks that seemed to compress his eye sockets. These were deep and curiously darkened, as in one of those wash-bears the Americans hunt. From the center of these pits shone pale gray eyes; an unsettling experience having those eyes look out at you, as if from the bottom of a well. Later I would learn that they could show sparks rising as from Hell itself when they stared at you after you'd done something stupid.

The first thing he said to me was a surprise, although now I think on it, nearly everything he ever said was surprising, one way or another. He said, "I knew your father."

"Did you, sir? Were you with the Kaisers in the Prussian war?"

421

"That is a stupid question, sir. The smallest cuirassier is twice my size."

I felt myself flush, and I stammered out, "I am very sorry, sir, to be sure. I meant no offense."

"None taken. Your father was a much larger man than you. I suppose you favor your mother."

"I believe so, Herr Oberst," I replied, a little stiffly.

"Yes, well . . . I was grieved to hear what happened. The association between your father and myself was brief, I should say, though warm. We were gallopers together for General Lacy, in the fighting before Prague and at Kolin in the Prussian war. He was senior to me and treated me with great kindness. I am of a mind to return the kindness to his son."

Here he picked up a paper from his desk. "This came in by post rider a few hours ago. The police ask all regiments to look out for several suspects, one a youth of just your appearance, an appearance, may I say it, impossible to conceal. You cannot return to Prague, it seems. What will you do?"

"I am not quite sure, sir," I answered. "I have . . . I am connected to a young person, whose interests I must consider. We had thought to go on to Dresden."

"And do what? Have you a profession?"

Of course, I was ashamed to say what I did to get my bread and stood silent.

He resumed. "I suppose you could seek a commission in the Saxon army, but how your ancestors would howl from their graves! My dear God, what a mess you young fellows get yourselves into! Paradowski and Waldstein will be safe in uniform, for if the emperor, God bless him, deplores dueling, I do not mind it in a regiment. It keeps the officers in sharp swords and sharp skills with blade or pistol, or else exceeding good manners and an eagerness to oblige. One is as good as another in an officer. And if these petty slights are not resolved, well, then upon a day when two men need at all hazards to work together, if there's bad blood between them, the whole regiment might be lost. By Christ, I have seen it more than once! Better that a few should go down from time to time in rencontres. The field of honor is a useful thing in an army, for subalterns can always be replaced, while victories stay lost forever. My advice is for you to join us. We depart for the east in three days' time and then you are beyond the reach of any police-president on earth."

I said, "Herr Oberst, I am truly grateful for the consideration, but my fate is not entirely in my hands."

He sniffed and said, "Your young person, eh? Well, you must do as you think fit." With that, he returned to his papers and I was dismissed.

After that I made my farewells to Paradowski and Waldstein, which took some considerable time, since they had to tell the whole story of the events at the Three Lions to their fellow officers, and wash the story down with many bumpers of wine. It was near sundown before I was able to get away. I mounted Kíslang and rode into Řepý. It was the usual Böhmer dorp, muddy streets and narrow stone houses, with but one inn. At that inn there was no sign of my carriage or Casanova or my darling. Inquiring of the inhabitants, I learned that the two of them had taken a meal, rendered Waldstein insensible with drugged wine, changed horses, acquired a new coachman, paid the former coachman in gold thalers for the rig, and the same to the hostler for the horses, and set off, for Dresden according to one, to Vienna according to another, while yet a third swore they had spoken only of Paris. They had my money, too.

Overcome with shame at my own gullibility, and anger at the two of them, I rode slowly back to the regiment, having purchased a bottle of slivovic before setting out. This was near dry by the time I reached the lines. I believe I fell off Kíslang before Colonel von O'Neill's pavilion. Paradowski put me to bed and in the morning, I humbly begged the colonel to let me accept his offer, and he brevetted me a cornet of cavalry, in lieu of commission. And that is how I became a soldier of his imperial majesty. What d'you think of that, sir?

Rudi finished the line he was writing and looked up. "It seems all one with your remarkable, I might even say, picaresque life, Herr Baron. But I am astounded that you let your Clotilde slip away so easily, that you did not devote your life to finding her."

"Well, you forget I was still a mere boy. I was not stupid, however, and this last betrayal I took as a sign of what I would have to endure from her thereafter. She well called me sherbet, for I was but an amusement to her, and ever would be. Standing there in the muddy street, the whole thing popped like a soap bubble."

"So you never saw her again?"

"I did, as it happens, twenty-five years later, in Paris, during the occupation. We were encamped on the Champs du Mars. Of course, the place was thick with grisettes and she was one of them. A fifty-year-old whore, missing teeth, her hair all faded, drunk. I gave her five francs, but did not indulge in her services; and if she recognized me—how could she not?—she kept her silence. *There* is a life for you!"

"As is yours, sir, if with a happier conclusion. My life seems a glide in a gilded barge over a smooth lake; yours has been more like descending a cascade upon a raft. My recent engagement in the great events of this revolutionary era has given me a keener appreciation of the delights of peace, nay, even of mild dullness. Soon, I dare say, I shall be as good a reactionary as you."

The baron gave Rudi a stern look and said, "As a soldier, I yield to no profession in the endurance of boredom. The life of a Prague clerk is a cavalcade of wonders in comparison to the life of a subaltern out on the frontier. And I wish to God I *could* make you a reactionary, if that is what you call a man who is loyal to his emperor and believes in the Christian religion. But I will not convince you, and meanwhile I am grown weary and dry. I will ring for cool beer from the cellar. Let us have some relief from these old tales

now, and let yourself imagine that the account of tedious gar-
rison duty over the next five years is droning on, like a dull
story half-overheard at a soirée. But for now you will tell me
how you do."

How I do, sir, is that I love my wife and yet I am in love
with a woman who is not my wife, who is in my mind at
every moment, who distracts me from my work, who makes
me a laughingstock among the idlers in taverns, who disgusts
me, who delights me. I dread to see her, knowing that the
sight of her, the smell and feel of her flesh, will take me over,
possess me like a succubus, and take me to a zone of passion
I have never been before, that I had not imagined to exist. In
her ecstasy, a spasm that goes on and on, (who could believe
how long!) she cries out vile curses in Czech, mixed with en-
dearments, with obscene urgings, and she never stops, she
always wants more. We could die tomorrow she says, this
could be the last of us. I wish often that it were. She chews
on me, she says she wants me inside her always, I have the
marks of her teeth and her nails on my flesh, her mouth on
my sex, it is purple as an aubergine now, misshapen and sore,
a strange and alien appendage.

I told her the cannibal kingdom story. Of course, she
said she would stay and be eaten, only providing she had me
with her behind the savage palisade. Suffering, ecstasy, the
two mixed together, and laughter too, gut-clenching hilarity,
for she is funny in a way I never thought a woman could be
funny, tales of the underside of life, of tavern-keepers,
hostlers, waiters, whores; my God, she can tell a story, and
then the dark tales, whispered into my ear when we are in bed
together in that wretched little room, covered in sweat, with
her hot small hand kneading my prick, tales of the Slavic un-
derworld, demon princes who suck the blood of little girls
and witches with chicken legs, and the hand never stopping
on the greasy length until it is astoundingly stiff once more
when with a cry she finishes the tale and drags me over her
with a squeal of lust.

Besides her, I do nothing, I eke out a few lines and
drill my futile little troop, fine boys, but all of us desperate for

a fight, we all feel something terrible in the wind, the tribes drawing their lines, civility and community, those brave ideas not tough enough to endure this accursed faction, and yet we swear there will be at least one body of men to fight and perchance die in defense of them. That would be a good end, to take a bullet for the revolution and not have to think about what I am doing to Berthe and the children. And you, sir, my deadly enemy, conspiring toward my ruin and that of all I hold precious; and yet, I have hardly ever met a man I like more, or whose respect I wish more to earn. This is how I do, Herr Baron: not well.

So Rudi thought; he said, "I am burdened and stretched thin, but holding fast. When the current situation is resolved and I can shut up here and return to my family in Vienna, I believe I will be fine. Naturally, should your memoir not be completed by that time, I would undertake to return here regularly to take down all you care to convey."

Here the servant Pavlic arrived with a pair of steins beaded with dew, from which both men took grateful draughts. When the man had gone, Rudi said, "If you care to resume, Herr Baron, I would like to hear some drone about the inception of your military career. For example, what became of Lennart when you entered service?"

"Oh, Lennart came with me, of course. I could never have done without him, and I almost did not join because, you know, he was huge, and when he went to the mustering sergeant, the man refused to read him in. 'This is fucking *light* cavalry, my lad,' said he, 'and you are a heavy if I ever saw one. Try the cuirassiers or the grenadiers.'
"I had to intercede with Colonel Max, and won my point by arguing that a man who could hold up the corner of a laden wagon while a wheel was fit on was a useful fellow to have along on a road march. So Lennart was mustered in, along with his horse, Onka, a gray mare who would go in traces and under saddle, and was big enough at over sixteen hands to bear his great bones. In any event, I would not have joined without him."

"Really?" said Rudi. "Was a servant so important?"

"You say that because you are bred a bourgeois and have no idea of the connection between master and man that can exist at an old-fashioned place like Pannau. It is not a matter of pay at all, but of mutual obligation and care. If I had a single crust, I would share it with Lennart as he would his with me. Our connection was more like a family relationship, and considering what my family was like, it exceeded in affection any I had enjoyed with those bound to me by blood."

"And yet you promised him that you would see him raised up," said Rudi. "This suggests that he, at any rate, wished to remove from the state of servitude. Did you ever keep that promise?"

At this remark there came over the old baron's face a look so dire that Rudi thought he was having a stroke—eyes shut, a gray pallor, trembles.

"Herr Baron, is anything amiss? Shall I call . . . "

The old eyes opened again, and flashed. "No, no, just a damned memory. I will relate how I kept my promise when the time comes. In any case, I took to soldiering as if born to it, which of course I was. To be paid two-hundred eighty-eight florins per annum, with more yet when on campaign, *paid*, I say, to ride horses, shoot firearms, and kill Turks—what more could any well-born boy of spirit ask? Looking back, I suppose I had declined entering the army in the usual way to spite my family, my aunt especially, who had condemned me as being mere food for powder. Well, so I was, but Providence had a hand here, for I think I would have made a very poor cuirassier, and I became, not to blow my trumpet over-loud, an excellent dragoon.

"I bid a sad farewell to Kíslang, for if I was food for powder, I resolved she was not to be. I had her sent to Wachtmeister Neckar, who had found new employment on an estate at Hartsburg, sending a note charging him to care for her and have her bred to a blood stallion, and keep the foal for himself, me paying all costs. That done, I had to buy uniforms and three chargers. I already had pistols and a saber. I feared I would have to go deep in debt for decent horses, but Lennart surprised me once again by producing a roll of thalers. It seems he had pinched it from my store, having sized up Casanova and being immune to his charms. I swear there was never such a fellow! Poor fellow! Poor fellow!"

The old baron drank some beer, coughed heavily into a great flag of a handkerchief and resumed.

Three days after we joined, we pulled up the camp and set out on the long road to our duty station, Usdin in the Banat. I made myself useful as a galloper for Colonel Max— there are so many messages attendant on a regiment on the march—for there were no vacancies for a cornet then in the troops. He said these would appear soon enough when we got to our station. "You young fellows die like flies out on the frontier," was his comment, which dismayed me not a bit, for I was eighteen and determined to live forever. As I have, of course.

Moving a thousand horses and near as many dragoons a hundred leagues or more, while keeping them fed, watered, healthy, and disciplined, is no small task. One moves not in some great cavalcade, of course, but along several slightly different routes, so as not to overwhelm the foraging capacity of a district. The regiment is dispersed somewhat as a result and there is a good deal of galloping back and forth with orders and reports. In this way I learned how a regiment is organized. I will explain. A regiment consists of eight squadrons, each of which has a hundred dragoons, five officers and fifteen non-commissioned officers . . .

"Forgive me, Herr Baron, but have I worked for the army for near fifteen years," said Rudi. "I know how a regiment of cavalry is organized. Each squadron has two flügel and each flügel has two züge, and so forth. All this can be dealt with in footnotes. The matter of your book is what happened to *you*."

"My, my, but you are testy today! Is that girl giving you trouble?"

"There is no girl and no trouble," Rudi replied sharply. "Please continue. Did anything of note transpire on your journey to the Banat?"

"Only the usual grinding misery—saddle sores and foundered troopers, biting flies and the runs; although we had less of that that the usual regiment, as Colonel Max had us dig latrines at each stop. The dragoons called him "Old Shit-Hole" and damned his eyes as they dug, but would have followed him through Hell's gate. In any case, we marched through the bright autumn, little rain, unusually good weather it was, and reached our station at Usdin. I suppose you know all about the Banat?"

"Nothing except that Prince Eugene took it from the Turks for the Empire and the Empress Maria-Theresa planted it with German farmers."

"Yes, that is what empresses do, plant farmers, and then send the poor miserable dragoons to watch over them. "

Look, sir, the Banat is your empire in small: well-watered, fertile, broad plains, high mountains, full of folk from different tribes, practicing different religions, speaking different languages, all looking for an excuse to cut one another's throats, and surrounded on three sides by implacable enemies. In the spring, along with the gentle rains come the bashi-bazouks, Turkish bandits who raid the villages, burning everything they can't steal, carrying off the youths and maidens as slaves, and killing everyone else.

I cannot erase from my mind the first time I saw a village that the bashi-bazouks had been at--they'd cut off the head of every grown man and woman in the village, and stacked them in a neat pyramid outside the church. The priest they had impaled. I spewed up my breakfast right there in the saddle. The stench . . . well, the sadder part is that after a few years out east, one no longer spews, or even much notes the vilest atrocities. More than once, we found a village burned, in the ashes of the church the inhabitants stacked like charcoal in a rick. You can't imagine the smell. When our Grenzers go into a Turk village it is the same, the mosque serves for roasting the poor devils just as well. But I was about to talk of the Turkish war and what we did in it, because six months after I joined, the Turks attacked Russia and since our emperor Joseph had an alliance with the great Catherine, we went to war as well.

We moved east with a rag-tag army made up of what forces we had on hand, under the command of a general who had last seen service in the Seven Years War and ordinarily did not rise before eleven in the morning. Colonel Max observed that the first rule of war was to quiz out where the enemy was likely to go and then arrive with one's army beforehand and make him fight you on your own ground. It was obvious that the Turk had to come through the Transylvanian passes, and just as obviously, at least to our colonel, the spearhead of their advance must come down the Danube at Orsova, because that was the only pass that had a Turk stronghold large enough to support an army.

We ought to have invested Orsova with our whole force and stopped up the Turks like a cork in a bottle. But in the event, that dotard general scattered our army across all the passes, in numbers too small to be effective, the Turks under Osman Pascha poured through the Orsova gap with twenty thousand men, beat us at Menhadika, and took nearly the whole of the Banat, while we ran like sheep.

Or not exactly sheep, I should add, at least not the Kinsky. We were of the rear guard, and we retreated in good order. At Jankahide on the Temes River, however, we turned and had a real battle. It was my introduction to war and there I first killed my man. Shall I relate it to you?

"I should like nothing better," said Rudi, but glanced at the mantle clock.

Observing this, the old baron remarked, "Yes, nothing so fascinating as old battles, related by drooling ancients, with the pepper pots standing in for hussar squadrons and breadcrumbs for the lines of infantry. Well, no pepper pots, for it was a simple battle, like all great fights, and I will tell it you merely to illustrate the genius of our commander. We were, as I said, the rear guard and the Turkish van was three *bunchuks* of *sipahis*, the cream of the Turkish cavalry, some four thousand sabers, well-mounted on the speedy little Arabs they favored and caparisoned with all the gorgeous pomp of the east, turbans worked with gold threads, silken cloaks, brocaded saddle-clothes, what-have-you.

They were not above two leagues behind us, our troopers were near blown and the men had been in the saddle almost without let for a month. I was still with Colonel Max, and of a certain morning I knew by the volume of orders I was sent to carry that something extraordinary was preparing. One of the people I carried them to was Paradowski, who had been promoted captain and was in temporary command of the first squadron, his superiors having fallen ill or died in battle. He read the orders and grinned at me.

"Well, we are to have the Tactic, it seems," said he. "You should remain with us, my dear, for it will be something to see, and you have not been blooded yet."

I protested that my duty was as a galloper and my post near the colonel, but he said in reply, "Max has other gallopers, and in any case, there will be no more orders until this affair is done. If it doesn't work, we will all be dead or en route to the galleys at Aleppo."

He spoke to his bugler, and the man blew a call I had not heard before. Immediately, one man from each züge trotted off to a line of willows and collected green branches. In a few minutes every man had a green sprig stuck in his helmet cover. I recalled then that time out of mind the soldiers of Austria have gone into battle with live green in their hats. No one remembers why.

Paradowski bade me ride alongside him, and as we trotted along I asked him about the Tactic.

"It is one of his fancies and we have drilled in it so we see the evolutions in our sleep. It is based on the idea that no one expects infantry to appear in a cavalry battle, but this is the great virtue of the dragoon …"

And with that he explained the colonel's plan. The land in this part of the Banat is rolling hills, which at the time, now late summer of the year 'eighty-eight, was covered in high grain. When one was within a dip it was impossible to see what was in the next dip, so that what we now did might have been considered an error by the enemy, which was what we wished him to believe.

So . . . we crossed the top of a little hill and we spied a vedette of *sipahis* upon the crest opposite. Blue sky, clear air, we could make out their faces across the little valley, and the devices on their guidons. Commands cracked out, bugles blew, and our squadron moved with practiced skill from a column of threes into two long lines abreast, as if to charge and envelope the vedette.

It disappeared, of course, and we pursued. Cresting the next rise we saw pouring toward us a vast mass of horsemen, flashing all the colors of the rainbow and making a noise such that if had you never heard it, it would be hard to imagine--the rumble of hooves on earth, the music of their horns, the shrill shouts of the Osmanlis, a sound that had terrified Europe for four centuries. Our bugles sounded too and every rider slowed and spun his horse in a neat circle so that he was retreating again, without stopping, except for a dozen or so riflemen, who sat up on their saddles and shot some of the most forward from their horses, to ensure a vigorous pursuit.

Now we were once again in column, tearing down the road, which descended to the river and ran alongside the stream. The river here was deep cut in its banks, with the road running between the water and the fields of ripe grain.

We had a lead of no more than a thousand yards and I knew the chase could not last much longer. A large body of cavalry will always catch a smaller one, unless it can find a place to hide, and there was nothing of that here, only the green water and the golden grain. Then, to my vast surprise, Mirek raised his sword and his bugler blew the halt. After that he blew column to the rear. The guidon and the head of the column, myself included, began to move back toward the oncoming Turkish horde. At that moment, another bugle sounded, and there came a great shout, "Dragoons, stand up!" I looked, astounded, for there, in three straight ranks along the right bank of the river was the rest of the regiment, a wall of infantry where no infantry should be.

On came the Turks, all unknowing, until a volley of five hundred carbines roared out. At the same time, number six squadron trotted out over the rise where they had waited concealed and set up a blocking position behind the last of the *sipahis*.

We now had over three thousand horsemen packed like meat in a sausage, and our carbines were turning them into something quite like mince. Of course they tried to cut their way out, front and rear, but the front on both ends was so narrow that they could not bring their greater numbers to bear. Of course, our rifles had accounted for most of their officers in the first minutes, a hole through every green turban, as we liked to say.

We had a nice melee on our side. A great Turk struck at me with his scimitar and I was able to parry and riposte to his face, which I split in two. I recall Lennart, who was my cover man, towering over everyone else on that packed road, whirling his saber in circles, lopping heads as if he were a boy knocking gooseberries off a hedge with a stick. I believe I accounted for two more men, but I could not take my oath upon it. Very few of them escaped, in any case, and there you have the Tactic.

"But how did you feel?" asked Rudi. "Your first real fight, your first kill . . .?"

"Why, I suppose I could make something up that would suit, but in fact, once you are among them, pistols going off in your ear, the rattle of the muskets, the shouts and screams, the ungodly sounds horses make when the balls tear their vitals, one remembers nothing of such affairs, although afterwards our imagination throws up a plausible tale.

See, it is all clear in my mind, I see his grimace as the blade goes in, although it could have been entirely different, and what I just related, that I have recounted to myself and others these fifty years, might be a mere phantasm. What I *felt*, since you ask, was the highest excitement possible in this life, and I do not exclude the act of love. Life shrinks to a fine glowing point, everything seems to slow down in the most peculiar fashion, and terror and exaltation combine in a way that I suppose is unique to the soldier; at least I have found it so, and I have hunted boar on foot.   Afterward, there is a kind of sorrow.   Though one might think oneself the paragon of humane sensibilities, would not harm a cat and so forth, it is undeniable that not ten minutes since, one has hacked the life out of several human beings. We never spoke of this, and I find I do not think it seemly to do so now. War is necessary for the defense of land and emperor, and certain men must kill other men in the process; or rather soldiers must kill other soldiers, for a soldier is not exactly a man when he is under arms, but the limb of an inhuman being, a being whose engine is duty, a being with no moral qualms about taking human life.   Your true professional soldier will slide easily back and forth between these states."

"What about fear?" asked Rudi.   "Were you not terrified?   How does one perform one's duties when death might come at any moment, when one is presented again and again with the death of comrades? I confess that this has always been my chief question concerning the military life."

"Oh, well, for the officer it is mainly breeding. From earliest youth one is imbued with the understanding that cowardice is so thorough a disgrace that death is preferable. It simply never occurs to a man to run. If it should happen, of course, they put you in a room with a loaded pistol and thus you gain nothing by your dereliction. And, as I say, in the thick of battle, one has not the time to dwell upon fear. That, I believe, is more common among those with a formal education, who live so thoroughly within their own heads. No, your Austrian officer is blithe in the face of death, gay amid the flying bullets, and oblivious to his own extinction."

To resume--such a vast loss of prime cavalry blinded Dervish Mehmed Pascha, the Turkish commander, although our army moved so god-damned slow ... as it happens, some months later the Russians, supported by a royal and imperial army corps, caught him at Focsani in Moldova and destroyed him. Well, I am not to rage over the stupidities of a half-century past. It was a wretched war, wretchedly handled. What I have described was our one great action; subsequently, as our reward for destroying a corps of cavalry, we were put to guarding transports during the siege of Belgrade. It seems that our colonel had been commanded by our general not to engage the Turks, so that in destroying them he had violated orders. Instead of a shower of medals, therefore, we were in disgrace. While half our army died of camp diseases before Belgrade, we conducted wagons down from Segedin, and made sure the bashi-bazouks didn't get 'em.

So to the tenth of September, in the year 'eighty-nine. We were a train of twelve wagons carrying ammunition and other warlike stores down to Belgrade from Segedin. I had under me a züge of the first squadron, my maiden command. Colonel Max allowed me this petty boon as a reward for my good service and for how I had comported myself during the fight at the riverbank. Three days out, at Becskereck, we received word that a large party of bashi-bazouks had crossed the Danube at Dubovacz and were terrorizing the country-side. As the Russians were far to the north and our own army was consumed with the siege, the commandant at Becskereck suggested I lager in the town until the raiders should be found and suppressed, but this I declined to do, thinking it dishonorable to shirk my duty for fear of mere bandits.

I recall Lennart remarking to me at the time that a siege was a long wait and so there was no urgency to our mission, and it would be an agreeable thing to spend a few nights in a town while the villains were chased from the region. I told him to mind his business, and that I knew my duty, if he did not. He answered, "Though I am taller than most without my head, my lord, still I would like to keep it on my shoulders. When the mice look for the cat they never send the mole as scout."

"What is that supposed to mean?"

"Only that we move snail-like through unknown country inhabited by brigands. Let us stop and send to old Shi . . . I mean Colonel von O'Neill, and ask him for a squadron or two to sweep the road before us, or at least move its position, so it can be easily called at need."

Of course, I should have thought of that before my servant did, and it irked me. I spoke with my one non-commissioned officer, Feldwebel Sebic, who was of the type that strives to discern the answer his officer desires and gives it with enthusiasm, and when I observed I had no wish to be stuck in some obscure town for who knew how long, he was quick to decide for pushing onward. But I sent three men out ahead as scouts.

We had hardly got on the move when one of these scouts, a fellow called Kubicek, came dashing back, all a sweat, his mount flecked with foam, to report that the next village on our route was deserted, the wagons and livestock missing, the doors of the houses barred. The men within earshot all stared at me. You asked about fear. Well, the men are often afraid, it is true, but discipline and loyalty to the colors and to each other keep them steady, if their officers show they know their business.

"Lager the wagons!" I ordered, and sent two riders off. One, Krupac, rode back to Beskereck and the other, Vaslov, to the Kinsky depot at Usdin, a longer ride; but I gave him my charger, Perseus, a four-year-old gelding with a remarkable turn of speed, and told him to kill the beast but get there in the shortest possible time.

Once they were gone, we drew the wagons into a circle atop a small rise in a field of ripe barley. I had the men slice the crop down with their sabers out to a hundred yards or so. Then we waited, me feeling something of a fool for my caution. The village could have been deserted because of a plague or there might be a harvest festival in another town-- such are the second thoughts of a commander and they are never profitable. I set the guard and there we spent the night. In the morning, I was awakened by Lennart at first light, seeing by his face that the news was not good.

"The wind is from the south, Herr Baron," said he, "and it carries dust."

Indeed there was a column of yellowish dust in the air on the southern horizon, and in less than an hour we could see its source: ten score or more riders, well-mounted on Arabs, wearing a mad variety of costumes topped by tall hats wrapped in scarves and beads. Their sashes held pistols and daggers and their hands curved scimitars and long muskets. When the first of them spied us, he gave a great cry, instantly taken up by the others, a sound like the shrieks of carrion crows above a dead thing. They charged toward us. I bade my men hold fire as they came closer and closer. When they were within thirty yards, the bandits began to fire their pistols and I drew a bead on a fellow on a fine white horse and knocked him off, at which all of my men started firing as quickly as they could.

The horde spurred their mounts forward in a rush, then swerved to race around the wagon lager in a continuous circle, screaming and shooting off their weapons, to no great effect. The fire of our Crespis was considerably more deadly. The first volley brought a dozen men or horses down and the second did better, and after a few circuits the brigands withdrew out of range. We had two riflemen with us, and after a few more of the wretches had fallen to their aim, they withdrew back to the road. I was feeling more confident. We had unlimited quantities of food, powder and ball. We had hogsheads of beer. Twenty against two hundred and some was long odds, but these men were not, after all, soldiers. Their game was raiding defenseless villages and I did not think they would press the matter in the face of imminent death. I had hopes too, that one of my riders had got through to Usdin or the Belgrade siege, in which case help would be on the way.

I was wrong. They wanted what was in the wagons and they had among them a body of *sipahis* with a *yuzbashi* in command. This personage now advanced under a flag of truce. We parlayed. He was a smiling, greasy fellow, fat, with a turban like a green pumpkin and a bold mustache. In crude French, he said that they had no interest in us, only in our supplies, and he was prepared to let us leave with our arms, mounted on our troopers, unharmed.

"That is a generous offer, sir," I said. "But I have a better one. Leave us, ride off from the Banat, and no more of your men will be killed. You have lost a score in ten minutes. At that rate, an attack of an hour or so will do for you all."

After some threats about our certain fate if I did not yield, during which he never stopped smiling, and seeing me remain adamant in refusal, he rode off with his fuglemen. Shortly thereafter some bashi-bazouks came forward and stopped just out of musket range. Two of them were carrying a long stout pole, sharpened to a point. The others supported a naked, bleeding man. It was my courier, Krupac.

The *yuzbashi* pushed forward one of his men, who spoke German. Perhaps he was a captive from a raid, poor fellow, coerced into turning Turk and preying on his countrymen. The man called out in a strong voice that they willing to let all of us pass freely, and that we would now see what fate awaited instead, if our officer did not listen to reason. He was. "Soldiers," he cried, "shoot the stupid boy of an officer and gain your lives! If not, share the agony of this one."

Then they impaled Krupac.

Do you know how they do it? First they use a knife to slash open the bowel and then they insert the spike of the pole into the wound, twisting and forcing it ever upward through the body, taking care not to pierce the heart or any other vital organs. They have experts at this, it seems. It took a long time and Krupac's screams were beyond anything I had ever heard out of a human throat. The point of the pole emerges right under the collarbone and then the pole is hoisted upright and its butt set in a hole previously dug. The screams if anything increased in volume and piteousness.

"Riflemen!" I shouted. "Penar and Hrubal!" Of course they were ready and in the next instant two shots stifled the screams. A great roar of rage arose from the horde. Then they all mounted and moved out of sight. From the plum orchard on the other side of the road came the sound of axes and breaking wood. We saw the smoke of a large fire. I should have anticipated their strategy, but I was a boy of eighteen, and my Feldwebel was useless.

Like most successful plans it was obvious in retrospect. They came at us out of the west, so that the sinking sun was in our eyes, a broad column of riders each with a torch in hand. We killed a good number of them, although two of our Crespis exploded from the hard use. Torches landed on and under the wagons and we were too few to fight both the fires and the Turks. I should have removed the powder kegs and buried them, I suppose, but in the event I did not. In a few minutes nearly all the wagons were burning and the horses in the middle of the lager were heaving at their lines and screaming in terror. Then the powder exploded, something struck me on the head, and when I regained my senses I was naked and hanging by my hands from a pole stretched between two plum trees. Next to me hung Lennart in the same condition. His body was covered in caked blood from several wounds.

The old man stopped, and sighed and stared blankly at the cold fireplace.

He continued in a smaller voice, "Do you know, Moritz, I have spent my lifetime trying to forget this day. I never speak of it, and here I am blabbing it out as if it were a tavern tale. No, no, I must collect myself and rest. But you will come tomorrow and then you shall hear all."

Twenty-seven

Shaken and faintly nauseated by the account he had just heard, Rudi walked away from Baron von Pannau's house as if in a waking dream, and it was some moments before he realized that someone was calling his name.

He turned and saw running after him a big youth he recognized, dressed in the blue coat of the Academic Legion. It was one of his boys--what was the fellow's name? Something ordinary and German--Schmidt or Muller? No, Vogel.

"Oh, sir, thank God I have found you," said the lad breathlessly. "You must come to the Carolinium this instant!"

"And why is that, Vogel? Fix your cravat and report properly!"

Vogel stiffened, fiddled at his throat, and said, "Yes, Herr Major. A message from Captain Popp, Herr Major. He says a mob has gathered in the Old Town. They have burned a shop and intend to march against the Jews."

"Oh, we cannot have that," said Rudi. "Have you transport?"

"A fiacre, sir, just there," said Vogel, pointing.

Oddly, Rudi felt a thrill of relief at the prospect of action. He clapped the boy on the back and said, "Let us make a brief detour to my home for my uniform and arms, and then into the fray!"

"You said you craved a fight, Captain Popp, and here it is," said Rudi to his second-in-command when they had assembled their company in the courtyard of the university. "Where are they rioting?"

"In Josefov, mainly, sir--the Guard is already there in strength. But there are roving bands all throughout the Old and New towns, seeking out Jewish homes and businesses and attack-

441

ing Jews on the street. The Tandelmarkt seems to be where they are gathering. One of the lads says they are distributing clubs and torches there."

"Then that is where we shall go. Have them fall in now."

When the company was stiffly at attention, holding their new, purloined muskets and looking as much like soldiers as was possible for a band with soft hats and assorted uniforms, Rudi put them at ease and ordered them to pull the balls from their cartridges, while he did the same with his pistols. He wondered if he should make a speech, but when he considered the shining eager faces before him, he decided that calls to martial valor would be otiose.

But he did say, "Gentlemen, we are going to preserve order and protect our fellow citizens. No one will load ball without my express order." Then he drew his sword and marched out of the gates at the trot, his company treading in step behind him, in column of fours, with their two drummers beating a tattoo. When they were well into the street, he ordered double-time, the drums beat a more frantic tempo, and they raced toward the Tandelmarkt.

As they entered the street that led to it, they heard a dull roaring, a rhythmic "hep hep hep" the traditional pogrom song, punctuated by shrill cries. Another dozen steps and the street before Rudi was filled with the mob, rough-looking men, with a scatter of bourgeois in tall hats, all carrying clubs, axes, bulging sacks, or torches.

"Captain, deploy!" Rudi cried. Popp snapped out a series of orders, and the company transformed itself, in a long-practiced evolution, from a column into three ranks, blocking the street. The mob slowed, then stopped, bemused.

"Fix bayonets!" shouted Rudi. There followed the martial sound of steel sliding on steel. Rudi stepped forward and pointed his sword at the mob. "You will drop your weapons and disperse! Now!"

Someone shouted a curse. A stone flew, then a hail of stones. A boy in the first rank cried out and went down with a bloodied head.

Rudi called out, in as calm and commanding voice as he could manage, "Front rank kneel! Present!"

To the mob he shouted. "By God, if you don't disperse this instant, I shall fire on you." He raised his sword high.

Someone yelled, "He wouldn't dare," and another, "It's just a bunch of boys, knock 'em over and let's get the Yids!"

A man came forward a few skipping steps with a rock in his hand, reared back to throw it, and Rudi called out, "Fire!"

The noise was tremendous, stunning, followed by shouts and screams from the targets, some of whom had been struck by burning wads from the blank shots. The smoke filled the street, obscuring sight and confusing the mob.

"Forward! Charge!" Rudi shouted, and without looking to see whether anyone was following, he pointed his sword and dashed into the smoke.

The mob broke and ran. Rudi spotted the fellow who had stepped forward with the rock and struck him on the head with the flat of his blade. The man went down with a cry, Rudi leapt over him, and in a few second the Legionnaires had driven the mob back to the square.

Which heaved with people, most of them spectators, Rudi saw, but small groups of men battered at the shuttered doors of Jewish shops, while others tried to set them ablaze. One house was fitfully burning already. From the upper story windows, the proprietors were throwing heavy household objects and items of inventory down on their tormentors: chamber pots, crates, andirons, barrels of herring. In the center of the square was a cart, with a man on it, haranguing the crowd, directing them to tear up the wooden stalls of the market to make weapons and arsonous fuel.

"Let us have another volley, Captain Popp," said Rudi, "and then we will take down that big fellow on the cart."

The guardsmen fired. The crowd howled and moved like a viscous tar away from the shops and across the square.

A shower of stones and bottles flew through the air. The mob coalesced around the cart, shouting defiance, and none louder than the big man standing atop it. The guard company formed line efficiently to the sound of their drums and with a cry ran at the crowd, bayonets flashing.

A wild melee ensued. The students thrust with their bayonets as they had been drilled to, and struck with their butt-plates; the crowd fought back with staves and stones. Rudi, jammed in the thick of the struggle, slashed with his saber at any man who dared raise a stick to him, at first with the flat, but in a short while, hardly noticing, it, he started to use the edge. Men fell before him; he stepped over their bodies, and moved on, ever closer to the man on the cart.

After some indeterminate passage of time, Rudi was sensible of a softening of resistance, as rioters on the edges slipped away. The student guards were young, vigorous, well drilled; the crowd was a mere mob, and most of them drunk and looking forward only to an innocent afternoon of Jew-baiting, with the promise of loot.

Rudi saw a guardsman—why, it was Vogel!--jump up on the cart and order the man to surrender. The big man turned and in that instant Rudi recognized him as Stefan Novak, whom he had last encountered with Sisi at the Sack of Meal.

Novak knocked the thrusting bayonet away with his arm, snatched the weapon from the boy's hands and swing the butt against his head. It made an awful sound. Vogel fell, gushing blood, to the floor of the cart. Rudi drew his pistol, aimed, and shot Novak square in the face.

That ended the riot. The big man was carried off, blinded, his face bloodied. whereupon Rudi turned to Captain Popp and said, "Take charge here, Popp. I must see to the safety of a friend."

In Liebig's apartment the windows had all been smashed, glass glittered on the floor, and when Rudi entered, after considerable knocking and calling out his own name, he was let in by one of the sisters, and found Liebig taking down the mattresses that had been propped up against the empty window frames. Sounds of wailing came from another room; there was a bearded old man Rudi did not recognize sitting in a chair at the table, his head buried in his hands, rocking slowly back and forth, as if at prayer.

"They were throwing torches and cobblestones wrapped around burning rags," Liebig explained, taking down a still-smoldering mattress and regarding it blankly, as if undecided whether it should not just be tossed down onto the street.

"Is everyone safe?" Rudi asked.

"Oh, yes. We are perfectly fine, as you see. My mother is in her room howling into a pillow, my sister Brisha has a cut from glass on her head, and Natalie is untouched but can't seem to stop shaking. The police, as usual, took their time suppressing the good-natured fun."

"It was not the police at all. It was me and a flying column from the Academic Legion."

"Well, then, *you* took your time!" cried Liebig, flinging the mattress aside. It released a foul stench of burned feathers.

"Don't be bitter, my friend," said Rudi. "Some disorder must be expected in such times, before the people perfect the habits of freedom."

"An excellent suggestion! I will not be bitter, nor wish for these God-damned Böhmers to have on their necks a boot heavier than that of the Hapsburgs. Habits of freedom, indeed! Well, if this is your freedom, the devil with it! A pogrom in the heart of post-revolutionary Prague! I would not have believed it, good little liberal that I am, had I not seen what I have seen. Those faces! Like ravening beasts. Oh, you will be happy to learn that one of those faces was Jasny's, our dear comrade."

"Jasny? In a riot? I can't believe it. He's a schoolteacher, for God's sake!"

"Oh, believe it, my friend. He was inciting them in the most grammatical Czech you ever heard." Liebig bent to pick up a lamp fallen on the floor. It slipped, the globe broke, and with a violent curse Liebig flung the base out the window.

The bearded man at the table let out a low groan.

"Well, despite this," said Rudi, affecting a cheerful tone, "I expect your brother will soon return. Have you had any news of him?"

Liebig goggled behind his smeared eyeglasses. Then he extended his hand, finger pointing at the miserable old fellow. "My brother? *There* is my brother, or what is left of him. That is what four years in Munkasch does to a man, although I believe Jews are singled out for special treatment. And this is his welcome home. I am sorry, Moritz, but I beg you to be off. I do not care just now to face any but my own people."

"Is there a casualty list?" asked Rudi. Someone had brought chairs to the Carolinium courtyard and the officers of Rudi's company and others of the Academic Legion were sitting there, while around the ancient quadrangle stood or sat or lay the Academic Legion, blooded now and sober with it, or giddy, according to temperament, filthy and exhausted, feasting on beer and provisions provided by the grateful Jews.

Rudi had been on his feet for more than thirty-six hours, racing from one part of the city to another, suppressing gangs of rioters, protecting the homes and property of their intended victims. Now he took the crumpled piece of paper from Popp.

"Seven injured? That is not too bad. Neuss's broken arm seems to be the worst of it, except for poor Vogel's noggin. How is he faring?"

"He is awake and sensible. A hard head, it seems."

"And among the people?"

"Thirty-two in the hospital, one dead."

"Not killed by us, I hope?"

"No," said Popp. "The regulars shot an apprentice they said was menacing with a firearm. A hundred fifteen in the town jail, including your Novak. It could have been much worse, that is certain."

"Yes. And among the Jews?"

"It is hard to tell. They are caring for their own, as they usually do. None killed, certainly. There is a great deal of property damage, I should think, looting and so forth. I dare say they will make it all back in no time."

"Not a helpful remark, Captain Popp," said Rudi with a snap.

"Sorry, sir. Here is a list of those imprisoned in the town jail for riot. What do you suppose will happen to them?"

"Fines for the prosperous, prison for the others. Or nothing at all. Who can tell these days?" He ran his eye down the list.

One name stood out. Rudi got up from his seat, swayed in a moment of dizziness, recovered, and said in a loud voice, "Gentlemen, I bid you adieu. I am going to eat, drink a great deal, and go to bed--in that order, I hope! I congratulate you on a fine action. You are a credit to your city and your nation, whose thanks you have earned in the days just passed. Long live Bohemia! Long live the revolution!"

He left amid loud cheering. This is glory, he thought, a thinner brew than was served in the Kinsky dragoons perhaps, but glory all the same. In a strange paradoxical way he was both wonderfully happy that he had been given the chance to risk his life with sword in hand and hugely reluctant to ever do it again.

The Knight tavern was full of men speaking loudly and with little substantive knowledge about the riots. A silence fell as Rudi walked in, reeking of martial puissance, and then the babble welled up again. Babka came to shake his hand vigorously and assure him he had the thanks, the eternal gratitude of all decent folk in Prague, for, you know, if they are allowed to despoil the Jews, who would be next?

Rudi said, "Who indeed? And since you have not been despoiled, I beg you, dear Babka, to let me despoil a capon and that creamed turnip and potato thing you do, and beer in quantities. And, I beg you, a glass of slivovic to start. Do you have any Pannau?"

They did, and in a few minutes Rudi was sitting at his favorite table, staring at a clear glass in which sat a crystal liquid exuding the scent of a hundredweight of plums that had died and gone to heaven.

"I will have one of those," said Paul Novotny, pulling the other chair out and sitting down. "I imagined you would turn up here sometime. I have been lying in wait, like a footpad."

Rudi shot his drink down his throat, shuddered, closed his eyes, and allowed himself delight.

"You have been through the wars, my lad," said Novotny. "You have dared the thing itself, red Mars in all his glory and terror. How do you feel?"

"Run over by a coach and four. But to tell the truth, arduous as it was, it was not precisely equal to facing Ney and the Old Guard in serried ranks. I have been hearing war stories from my old baron, about what our men must do to hold the empire, and what they suffer in the emperor's service. The most hellish thing you can imagine, or perhaps beyond . . . suppressing a gaggle of louts is nothing to it."

"Nevertheless you look like one fled from the field of Austerlitz. Here, Helen!"

Babka's girl came over and Novotny directed her to bring two more drinks and a basin of warm water and a soft rag. This delivered, Novotny rolled back his cuffs and said, "You are black as the ace of spades and are frightening the children," and over Rudi's protests cleaned his friend's face with remarkable and unexpected tenderness. It is from wiping his children's faces, Rudi thought and was at once seized with such an awful longing for his own hearth and the presence of his own two that tears sprang from his eyes, and he was happy that his face was already wet, to spare him the shame.

The meal came and Rudi fell to like a carter. Novotny talked about the riots. He himself had been in Josefov, where the trouble had been worst, and he had actually seen the ap-

prentice shot down. He was composing his story just then—
he opened his notebook to show how far he had progressed--
and asked Rudi to recount his experiences at the Tandelmarkt
and beyond.

Rudi told him, between mouthfuls.   Always an
interesting experience, being interviewed by the press. As he
spoke, the incomprehensibility of military action spun into
coherent narrative, and he realized that this was how history
would be created henceforth, a participant of some signal
event speaking with a journalist. He tried for the truth, of
course, but the truth was all shouts and pounding feet and
swinging arms, cries of pain and rage, Novak's face vanishing
in smoke.

"You didn't kill him, please God?" Novotny said.

"No. The charge was blank, but at close range it had
to be most unpleasant. He was blinded for the moment, at
any rate, and my boys dragged him to earth and bound him
up, which I doubt they would have been able to do, had he
not been so disabled. The man is a very bear. I'll tell you
something else, but you must not print it. Agreed?"

"It will be off the record, my friend."

"At the moment I pointed my piece I had entirely
forgotten whether I had drawn the ball. Imagine that! Yet I
pulled the trigger."

"Well. We never know who we are, or what we will
turn into, I should say, in the grip of extremity. What else?"

Rudi said what else, a tale of short, violent encounters
with roving bands of drunken fools throughout much of
Prague, and he related the story of what had happened to the
Liebigs.

"He had some things to say about the Czechs, I'm afraid,"
Rudi added.

"Then we are even. Let us have no more bad feeling
between our nations from this day forward." Novotny finished his drink in a gulp, his hand came up, as if by instinct,
to order another, but he checked it, sighed, and said, "I must
recall I am an ex-sot. It is amazing, you know, how many

florins accumulate in one's purse when one does not spend all of them on drink. This I owe to you, my friend."

"To me?"

"Of course, you. How many times have you lectured me upon improvement! Get a job, Novotny, do not insult employers, Novotny; don't spend every spare kreutzer buying liquor for yourself and your low companions, Novotny! I took it to heart at last, and here I am, a new man. Who has no friends and lives the respectable life of a grocer."

"You have *me*."

"I do indeed, but you will not copy me, and take *my* advice, for the improvement of your own prospects."

"What advice?"

"You know very well what advice. After the cartoon? And yet you keep to her bed—the whole town snickers at it. Christ, Moritz, for an intelligent man . . . I bring it up now, not to nag, but because she has just this minute walked into the Knight."

Rudi twisted around in his chair and saw Vasová threading through the tables, a fraught look on her face. He realized that for the duration of the recent action he had not thought once about her; but now it all came rushing back into his mind, like the return of a toothache that had been checked by oil of cloves.

He rose quickly, intending to offer his chair, but she threw arms around him and dotted his face with kisses.

"By Christ, I am happy to see you!" she said. "I was mad with worry. I heard the students were fighting in the Tandelmarkt, and I rushed there, but you had already gone. Are you hurt at all? By the Virgin, you look a wreck. I would have searched for you further, but then I heard that Anneke had been hurt, so I dashed back to the tenement. Come here, you wretch!"

Rudi saw that the girl had come into the tavern, but was hesitating at the head of the room. She marched forward with lagging steps, head unnaturally high, as if taking her place at the wall in front of a firing squad.

"Horrible child!" Vasová went on, "Do you know what she did? Let me sit down; I am entirely done in! And a schnapps, if you please. No, you may not sit down, Anneke, you must stand like a prisoner in the box. Well, you know how this whole affair started? No? It must be the day before yesterday. A certain Ferdi Dugaš, an idler, took a roll of silk ribbon from Edelstein's on the Schwefelgasse and refused to pay for it, for he said Edelstein had been cheating him on length for years and this was only right. Edelstein's two sons grabbed him and wouldn't let him go until he paid. Ferdi yelled murder, a crowd came, stones flew, the Edelsteins dropped their shutters, retreated to the upper floor, and threw old junk down on the crowd. The crowd grew and brought all the ruffians in the Old Town out of their stews and the attack on Jewish shops became general. And then . . . "

"Stop--let me get this down," said Novotny, scribbling.

"Why? It is not important. Anyway, the riot spread to the Tandelmarkt and into Josefov, because rumors started that the Jews were pouring buckets of vitriol from the rooftops and some evil children, hearing this, smeared oil and lampblack on their faces and went about screaming that the Jews had burned them up. This one among them, I am sorry to say. Why ever would you do such a wicked thing, Anneke? And why against the Jews? Has not Frau Grossbart fed you a thousand times? Is she not a Jewess? Speak, you monster!"

"They oppress the Czechs," said the child in a small voice, though her tone was defiant.

"How do they oppress us? By selling us food and clothing? By giving us employment? Tell me, did you ever see a Jew policeman, or a jailer, or a judge, or an official? *Those* oppress us, you ninny, not the Jews."

"Steinmetz, the landlord, oppresses us. You said he was a dir . . . "

Vasová clapped her hand over the child's mouth.

"Never mind that. Have you eaten? No, of course not, poor thing. Go ask Pan Bobka to give you some soup and bread! Go now!"

She pushed the child away, but Anneke stopped, turned and said, "You promised we could go to Petřín Hill today and fly kites."

Sisi raised her eyes to heaven and said, "Oh, my little goose, I cannot. I have to finish my article and I cannot afford a kite today."

"It is only one kreutzer. Ask Moritz! He is rich as God, you always say."

"What is the article?" asked Rudi mildly, and to change the subject.

"Bohemian dancing, would you believe? For the *Tisk*. This is what I have come to."

"Write your article," Rudi said. "I will take her kite flying on Petřín. In any case, you would not be permitted to cross the bridge. Travel is shut down entirely because of the disturbances, but my epaulettes will pass us through. We shall take a fiacre."

"We will fly a red-and-white kite, in honor of Bohemia," cried Anneke. "Can we, Moritz?"

"Yes, and we can write upon it, 'Down With the Empire,' if you like. Go now and get your meal!"

Sisi Vasová gaped at him in speechless wonder. On Paul Novotny's face, however, was a bleaker look, as if he had just seen someone fall from a window.

In the days when he toiled at the courts, Rudi would sometimes leave work and climb this hill, past the vineyards to its rocky crop. It was a favorite place of both his children. The height, near a thousand feet, suggested removal from the ordinary concerns of the world, and it was pleasant there, cool in summer and clear when Prague smoked in the winter. It was an odd thing to do when he was as exhausted as he was now, but he had been seized by an intense and undeniable desire to get away from both Vasová and Novotny, and this had presented itself. Besides that, he rather liked the strange child, so different from his own, but still a child who reminded him of times spent with his Reni and Fritz, like a smudged engraving of a familiar and beloved landscape.

He bought her a kite from the stall there, allowing her the choice. She chose the largest and most gaudy and she did write "Down with the empire" on it with Rudi's pencil, and also "Bogomila."

"Why do you write Bogomila on your kite?" Rudi asked her as they walked up the slope. "Is she a friend of yours?"

"No, silly, it's the kite's name," Anneke answered. "It has a name like our boat—our *secret* boat, you know, and I am not to tell anyone. Can you help me to tie on the string? My knots always fail."

Later, when the kite was launched rattling into the sky, he stood on the rocky peak of the hill; the wind that flew the child's kite disarranged his hair, and he took great draughts of the pure gust into his lungs. A bird, a black crow, flew below him, and beyond its wing lay the city of Prague: the twin pointed spires of the Týn church; the great palaces, Wallenstein, Kinsky, Kolowrat, Clam-Gallas; the town hall; beyond that the yellow block of the flour depot, and his own, imperceptible home nearby. Beautiful; but there was another way of looking at it. Most of Prague was within easy cannon-shot of where he stood. It was perfectly clear that who held Petřín held the city and its fragile revolution in his fist.

Rudi was seized with a terrible impatience then, for what he did not know: the urge to do something about this awful vulnerability, perhaps? He wanted to leave immediately, to grab someone by the lapels and shout, look, look, you fool! But the child was having such a joyous time with her kite, dashing back and forth across the sward with the flag of her nation high above, yelping her glee. He sat down against the hollow rock, felt the sun on his face, smelled the spicy scent of some flower he could not identify. Berthe would know, he thought, who knew the names of all the flowers and trees. In a few moments he slipped into an exhausted sleep.

The girl shook him awake; a tree had claimed her kite and there was nothing to be done, and she accepted this with good grace. The sun had dropped low, so that its slanting rays turned the city into a stage set, and gilded the red tiles of the roofs and towers. She held his hand as they walked down the hill before long shadows to the cab rank on Karmelitengasse.

"I do not often take cabs," she observed as they passed through the cordon of troops guarding the bridge, "they are oppressive."

Regular troops, thought Rudi, not the National Guard. Was it a sign? Of what? He had no idea.

He said, "Then I appreciate your indulgence. But surely the cab drivers must earn their bread. And the horses must have their oats."

"True, but then everyone should have a cab, and not just the rich bourgeois. After the revolution it shall be so." She yawned and closed her eyes. "After, all will be so wonderful and free," she murmured.

"I have many learned friends who would concur," said Rudi, and watched the child collapse into sleep upon his shoulder.

"You are the best man in Prague," said Vasovà when she returned from the alcove in which the child slept. "No one else I know or even imagined would have taken a child not his own to a park after fighting a battle all day and night."

I am the worst man in Prague, he thought to himself, but made his face smile.

She slid into his lap and kissed him. Her rose scent was tainted by the prevailing stink of the recent fires in Josefov, a few streets distant. She was wearing a thin robe printed with cabbage roses, her usual attire when writing. Beneath it, not a stitch.

"Did you finish your article?"

"Yes, and copied it out fair. I feel like I need a reward for all that wonderful exegesis of the polka, scočná and furiant, and you must have a reward for being the best man in Prague and protecting the poor Jews and so forth. Perhaps this reward will be the same thing?"

"That would be most convenient," said Rudi.

"And efficient," she said, reaching beneath her thighs, clever fingers undoing, unbuttoning, exposing, massaging. A quick motion, a small cry, and she was on him, hot and slick around his sex.

"Oh, this is wonderful," she said into his ear between her gasping breaths, "I swear I have never had anything like this, I feel you stabbing up, it is touching my heart, it is killing me, oh!"

She tangled her hands in his hair and clasped her mouth upon the side of his neck, her teeth digging into his skin, strangling her cries so as not to awaken the child. After that she moved more violently up and down on the flesh that joined them, speaking into his ear, interrupted at intervals by her muffled ecstasies: I love you I hate you kill me I can stand it I am lost this is wrong this is right, have you ever had this before do you have it with her does she do what I do? Oh don't answer, it is wrong to ask, you will leave me, oh never leave me, though you must, I know it but not now, stay longer, a little longer, will you leave me, will you, will you?

"Not while this is going on at any rate," he said.

She laughed and laughed at that, and through her laughter, she said, "Then I will make it go on and on and never never stop, no never."

But it did and he was granted a few moments of oblivion, in which he did not think about Kunningshelm or cannons on the Petřín heights.

"Well, Moritz, you look like you have been to the wars," said Alderman Borosch, as Rudi entered the corporation chamber in the town hall. It was only the tenth or so time the phrase had been used, for Rudi only had one uniform and though Gregor had sponged and darned late into the night, the equipage no longer looked shop-new. No one except the banker Maisel mentioned his part in the broils of the past two days, and in doing so assured Rudi that his acts would never be forgotten.

The Burgomeister opened the meeting. Rudi had hoped that Count Thun would be there, but the governor had begged off, pleading a conflicting meeting with the Estates. Mohlmann was a competent burgomeister, reasonably honest and efficient, who could be trusted to keep the streets swept, the lamps lit and the drunks jailed, but he was not the one to take any action that he had not taken a thousand times before.

He was even more cautious—they were all cautious—because of the riots, for while they had cheered the institution of a new order, and while freedom and constitutions and newspapers were all very well, it remained essential that their property not be put at risk. So Mohlmann and the others in the town council and the provisional government—the same worthies occupying seats in both—once again did not welcome Rudi's proposal that the National Guard occupy the Petřín hills to forestall any attempt by imperial troops to emplace guns there.

"Gentlemen, I suggest you remember one thing," he said to them. "This revolution was carried out against a form of government that still exists. It has not gone away. It hates what we have done here and would dearly love to return affairs to the status quo ante March 13 of this year."
(Cries of no, never!)

"It has an army that is intact. We have a small and ill-armed national guard, which is commanded by a senior officer of the imperial and royal army who is not famous for his liberal views. Will he step in to resist if the army decides to emplace guns on the heights? I very much doubt it. And once guns overlook the city, there is no longer a revolution."

A dozen voices spoke at once. Mohlmann banged his gavel and when the hubbub receded, said, "Herr Moritz, surely this is alarmist. Do you really suppose that the army, *our* army, after all, would menace a peaceful town with artillery? The idea is preposterous."

"It is not preposterous in Italy or Hungary," replied Rudi, "Towns have been bombarded there. Truly are cannon called the ultimate argument of kings."

"Yes, but really, Moritz," said Lörner, "those countries are in rebellion against the empire."

"And we are not? Have you all forgotten 'forty-four?'"

"We were not bombarded in 'forty-four," said Maisel.

"Because the revolution failed in 'forty-four. Forty-four was an affair of gendarmes. But we have *succeeded*! We have made a revolution and now we must defend ourselves against the counter-revolution that is sure to come. And the key to that defense lies on the heights, on Petřín and Vyšehrad."

"What, Vyšehrad too!" cried Lörner. "You want us to seize an imperial fortress? Have you gone mad? Gentlemen, we all appreciate Herr Moritz's services I am sure, but I would remind him that our revolution was a peaceful one, a revolution of law and order. I would further remind him that we have a governor, who commands both the regular military and the national guard, and that this governor, Count Thun, is entirely in agreement with the agenda we have laid out over the past months. Any move by the provisional government or its agents to occupy the heights would be regarded as an unbearable provocation. Can anyone imagine our good Count Thun ordering the bombardment of his native town?"

Someone giggled. Then everyone burst into laughter, except for Rudi, who sat with a face of stone.

"You are in a black mood this afternoon, Herr Moritz," observed Hans von Pannau. "I pray it is not a trouble in your family?"

"No, no, merely politics. A gang of fools will not do as they ought."

"It is often so with fools. This is a good argument for autocracy, you know, for with it one only has to deal with a single fool, and he cannot see everywhere. And sometimes God may place a genius on the throne."

Rudi, however, was in no mood to be drawn. He arranged his notebook and said, "Sir, we left you and Lennart hanging from a pole in the camp of the bashi-bazouks. Pray continue your narrative."

Yes, poor Lennart. As we hung there, I heard him say, "Baron, dear, all things taken together, it is my opinion we should have gone for billiards in Dresden. But as my old Mam used to say, make sure the bucket is under the tit before you squeeze. It will take some doing to get you out of here, I think."

"Do you have a plan?" I asked.

He said, "A plan's as good as a fan to a dead man," and began to swing on his bonds, until he was able to grasp the pole. Have I said how strong he was? There was a steel-yard in the depot at Ustin that we employed to weigh grain sacks, and once, on a bet, he sat on a horse beneath it, with his ankles tied under the horse with a girth and he was able to touch his chin to the bar, hauling the horse clear off the ground.

I wander. Once, as I say, he had gripped the pole, he brought himself up to the straddle and then he chewed through the ropes. He could chew through anything; I once saw him bite through a horseshoe nail. He dropped free and whispered, "Now I will get us a blade, sir, for your ropes and to cut us out of here."

He vanished. In a few moments I heard a scuffle and a strangled cry, and there was Lennart grinning up at me with a scimitar in his grip. But alas, he had taken too long about the ropes, for dawn was already breaking, the fallen guard was found, the alarm was given; I heard the shouts and the running of many men, and in a trice we were surrounded. I think he would have accounted for half the villains if they had allowed it. But after losing a near dozen to his sword, they shot him down. Then they impaled him. Oh, yes, as I looked at him screaming on his pole, I be-thought myself of the promise I had made him years ago, that I would see him raised up, and would have wept, had I not had to show a face before those devils.

Then they prepared a pole for me. Their impaler was an old man, three teeth in his mouth and a leather face, mumbling to himself as he examined the place he was about to cut. You understand I was being gripped, arm and leg, by eight men, four on a limb and my legs spread near to cracking. He leaned over me and gripped my privates, clearing the way for his vile cut. I closed my eyes. The next moment I felt a wash of hot liquid on my belly and I thought he had done me. But then there was the sound of a rifle shot, a fusillade. A weight fell upon me. Opening my eyes, I found myself face to face with my would-be impaler, his brains bulging out of his shattered forehead. Another man fell on top of me, after which I saw nothing, but I heard hundreds of shots, shouts, the clash of steel, the death-screams of men and horses, all the dreadful music of battle.

These faded. I saw light again as the bodies covering me were pulled away, and there was Paradowski. Vaslov had gotten through to Ustin the previous evening and Paradowski had ridden breakneck all the night through with two squadrons to surprise the bashi-bazouks at first light. Little men on small fast horses, riding like the wind—it was the Kinski's raison d'être, and it had saved my life.

"Are you all right, Hans?" he asked and I cried, "For the love of God, take him down!"

They did, and I held Lennart's suffering body in my arms, and wept like a child. He was still alive. The fiends do it so a man can stay alive for days. He was screaming of course, great hoarse cries like a gutted horse, and he did not know me. I asked for a knife then. I kissed him and cut his throat and he passed away in my arms the next minute.

That moment ended what remained of my boyhood. The iron passed into my soul and any mercy I had in it leaked out onto the bloody earth. My tears, that had soaked

Mirek's tunic, ceased, and I swear that I have not shed another since, not even at the death of my wife and her child.

"You married?" asked Rudi, his pencil suspended.

"Yes, but all in order, all in its proper place," said the old baron, and continued.

I demanded clothing; they found me breeches and a shirt. I demanded a saber. They found mine in the tent of the *yuzbashi,* who had survived, though wounded. He was still smiling that peculiar smile when I struck off his head. I had the head taken along, buried and then, when cleaned, made into a drinking cup. It's in the beer cellar, if you would care to see it.

"Not just now, Herr Baron. Pray continue."

We killed all the other Turks that had survived, including the boys, catamites in the main, but that was how we did it in the Banat. Perhaps fifty of them had fled, but Paradowski sent a column south under Hoth, and the fleeing horsemen ran into their ambush. None escaped, I believe.

Later, we organized a punitive expedition. We crossed into Servia and burnt a dozen miserable Turk villages, slaughtering all the inhabitants we could catch. If I listed the atrocities I witnessed your hair would turn snow-white, so I will pass by that period in decent silence.

Only . . . the hatreds that rive this empire, of people for those who speak a different tongue or hold to different customs, is beyond the imagination of you liberals dwelling in the peaceful towns. You simply have no idea. It is only the Hapsburg fist that keeps them from each other's throats. Let that fist but slip—which I believe is your entire program— and the nice practices of the military frontier will come home, even to Prague and Vienna.

I see by your face that you think this the ravings of a superannuated brute from a fiercer age. But it is so, Herr Moritz, it is so. Loyalty to the crown is the only hope you have.

Well, let us leave that for the moment. The Kinsky was then transferred to the Austrian corps supporting the

Russians on the Moldovan front, where we beat the Turks at Focsani, as I have told. Belgrade soon fell and the war ended. We lost thirty thousand men in it, mostly from disease, including the Emperor Joseph, who could never keep his nose out of anything, and insisted on leading the army in person. Also dead was Conrad Franz Graf von Leiningen-Skorczy, father of my boyhood tormentor and my nemesis in Prague, who loyally followed his emperor to the Danube swamps and succumbed to the same miasma. So I could have returned to my former life, but I felt that it, like my life at Pannau, had been destroyed by events. I was no longer the billiard sharp and rake; I had become something harder and grimmer, a royal and imperial dragoon, and that just in time for the greatest war in history.

I suppose I must consider myself fortunate, despite all that had befallen me. I had comrades, and a regiment to be proud of, and one friend of the heart, something no man can well do without, and a leader I would have followed anywhere. This is all a soldier needs besides bread and beer, horse and steel, shot and powder.

I was content to go where I was ordered and fight who happened to be the enemy of the day. Perhaps you would not care for such a life. It had little of the freedom you seem to prize above all other goods, and yet I believe we were all of us as happy as the general lot of men. This is a puzzle you should consider before you shove your freedom down the throats of those who have not asked for it. You may be disappointed with the uses to which they put their new toy.

Freedom had by that time broken out in France, and in 'ninety-three, as is well known, we Austrians joined with the Prussians, some petty states, and a few thousand French nobles to go to Paris and put an end to those capers, restoring to the French bastards their rightful monarch.

The old soldier ruffled through the maps that lay before him on the low table. The two men were in the Green Room, and Rudi's eyes kept shifting to a peculiar painting above the mantle. A lovely woman sat with a boy, who held his hand out to a spaniel. What attracted his eye he could not have said, except that after the Baron's oblique mention of a wife, he was mad with curiosity to find out the identity of the subjects. An importunate rapping of the old man's knuckles brought him back to the present, or rather to the past: the year 1793.

We marched out of Coblenz in August in rain. In fact, I believe it rained every day of that damned campaign, and chill fog when it stopped. It was the Prussians' show, the great army of the great Frederick, commanded by the Duke of Brunswick, Frederick's cousin, and we made up part of the Austrian corps under Clerfayt.

I was aide-de-camp and galloper for Colonel Max.

Brunswick was a good enough general for his time, but his time was past, as events proved. You know how the battle we fought that year turned out. We dragoons played little part; it was an affair of guns, not cavalry. The French foot and horse were not up to much at the time, but their artillery was the best in Europe.

One curious incident sticks in my memory of Valmy. We were stationed on the Prussian right, on the crest of a hill looking across a sloping mead at the hill opposite, where the French batteries were blazing away at us, balls whizzing by and so forth. The ground was sodden, which was good, because the balls struck and mired themselves, rather than bowling along doing destruction on the bounce. Then, from the Prussian lines came a lone rider, trotting across as if on a ride in the Prater.

Every one of the officers present had their glass upon the figure, around whom the French balls were flying, sending up great columns of mud and water when they struck the earth. I did not have a glass, but I heard one staff colonel say,

"That fellow is the savant who travels with the King of Prussia, you know, the poet, von Goethe."

To which my colonel replied, "I believe you are correct, sir, it is indeed the poet. But the French are finding the range and if he does not remove from where he is, he will be a dead poet." He turned in the saddle and looked at me. "Pannau, trot down there, if you would, and escort that lunatic back to the Prussian lines."

I dashed off breakneck, although it was hard going with the mud. I could hear the hum of the balls as they flew overhead on their way to our batteries. I had been shot over by cannon at Foscari, but it was nothing like this, an almost continuous roar of guns, a river of cannonballs, you could see them as dots against the leaden sky, like great horseflies over a shit-pile.

I reached my man, who was jogging along and looking around him. To my amazement, he stopped his horse, took a notebook from the pocket of his redingote and proceeded to scribble in it.

"Sir! Herr von Goethe!" I cried. "We must go back to the lines, sir. It is not safe out here."

He smiled at me, saying, "Oh, they won't shoot at me. I am a civilian," and continued his writing. "You know," he said, "one has read about war, but it is not quite the same, is it? One would never, without experiencing it, have imagined the sound of a cannon ball flying overhead. One never hears anything remotely like it in peacetime."

A ball flew directly at us, though a little low. Had the ground been firm the pair of us would have been destroyed, but as it was the shot struck, skipped, and buried itself not five yards away, sending its filthy spire high above our heads.

I rounded on him and cried, "By Christ, von Goethe, this is the second time you have tried to kill me--first with that damned Werther of yours and now here. You are ordered back to the lines instantly. Now go, you fool!" With which I brought my crop down on the haunches of his mare, and off we went.

That was the famous cannonade of Valmy. Brunswick made two half-hearted attacks, then gave up the fight. We disengaged; the French rebels were able to boast that they had beaten legitimacy's best, and the next day Paris deposed the king and declared a republic. Colonel Max kept muttering about the end of the world and drank more than was his wont.

"We can stop here, if you like. Our next few meetings will be all war and bloodshed. I will give you, in fact, a portfolio of notes I have from time to time written down. Colonel Max was always doing so. Write it down at the moment or as near as you can manage, is what he used to say, for your mind will write its own false story after very little time has passed. You will find it all there: Fleurus, Lodi, Marengo, Ulm, Austerlitz, the cavalry battle at Liebertwolkwitz before Leipzig, the overthrow of the monster, all of it. What I *will* tell you, however, is not something I ever cared to commit to writing, until now."

Twenty-eight

Rudi avoided Vasová that evening, dining at home and working late on the Bohemian constitution. He slept badly, amid nightmares seasoned with the horrors of which he had heard that day. After putting in a scant few hours at his office, he changed into uniform and inspected his troops, after which he hurried to the von Pannau house, anxious to be allowed to write down what had never yet seen paper. The baron was seated where he had been the other day, a large map spread out before him. He looked briefly at Rudi's uniform and ran his eyes up and down, as if in service of an ancient instinct of military inspection. Then he began.

I mentioned the fight at Fleurus: an important battle, another botch by one of our wonderful field marshals, and like Valmy, one that changed the world forever. Fleurus came some nine months afterward and lost us the Netherlands, also forever. The French under Jourdan and eighty thousand men moved to take Flanders and invested the fortress of Charleroi. The Dutch chased them away, but they came back, and on the morning of the fight we had no idea whether the fortress lay in our hands or theirs. We were with Beaulieu on our extreme left, facing the French under Marceau.

Now our colonel used to say that in almost every fight, there is a time when the tide of battle turns upon the actions of a small number of determined men at a particular point in space and time, affecting many times their number and even changing the fate of nations. It is therefore the responsibility of every commander to discover where that point in space and time is, and to go there.

Early in the day at Fleurus, we were able to push in the French right, and some of their formations broke entirely, with Frenchies running pell-mell toward the river, or into the forest. We were ordered to pursue, which we declined to do, for our colonel had other plans.

He had of course pushed vedettes out since dawn, gathering intelligence of the enemy and of the terrain. One of them had found a boy who knew a trail through the Copieaux forest, and in a flash Colonel Max sent the whole regiment into the woods, a fearful risk, as horsemen are near helpless in close-grown forest. But the boy was true and we emerged in the French rear astride the only road that led between Charleroi, where the French had their reserves, and Marceau's crumbling position.

Colonel Max sent gallopers back to Beaulieu and Coburg, telling them that he had found the key to the battle, and he would undertake to hold the road until infantry and guns in strength should arrive, for we had it in our power by so bold a move to turn the French flank and roll up their whole army like a ball of twine.

I need hardly add that such an evolution was far beyond the imagination of any Austrian general of that period. The request was denied and we were ordered to go chase Marceau's broken formations.

"How unfortunate that this order was delayed or lost," said Colonel Max, when these decisions reached him, "but such things happen in war. Failing any direction from higher headquarters, I will make a stand here and attempt to at least delay the movement of reinforcements to the French right."

No sooner had he made his dispositions than a regiment of French infantry came marching into view, from the French reserve under General Hatry east of Charleroi. They found their way blocked by four squadrons of the Kinsky arrayed in four ranks. I had received permission to ride with the first squadron, next to Paradowski, and I watched as the French, halting at a distance some three hundred yards from us, quite properly formed square and prepared to receive cavalry. They must have imagined the danger to be slight from a single regiment, for, as was later discovered, they knew an infantry brigade was coming along behind them.

Imagine their surprise then, when at the sound of a bugle, our other two squadrons, including every one of our rifles, stood up from the young grain on one side of the road, and emerged from the woods on the other, and gave them three volleys. The riflemen accounted for more than half their officers. It was not then the custom to target epaulets, but our colonel had told us that rebels against their king could not be considered proper officers and should be treated like Turks. This done, we charged.

A cavalry charge against a square of infantry is a rum thing, you know, and almost always futile, for the mathematics are against it. Consider that one side of a regimental square has near two hundred fifty muskets. In the hands of steady infantry, these can fire four shots a minute, and a man upon a horse is an unmissable target.

We advanced at the walk for a hundred yards; then the bugle blew for the trot. Truly, nothing I know is so beautiful as light cavalry at the trot, the helmets rising and falling in waves like the sea, and the sound like the sea as four hundred sabers leap from their scabbards at once. There is pathos too, for one understands that all these perfect bright uniforms and these well-groomed horses will many of them go down in the next seconds, falling into mud, gore, pain and death.

"But Herr Baron," Rudi objected, "how then can you call it beauty? Why is it not the *ruin* of beauty? All those young men driven to their deaths, most of them, I wager, not having an idea in their head of why they must die."

"Well, sir, ideas are not of much use to a dragoon. Yes, they die, but they die in glory. We all owe God a death, you know, and He wisely offers some lucky ones a choice of what kind. Is it better to die a demented toothless sack of bones after a life of desperate hard labor with but a few coarse pleasures? Or to perish in an instant in the full vigor of youth, dressed in bright colors, mounted on a brave horse, with steel in your hand and a grin on your face?"

Rudi found he had no ready answer to the question, and the baron continued.

And there was glory aplenty that day! At a hundred yards out we began the gallop. A cavalry trooper at full tilt will cover that distance in ten seconds. A steady infantry will hold fire until five of those seconds have elapsed and then send two hundred fifty balls at you, and in that storm of lead a good part of your first squadron will go down in a tangle of kicking, screaming horses and dead and dying men, forming a barrier to the next squadron, for a horse will balk at running over such an obstacle. The force of your charge is thus diminished and the enemy has the chance to put another volley or two into the second squadron, and then you are sunk; which is why dragoons should not charge an unbroken square of steady infantry.

But we had unsteadied them as I have described. Most of their officers were down, and they were looking at a great wave comprising seventy tons of horse and rider coming toward them at thirty miles an hour. This last five seconds is where a Rittmeister earns his pay, for he must in that tiny instant see where men are wavering, turning their backs, not pointing their pieces. We were all screaming 'Nederlands' at the top of our voices, and now Paradowski spurred his charger ahead of the line and struck out for a particular section of the French square. We received our volley but it was a weak one.

Paradowski had dropped his reins and had his pistol out in his left hand, and remarkably in that moment he snapped his head around and looked me in the face. O what a sight! His handsome visage was transformed, god-like, as if the entire force of his life was refined to a single shining point. This exaltation, sir, is what we call glory and this instant is the only shop where it is for sale. You may say, death is also on offer there, and that death is horrible and so there can be nothing connected to it but is polluted by the contact.

Every man and every nation must decide if that is so. As for me, I know there are two sisters, one hideous, one beautiful beyond dreams, death and glory. You cannot have one without the other. That is a dilemma of mankind. But I cannot conceive living in a world without the possibility of glory.

Well, not to go on tediously. We hit them and they crumpled like tissue paper. You see, no infantryman will stand in front of a charging horse. They must quail and make way. Your pistol takes the man on your left and your saber strikes down the man on your right. Then you are through and into the square and you all race to where the standards fly and the commanders are and you do slaughter there and then dash on to strike the opposite side of the square, taking the soldiers in the rear, and then your second and third squadrons come in at an angle on either side. In a few minutes an infantry regiment has turned into a maddened rabble running this way and that, desperate to escape the ring of horsemen and the terrible rise and fall of the sabers.

The slaughter had almost finished, only a few infantry escaping to the shelter of the woods, when Paradowski hailed me, looking like the God of war, his teeth flashing in his powder-blackened face. His saber dangled from its knot, the whole length clotted with blood and black with blood too was his sleeve to the elbow, a few scarlet marks even upon his cheek, as will happen when you strike off the head of a foot-soldier.

He said, "How now, Pannau! Is this not a red-letter day! I do not believe that a regiment of light dragoons has ever broken a regimental square before. We have made history!"

As he said that, there came some shots from the edge of the wood—what, have I said something disturbing? You look like you have bitten into a sour plum.

"I suppose it is this talk of slaughter, casually described, like the account of a fête. And I admit to a greater repugnance, shameful as it is for a confessed liberal, toward the killing of Frenchmen than of bashi-bazouks."

"No soldier thinks so: an enemy is an enemy. Had it not occurred to you that even war in civilized Europe is a brutal business?"

"Yes, one knows it in general, but the specifics . . . they make me shudder."

"They make *me* shudder, sir! But as to your specifics, your hand-to-hand melee is very so *very* specific, a man against a man or two or three. Time stretches out in the most peculiar way and burns itself into your memory, like scorching a paper under a glass with the sun's rays. I remember the face of every man I ever killed, except for the ones I shot in the back."

"But how did you stand it, sir? Forgive my presumption, Herr Baron, but you do not appear to me to be a man of coarse sensibility. Your life is all fine sentiment and deep feeling."

The baron showed the tooth-concealing grin that served him as a smile. "I will take that as a compliment, Herr Moritz. You have a good deal of penetration, I find. You have asked that question before now and I will give you the same answer: it must be done. The nation must be defended from those who would conquer it, and this necessarily involves killing large numbers of men. It is our duty as soldiers of the crown. And there is honor. Some men can do horrible things in the name of duty and honor. Others cannot. I, of course, am a man who can,. And you are another, sir."

Rudi stared. If the old man had started dancing a minuet he could not have been more surprised. At the same time he thought it the greatest thing anyone had ever said of him to his face.

"How can you know that, sir?" he asked.

"Oh, merely forty some years of experience in judging men, at the risk of my own life and those of my dragoons. Ten thousand times I had to judge if a man would break or stay. It is odd. You were not bred to it at all, yet you know duty and honor."

"Herr Baron, that is a flattering thing for you to say, but I can hardly think how you formed such an opinion on the evidence of our brief colloquies."

"Hmm. Well, the fact is, sir, that I know a good deal about you. I suppose I know nearly everything about you."

Rudi stiffened. "What do you mean by that, Herr Baron?" he asked, in a tightly controlled voice.

"Just that you have been watched, sir. Investigated, in a word. Surely you expected this, carrying on as you have."

"You have been *spying* on me?"

The old man uttered a sigh. "I had thought to delay this until after my whole story had been told, but I suppose I must confess all now, or you will dash away with your outrage and I will have no one to hear my story to the end."

"Oh, I do assure you, sir, Prague is full of people who can listen and write."

"But only you will serve. Tell me, did you wonder why I chose you of all these notional literate fellows? Or paid you such a princely sum for what is after all a clerk's position?"

"Yes, I did wonder," Rudi admitted.

"And your conclusions?"

"That you are a conniving old reactionary and you wished to suborn a leader of the revolution, although what advantage you might gain by this effort I cannot yet determine."

There occurred a short pause, and then the baron burst into choking laughter. After coughing into a large handkerchief and wiping his eyes, he said, "My God, so you thought that, did you? I am afraid that suborning revolutionaries is not any longer in my department. It never really was; shooting them, yes, but I am far too unsubtle for the *suborning* trade. No, my interest in you is far more personal. I ask you to recall a night when your friend Novotny encouraged you to attend the baths. It was at the end of February."

"Yes—what of it?"

"You were observed. Part of the observer's brief was to note down any distinguishing marks on the subject, marks normally obscured by clothing. You have adverted before to a brown mark at the base of your spine. This mark was noted and, in the course of time, described in a report that happened to cross my desk. You will recall asking me how my father knew without doubt that I was his child and not some other man's, and my answer, the small brown blemish we call the wolf mark. I had it and so do you—by report. You will do me the favor of exhibiting it."

"What, now?"

"This instant, if you please," said the baron, in a voice so commanding and with a gaze so fierce that Rudi found himself obeying, like a man in a dream. He removed his tunic, lifted his shirt, loosened his trousers, and turned his back.

"Yes, indeed," said the baron. "A very well-formed wolf mark. No, do not ask questions just yet. When you have put yourself in order, go to that desk!" The baron pointed to a handsome mahogany campaign desk standing to one side of the fireplace. "In the center drawer you will find a file, in which lies a document that will be of some interest to you."

Rudi did as he was told, returning to his seat with the file. It proved to be a certificate attesting to the marriage on the fourth of October, 1813, of Cornet Karl-Franz Victor Johann Freiherr von Pannau-Kinsky to Caroline Augusta Hetzen, spinster.

"What does this mean?" said Rudi. "I don't understand . . . That is my mother's name. But this is impossible. She married my father in December of 1813."

"Indeed she did. But not before contracting a previous marriage with a foolish young officer, who died two weeks after the wedding, at Leipzig. They were wed just long enough to leave her with child. That child is you. That young officer was my son. I am your grandfather."

"Impossible," Rudi repeated. His head swam, and he had some difficulty keeping himself erect in his chair. But, of course, it was not at all impossible. It explained a great deal: the baron's interest in him, the lucrative employment, the pervasive sense that he was not one with the Moritz clan.

"I see you are shocked," said the baron. "Well, it is disturbing to discover you are not the man you thought you were, but this must be a continuous discovery for any man of parts, if not usually in quite so dramatic a fashion. In any case, you may now style yourself Johann Rudolf Freiherr von Pannau-Kinski. As I have said, all males in our direct line are barons of the empire. I bid you welcome to our clan, Herr Baron."

"This will destroy my family," said Rudi in a low voice, as if to himself.

"It will do no such thing. Your mother may be taxed with an absence of grief, or a too-easy eye for the main chance. But she could not have known of her pregnancy at the time, and if she concealed her brief marriage from your-- I suppose we must now call him your step-father--that is hardly a hanging offense. Moritz will be glad enough to have a baron in the family. Your relations with him are in any case not warm; this news will hardly break his heart. Your wife may enjoy being a Baronin, and your little boy is now a baron too. I think it's rather like a fairy tale, don't you?"

"I think it is horrid. To be one man, with a family and a heritage, however humble, and then to discover you are someone else? How can one bear it?"

"Oh, one can bear all sorts of surprises, sir. If you take up your pencil again, I will relate to you a surprise I had to bear, compared to which yours is a bagatelle."

When Feldmarschall Coburg learned Charleroi had fallen, he lost interest in the battle and ordered a withdrawal. I thought our Colonel Max had been angry after Valmy, but his rage then was nothing to his rage now. To his staff assembled after the battle, he declared, "By Christ, we could have drowned the baby at Valmy, and we could have strangled the infant in its cradle today. But when this revolution grows into the strength of manhood, as must soon happen, all the royal armies in Europe will not check it."

I heard of this later from Silmaringen, who happened to have been present. I was otherwise engaged at the time. Did I say there were shots from the infantry stragglers? Yes, and this is why, as grim a business as it is, you must kill or make prisoner every member of a broken square, for you must never leave muskets at your rear when you withdraw.

I saw Paradowski fall, struck in the back. I rushed to his side and found the ball had entered at the point of the shoulder blade. My heart sank, for such a wound was almost always mortal. He had fallen on his face and when I turned him over I saw that the shot had gone through-and-through, a great hole high in the front of his tunic, near the collarbone. He was awake and writhing, his handsome face contorted to a gargoyle's mask. I shouted out, "The Princess has been shot! First Squadron to me!"

Instantly, or so it seemed, he was lifted and tied across a saddle face down. We departed that place, to the doleful sound of shots as dragoons put down the wounded horses and killed the infantry stragglers.

At this time the office of regimental surgeon was not common in our army. The wounded were left on the field, or in the care of friends. Mirek had many friends. We took him to a farm cottage on the other side of the Copieaux Wood, though we had to fight our way through random French detachments to get there. I suppose the unluckiest Frenchmen that day, save those of the regiment we had destroyed, were the ones who tried to stop us.

The house was a large one, almost a small manor house, and we took him to a room upstairs and laid him on a bed. His servant Wojtek was sent for, arrived, and took charge of my wounded friend, while I dashed off on horseback to find a medical person.

The road leading from Fleurus was thronged with carts, carriages and trudging peasants fleeing the battle. From a party in a calash I received the intelligence that the convent of St. Blaise in Gembloux had established a temporary hospital and that a Dr. Etienne Gerard was treating wounded there.

I rode with my saber in hand and those who could leapt from my path. I suppose I did for a number of domestic fowl and some dogs en route, but arrived at St. Blaise late in the afternoon, it being still light.

Wounded were coming in from both sides, the French under a flag of truce, of course, and the white habits of the sisters were no longer white down the front, but carmine. Dr. Gerard was attending a private soldier when I accosted him and demanded that he come at once to save my Mirek. He smiled and said that it was quite impossible for him to leave his patients here, and when I pointed my pistol at him, he actually laughed in my face, saying, "Young man, feel free to shoot me, but if you do many of these poor fellows will die and your friend will die as well, whereas if you bring him here, he may have a chance. Where did the ball enter?"

I described the wound as well as I could, and he responded, "Through and through is good news. It means we will not have to probe for the ball; also, if he did not perish at once from exsanguination, it means that no major vessels were severed. Thus the primary danger is mortification. Place him on a litter between two horses or find a carriage and bring him here. If he survives the journey he may live. Or you can shoot me. In the meantime, I must attend to this man's jaw."

He turned away. I did as he said, of course, nor will I dwell on the details of that dreadful passage. Suffice it to say that it failed to kill him.

So now we are at the convent. There was a ward for officers, with a bed for each and drapes separating the beds, one from the other. I waited, pacing in the hall outside, thinking that God could not be so cruel as to deprive me of Mirek and Lennart both. I went to the chapel and prayed on my knees, which I had not done since a child, when Ljuba, Lennart, and I said our prayers together at night.

When I returned to the officers' ward Dr. Gerard was just emerging, wiping his hands on a bloody rag, and shaking his head, a bemused expression on his face.

"Oh, Doctor, tell me he lives!" I cried.

"Well, always saving putrefaction, the wound does not appear to be mortal."

I thanked God.

He went on, "There are two interesting aspects to this case, Herr Leutnant. The first is that the ball struck the proximal margin of the scapula and instead of smashing down into the chest cavity and destroying the heart or lungs, it travelled upward instead, breaking the clavicle and exiting above it, entirely missing the subclavian artery, a stroke of fortune I have not often seen. Your comrade is extremely lucky."

"This is so, doctor," said I, "for no one in our regiment has placed himself in more danger, nor, before this day, had he received so much as a scratch. But what is the other interesting aspect?"

"Oh, only that your captain is a woman."

I stared at him. "I don't understand," I said.

"That the human race is divided into two sexes? Well, it is so, and your captain is of the opposite one to you and me, although perhaps I should not be so assuming in your case. She was tightly corseted, and when I cut off the restricting garment, out popped two female breasts, small but well formed, perfectly normal. Upon further examination I found the usual female pudenda, also normal--not a hint of androgyny in the clitoris, for example. A woman, without question; and I took the liberty of determining that she is *virgo intacta*. Now sir, if you will excuse me, I have other patients to attend to, most of them not as lucky as your friend."

I went instantly to where Paradowski lay. His Wojtek was with him, tears streaking the grime on his face as he mopped his master's brow with a cloth. Mirek was covered with a sheet, but it was soaked with sweat and the contours of his body were perfectly apparent. I looked at his face and then at Wojtek's.

Do you know how it feels when you awake in a dark room at home and you imagine a stranger standing there, and you feel a pang of fear? Then, an instant later, your vision undergoes a kind of jerk and you realize it is only your old

bureau or a coat upon a rack? It was like that. Of course I
saw then that what I had seen as a handsome man was actually a beautiful girl and that Wojtek was naturally enough a
woman as well.

"Who is she?" I demanded. I spoke in Czech and the
servant answered in a mix of that language and Polish.
"Ana Miroslava Paradowska, your honor," she answered.
"From Zamocz, in Poland."

She told me the story without much urging, as people
will when a secret long held has been exposed. Wojtek (born
Wanda) had been raised as a body servant to the *szlatcha*
maiden, as Lennart had been with me. The father was a major in the Army of Poland and not a very good man, a drunk
and an inveterate gambler. He fought with his wife ferocious-
ly about his drinking and debts, and beat her too, which was
one reason why she took lovers. Her death had occurred just
as Mirek had described, and after that, the father had more or
less sold his girl as bride to one of his cronies, as payment for
a debt incurred at faro. Rejecting this wicked arrangement,
she plotted her escape, with Wojtek or Wanda helping the
conspiracy. She was seventeen when she slipped across the
border into Austrian Galicia and presented herself as a young
man to the first cavalry regiment that passed, which happened
to be the Kinskys.

"But how is it possible for a young girl to be . . .
him?" I protested. "The rider, the swordsman? The bravest
of the brave?"

"I hope you don't think women lack bravery, your
honor, for if they did there would be no longer a human race.
 But as for her . . . one day when she was about three, her father and mother got into one of their fights, terrible it was,
sir, things flung, blows struck. He beat her to the floor. She
said he couldn't fuck worth a damn, begging your pardon,
your honor, but you asked for the tale. He couldn't fuck a
woman as she deserved, so she had fucked all his friends. I
don't know if it was so, but women will say things like that to
men they wish to hurt. At the time the baby was in its cradle

and crying hard and my mother went to pick her up--I was not more than six myself, and my mother was wet-nurse and nursery maid to the baby. But he knocked her out of the way with his fist, snatched up the little mite, and threw her out of the window. But the Holy Virgin saved her and made her land, not on the hard ground but on the drum."

"The drum? What drum?"

"A kettle-drum, your honor, of the regimental band that was marching by at just that moment. She bounced and the drummer snatched her out of the air. I didn't say--this happened in the cantonment of the Danielski Regiment at Krakow. Of which my father was a sergeant major. Thereafter, she was raised, you could say, by the regiment, for the soldiers understood that she had been rescued from death by no earthly power."

I recalled then how we had shared wonderment on the day that we had both been taken in hand by sergeants and trained from an early age in horsemanship and weaponry.

So he became a soldier in the Austrian service and not once did anyone question his manhood, or, if they dared to call him effeminate, quickly regretted it, either in this world or the next. But now he lay as one dead. I found a chair and sat next his bed and hardly left his side for three days. Eventually his wound expressed laudable pus. The doctor pronounced himself satisfied. Man or woman, my friend would live.

On the afternoon of the fourth day, Paradowski opened his eyes. Seeing me, he blushed red and turned his head away.

After a long silence, he spoke. "You must despise me now."

"Why should I? You are the bravest, most decent man I know, and the best friend and companion I have ever had. That you are a woman hardly signifies. It is as if you had lost a leg in battle, a trifle."

"No, no, I fear it can never be the same between us, now I am exposed."

"You must put your mind at rest on that score, my dear Paradowski. You are hardly exposed. Wojtek has always known, the doctor is confidential and indifferent. He would never tattle the private affairs of a patient. The nuns will be quiet as . . . well, nuns. And I would die before betraying you."

"Then what do you propose?"

"Only that you regain your strength and, when fit, rejoin our regiment."

"It can never be the same," he repeated, and again turned his head away.

"You are correct," said I. "Henceforth, you will embroider cushions and dream of satin gowns. You have been many things in my sight, Paradowski, but never a fool. Please to not begin now!"

He sighed and made no response.

"But here is a happy thought," I said, "it will be a long war, and I am sure to stop a bullet, and then all will be as it was before. No one who matters will know your true sex. By the time you are promoted major general, this little mishap will be entirely forgotten."

At first, no reaction, all mum. Then some little sounds. He shoulders began to shake. I supposed he was weeping, and my heart sank, but then he turned his face towards me and I saw it was convulsed with hilarity. I started to laugh as well. We both laughed until the tears came, a sound unprecedented in such a place. A nun peered in and I said, between guffaws, "It is nothing, sister--my friend is happy to be still alive!"

"I am in agony, you bastard," he managed to say. "How could you make me laugh so! Oh, Christ, it hurts, ha ha ha ha!"

When we had recovered somewhat, he said, "Well, I cannot be too far gone. And assuming I will be well enough to ride and fight again, how do you propose we rejoin the regiment? I notice you are no longer in uniform, which cannot bode well for our situation."

"Yes, it is moderately dire. The French have Gembloux, and Coburg has withdrawn over the Rhine. There are French military surgeons here now and French soldiers guard the grounds. I sent Wojtek out to the town to buy me a coat and pantaloons and round hat, and I also had him buy some necessaries for you and himself, for it is impossible that three men of military bearing will be allowed to walk through the French lines. You will recall Prague and old Casanova's strategy. I believe it will serve once more. We speak French and no one will mind a married couple and their maidservant traveling to Brussels. I fear it is our only way to avoid a French dungeon."

"What an odious notion!"

"To be sure. The alternative is three men, one wounded, unarmed but for a saber and a pistol, with only one horse and little money, trying to slip through the entire French army."

"Yes, of course you are correct, but it galls me nonetheless. And in Brussels, what then?"

"We will find a place to stay; we will feign the character of a respectable married couple of some means, with a servant."

"But we have no means."

"Oh, as long as there is a billiard table or two in Brussels, we shall not lack for gold. When we have gathered enough to fund a journey, the border at length becoming more peaceful, we will slip across the river and make our way to the regiment, appearing transformed, it goes without saying, into three dragoons escaped the French. What do you think of that?"

He replied sourly, "I think you would not be so jolly in your stratagems, were you the one who had to wear a gown and bonnet and be a woman."

This plan working as I had proposed, we were in Brussels by the end of July, occupying the second floor of a decent town house behind the Grand Place. There were billiard tables enough in the district and I prospered even more than I had before. They never imagine that someone with an aristocratic air can beat them, but, disbelieving, come again and again to be sheared.

Our domestic arrangements fared less well. You know, life is made much easier as it is repetitive. One doesn't have to work out every morning how to put on one's breeches or saddle one's horse, and today is nearly always a good precedent of tomorrow. But our case was different. It has not frequently happened that a man, accepted as a man over years by his dearest friend and all his comrades, a man moreover of particularly manly parts, a bold dragoon, a devil with a sword, a famous topper of girls, becomes overnight a woman. And not only that—a woman living as the supposed wife of that same dearest friend--well, my point is that there are no manners that cover the situation.

The billiard shark of necessity plies his trade at night, so I had scant daily commerce with my friend. I would return to our apartment late, sometimes by the faint light of dawn, often to scenes of chaos, broken crockery, stains on the wallpaper from thrown vases, and Paradowski stalking about, raving. His habitual garment was a wine-colored velvet dressing gown, for he eschewed all female dress, and, of course he never went out at all. When I entered he would howl at me, demanding of me why I had not let him die, asserting that languishing in a French prison would be preferable to his present jail. More often than not he was drunk, on gin, no less.

I avoided his blows, spoke soft words, recalled for him his true character, made him eat a bite of something, and at last, after his rage had burned out, put him to bed. I lay down beside him, for we had only one bedroom in our establishment, and fell myself into exhausted slumber. The next afternoon I would bathe and dress and slip out, and the same again upon my return.

You will understand that a woman of our class has nothing to do all day, and the contrast between her life and that of the man Paradowski had been, the life of a dragoon officer on active service, could hardly have been more extreme. I forbore to suggest that he take up lace-making.

I should add that all was not hideous with us. We had long conversations, I recall, in which we shared boyhood stories, much like the day we had met, and I cherished these. I also learned how he had carried off his imposture. If one is in the field, for example, at a halt, all dismount, retreat to a convenient wood-line or verge, and answer the calls of nature. Many a time had I stood with him, almost near enough to touch, and watered the moss, or pissed off a bridge, and at those moments it is impossible not to catch sight of the source of the stream. He had the repute in the regiment of being unusually endowed in his organ and I confirmed that with my own eyes. But what I had observed, it seemed, was an appliance, made of leather and papier mâché, appropriately painted. He had in Wojtek's keep a dozen of these and a pig's bladder attached to his female parts with sticking plaster. When in use this was connected via a nozzle of gutta percha to the appliance to produce a satisfactory, even dramatic, squirt. His monthly courses were slight in the main and easily concealed.

"But what of the girls, Paradowski?" I asked. (We were drinking at the time: gin for him, hock for me, and he was at the convivial stage. I intended to retreat to the billiard rooms before he advanced to the next one.)

"What of them?"

"Your reputation as a lover. How did you bring it off?"

"Oh, I brought them off well enough," he answered, laughing. "It is not difficult, and hardly any men know the secret. It helps to have a woman's body, curse it as I might. You would be surprised at how few men possess the art, or even know what women are capable of under the sign of Venus. The excuse I offered to respectable girls was consideration for their honor and in aid of avoiding scandal. How very grateful they were! As for the harlots, I put out that I had an injury from the wars. To make a woman howl with pleasure with one's hands or mouth requires only good will and the knowledge that it is possible."

"You speak of Sapphic practices?" said I.

"Call it what you like—it served, and enhanced my deception. Although the generality of men are so easily deceived, it was scarce necessary."

"But what of your own pleasure?"

He shrugged. "My appliances served in another fashion. But this grows tedious, my friend. Tell me more about Pannau instead."

So life went on. The font of my prosperity was the ruck of French officers that filled Brussels, in the main jumped-up bourgeois or peasants, all stuffed with the prodigious loot the war had afforded them. I was happy to relieve the rogues of some of this, but on one occasion, a major named La Forgue complained, after I had stripped him bare, that no man could win so consistently at billiards without recourse to cheating. A gentleman in attendance, a decent sort, agreed to be my second. I returned to our apartment to inform Paradowski and to put my affairs in order, as one does in such circumstances. He seemed indifferent, nor was I surprised at this, as we both had gone out so often.

The dawn breaking soon after, I met my second, we repaired to a grove at Laeken Park and I killed La Forgue with my father's excellent Hauschka pistol. That done, my second graciously offered to buy me a breakfast, and afterward invited me to a *hotel particulaire* for a game. As such things will, the game dragged on into the night, we players feeding on sliced meats held between pieces of bread, a meal I had never had before. It is an English invention, I believe.

Returning to my dwelling-place, I was met at the door by Paradowski, red-eyed, cheeks bathed in tears. When I had not returned, he had sent Wojtek out to inquire in the taverns, and he had come back with the news that there had been a duel at Laeken and the foreigner had been killed. It never occurred to either of them that to a Belgian both combatants would have been foreigners. He had thought that I lay dead.

Tears burst forth anew and he threw his arms about me, saying he had feared me slain and that, so thinking, he no longer wished to live. Now here is the most peculiar thing. I had seen Paradowski weep before. When he held me in his arms at the Turkish camp after Lennart was killed, he had mingled his tears with my own. But those were the tears of a comrade. These were not. You will hardly credit this; I can scarce credit it myself, but for the first time, after months of cohabitation, it struck me that I held in my arms not the man I loved, but the woman.

The woman he had become felt it, too. Our eyes met, and there it was, a look that once seen is never forgotten. We stumbled to the bedroom. There, on the very bed we had lain in for so long as comrades, we became lovers. I cannot tell you how strange it was, that fierce coupling. When Lennart and I were boys at Pannau, we once captured a fox kit and thought to tame it, but try as we might, it would not yield to domesticity, snapping and growling whenever we extended a hand. In the end we gave it up and knocked it on the head. But the look on its face, the animal fierceness in its eyes, compounded of fear and brute courage, was just what I saw in Paradowski's as we made love.

Not a word was spoken between us on this aspect of our connection, then or later, although we threw our flesh together every time I sought my bed at dawn. Christmas came, and the New Year, and a few days afterward he informed me, pale and shaking with terror, that he was with child.

When I recovered from my shock I proposed that we must marry.

"Nonsense!" he cried. "I will never be a wife or mother. I will bear this as I bore my wound, and afterward there are foundling hospitals."

But I swore I would die before a Pannau child was raised by strangers, ignorant of his birth, nor would I suffer a child of mine to wear the shame of bastardy. We quarreled for a week and I wore him down. He cried much. Once we fought with our fists like boors in a country stew. At last he agreed, with the proviso that it not be in a church but only an atheistical performance at the mairie, under the tricolor, as recently instituted by the conquerors. It seemed fitting.

I suppose I am bred to patience and forbearance, as you will understand, who know all concerning my early life. There is no need to rake over the details. He was not happy, and he could not bear to have happiness around him. I proposed a change of scene, for I was becoming rather too well known in Brussels. I obtained forged papers and we crossed into Germany that spring, spent a few months in Dresden, and then removed to Prague. I had a good deal of money by then and was able to purchase a house. This house, in fact.

In a bedroom upstairs--I could show you it, if you like--my wife entered labor on the fifteenth day of August, 1795. He bore it like a dragoon and the next day was delivered of a healthy boy, with the mark of the Pannau men on his little bottom, whom we christened a week later just next door at St. Thomas Church. We named him Karl-Franz Victor Johann."

Rudi recalled the name next to his mother's on the marriage license. "Good heavens! Do you tell me...?"

"Of course. He was your grandmother."

Twenty-nine

Rudi walked home in a daze, bumping into people on the bridge, turning down the wrong street, gaping and stammering excuses at the strange parlor maid who opened the door at which he had wrongly knocked. For a time he stood on the alien pavement, breathing like a horse dragging a cart uphill, trying to recover himself. But who was himself?

During that dreadful walk, his mind had chased itself down a dozen blind corridors. Could it be a mistake? Could it even be a *plot*? Could the spider baron have concocted this story to unman him, to bring him across to the side of reaction? No, that was absurd, no one would do that, and besides, he *believed* von Pannau. The man was wrong on every conceivable issue, but he was true to his idea of honor and his sense of family was sacred. A forged marriage certificate, allying his only son to a bourgeoise, and all to subvert a minor liberal? The notion was absurd, believing it a symptom of lunacy.

So I am a baron of the empire, Rudi thought, and all my life I have been working toward the destruction of my own class. It is hilarious. He laughed out loud in the street and had to make an effort to bring himself under control again, as passersby avoided him and gave him looks. In turn he avoided looking into the faces of his fellow citizens. They seemed menacing, distorted. Perhaps *they* were not what they seemed, either.

I am going mad, he thought, this is what insanity is, after all: when we lose contact with our inner selves and become prey to the demons of fantasy.

He found his house, found his room (oh, wonderful consistency!), stripped off his clothes, gripped his servant by the arm and peered long into his face. Yes, Gregor was the same. He would be shocked if I kissed him in gratitude, so I forbear. Oh, Gregor, you are servant of a nobleman now, if you but knew it. How you would preen in the tavern! But you mustn't know. This is the worst part. There is no one with whom I can share this revelation. My friends would mock me, despise me.

Berthe? Oh, by the way, my dear, you are a baronin. Berthe as a baronin—the thing was nonsensical. Easy enough in novels—the secret papers discovered, the deserving girl elevated, or the boy, and life goes on, though they live in a palace and people bow and scrape. But not in real life. Worse: von Pannau was wrong about the Fathers. My father—who I must now call my stepfather—would see it as a swindle, a fraud, a cuckoo placed in his nest, and the comfortable happy marriage with Caroline Augusta would be over.

I could tell Sisi. Yes, my girl, yet another person arrives besides the two already occupying my skull. Besides the decent bourgeois husband and the rake of the revolution comes now Baron von Pannau-Kinsky, the heir to an ancient name, proud and dripping hauteur. Not to mention the dragoon *grandmother*! Sisi would split her sides laughing. Odd, I have heard of people being shattered, and this is what it is like, although I suspect few have been shattered in quite this way.

Stop thinking about it, you dolt! What is sure? The work. This revolution. To work then, and let the fragments of the former man fall where they may!

The next day, Rudi appeared early at his office and worked assiduously at his papers, mechanically, like the clockwork Turk, suppressing thoughts of barony. The Menninger affair was slowly resolving itself; most of the muskets were accounted for and Rudi had a fair idea of what had happened to the ones that weren't. Jiskra and his cronies had them, location unknown. Havel was his usual efficient, silent presence, except . . .

"Havel, have you been consuming fish?"

"No, sir. Do you mean here in the office?"

"Yes. You stink like a fishmonger."

"I am very sorry, Herr Amtsrat. I . . . it was yesterday evening, sir. I went fishing at Venedig with some friends. We caught a tench and I cleaned it. I am afraid I did not wash my hands thoroughly enough."

You're lying, Rudi thought, but dismissed the lad with a motion of his hand. I have to find those damned guns.

At three, Rudi left for home, donned his uniform (why did he not have another one? This to-ing and fro-ing had become tedious) and took a cab to the house on Wammelgasse. I am going to my *grandfather's* house, he thought during the ride and the thought rattled maddeningly in his head.

When he arrived he saw the baron's carriage waiting in the street, and when he was ushered in he saw that its owner was fully dressed in a dark suit and an old- fashioned blue redingote. He carried a tall hat. The clothes had been cut for a larger Hans and he looked shrunken within their folds.

"Good day to you, Herr Moritz," said the baron. "Although I suppose I must call you Rudi now."

"You may, sir. But it will take some time before I am comfortable addressing you as grandfather. You will forgive me: I have not yet recovered from the shock."

"As you wish. But I recommend you summon up enough family feeling to greet your cousin with due cordiality. You may wonder why the carriage waits and why I am dressed for the street. I suppose you still require a horse? Yes? Good. We are off to the castle, the riding school. If we cannot find a decent mount for you there, I am a Mussel-man. Give me your arm!"

Rudi helped the old man into the berlin. When they moved off, Rudi asked, "You mentioned a cousin, sir. What cousin is that?"

"Your cousin Alfred Candidus Ferdinand, Furst zu Windis-chgrätz."

"What! The Butcher of '44 my cousin!"

"Yes. You'll like him, I'm sure. He has wonderful manners; although I would not call him that to his face."

"Tell me how am I his cousin!"

The old man seemed not to hear him; he looked out the window as a man lost in the desert might stare at the sudden revelation of an oasis.

"I see the world is still here," he said. "The whores still work this end of the bridge, and I swear that sausage vendor in the tall white hat was here the first time I ever saw the town. He would be a hundred and twenty now, I suppose. As to your relationship—his mother was of course Maria Leopoldine, Herzogin Arenberg, a famous beauty of my day. My grandfather's middle brother married Marie Angelica von Kuenenhauer. They had two daughters, the eldest of whom married Archduke Arenberg, whose daughter was that Marie Leopoldine, the current Prince's mama. There are other connections, but that is the most direct one. We are all of us cousins, you know. You cannot escape your blood."

Rudi said nothing: it was his turn to stare out the window. He had drunk three glasses of slivovic prior to setting out for his grandfather's, something he had never done before, and it depressed his spirits. These were not improved when his grandfather sniffed loudly twice and exclaimed, "Good Christ, is that you? You smell like a still-house. Are you drunk in the morning?"

"I had a glass of Pannau, as I believe is my birthright. Make light, if you will, sir, but I have grave reservations about meeting this prince, cousin or no."

"That is because you place the politics of the moment before family, sir, which is the wrong way about, in my view. Politics passes; family is eternal."

"A good maxim, sir, but if I were to discover that you were cousin to Bonaparte and brought you to him, to shake his hand and smile, you might experience something of what I now feel. I rather wish I *were* drunk, to be frank."

The old man sniffed once more and remained silent for the remainder of the ride.

Although Rudi had been to the Bohemian Chancellery at the Hrad any number of times, he had never visited the riding school. The carriage wound up the steep road on the north side of the Hradčany, past the Matthias Gate and over the Staubbrucke to the immense L-shaped building that the riding school had occupied for nearly two centuries. They drove through a gate capped with the Hapsburg eagle and flanked with reliefs showing prancing horses, Turks (in defeat), and bold cavaliers, and arrived at a broad graveled yard. Rudi helped his grandfather down from the carriage and offered his arm. After a moment's hesitation, the old baron took it.

The yard was busy with the business of horses, officers riding out or returning, the parade of fine animals led by grooms, while the air was full of boisterous talk and the simple music of horseshoes crunching gravel and the echo of this sound from the stone walls. Rudi cast his eye over the moving animals: he could not tell one horse from the other with respect to breed or, without a discrete peek, sex, not to mention discerning any quality considered useful in a horse.

Guided by the older man, he entered a building redolent of horse, hay and grain, that interesting smell that never appeared anywhere but a stable, then proceeded down a corridor and into a vast, open oval room, high-ceilinged, and floored by an earthen ring in which several riders, young officers in white tunics, were going round and round. Galleries for spectators rose on three sides. In one of these was a group of officers, among whom, Rudi saw General Prince Lobkowicz.

"Ah, there is our Windischgrätz," said Hans, and steered Rudi up some steps and down the aisle of that gallery. As they did so, a tall, slender officer detached himself from the group and came toward them, smiling. He was taller than Rudi and far taller than Hans, dressed in the white uniform of a field marshal, his chest sparkling with orders.

"My dear Pannau," he exclaimed, holding wide his arms and enfolding the old man in a warm embrace. "How good it is to see you again! I had heard you were ill, and only the press of affairs kept me from a visit. But you are recovered, I see."

"All too temporarily, I fear," said Hans. "But I seize the day. Prince, allow me tp present to you my grandson, your cousin, Rudolf, Freiherr von und zu Pannau-Kinsky. Rudolf, this is your cousin, Alfred, Furst zu Windischgrätz, field marshal of the royal and imperial army."

Rudi made a stiff little bow. Windischgrätz beamed and held out his hand. With a sick feeling, Rudi found himself offering his own, and made himself look the man in the eye. A face made of vertical lines, like the architecture of a former age: a blade-thin nose, grizzled side whiskers, a high unwrinkled forehead, and small, deep-set, intelligent blue eyes. The only horizontal element was a stiff military mustache.

"I am happy to meet a relative of whose existence I was quite unaware until just the other day," said the Prince. "I dare say it is too late to send you a silver christening cup? Ha ha!"

"I fear the birth notice was misplaced, my lord . . ."

"*Cousin*, please! No need for formality within the family. It was Lobkowicz over there who tipped me wise to your existence. I immediately sent a note of inquiry to Pannau and here we are. I am delighted to know you, although old Lobkowicz over there says you aim at the dissolution of the empire and the conversion of its army into mere rabble. I am sure that's not so. My princess will be delighted as well —she is always talking of new blood in the family. I'd like to know what is the matter with old blood, eh, Pannau? I daresay she will be organizing a ball if I am not careful."

"Do you intend to stay long in Prague, cousin?" Rudi inquired carefully.

"Oh, well as to that, I am not in Prague at all just now." He held a finger to his lips. "Just a whirlwind visit of inspection, so to speak. I will not officially arrive until the eighteenth of this month."

"To what purpose, if I may inquire?"

"I beg your pardon, cousin, but you may not. It is all some tedious reason of state, but the Hofburg thought it best to keep my visit and purpose a bit foggy, if you understand me. The times and all. But I have heard great things of you, cousin. Not from Lobkowicz, unfortunately, but from others. You behaved splendidly in putting down these riots, just as a von Pannau should. Lobkowicz ought to have thought of a flying column, but innovation was never his strong suit, poor fellow." He turned to Hans. "But let us speak not of slow generals, but of fast horses. You said in your note you were in the market for one."

"Rudi is, rather. This young man's duties in the National Guard apparently require a charger, and since we were coming here to meet you, well, two birds with one stone . . . ."

"Oh, nothing simpler," replied the field marshal. "As a matter of fact—you don't mind a Lipizzaner, I suppose?"

Rudi nodded, and said, in a voice that seemed not his own, "Oh, yes, cousin, a Lipizzaner would do."

"Then I could let you have my Gitano. Six-year-old gelding, sound of limb and wind, a very fine goer—a white coat if that suits? He's normally at our place in Styria, not ridden enough and getting fat. Fortunately he's coming up to Prague with the rest of our lumber, so I could let you have him early next week, say. How would that be?"

Rudi mumbled his agreement. He had enough of his stepfather in him to worry about the cost of so aristocratic a beast, and enough of his newfound grandfather to know not to ask. The three parted with the expression on Prince Windischgrätz's part of pleasure at making young von Pannau's acquaintance, assurance that he would send word upon the arrival of the horse, and hopes of greater familiarity in future.

As the two von Pannaus walked out of the hall, the elder remarked, "You did well. He liked you, and he does not like many. His condescension in the face of your bourgeois manners was exemplary, I thought."

"I am glad you think so. As for myself, I feel nothing but contempt for the way I behaved. Now I am to ride the horse at whose feet perhaps fell the martyrs of 'forty-four. Perhaps his very hooves waded in their gore."

The old baron tutted and said, "What a fantastic fellow you are, Rudi, to be sure! As I recall there was not much gore in 'forty-four. It was mainly a matter of drafting obstreperous young fools into the army, where I wager they learned what real oppression was and became more able to contrast it with the mild and beneficent rule of our gracious king and emperor."

"I believe I must change the subject, Herr Baron," said Rudi in an unnaturally calm voice. He was thinking of what Josef Liebig had become under that oppression. "Shall we return to your house and continue our dictation?"

"We shall continue, but not to my house. No, I am out and about for the first time in years, or so it seems. I wish to spread my crumpled wings for a while yet. Do you know what I would like to do? You will never guess!"

"Visit the Mounted Man?"

The old baron's mouth dropped open for a moment, and then he laughed long and loud, his voice bouncing around the vaulted stone corridor through which they passed in a manner that was almost disturbing. Too long and loud, apparently, for he was seized by a coughing fit that doubled him over and brought tears to his eyes.

When this was done with and he had put his handkerchief back in his sleeve he gazed at Rudi fondly and said, "My good Lord, I haven't laughed like that for a long while. You do me good, grandson! But no, you shall never guess it. I wish to see a railroad train. I have never seen one, much less ridden upon such a thing. But I understand they run only at certain times."

A look had blossomed on his grandfather's face that Rudi had not seen before, one of innocent delight, as if the lost boy was peering up from beneath the scarred surface the old monster presented to the world. Rudi was touched by this apparition, so that he smiled broadly and replied, "Nothing easier to arrange, sir. The night train leaves for Vienna at ten past six o'clock today. It could carry you to that city in time for your supper tomorrow."

"But surely the train stops before Vienna. I would not like to go all the way. One can dismount, I suppose?"

"Of course. We could ride to Béchovíce station, and return by coach, or you could send your carriage ahead and return thereby."

"What is the time now? I had a watch once, but it stopped, and I let it, having lost any interest I ever had in the passing hour."

Rudi consulted his Breguet hunter. "It is five past four."

"Splendid!" said Hans. "Then this is what we shall do. I will order Pavlic to take the berlin to Béchovíce, but first we shall find a tavern, a low one by preference, near the train station, and I will eat a dish of hot, greasy blood sausage, sauerkraut and goose dumplings, with black bread and butter, and a pint of black beer, and beer-cheese with onions. If I should expire from this, be so good as to have me interred in the crypt at Pannau. If my doctors are in error, however, then we shall travel on the train."

Shortly thereafter, the old baron was enjoying the meal he had described in a tavern hard by the train station called The Fishing Cat. The other patrons were railway workers, freight heavers, porters, and third-class passengers, and these stared without embarrassment at the two gentlemen, especially at the one dressed in the fashion of the former age.

"I love this food," said Hans, taking a comfortable draught from his stein. "I was raised on it, you know, and my bones require some from time to time. Your Frenchie chefs are all very well, but one does not have enough to chew upon, and one is never quite full. How do you find it?"

"It is certainly *filling*," said Rudi, and stifled a belch.

"Not to your taste, eh? We have spoken before of the connection between peasant and noble, from which the bourgeois is excluded, and here is a fleshly example. Well, never mind. Do you have your notebook? "

Rudi pushed aside his half-eaten dinner and took out his writing implements. The old man finished his beer, signed for another and commenced.

Mirek (or Mira) wouldn't nurse the babe at all, wouldn't comfort it when it wailed, resigned all the sloppy parts of infant rearing to Wojtek, who immediately went out and found a wet-nurse, a girl just in from the country. Her name was Vizla: large, moon-faced and silent, with immense ever-flowing breasts for her own babe, and our own Karl-Franz.

I fear Paradowski lasted just three months as Mira. I came home from a night at my trade to find him gone, and Wojtek with him. There was a note left by a folded pile of women's clothing saying that he was off to Poland to join their army. He said he did not regret our association; indeed it was the dearest thing in his life. But he could no longer live with his heart riven between his love for me and his destiny, which was to ride and fight and lead men into battle. He had got news from his native country, letters I had not seen, warning that Poland was in danger, that Prussia and Russia might seize upon the current broils of Europe to devour the last slice of his native land. If his sword could help stop this, his honor as a man compelled him to go. He actually used that phrase.

Well, naturally, I had known it couldn't last--did I not love him and know the secrets of his heart? Had I not caught him out, ludicrous in that dressing gown, practicing passes with my saber? How we do conceal from ourselves what we do not wish to know! I confess I wept like a babe in arms, my cries joined by those of my son, your father. To be deprived at one blow of my dearest comrade and the mother of my child! No one has ever borne such pain, I believe. I recovered, however, and then was glad that he lived still and had not put a ball through his head on account of what he must have considered abject shame.

I never saw his face again, I believe; the possible exception comes later in the story. He wrote from time to time, perhaps once a year. I never replied; what was there to say? Nor did he once inquire about his child. He was involved in the Kościuszko affair and later joined General Poniotowski in exile. When Poniotowski joined Bonaparte, he did too, and the letters ceased.

From time to time I dreamed of him lying dead on the road back from Moscow, his beautiful body frozen in a ditch, or pieced by a Cossack lance and dying in some Ukrainian field.

Another year turned, and in the autumn of '96, my brother, out hunting deer, tried for a hedge too high for his horse and smashed his skull against a tree, leaving Pannau to a new count, Friedrich Anton Ludwig, the twenty-eighth of that line, aged seven years.

I immediately left for Pannau with my son, his nurse, and a manservant I hired for the occasion. The funeral was passed with all customary pomp, lacking only the deep sorrow that had accompanied my father's passing. Anton had not been a success as count, I am afraid. Of course, I knew all the servants from old and I was fully informed of his behavior. He had treated his wife with cruel disdain and had terrified little Fritz and his sister Sophie with his violent rages.

I stayed after the funeral guests had departed, to comfort the not particularly grieving widow. Did I say that it was Anton who married Marietta? Yes, that is why it was so embarrassing to all parties, my love for Marietta, for he had begun to court her secretly and proposed a match to her father as soon as he discovered my interest in her. You would not think that a man would arrange his intimate affairs chiefly so as to discommode his brother, but there it is. I had no idea he even knew her. Poor Anton! I would have loved him, had his hate not thrown up such a barrier between us. That is the saddest thing on earth, to die unreconciled with a heart full of bile!

Well, a county cannot be ruled by a woman of Marietta's mild kidney in consort with a seven-year-old, so I stayed and became Count of Pannau in all but name a year later, after I married her. You will call me a bigamist, but I did not feel so, owing to the peculiar nature of my liaison with Paradowski. Besides which, one cannot consider a connection blessed only by some atheist functionary as binding. I explained my little boy as the result of a marriage to a Polish noblewoman, lately dead, which for all I knew was true. Marietta did not press me for the details.

I suppose it was a good enough marriage, though short. I no longer loved her with my boyish passion, for after my experiences with Clotilde and others, many others, I found her somewhat slight, and entirely uneducated in the ways of love. Anton had hardly come to her bed at all, preferring his peasant doxies, but I was able to repair the damage, with some enthusiasm, for she was still as beautiful as I recalled, and more than willing to learn. I loved her too for the way she took Karl-Franz to her heart, and I became a second and better father to her own little ones.

The portrait you have seen in the Green Room is of her with Karl-Franz, painted when the boy was about four years of age. How she looked then was how I recall her, for in that same year Bonaparte invaded Italy and I was called again to the colors. I left Pannau in the charge of its lord, then rising thirteen and a decent lad, the only boy whose breeding I have had charge of, and I am content to know that, as a father, I am no monster at least. Count Fritz was a good count, too, kind and of the improving sort. Pannau prospered under him. I also left a baby in Marietta, which had a less happy outcome. Oh, that bell just now was the quarter hour, I believe. We should make haste to the train.

Soon they were on board the train, rushing through the outskirts of Prague. The old baron grinned like a lad, looking at the blurred landscape, exhilarated by the speed.

"Why, we are going as near as fast as a horse at full gallop! What a wonder! And not a breath of wind inside.

How can it be? Oskar would know, but he died in the year sixteen, poor fellow."

Rudi supplied the answer, and afterward they talked about railroads and Rudi's family and the family of the Count in Pannau, amiably avoiding politics, until Rudi said, "Herr Baron, we are coming into Béchovíce now and will have to suspend our conversation. Shall we return to your house, or will you wish to adjourn until tomorrow?"

"Neither," said von Pannau, "Rudi, listen to me now. I have something to give you and something to tell you."

The old man reached into his waistcoat pocket, brought out a lump wrapped in tissue, and handed it to Rudi. Confused, Rudi unwrapped it and found a gold seal ring with the arms of Pannau-Kinsky engraved on the face.

"That belonged to your father," said Hans. "I took it from his dead hand at Leipzig. It is your patrimony, along with the saber he carried, which is already at your side. Such are the signs and accouterments of honor. Though you are not bred to them, I believe your blood is true, and you will behave according to its dictates."

Rudi felt tears prickle at his eyes. He said, "Thank you . . . grandfather. Is that what you wished to tell me?"

"Not at all. It is this: you must stay on the train."

"Excuse me?"

"You must remain on the train until Vienna and then go to Kunningshelm. Forget Prague and its troubles, enter a different life in the bosom of your family."

"Are you serious, grandfather?"

"I have never been more so in my life."

"But why? And *how*? I cannot just leave. I have a house, I have responsibilities to the revolution . . ."

"The revolution is finished, my boy. It will not last another month. And the Hofburg will wish to make examples of its leaders."

An inane spasmodic laugh burbled up in Rudi. "The Hofburg! The Hofburg is in the hands of the people. The emperor is captive, or near enough. The streets are controlled by student militia. The revolution is as secure as the one in Paris."

"My dear boy, the royal and imperial government is often slow off the mark, but we have been putting down rebellions for a very long time. And we are not Paris, nor yet France. I have tried to explain this to you, but you don't listen. Just consider this: two hundred years ago exactly, the people of Prague marched out on the Charles Bridge to fight the Swedes, the best soldiers in Europe at the time, the victors of Breitenfeld and Lützen. The whole people came out to stand by Colloredo's musketeers--Germans, Czechs, even the Jews were valiant. And so I ask, have you that unity now? Will the whole population of Bohemia rise up and defy their lawful monarch? Will even Prague rise up?"

"Many will fight to preserve what we have gained, sir," Rudi replied, "and among them will be me. But what have you heard? Will the army dare to attack? Or if so ordered, will they not refuse? Such demurs have happened in France."

"But in France they are all Frenchmen, by God. Why can't you see this? No soldier wants to shoot people who are like him, who speak his language and so forth. But ask a Grenzer from the wilds of Croatia to shoot down a Viennese student and he is only too glad to do it, as your own countrymen are happy to help Radetzky send Italians to hell. Look here, why did you think I took you to see Windischgrätz?"

"Because you desired to introduce me to a cousin, I supposed. And the horse."

"Don't talk nonsense! It was so that you could take his measure, and see that he intends to stay. He waits, you see. He waits for some outrage, worse than those Jew riots, and the outrage will come, or he will provoke one, and then it will be over in a day or two."

"I do not think you are right, sir. The revolution has its turmoils and spats, but the desire of the people for freedom is as solid as these steel rails on which we travel. They will defend it, against the army if need be, and I am honor-bound to be among them should that happen."

"It is never honorable to defy one's lawful king," replied Hans, snapping; after an interval of unpleasant silence, he added, "But I see I speak to a wall. You know, there is a kind of gentleman whose pursuit of honor is unreasonable because it arises not from knowledge that he *is* a gentleman, but out of fear that he is *not*. You are one such, because of your breeding as a bourgeois, and Paradowski was another, because, although gentle, he was not a man at all."

The train slowed, its brakes squealed, and it rumbled and clattered to a stop. The old man rose slowly to his feet, leaning upon his ebony stick. He said, "I hope I may see you again, if you stay in Prague, as I pray you do not. One last time I implore you--stay on the train!"

Rudi rose, however and followed his grandfather out into the corridor, moving like a man in a dream, chained, as he now realized, to his fate.

Sisi Vasová laughed long, cawing like a crow. "That is a charming story, Moritz. How remarkable that he should think you would fly away from your life at his beck! One hears many similar tales when one labors amid the soiled sheets and chamber pots of a great hotel. It is the result of freedom, I believe, the sense that the little particle before the name allows one to do anything one desires as long as one maintains the grave and dignified public face. We artists are the only other class that enjoys similar freedom, the difference being we have no dignity and don't give a tiny shit about who knows of our excesses. But pity the poor little bourgeois, who think of nothing but reputation. That and money, of course."

"It is different now that we have had our revolution," replied Rudi wearily, "and furthermore . . ." He hesitated a moment. Oh, why the devil not?

"Furthermore, he says he is my grandfather," and he told her the whole strange tale. She laughed throughout and clapped her hands in delight when it was done.

"It is perfect," she crowed, "something right out of myth. Dear Moritz, I knew you were a magical creature the moment I first laid eyes on you. The noble cuckoo child, raised by peasants, who grows up to manhood all unknowing and overthrows the king that sired him. It will make a wonderful play—in fact, it is operatic!"

"In the first place, the Moritzs are hardly peasants and I am hardly a king's son. And I would be displeased if this story were widely known."

"Oh, don't be prosy, my love! You are a poetic being. And you know very well that if you tell a tale to a writer, it is like pouring grain into a mill. It will come out by and by to make her daily bread."

This conversation took place in her bed. Rudi had gone to the tenement directly from his grandfather's house, where the carriage had left them after the trip from Béchovíce, which passed in desultory conversation.

"Even if it embarrasses me?" he asked.

"Bah to your embarrassment! So you are a baron! You said yourself we have had the revolution and now such titles signify little. Even if they did, there is nothing to stop a noble from being a revolutionary. Look at St. Juste, at Phillipe Egalité! It will be a one-week's sensation in any case. The important thing is that you are here. How happy I am you did not stay on the train! Think of all the benefits of freedom you would have surrendered." She threw a thigh over him as illustration, and slid her hot flesh slowly back and forth over his sex.

"I appreciate them, of course," he replied, "although the revolution has not, sadly, transformed me into a boy of eighteen. I am spent, alas, and I must leave you, unless you want your friend Novak to spend another night in the cells."

"You will release him! Oh, you wonderful man!" She slid neatly on top of him and covered his face with kisses, then his neck, then his chest and belly. But he put his hand on her head and stopped the planned descent, thinking how remarkable it was that one could, at last, have a surfeit of even this.

"No, let me go, devouring creature! It is nearly eight and I must be at the jail when the shifts change. The warders will be anxious to get home to their supper, and will not question too closely a paper that releases certain malefactors to the custody of the National Guard."

He slipped from bed, washed at a basin and pulled on his uniform. As he was kneeling to recover his sword, he caught the waft of an odor of fish. It came from her shoes. He picked one up and removed from its heel translucent herring's scale.

At the city jail, where he appeared some time later in a uniform as fresh as his valet's skill could make it, Rudi was amazed at how packed were the cells. It seemed that here, as in France, the expansion of freedom for the many required that some lose their freedom entirely.
But this must be a transitory condition, he thought. The people must learn to conduct themselves under the new conditions, without a police boot ever upon their necks. It was natural that some would take advantage of this and run riot.

He found the giant Novak in a cell meant for four that contained a dozen. A filthy bandage girdled his head and both his eyes were blacked. From these Rudi received a baleful look and from the bruised mouth a curse.

"Come to finish the work your boys started?"

"I've come to get you out," said Rudi. "Warder, unlock the cell!"

The man did so, reluctantly, it seemed, and backed quickly away.

"I want no favors from you, *skopčak*," said Novak.

"Oh, be assured it is no favor from me. For my part, you could rot here forever. But Sisi speaks well of you . . ."

"Oh, so it's a favor to your dick."

"Don't be an ass, Novak, and come out of there! Think of your family!"

Another voice, a familiar one, spoke up, and from the crowded cell a disheveled figure pushed forward.

"Moritz, for the love of God, get me out of here!"

"Good evening, Jasny," said Rudi, "I am sorry to see you here."

"It is all a misunderstanding, Rudi," said the man. "Your bully boys seized me as I was about my business and would not listen. I told them I was a school teacher."

Novak laughed and said, "That in itself would be a good enough reason to lock the fool up, but he was flinging stones at the Jew windows with the rest of us."

"It was only one little stone," said Jasny. "I was swept up in the moment. You know how it is . . . "

"In fact, I do not," said Rudi "Stoning Jews? Is that why we made this revolution? So you could proceed to justify our oppression by rioting in the streets? Have you gone insane?"

"At least I know who my people are," said Jasny sullenly. "At least I do not pretend to be a revolutionary while leading a band of Cossacks bayoneting decent Czech patriots in their own town."

"Oh, Jasny," said Rudi with a sigh, "look at us! Look what we've become! We are liberals, Jasny. We believe in the rights of man. We believe that all are equal before the law. How then can you support joining a mob to despoil and injure your fellow citizens?"

"The Jew is not my fellow citizen. The Jew is a vulture preying on the people. The Jew is the very spearpoint of German oppression, and never will we rest until the true revolution has come, and that yoke is off the shoulders of the Czech people."

Rudi addressed the warder and pointed to Novak. "This man is to be released, by order of the National Guard. If he refuses, throw him out on his ear. As for this one, I wish to question him on matters regarding the security of the state. Please to provide me with a suitable room!"

The room was bare, small and filthy, with a single barred window up high, and black spatters on the walls that might have been old blood.

"I will come straight to the point, Jasny," said Rudi when they were alone, and the door shut. "You know very well that if you come before a magistrate on a charge of riot . . ."

"I was not—"

"Yes, you were. Liebig saw you trying to burn his house down. Please be quiet! If you are charged, you will lose your place as a schoolteacher and you will be ruined. I am inclined to get you out of this trouble before that happens, but in return you must tell me where you have stored the guns."

"It is true, then, God damn you! You have been a police agent all along."

"Believe what you like. Where are the guns?"

"Go to hell!"

Rudi flung open the door. "Guard!" he cried. To Jasny he said, "You have one minute. Tell me now! Save yourself! This is private and between us. No one will ever learn you spoke to me . . ."

The guard appeared at the door. Rudi held one finger up to detain the man and moved so that his face was inches away from Jasny's. "Well?"

It was clear to him that Jasny was no longer thinking about revolutionary martyrdom, but about what his family would say, if he was imprisoned not for politics, but for arson and riot, and thereby lost his position. His face was cheese-colored and slicked with fine sweat. "I tell you I don't know! I overheard Paul say something about a place on the river, near the canal. But I swear to you, Moritz, I don't know anything else."

"You do. by God! You know who Jiskra is, though. You used that name when you involved young Havel. Jiskra is the originator and organizer of the plot to arm workers, isn't he? Damn you, Jasny, answer me!"

After a moment, Jasny nodded. "That's what Novotny said when he got me into it."

"I thought so," said Rudi. "The mysterious Jiskra! Who can he be? Not Paul—his literary style and Paul's are entirely different, and it beggars belief that if Paul could write like Jiskra does he would not use that brilliance himself. Not you, obviously, and not Liebig. Yet Jiskra is the key to this whole plot. I must find him, not only to forestall a catastrophic rebellion, but also to look him in the eye and demand to know why he wrote that disgusting thing about me. And failing a suitable answer I will see his blood. I will call the swine out. Oh, and there is yet another reason. I wish to know how a man that brilliant could yet be so irresponsibly stupid. It defies my sense of human nature. Give me a name, Jasny and I will see you walk free this minute!"

He watched Jasny's face contort in an agony of indecision and felt his own throat fill with bile. I am become my grandfather, he thought, a tormentor in the service of the state. But I must have that name!

Jasny remained silent except for a low groan. Rudi said, "Then farewell, Emil.

Believe me when I say I bitterly regret the loss of our friendship."

He turned to leave, but as he called out to the warder, Jasny cried out. "Wait!"

"Yes, what is it?"

"Novotny knows. He said he was meeting Jiskra at a tavern in Josefov, tonight at ten. The Sack of Meal. It lies at the foot of . . . "

"Yes, I know where it is," said Rudi. The warder had appeared at the door. Pointing to Jasny, Rudi said, "This man is to be released at eleven o'clock and not a moment before, by order of the National Guard." He left the cell without another look at the prisoner.

Rudi raced home. Once there, he dismissed the servants to their beds, and told Gregor to assemble a full suit of clothing and deliver it to the Demeril Baths at the Rossmarkt. His tone was such that no questions were asked. Then he stripped naked, donning his dressing gown. Berthe kept a bag of old clothes too worn to be respectably mended, and in this he found an old shirt of his and pair of trousers upon which he had spilled a bottle of ink. He located the ragged straw hat that little Fritz used for dressing-up and descended with this and the old clothes to the kitchen, where he rendered them filthy with coal dust and kitchen grease. He did the same for his hair, face and hands, and put on the clothes. He found the cook's rum bottle and splashed the liquor liberally all over him. On his feet he wore carpet slippers, similarly dirtied, and wrapped with greasy kitchen rags. Taking up one of the stout ash poles that the servants used to stir the washing, he left his house through the tradesman's door.

Half an hour later Rudi sat amid filth against a wall on Heiligegeistgasse across from the dark, cave-like opening that led to the Sack of Meal. In the last ten minutes he had discovered that among the miserables he was accounted something of a swell, since beggars, scenting the alcohol on him, assumed that he possessed drink or the coin to buy it, and he had to menace a few of the more importunate ones with his stick.

Novotny came up the street just before ten and entered the tavern. Rudi waited for ten minutes and then went in himself, with the hat pulled down low on his face. The place was not crowded this late, its usual clientele not having enough money to drink more than a few hours after work, so Rudi had a clear view of Novotny and his companions. He had thought that he could get close enough to eavesdrop, but when the barmaid saw him she let out a cry and the barkeeper cursed and ordered him out of the place, brandishing a cudgel to support his demand. Rudi retreated, but not before determining that the two people with Novotny were Stefan Novak and Sisi Vasovà.

Later, soaking in perfumed steaming water, he considered the meaning of what he had learned. Sisi was clearly in it up to her eyes, but he had known that already. The child

Anneke had given him the name of a "secret boat" the *Bogmi-la*, and this must be where the weapons were stored. A fishing boat, obviously, which explained the fishy stink he had noticed about Novotny and Havel in recent days, and that fish scale he had found on Sisi's shoe. The most surprising thing was to learn that Jiskra was Novak.

Clearly the man was living a lie, a brilliant writer posing as a low brute. How could he bear it? But the moment the thought appeared in Rudi's mind, he had the answer, and felt a stab of shame. He knew very well how a man could live two lives. And what could be a better disguise for a revolutionary intellectual than to pose as a heaver of sacks. Rudi had heard that this was now quite the thing in Russia: educated young people, surrendering their easy lives to dwell among the peasants, sharing their suffering while raising political consciousness among the masses. Apparently, in at least this instance, the practice had come to Bohemia.

Mixed feelings now—the man was a monster, no better than Bors, and yet . . . to give up everything for an ideal was surely worthy of admiration. Could he have done such a thing himself? Well, he just had, if only for a few hours, and there was indeed something horribly appealing about descending to the depths. Rudi thought now about what the baron had said regarding war, that somehow entrancing mix of horror and delight. Was this essential to the human creature, or could it be trained out by education? He would have to ask Jasny, he thought for an instant, before he recalled that there was no more Jasny, that the supposedly enlightened former friend had been jailed for participating in a Jew-baiting riot.

You think you know everything, but we really do know everything—the words of the Fathers came back to him. Perhaps they were right, and perhaps the baron was as well. Could the entire liberal project be inherently flawed, had his life been a grotesque error?

Oh, how I envy the certain, the righteous, the fanatics! he thought. Myself, I am doomed to be a man of bits and pieces, stumbling through dark passages, uncertain if I do more harm than good, like the shambling creature of local legend that long ago a wizardly rabbi of Prague had formed from clay.

He plunged his head under the water. My new grandfather is right about one thing, he thought as he blew out bubbles: honor exists and I have it. I did not stay on the train; I will lead my brave lads until the end; and I will foil that accursed plot to foment a class war in my land.

Some days later, on May 15th, news reached Prague that the students who ruled Vienna had stormed the palaces of government demanding universal suffrage and a unicameral parliament, in which the aristocracy would not be welcome. On the 18th came the even more shocking news that the emperor and his family had slipped out of the Hofburg by night and were now at Innsbruck, surrounded by loyal troops.

As for Prague, Rudi observed that the mood of the city had changed, as had its appearance. German flags and bunting disappeared from certain streets. In whole districts there was no trace of the black, red, and yellow; only the red and white of Czech nationalism was seen. These colors also adorned the biceps of Czech militiamen, who were marching and drilling in the parks at all hours of the day. Few of them had weapons as yet, and Rudi wondered when the stolen muskets would be distributed. He had to act before that, but how?

There were more riots in the third week in May, and once again Rudi found himself leveling bayonets against his fellow citizens. On a day following a night of disturbances, he sought out Paul Novotny, finding him at his usual place at the Knight.

Novotny rose to his feet and bowed low.

"I am honored, Herr Baron," he intoned.

"She told you."

"Of course. It is all over town. I laughed tears when I heard, but I was not surprised."

"Were you not?"

"No. There has always been a certain something about your mien, a punctilious reluctance to get your hands dirty, a arrogant paternalism in your politics that carries the odor of the Hofburg. Oh, why can't the silly nationalities simply get along under our masters' beneficent rule?"

"Thank you, Paul. Perhaps, like Jasny, you no longer wish to know me."

"Oh, don't be absurd. I love you like a brother. It did not check me that you were filthy rich, and it will not affect my regard that you are noble. But the time for such amelioration is past. It is a pity you were not a baron when it meant something. Does he care about you at all?"

"He urged me in the strongest terms to leave the city. He thinks the revolution is done for."

"Perhaps you should take his advice."

"Perhaps I should go fishing instead," said Rudi. "We could both go fishing. We could hire a boat, a large one with plenty of room."

Novotny gave Rudi a long, considering look and replied, "I get sick in boats."

"Too bad then. It is true that some boats, are extremely dangerous."

Novotny stared at him, his face unnaturally stiff. After a brief silence, Rudi added, "In any case, I shall not desert the revolution and all we have worked for."

Novotny's face relaxed into its usual expression. "I fear the revolution is deserting us, my friend. All any Czech can talk about now is the Slav Congress, as if a gathering of philologists and scruffy radicals from the barbarous east will wreak a miraculous transformation. Suddenly, there will be no more Germans in Bohemia and freedom will ring. You have always said that I had a sour view of political humanity, but even I have been surprised by this. Whence comes this rancor? Why do two of your oldest and dearest friends, intelligent and educated men, make war? Why does a fellow who has shared his district with Jews his entire life, without a cross word, mind you, suddenly feel that he cannot for another minute breathe the same air as the Hebrew? It is a mystery, my dear, but one that becomes more common as the age progresses."

"My grandfather would say it is no mystery at all, but the natural result of throwing off the benign rule of the house of Hapsburg."

With a chuckle, Novotny said, "I detect that you may be beginning to think him correct."

"Never! I think, however, that we are mere babies at this work of politics. We thought it simpler than it is. Now we know we must work harder, bury our differences, present a united front to reaction."

"I take it you were not at the Verein meeting last night."

"No. I am not of the Verein, no more than I am of the Slavia militia. Why, what was the result?"

"There was none, for the meeting did not take place. It was intended that some of our expert Germanic liberals from Vienna should explain to their Bohemian cousins how to organize the voting for the Frankfort parliament next week. I was there for my newspaper, notebook at the ready, but no sooner had Lörner gaveled the meeting to order when the doors burst open and a gang of Czechs rushed in with their faces wrapped, carrying clubs and iron bars and bottles and drove out the Germans, breaking everything they could in the process."

"My God, those mad fools!" cried Rudi. "Was anyone hurt?"

"Only in their dignity and some articles of clothing. Hats were crushed, I believe. I sang *Kde domo muj* at the top of my voice to keep from being savaged myself. You will be happy to learn that your old friend, Big Steffi Novak, was there, leading the fun. I understand it was you who had him released."

"I did. I suppose I should regret it. But I did not then know who he really was."

"What do you mean?" asked Novotny.

Should I tell Paul what I suspect? thought Rudi. Of course not, for he would immediately run to Jiskra né Novak and tell of it, and then he would be on his guard. No, I must keep this close, and here is another result of our revolution, that I must be on my guard against my closest friend.

"I meant," said Rudi, "that I did not realize he was a professional rioter."

"Well, Count Thun has released them all now, as a gesture to the Czech community. You see how well that turned out. But I require some information from you, my friend. That is how it works with us journalists: we give a little news and in return demand a little more. What do you make of these rumors that Prince Windischgrätz is back in town?"

"They are rumors no more. He is. In fact, I met him, on the introduction of my grandfather. Apparently he is a cousin. I am buying his horse."

Novotny turned his eyes to heaven and said, "You rend me, sir, between my lust for a story and my friendship. This is an item that the world is not ready to hear: prominent liberal bound by blood to the Butcher. Rides the steed the monster rode while sabering patriots."

"Oh, print what you like. I cannot bring myself to care much."

"You ought to care, if you value your windows and your skin. What are the prince-butcher's plans, do you know?"

"He did not vouchsafe them to me, unfortunately, but what other plans could he have but crushing the revolution here? And the sort of disturbances you recount are all the excuse he would need. Why, our governor is establishing a junto--an executive council of four Germans and four Czechs."

"Yes, all revolutions must have a junto, or history will not regard them seriously. Do you think you will be of its number?"

"No. Trying to make peace between the nationalities is the quickest road to unpopularity with both sides. I am done as a politician in Prague, I fear."

"Then why not leave?"

"Now you agree with my grandfather! I cannot just abandon my Legion boys, Paul, and perhaps I can do some good still. If we can just keep our heads and show no outright defiance, if we can establish a constitutional government that peacefully rules this kingdom in loyalty to the empire, we may just manage. If the idiots can keep their heads ..."

"Faint hope of that, my friend," said Novotny.

"Agreed. But faint hope is better than no hope. I will stick it out, come what may."

Thirty

Rudi went home and wrote another letter to Berthe, in which his fragment of hope was made manifest, in which he limned the Prague of his desire rather than the one that lived in the sullen streets. If only, he wrote, you were by my side, if only fate had not parted us. It is only since we have been separated that I have recognized my utter dependence upon you, my love. Without you, I am half a man, nay less, for a man is as nothing without his soul, and you, precious darling, are my soul.

And on and on in this vein, counting the minutes until they could be together, ever in my thoughts, and so forth, so that actual tears fell from his eyes and smeared, in two places, the black ink. He omitted any revelation of his newly acquired nobility. There would be plenty of time to puzzle out the introduction of this revelation into the Moritz clan.

Now he took another piece of paper, but his pen hesitated over the page. It dried. He dipped it again. Was he doing right? Was this a betrayal of the revolution or its salvation? No, he would not write an anonymous note. He would brave the consequences in a face-to-face meeting. He wrote briefly, folded the paper and sealed it with his father's seal.

Gregor came at his ring, took the letters and handed him a note. It was from Prince Windischgrätz's man-of-business, informing Rudi that the gelding Gitano was presently stabled at the Pachta palace, available for inspection at short notice, if the noble gentleman would care to name a time to meet at the riding school. He begged to inform the noble gentleman further that the sum of three hundred florins was the purchase price of this animal, payable at the noble gentleman's convenience. A paper attesting to Gitano's blood-lines was appended.

Rudi whistled and felt a pang in his vitals when he saw this figure. He had earned twelve hundred florins a year as a lawyer. He had nothing like that sum in savings. Then he had a happy thought and quickly wrote out two notes, one to the Prince and one to his grandfather. Some hours later, the servant returned with replies. Rudi dressed in his uniform, girded on his father's saber, and left by fiacre for the riding school at the Hrad.

The Prince and Hans von Pannau were already there, standing on the sand of the ring, as was the horse Gitano. His grandfather greeted him cordially; if he was disappointed with Rudi's continued presence in Prague, he showed no sign of it. The two older men spoke of horses for some time, in the manner of those raised among them. Rudi had the sense not to attempt a contribution. It was curiously comforting to be ignorant of such matters, to rely on his grandfather's vast experience of things equine. It was like a retreat to a boyhood he had never had, and a relief from the awful weight of the expertise on law and politics that had lately over-stuffed his brain. He walked around the horse, he felt its limbs and patted its flanks, and in short did what he had seen others do. He looked the horse in the eye, but thought it unseemly to look in its mouth, nor did he know what one was supposed to see there.

"May I ride, sir?" he asked Windischgrätz.

"Of course. That is why we are here."

Rudi adjusted the stirrups and climbed into the saddle. He surprised himself by not feeling at all nervous. It was rather like a dream. He put the horse through its paces. Gitano, he found, was everything his noble owner had claimed, wonderfully close-coupled and exquisitely alive to the helps. He trotted back to where the two stood and declared, "He is a marvel, sir. Perfectly satisfactory in every way. I can hardly bear to get down."

"Then don't," replied Windischgrätz. "He is yours. Ride him away with my best wishes."

"I would, Prince, but I have nowhere to ride him to. My establishment is not equipped with stables, and there is too much furniture in my parlor for him to stay comfortably. I will have to see about his keeping hereafter."

The Prince frowned up at him briefly, as if not quite grasping that there were men admitted to his conversation who did not have stables, and then brightened. "Not at all, cousin! He shall remain at Pachta until you make arrangements. Do not hurry yourself at all in that regard, I beg you."

A young aide-de-camp strode up at that moment, and required Prince Windischgrätz's attention. When he was a little distant, Hans said, "Well you have a seat, sir, and a good thing, for I believe I would have perished with shame had you proved a flour sack. A fine animal this; I congratulate you."

"And I thank *you*, sir. I will, of course, pay back your advance when I am established in Vienna."

"Oh, tut-tut, I am happy to do it. It is the great plea-sure of grandsires to lavish treasures on their offspring, and I have not lavished much in your case! Well, off with you now. And do me the service of informing Pavlic as you leave to send the chair for me. My limbs remind me that I will never see the vigor of seventy again."

Rudi walked his horse out of the ring and down a stone corridor. He saw Pavlic there with a sedan and two footmen and, after conveying his grandfather's order, rode on. The innards of the riding school, he discovered, were something of a maze, and he soon became lost. A passing groom pointed out to him where he had gone wrong and he reversed direction. After some minutes, he found himself in the corridor that led back to the riding ring, and again re-versed, containing his irritation. Why were there no signs?

He had gone just a few paces when he saw a priest emerge from a side passage, slide along the wall to avoid the horse, and hurry toward the ring. Odd to see a priest in a sta-ble, Rudi mused, and the man's face, or what he could see of it under the broad hat, had a familiar look. Or it might have been the walk, the posture--perhaps a curate at St. Jacobus? A very striking face, actually. He grew distracted with trying to recall where he had seen the man; the horse felt his distraction and stopped walking. The hoof beats ceased their echoing clack in the stone corridor. Rudi looked over his shoulder at the retreating black figure; and the man, who must have heard the horse stop, turned and stared back at him.

In the instant, Rudi recalled where he had last seen that face. He turned the horse so violently that it nearly stumbled on the flagstones, but he collected it neatly, and charged toward the man in priest's garb: Bors.

Who drew his fearsome pistol from underneath his soutane and fired, the sound tremendous in the narrow passage. Rudi felt a blow against his left shoulder, but spurred his horse onward, managing at the same time to draw his saber. Bors aimed his pistol again, but seemed to quail at the sight of the onrushing horse and rider. He turned and fled. No more than twenty feet separated them when Bors burst into the horse ring. Rudi shouted a warning. The officers around Windischgrätz looked up in dismay. Bors leveled his weapon and began a rapid fire—one, two, three shots rang out before Rudi's saber split open his head.

"And what happened then?" asked the old baron. Rudi was reclining on a chaise in his grandfather's green drawing room, his shoulder smarting under a new bandage. The ball had carved a deep groove in the meat above his collarbone, but he was otherwise unhurt.

"I dismounted and looked at the assassin. He was lying face down and the back of his skull was in pieces with the brain bulging out and there was an immense pool of blood. I sank to my knees and was sick. It was shameful, but I could not help myself. I had never . . . that is to say, I had never seen a man killed so. And to think I had done it!"

"Oh, it is far from uncommon, my boy. A good deal of vomit litters the field of battle, along with the more picturesque gore. And shit too, to tell the honest truth. But you did well. As I am always telling you, blood will out. You are a true Pannau and you have killed your man in a noble fashion and saved the life of a great personage. A pity you are not in the army--you would have a fine ribbon for your coat. He is the most dangerous enemy in the empire and the stoutest friend. By God, I wish I had been there to see it! What is that face? You look like you had bit on a bad egg."

"It is how I feel at this moment. I am not feeling as Rudi Moritz should feel, having just split a man's skull with a saber. My God! Even saying the words—not words I had ever imagined coming from my mouth. Yet I am filled with an uncanny terror that seems unconnected with that violent act."

"Oh, as to that—you feel you are turning into *me* and it frightens the daylights out of you. I have told you before now that blood will out, and now you see it. Do you imagine that the little Prague clerk that was Rudi Moritz but a month ago could have done what you just did? And the Böhmer mistress, too, although I must say that after La Daumer I stuck to my own kind. The world is full of complaisant husbands, you know, and a girl of your own class will always give less trouble in the end."

"I married my sister," said Rudi without thought.

"So you did, sir, and you were a happy man then, before you took up this wretched business of politics."

"Thank you for that observation, sir. Perhaps we can changes places and you can take down my memoir."

"Oh, your story has too many chapters to come, my lad, that I will never see. But you are out now in the fullness of your blood, and never will you stuff yourself back in the sausage of the man you once were. Now, I had wanted to continue *my* story, which, as I recall, we left in an interesting place, but I suppose you will want to go home."

In his dressing gown, in his study, Rudi transcribed his notes of the recent interview from the legal shorthand of the notebook into proper German prose. As he did, he unconsciously improved the flow of the old man's monologue, cutting out the repetitions, rearranging events, polishing phrases. He never invented incidents, but he gave the narrative more coherence than it had when the actual words dropped from Hans von Pannau's mouth. He enjoyed this, just as he enjoyed inventing a smooth transition to a more liberal society in Prague in his letters to Berte.

He finished the transcription, had a drink of slivovic, and launched into another letter. A familiar thought floated into his mind: if Berthe were by his side as she ought to have been, he would not have become involved with that woman. These were ignoble feelings, he knew, but he had proved himself more than ignoble; he had a tendency, common to those skilled with words, to invent for himself a more comfortable reality than the one he actually inhabited, sculpting the narrative of his life as he had just shaped that of his grandfather's.

Rudi's composition was interrupted now by a commotion, a shouting voice from the street, a pounding on the front door. In a few minutes Gregor appeared.

"It is a man, sir, a gentleman with a great beard, pounding his stick on the door and demanding to see you. I said you were already in bed, but he would not leave. Shall I call for the guard?"

"As I *am* the guard, that would perhaps be superfluous. I will see what he wants."

The man was Bakunin, and he was drunk. "There you are, monster!" he shouted when Rudi appeared. "Traitor who disguises himself as a revolutionary to overthrow the revolution from within. Vile worm, who has not the courage to show his true colors. Murderer of the one true revolutionary in Prague . . ."

"I am sorry about your friend," said Rudi, " but he was on a mission of assassination, and I could not permit it."

"Oh, yes, your bourgeois values! Let us see where they are when the tyrant you rescued unleashes his troops on the people. Can you really mean to justify the salvation of Windischgrätz? Windischgrätz, that murdering demon of reaction! When he sends out his booted hirelings to massacre the people crying for their rights, will you be there with your saber to strike down the assassins of the proletariat? No, you will not, you swine Moritz! All Prague will know you by the name of Judas Iscariot!"

"I am sorry about your friend," said Rudi again, "but a revolution that is advanced by assassination is not an enterprise that I want any part of."

The Russian swayed and a heat seemed to come from his face, as if he were a pot jiggling on a fire far too hot. "If you believe that," he roared, "then you are not only evil, but stupid."

"Be quiet, you fool," shouted a woman's voice from a window on the other side of the street. "Leave Herr Moritz alone!"

"I will not," Bakunin shouted back. "I have not yet catalogued all his infamies."

But other neighbors began to shout similar imprecations and then came the flung chamber pots and crocks full of kitchen-filth. Bakunin withdrew, shouting about the need for the re-education of the common people.

Rudi bowed to the street and went back into his house. He felt curiously light-hearted. Of course, Prince Windischgrätz would try to crush the revolution: that was his function, as it was Bakunin's to spout anarchist nonsense, and Rudi's to defend what was left of the revolution, with his blood if required. They were all like puppets in a show, with fate pulling the strings. It was a curiously comforting feeling; Rudi went to bed with it and slept like a lamb.

The next morning, he pulled on boots, breeches, and a short jacket. Taking a low hat from the rack and, after a second's hesitation, Liebig's sword-cane as well, he walked out of his house and across the few streets between Zeitnergasse and the Fruit Market, where lay the Pachta palace. He was conscious of a certain embarrassment; walking the streets dressed for riding announced clearly that while the gentleman might own a horse, he certainly had no stable on his property.

This was compounded when he arrived at the Pachta and had no notion of where the stables were kept. Should he knock at the front door? Was that done? Or should he try to search out the stables himself?

At that moment a revelation struck him. All these thoughts were the thoughts of a bourgeois, this terror of doing the wrong thing, of losing one's place on the ladder of society. But he was a baron of the empire! He could walk through the streets dressed any way he pleased and not care what anyone thought; he could knock on the door of any prince in the land. This is what it *feels* like to be noble, he thought, to not have to consider the opinion of anyone, as long as your honor is intact. He laughed to himself. It has taken a revolution to make me into an aristocrat, he thought, and knocked on the door.

It was opened by a man wearing livery and a white periwig.

Rudi said, "I am Baron von Pannau. Kindly direct me to the stables!"

The footman bowed gravely and said, "Welcome to Pachta, Herr Baron. Her Grace gave instructions that you should call upon her whenever you arrived. Please to follow me."

The man led him to a splendid room, where stood a tall woman, dressed in riding costume. With a bow, the footman said, "Your Grace, the Herr Baron von Pannau."
The woman smiled, and extended her hand. Rudi bowed over it and kissed it, as if he had been doing it all his life. In fact, he had never been *tete à tete* with a woman of the aristocracy before, Madame von Silber not really counting.

"I wanted to meet you, Baron, even before you saved my husband's life, an act for which you have my deepest gratitude."

She had a low voice and spoke with a rich Hofburg accent, the syllables drawling and the words falling away at their ends.

"It was only my duty, Princess. But why had you wanted to meet me?"

"Oh, you know-- a von Pannau who is a revolutionary. It is remarkable! I hardly know how to put it--like . . . dry water? Boiling ice? I knew you would be by soon enough to ride Gitano, and I hoped you would come in time for us to ride out together. I invariably take horse at this hour, and so we shall now ride, and you shall tell me why you have decided to do this remarkable thing." She smiled, an expression that softened the severity of her long, boney face. She was younger than the Prince, perhaps forty, with bright blonde hair and small, deep-set cornflower eyes, a straight nose and a pendulous lower lip of the sort common among the high nobility of the Hapsburg lands.

They mounted and rode across the bridge to Petřín. Rudi was conscious of the walking people looking up at them, their faces registering admiration, envy or resentment—or so it seemed. For himself, he found he was deeply happy. It was extremely pleasant being an aristocrat. It was a happier state than being a worker, for obvious reasons, but it was also happier than being a bourgeois, even a bourgeois with more money than most aristocrats. The purpose of any real revolution must therefore be to make everyone feel like he did now.

How this could be accomplished occupied some thought as he trotted along next to the Princess Windischgrätz. Could it be that Bakunin was right in some way? Yet, how could society exist without some ordered hierarchy? He became less happy; he turned his thoughts to the princess. She was a fine woman, not near as lovely as his Berthe, but she had something fascinating about her that he could not quite name. A perfect confidence that she would receive respect and good wishes from everyone she encountered? Whatever the cause, it seemed to give her a freedom that he envied.

They finished their gallop and walked their mounts side by side, the Princess chatting away. Her conversation was horses, her lands, the poverty of their estates, the difficulties presented by servants nowadays, and the intimate imbroglios of the nobility. The last of which she presented with such wit and insouciance that Rudi wondered if she was considering an imbroglio of her own!

This thought made him laugh out loud. Fortunately, the Princess was finishing a tale about a nobleman of excellent family whose wife, discovering him *in flagrante* with a mastiff bitch, had exclaimed, "What, are there no more peasant girls!"

"Truly, men are dogs," observed Rudi and the princess's laugh rang out deep and free through the woods.

Later, after the princess had given him coffee and nothing else (how peculiar that aristocrats did not think to feed one!) and he was walking home, he found his recent euphoria quite evaporated. I am mad, he thought. I am running out of money, and I have just contracted a huge debt for that damned horse. A wonderful horse, true, but he was feeding Sisi and Anneke and often their neighbors as well, a steady drain of florins, and buying up slivovic, gallons of the best--Pannau when he could get it. It gave a him a keen and primitive pleasure to know that his ancestors had planted the plums from which this elixir was made. Or the peasants had, he supposed.

Sisi. Everything would be fine without her, he thought, even as he despised himself for so thinking. Not a day passed but he was at the point of sending her away. But in the night he re-discovered why he could not. He recalled reading Byron at eighteen and swearing to himself that he would lead a Byronic life, as being the only life fit for a true man. Now he had it—revolutionary! aristocrat! libertine!--and how did he like it? Not much, it seemed. Perhaps Byron had something he himself lacked. He must re-read the poet. He read English well, although he rarely had a chance to speak it. Czech he spoke ever better, was now nearly fluent in it, but not the Czech of the philology professors. Pillow talk had given him the true demotic Praguer dialect. Meanwhile, he found himself living like a goddamned noble, with a white horse and a Böhmer slut. He thought of what his grandfather had said about becoming him and laughed out loud.

On May 19th, Prince Windischgrätz took formal charge of all military forces in Bohemia. No one knew if this was on orders from Vienna, or from the court in Innsbruck, or merely a coup by the field marshal, but Lobkowicz immediately put the National Guard at the disposal of the new supremo, and the thing was done. Liberal Prague voiced its objection in press and pamphlet, to no effect whatsoever.

The rage of the population coalesced and found its most violent expression among the young: the apprentices and, especially, the students. The next day Rudi arrived at the Carolinium to find the courtyard packed. A young man with a straggly beard was up on a table haranguing. This was Karel Sladowsky, a student from Vienna, who had recently arrived and had taken over the leadership, such as it was, of the students of Prague. The burden of his argument was that they could do what the students of Vienna had done: face down reaction, demand arms, take over public buildings, and advance the revolution to its next level, although he did not specify what this might be. He was cheered to the echo.

Rudi saw Andrej Popp in the crowd and approached him.

"What do you think of that, Popp?"

"It's inspiring," said the young man, with a glow in his face. "Could we not do as they have done in Vienna?"

"Possibly. But in Vienna the students confronted a dithering government headed by an idiot emperor. Here we confront Field Marshal Windischgrätz, who has never dithered in his life. How many men remain in our flying column?"

"Fewer than fifty, sir. Some left the city when they suspended lectures, and others have gone over to the Slavia militia."

"Well, don't look so down-hearted. It is not your fault. But would you do something for me? Go out to the various militias and find out how many pieces are in their hands."

525

"Yes, sir. But, sir, Sladowsky says if we march on the Butcher's headquarters and demand arms, he cannot refuse. They did not in Vienna, after all."

"Sladowsky has never met the Prince," said Rudi. "I have. Provide me that inventory, and I fear what you discover will be the only arms we shall ever have. That little expedition that won us our new muskets cannot succeed again, now the Prince is in control."

"Do you think it will come to a fight, sir?"

"You asked me that once before. Then I thought not. Now I am not so sure. It may be that the regulars will not fire on their fellow citizens..."

Rudi offered a smile he did not feel, clapped the young man on his shoulder, and departed.

The next day, Rudi was seated in a pew in St. Vitus Cathedral, in the heart of Hradčany Castle. Spring sunlight fell through the great rose window and painted the stones of the floor and walls with vivid hues. For the first time, Rudi considered what it would be to accept that the purpose of the place had the same reality as the colors. He found he could not. Some element in his soul must be missing. He wondered about that too, and this idea led to another: could believers and unbelievers ever be truly united in a state?

While considering this interesting and insoluble question (insoluble as all the others that now dominated his life) he heard the sound of a person sliding into the pew just behind his, and a familiar voice.

"A good choice of venue, Rudi. It is the least likely place in Prague to find a liberal."

"Good day to you, Wulfi. Thank you for coming."

"Of course I came. In your note you said you had some intelligence to convey."

"Yes. I believe I have puzzled out where the people who stole some twelve hundred muskets are hiding them. I will tell you, provided you promise me on your word of honor that you will conduct no investigation into who perpetrated the theft. I want the weapons and gunpowder returned to the army and kept out of the hands of radicals, but I will not have any arrests."

"An interesting proposal. Of course, I could arrest *you* for concealing evidence of a crime against the state."

"Go ahead. In which case, I will stay silent and someday soon you may see twelve hundred workers armed with the latest model muskets on the other side of the Charles Bridge. I would be happy to explain upon that day how you allowed it to happen."

"Yes, I suppose you would. You know, I learn with interest that we are no longer relatives--Baron. That must have been a shock. But barons are not immune from arrest."

"Don't play, Wulfi. Do you agree or not?"

"Did you know gunpowder has a distinctive odor that dogs can detect? We have dogs especially trained to seek it out. I might find the cache myself, without your conditions."

"I believe our clever radicals have taken your dogs into account. You will not find this place by tracking odors, I do assure you." Rudi turned in his seat and stared into Speyr's face. "Well? Do I have your promise?"

The policeman grinned; it was not a pleasant sight. "Oh, well, we have a fair idea of who they are anyway. I dare say they will commit some other crime and we can gather them up at a later date. So yes--you have my word they will be held harmless for this adventure."

"I will hold you to it. The weapons and powder are stored on a fishing boat moored on the river below the canal. The boat is called *Bogomila.*"

"And you know this how?"

"Fish. And a kite," said Rudi. "Don't forget your word." He rose and walked out of the cathedral, leaving the policeman staring in bafflement.

That night, Rudi sought out Sisi Vasová at her apartment. She was alone, writing. She was at her table, which was strewn with scribbled papers. She frowned when he entered and gathered them all up in a rush, jamming them into a satchel, while he tugged at her clothes. In a few moments, her resistance faded, and she allowed herself to be carried to the bed, and subdued with kisses. The usual followed, in an unusually delicious fashion.

After the yells and sighs, she pouted. "This demonstrates how little you regard me as a thinker. My thoughts on school reform are quite blown from my head."

"They will return along with detumescence, I dare say."

"*You dare say*, pah pah pah! You have become more lubricious since you became a baron, my dear. It is no surprise. I was debauched by an aristocrat, did you know that? Yes, a count. I was by then a waitress at the Rialto in Pilzn. I was sixteen and still in school. He invited me for a carriage ride. Of course, I said yes; I had never been in a carriage before. We drove through the park of his estate; he had a flask--cognac! The first time it passed my lips, that divine substance. You must buy me a bottle of cognac, Moritz, it is the done thing for the Böhmer whore. Well, after that he made quick work of me, up with the skirts, the thighs pried apart, and there it was done. I was amazed it was such a nothing: all the talk, all the warnings, and just this."

"Yet," Rudi said, "you improved it far beyond a nothing thereafter, upon my own witness. And you are not my Böhmer whore."

"No? Then what am I?"

"You are my dear and esteemed colleague and comrade in arms, with whom I am having a passionate affair."

Her mouth hung open for an instant, and then she let out one of her great laughs. "By Christ's royal ass, Moritz, I tell you there is not another man in Prague who could have produced that sentence! It warms me more than cognac. Well, do you have another shot in the locker?"

He did. After that, lying in her arms he said, "Do you trust me?"

"With my life."

"Then tell me who is Jiskra?"

"First, tell me why you want to know."

"Because he is the most dangerous man in Prague. He is brilliant, daring and unprincipled—a deadly combination. If anyone can engineer an outrage that will bring the army down upon us, it is he. Therefore, I must find some way to locate and forestall him. Perhaps even now he will listen to reason."

"Nonsense! You are simply enraged at him because of that silly lampoon he wrote on us."

"And are you not?"

"No, because I am shameless, and don't care who knows that you inhabit my bed."

"You are mistaken, my dear. I think not of what he has done, but only of what he might yet do. Look now, I have a suspicion. Will you at least confirm that I am correct?"

"What suspicion?"

"That Jiskra is Novak." As he said this, Rudi studied the face on the pillow inches from his own. He observed a brief passage of shock run across it, quickly converted to a grin and then one of her hearty laughs burst out.

"However did you guess, love?"

"Never mind that. Can you arrange a meeting?"

"I can try. He doesn't like you at all."

"The feeling is mutual. I hate to leave you now, but I must."

A final kiss, and then he was out of bed. When he had washed and dressed, he sat next to her, held her naked shoulders in his hands, and looking into her eyes said, "Sisi, listen to me and do not ask me any questions about what I am about to say. Stay away from the boat! The *Bogomila* has been compromised. Tell Novotny and Havel and any of the others the same!" Before she could do more than let out a startled cry, he had left the room.

For the remainder of May, Rudi withdrew from active politics, and all around him a peculiar stasis seemed to grip the city. There was no news about any seizure of weapons, but without fuss the paperwork shadow of twelve hundred and eighty-two muskets and four hundredweight of gunpowder appeared in Rudi's office. A hundred or so muskets were still missing, but the danger of a massive armed insurrection seemed to have disappeared. No one had been arrested. Rudi felt he had behaved credibly enough, and thereafter lost what little interest he had retained in his official occupation.

Each afternoon, having spent a few ceremonial hours at his desk, he rode out with Princess Eleanor and drank coffee with her afterward. These hours were like a visit to the world his grandfather had described, for he had never met anyone (not even Berthe) as politically innocent as the princess. The tumult of the French Revolution might never have happened, for were not things all repaired? The proper kings were back on their thrones, except in France, but the French had been quite ruined and no one looked to France anymore; German culture had now exceeded anything those benighted people had to offer. Bonaparte she knew of, but as a figure from myth, useful only to frighten children. It was enormously relaxing to be in her presence, like getting drunk, without the ill after-effects. They had graduated from the hand-kiss to the embrace and the kiss on both cheeks.

His only quasi-political activity was a series of articles he wrote, in Czech, and published under the pseudonym *Vile* in the newspaper *Česka Vičela*. He meant them as parody--the pseudonym referred to a kind of tricky wood-spirit out of Czech folk tales--mocking the extreme sort of Czech patriotic nonsense that appeared all too often in the current journals and street pamphlets. Vile demanded the elimination of all things German, not only the language but also beer and sausages, as well as unification of all Slavs, including the Red Indians of America, who by their language and free spirits were shown, in a burlesque of mock-scholarship, to be brothers to the great Slavic nation.

These bagatelles gave him pleasure and, he thought, did no great harm. He stopped writing them when letters started appearing in the paper, praising Vile as a true patriot and supporting his proposals. After that he took the notes and drafts he had made for the Bohemian Constitution and handed them to his cook, to line pans and start fires.

During this time, the self-proclaimed Böhmer whore was less available than before; she had become an important organizer of the Slav Congress scheduled to open on the second of June. The hotels had already begun to fill with delegates from abroad, Russians, Ruthenians, Slovaks, Croats, Serbs. Sisi had great hopes for it, an enthusiasm he did not share. Rudi both burned for her and was relieved when his proposed assignations were rejected.

On the twenty-sixth, the election to the all-German parliament was held. Virtually no one in Bohemia, Czech or German, bothered to vote. Divide and conquer had worked again. On the twenty-ninth, a Monday, Rudi received an un-expected message from the Hrad. The governor, Count Thun. requested an interview. Once there, he was led, not to the great official room where he had been before, but to a smaller room in the precincts of the Bohemian chancellery. It was the sort of place where a meeting with the governor might be kept as private as anything ever was in that beehive of gossip.

The governor rose from his chair to greet Rudi and offered his hand. When they were both seated, after the usual chat, Thun came to the point of the meeting.

"Baron, I assume you have heard of my plan to form a provisional government."

"Only rumors, my lord."

"Well, it is so. The letter to the Hofburg has already been drafted. There will be a council made up of myself and eight members, four Czech and four German, aristocrats and commoners. You know very well that we cannot govern Bo-hemia through the National Committee. The only thing they can agree upon is the color of the cockades the police must wear in their hats. Beyond that, the situation in Vienna dete-riorates by the day. The army has the emperor walled off in Innsbruck and Latour and his camarilla of reaction are in charge in Vienna. I do not know how long Pillersdorf can hold on as premier. We simply must have a functional government here in Prague or all is lost."

"I see that, my lord. But what of Windischgrätz? Will he accept orders from the provisional government? He seems to be a force unto himself."

"He says he will. As long as the hotheads do nothing requiring what he calls a firm hand. And as long as there is no serious move to separate Bohemia from the empire. All now depends on showing the world a functioning, loyal government. I presume you agree, baron."

"With all my heart, sir!"

"Then see what you think of my choices. Here is the list of the eight."

Rudi took the paper the Count handed him, read the names on it and handed it back.

"I am honored, my lord, that you should include me, but I must decline. I have decided that my future lies not in Bohemian politics but in Vienna with my family."

"In Vienna? Have you been offered something in government?"

"No, my lord. I don't know what I will do. Perhaps I will join my stepfather and father-in-law in the enterprise of railroads."

The governor could not hide a startled look, as if Rudi had announced a preference for hoeing potatoes. "Really! Railroads? A man of your . . . well, I mean to say, that is too bad. I suppose it will have to be Borosch after all."

"What, Borosch!" cried Paul Novotny, his pencil poised over his notebook. "God save Bohemia!"

"I think him a very good choice," said Rudi, who had come directly from the Hrad to the Knight. "He gets along well with everyone."

"Yes, because he wholeheartedly agrees with everyone he meets, regardless of any substantive position. Well, well, so the provisional government is a reality after all. What a

Mayfly is our revolution! It took the French three years to go from a popular assembly to a Directory; we have managed it in as many months. I hope it will serve, but alas, the only Bonaparte on the scene is playing for the other side. You say Windischgrätz approved of this scheme?"

"So the Count implied. He could hardly oppose it publicly. There is something a little irregular about his own position, I believe."

"Yes, he is a tool of the camarilla, the bastards, and the way Radetzky is flinging the Italians about now, they will soon be able to turn their military attention to us. How many troops do you suppose are at the Prince's disposal now?"

"Too many--five or six thousand bayonets and near two thousand sabers."

"And on the side of the revolution?"

"I had my captain ask around the town. He says there are just under three thousand actual muskets, besides an unknown number of pistols, fowling pieces and various other lethal hardware in the possession of the various militias. I don't count the National Guard on our side as long as Lobkowicz commands it. They will remain hostile neutrals in any clash."

"There *will* be a clash," said Novotny. "Sometime during this Slav Congress, some maniac will declare a Slavic Republic free of the empire or some such nonsense and the troops will march."

"You sound like you are looking forward to it."

"As a citizen, not at all." He flourished his notebook. "As a reporter, I dote on the notion. It will be the most excellent copy. By the way, speaking of doting, your inamorata was just in here, seeking lodging for her Slavs."

"I wish you would not call her that. In any case, that is yet another reason that it is well I am quitting Prague."

"She will take that badly, very badly, you know." Novotny's tone turned grave. "I have seen her through a number of men, and thought her a butterfly, but with you it seems different. She is serious about you."

"I can't help that. She has known from the beginning it could not last and she has known for weeks that I am planning to leave."

Novotny touched a finger to his temple. "Here she knows." He moved the finger to his breast. "Here she does not."

Rudi left the Knight and walked through the town square, thinking about what Paul had just said. Head and heart, the old story with women, or at least women of the class Sisi belonged to, and the type--the artistic type, and devotees of Romance. He wondered if the Princess Windischgrätz ever had a conflict between her head and her heart. Somehow, he doubted it, and the same was true of Berthe. She was one thing all the way through. Sisi, on the other hand, could be four things at once: a maddening woman.

He felt his arm gripped in a too familiar way and heard a familiar laugh and there indeed was the maddening woman herself, linking her arm through his.

"Remarkable!" he said. "I was just this moment thinking about you."

"I am not surprised," said she, kissing him on the cheek, "I expect you to think of me nearly without cease. Come along with me. I have to deliver these receipts to the committee. They have put me in charge of finding lodging for the delegates, which is only natural, me being a woman and an experienced chambermaid. How I would like to see that revolutionized someday!"

She was in the highest spirits and dressed in unaccustomed finery—a dove gray day dress of fine wool with a line of ribbon bows down the front and a short jacket with velvet lapels. She wore a bonnet of lacquered straw instead of her usual turban or nothing on her head.
That is a handsome dress, Sisi," he said. "The folk-tale trade must be booming."

Laughing, she replied, "Oh, this old thing? It is on loan from Friedmann's, so I may meet and make arrangements for our distinguished guests without scandal. Saving my expression and my tongue, I believe one might take me for a spoiled bourgeoise. Porters scurry at my beck. It is a lark, my dear!"

They were walking on the south side of the square, passing the café called the Angel and the long line of carriages that waited outside, for it was a tradition of the town's *gratin* to take tea and cakes there in the afternoon.

"Shall you buy me supper someplace nice tonight?" Vasovà was saying. "I have been living on crusts since this business began."

Rudi was about to answer, when the Angel's doorman threw open his door and bowed low, revealing two women dressed in fashionable light summer frocks and straw bonnets. To his shock, Rudi found himself looking into the face of Princess zu Windischgrätz.

"Ah, Baron von Pannau," she cried. "How charming to meet you! Allow me to present my cousin Sophie, Gräfin von Keyserling. Sophie, this is my riding companion, Rudolf Freiherr von und zu Pannau-Kinsky, of whom I have spoken."

He greeted the princess, greeted the countess, kissed the proffered hands, attested his enchantment. The princess turned her eye upon Vasová.

"And this must be the Baronin von Pannau," she said smiling.

At this, Vasová dropped a low curtsey that would not have been amiss at Schönbrunn, and said sweetly, "Oh, not at all, your serene highness. I am only the Böhmer mistress."

The princess retained her smile and observed, "And isn't this weather glorious? So clear and not a bit of oppressive heat! But we must be getting on, dear baron. Charming to have met you. I will await our next ride eagerly."

The two noble ladies swept on to their carriage, an open landau with the Windischgrätz crest on its varnished side.

"Sisi, did you have to?" said Rudi when they had passed.

"I did have to. I am never other than I am, unlike some people. Which princess was that? One meets so many princesses it is hard to tell one from the other."

"That was the Butcher's wife, as a matter of fact."

"Was it? How odd! One never thinks of monsters enjoying domestic felicity. One hopes that her talk of riding referred to an actual horse and was not a figure of speech for something else. Or perhaps not; it would be delicious if little Rudi Moritz was cuckolding the Butcher."

"I'm afraid the princess regards a mere baron as only barely human."

"Then you don't know what every servant knows. I wish I had a kreutzer for every fine lady who fucked a footman. Then I might even afford this dress. Farewell, my dear, I am off on the people's business."

In a moment she was lost in the crowd.

Thirty-one

The next day, Rudi took his ride as usual with Princess Windischgrätz. She did not advert at all to their meeting the previous day, nor to Sisi. How wonderful, thought Rudi, is the amnesia of the high aristocracy. Certain unpleasantries could not possibly occur and therefore did not, and the fortunate life continued unaffected.

Upon returning to his study, Rudi found Sisi Vasová comfortably ensconced in his chair, reading through copies of his letters to Berthe and her responses, which he had arranged by date in his cardboard portfolio.

"How the devil did you get in here?" he demanded. "And how dare you read my private letters!"

"Ah, dear Rudi, you really are a swine. I have called you the best man in Prague, and you are, but you are still a swine, even if you are the swine least encrusted by filth. Your heart is always with her, as you say here, even though your *churak* is with me. Truly, I am dying to meet the woman who possesses your heart. Perhaps she will tell me the secret when she arrives. We will sit together in her little white bedroom and discuss . . . oh, all sorts of things."

"Don't be stupid! She is not coming here. I am going to her, and not a moment too soon!"

"Not coming? Off course she will come. Oh, Rudi, my dear fool, how is it that you are such a wonderful lover and know so little about the hearts of women? If I was many miles away from my husband and received from him letters such as this, I would imagine only two things. That he was dying without me, in which case it would be my duty as a wife to rush to his side, come what may. Or that he had taken a lover and that guilt guided his pen, in which case I would rush to his side all the faster. Oh, she will come, never fear!"

"Nonsense. You are a very silly woman if you think tricks like this invasion are endearing. Again I ask, how did you get in here?"

"Why our little Lidunka, of course. She would sell her mother for cream cakes. I have quite corrupted her."

"She shall be dismissed immediately."

"You would do that? Throw a child into the street in a fit of pique? No, you are too kind by far. And she is so proud of her new shoes. It would be a pity to see them sold for bread. No, Lidunka will stay, I think. But I will go, my dear swine."

She rose, gathered her bag and bonnet, and said, "By the way, Big Steffi sends his regards, and says he will meet you. He wishes, however, to know what you wish to discuss."

"Thank you, my dear. Tell Herr Jiskra that the subject will be the defense of Prague and the revolution," said Rudi. "Let it be tomorrow, when his work is done, at the Sack of Meal. And let him come alone."

After Vasová left, he moved to the cabinet where he kept his files and pulled out a map of Prague. Working with a straight edge, compass, and dividers, he made notes directly on the map with a pencil, taking some hours at the task.

The next day, June the second, Rudi went as usual to the Pachta palace and rode out with the princess. She complained about the dullness of the town, its inferiority to Vienna. "Why, it is almost like being in the country!" she declared. "And the people! Their manners, even those of rank, are abhorrent. One does not know where to look sometimes. And the Prince works so hard, you know, always at his office, and the people are so ungrateful! Do you know, a boy threw a stone at my carriage the other day! A stone! And one cannot find a decent gown—one might almost be in *Gratz*. I thought of giving a ball, but who is there to invite? No one."

Rudi objected that Prague was full of brilliant and interesting people.

"Oh, *people!* I meant people one can know. My husband always says that the human race begins with the barons. Below that, well..."

Rudi changed the subject to martingales--one sees them so infrequently on horses nowadays and why did her serene highness think that was so?

When they came to Petřín, Rudi suggested climbing the heights for the view. There were cavalry there, and as they approached, a young captain rode out to meet them on the road and, with apologies, suggested that they take another route, as military exercises were in progress. It would be dusty and unpleasant.

Through the trees, Rudi could see men at work, sappers by their uniforms, carrying baulks of timber, digging pits, and clearing shrubbery. His heart sank; even to his untrained eye, it was obvious they that were preparing emplacements for siege guns.

He was so silent on the way back, that the princess politely inquired if there was something amiss. He excused himself and said he had a headache.

"Oh, headaches! They are my cross as well. I will give you chamomile instead of coffee. I find it sovereign for headaches."

At home waited another long letter from Berte, in which she waxed more emotional than was her wont. No gossip and children's doings, or but a little. She said that his letters filled her with joy and that she now felt their parting had been providential, that the separation had proved to each how much they loved and needed one another. She confessed herself delighted, however, that it would very soon be at an end.

He kissed the letter and cursed himself for a villain. But she was correct. The present crisis could not last. The irritation of the Czechs would be diverted by this Congress they were putting on, there would be volumes of hot air expended instead of gunpowder, the Germans would remain docile, the provisional government would take hold, peace would reign, if only the hotheads could be contained, and he could slip away in good conscience.

Novak was already there, alone in a dark corner, when Rudi entered the Sack of Meal. The place was crowded but the other five chairs at his table stood empty. Rudi sat in one.

"Have you any weapons?" Rudi asked without preamble.

"You come to the point, don't you, Moritz? Or should I say, my lord?

"Moritz will do. Well?"

"Why is it your business?"

"Because Windischgrätz waits for some sort of emeut, an uprising--Czechs against Germans, workers against students, it won't matter. This disorder he intends as a premise to crush our revolution. He will soon have cannon emplaced on Petřín. I have seen the preparations and I do not doubt they are doing the same at Vyšehrad. This emeut must not occur."

"Maybe it should. We have arms: powder and shot in plenty, but not enough muskets. We had some stolen but they got discovered. Can you get us some?"

"That is not the *point*, Novak. There cannot be an uprising now. We must have peace until the provisional government has started to function. If we have peace, Vienna cannot but accept the provisional government as legitimate, and they will pull Windischgrätz's teeth. In effect, the revolution will be won."

"Yes, won for you and your kind, and us still with nothing. Will we have the vote? No! Will we have bread for our children? No! What does it matter to us if the boot on our neck belongs to a king or a fat merchant? Our face remains in the mud."

Rudi sighed. "But if the principal of autocracy and the practice of aristocratic rule is not broken, your people will have no hope at all. If the bourgeoisie have the vote, universal suffrage cannot be far off. If they do not, it is not simply far off, but impossible. Look here, Novak, I did not come to argue politics with you, about which we never shall agree, but to put forth a proposal. Look at this map! In a few days, or even as we speak, there will be siege guns emplaced here and here. I have marked the ranges of the largest gun likely to be employed, the eleven pounder. You will notice that there is a small area of the town out of the range of these guns either on Petřín or at Vyšehrad. What lies in the center of that zone?"

He pointed. Novak said, "The flour depot."

"Yes. A large stone building that also commands the most important intersection of streets in the city, Kolowratsgasse going roughly north-south and Zeletnergasse going east-west. Army General Headquarters is on Zeletnergasse, *here*, and this will help isolate it. If the Carolinium, the town square, and the Clementium are also fortified, we will have a little quadrilateral, with interior lines, in which our few firearms can hope to stand off any assault that may come."

"Why should I trust you?" said Novak. "You ride horses with the Butcher's wife every day. Why should I believe this is not a trap cooked up by Windischgrätz? Anyway, first you say we must do nothing, and now you are planning for a battle. This looks like provocation to me."

"I meant it would be wise to prepare for an attack I hope will not come."

"We don't need the help of the bourgeoisie. There are five thousand workers at Karlin who will come to the town at need."

"And what will they fight trained infantry with? Posters? Crowbars?"

Novak picked up the map and slowly crumpled it into a ball. He said, "Even if we fight with our teeth, we do not need your help."

"Oh, for Christ's sake, Novak, or Jiskra, or whatever you want to call yourself! Can you not end this charade of being a moron with a strong back? Surely you can see this the only faint hope we have? And you know me, you know what I have written and my character. You cannot imagine I would be party to this kind of provocation!"

The big man rose and stared at him. His eyes held nothing but dull rage.

Rudi watched him walk out, and shouted out after him. "For God's sake, do not try to fire out the windows! Block them up and make loopholes in the walls!"

The man kept walking and a heavy pall of despair settled in Rudi's heart. He could have the man arrested, but that would do no good at this stages of events. He was needed to defend the flour depot. So much for the rule of law.

During the succeeding days, Rudi traveled the city on his wonderful horse, in his uniform, seeing various people—student leaders, National Guard officers, the leaders of the Slavic militias—in an attempt to forge a unified command. In this he failed. No one he talked to was interested in cooperating, and no one thought an Austrian general would ever order the bombardment of Prague. Yet Rudi persisted: up to Petřín, where, as he had predicted guns were being emplaced, over to Vyšehrad to see the other cannon, along the walls and the river embankment, threading the streets of the old town and the new, devising in his head a plan of defense that would never be realized.

He now kept his horse in a livery stable on 14 Zeitnergasse, a few yards from his door, and did not ride out with the princess any more.

On Monday, the fifth of June, a summons from grandfather interrupted this military fantasia. He had hardly thought of the old man at all during that time, and the memoir writing seemed part of a vanished life, nearly a dream.

"My, but you look wan, my boy," said the baron when Rudi entered his room "I swear you have aged two years in a fortnight. I hope it is not illness; or venery."

"Neither, grandfather, I assure you," Rudi replied in the tone used to change a subject. Extracting his notebook from his portfolio he asked, "Shall we begin?"

Where were we!? It has been some while. Yes, I have mentioned I married Marietta in '97, in May at Pannau, very pretty, blossoms in the air and so forth. We had music. She insisted and I could not deny her. We had the summer together and it was a very good time; I thought perhaps she tried to repair the past. You cannot, but you can learn from it, if you dare. What had fascinated me as a boy was gone, but the boy was gone, too. I felt badly for her and wished to make her happy. That is not love, that is not what I felt for Paradowski, but it is also not nothing.

She was an excellent gräfin, by the way, and as I said, Pannau came to life again under her sway, which was a great relief, it having languished for many years under a solitary melancholic and then a violent boor. I sent to Wachtmeister Emil Neckar and brought Kíslang back to Pannau, which gave me a great deal of pleasure.

In November, this idyll ended when a messenger arrived, informing me that the regiment was about to join our forces facing the French in three days' time and requested the pleasure of my company. We had been trounced by Bonaparte at Rivoli and he was coming for Vienna next. The Hofkriegsrat was screaming for any man who could ride and swing a saber.

As it happened, we didn't have to fight. Bonaparte at the time had a better sense of his luck than he did thereafter and asked for terms. We gave him all our lands in Italy and the whole of the Netherlands, which hardly sated him, since he then went off to conquer Egypt. We licked our wounds, hardly imagining there was much worse to come. I went back to Pannau, and in February a daughter was born to us dead, and took her mother with her after a week of agony.

I confess that her death did not shake me as hard as it did the children, including your father, for he had formed a bond with her, though a little mite. Hansel, we called him: he cried and cried. I suppose I had become immured to suffering and loss by then. It is a common danger among soldiers, I fear, and I had endured more loss than many, on the field and off. At the funeral I took my Aunt Fredi aside and asked her to come to Pannau, to raise the little Count and his sister and also my Hansel. Her Oskar was gone to Jena for his studies and her daughters were all married off and she doted on being in charge of things. Until Karl-Franz's majority she would, in addition, be virtual Countess of Pannau, which I believe was the final inducement, for she loved rule above all else.

I saw your father only on leaves from the wars, and the wars dragged on, as you know, near twenty years in all. We treated each other as was proper, and I suppose his childhood was better than my own in that regard, since I did not absolutely ignore him, and his relations with his cousin, Count Fritz, were cordial as far as I could make out. But he was undeniably second to the young count about the place and this bred in him an ambition to distinguish himself in some way. Which he did, poor lad.

The old baron lifted up a thick, leather-bound volume that lay on a table near his chair.

This book is our regimental history. It will tell you more about the famous battles than I could, for a lieutenant of dragoons sees only what is before him and has all he can do to manage his horse and his troop.

Colonel Max died at Wagram, struck by a cannonball. I suppose his heart had died years before, although he concealed it well. Promotion was denied him, of course, and he remained a mere colonel while men far inferior to him became field marshals. And as he had predicted after Fleurus, war itself had changed, now it was all about massed battalions and vast numbers of cannons. The little Austrian army in which he had been raised had become obsolete. So I lost my second father, never having had much of a first. A year later, I inherited what was left of the regiment.

Yes, they all died, in the end, all that merry group that used to go to the Mounted Man, all of Paradowski's friends and mine. Hoth died at Marengo, Silmaringen at Ulm, little de Cavriani perished at Hohenlinden in those terrible close woods the idiots sent us through. Cannon fire got him. He was just twenty-five. Fritz von Waldheim received a small wound in his foot at Aspern that festered and he passed from this world raving in a monastery fitted out as a field hospital. Oh, read it, read it, my boy. It is a long sad story. But we got the bastard in the end.

"When did my father join the colors?" asked Rudi.

"At eighteen or so. He was always of military bent, and, as I have said, he wished to gain distinction in my eyes, who had before this paid him little attention on account of my long service. I brought him into the Kinsky as cornet, although it is not regular. He was a fine young officer for the month or so he served before Leipzig."

Now as to Leipzig. You should recall that Leipzig lasted three whole days and contained battles that by themselves would have been among the greatest battles of the war. Dölwitz was but the first on the southern edge of the fight. I will not detain you with the details, they are all in the book— suffice it to say that the French had fortified a mill and a manor that we had to carry. The place was held by some regiments of Poniotowski Polish corps. Examining their dispositions with my telescope I received the great shock of my life, for my glass picked out, under a schapska helmet, a face I knew—Paradowski. I cannot now recount the feelings that arose from this sight, relief and horror and love all mixed in a posset. Perhaps no man alive ever had such a feeling! But more powerful than these feelings was my duty, and I ordered my people to the attack.

All morning we assaulted both buildings until at last they were pushed out and the black eagle flew over the spire. Then they came back with their reserve companies and we in turn were forced to retreat. By this time we were all fighting as infantry and I had lost a fifth of my men. Even the hussars had dismounted and were firing their carbines.

Such a battle, when both sides are courageous and unyielding, must be decided by who runs out of ammunition first. In this case it was us and we had to withdraw. I sent to corps begging for artillery. It came, for we had many more guns than the French for the first time in the war, six batteries of twelve-pounders, well served, and their fire reduced the two strong points to rubble. We remounted and occupied the village.

I never saw such a sight in all my years at war. The pile of stones that had been the manor house was stuffed with corpses and parts of men, like raisins in a cake. In what remained of a room there, no bigger than the one we sit in, I counted fifty dead, Polish and Austrians all mixed together; the blood on the floor slopped over the toes of my boots. One of them was your father, still with his sword and pistol gripped in his dead hands. I kissed his face and took away those implements of war, that he had used but once and would never require again. And the ring you now wear.

The old man went to a desk and removed a much-scarred dark wooden box from a drawer.

"I doubt if I will find a use for these anymore and they may serve you, I hope, as well as they did me."

Rudi opened the box. "These are the pistols your father gave you."

"Yes. Rifled and astonishingly accurate out to fifty yards. You can stand against a musket at that range and kill your man."

"I thank you once more, sir, with all my heart. But tell me, did you ever find Paradowski again?"

"Never. And I am not even sure it was him, not at that distance through a glass. The notion that it might have been, and that he might have shot his own babe—it is too horrible to contemplate. But I suppose you are still involved in these broils I hear of."

The abrupt change of subject shook Rudi and he could supply only a halting answer.

"Yes . . . that is to say, I hope that all will keep their heads and that the broils will diminish."

"They will not. As we speak, Windischgrätz is leading a grand parade of his troops through Karlín."

"My God! That will drive the people into a fury."

"That is the plan. It is an old trick. I used it myself in Parma years ago. The message is, oh, you lowly, bow the knee, for I have the power. It is a fair warning, but the fools never seem to take it."

"The desire for freedom does not seem foolish to me."

"Yes, well, there we differ. And even you must deprecate the uses to which the freedom desired has been put, here in this city. No sooner do you tell a man he may do as he wishes than he joins a mob whose purpose is to gain advantage over those he marks as in somewise different. It was ever so, back to the Greeks and ever will be so. In the meanwhile, you bid fair to wreck the only government that can balance the rivals of Europe. Your face takes on that mulish cast, I see, although in your heart you know I speak the truth. Tell me, what do you imagine we have been doing together these weeks?"

"What do you mean, sir? I have been taking down your memoirs."

"Bah! As to that, I bid you consign your notebooks to the flames. The only purpose of these conversations was to teach you the lessons of my life so that you might apply them to your own. Do you know what is the problem of the human race? It is that the young do not study the lives of their forebears and take advice from their mistakes. Every generation thinks it has discovered something new, to which the experiences of the past do not apply. Mine was no different. We believed in romance as you believe in liberty, and what was the result? That I wished to hang myself at age seventeen? That you promise the people liberty? It is sure that this promise will be like mine to poor Lennart, to raise him up. You heard the result."

"I am sorry that your experiment has been a failure then," said Rudi, and could not keep the bitterness from his voice.

"No, in one respect it has been a success. I have ruined you as a revolutionary, I think. There is a bleakness about you that you did not have when first you came to me. Your giddy mania has quite departed, I am happy to observe. I have told you this before now: aristocracy lay as an ember in your blood and I have blown it into flame. Your action in revealing the hiding place of the stolen arms proves it."

"You know of that?"

"Yes, you never listen to me: I say again, there is little I do not know of your doings. May I offer you two bits of advice?"

"Of course, sir."

"The first is to leave here. Stable your mount, and take the train to Vienna."

"You know I cannot do that."

"You feel honor-bound to continue your struggle?"

"I do. This is your firmest teaching, after all—that honor binds, even when good sense and self-preservation argue an opposite course."

"Yes, I am cut by my own blade there. It is too bad, too bad. I got to you too late, it seems. Well, sir, in that case, my second piece of advice is that when you are on foot and confronting a mounted swordsman, you must not try to duel with him, but strike at his horse's head as hard as you can with your sword."

Hans closed his eyes. "Leave me now, if you please. This has been an unusually tiring colloquy. I worry about you and that is exhausting. I have grown unused to worry of late; freedom from worry is one of the rich gifts God offers to dying men. You must have a care, my boy, in these coming days. And mind about the horseman!"

Out in the street Rudi looked up at his family's crest and read the words engraved there., the reading blurred by tears. My Honor Is Called Loyalty. How simple! How stupid! Yet they gripped his heart with a force like the most passionate love. He mounted Gitano and rode back across the bridge to meet his undesired fate.

The next evening the students held a rally at the Wenceslaus Baths to protest the Karlín military demonstration and its author. Arriving at the hall, Rudy was struck by the difference between this meeting and the one held here months ago to discuss the petition to the crown. This crowd was composed in the main of students, with a scatter of apprentices, and the few notables in attendance, like Palacký and Trojan, seemed symbolic, like the plaster saints at a village festival. The youthful faces were lit by anger and the mad courage of the young; it was noisy, with little groups of arguers forming and reforming, and the air was full of thrown objects—crumpled paper, spitballs, pieces of fruit.

As he moved through the crowd, Rudi heard a murmur of disapprobation in his wake, remarks about his ancestry, his connections with the Butcher, his treasonous behavior. Karel Sladowsky was at the podium declaring that the people would never stand for these provocations, that the Butcher could not remain in command, that protestations should be made to Vienna, demanding his immediate removal. These points each engendered loud cheers and cries of "Down with the Butcher!" and a chant that went on for minutes: "Windischgrätz out! Windischgrätz out!"

Sladowsky then yielded to a portly youth in spectacles who urged that the students demand arms from Windischgrätz, as was done in Vienna in the great days when the revolution was new. If the people were properly armed, he argued, there would be no need for soldiers in the town. Raucous cheers greeted this announcement, but Rudi laughed aloud.

"What lunacy!" he cried. "You demand the man be dismissed and then you beg him for arms? You will get no arms. In fact, he is bound to try to strip you of the arms you already have. Idiots! Don't you see the difference between Vienna in March and Prague in June? The Prince means to destroy the revolution, *tout court*, and waits only for a convenient excuse. And you still imagine you are in control?"

Rudi was now surrounded by a circle of hostile faces, some people climbing on chairs to see who was uttering these blasphemies. Someone shouted, "No one can stop the revolution!" and others cried out against him personally, naming his crimes: assassin, bourgeois tool of reaction, traitor, aristocrat, defeatist, provocateur. A chant, "Down with Moritz, out with the traitor!" began and soon Rudi confronted a squad of youths with the red-and-white armbands of Svarnost, a Czech militia. They grabbed him and dragged him from the hall amid a storm of curses, kicks, pelting food, and spit.

He had lost his hat. With a handkerchief, he cleaned off the worst of the filth and walked across the square to the Red Goose. On the third floor he took a seat and ordered a bottle of Pannau slivovic. He drank seriously and steadily and in less than an hour was in that interesting state where one can still talk coherently but is not responsible for what one is saying; the dark thoughts within are spread out for public view, and one will not remember the next day what they were.

Paul Novotny sat down across from him. Placing a beer stein on the table, he poured a short tot of liquor into his drink, took a long draught, grinned broadly, and said, "'Prominent liberal expelled from meeting amid jeers.' That might do very well at the head of the column. Or, 'Butcher's cousin exposed by revolutionary students.'

It is certainly a far cry from the last time we met at the Baths, only three months ago."

"Yes, I was just thinking that. it is like a nightmare in which the familiar objects of one's bedroom take on aspects of the horrific. I think I'm going mad, Paul. I see what must be done so clearly, and yet no one listens to me. They keep on with their stupid ways, heedless, marching toward destruction."

"If that is true, it would suggest you were not destined for a career in politics."

Rudi let out a guffaw. "Yes! Why did I not think of that? What a penetrating insight, Novotny! However do you do it?"

"My friend, when you become nasty and sarcastic, I know there is something really wrong with you. *I* am the nasty and sarcastic one. What is it? I would wager La Vasovà has some part in your troubles, because for the last few minutes you have been speaking to me in almost perfect Praguer Czech, where we have never once had a conversation in Czech before."

Rudi laughed again. "Yes, a small souvenir, and were the revolution to start afresh, I dare say I could rouse the Böhmers in their native tongue. But in truth Vasovà is only a tiny part of it. The greater part is what I just said—my political impotence, the frustration of all my hopes . . . and other things, things I am ashamed to own. Ah, at the mention of things hidden, you look at me with your inquisitive look. How remarkable that someone as debauched as you have been, and as cynical, could hold on his face that look of intense but innocent fascination!"

After a second or two of staring, they both began to laugh and the laughter went on for some minutes, drawing looks from the other patrons, although the venue was famously not one in which odd behavior attracted much interest.

"God in heaven," said Rudi, as he wiped his streaming eyes, "I have not laughed like that in a while. I believe the last time was with Vasovà."

"Yes, she does make one laugh," Novotny agreed.

"But it's not mere wit. There is a deep joy about her that is connected in some way with her suffering. Her humor arises from that, too. Her passion as well, I suppose. I never experienced that kind of thing before."

"Yes. It is why you all have Böhmer mistresses to go with your proper German wives. Rest assured, you were not the first, nor will you be the last.""

"That was a hateful thing to say. I should call you out. In fact I have a pistol on me. I would like to go out once, although it shames me to say it. Not with you, necessarily. This is my grandfather's pistol, got from his father, and now mine."

He pulled the weapon from his coat pocket and laid it on the table. Paul picked it up and sighted down the barrel, as people do.

"A Hauschka! My word! I am not nearly of rank enough to be shot by such a pistol." He handed it back. "So, my dear, what will you do, now that you are, as you say, impotent in politics?"

"I will get drunk. You see, I have well started. When I am not drunk, I will organize as much resistance as I can, and keep order where I may. You should be interested in this as a matter of historical record."

Rudi took a folded piece of paper from his coat and handed it to Novotny.

"A city map? What am I looking at?" asked Novotny. "My plan of battle. The strong points that will exist if it comes to a fight are marked, but as you can see there are deep gaps and no defense in depth at all. If only . . . but it is too late now."

"Then why . . ."

"Because I am a prisoner of my fate. It is curiously relaxing. I have become like the sages of the east, accepting all things. It is odd, Paul, but I never thought of owning a pistol in Prague. Now I have three of them, and two swords, with one of which I have recently killed a man. And I will be immensely surprised if this month ends without sword or pistol striking at human flesh. It will be a fiasco. But I will stick it through. "

During the remainder of that week, Rudi continued to patrol the city with his little army. Some men drifted away, he gained others, and at last made rough agreements with other National Guard commanders, who were, like him, suspicious of Prince Lobkowicz's intentions and loyalties, and who would aid in defending the city if the army attacked. Rudi estimated that there were perhaps five hundred guardsmen so inclined.

Meanwhile, the city filled with regular troops. One saw them everywhere, infantry marching to the beat of drums, cavalry squadrons in all the squares, in the parks, walking in columns of twos down the major avenues.

Rudi's men had strict orders not to challenge the regular army or to respond to provocations, but others were not so careful. On the Saturday, in a public park by the riverside, someone fired a shot. Troops rushed through the park with bayonets fixed, terrifying hundreds of people, some of whom endured rough handling. A boy was arrested with an old flintlock pistol. When Rudi heard of this, he exclaimed to his officers, "Stupidity! When the ax finally falls, it will be foolishness like that which precipitates it."

A young man said, "If it must come, let it come soon. We can fight them--and win!"

Rudi frowned at . . . was his name Settelmeyer? He'd tried to recall the names of all his men, but they kept coming and going and it was difficult.

"Winning is, I believe, beyond us," Rudi said. "At this point I should be happy with mere survival, and hope that Count Thun can work some political magic with his new provisional government so as to relieve Windischgrätz and gain full recognition at Innsbruck."

"Not Vienna?" asked one.

"No. Windischgrätz does not give a fig for anything out of a city dominated by students. Only a direct order from someone who speaks for the emperor will winkle him out of here. But if we hold out for a considerable time, the people, and I mean all the people, all ranks and nationalities, may rally behind us, which will strengthen our count's hand. In any case, it will be a very close-run affair, and the longer it is delayed, the better. Pray there are no more fools with pistols!"

Thirty-two

Prague awoke on Whitsunday morning, the eleventh of June, to find the walls of the town plastered everywhere with posters printed in red. These demanded the removal of troops and the dismissal of Windischgrätz, and promised violent upheaval if not. The soldiers were ordered to tear the posters down, and they did, but as soon as they had moved on, gangs of students and schoolboys with ladders and paste-pots put them up again.

Meeting in the Aula of the Carolinium that evening, the students decided that instead of another meeting there would be an open air Mass the next day, Whit-Monday, in the Horse Market Square. Rudi, there observing, noticed that the students organized themselves easily to prepare for this event, breaking into committees to find a priest who would do it, preparing for food and decorations and the supervision of the crowds. It was all a kind of huge party for them, he thought, a way to spend the summer as heroes instead of returning to the dullness and restriction of family life.
Still, Rudi let Andrej Popp volunteer the Academic Legion to protect the event.

Whit-Monday dawned clear and mild. By the time the introit was sung the crowd had packed the vast square to bursting; miraculously, no soldiers appeared during the Mass, although they had been quick to disperse any gathering during the previous week. Rudi sat on Gitano, his men in ranks behind him, and watched the throng. All the women were in white, as was the custom of the day, and most of them carried bouquets or had wreathed flowers in their hair. It was almost possible to forget for one hour that Prague was within a whisker of being a city under siege.

Ite missa est.

No sooner had these words left the mouth of the priest than a cry went up, and reverberated through the thousands, that the assembly should move to Zeletnergasse and demonstrate before Windischgrätz's headquarters. Rudi cursed aloud, but he was powerless to stop the movement of so many: it would be like trying to stop the tide with a pail. What he could do, he did, which was to maneuver his horse and his few dozen troops to a position near the front of the march. They were far from being the only armed men in the crowd, however; the Czech militias were out as well, and odd groups of men brandishing old muskets and fowling pieces.

Down the length of Zeletnergasse they marched. A choir started singing *Kde domov můj* and the crowd took it up, as they had on the day of the constitution, when hope still shone brightly upon Prague. From horseback, the flowered crowns of the women made it appear as if a garden had gone roaming.

As they passed Koniggasse, they got their first glimpse of the troops arrayed in front of the headquarters building. The guard was being changed. Rudi saw their officer hesitate, and then make an urgent decision. He truncated the ceremony, dismissed the old guard and sent the new guard around the corner, leaving only two sentries in front of the massive building. The crowd cheered and moved forward, carrying Rudi and his men within it, quite helpless, like chips on a torrent.

Then, from one of the smaller streets leading south to the Fruit Market, came a pair of closed carriages. These drew up before the entrance to headquarters and from the first one stepped forth, astoundingly, the Field Marshal Prince Alfred zu Windischgrätz, dressed in full military glory, plumed hat on his head, ribbons and medals shining. The singing stopped abruptly, replaced by a great roar of outrage.

The Prince paused while the carriages emptied of their passengers, who proved to be the German burgers of the Verein.

Screams of "traitors!" Cries of "get the Butcher!" Then came the sound of drums and tramping feet, barely to be heard above the roaring crowd. But Rudi heard it and quailed as, from the direction of the Ziegengasse barracks came a company of infantry, arriving at the worst possible moment. They were grenadiers, large men made larger in appearance by their tall black bearskin shakos. They had red facings on the collars of their white coats, so Rudi could identify them as members of the 18th Infantry. Bohemians. The Prince stared at the crowd with cool contempt, then proceeded into the building, followed, with unseemly haste, by his Germans.

The grenadier lieutenant halted his company. The crowd surged forward unwillingly, it seemed, but helpless before the crush from behind, moving ever closer to the soldiers. Rudi screamed himself hoarse, urging the people to turn around, to go back, but even if they had heard him they were helpless to obey.

The grenadier officer shouted, "Form line!"

The well-drilled troops swiftly transformed themselves from a column of twos into a line of three ranks blocking the avenue. The crowd closed the distance between the now terrified women at the front of the mass and the waiting soldiers. There was a shot from somewhere in the mob, then another.

"Order arms!" cried the lieutenant. The muskets left the shoulders of the grenadiers all at once and their butts crashed with a single sound against the cobbles. Rudi's horse, pressed uncomfortably by the throng, was shying and tossing his head, showing the whites of his eyes

"Load your firelocks!" ordered the lieutenant. A tinny clicking sound as the ramrods flew down eighty gun barrels. "Front rank, kneel!"

The lieutenant stepped forward and ordered the crowd to disperse. Rudi could see he was hardly more than a boy, the same age almost as his own lads. In answer came several more shots. By now almost everyone at the front of the crowd was struggling to get away, an impossible task, for the pressure from behind was undiminished. Another shot. A grenadier cried out, and fell backward. The lieutenant strode with quick steps to his post on the right flank of his line, drawing his sword as he went and raising it high.

"Present!" Up came the muskets, pointing. Down came the sword. "Fire!"

The sound was like a blow to the head, the street filled with smoke. Panic now truly gripped the throng—the screaming was continuous, shrill and maddening. Rudi put the spurs to Gitano, heedless now, knocking people out of the way, surging to the open space upon which lay a dozen people, dead or wounded, the white dresses of the women soaked red, the flowers scattered in widening pools of blood. The grenadiers were reloading. Rudi advanced far enough so that he could address the grenadier lieutenant.

"For the love of God, sir, withdraw! I will disperse this crowd, if you but give me time. But withdraw, or more of your men will be shot and you will perpetrate an infamous massacre of harmless women." The lieutenant's face was flour-white, and he hesitated; but the presence of an authoritative officer on a horse had the desired effect, no matter that officer was a mere guardsman.

"Attention! Shoulder arms! About face! By column of twos, forward march!"

The drums beat, the grenadiers marched back the way they had come, with the bandsmen bearing the wounded along.

Rudi had his men tend to the fallen, of whom there were several dozen. They searched for the men who had shot at the troops, but these had vanished down the alleys with the fleeing crowd. The Legion marched over crushed flowers back to the Carolinium with loaded muskets and fixed bayonets. From disparate quarters of the city came the crackle of small arms.

The barricades went up quickly, and by Monday night there were nearly four hundred throughout the city, almost all of them in the Old and New Towns, for the Little Quarter on the other side of the bridge was too heavily manned with troops to allow such activity. In response, Windischgrätz sent four regiments of infantry and a regiment of dragoons into the city and began methodically to dismantle the barricades. His officers broke up the Slavic Congress, expelling the foreigners and arresting the Austrian subjects.

Rudi took his little force to the Carolinium and tried to order its defenses. Meanwhile, the radicals in Prague flocked to the Clementium and established there the headquarters of the true revolution. Forty-eight hours passed. Delegations went back and forth between Vienna and Prague. Prince Windischgrätz blithely ignored all notices and petitions and brought in more soldiers from the Bohemian forts.

On the morning of June 14, Rudi stood in the library of the Carolinium pointing to a map of Prague spread out on a table. The place was lit only by candles and odd shafts of sunlight, for the students had pushed loaded bookcases in front of the tall windows to keep out the bullets.

He was not entirely in command here. No one was, which was the problem. His flying column followed his orders, as did some of the other student leaders, sometimes, but others did as they pleased and argued things out at great length when there was disagreement.

Now Rudi pointed at his map and said, "As far as we have been able to determine from the messengers getting through the military cordon, these are where barricades exist at present. Almost all of them are useless—in the wrong place or far too flimsy. One of our wonderful student leaders, I understand, set up his barricade on the square near his home so his mother could cook him lunch. There remain perhaps a dozen barricades that are significant, including this one, the one at the Clementium, and those around the flour depot. These control the north-south routes through the city and there are a few others on the east-west axis as well. The army will concentrate on clearing these and I cannot imagine that it will take them more than a few days."

Examining the young faces around the table, he saw he had dismayed them. Well, too bad! They deserved dismay.

A student, Mohlen by name, a chemist, objected. "That is defeatist, sir. When the people see how we are resisting, they will flock to join us. And the soldiers cannot continue to fire on their own people. We will appeal to their honor and patriotism . . ."

"Yes, that might have happened, had we prepared, had we been united, had we possessed a plan of resistance. But there is no plan, because in order to have a plan, you must have a planning body with command authority. In the end, you must have someone who can say do thus and so and have people who obey that order. But this was found to be against revolutionary principles, and so we had everyone doing as he pleased, so as to be able to sport different colored ribbons. No, we have no plan, but let me assure you that Prince Windischgrätz does, and he is executing it right now. Do you hear that cannon? That is a barricade blown to flinders. It is simply a matter of time before our turn comes."

A student said, "But the people *are* behind us! The girls at the convent school next to the university have thrown all their furniture out the windows to use as barricades, and the Franciscans have offered food and medicines."

"I stand corrected," said Rudi. "We cannot help but triumph, since it is well-known that the dressers and desks of little girls are proof against cannon shot of any caliber."

"Then why the devil are you here, if you believe that?" demanded Mohlen. "Why don't you just go home and stop spreading discouragement?"

"I am spreading realism, sir, and if it is discouraging, that is simply the nature of the existing case. I am here because it is my duty to see the revolution into its final stages. Beyond that, I am here to spill blood, my own by preference and that of the enemy, because only the spilling of blood can sanctify an idea and make it a part of history. We may fail. I believe we *will* fail. But because we spill our blood, Bohemia can never forget us. Years from now, even centuries, our deeds will live and therefore so will our ideals ... yes, Heinie, what is it?"

One of the gymnasium boys who served as messengers had clattered in and was demanding Rudi's attention.

"Sir, there is a . . . a little girl here. She says she is from the flour depot and asks to see you. Shall I send her away?"

"No, bring her in."

It was Anneke, now with a red-and -white cockade fixed to her untidy locks and a similar brassard wrapped around her thin right arm.

"Well, Anneke, how are you enjoying the revolution?"

"Very much, dear *skopčák*, although I wish to have a firearm and no one will give me one. It is unfair and un-revolutionary to deny me."

"But you are a messenger, which is a vital function in a revolution. And do you in fact have a message?"

The girl reached into some recess of her soiled garment and drew out a folded paper. In familiar handwriting, it read:

My Dear R, can you spare a very little keg of gunpowder? We have bullets enough. Isn't this a relief? Love always, V.

"The flour depot wants gunpowder," Rudi said in answer to the inquiring faces.

"Why should we give any powder to workers?" said a philosophy student. "We have little enough for our own needs."

"Because if the depot falls, the other barricades will be even more useless than they are. Look at the map, Neckar! To the chemist Mohlen he said, "Do we have a keg to spare? Excellent. Please prepare one and some slings to carry it with." He asked Anneke, "However did you get through, my dear? The streets are full of soldiers."

"It was simple. I used the alleys and people let me through their houses and out the back doors. It is how they remove the filth and night soil and the God-damned *skopčáky* know not these ways."

"Yet at least one God-damned *skopčák* soon will," said Rudi, "for I intend to come with you and carry your gunpowder."

"I knew you would come," said Vasovà. "And I am ridiculously pleased when my judgments are proven correct. Was it very difficult?"

"Not at all," Rudi answered. "The little vixen knows the routes well and there was only a small open area covered by enemy guns before we reached your barricades. You have the handsomest barricade I have seen, by far."

"Yes, because we have all these bags of flour. Wetted and let dry they become impervious to bullets. Behind walls of bread we fight and die for bread and life. There is a poem in that, I believe, which I will not get to write."

"Why will you not?"

"Oh, because this is the end, my love. I can feel it in my bones, and I am never wrong. I regret we will not lie together again. That is over too. Don't you feel it? Because death has a prior claim on our bodies, the passion drains away. I have but one regret—that I did not have the opportunity to speak with your Berthe."

"What would you have said to her?"

"Oh, when this is over, the gossip about you and me will hang in the air like the stink from burning Prague, and it will mar your happiness. I would tell her a tale that would ease her mind. I am excellent at that, as you know. I will paint a picture of two stout revolutionary friends who never shared more than a chaste kiss or two. Thus you will be happy again, which is my chief desire now."

Rudi did not know what to say to that. She spoke on.

"You see I am making cartridges. I always had clever hands. Watch how it is done--the paper curved into a tube, the bottom crimped just so, a measure of powder, then the ball and another crimp. There, that is one more, and may it strike down a soldier! They had me tending to the wounded, but I could not bear it. When the blood gushed, I became ill and had to run outside and spew. Shameful! But I am a good cartridge maker. "

"This seems a well-ordered enterprise," said Rudi, looking around the chamber. Women and a few girls were making cartridges at long tables, and boys were running about delivering paper, shot and powder to each of the workers and carrying off the finished ones to the fighters.

"Yes, Novak has a genius for this sort of thing. And yet he had no education at all, he spent his life lifting heavy weights from one point to another, a donkey's life, the life of a Czech peasant."

Rudi was looking at a sign posted on the wall. It was written in a crude hand and contained any number of grammatical mistakes and misspellings. It comprised a set of regulations for the magazine and was signed "S. Novak, Comander."

The fellow is clever to the end, Rudi thought, disguising his style to match his workman's persona, and then in an instant it struck him how unlikely that was. Jiskra was a wonderful writer and intelligent enough to know how perilous was his situation. That being so, would he not have simply dashed off such a notice in perfect Czech? What was the point of further dissimulation? The answer was clear: there was no point at all and therefore Novak was what he seemed, an intelligent but uneducated Czech workingman, which meant that he was *not* Jiskra, which meant...

He laughed out loud. He laughed so hard he had to lean his shoulder against the wall.

"What's so funny?" asked Vasová.

"This notice. Your Novak wrote it, I suppose. Yes? Direct, competent, but with many errors of usage."

"Do you mock him?" she said, a frown appearing on her powder-smudged face.

"I mock only myself. I failed to see what was before my eyes. How typical of Baron Rudi von Pannau! Jiskra is you, my dear. It was you who organized the theft of those armaments and you who wrote those inspiring and brilliant articles and you also who composed those scabrous verses under that vile cartoon. What, you blush! Something I had never thought to see.—but tell me, why ever did you write it?"

She sighed and answered, "Oh, it was partly nagging from Novotny and the others. Was I true to the revolution or to my lover? And then it is a common thing among we mistresses to wish to hurt the men who fire us with a passion in which there is no particle of hope. A shop-girl driven mad might use fire or vitriol; I used ink. Do you forgive me?"

"Of course I do. Believe me, any anger I had toward the author has quite burnt up in the general conflagration of everything now proceeding around us. And believe me also that I wish that things had been otherwise with us."

She seemed not to hear this last. In any event she made no comment about it, but said in a light tone, "Yes, this conflagration. How do you fare in it, my dear? Your cousin the Butcher is active, it seems."

"He is. It is all a matter of arithmetic now. He has ten thousand muskets to our three thousand. It is a mere question of time."

"No hope at all?"

"None."

"Novak still believes there will be an uprising of workers."

"Novak is a fool, though brave as Samson. Like his Biblical precursor, he will see this temple collapse about his ears, although I note he has at least stopped the windows and made loopholes in the walls. A pity he did not take my more important advice."

"You doubt the intent of the workers?"

"Their intent is by the way. For three months we have dwelt happily in a cloud-cuckoo land of manifestos and petitions and wrangles about cockades and school-books, and when any pointed to dangers we sang tra-la-la."

"We stole a thousand or so muskets," she said, "But someone betrayed the location before we could move more than a handful, which you see here in use."

"That was me," he said.

"And why would you do something like that?" she asked, without heat. She seemed merely curious.

"Because those weapons were not meant to defend the revolution of the whole people but to strengthen a faction. I stole a hundred or so muskets myself, for the Academic Legion, a lawful body responsible to the Provisional Government. If we could have forgotten our class and national differences and formed a common defense, I would have stolen ten thousand more. As it was, those weapons would have fomented civil strife and in any case, twelve hundred would not be nearly enough to make a difference."

She smiled at him then, that familiar dazzle. "It hardly matters now. How interesting that all our betrayals become insignificant at the end! What I would really like to do, when the cartridges are all filled, is to lead a charge of bayonets. Will I have to loosen my stays? What is the done thing? Perhaps I should bare my breasts to the shot. Would that distract the enemy for a vital moment? The tits that won freedom for Prague! I can see the bronze statue now, in the Horse Market."

They laughed together briefly; then he kissed her on both cheeks and departed. Strangely, though he still cared for her, he no longer felt any desire. She was right. The thing had passed: Mars in the ascendant, Venus sunk low.

It was just after their scant evening meal that the inhabitants of the Carolinium noticed a diminution in the sounds of gunfire. By eight, the town was entirely silent save the usual domestic noises. Looking out through their barricades, Rudi and his men saw that the troops who had been standing guard across the street had gone. Messengers arrived with the information that the troops were marching out of the Old and New Towns. Sustained cheering broke out. Popp ran up to Rudi, his face shining. "Sir, we've won! They've given up!"

Rudi had not the heart to disabuse him. Nor had he time to consider what response to make, for, as he observed the now deserted street, he noticed a familiar figure hurrying toward the university building. It was Gregor, his servant.

Rudi ran toward him.

"What is it, Gregor? Trouble at the house?"

"No, sir; only . . . I am to inform you that madame has returned."

Rudi took to his horse.

He was stunned but not entirely surprised. Of course Vasová had been right.

After their embrace, he said to her, "I knew you would come."

"Oh yes?" replied Berthe, "But it is still a surprise, isn't it? I sneaked away and will be in disgrace forever, should I be found out. I left in disguise, can you imagine! Fortunately the Fathers are visiting at Innsbruck and so I will be back before they return. And I hope to bring you with me."

"Ah . . . Berthe, my dear, did you not notice anything amiss while you drove here from the station?"

"No, the fiacre had its hood up, and you know you can never see anything through those little windows. Why, what is wrong?"

"What is wrong is that this city is in the midst of civil war. There are barricades up, shots fired, people wounded. It's possible that there will be a bombardment."

She stared at him, and over her face came a look of desperate sorrow. "Oh Rudi, all your dreams! Oh, you must be so awfully unhappy."

Rudi felt his throat contract and tears start in his eyes; this was too much, this was a love he did not remotely deserve. He turned away for a moment to compose himself, made himself wear a smile that he was sure must look ghastly and false, and said, "It is true. But now I have seen you, I cannot be very unhappy. And I shall leave with you as soon as ever I can."

She embraced him, weeping softly into his tunic, and they stayed like that for many minutes, silently.

He drew back at last, and said, "I must return to my responsibilities now, and you must stay here and wait for me. But Berte, dearest, do heed me, for this is very important. If there should be a bombardment, you must put out all fires in the house and you and all the servants must stay in the kitchen. As it is below ground you will be safe from any errant shell."

"I am sure we will be perfectly safe," said Berthe. Tears stood out on her eyelashes like tiny jewels. "Who would want to toss great cannonballs at *us*? But Rudi, why must you go?"

"Because I must, my love. There are people depending upon me to lead them, men whom it would be dishonorable to desert. This will not last long. We will be back in Kunningshelm soon and have summer there. I have a new horse."

"But what is the fighting about! Can you tell me that? Why would our own army rain bombs on the heads of ordinary people?"

"Oh this is a long story, my love. But in the end it is little different from when Fritz takes Reni's doll out of spite, and Reni screams and kicks Fritz and Fritz throws the doll at her head. Both of them are howling and red-faced with tears and breaking one another's favorite toys when Hana comes in and pulls them apart and settles the issue. Fritz, you must not take your sister's doll! Shame on you! And you, Fräulein, you must not kick. All is settled before supper. But here, unfortunately, there is no nursemaid."

"At last I understand politics," said Berthe with a laugh. "Although you tried, my love, did you not?"

"I did," he said. "Goodbye now, my best dear!"

He kissed her soundly on the lips and left.

Back at the university library, Rudi found Andrej Popp and led him into a quiet alcove.

"Listen to me, Andrej, and please to not interrupt, for I am going to tell you something you will not wish to hear. We must evacuate the Carolinium. "

"What! Impossible! The university is the ..."

"I said, do not interrupt! Yes, the university is the spiritual home of the student movement, but its very design dooms it as a bastion. It reflect the ideas of enlightenment, you see--large windows, many doorways, separate buildings for the different fields of learning with spaces between them, and so on. Do you follow? A company of grenadiers could clear it in half an hour against any resistance we are likely to muster . . ."

"We are not afraid of grenadiers."

"Oh, Andrej--no one doubts your courage. I speak only as a tactician. Think! These are men trained to take mighty fortresses defended by cascades of grapeshot--university buildings guarded by a few muskets will pose no challenge, once they are unleashed. The Clementium, on the other hand, reflects the Jesuits, the shock troops of an embattled alien church: a virtual fortress, thick-walled, small windowed, with that line of gables on the roof that are practically crenellations made for defense. Invaders penetrating the outer wall would be trapped in one of the four courtyards and subject to plunging fire from all sides. Most important, Andrej, the Clementium commands Karlgasse and the foot of the Charles Bridge. They cannot send troops and supplies by the bridge as long as we hold the Clementium."

"But, sir, the radicals hold the Clementium. Sladowsky and all of them. Will they welcome us?"

"Oh, believe me, we shall see a time when they will welcome anyone with a working musket and ammunition, be he ever so reactionary. Now. Here is what we must do . . ."

At eight the next morning, Prince Windischgrätz gave the order for the bombardment of Prague and the great guns on Petřín and at Vyšehrad opened fire on the defenseless town. From his perch in one of the bell towers of the Clementium, Rudi could actually see the flight of the bombs, fine black lines sketched against the pale blue sky followed by smoky tails from the burning fuses. Each black line descended and brought forth the startling shock of an explosion and a gush of black smoke as the target burned. He had a telescope, but he put it aside when the tears he could not seem to stop obscured his view.

He had made the transfer from the Carolinium discretely and successfully, moving his eighty or so student-soldiers out during the night, carrying all they could of warlike stores. Fewer than fifty declined to leave their university, and Rudi prayed that they would surrender at the first shot. The radicals had not exactly welcomed Rudi and his people, but Karel Sladowsky had convinced his comrades than any musket was a radical in these desperate hours.

It turned out that Bakunin too had taken refuge in the Jesuit foundation, apparently agreeing that if their doctrines were suspect, their walls were not. The Russian anarchist had spent the previous night arguing that the withdrawal of troops provided an opportunity to declare a revolutionary regime for the city, with dictatorial powers, and this idea was debated with all sincerity for hours by the radical students. Rudi listened, but declined to participate. He saw the Russian was enjoying himself and keeping the young men from thinking overmuch about the morrow. It was exactly like an old nursemaid telling fairy tales to children during a thunderstorm, Bakunin's broad face all aglow with enthusiasm.

When Popp had inquired of him what he thought of the idea, Rudi had replied, "An excellent notion. But I have a better one. I hereby declare myself Holy Roman Emperor. Would you like to be Pope, Popp? Of course you would! There, it is done. Go forth and rule!"

Bakunin refused throughout the evening to acknowledge Rudi's presence. The Russian had a wonderful talent for eliminating any unpleasant reality from his consciousness, and Rudi wished he had a little of that gift himself.

Reality, however, pressed in without mercy. Rudi now observed a black dot hanging in the sky rather than the usual line and it took him a moment to understand what it meant-- that a shell was rushing directly at him. He shouted a warning to the men on the roof below and ran in leaps down the narrow spiral stairs. He heard a great thump and the sound of something heavy rolling on the roof tiles. A half-second of hideous waiting silence; then came the blast. Plaster and bits of old swallows' nests showered on his head as he ran through the attic to the gable where the shell had exploded.

The attic, once a dormitory when the place had been a Jesuit seminary, was now used for storage and contained huge piles of mattresses, books and furnishings. One edge of the ceiling now showed blue sky through a wide jagged breach, and this hole was busy with men passing down the wounded. One of these, Rudi saw with a shock, was Liebig. His comrades laid him down on a dusty mattress with a thick volume of theology for a pillow.

Rudi knelt, took Liebig's hand in his, and said, "What are you doing here, Liebig? I had no notion of you being of our company—I would have sent you away. My God, you are the sole support of your family."

"I had to . . . sometimes one cannot do the sensible thing. Am I badly hurt? I am not in much pain, but cold."

"We will see you mended, dear friend. Just rest a moment and we will carry you to the infirmary."

"Now they can say even the Jews fought, as in 1648. Isn't that a silly thing to die for?"

"You are not going to die, Liebig," said Rudi and shouted for a stretcher.

"Stupid," muttered Liebig, "too cold. Could you possibly find a blanket?" His mouth gaped, he coughed, a gush of blood emerged, his head fell back upon the volume, and he passed. Rudi tried to feel something and could not. He recalled his grandfather's attitude toward the death of comrades and thought, once again he lives in me, I am achieving his simplicity of thought. *My honor is called loyalty.*

How relaxing, after being so long in fragments! Yes, this battle has won me myself again, I am clean once more, and, should I survive this, I can start my new life with a clear conscience. Perhaps others have felt the same, and perhaps this is why there are so many wars.

At one o'clock the barrage ended. Only a few shells had struck the Clementium, and these had caused no further casualties. Rudi raced through the building, checking on preparations, making sure there were fire parties assigned to the different sectors of the place and that the barricades and the rooftops facing the bridge were manned and supplied. He did all this because he could and because no one else was doing it. Sladowsky, the nominal commander, was closeted with a few others preparing a petition to Vienna demanding the removal of Windischgrätz and a new election based on universal suffrage. Sounds of shooting could now be heard from different quarters, as the troops returned to finish the work of suppression.

On a darkened stairway during this time, Rudi passed a party of men carrying sacks of cartridges, and saw that one of them was Havel.

"I am surprised to see you here," said Rudi. "I would have thought you would be with the Czech militia."

"I am," said the clerk, pointing to a red-and-white brassard. "We were chased out of our barricade. Some of us heard the old Clementium still held and we made our way here. I am happy to see you, Herr Amtsrat."

"You need not call me that anymore. I believe this present business will tend to disqualify me for a post under the government. But why are you happy to see me?"

"There was a rumor that you were working against the revolution."

"Dispelled, I trust?"

The lad grinned, a bright line in his powder-smeared face. "Oh, yes, sir," he said and then was off up the staircase.

Outside, they had thrown a barricade across the Karl-gasse, made largely of carriages and cabs overturned and stuffed with cobbles and bricks. Rudi had placed Popp in command of it.

"Anything of note, Captain Popp?"

"Firing from the direction of the Carolinium, starting half an hour ago, and a few cannon shots as well. No, listen-- it has stopped."

"Thank God for that. They were intelligent enough to yield the place without a bloodbath. Now it is our turn. And we will not yield so easily "

As if to illustrate this remark came the sound of drums and hoof beats and a rhythmic tread. Rudi climbed atop a phaeton hulk and used his telescope. When he jumped down he said, "It looks like two grenadier companies, a battery of horse artillery and a troop of hussars. We shall have a busy afternoon, Herr Popp. Unless you would like to help draft the petition?"

"Never in life, sir," answered Popp with a grin. A moment later, though, his face showed alarm. "Look, sir, there is that child again!"

Anneke had emerged from a doorway on the east side of Karlgasse and was dashing toward their barricade.

Rudi climbed upon a carriage wheel and shouted, "No, Anneke, no! Into the doorway—hide yourself!"

The child ignored his shout and kept running. The lead hussar spurred his horse into a trot, easily overtook the girl, and struck her down with a blow of his saber.

Rudi leaped into the road, drew his grandfather's pistol and shot the hussar through the heart. The other hussars spurred toward him. Rudi ran to the child, threw her limp body over his shoulder and raced back to the barricade, hearing the sound of hoof beats coming ever closer behind him.

He was twenty feet from the barricade and knew he could not make it in time; so he stopped, put the child down, drew his sword, and, as the hussar came rushing up, swung his blade with all his strength at the horse's head. An immense blow lifted him from his feet and flung him to the cobbles. As if in the distance he heard a volley of muskets, shouts and screams. He felt himself lifted by many hands over the barri-cade and then placed on the ground.

When his head stopped swimming and his vision cleared, there was young Popp, looking stricken.

"Are you all right, sir? When the horse knocked you over, I thought you . . ."

"I'm fine—how is the girl?"

The man's expression told all. "The skull was completely broken, sir. Death on the instant. She had a mes-sage in the pocket of her apron, sir."

Rudi read from the crumpled, bloodstained scrap:

under heavy attack, infantry and cannon--we hold out. Send medical students, and supplies, we have many wounded. The revolution is dead; long live the revolution! V.

Thirty-three

For the remainder of that day the students behind the roof gables of the Clementium maintained a brisk exchange of fire with squads of grenadiers emplaced on the roofs and at the shattered windows of the upper floor apartments of the building on the opposite side of the Karlgasse. From the barricades Rudi could see the troops waiting out of range at the head of the street, before the Clam-Gallas palace. They could not move their cannon down to blast through the barricades and the main doorway so long as the students could fire down on them from the roof. They had tried once; evidence of failure in the form of dead horses lay on the street. They were not being particularly aggressive, and Rudi wondered why.

The air went blue, the street faded into shadows, and the firing ceased. They could hear the sounds of departing horses, men, and cannon.

"They are withdrawing. Another cannonade?" said Popp.

"I would not bet against it," said Rudi, "and this time we shall be a prime target."

"The Franciscans have brought food. Would you like to get something to eat, sir?"

"You know, that is interesting. I literally cannot recall my last meal. Yes, I believe I will have a bite. Oh, have one of the chemists make up some fire-pots. Toss them into the street at intervals. Let us not have any sneaking guns with muffled wheels in by night!"

Rudi was in the refectory with a plate of stew when a messenger from the Old Town Square barricade came in, shouting, "They have killed his wife! Princess Frau Butcher is dead."

Rudi put down his fork, and with bile rising in his throat approached the messenger, a ragged street boy not much older than Anneke.

"Who has been killed?" he asked.

"Why, the Princess Windischgrätz. They were shooting back and forth in front of the High Headquarters. The silly woman stepped to the window to see what was going on, and bang! Right through the neck. Wish I was the one that got her, the stuck-up bitch!"

Someone said, "Well, we're in for it now. If he was a Butcher before, he'll be ten times worse in revenge."

Rudi turned on the man, his face gone white. "No, sir, you are quite mistaken. On the contrary, Prince Windischgrätz will make every effort to be mild, so as not to prompt any such inference. He does his duty, sir, and only his duty. There is nothing personal in it at all."

Everyone stared at him, as if he were speaking some unknown, antique tongue. He walked out of the hall, back to the barricades.

"Was the supper good?" asked Popp.

"I don't know. I lost my appetite," Rudy answered curtly, and sat down against a wall, his head in his hands.

The Princess and Anneke, the highest and the lowest, sisters now in death, he thought. Each lovely in her own way, each dear to me, each one a fool, according to her station. How God must be laughing! What more hideous acts will befall us before this charade is done? The next time I look into a mirror I will see the hardness that so shocked me in my grandfather's eyes appearing in my own.

At nine p.m. precisely the cannonade resumed. Rudi returned to his bell tower, although his men pleaded with him not to expose himself so. He found he did not care. Horror saps our will to live, he thought; enough of it and life turns foul and one is, if not anxious to leave it, at least indifferent to one's immediate survival.

It was a spectacular view. At night, the shells as they flew made bright trails of sparks across the blackness, and when they landed threw up livid flashes, like red lightning. Many of these landed on the Clementium--as he had guessed, it had become a prime target. Most landed in the courtyards. He heard the singing of the fragments and the crash as they struck the walls. But many shells fell also upon the roofs, making them untenable for the musketeers and starting fires throughout the structure. The students became firemen, struggling to keep the flames from lighting the roof beams and the masses of books. No more torches fell into the street; rather an obscuring smoke filled it, enabling the soldiers and their cannon to move down Karlgasse unopposed except for blind fire from the barricades.

The barrage lasted four hours. Rudi could see, and the sight caused no emotion besides a curious cold deadness in his heart, that the flour depot was burning like a bonfire, great flames shooting up, turning the clouds above into a bloody pall above the wounded city. They must have brought cannon down the river on barges to bring the depot under fire, he thought. Yes, it turned out to be about cannon after all, dear Kalo. You were right, and I was wrong.

Near midnight, by the light of a torch, in the shelter of the tall main doorway, under the carved saint, Rudi dismissed his little troop.

"Gentlemen, we have done all we can. I now sound the *sauve qui peut*. It is the call given when honor demands no more, when further resistance yields only a useless effusion of blood."

Cries sounded, of "No, no!" and "We shall fight on!" Some of the men—many of whom were, in fact, boys-- burst into tears.

Rudi shouted for silence, and when it fell, said, "You cannot fight on, gentlemen. The dawn will show a battery of cannon pointing this way, and the buildings opposite crammed with an assault battalion. They will have this barricade and the great doors in pieces within ten minutes, and then they will come in with the bayonet. Go to your homes, my valiant lads, go home and live! The revolution is over, except in the heart of Bohemia, where what you have done will live forever. Now go home!"

They drifted away. Most of the radicals had left during the bombardment, which Rudi thought indicated something, but at the moment he could no longer form political thoughts. His horse had been kept in the Clementium's own stables, along with the horses that pulled the chancellor's carriage, and Rudi was happy to see the animal had survived. He fed it some grain, talking to it conversationally, like a madman or, he suspected, his grandfather. It seemed a reasonable activity at that moment.

At last he rode out of the Clementium on the Plattnergasse side, where there were few soldiers. A body laid on the street, an apprentice lad, just a dark shape with a halo of glistening blood around the broken head.

No one stopped Rudi, nor did any of the many troops he passed along the way bother to halt a major of the National Guard mounted on a particularly fine steed. They saluted him, rather, which Rudi considered the final joke in this farce.

He returned Gitano to the livery stable and walked down Zeitnergasse to his house. The street was filled with people, many of whom murmured and crossed themselves when they saw him and made way. Among them was Herr Trevigliani, who stood outside his shop with his wife and children. They were all wearing black and this black was speckled with white dust. Frau Trevigliani was sobbing into a large handkerchief.

"Why, Herr Trevigliani, what has happened?" Rudi asked. The air smelled of burning, a more intense odor than that which hung over the whole town, as if every housemaid in every home had burnt the toast.

The stationer opened his mouth to answer, but nothing emerged.

Gregor was waiting in front of Rudi's door, in his shirtsleeves, looking as Rudi had never seen him look before, his linen black with soot and his face smeared with the same.

"Gregor? What has happened?"

The servant cleared his throat heavily. "Sir . . . I regret there has been an unfortunate incident. During the bombardment last night, the house was struck by a shell. The mistress was, ah, affected by the explosion."

"What! But I told her to stay in the kitchen. Where is she? Is she hurt?"

"Sir, we were all in the kitchen as you ordered. We heard the bombs exploding nearby. Then we heard a pounding on the servants' entrance. I went to open it and found a woman there. She announced herself as Svetlana Zbyhneva Vasovà and demanded to speak with the mistress on a matter of utmost urgency. I was not going to let her in, sir. She was covered in ash and bleeding on her head, not the sort of person . . . but the mistress came to the door and made me admit her. They spoke for a minute and then mistress led her out of the kitchen. They must have gone upstairs. Then the bomb . . ."

"Gregor, where is my wife?"

"In Herr Trevigliani's shop, sir. We laid her there, her and the other lady. And the girl, Lidunka."

"Who?"

"The kitchen girl, sir. She ran out when the bomb exploded and went up the stair, just as the whole floor collapsed. I am sorry, Herr Moritz. They were all three beyond help when we pulled them from the ruins."

"That's impossible," said Rudi. "She was supposed to stay in the kitchen."

He spun away, ran past the Trevigliani family, and entered the shop. Three trestle tables stood on the shop floor, of the sort used by the greengrocer down the street to display his produce. Three forms lay under white sheets, one smaller than the other two. One little foot extended beyond the sheet covering this last, upon which was a brand new shoe, its sole barely marked by wear.

Rudi was conscious of a high-pitched moaning sound, without quite understanding that it came from his own throat. He pulled back the sheet.

It was impossible to tell the two faces apart; both had become hideous blackened masks, with grinning white teeth, although it was just possible to discern that one had blond hair and the other dark. It seemed to Rudi then that the blackness rose from the scorched flesh and filled the world. He felt himself falling.

When next he saw light it was the light of day, the sun streaming into his eyes from a strange, irregular patch of sky above him. The patch was surrounded by dark shapes that he could not at first make out. After a few moments, he understood that he was lying on the sofa in his parlor and that the light was coming from a hole in the roof, exposed by the great gap blown in the ceiling. Black jagged beams stuck down through this hole like giant jackstraws, together with chunks of plaster, lathe, and a flap of his bedroom carpet.

"Here, Herr Moritz, have a drink of this."

Herr Trevigliani was hovering near, extending a small glass of clear liquid.

Rudi drank it down. Pannau slivovic. He held out the glass for another and drank that, too.

He said, "I only wanted to read a newspaper. Was that so wrong?"

Herr Trevigliani made no answer.

Rudi looked around the wreckage of his parlor. A beam had crashed down upon the piano, breaking the keyboard, leaving a scatter of ivory, bright amid the charred fragments.

"Berthe will need a new piano," he said. "She will want all the keys to play her Mozart. Did you know, Herr Trevigliani, that my grandfather knew Mozart? Although it should have been Berthe who knew Mozart, but she was too young."

After his arrest, everyone treated him with the utmost gentleness, clearly on orders from above, although he was unaware of this, or of anything, really, except the phantasms of his wife and Vasová, with whom he kept up an intermittent conversation.

The cell was a comfortable one, in the section of the Dalibor Tower reserved for prisoners of rank, and looked as if it could almost be a room in a mediocre provincial hotel. Rudi was never afterward able to say what the first week of his captivity was like. It seemed to him that he awoke one day knowing who he was and where he was and what had happened on the night of the 15th of June. He wept for a day and a night, until he was hoarse with it, until his eyes were swollen and his pillow sodden.

Then he was himself again, although what that was remained to be seen. He called to the jailer that he wished to be shaved and they sent a man in to do it, and another man came with a change of clothing, well-fitting garments that he had never seen before. The next visitor was Major Wulf-Eric Speyr.

"Rudi, I am sorry for your loss," said the policeman by way of greeting. "I was extremely distressed when I heard, as was my family. A splendid woman . . . well, you know how I always felt about her. A terrible thing."

"Thank you, Wulfi. I presume you are here not as a friend, however, but in your official capacity."

"I am, unfortunately, but let me assure you of my continuing friendship."

After a pause, Rudi nodded and the policeman continued.

"I shall come to the point. Martial law has been declared in Bohemia, and they are trying revolutionaries by court martial. The army, which is in entire control of the government for the moment, is desirous of holding up for especial punishment those citizens who actually fired upon soldiers from the barricades or elsewhere, and among these, they single out those who can be shown to have killed his majesty's soldiers."

"Among these being myself, of course."

"So it appears. Rudi, you do have a talent for the most awful scrapes, I must say! In front of a hundred reliable witnesses you put a bullet through a hussar officer, and not just a hussar officer, but Captain Wilhelm Franz Nepomuk Freiherr von Khevenhüller. The family is close to Latour, the Minister of War, and they want blood. It is very bad."

"Hanging, do you suppose?"

"Someone must pay for all the death and ruin, my friend, and I imagine that hanging a baron makes a nice point. What would save you, of course, is if you made a public apology for your misdeeds, said you were led astray by this one or that one, expressed your complete loyalty to his majesty, and, to show the sincerity of your repentance, provided us with the names of all those who fired upon troops during the disturbances. I believe that would save you."

"Bring on the hangman!" said Rudi, and laughed.

"Seriously, Rudi, only a few names would suffice. We know them already, of course, but coming from you . . . You understand how these things work."

"May I see my children?"

"I suppose that if you cooperate in the way I have described, all things are possible."

"You know, Wulfi, one feels the small cruelties of the state even more keenly than the great ones, simply because they seem so gratuitous. Letting a condemned man hold a child in his arms--what harm could that do to the house of Hapsburg? And yet such deprivations are common, as you have just confirmed. Let me make myself clear, Herr Major: I will never do as you ask, though you kill me for it. This tiny, ridiculous scrap of honor is worth more to me than my life by far."

Speyr exhaled a dramatic sigh and stood up.

"Well, if you are determined to remain a fool to your last moment, there is nothing I can do. My God, Rudi, when I think of all the promise that clung to you when we were boys! How did you ever make such a confounded mess of things?"

"I wanted to read a newspaper without someone like you saying yea or nay."

"I am sorry for you, then. Will you shake my hand?"

"Of course, Wulfi. I bear you no personal ill will. We are all victims of our fate and we must all bear it as well as we can."

They shook hands. Speyr's grip was warm, and he clutched Rudi's forearm with his other hand. Rudi said, "I wonder what became of Novotny. Do you know?"

"As a matter of fact, I do," said Speyr after a short pause. "He is here."

"Under what conditions?"

"Arrested and condemned. He was leading a rabble of workers from Karlín who were attempting to enter the city. He shot a soldier dead . . ." The policeman shrugged. "His case is the same as yours."

"Not quite, I think. May I see him?"

Speyr thought for a moment and answered, "Yes. I will have you conducted to his cell. Perhaps he can talk some sense into you. I will call a warder."

He left. Rudi looked down at his arm where the other man had gripped it. There was a small white mark showing bright against the dark cloth. Rudi now recalled having seen a similar one not too long ago, and his heart seemed to freeze in his chest when he realized what the little mark must mean..

Novotny's cell was on a lower level of the fortress and was not nearly as comfortable as Rudi's. A wide plank suspended by chains and covered by a thin, dirty blanket served as a cot. A tin bucket and a wooden stool completed the furnishings. Wan light fell from a barred slit high up on the wall. Novotny was sitting on the cot when Rudi walked in.

He looked up and Rudi saw that the whole right side of his face was purpled with bruising.

"Ah, you live still," said Novotny and rose slowly to his feet. The two men embraced.

"I do, but not for long, it seems," said Rudi, taking the stool. "They are being harsh with anyone who shot a soldier, a category that apparently includes you. I was surprised when I heard of it--you were supposed to be an observer only, were you not?"

"Yes. I suppose it was the passion of the moment. I was marching with a large party of workers, men and women, from Karlín. Just outside the Hofs Tor they sent cavalry to oppose us and there was shooting. Very few of the workers had firearms, just tools and iron bars. The cavalry charged. People were being trampled on and hacked with sabers. I thought to myself, ah, at last, this is the thing itself, what lies beneath all the fine words--tradition, honor, order, aristocracy, the rights of property--a paid assassin upon a horse chopping at the face of a helpless woman who earns four kreutzers a day sewing coal sacks for the railroad. I can't recall where I obtained my musket. Did someone thrust it into my hand? Did I pick it up from the ground? Perhaps I brought it with me. I honestly cannot recall anything before the attack. I do remember shooting that bastard off his horse. It was a miracle that I hit him--can there be a miraculous murder?--for you know I never shot a musket in my life before that. And my life is forfeit because of it. It would be hilarious if they were not actually going to hang me. Maybe it is hilarious even so."

"I had not meant to kill either," said Rudi, "not in my heart, although I was responsible for a military resistance, and it was inevitable that I would kill or cause others to kill. An absurd self-delusion. My grandfather pointed it out to me, but I ignored him. I shot my man after he cut down a child I was fond of. We shall be revolutionary martyrs of Bohemia, famed in song and story together."

"There may even be a statue of both of us, arm in arm, facing the glorious future."

"Yes, unless the truth gets out," said Rudi, with a searching look at his friend.

"What truth is that?"

"Oh, Paul, can we not be frank with one another in these final moments? *You* are the police spy. You have been working against the revolution from the beginning."

Novotny's eyes grew wide. "What? Have you gone mad? Liebig was the spy. I explained that to you, but you . . ."

"Liebig died for the revolution at the Clementium. He was no spy. But he was the most intelligent of the four of us, and he knew you were the one. I didn't want to believe it, and I did not until I found that spot."

"Spot? What are you raving about now?"

"I found one on my own coat, too, and that is how I made the connection. Look," he said, extending his arm. "Here is another. Major Speyr has a habit of clapping his good comrades on the shoulder and as he uses pipe clay to cover the ink stains on the cuffs of his uniform a mark is sometimes made on the dark cloth of a coat. I saw such a mark on your shoulder once when we met in your office. You explained it away as whitewash, do you recall? And the last time we met at the Knight we discussed my pathetic plans to defend the center of Prague. It was hardly worth the betrayal, we were so weak, but it must have helped the Prince dispose his troops, and so crush us in a mere six days. Who knows, if it had lasted longer, a dozen things might have been different. The National Guard might have changed sides at the sight of a more effective resistance and . . . well, no matter. I have no regrets concerning my actions.

"But you! What are you doing here, a condemned man? Your side won! What possessed you to pick up that musket? Come to that, why did you conspire with Sisi and Jasny and Havel to steal those muskets? Yes, I know about that too. Was it to launch a provocation? Or did you truly hope to arm a workers' revolt?"

Novotny rose from his pallet and began to pace the narrow confines of the cell. "I did what I did," he said. "It doesn't matter now."

"It matters to *me*!" cried Rudi, shooting to his feet and grabbing Novotny by the shoulders. "Listen to me, you wretch! Berthe is dead, Vasovà is dead. The revolution is dead. I have lost everything and am likely to be dead too, soon enough. But while I draw breath I demand to know why my best friend, whose dreams of a better world I have shared for near twenty years, betrayed all he professed to believe."

"*Believe*, you say! Let me explain something, Herr Baron--these fine liberal *beliefs* are a luxury, like white bread. When your children have no bread at all, you do what you must. Have you seen the families out past Karlín, living in holes they have scraped in the railway embankments, their little ones roaming the lines, picking up bits of coal to sell? No, you have not, nor have you lived with the terror that your family would end up in a hole and your children . . . no, you cannot possibly understand what drives a man like me to take a policeman's bribe, and turn traitor. It hollows you out, you know, that sort of life, nor can any amount of beer and brandy fill the hole. And when the opportunity arose, your little Czech clerk and his access to those requisitions, I took it, because I wanted to get back at those grinning swine, Actually, Sisi had the idea first. It was her courage that emboldened us, I wanted to sow chaos in the streets, I wanted you and your class despoiled, your houses burned, your factories and warehouse wrecked. I wanted to make Prague into the image of my soul."

Rudi dropped his hands from the other's shoulders. "It was about *money*? But you had a position, you were an editor . . ."

"It came too late. The hooks were already deep in my flesh. Before you arranged for your Jews to fund me, I never earned enough from writing to support myself. Do you know why? Because, dear Rudi, I am not good enough to earn a living as a writer. Liebig was right--I produce a thousand words of light drivel and I am depleted. You are the writer, my friend, you and poor Vasová. I suppose you know she was Jiskra. Of course you do, you who are so, so clever." Here a burning look from those peculiar bulging eyes. "How did she die?"

Rudi told him.

"Characteristic," said Novotny. "She truly loved you. I would have given up everything had she looked at me the way I saw her gaze at you. But I was unworthy of it, being hollow. And now my children will sleep in holes after all."

"They will not. I will make provision for them out of my property. For them and Liebig's family. The house is ruined but the lot alone is worth ten thousand florins. And there is the Pannau money, too. My grandfather will arrange it. "

Novotny stared at him. "Why?" he asked in a failing voice. "After what I have done?"

Rudi shrugged and answered. "Because it means that a small good may be rescued from this farce. They are innocent, after all."

Novotny seemed to deflate and collapsed upon his cot, face turned toward the wall. "Go away," he said. "I hate you."

When he was back in his chamber again, Rudi called for paper and pen. During the following hours he composed letters to his children, explaining what had happened to their mother and father, and why, and attempting to condense for them all he had learned from his sorry existence, in hopes that they would forgive him and avoid his mistakes. He found it a task more difficult than drafting the constitution of Bohemia. Balled-up discards littered the floor of the cell.

He then disposed of his property as he had described to Novotny, and reflected that it was perhaps the last legal document he would ever compose. He had just written out the fair copies when the door opened and two green-coated dragoons entered, carrying a sturdy armchair. In the armchair sat his grandfather.

The men placed the armchair in the center of the cell and departed.

"You should have stayed on that train," said the old baron.

"You are right, grandfather, as my step-father was correct about the role of artillery in the revolution. I have been wrong about everything. Do you come to gloat upon my ruin?"

"That is insulting."

"Forgive me, then. A certain callousness has crept into my being. Why then are you here?"

"To find out how you do, of course. You are my only grandchild—where else would I be?"

"I don't know how I do, sir. I don't know who I am. I was a man with a family I loved and a mistress I adored and a faithful best friend and they are all gone and so that man has vanished. I am nobody."

"You are a von Pannau still. I expect your situation has been explained to you?"

"It has, sir. I hope that you have not come to convince me to save my neck by betraying my friends."

"You still refuse, then?"

"I do. Our honor is called loyalty."

A wintry smile flashed on the old man's face. "I told them you would not. Never has a von Pannau broken trust, and you are, at the end, a true son of our house. I wish to God that you had placed your loyalty with your king and emperor instead of with that gaggle of fools."

"With the greatest respect, grandfather, the system you prize is doomed. Freedom, once tasted, cannot be banished from the hearts of men. That we misuse it, and by Christ we do, is neither here nor there. We shall learn."

"Allow me to doubt that. I understand you have been to see your Novotny. Whatever possessed you to make a friend of him?"

"He was different when young. And as you should know better than any man on earth, even a friend of the heart can be other than what he seems. I thought again of your cannibal story, you know. It seems we in this modern age have invented another choice besides daring escape or resting in comfort and being eaten. It seems there are certain men who eat up themselves, and he is one of them. So I am to hang. When will it be, do you know?"

"Oh, don't be stupid, Rudi! A von Pannau does not hang for treason, not under the sway of the Hapsburg at any rate. They owe us far more than they can repay. And the current military dictator of Bohemia is your cousin. Have you even now learned nothing about how things are done in the empire?"

"More than I wished. What will my fate be then?"

"You will be transported as a common prisoner to the fortress of Olmutz. There, after a certain interval, it will be given out that you were hanged for your crimes against the state. A corpse will be obtained and, under your name, will be buried disgracefully in a potter's field. Thus ever to traitors! You will be secreted out of Olmutz by night, placed on a train, under guard, and conveyed to the port of Trieste, where you will board ship, still under guard, and be conveyed to an American city, New York, perhaps, or Philadelphia. I have arranged for a draft to be waiting for you at a bank there. You will not be rich, but nor will you starve. The condition attached is that you make no attempt to write or make your existence known to your children. And be warned: if you ever return to the empire, you will be taken up and done away with, in earnest this time. The empire may forgive, but it does not forget."

"I see. Well, a martyr to the revolution is not such a bad fate, and the reality accords well with the rest of my fraudulent life. It pains me, though, that I will never see you again. You are wrong on every detail of life, but I find I still love you. I am afraid your memoir was consumed by flames."

"Oh, damn the memoir! As I have already said, you were always the only intended reader, and part of me will live on in you, much as you may despise it. I pray you will not despise it all, however."

"Never! But, you know, they will not care a whit for your aristocratic name in America, grandfather. That is why I I believe I shall enjoy the barbarous society of that land, as much as I can enjoy anything."

"Pah! You imagine you will sink into the *canaille*, but you will not, unless you destroy yourself with vice. The mark is upon your skin and upon your spirit and you will not escape your fate. I wonder, do they get the news in hell? If they do, and if I should hear you have become a colonel of dragoons suppressing damned rebels, I will laugh my head off."

Rudi chuckled at this, and then cut it off short, abashed. He could still laugh?

His grandfather seemed to catch his thought. "Yes, you are shocked you laugh after what has befallen you. We laughed all the time during the war. I never laughed so much before or since. One day you see some dear companion chopped in half by a cannonball and the next day you're splitting your sides over some fool getting a foot stuck in a bucket. It is a mark of your quality that you laugh at fate. The *canaille* are always bemoaning theirs, no matter how rich they wax."

"Well, we shall see how I fare in a land without rank. But will you do me a final favor, sir? These two letters are for my children. Deathbed missives you may call them. I cannot bear the thought that I will leave them with nothing of myself. You will understand this more than any man alive, and so I beg you to let them rest with some responsible person, to be conveyed to them when they are of age. And this paper disposes of my property to some innocent victims of the rebellion. I charge you to see the provisions are carried out."

Rudi proffered the letters and the old baron took them without a word. Rudi observed that his eyes shone with tears.

"Ah, me!" sighed Hans, "My heart has been broken so many times! Thank Christ this must be the last of it. I intend to remove to Pannau, for there is nothing now to keep me in Prague. I shall dwell for some little time in the apartment once occupied by my dear Wolanska. There will be a bequest when I die, covertly, of course. You can buy a railroad of your own if you like."

"Thank you, grandfather; and that advice I will take. One question more. When you discovered my identity, why did you not come forward to be part of our family, to play with your great-grandchildren and come to love them and their mother? Why was that?"

"Pride," said the old man. "The black side of the coin, of which honor is the bright face. It has been the ruin of both of us, I believe. And now, farewell, my dear child, and may God protect you. Sergeant!"

The soldiers came in, lifted the armchair and carried Baron Hans von Pannau-Kinsky out of Rudi's life.

Epilogue—Fifteen Years Later

He found the colonel sitting in a canvas chair with his face turned toward the sun, his eyes closed. Except for the regimental colors standing cased nearby and a soldier at a folding table outside a large, dirty tent, there was no sign that he was in a regimental headquarters--no formalities, just a tired man with mud-caked boots in a canvas chair.

The young officer came to attention and saluted, saying, "Second Lieutenant Jerome V. Kincaid, reporting as ordered, sir."

The colonel opened his eyes and after a moment's pause, sketched a salute.

"Welcome to the First Pennsylvania Mounted Infantry, Lieutenant. What does the V stand for?"

"Sir?"

"Your middle name, Mr. Kincaid."

"Oh. Vesey, sir. From my mother's family."

"And from where do you come to us?"

"From West Point, sir. I have just graduated from there. And Doylestown before that."

"I see." The colonel stood and stretched and put on his cap. "Well, I cannot meet you properly now, as I am just off to division. Captain Pike will attend to your immediate needs." He signaled to a black man, who came forward leading a horse, and the colonel rode off.

Captain Pike, a plump, rubicund fellow of five and twenty, languid, loquacious, but reasonably efficient, arranged a servant, remounts, and weapons for the lieutenant, and brought him au courant on the doings of the First Pennsylvania M.I.

"We're using the Spencer carbine, now, all the regiments in Gamble 's brigade got them. Ever use one? Well, it's easy as slipping in the mud. Brass cases, don't have to bother with no cap--the cap's right on the end of the cartridge. Seven rounds in the tube magazine, crank the lever and you're ready to shoot. We all use 'em--officers and men alike—colonel's orders. The colonel likes to lead from the front. I expect you'll start as aide-de-camp, so's he can inspect what you're made of close up. I guess you ain't seen the elephant yet?"

"No, sir. But I did expect to be with the troops. I mean to see action."

"Oh, never you fear about that, not with the colonel. I said he likes to lead from the front and he makes sure we *are* at the front. Do you realize, Mr. Kincaid, that you are standing at the very tippy tip of the Army of the Potomac? There ain't nothing at all yonder to the west or north of us but Rebs. He's a square-head Dutchman, you know, but I reckon you sussed that out from the way he talks; and not one of our Pennsylvania Dutchies, neither. He's from the old country, one of them Forty-eighters, don't you know, and he has his ways. Don't you dare rough a horse where he can see you, that's one thing he can't bear. Nor abuse a darkie. He's got a darkie servant--well, I guess more than a servant, for he takes him as cover man. I wouldn't like to trust my back to a nigger, but Wallace is a little unusual. I mean for a darkie. Fights like a sunuvabitch too, although servants ain't supposed to ride cover according to regulations. Latrines, that's another thing the colonel dotes on. The men call him Old Shithole."

"Do you mean to say they despise him?"

"Oh, Lord, no. The opposite. They'd follow him right through Hell's gate. But he makes them dig latrines more than they'd wish, and use 'em, too. It's one of his foreign ways, is all."

Several hours passed, in which Lt. Kincaid worked on a letter to his father, and then the colonel returned and summoned all his officers to the headquarters tent.

"Gentlemen, General Buford has entrusted Brigadier Gamble's brigade to lead the advance," he began, "and Brigadier Gamble has entrusted us to tip the spear. As per usual. We shall depart in two hours, proceeding north on the Taneytown Road to occupy the high ground west of the town, with the purpose to hold it until General Reynold's infantry corps can come up. Major Dugan will distribute sketch maps on which the positions of your squadrons are marked. Are there any questions?"

A troop captain asked how long they would have to hold the ground.

"Until we are relieved or dead. The rebels cannot be allowed to occupy those ridges. It is they who must struggle to pry us off and not the other way around. Do you remember Fredericksburg?"

A mumbled groan came from those who had been there.

"Yes. Now we will hold the heights and Lee must advance against us."

Another question: do we know where the Rebel army lies?

"To the west in the main, with Ewell's corps to the north. But it does not signify, for Lee must have Gettysburg if he is to advance, and we plan to be in his way. He will be attracted here as a nail to a magnet. Remember to draw extra ammunition, all you can carry. Major Sommers, have your guns forward in the column of march, if you please. I want them well advanced on McPherson's ridge. Thank you gentlemen. Mr. Kincaid, you will remain."

"Take a seat, Mr. Kincaid, and tell me about yourself."

Both men sat on canvas stools and Kincaid did so, with increasing ease. The colonel asked few questions; in the main he seemed interested in Kincaid's family life, his parents and siblings, his home and friends, and his political stance, especially his attitude on the Negro question. Kincaid responded that his family had long been for abolition and staunchly Union, and that seemed to please the colonel very well. He wanted to know why the young man had chosen the cavalry, and how he regarded the art of riding, and these answers seemed to please him too.

"Very good, Lieutenant, I think we shall get along well enough. You seem to be well bred and eager and responsible to your duties. That is all I require. Your valor we shall take as given. Sergeant Pratt!"

A tall man wearing a huge black mustache and the stripes of a sergeant major came through the flap that separated the tent into two sections.

"Sir?"

"Sergeant-Major, this is Mr. Kincaid, who will be my aide-de-camp. Take him along the lines and introduce him to the squadrons. Remember we depart in two hours. Carry on, sergeant!"

Sergeant-Major Pratt and Kincaid walked through the encampment of the regiment, stopping at the various squadron command posts to introduce the new aide-de-camp to the squadron commanders, men in most cases only a year or so older than Kincaid himself, but with a certain chill and faraway look in their eyes, as befitted men who had seen the elephant many a time. Kincaid felt like a schoolboy on the first day of term. The men he met were polite but not friendly. Unlike Captain Pike, Sergeant-Major Pratt was economical of speech.

But after a particularly long period of silence, they having just inspected the horse lines, Lieutenant Kincaid made bold to ask a question.

"Sergeant, the men seem unusually quiet. Are they of low spirits?"

"No, sir. The morale of this regiment is excellent, I should say. But they know there will be a battle tomorrow and that lowers their tone a bit. It is only natural. And they are tired, sir. The colonel works them hard, and they had the devil of a hard fight at Hanover this past week and have lost some comrades."

They proceeded to another encampment and introductions, after which Kincaid asked, "Yet I find there is something odd about the way the men regard me, as if I am an object of pity. Is there something amiss in my turn-out or equipage?"

"No, sir," said the sergeant. "It's only that you are the colonel's sixth aide de camp in as many weeks."

"Oh? Is he so hard to please?"

"Not at all, sir, although he likes a clean camp and the men looking like soldiers of the Army of the Potomac and not a gang of bummers. But not unreasonable compared to some I have known, except in the case of the shit holes. No, sir, it is just that the colonel likes to lead from the front, and the aide de camp is always at his right flank rear. The colonel is keen for the thick of the fight, as you might say, and it do get tolerably warm thereabouts."

"Do you tell me they were all killed?"

"Not all of them, sir, by no means. But rendered whores dee combat, as we call it."

"I see. Captain Pike has told me that they would follow Colonel Panow through the gates of Hell. He must be an unusually fine officer."

There came a long silence after this remark and Kincaid wondered if he had said something amiss, but the sergeant finally responded, "He is a remarkable man, sir, I suppose he is the most remarkable officer under which I have served this war. We have been together since Antietam. You know he was a real duke or some such, back in Germany?"

"I did not. That *is* remarkable."

"Yes, sir. But no airs and graces, not him. Why, he don't touch a drop of food less'n every last man of his has been fed. I will tell you a story, sir, if I may. We had captured a Reb colonel at Brandy Station and Colonel Panow invited him to a sit-down dinner, with wine and all, and a turkey his man Wallace had picked up somewheres. That's another thing, sir, he treats Wallace like a white man, and you best do the same, sir. The Reb colonel insulted Wallace, and Colonel Panow, why he just went after that Reb something ferocious, and the Reb says that's the trouble with you Yankees. You have no idea of the proper relations between a gentleman and his servants. And he goes on about how the niggers is happier so, and how slavery is so almighty great, and gassing away like they do on that subject: us Yankees don't know nothing about true aristocracy, we're all a bunch of feather merchants.

"Well, nothing was said for a minute and I get up and peek through a hole in the flap to see what's what, and I see Colonel Panow standing up and I see him take a silver case from his breast pocket and hand a card out of it to the Reb and the Reb reads off some Heinie name, a real long one like the quality have over there and says, "Uh! Why anyone could have a card like this printed up.""

And Colonel Panow says he has insulted his honor, and if the Reb wasn't his prisoner he'd call him out and shoot him dead, but in any case, he would look the bastard up after the war, if they was both still living, and kill him then. He calls out for the sentry and says the Reb was no gentleman and could not have a seat at his table and to take the Reb prisoner back to the cage, and no milk puddin' neither."

He paused and added;

"That's another thing about the Colonel, sir. He does hate a Reb. I ain't too partial to the sumbitches myself, sir, but the Colonel just purely *hates* 'em. Disloyal swine, he calls 'em. *Schvine*, like he says. Loyalty, that's a mighty thing with the Colonel. Any man who works for him, sir, needs to keep that in mind."

Lieutenant Kincaid agreed upon the importance of that virtue, and about the remarkable nature of his commander, as evinced by the sergeant's tale. The sergeant, however, seemed abashed by his unaccustomed loquacity and was moodily silent for the rest of their time together.

During their ride north, the 1st Pennsylvania Mounted Infantry encountered a group of riders that proved to be

General John Buford, commander of the 1st Cavalry Division, and his staff. Colonel Panow left his post at the head of his men for a brief conversation, during which, as Lieutenant Kincaid observed, the colonel said something that made the general laugh out loud.

The column proceeded on at a good pace. Kincaid was in his assigned position a little to the rear of the colonel, on the right, just in front of the color party. To Kincaid's surprise, the colonel motioned him forward.

"I have been derelict, Mr. Kincaid," he said, "for I have not instructed you in the duties of an aide-de-camp. There are three. The first is as galloper. You must carry orders--in memory, for we do not like it when written orders fall into the hands of the enemy--and convey them clearly and with my authority to my subordinate officers; as well, you must ride out and be my eyes when necessary, bringing intelligence back to me. The second is to keep your eyes and ears open when I make my dispositions and plans. Then, when I am shot dead, you may convey to Major Haines or Major Franklin my last thoughts, when one or the other takes command of the regiment. Can you do that?"

"I will do my best, sir. What is the third duty?"

"Why, to make me as comfortable as possible, securing the most luxurious billets and gathering the choicest viands for my table. That is by far the most important duty. You must take advice in this from Wallace here. He will make you a dog-robber, as they call it, if you have the talent. Ah, this is a present example. We hear now this firing up ahead and wish to learn what it is. You must ride fast and come quick right back to tell me."

Kincaid spurred his horse and raced to the sound of firing with pounding heart. By the time he reached the sources of the shooting, however, the skirmish was all over. A vedette of the Pennsylvanians had run into a patrol of Confederate infantry, shot some, captured two, and scattered the rest. Kincaid garnered what intelligence the lieutenant in charge of the vedette had learned and rode back to his colonel.

Who listened to what he had to say, and then fixed him with a stare that riveted the young man's attention.

"Mr. Kincaid, you will ride to inform Brigadier Gamble and General Buford that we have made contact with the advance guard of Lee's main force, under Heth, and that I have refused further engagement and am moving with all speed to our designated positions. Their infantry is uncovered by cavalry. Repeat that! "

When Kincaid returned to his post, his horse all a-lather, and had conveyed what the two generals had said in reply, the colonel asked him, "And do you know the meaning of this intelligence, Lieutenant?"

"We will be there before Lee's infantry."

"Yes. And?"

Kincaid thought for a long moment, and then hazarded, "And because he has no cavalry shadowing us, he will not know who opposes him or their strength."

"You have it right. We will occupy our ridges and the whole of Lee's force will have no thought but to push us off. They will send skirmishers in triple lines against us and when we fire down at them, they will not see us, because we will not have to stand up to reload, and so they will think that instead of a regiment of horse, there is a brigade of infantry against them, for we can throw bullets as much as a brigade of Springfields. This will confuse them, which is always a good thing in war, to confuse the enemy. And we know that Lee has thrown away his cavalry, so he does not have enough intelligence about us to invent a good plan of battle."

He paused and gave a tight-lipped smile.

"I think, Lieutenant, that this is the most interesting battle I have ever been in."

Later, the colonel said, "You know, I have a son of about your age. Fritz is his name."

"Yes sir?" Said Lieutenant Kincaid. The two men were standing at the regimental command post, set in a little hollow on Herr Ridge, looking west.

"And fortunately, he lives in Austria, so does not fight in a war, like you."

Kincaid waited, but apparently the colonel had nothing more to say about his son. After a silence the colonel laughed out loud.

"You wonder why I laugh, Lieutenant?"

"I am glad the colonel is happy," said Kincaid.

"This morning I was brevetted full colonel. I am now in truth a colonel of dragoons suppressing damned rebels. My grandfather is laughing his head off in Hell."

The lieutenant waited, but there was no explanation for this odd statement.

They heard running steps and presently a private burst into view.

Breathless, he called out, "Colonel, sir, Mr. Newton's compliments, and he says the pickets are pushed in and the Rebs are coming up in force."

They went forward to take a look. Three lines of skirmishers, as the colonel had foretold, marched forward with banners flying and the sun glinting on their weapons, their faces hidden behind slouch hats and caps. As they came closer, they began their famous yell, and the 1st Pennsylvania Mounted Infantry opened fire with their Spencer rifles.

Upon the Confederate regiment of perhaps six hundred troops now fell in the next twenty seconds over four thousand bullets. The Confederate regiment disappeared; where there had been three lines of living men there was now only a long heap of dead and wounded, with a few lucky straggling survivors retreating down the hill. The 1st Pennsylvania let out a peculiar cheer.

Kincaid asked Sgt. Pratt "What are the men shouting, sergeant?"

"Never-learn? Oh, we always cheer that. It was something the colonel was yelling when we were running through the orchard at Antietam and we all started to do the same. He thought it was a good enough yell. Here they come again."

601

The Confederates now sent two regiments at once, and when these met the same fate as the first, the Rebs brought up their cannon.

Kincaid had just thrown up his breakfast because of seeing Sergeant-Major Pratt die. The sergeant-major was standing right next to him, and had just told the color party not to hang back so, when a cannonball whipped off his head, splashing Kincaid from face to breast with gore.

The colonel called out, "Mr. Kincaid! We will now withdraw to McPherson's Ridge. They have the range and it will soon be too hot to remain. Please go along the line and inform the squadrons to withdraw stepwise, starting with Second Squadron. Have Major Sommers continue firing canister until the last moment. Repeat!"

They pulled back and the Rebs swarmed after them thicker than ever, for there was most of a corps coming against them. By that time Kincaid had his own Spencer and was killing men one after another, knocking them down like crows, or targets at a fairgrounds, and right next to him the Colonel was doing the same. They kept coming though, it was like sweeping back the sea with a broom, and here came the cannon fire again, the hum of the balls passing, the screams of men when they were hit, the solid crack when a ball struck a tree trunk.

Every moment Kincaid thought this could not go on, there were too many of them, and his gun barrel was starting to glow red. But gradually, over some minutes, he became aware that the firing from the Union side had both increased and changed rhythm, and when he looked about him he saw that the two men on either side of him were shooting Springfield rifles. Reynold's infantry had arrived.

Some weeks after this, Kincaid wrote to his father about his experiences on that first day of the Battle of Gettysburg:

It is generally agreed among us all, and not just in the regiment, that had Buford's Division not held up the enemy until the infantry of the 1st Corps arrived, the Rebs would have taken over the high ground, and later won the day, for, as they broke against our defenses, so would we have broken against theirs. I think further that had we of the 1ˢᵗ Penna. not held, then the brigade and the Division would not have either, for we were in the thick of the thick of it.

And I suppose one might even say that we would not have held without the Colonel, who throughout the whole affair was just where he ought to be, lending his own rifle fire when needed, encouraging, rallying, and being entirely the spirit of the fight. He seemed to me like a warrior from another age, a Frederick, a Prince Eugene, in small. We Union men can fight, of course, and our bravery is without match anywhere. But we are civil at heart. He is a soldier bred in the bone. I saw his face in the midst of the fight and it seemed to me that he was having the time of his life. How strange it would be if fate had brought this one man across the seas for just this purpose, to save the battle, and throw back the slave power in its pride and rescue the day!

He has that air of effortless command that I suppose comes of his aristocratic birth, which I have noticed also among the Reb officers we have captured. They are men brave to a fault, sensitive to honor, chivalrous. It is admirable although it must originate from domination over a servile race. I would be glad if we were as noble as they, without the vice of slavery. How this may be accomplished is a question for future ages, I suppose. Yes, they exceed us in nobility. But we licked 'em.

NOTE TO THE READER

SPOILER ALERT. Please read no further if you intend to read this book. If not, or if you've finished it, read on!

Historical novels, of course, mix real and imaginary events, yet some of the historical events described in this novel are so bizarre that they could never be used as fiction. In a sense, they are unimaginable. For example, the world of gentility during the *ancien regime* was remarkably small, and it was possible for a mountebank like Casanova to know face-to-face a good proportion of the great personages of Europe. My chief character was meant to portray the range of connection of a typical gentleman of the late 18th century. It may seem Zelig-esque, but it is not.

Goethe really did ride out on the battlefield during the Cannonade at Valmy and had to be rescued by an officer, but not my officer, who is fictitious.

Casanova really was a close friend of Lorenzo Da Ponte, the librettist of Mozart's *Don Giovanni*. That Casanova himself worked on the libretto is an unconfirmed but persistent item in the scholarship of the opera. Casanova really was at the premiere.

Mozart actually was a billiards fiend.

Aficionados of Isak Dinesen (and who is not?) will recognize the Hugh of Scotland cannibal story as a modified version of one found in her *Winter Tales*. As it happens, the author sat next to Baroness Blixen at a concert in France in the middle of the last century, and through mystic arts was able to return to his former self and ask permission, which was graciously granted.

The events in Prague between March and June of 1848 happened as described. Bakunin was actually in Prague at the time. I have stolen some accomplishments from real people and attributed them to fictitious characters, in service of the tale.

Princess Eleanor zu Windischgrätz really was killed by a bullet from the street during the rebellion in June, 1848.

There is a good deal of anti-Semitism depicted in this book, reflecting the language and mores of the times, but also to make the point that this era and this region were the time and place where modern race-based anti-Semitism (as opposed to the old religious kind) was born. Here is the seedbed, also, of the Shoah.

The repulse of the Confederate assault on the high ground west of Gettysburg on July 1, 1863 by John Buford's 1st cavalry division, some armed with Spencer repeating rifles, is historical fact. They did hold off a vastly superior number of the enemy until the lead corps of the Army of the Potomac could come up and occupy the high ground with infantry, one of the many times at Gettysburg when the action of a small number of determined men saved the victory for the Union.

Readers who find it hard to believe that a woman could pose as a man and have a career as a soldier should read *The Cavalry Maid*, a memoir by Nadezhda Durova, who ran away from home to join the Tsar's army, fought with distinction as a uhlan during the Napoleonic wars, was wounded at Borodino, and served as aide-de-camp to the legendary General Kutuzov. When she reverted to being a woman afterward, she was famous throughout Europe.

The author would like to thank researchers Jeffrey M. Horton and Ann Weber for their invaluable help in seeking out historical details from the two eras in which this novel is set. My twisting of the facts when necessary is not their fault.

Made in United States
North Haven, CT
03 March 2022

16757661R00339